RAVENS
OF
WINTER
BOUND TO THE FAE
4-6
EVA CHASE

Ravens of Winter: Bound to the Fae - Books 4-6

2 in the Bound to the Fae Box Sets series

First Digital Edition, 2022

Cover design: Malice & Mayhem Book Covers

Case design: Story Wrappers

Front character art: Monsterlab

Back character art: Kalynne Pratt

Ebook ISBN: 978-1-990338-91-5

Hardcover ISBN: 978-1-990338-92-2

ROYAL MATE

BOUND TO THE FAE #4

CHAPTER ONE

Talia

This night should be a time for celebration. The arch-lords of the summer fae just welcomed one of the men I love to rule alongside them. Minutes ago, the field around me was full of dancing and laughter in honor of his coronation. And I had a promise from all three of my lovers tingling giddily through me. The air itself felt full of joy.

Now I'm backing away through the crowd with my stomach twisted and my thoughts scattered by a surge of cold horror. Not because of the arrival of the five Unseelie arch-lords with huge raven-like wings jutting from their backs, as unsettling as they are as they stare down the Seelie trio. Something much worse is happening *inside* me.

A voice—a vibrant tenor, unmistakably male and shocked—peals through the searing gap that seems to have opened down the center of my being. *Where are you going? We have to— We must speak.*

No. No, no, no. I'm incapable of anything other than that repeated but probably futile denial.

No one else can hear his words, just as no one else could sense the burning jolt that tore through me when my gaze collided with that of the youngest of the winter arch-lords. The space that opened up inside me conveys not only his voice but also a wave of inexplicable impressions: the sight of my slim, pink-haired form vanishing amid the bodies of the gathered summer fae, the flex of unfamiliar muscles and the wash of the warm breeze tickling across feathers attached to those limbs, a stutter of a pulse that's beating even harder than mine.

I don't want this. I need it to *stop*. But the flood of sensation only swells, upending my own awareness. My feet stumble under me, a pang shooting through my warped foot. My elbow bumps one of the other spectators, who jerks back with a frown.

I have to get away. Maybe if I go far enough, I can outrun this awfulness?

Please, come back. I know you must be startled too, but—

Spinning around, I stop paying attention to his words, thinking of nothing but propelling myself in the opposite direction. My balance is off; the ground seems to sway. A hand catches my arm, and I flinch, striking out instinctively.

"Whoa there." It's not an enemy—not *him*—but Astrid, the fae warrior woman who's acted as a sort of bodyguard when the lord of my pack and his cadre can't watch over me themselves. Staring down at me, she blocks my reflexive jab easily and gently. My awareness of her is fractured by other scenes from an angle another pair of eyes are seeing from: the semi-circle of gathered Seelie. The line of Unseelie arch-lords beside—beside him, not me—

Astrid's steady voice breaks through the stream of clashing images. "What's wrong? You don't have to worry—the ravens can't attack us. They'll have taken their vows to come through the border here by the Heart."

I'm not worried about that kind of attack. A totally different sort of assault is already underway within my mind and body. I close my eyes, but that only brings the invading impressions into sharper clarity.

I wrench my eyelids open again with a wild shake of my head. A ragged plea spills from my lips. "I have to get out of here."

Astrid may not understand what's going on, but she knows she's meant to protect me. Without arguing, she adjusts her grip on my arm so she's partly supporting my weight and ushers me toward the Bastion. The gleaming, gold-veined walls of the building where the Seelie arch-lords conduct their business no longer reassure me with their warmth. Somehow I don't think they'll provide enough shelter.

You must— Wait. We can talk about this like reasonable—

No! I think at the voice with a more emphatic burst of panicked resistance. *No, go away, stop, get out of me.*

I've never experienced anything like this before, but I've heard it described. This splitting down the middle, this rush of another person's awareness sweeping in—it's how a soul-twined mate bond feels when it sparks. But only true-blooded fae are supposed to make soul-twined connections. And I'm not fae at all, except for the tiniest trace somewhere in my heritage. By every measure that matters to the folk around me, I'm human. This is impossible.

But then, other things about me have been impossible since the moment my path crossed with the fae in violence and bloodshed and the murders of my family nearly ten years ago. Why not this too?

Oh, God, I don't want to think that. I just want this unwanted invasion to be done.

We duck through one of the shadowed doorways. Footsteps thump after us. I flinch again, but when I look up, relief washes over me. August, the lead warrior of our pack and the tenderest of my lovers, is hustling over to us, his boyishly handsome face tensed with concern. Astrid must have managed to signal him while she was leading me here.

"What's going on?" he asks, grasping my shoulder. "What happened to you, Talia? What do you need?"

The impressions rising through me have jumbled into some sort of commotion—urgently spoken words, a glare, a flash of frustration. *Come back*, the voice demands, but then it falls away as if the man out there is distracted by whatever's going on around him.

I gulp for air. "I don't know. I—I think— It doesn't make any sense."

August gathers me in his arms, tucking his chin over my head. His hand strokes up and down my back. An uneasy twinge I've never experienced in his embrace before runs through my gut. A flare of hostility carries through the connection—

And then it's gone. *He's* gone. But I'm not the same as I was before. The seared-open space inside of me echoes with the sudden emptiness. I can't shake off my awareness of the Unseelie man's absence, as if he's carved a mark inside me that will linger no matter where he goes.

No. I clench my teeth against a sob. August hugs me tighter, murmuring reassuring words, and my stomach knots with an ache so sharp I shudder.

How can I tell him? How can I tell any of them after they just offered me so much devotion, even committed to making me their mate?

I love the three fae men who've become my saviors and protectors, and they care for me so much in return, as impossible as I thought that would be too. I'd never been happier than I was moments ago in this building when they swore they'd find a way to make our shared relationship official in the eyes of all their peers.

And now this—this whatever it is—has betrayed them and me.

"Just tell me when you're ready," August is saying.

I swallow the lump that's filled my throat. My voice comes out thin and scratchy. "I—I don't—"

Two more sets of footsteps ring out across the stone floor. Sylas, lord of our pack and newly proclaimed arch-lord, and Whitt, his spymaster, stride over to us. There's a storm already brewing in Sylas's mismatched gaze—one eye dark as chocolate and the other one ghostly white amid the scar that cuts through his brown skin. It turns even wilder when he takes in my expression.

"Did they injure you in some way? If those blasted ravens—"

"No," I say quickly. The last thing I want is for his first move as arch-lord to be charging back out there to start a full-out war. He became arch-lord partly to *prevent* all Seelie kind being sucked into an even more massive conflict against the Unseelie, who've been launching raids along the border between the summer and winter realms for a few decades now. "I—"

My voice wavers with another burst of sensation from deep within, this one more like a brief punch than a flood. A harsh female voice rattles through my mind. *–can't seriously be saying that—* It comes with a clenching of loss and dismay, a glimpse of pale walls and fierce eyes, and then it's gone again.

The connection hasn't been broken. The Unseelie man on the other end of it must be shutting me out—or at least trying to.

I lean back against August's brawny frame, inhaling slowly and scrambling to regain my bearings. I can't hide this problem, and I sure as hell have no idea how to deal with it on my own. Bracing myself for my lovers' reaction, I force out the best explanation I can offer.

"I was in the crowd, watching the Unseelie arch-lords for any clue about why they'd come. And then—the one at the end of the line, the younger man—he glanced toward me, and our eyes met, and—" My chest hitches. I gather myself and press onward, quieter than before. "It felt like I was being seared apart inside. And I started seeing what he must have been seeing, feeling— I heard his voice in my head."

I press my hand to my temple. It *is* my head. I can't even explain how wrong it feels to think that someone else could slip into it like that. How many of my thoughts did the Unseelie man catch?

August's arms tighten around me. Sylas and Whitt are gaping at me, Sylas's stance gone rigid, the color draining from Whitt's tan face. The fae lord speaks first. "You can't mean…" He doesn't seem to know how to go on.

"I know how impossible it sounds." I cringe, misery coiling all through my abdomen. "I know it shouldn't have been able to happen. I wish it *hadn't* happened. But that's—"

"Wait." Whitt's tone is taut and urgent, with a thread of the anguish creeping into his ocean-blue eyes. "If that kind of bond has formed between you and one of the Unseelie arch-lords—he'll be able to see and hear all this through you."

I stiffen. The winter fae could be spying on us, on the Seelie's newest arch-lord, through me. We haven't said anything it'd hurt for them to overhear, but if he can read even my thoughts…

"How do I stop it?" I blurt out.

Even as I speak, another flash blazes through my mind: cold, raised voices clashing, a gleaming silver table. It snaps away as quickly as it rose up.

I shiver. "I think *he's* trying to stop it. At first so much was coming at me from him, and now it's mostly cut off. I just feel kind of… empty."

Sylas grazes his fingers over my head, but his expression is too grim for me to take any comfort from the gesture. "That serves us well. No doubt he's as worried about you reporting what goes on in the winter realm back to us as we are about the reverse. The arch-lords left rather abruptly—it did seem that one raised some kind of issue with the others—but they'd already started making demands of other sorts that we weren't interested in entertaining. I can't imagine they were expecting a sudden soul-twined bond to take hold during their foray here."

He's said the words I hesitated to. *Soul-twined bond.* I'd already thought them, but hearing the fae lord voice them out loud brings the full impact of the situation crashing down on me.

I rub my hands over my face. "How could it have happened?"

If it was going to happen, why couldn't it have been with one of the men around me—the men I already love so deeply?

"I don't know," Sylas says, softly if a little raggedly. "But first let's give you whatever measure of control we can over the connection. There are ways to tune out a soul-twined bond, as I know too well. Are you ready for me to talk you through it?"

I can't imagine what a frantic mess I must look. I lift my head as straight as I can and nod.

"All right." He takes my hand, and August releases me so Sylas can guide me to sit cross-legged on the stone floor across from him. The fae lord lifts his gaze from me for only a moment to his cadre-chosen. "Make sure we're not disturbed."

August moves to the hall we entered from, Astrid taking the initiative to do the same at one of the other doorways to the room. Whitt stays poised over Sylas, crossing his arms tightly over his chest.

Sylas grips both of my hands in his. "You want to pick some element or material you feel closely connected with. I used living wood. Whatever speaks to you the strongest, picture it sealing over the space inside you, blocking anything that would try to travel through either way."

I wet my lips. "Does it have to be something you're magically connected to?" One of the other impossible things about me is that despite being human, I've managed to wield a few true names like the fae do, conjuring and manipulating things with them. But my skills are weak, and I don't have many options to draw on.

Sylas's gaze flicks to Astrid, who doesn't know about my fledgling powers, but he seems to decide that if she follows this part of the conversation, there's no harm in it. "I expect that's more likely to form a strong barrier, yes."

Then I'm choosing between bronze, light, and air.

I close my eyes, thinking back to the times when I've called to them, and the answer comes to me faster than I expected. Bronze has defended me and air has brought information to me, but light is the magic of my heart. The power fueled by the joy I feel when I'm with these men.

If anything can shut out this unwanted intruder, that'll be it.

I imagine the light I've summoned between my hands with its true name and the brilliant sun streaming over the castle in our home in Hearthshire. The way August's face lights up every time I tell him I love him, the playful spark that so often dances in Whitt's eyes, and the heady warmth that passes from Sylas into me with his touch. All those glowing sensations wrap around my chest and spread through my limbs.

Collecting that impression of brightness, I picture it pouring into the gap that's split open inside me. I will the warm glow to thicken until it's an impenetrable mass of light.

The impression of emptiness fades. No further flickers reach me from that other mind. I feel… almost complete again as I am.

A shaky breath spills out of me. "Okay. I think—I think I did it."

"Good." Sylas squeezes my fingers. "It'll take practice to perfect it. You'll need to stay watchful and notice when any awareness from the other side begins to seep through. But with every breach, you'll get better at telling whether you've gotten the seal solid."

I meet his solemn gaze. "This isn't a real solution, though, is it?"

His jaw tenses. "No. It's a temporary fix. The rest…"

He glances up at his spymaster. Before they can discuss the subject any further, a voice carries down the hall.

"Sylas?"

It's Celia—his new arch-lord colleagues must want to discuss the visit from the Unseelie. They don't know about me yet—about what happened to me. What will they think when they do?

Sylas grips my hands firmly as we stand together. "Over here!" he calls, and turns back to me. "You'll go with Whitt and August while I see to other business—I'll be back as soon as I can. We won't mention this to anyone else until we know our next steps."

That reassurance only soothes my nerves a little. As the fae lord goes to meet his fellow arch-lord, giving a few quick instructions to his cadre on the way, I hug myself. The glowing patch inside me wavers. With a hiccup of my pulse, I gather more light together, putting all the power I can summon into it.

What next steps can there be? My soul is somehow intertwined with one of the Unseelie—one of the leaders of the raven-shifting winter fae who've been attacking the Seelie since before I was even born. No matter what benefits my blood offers the summer fae, no matter how much affection my lovers have for me, I can't picture any solution that won't come with a whole lot of pain.

CHAPTER TWO

August

As I stalk from one end of the make-shift office to the other, I can barely rein in my wolf. It stretches within me, fangs gnashing and claws raking, every nerve reverberating with the desire to leap free and launch myself at the mangy raven who somehow twined himself with Talia's soul.

I love her. I meant to make her my mate. The thought of losing her to anyone, let alone the wretched Unseelie, brings a roar to my throat even while she's sleeping just down the hall. If the feathery bastards actually try to take her away from us…

The only things holding me back from unleashing the beast inside are the fact that murdering an Unseelie arch-lord would ruin all of us, not just Talia—and the possibility that severing her from a soul-twined bond that's already formed might hurt her even more than *I'm* hurting right now.

"We can't throw her into the winter realm," I say, unable to restrain the growl that creeps out with the words. "None of this makes sense. She belongs with *us*."

Whitt's voice comes out as strained as it is dry. "The bond would appear to indicate otherwise." His face is drawn where he's propped against the rough desk Sylas has been using for work while our castle here by the Heart is still in the early stages of construction. The tart scent of fresh oak sap laces the air.

I don't think either of my older brothers are any happier than I am with the situation. Sylas stands next to Whitt, his arms crossed and his unscarred eye smoldering with dark emotion. "We aren't sending her anywhere until we have a better idea of how this happened. And not even then, if I have any say in it."

I stop, swiveling toward them. "*She* should have the say—and she doesn't want it. You saw how upset she was."

Sylas steps forward to set his hand on my shoulder. "I did, and that's why I'm going to do everything in my power to get to the bottom of this."

As always, my lord's steady authoritative air helps settle my temper. If anyone can find a solution, it's him.

But what if no one can? What if Talia is doomed to be tied to some vicious winter fae for the rest of her life?

As soon as Sylas lowers his hand, I start pacing again, unable to keep myself in place. Wary of what might spring free of me if I did.

Whitt swipes his hand over his face. Afterward, his expression only looks more uneasy. "We've always known she's more than a regular human. The way her blood counteracts our curse, and her minor capacity for learning true names. But for a soul-twined bond to grip her—that's an immense escalation. Most *fae* don't experience that."

Sylas inclines his head in agreement. "I can't see how Nuldar's statements shed any light on this development either. A trace of fae blood in her ancestry and a coincidence of synchronicitous timing might explain her connection to the curse, and that connection could conceivably have allowed her to tap into a small amount of the Heart's power. But as you say, for a soul-twined bond to form… and with an Unseelie, no less!"

A miserable thought occurs to me. "The sage never said the fae heritage she got through her great-grandmother's line was Seelie. For all we know, the trace she has is winter blood."

"But for her to be connected to *our* curse—" Sylas cuts himself off with a violent shake of his head. "No, there's no debating it. It remains a mystery—far too much of one for us to draw any real conclusions."

He glances at Whitt. Things have been tense between them for the past few weeks because of a horrible admission Whitt made that I don't want to think about right now, but in this moment, with a much more urgent concern in front of us, any hesitation Sylas felt before has fallen away. Say whatever you might about Whitt's behavior, there's no doubting his skill at his work.

Sylas motions to him. "Have you ever heard any report, current or historical, of *any* faded fae having a soul-twined bond come upon them?"

Whitt grimaces. "Not one that I can think of—and while I don't expect my mind has held onto every story that's reached my ears, one like that would have been remarkable enough to stick."

My hands ball at my sides, the claws I can't quite will back pricking my palms. "Should we go back to Nuldar and request another audience? Before we only asked him about her connection to the curse."

"He's never had patience for those who fail to ask the 'right' question the first time, and after that first answer, I have my doubts about whether we'd glean much more from him anyway." Sylas pauses, his gaze going momentarily distant. His mouth curves with a frown. "There is another way we could discover more about her history and how her soul might have become intertwined with fae kind."

Whitt stiffens just slightly. Between that and his frown, I can guess he knows what Sylas means and that I'm not going to like it. Still, I have to ask. "What is it?"

Sylas gives me a pensive look before answering. "We could bring her to the Pool of the Clouded Past and see what it shows her."

"The—" My hackles rise even though *he* hasn't done anything to offend me. "We'd have to go back to Thundervale."

He nods grimly. "And request permission from its lord. I know you have unpleasant memories there. If you'd rather not—"

"No, I'll go. Talia needs all of us." I'm not going to abandon her over my own past ordeals, even if the thought of returning to that place makes my chest constrict.

All three of us are incredibly familiar with both the domain of Thundervale and its lord… because we all grew up there, and Lord Eldris is our father.

The closer the carriage brings us to Thundervale, the tighter my ribs seem to compress around my lungs. I sit in the bottom of the vehicle next to Talia, my arm around her, sheltering her from the whipping wind. At least I *can* shelter her from that when there's so much else I can't.

We've made the journey to Thundervale at a swift pace so that we're not keeping Sylas from his new duties as arch-lord for very long. He told his colleagues that the trip was to gain insight into a matter involving both the curse and the Unseelie, which is technically true.

Whitt volunteered that he and I could escort Talia on our own, but our lord vetoed that idea immediately. I'm not sure how much it was because he wants to hear Talia's account firsthand and how much because of the brightly brittle note in Whitt's voice that suggested if left to our own devices, the two of us might unleash so much of our honest opinions on our father that we'd never get to the pond in the first place. The man's love of criticism has never extended to any aimed at himself.

I suspect I'm going to spend the better part of the initial meeting biting my tongue. It's been a long time since I thought of Lord Eldris as anyone I'd want to call Father. In my head, he's not so much a father or a lord as the man who ordered my mother's death.

Even a century and a half later, the memories rise up with brutal vividness: her screams and his guards' claws gouging into her flesh, my muscles straining against my father's magic as I struggled to spring to her defense. A "lesson," he called it. All it taught me was never to trust that anything I cared about would stay safe in the presence of that man.

And now we're taking Talia straight to him.

I must be letting too much of my discomfort show. Talia adjusts her position in my arms so she can peer into my face. "Are you worried about seeing him?"

A flash of regret passes through me that I shared so much of my history with her. Not because I don't want her to know me in every possible way, but because it gives *her* more reason to worry about this trip. But then, maybe it's better that she knows the darkest side of the man she's about to meet.

"I don't enjoy having to see him or speak to him," I say over the warble of the wind. "And I'd rather you never had to come anywhere near him. But he's proud of Sylas, even though Sylas struck out on his own rather than waiting to continue the Thundervale legacy. He respects him. I don't think he'll challenge Sylas's authority or act against us in any way."

And Sylas will be on his guard just in case I'm wrong. Our father may respect *him* as his true-blooded son, but Sylas didn't turn a blind eye to how things were run in the domain while he was coming into his own. I never told him exactly what went on with my mother, but he found me during the anguished rampage I went on through the woods afterward, cooled me down and comforted me as well as he could without demanding anything from me. I'm sure he gathered enough from other witnesses to put the pieces together well enough.

He told me once that the day when he heard Eldris had ordered my mother's murder was the day he decided for sure that he was leaving Thundervale. And as soon as I was of age to officially join his cadre, we left that place behind. I've only been back a few times in the many decades since then when official business required it, and not at all since our banishment.

Talia shudders and squeezes my arm in sympathy. "I wish we didn't have to come anywhere near him. Do you really think this pool will tell us something that could help with the soul-twined bond—or at least explain how it happened?"

I make a face. "I don't know. Like the sage, the sorts of responses it gives aren't always straightforward. You have to word your requests carefully. But it does at least show a literal representation of whatever past moments you're able to summon to the surface." My lips slant into a half-smile. "I'll admit there were a couple of times I used it just to find out where I'd left some object or another I'd misplaced."

Talia laughs. It's a beautiful sound, over far too quickly as the weight of everything she's struggling with descends on her again with a shadowing of her eyes. She tucks herself closer to me.

"Is your barrier against the soul-twined connection holding?" I ask.

She nods. "For the most part. I have to stay focused and keep bolstering it. Every now and then if I'm distracted, bits and pieces trickle through. He's been trying to talk to me."

I hug her and kiss her forehead. "You don't have to listen to him. The bond doesn't give him the right to demand your attention."

It just means it's much easier for him to make demands of her anyway. The toll her efforts at fending off the Unseelie arch-lord are taking comes through in the thread of weariness in her voice, the way she sinks into my embrace rather than insisting on holding herself straight and strong.

I grit my teeth in frustration. I should be able to protect her better than this. But the best I can do is stay beside her while we carry out this quest. I just hope something useful comes of it.

The carriage slows. We're almost there. I lift my head and catch Whitt's gaze. He offers me a crooked smile that's closer to a grimace. Eldris might have gone easier on him as the child of a fae dalliance rather than a human one, but my oldest brother has never made his disdain for our father's tyrannical habits a secret. For all the ways we're different, there's something reassuring in knowing we're united on that one subject.

It probably is a good thing Sylas insisted on coming along. If Eldris made one cutting remark about Talia in front of just the two of us, he might very well have ended up equally lashed by Whitt's words and my claws.

When the carriage comes to a halt, Sylas hops out alone, as we planned. I ease onto one of the benches, keeping an arm around Talia, and watch my lord stride up to the castle.

True to Eldris's magical affinities for plant life, which Sylas inherited a fair amount of, the massive structure is constructed out of interwoven vines. In the time since I was last here, they've darkened from green to brown and melded together at the edges with age.

They aren't the only things about this place that have altered as they've gotten older. The man who marches out to meet Sylas is grayer and more weathered than I remember, the dark purple-brown hair Sylas also inherited grizzled along his temples and through his short beard, new crow's feet lining the skin at the corners of his eyes. Eldris smiles the same way as ever, though—wide but thin, as if he doesn't quite trust anyone enough to offer a glimpse of his teeth.

The smile he offers Sylas does reach his eyes though, with a gleam of the pride I told Talia about. "My son, now Arch-Lord Sylas. I wish I could have come to the crowning, you know—there were just too many things that needed my supervision here. I'd have arranged to come to you to offer congratulations as soon as I could."

We all know that "as soon as I could" means never. I'm not sure Lord Eldris has left his domain in the entire time I've been alive. He rules with a tyrant's fist—and a tyrant's fear of how his pack might revolt if he gave them any room to breathe out from under his thumb. From what I've gathered based on Whitt's and Sylas's stories, that paranoia has only grown as his cruelty did in the wake of his soul-twined mate's departure.

When I was younger and I heard people refer to how much milder Eldris's temper was when he had Sylas's mother by his side, it made me angry at her for leaving. Now, with an adult's perspective and the understanding that a milder cruelty still wouldn't offer much happiness, I can't blame her. After all, we left as soon as we easily could too.

"I'm glad to receive those congratulations now," Sylas says evenly. "Unfortunately this matter is too urgent for us to enjoy a full visit. Do we have your permission to journey to the Pool of the Clouded Past?"

Eldris dips into a small bow, remembering a little late the extra respect he owes Sylas's new position. "Of course. I wouldn't deny an arch-lord or my son."

Not that son, anyway. His gaze slides over the carriage, taking in Whitt in his careless pose by the bow, me on the bench, and Talia next to me. A different sort of gleam lights in his eyes, one closer to greed.

"Is that the human of the cure?" he asks without any sign that either of us with her deserve his acknowledgment.

Talia's stance goes rigid. I react automatically, even though inside I'm recoiling at the sight of my father. I get up and step in front of her to fully shield her from his view. My fingers curl over the sides of the carriage, gripping it hard. Just shy of digging my claws into the wood.

Let him look at *me* all he likes. I can hold my other urges in check, but I'm not letting him subject her to his malicious stare.

Sylas's voice goes firmer. "It is, and she is part of our business here. We'll take our leave of you. I assume we can count on being undisturbed?"

Eldris scowls at me, and I stand there immovable, glowering right back at him. After a moment, he jerks his gaze back to Sylas. I get the sense he's bitten back a few things he might have wanted to say to me if he weren't faced with the son he actually values with all the authority that son now wields.

"I'm pleased I could be of service," he says, only a hint of annoyance leaking into his formal tone. "You will have the pond to yourself."

He draws back, and Sylas returns to the carriage. I stay where I am, poised in front of Talia by the edge of the canopy, until the vehicle glides forward and Eldris hustles back into his castle.

That's one minor challenge we've dealt with. There's far more than I'd like to measure still ahead for us to tackle.

CHAPTER THREE

Talia

As Sylas directs our carriage toward this magical pool, my brief observations of my lovers' father replay in my mind. I've heard enough about him to know I wouldn't want to spend any more time around him than I have to, so I should have been prepared, but my skin is still crawling from the brief encounter. The way he spoke to Sylas with no trace of genuine fatherly warmth—the way he totally ignored his other two sons while they were right there in front of him—and the cool calculation in his expression when his gaze settled on me…

A shiver passes through me. August sits back down beside me and tucks his arm around my back. The tightness of his mouth shows that he didn't enjoy that interaction any more than I did.

Whitt leans back against the wall of the carriage, turning his face to the wind so it ruffles his sunkissed-brown hair. "Looks like the joys of fathering an arch-lord didn't distract the paternal pissant from his obsessions for more than an instant. Here's to another century or so before we require any further dealings with that dung-heap."

Sylas shoots him a chiding glance, but he doesn't dispute Whitt's commentary. He's told me he couldn't call the man I just saw a bad father as far as he was concerned, but I know he hates a lot of things about the ways their father has ruled.

Nevertheless, they all handled the conversation with poised control, none of them sinking to the other man's level to show their contempt in return. Lord Eldris might have fathered them and had a hand in raising them, but they've clearly risen far above anything they could have learned from him. Thinking of their strength, I reach to squeeze August's hand. After what that man did to his mother, this meeting must have been hardest for him out of all of them.

"You could put out a word surreptitiously via your typical methods," Sylas says to Whitt. "See that anyone who'd rather not remain under his tyranny knows they'd be welcome at Hearth-by-the-Heart."

Whitt inclines his head with the faintest of smiles. "I'll make sure the word gets out without him catching wind of it."

I guess our current pack-kin must mostly be fae who left with Sylas and his brothers when they founded Hearthshire. The others must not have disliked Lord Eldris's approach enough to switch their loyalties, but maybe a few of them have changed their minds in the time since. Our pack must be awfully small for an arch-lord. The men have said their numbers dwindled after they were banished, and I've seen how many people arch-lords like Ambrose had at their disposal.

Sylas urges the carriage faster again, and I tip my head against August's shoulder. The wind ripples over my hair—and a fragment of a forceful voice breaks through the mass of light I've pulled together inside me.

—have to listen to me. We can't just—

My pulse hiccups. Closing my eyes, I wrench more of the glowing sensation into the center of me. Let it burn out any impressions trying to slip through and seal over the hole inside me.

I focus on that place until the light feels like a thick, solid thing, a wall as blazing as the sun. It's only when I open my eyes that I feel the sweat that's broken out on my forehead, cooling my skin.

August rubs my arm. "He tried to reach you again?"

I nod, too exhausted in that moment to form words, and snuggle close to my lover. How much longer am I going to have to fight this connection?

How much longer *can* I fight it before I'm completely worn out?

August holds me tight until the carriage slows. We've passed into a stretch of pinkish rocky terrain dotted with tufts of sea-green grass that glitters when the sun's beams hit it. A faint ozone-y scent lingers in the air as if a thunderstorm has just passed, though there hasn't been any rain.

The pool lies directly ahead of us, an oval of water surrounded by a glossy stone bank. The pond's surface is so smooth it looks more like a mirror reflecting the sky above than anything I could dip my hand into.

As I watch it, a breeze trickles across it, rippling the reflection. The water returns to stillness just moments later. It's so eerie, the hairs on the back of my neck rise.

We walk up to it, our boots thumping on the hard ground. Sylas motions for me to sit at the narrowest point on the oval, right at the water's edge.

"Each person can only see their own past, and the pool will only show what you ask it for, however it can best interpret that," he says. "You'll have to look and tell us what you observe."

I inhale slowly, bracing my hands against the marble-like surface beneath me. "And I should ask about anything to do with the fae—any ways I might have been influenced by magic without realizing it?"

"Exactly. But follow your gut. You know your life far better than any of us. There's no limit to how much the pool will show you if you keep making new requests, so take your time and try anything that occurs to you."

"All right." With my legs crossed, I scoot a little closer until my knees jut over the pool. Then I lean over to peer into the motionless water.

My face stares back at me, even paler than usual with dark smudges beneath my eyes. I didn't sleep much last night, jerking awake every hour or two with fears that my barrier of light was failing, building it back up before I could even start to relax again. Not even seeing the dark pink hair August gave me months ago with a combination of magic and fruit-based dye raises my spirits. I tuck a few stray strands behind my ear as I decide where to start.

Why not go back to the beginning? The sage said that my connection to the curse was something passed on through my family. Were there signs of it when I was born, when I was so young that I wouldn't remember?

"Show me when I was first born," I say to the water.

A shimmer skims across the pool's surface, and my reflection falls away into darkness. But no other images emerge. I'm just staring into flat blackness.

I frown. "It isn't showing me anything. It's just gone dark."

Sylas hums, peering into the pool from beside me even though he said he wouldn't be able to see what the water presented to me. "Perhaps it's taking your statement a bit too literally in the sense of when you'd be considered fully 'born'?"

Nuldar's words come back to me. *She started in darkness. Then she came out into the light.* Is the pool being equally obtuse?

"Show my mother holding me when I was a baby," I say, and then quickly add, "less than a month old. When it was light out." Hopefully that narrows it down enough.

The darkness pulls back. And there before my eyes is Mom, swaying from side to side and back and forth in a wavering circular motion. Pale sunlight spills over her from a window beyond my view. A round head with a smattering of brown hair pokes from a tightly wrapped blanket in her arms.

My chest hitches. That's me. That's me with my mother. I can only see her profile, and she's younger than in any of my memories—but I'd almost started to forget what she looked like in all the years since then. This glimpse of her brings so many moments with my family back into startling clarity.

She looks tired, her dark hair rumpled and her eyelids drooping, but she's smiling at my infant self. There's a joyful glow in her face that wrenches at my heart. I find myself blinking hard.

It's been almost a decade since I saw that smile aimed at me, heard Mom's soft laugh or the tsk of her tongue. I have the wild urge to throw myself into the water as if I'd somehow crash into her embrace.

But she's not really there. She's not really anywhere. Aerik and his cadre tore her to pieces along with Dad and Jamie.

My hands clench the rocky lip of the pool.

"Do you see something now?" Sylas asks gently.

Right. I'm here for a reason, not just to reminisce about what I've lost. I clamp down on the rush of emotions and study the image as well as I can. My voice manages to come out steady. "Yes. My mother, holding me. Rocking me to sleep, I think. She had this funny way of doing it—she told me that the first couple of weeks I cried so much she was afraid I had colic, but she tried all kinds of things and finally found this specific motion that calmed me right down."

My lips twitch at the memory. Whenever I started complaining too much when I was older, she joked that she'd have to scoop me up and give me a good rocking. *If it worked when you were two weeks old, I'm sure it'll work now.* In my protesting or laughter, I often forgot whatever I'd been whining about.

August has hunkered down nearby. He strokes his hand up and down my back. Sylas's jaw clenches as if he hesitates to press further, but he goes on anyway. "Is there anything unusual that you notice?"

I peer at the image as intently as I can, keeping a tight hold on my emotions. I can only make out hazy impressions of the room around my mother and me, but it looks like an ordinary children's bedroom. Nothing strikes me as odd about her or me. "No."

I feel more than see Whitt come up behind me. "Ask it to show you one of the times when you were crying, like you mentioned."

Does he think there's something odd about that? I fix my gaze on the water, letting go of the desire to just keep staring at Mom as she is there now forever. "Show me when I was with my mom as a baby crying."

The image wavers and bleeds into another. My mom is hustling me into the house, bundled up in a stroller. The pool doesn't emit any sound, but it's obvious from the ruddiness of my infant face and the shape of my mouth that I'm wailing my heart out. Mom's lips form a shushing sound as she scrambles to undo the straps.

There's still nothing remotely magical or otherwise strange about the scene. I shake my head in anticipation of Sylas's question.

At the edge of my vision, he glances toward Whitt. The spymaster must be satisfied, because Sylas gives the next instruction. "I'd say focus on asking about the fae influence in your life next."

That sounds reasonable. I watch Mom tucking my infant self into her arms for a moment longer, absorbing every detail of her I can make out, and then force out the words to send her away. "Show me the first time I was affected by the fae."

The previous scene is swallowed into the same blackness my first request brought. I wait a few seconds, but the darkness doesn't change. "Nothing again," I say. "I guess the first time I was affected was before I was even born. Um, show me the first time I was affected by the fae *after* I was born."

Only more darkness, stretching across the pool. I knit my brow. "Still nothing. Maybe that means I wasn't ever directly affected, however it's interpreting that word?"

Whitt lets out an irritable sound. "So convenient, these wizened sages and magical places. Try phrasing it as when you first *saw* a fae, so we'll know there should be a visual."

I give the water my best *You'd better start behaving* glare. "Show me when I first saw a fae."

The darkness shatters apart into a dimly lit scene of a preteen girl giggling as she jogs between a couple of trees—just as a massive furred shape leaps out of the shadows.

My heart hurtles into my throat. I choke on it, my breath fading to a rasp with the constricting of my lungs. Icy panic clutches my chest.

I squeeze my eyes shut, but it's too late. I've already watched the beast with the tawny fur sink its jaws into my 12-year-old self's shoulder where scars still mark my skin today, seen the shriek in the contorting of my mouth, and caught the gangly figure of my eight-year-old brother just coming into view with another monstrous wolf charging straight toward him.

"Talia!" August says, alarm ringing through his voice.

I'm rocking against his supporting hand. My breath is still seeping out of me in gasps. I press backward into his touch harder and slam my palms against the smooth stone, training every bit of my attention onto those solid surfaces.

This is what's real. This is what's now. The rest—the rest is done. It's over with.

It's running through my mind so vividly the scars on my shoulder sting.

Other hands rest on my back, my head. Sylas's steady baritone breaks through the haze of panic. "We're here with you, Talia. No one can hurt you. Whatever you saw, it won't happen again."

I manage to drag in a deeper breath. The images retreat but don't fade completely.

And then another voice splits through them from within. *Talia? What happened? Are you all right? Please, if you would just speak to me—*

The Unseelie arch-lord—in my fluster, the light walling off our connection faltered. How much of my distress did he feel? If it was even half of it—

I don't want this total stranger, this enemy of my lovers and my pack, seeing so much of me. My body recoils from the inside out.

No! I shout at him inwardly, and visualize every particle of light I can summon swelling through my torso, blocking him out.

When that's done, I open my eyes, dragging in another ragged gulp of air. I'm not rocking anymore, only trembling. I can't tell how much that's from the aftermath of the scene the pool showed me and how much from the effort it took rebuilding my inner wall.

Then one new fact catches up with me, hitting me hard enough that I speak without thinking. "He knows my name."

Sylas brushes his fingers over my temple. "Who? What did you see?"

"It's not— There was nothing useful in the pool." I make a rough gesture toward the water. "It was the night when Aerik attacked me, just like I remember it, nothing I'd forgotten. I'm sorry. I should have realized I might see that—I should be able to handle it better—"

Whitt's knuckles graze the back of my neck as he gives my hair an affectionate tug, cutting off my apology. "You don't have to be that mighty, Talia. No one here is going to blame you for carrying scars inside any more than we do the ones on the outside."

Will I never be able to recall that horrible night without a panic coming on, just like the marks on my shoulder will never disappear? The thought makes my stomach twist, but I haven't actually answered Sylas's question yet.

I look up at the fae lord. "When I panicked, the barrier I put up over my soul-twined connection weakened. I think the Unseelie arch-lord felt some of it. And he tried to talk to me again—he used my name."

No sign of concern crosses Sylas's face. He simply drops his hand to caress my cheek. "That's not surprising. If he didn't hear it when we were first determining what had happened back by the Heart, he might have just now. You couldn't expect to keep something that basic from him for very long."

Right. Because fae men destroyed my past life, and now another is attempting to take over my current existence. My throat tightens all over again.

I draw my knees up to my chest, hugging my legs. "If Aerik's attack was the first time I saw any fae, what else can I ask?" What if it all goes back to my great-grandfather and whatever fae heritage he had?

Whitt's hand goes still against my spine. "I think we've put her through enough, don't you two?"

Sylas pauses. "Now that we've come all the way out here, we should try everything we can think of."

"What else is there? We've already forced her to re-experience the worst moment in her life." Whitt leans in to press a kiss to the back of my head. I reach to twine my fingers with his. There was a rawness in his voice that reminds me he had to dredge up what might have been the worst moment in *his* life not that long ago.

I defended him then, and now he's trying to protect me.

"It's all right," I say quietly. "I want to give it my best shot. I'll just be more prepared this time—if it looks like I'm going back to the attack, I'll look away."

The spymaster lets out a soft growl. "Fine. Do what you have to do. But something's occurred to me that might work better."

August perks up. "What's that?"

Whitt is silent for a moment. "It won't be easy or fun. But it doesn't matter *why* this happened if we can make it so it never happened. I may know of someone who can break a soul-twined bond."

CHAPTER FOUR

Whitt

I know we've almost reached the spot when the humidity gets so thick the air might as well have turned to soup. This section of the fringes is a swampland, and the closer we get to the outermost edges of the Mists, the more the slimy water beneath our carriage seeps up from the ground to saturate the space above. It carries a scent like mildew and algae that makes me wrinkle my nose.

I'm going to need not one but several showers the moment I'm back at the castle.

Talia peers into the drifting fog. A shiver she can't hide runs through her delicate frame. "There's a jail around here somewhere?"

"Not a jail." I scan the hunched, half-submerged trees and the bubbling patches of water. "She's a solo prisoner. The lord she offended had a grave enough case that the arch-lords agreed to not only banish her out here alone for the foreseeable future but also to place her under indentured servitude."

"Servitude doing *what*?"

"There are fish that live only in this swampland that are a delicacy among the fae, brought out for special occasions. From what I've heard, they have her hunting them, with a certain quota to be met each month." I grimace. "It won't be pleasant work. There's a reason they're a rare delicacy. As far as I know, no fae has ever been able to 'commune' with them well enough to learn their true name, and their scales repel magic. No one much enjoys going up against their many sharp teeth."

Talia outright shudders. "How long has she been stuck out here?"

"Coming up on four centuries. I wouldn't be sure she's even still here if it weren't for the barbtooth filets that were included in our glorious leader's coronation feast."

Reasonably sure, anyway. And I'm less certain of how exactly we'll find her. I murmur a few words designed to resonate with any magic around us, since presumably the woman has used her skills to build some sort of shelter and other amenities even if they won't help her with her duties. A faint twinge leads me to redirect the carriage.

Talia pulls back from the bow to sit on the bench across from me. We've drawn back the carriage's canopy, since the hazy sunlight that filters through the overcast sky and the fog gives the impression of dusk even though it's mid-day. She closes her eyes for a second, I suspect adding to her internal defenses. My fingers clench around the rim of the hull.

When she opens her eyes again, she looks at me far more wearily than I'd prefer to see. "And this is the only fae who's ever managed to break a soul-twined bond?"

"To the best of my knowledge. I only have it on third-hand authority that breaking a bond was her crime. The lord and his lady in question stayed on as mates and acted as though they were as bonded as ever until their deaths. The exact matter they brought before the arch-lords was kept quiet. But you know I have many sources always on the lookout for those with loose tongues."

"What did your source say happened?"

"He mentioned that someone or other claimed that the woman we're seeking was in love with the lord. She was supposedly so jealous when he found his soul-twined mate that she went to excruciating lengths to discover a method that would shatter that connection." I cluck my tongue. "I can't imagine the depths she must have stooped to —or whether she still thinks it was worth it."

Watching Talia, I can't hold onto the nonchalance I put into my tone. Her suffering is no laughing matter. I've kept the tension wound through my innards at bay by focusing on the schemes we've come up with to help her, but in moments like this, when there's nothing to do but wait for the current scheme to come to fruition, I can't tune it out completely.

I'd like nothing more than to wrap my hands around the neck of that blasted bird-brain arch-lord and squeeze until there was no soul left for her to be bound to.

Talia holds my gaze with such a pensive cast to her eyes that when she opens her mouth to speak again, I ready myself to tackle some new calamity.

"Are you doing okay?" she asks.

I blink at her, momentarily struck speechless with surprise. "I'm pretty sure I'm the one who's supposed to be asking *you* that question."

Her mouth twists. "I just mean—I know you were still dealing with having all that stuff about Isleen brought up after so long, and things have been tense between you and Sylas. Just because we have other problems doesn't mean yours don't matter anymore."

The mention of my relations with my lord's late soul-twined mate and his feelings about that encounter stirs up a clash of emotion that's becoming unpleasantly familiar. But it only lingers for an instant before the deluge of awed affection that sweeps through me at the same time washes most of the rest away.

I appear to have lost my capacity for words completely now. I reach out to Talia, and she comes to me without hesitation, slipping into my embrace with her head against my shoulder and her legs tucked over my lap as if she were made to fit against me. Hugging her, I dip my head to inhale the tartly sweet scent of her.

This incredible woman. Worried about *me* while she's grappling with a disaster none of us can protect her from. The jolt of shock that hit me when she first told me she loved me seems absurd now. That love radiates from her with every gesture from the squeeze of her arm around my chest to the kiss she brushes to my jaw.

She's seen every part of who I am, including the bits I never wanted to show her, and she's stood by me when even I wouldn't stand for myself.

A large part of me is still far from convinced that I deserve anywhere near the compassion she's shown me, or that the drugged tryst I tumbled into with Sylas's mate isn't my crime but only Isleen's—that I haven't fucked up in *some* way beyond what any rational being would respond to with mercy. I've been carrying the guilt for so long that it's grown roots all through me, and tearing them up has unearthed all sorts of other uncomfortable pangs.

But I'm still here. Sylas hasn't seen fit to cast me out or rend me apart after hearing the full account, and he's possibly the most rational fae in my acquaintance. If I didn't know better, I'd be inclined to say our mighty human has cast a spell over us all that included saving me. There's no denying there's some kind of magic to the feel of holding her against me.

I've never given much thought to love. After the first few rounds of temptresses hoping to score a prized position in Sylas's court through their association with me, I dismissed the possibility as something that wouldn't factor into my life, and I can't say I've anguished over that decision. But now…

What else could I call this unceasing welling of affection and desire from some spring deep inside me? The thought of a wretched raven having any sort of claim on her brings my wolf lunging to the surface.

Talia was meant to be our mate, *my* mate—to stand by me and my brothers for decades more to come. Longer, if I have any say in it with the magic this world can offer.

And even if not that, she deserves so much better than to be torn in two from the inside out by a murderous villain who probably has ice in his veins.

But Talia isn't thinking about any of that right now. She's still worrying about me. She strokes her fingers down the side of my neck, waking up a heat much more pleasant than the sticky humidity wrapped around us. "You haven't answered me. Are you okay?"

She's incredible and also incredibly stubborn. I let out a rough sound and lower my lips to kiss her temple. "I expect it'll take some time getting to 'okay,' but at least I *can* get there properly now that those secrets are out in the open. I still—" Just talking about it revives the clashing emotions. "I have many regrets that I haven't fully come to terms with, and I can't blame Sylas for feeling betrayed that I kept so much from him even if he absolves me of my greatest theoretical crime."

Talia nuzzles me. "I don't think he'll hold that against you for very long. It was understandable that you didn't know how to bring up the subject."

"I suppose. But also… somewhat bizarrely, I find I'm a little angry with *him*. Which isn't exactly fair, because I should be glad the idea that I'd have been involved in Isleen's unfaithfulness was so unbelievable to him that he never considered it, but if he'd simply dealt with *her* betrayal to begin with, it could have all come into the open so much sooner."

"I think he's pretty angry with himself about that too."

"Yes. Well. And as I said, it's hardly fair. But that feeling is there along with everything else. I suppose it's just a matter of continuing to go forward and work together until the broken edges of this division between us smooth out and fit back together more easily again." I pause, considering. "I don't know exactly how long that'll take, but we do have a long time. I trust that we'll get there."

"Good." Talia brushes one more kiss to my cheek and then turns her head to glance out over the swamp.

We both spot the light at the same time—I can tell from the tensing of her body. It's only a reddish glimmer through the fog, but it's no natural part of the landscape around us. We've found our fae convict.

Talia eases away from me so I can stand. I walk to the bow, adjusting the carriage's path with a gesture of my hand. I assume a casual stance, but my spine has gone rigid.

I don't expect what we find here to be pretty. I'd have embarked on this journey alone if Talia hadn't insisted with that stubborn spirit of hers on keeping me company. *You're doing this for my benefit*, she said. *I should be there.*

The fog thins to reveal a patch of solid, muddy ground holding a shack formed out of woven reeds, which sag here and there with patches of rot. The reddish light is a magically-charged fire flickering in a ring of stones near the door. As I motion the carriage to a halt, a figure emerges from the shack with a combative stride and a spear clutched in her hand.

It's worse than I anticipated. Four centuries in this fringe swamp wouldn't do anyone good, and it's clearly punished the woman before me in all sorts of ways. The deep, angry scars of piercing teeth mark her limbs, even her chin and cheeks. One of her ears is outright missing amid the ragged strands of her hair, and she's lost three fingers and more than half of her nose as well.

But perhaps the worst is that the same rot that appears to be spreading through her home has infected her as well. Dark brownish-green hollows seep into her bare arms, calves, neck, and face alongside the scars, as if the swamp has made her its home as much as the reverse. My gut recoils.

The woman raises her spear and snarls. "You're not the usual one—and it's not the right time. What do you want here?"

I hold up my hands in a gesture of peace. "I'm not here to make any demands or cause you any trouble. I simply have a few questions to ask. And I've brought gifts to compensate you for your time."

I bend down—carefully, so as not to appear threatening—and raise the large basket some of our pack-kin put together without knowing its destination. The woman's bloodshot eyes rove over the block of cheese, the fresh-baked pastries, the gleaming mirrornuts, and the bottle of dusk-apple wine.

As much as the fish she catches are a delicacy to the fae who can afford them, the common foods I've brought will be a treasure to her. Her diet won't have been comprised of much more than aquatic creatures and swamp plants in close to four hundred years.

She licks her mottled lips, revealing a flash of fangs. Then she turns the spear so she's holding it like a staff rather than a weapon, her fingers clenched around it. "What do you want to know?" Her gaze flicks past me to Talia still crouched on the bench.

I snap my fingers to bring her attention back to me. Better we get this over with quickly. "I've had it that the crime you're being punished for involved the severing of a soul-twined bond. Is that true?"

The stiffening of her posture suggests it is, but her lips press flat too. She glowers at me. "I'm not to speak of my crime."

I wave her objection off. "What can they possibly do to you that's worse than this? Besides, I come on the request of one of the arch-lords as his cadre-chosen." I produce a token from my pocket that gleams with a power only those with the closest bond to the Heart can access.

The woman studies it for several seconds. Her shoulders come down. She eyes the basket and then my face. Her voice comes out much less strident than before. "All right. Yes. What about it?"

"I want to know, if an arch-lord requested it, if you could do it again."

Her jaw slackens. She composes herself again with a shake of her thin frame. "Your lord wants me to—to break another soul-twined bond?"

"Perhaps. It depends somewhat on the process involved." We're assuming it would be much more expedient to have someone who's learned the magic already carry it out rather than asking her to try to teach something so obscure and presumably difficult to one of us.

"Well, I—I suppose I could. I believe I remember all that's required, or at least how to remind myself. There hasn't been much to think about out here other than my life before." She rubs her mouth. "You can tell your lord it could be done, but he may not like the results."

I raise my eyebrows. "What do you mean by that?"

"The only method I found—and I did try—I didn't *want* to hurt him…" She pauses, her gaze drifting away, and then appears to gather herself. "It's very painful for both parties. Neither… Neither may come out as whole as they were when the bond formed. I think something in each goes into the connection and then is burned away with it."

A chill prickles down my back. I don't like the sound of *that* at all. Although— "What if the bond hasn't been confirmed and consummated yet?"

She lets out a hoarse bark of a laugh. "The magic I know won't work at all then. It draws on the power of the bond to turn it around on itself… If the connection isn't fully formed, I won't have anywhere near enough energy to apply. It's a close thing as it is."

"Ah." My heart sinks. I grope for another question or suggestion, but her last statement cuts off most other avenues. The only thing left to ask is, "Would you need anything other than the presence of the bonded pair?"

"There are a few supplies, things I'm sure an arch-lord could arrange." Her expression turns more calculating. "Better I don't spell too much of it out for you or I'll have nothing left to bargain with, will I?"

A fair point. I direct the carriage a little closer so I can hand the basket to her. "Thank you. I'll return should we decide we're in need of your services, and I'm sure if we are you can expect a far more extensive reward."

She snatches the basket and hurtles into her shack. As I back the carriage away and turn it to leave, the sounds of teeth gnashing into the gifted food carry through the frail walls.

I wait until the shack and its occupant are well behind us and the carriage steady on its way before I return to Talia's side. She's staring straight ahead, her eyes unnervingly glazed, her hands twisted together in her lap. For an instant, I think she may be caught up in some sort of vision through her soul-twined bond, but her gaze slides to me when I join her.

Her voice sounds as brittle as charred paper. "What does it mean to confirm and consummate a bond?"

Of course she has to ask that. I swipe my hand back through my hair, my stomach knotting. "There's a brief ceremony in which you acknowledge and accept the bond with words and magic. And then you accept your mate with your body as well. Only after both happen is the connection complete."

A tremor runs through her. "It gets even *stronger* than this?"

I have no idea what she's already experienced. I ease my arm around her shoulders, hating how poor a comfort the gesture must be. "Sylas was still able to dull his. From what I understand, it gives you a greater ability to convey thoughts and impressions you *want* to pass on, and brings those of your mate into greater clarity when you focus on them."

Talia nods, a defeated motion. Her arms come up to fold over her chest. Her whole body closes in on itself: her head drooping, her jaw clenching, her shoulders drawing tight, her knees pressing together. Trying to hold in what a moment later comes spilling out anyway.

A sob wrenches from her throat. She claps her hands to her face, but the sudden flood of tears streams past them, down her cheeks and her wrists. Her gasps for air shake her entire frame.

Her misery tears right through my chest. I scoop her up and hug her tightly against me, caressing her hair, absorbing her weeping as well as I can, which isn't very well at all. I can't remember the last time *I* cried, but tears prick at my own eyes on her behalf.

I've never seen her break down like this. Even when she was huddled in Aerik's horrid cage, even when she had to come face to face with that prick and his minions afterward, even when the arch-lord whose place Sylas took threatened to use her as breeding stock—throughout all the torments and indignities she's faced in my presence, she's never bawled her heart out as she's doing now.

Seeing just how much anguish she's been holding in, I realize I didn't appreciate how much strength she's been expending over the past few days. My fangs emerge, gritting against each other with dark thoughts of all the many ways I'd like to apply them to the feathered bastard who's brought her this low.

The only words I can think of to say, nowhere near adequate, tumble out of me in a murmured string. "I've got you. *We've* got you. Whatever we have to do, we'll figure it out. None of us is going to leave you while you're facing this."

Talia's breath hitches. She paws at her eyes, but the tears keep gushing out. All I can do is hold her and murmur those pale reassurances to her over and over until the torrent finally ebbs.

When her sobs have dwindled to sniffles, she cringes against me. "I'm sorry," she whispers hoarsely.

Somehow the apology makes me twice as furious as before. I kiss the top of her head, hugging her with all the adoration I have in me. "*You* have nothing to be sorry for. By all that is dust, mite, it's a wonder you've held yourself together as well as you have up until now. Not one bit of this changes how mighty I think you are."

She manages a short, watery-sounding laugh. "I just—after all that time with Aerik, everything I've been through since then was at least *better*. It was hard to get too upset when I knew how much worse I'd endured. But this…"

Her voice breaks, and she pauses, swallowing audibly. "It's like I've been caged all over again. Except even more than before, because it's not just my body that's trapped but my mind, my soul—there isn't any part of me that can get away. Not when the person I'm trying to get away from can reach me from right inside me. And to have any chance of getting out of it, I'd have to let him in even *more*. We don't even know for sure that I'd survive the magic she was talking about if it'd hurt even a true-blooded fae."

All of that is true. None of the anguish spreading through my own body can change it.

I love this woman, and I might lose her.

I hold her and press my lips to her forehead, hoping she's taking at least a small measure of comfort from my embrace. "Whatever it takes, whatever I have to give, I won't stop until I've done everything I can to figure out how to get us out of this catastrophe."

Heart help me find the way to protect her as much as she's been here for me.

CHAPTER FIVE

Talia

The grass ripples around me in a sunlit field, the scattered daisies swaying with the breeze. Pale glimmers drift on the currents. It takes me a moment to recognize them as snowflakes, impossibly tumbling down from the clear sky.

This is a dream. The awareness of that fact creeps up over me as I turn on my feet, taking in the hazy sensations, the lack of pain in my foot even though I'm not wearing my brace. It's a *good* dream for once, without vicious teeth or splattered blood, just me and—

My legs stiffen in mid-swivel. I back up a step, staring at the figure who was standing behind me: the Unseelie arch-lord who's been invading my mind for the past few days.

Maybe this is a nightmare after all.

But the fae man doesn't make any move toward me, just gazes at me from where he's poised several feet away. His posture is straight and formal, but his expression looks more concerned than hostile. If he's angry at me for how much I've been blocking him, he isn't showing it.

My heart thumps against my ribs, but it is only a dream. He can't hurt me. So I hold myself in place and study him like he's studying me.

His bronze-brown skin is as smooth as I remember, broken only by the darker lines of the true-name tattoos that unfurl up from the corner of his jaw, down his neck, and across the backs of his hands. No hint of gray shows in the blue-black hair that curls around the peaks of his sharply pointed ears, but I get the impression he's a little older than I assumed when I saw him next to his stately colleagues. Older than August or Arch-Lord Donovan at least, maybe closer to Sylas's age. There's a solemnity in his dark eyes and the set of his jaw that suggests a certain amount of experience—and not all of that experience good.

He's dressed less formally than he was when I saw him before. Ivory trousers and a trim, dove-gray tunic with just a smattering of silver embroidery clothe his tall, lean frame, which is less brawny than my wolfish men but emanates understated strength.

He doesn't have his expansive raven-like wings out now. I guess the Unseelie probably keep those restrained most of the time like the Seelie do their fangs and claws, only revealing them to threaten or intimidate.

In that way of dreams, I simply know that he's dreaming this too—that we're still far apart in actuality. He's slipped his way through my barrier of light into my mind yet again.

My shoulders tense. I close my eyes, willing myself to wake up so I can rebuild that wall, but nothing happens. The falling snow tickles my arms with specks of cold. The summery breeze licks over my skin, warming me again.

"Talia," the Unseelie man says quietly, his voice cool and as smooth as his burnished skin. "I know you must be startled by this connection. I am too. But the bond is there. We can't simply dismiss it. I believe it would do us some good to talk it over—to see what we can make of it."

I raise my eyebrows at him defiantly. "Did you make this dream happen because I wouldn't let you in while I'm awake?"

He shakes his head in a subtle movement. "I wasn't expecting to meet you like this either. But with the bond tying us together, it isn't surprising that we'd find even some of our dreams merging."

Frustration grips me. I cross my arms tightly in front of me. "I don't want this. I don't want *any* of it. You hate the Seelie. You've been attacking us—your people have *killed* my pack-kin."

The fae man's mouth tightens. "I—" He pauses, looking as if he's holding back a frown. "You were with the new Seelie arch-lord—Sylas. You're of his pack."

"I am." It's true enough. He doesn't need to know exactly what role I play in that pack or among the rest of the Seelie. If the Unseelie knew just how valuable I am to their enemies—

I clamp down on that thought with a shiver. What if this man can pick up on my thoughts as well as what I say out loud?

He doesn't give any sign that he's noticed my concern, though. "If the arch-lords brought on your lord to replace the one they lost, then they must have trusted him. Has he said anything about a note of warning?"

My pulse hiccups. Sylas told us that the arch-lords had gotten a note that appeared to have been left by someone from the Unseelie side, warning them about the raven shifters' plans for an attack during the full moon. Whoever did that went against their own rulers to help us, whether they regret that now after the summer fae were able to beat the Unseelie warriors back or not. Is the arch-lord attempting to figure out who betrayed him?

"I don't know everything the other arch-lords have shared with him," I hedge.

"Well—perhaps you could speak to him about it, and he can confirm. I don't agree with many of the tactics my colleagues have been taking, but my vote is only one out of five. To strike out when you couldn't even defend yourselves…" He gives that little shake of his head again. "I couldn't let your people face it unaware."

My jaw drops. "*You* left the note?" I realize after the words have already spilled out that I've just admitted to knowing about it, but I'm too overwhelmed by shock. This man, this *arch-lord*, warned us against his own people?

He inclines his head. A glimmer of what might be pain shines in his eyes. "I did. I didn't anticipate the results being quite so catastrophic for our own, but—they wouldn't listen when I made my case against the assault. There was going to be too much blood shed either way. As much as I hated to see the results, we brought it on ourselves by sinking so low."

As I take that in, a sudden prickling of guilt fills my stomach. All the horrible things I've thought about him, all the assumptions I've made… but how could I have known?

My arms loosen where I was hugging myself. "Thank you," I have to say.

A muscle at his jaw ticks, and it occurs to me that he's just revealed a secret to me that could end his entire career, if not his life, if his fellow arch-lords found out. Not that I have any means of telling them or any desire to. But he doesn't know me that well yet.

And still he trusted me enough to say it. Because earning *my* trust meant that much to him.

"Obviously you should ensure that information doesn't get back to any of my brethren," he says, a little stiffly. I think he's trying to avoid showing how precarious a position he feels he's put himself in. "It would be to your people's benefit as well as mine if I could continue to speak up for a more peaceful resolution to the present conflict."

"Of course." I open my mouth and close it again, unsure of what else to say. Even if he isn't a monster, I don't want to be tied to him like this. Can't he understand that?

No, he probably can't. He'll have lived his whole life as a true-blooded fae knowing that he'd meet his soul-twined mate eventually. He was ready for this, maybe even looking forward to it.

Whatever he imagined, I know I can't possibly be it.

He takes a step closer, and I manage not to shrink back. "Talia," he starts, and I'm struck by the discomfort of how familiarly he says my name, as if I offered it to him rather than having it stolen out of my awareness.

"I don't even know *your* name," I blurt out.

He blinks, looking briefly taken aback, but his cool composure returns a moment later. "Corwin," he says. "Corwin of Heart's Cadence. I apologize—it is… strange, feeling so close and yet knowing each other so little."

No kidding. But the fact that he's acknowledged the strangeness lets me relax a smidgeon more. I try out the sound of his name. "Corwin. Yes, it is strange."

A different sort of light flickers through his face, something hopeful if fleeting. "I don't want to tear you from your home. I don't want… I don't want this unexpected bond to harm either of us. But can you see that it could be a good thing for both our peoples? A chance to find more of a common ground, to ease the tensions—build a bridge between summer and winter, a demonstration of unity. I think that's worth giving a try."

A lump rises in my throat. He makes it sound so easy. He has no idea—there's *so much* about my life he doesn't know.

Corwin steps even nearer. "All I'm suggesting is that we give it a fair chance. See what comes of it. I understand there would need to be compromises made, but that isn't impossible."

He raises his hand, his fingers grazing my forearm, and a jolt of sensation shoots through my nerves like a burst of sparks. I gasp for air, half of me compelled to lean into his touch, the other half gripped by the urge to wrench myself away.

From the widening of Corwin's eyes, I don't think he was prepared for this either. Emotions that aren't mine trickle through the turmoil rising inside me: uncertainty and alarm but also a glimmer of joy.

That last impression brings me back to myself, to the echo of joys past it stirs in me. I jerk my arm away, stumbling backward, my heart outright hammering now.

"I can't— It isn't—" I heave in a breath, fighting to get my protest out with some kind of coherence. "It isn't just about giving this a try. I already—there are people here I love. I don't want to leave them. We were going to be mated…"

I trail off at the flinch Corwin doesn't manage to restrain. He masters his expression an instant later, but it's too much—the pain my admission caused him echoing into me, the fact that we're twined enough to be having this conversation at all. Driven by instinct and panic, I whirl around and fling myself away from him—

—and wake up with a hitch of breath in my bedroom in Hearthshire.

I'm not alone here either, but at least my present company is much more wanted. As I sit up, clutching the covers around my legs and swiping my hand across my eyes, Sylas rises from the armchair across from the bed, his massive form unmistakeable even in the thin moonlight that's the room's only illumination.

"Are you all right?" he asks. "You didn't sound distressed, but you were murmuring in your sleep—I was keeping watch in case one of your nightmares took hold."

"I—" I cut myself off, at a loss for how to explain what just happened while my mind is still whirling. Reaching inside me, I summon up another shield of light to block off my connection to Corwin. I'm not sensing anything from him right now—maybe he's still sleeping—but even if I find him less horrifying than before, I don't want him sneaking peeks into my thoughts or my conversations.

"When did you get back from the Heart?" I say instead. Whitt brought me to Hearthshire on the fae lord's orders—we agreed that I'd feel more secure on familiar ground rather than in the unfinished rooms of the castle still under construction. Sylas, of course, needs to uphold his new duties as arch-lord. My situation has already disrupted that transition plenty.

"About an hour ago," he says, which judging by the dark sky beyond my window means he traveled through the night. "As soon as I could reasonably get away. Whitt said that your venture did not prove as helpful as we'd hoped."

A broken laugh falls from my lips. No, it didn't. Not at all. But thinking about it brings a fresh burn into the backs of my eyes. I'm afraid if I try to say much about it, I'll burst into tears all over again. It's bad enough that I melted down in front of Whitt. I have to hold it together better than that.

I'm *stronger* than that. I know I am, as helpless as I felt after hearing what that unsettling fae woman had to say about breaking the bond. And really, talking to Corwin in the shared dream has left me calmer as everything he told me sinks in.

I hold my hand out to Sylas, and he sinks onto the bed next to me, opening his arms so I can tuck myself into his embrace. I lean my head against his solid chest, absorbing his warmth and his smoky, earthy scent. The words work their way up my throat.

"I had a dream with the Unseelie arch-lord. He was dreaming it too. We talked a little."

Sylas hugs me closer. "If he threatened you in any way—"

"No. He was actually very… kind about it. It was important to him that we talk, but he didn't try to push for anything else." I pause. "He knew about the note that warned the arch-lords about the full-moon attack. He said he's the one who left it for them, that he's been trying to convince the other Unseelie arch-lords to stop the fighting. It sounded like he was telling the truth. I mean, he couldn't have known about the note otherwise, right?"

Sylas hums, a rumble reverberating through his chest into me. "If they caught the one who betrayed them, they might have found out. He could be using that knowledge to convince you to trust him. Did he phrase it in a way that only *implied* he sent it, or did he say it outright?"

His voice stays mild, just stating a possibility rather than insisting on it. I think back to the dream. The details of it are already turning foggy, but nothing about Corwin's demeanor gives the impression of deception. He was nervous and trying to hide how nervous he was making that admission.

And fae avoid lying, especially when close to the Heart. Apparently saying something false can damage their connection to the Heart's magic. Corwin didn't say he left the note in so many words—I was reading between the lines—but he confirmed it openly, and he said lots of other things directly stating that he disagreed with how the other arch-lords are handling the conflict.

"I believe him," I say. "I could be wrong, but—everything about it felt true."

"I suppose there's some comfort in knowing the one you've ended up tied to has less hostile intentions toward us than many of his brethren. Did he say anything else?"

"He told me his name—Corwin. And that he wanted us to try to see where the bond could take us. He thinks it could be a way of ending the fighting, like a bridge between the summer fae and the winter fae."

Sylas rests his chin against my temple. "And how do you feel about that?"

I grimace. "I don't know. It's a nice idea. But… I'm happy here. I don't want to give this up. I don't want to give *you* up." I hesitate with a wince. "I kind of told him so. That I had someone—or someones—I'd already meant to take as mates. He definitely didn't like hearing that. Then I woke up."

"Did you say anything about what you mean to the rest of the summer fae?"

I shake my head. "I didn't mention anything about the curse. I tried not to even think about it. He didn't seem to have any idea." But that is yet another complication.

Sylas is silent for a stretch, just holding me, his thumb tracing a curved line up and down my arm from shoulder to elbow. "I don't like any of this," he says finally. "I hate that you've found yourself in this position, and I hate that I haven't found any way to get you out of it. Whatever you decide will be your free choice. I'm still committed to that, even if it takes you away from me."

The rawness in his voice makes me lift my head. He sounds as if he expects me to leave even though I just told him I don't want to. "Did something happen in your meetings with the arch-lords? Do you think I'm in more danger here?" That's the only reason I can think of that he'd suggest even vaguely that I should leave.

"No. I—" He lets out a strained huff. "I don't know if I should tell you this. I've always kept the knowledge to myself, so as not to influence—but I don't want to keep anything from you either." He eases back far enough that I can see his face. "You've never asked how I got my scar."

I'm sure he has others, but it's clear he's talking about the most visible one that cuts through his ghostly eye. I've wondered enough times, but— "It seemed like a pretty personal question."

He chuckles with a hint of genuine emotion despite his still-somber expression. "I'm not sure we can get much more personal than we already have, my love."

Those last two words provoke a flutter in my chest, even though he already declared the depths of his affections the night of his coronation. It's still a little hard for me to believe that this powerful, magical man loves *me.*

I squeeze his arm where it's wrapped around me. "How did you get it, then?"

Sylas's mismatched gaze drifts away from me, going distant. "When I was what a human would consider an adolescent, still finding my footing within my father's domain, a small group of Murk got it into their heads to stir up trouble for the sentries watching over our borders. I volunteered to deal with them. I was… somewhat overconfident in my abilities and how easily a pack of rats might be subdued. I located the den they'd made and came at them alone."

I trace my finger along the pale, jagged line that marks his cheek. "And they did this?" I haven't encountered any of the rat-shifting fae called the Murk yet, but from the way I've heard the Seelie talk about them, they distrust them even more than the Unseelie. The winter fae they at least see as equals, if enemies. The realm-less fae that lurk around the edges of this world and the human one, they talk about with disdain as well as animosity.

"They nearly ended me. Three of their number I dispatched quickly enough, but the fourth had more magic than I'd bargained for. She threw a curse at me that would have killed me if I hadn't managed to deflect it at the last second. As it was, it still caught the side of my face rather than burrowing right into my brain."

I shudder. "That's awful."

"My own fault for going in too cocky." He dips his head to nuzzle my temple. "But whatever the spell would have done to my mind, it had something of an odd effect on my eye. I can't see in the regular way through it—in that sense, it's essentially dead. But here and there it shows me brief images from the past or the future or hints at a reaction someone is holding in. Sometimes literal, sometimes more the gist of a situation. It can occasionally be useful, but often I'm not sure enough of the when or how to make use of those impressions."

My thoughts slip back to the comments that got us started on this tangent. "Did it show you something today?"

"Yes." He inhales slowly. "When I left the Bastion after my last meeting with the arch-lords, I got a glimpse of you, walking toward the border right by the Heart as if you were going to pass through."

My stomach twists. "And that couldn't be from the past, because I've never gone through before."

"Exactly." He turns me to look at him straight on. "I don't know how far in the future that glimpse might have come from, what might have led to it, or whether it's unavoidable. Don't make any decisions based on that." His tone turns vehement with a trace of a growl. "As long as you want to stay here, I'll fight for you with every shred of my being."

An answering emotion floods my chest. I grasp his shirt and burrow my face against his neck. "I love you."

I wish that was *enough* of an answer. Not that long ago, I thought the only thing standing in the way of my staying with the men of Hearthshire was that they'd never return my feelings as strongly. Now…

Now I'm no longer sure that even a fae lord's love will be enough to save me from whatever awaits us.

CHAPTER SIX

Sylas

Stepping into the Bastion of the Heart used to fill me with a sense of wonder. To some extent, the sandstone walls with their glowing veins of gold that pulse in time with the energy flowing from the Heart still do. But as I stride through the halls to the central meeting chamber on an urgent summons from the two arch-lords who are now my colleagues, that awe is dampened by a sinking sense of dread.

These days, the weight of my multiplying challenges and responsibilities doesn't leave much room for wonder.

Celia and Donovan are huddled in quiet conversation by Celia's throne. A few of their cadre-chosen stand at a respectful distance. With August stationed in Hearthshire to watch over Talia for the day and Whitt off making more inquiries, I've brought only Astrid with me—a loyal warrior but not official enough to be allowed into the room for whatever discussion we're about to have.

I make a brief gesture to her, and she stops without hint of protest to wait in the doorway in case I have need of her. As my fellow arch-lords glance up to mark my strides to meet them, I feel my lack of support with a prickle down the back of my neck.

It's the risk you take, setting off to found your own domain rather than lingering to take over from your parents. Split the pack, and you end up with one much smaller than you'd have been able to call on otherwise. Hearthshire was growing well in those early decades, but the banishment set us back to even worse numbers than we'd had when I first struck out on my own. And I couldn't justify asking any of my pack to make such a heavy commitment as adding to my cadre when I hadn't even been able to hold onto our home for them.

Something I'll have to put a mind to changing… once I no longer have quite so many other pressing concerns on my mind.

Celia and Donovan turn toward me as I reach them. It's easy to discern that there's been bad news. Despite her advanced age, Celia has never lacked for energy, but today her ebony face looks tired. Donovan's mouth slants downward. He rakes his hand through his flame-like hair with a jerk of his arm.

"Has some new trouble arisen?" I ask, tamping down on the urge to add a frustrated *What now?*

Celia draws her willowy frame up even straighter. "We've had word from the Unseelie arch-lords. They're threatening an assault on our own domains."

I blink at her, the statement so bewildering it takes me a moment to regain my composure. "On *our* domains—around the Heart? They'd have a hard time reaching us from any place they could cross the border without taking the Heart's vow."

"They say that circumstances will allow them passage without the vow," the younger arch-lord says, his voice strained. "That keeping one of their soul-twined mates from her bonded partner is in defiance of the Heart, and the Heart will allow them passage to rectify that offense."

Every muscle in my body tenses. It is true—there is a minor loophole in the spell the summer and winter fae created together all those centuries ago. If we committed a severe enough crime against the Heart's will, it would let their warriors pass through without their oath to do no harm. We could still defend ourselves—we have no shortage of our own warriors, after all—but imagining how they might ransack the sacred lands here brings my fangs springing forth.

"We haven't been *keeping* Talia from him," I retort. "She has her own mind—she doesn't want to go to him."

Celia sighs. "And we don't particularly want her to go either, considering her role in defying our curse. The entire situation is incomprehensible. Are you absolutely certain that it's a soul-twined bond and not some awful magic they cast on the girl?"

Of course she'd only think of what Talia can offer through her blood, not anything else. But then, that's exactly why I haven't told my colleagues about my intention to take the woman I love as my mate. Until I *can* do that, starting what will likely be an argument over it will only be another complication.

I'd rather not even have told them about her soul-twined bond, but after our initial attempts to overcome that problem failed, I couldn't keep the information from them any longer.

I gesture toward the Heart. "The Unseelie wouldn't be able to say we're keeping his soul-twined mate from him if that's not the case. *That* would be an immense offense against the Heart—can you imagine the consequences of a lie so immense?"

Donovan rubs his narrow chin. "And you haven't found any explanation for how this could happen to a human or whether it could be undone?"

I grimace. "Our efforts have brought little result. The only possible solution we've come across requires that the bond first be consummated, and it might very well kill Talia in the breaking of it. Do you really think the Heart will allow them to attack us when the choice is hers?"

Celia gives me a measured look. "Soul-twined bonds are one of the Heart's greatest gifts to us. To deny one… I don't know how this would play out. She isn't making the choice entirely for herself, is she? I find it hard to believe that your cadre-chosen who's so enamored with her hasn't swayed her on the matter at all."

It *is* impossible to know exactly how the Heart will react to these circumstances. None of us would have believed it would ever create a bond between fae of opposing seasons, let alone bestow one on a human. The Unseelie might attempt an assault and be pushed back—or they might descend on us like they did on that full moon night several weeks ago.

There would be no withdrawing to a defensive position and regrouping. We'd be locked in an unceasing battle to the death until one side or the other came out on top. If we lose these lands, our connection to the Heart will falter, and our magic alongside it. Once the Unseelie gain that foothold, we may never regain it.

But to lose *Talia*… I have to hold in a snarl of defiance. Fury reverberates through every nerve in my body at the thought.

I rein in my temper, though I can't quite keep the edge out of my voice. "What do you suggest, then? You can't mean to give up our only current means of controlling the curse. Especially when she *wants* to remain with us."

"You're a skilled negotiator, Sylas," Celia says evenly. "We saw that when you made your appeal to us to protect her position with you. If she spends a short amount of time with her mate and rejects the bond with no influence from us, then her will in the matter is undeniable. I say we have her make whatever arrangements you need to through their connection to ensure her safety and her return to us should she wish it—and to keep our secrets uncompromised."

I probably could ensure that with an oath or two solidifying the promise. My heart balks at the idea, though. I keep my mouth shut for a moment, lest the anger burning through me sear from my tongue into my colleagues instead.

Celia is right. I know she is, as much as I detest the fact. And when I accepted the role as arch-lord, I made a graver commitment to my people—to all the Seelie—than ever before.

Either I fail as a mate-to-be or I fail as leader of my people. One injures at worst four of us, the other thousands. May maggots eat those raven bastards.

"I'll put it to her," I say. "I won't force her." But I already know how she'll answer if she knows the potential disaster we face, don't I?

Talia should know just what sort of man she'll be dealing with on the other side. My gaze flicks between my fellow arch-lords. "Did the threat come from her mate—the one named Corwin?" If he thinks he can go from making a plea for peace in her dreams last night to calling for war less than twelve hours later—

But Donovan is shaking his head. "It was from the woman who spoke for them on your coronation night—the one who seemed to carry the most authority if not the most seniority—Laoni?"

Then there's no telling how much Corwin was or wasn't directly involved. "And you agree with Celia's proposal?"

The younger arch-lord has been my greatest ally outside of my pack. He supported my return to Hearthshire whole-heartedly, let me into his confidence when he came under attack from the arch-lord before me, and put me forward as Ambrose's replacement. His pained expression tells me he knows more than Celia does how much this means to me. But he tips his head in acknowledgment anyway.

I can't even blame him.

I force my hands to unclench so I look reasonably in control of myself. "All right. I'll think on it and speak to Talia. Inform the Unseelie that the mate in question is coming to *her own* decision on the matter, and that it'd be an offense against the Heart to rush the acceptance of the bond."

As I march back to the hall, I hold my rage in check, but only by a thread. Astrid falls into step beside me, alert enough to my mood to stay silent.

The beaming of the sun feels like an insult to the turmoil inside me. I turn to Astrid. "Whitt was making use of the library at Blossom-by-the-Heart. Find him and inform him that I want him to look into every obscure detail he can find on oaths, especially as it regards the Unseelie."

She bobs her head. "Is there any way I can assist after that, my lord?"

Turn back time so I never became arch-lord after all? I grit my teeth, knowing that even if such a thing were possible, even if I'd actually ask for it, it wouldn't solve anything. I'd know what I owe my people regardless of my title.

Blast it all to dust.

I nod toward the border. "Keep a watch by the Heart for even the slightest sign of Unseelie intrusion, however innocuous. Report back to me if you see anything at all."

She grins tightly but fiercely, showing her fangs. "If they show more than a beak, I'll happily tear their feathered heads off as well."

I watch her set off and then stalk toward the half-finished castle in my newly-granted domain. She's done well, this loyal warrior who's followed me so far—protected Talia when I couldn't be there.

As much as any of us have been able to protect Talia in the end.

The several pack-kin with the true names needed to construct the castle and its furnishings are gathered around one of the outer corners, coaxing the massive fused tree trunk there into the shape of a ballroom. As if we'll have anything to celebrate anytime soon.

I swallow my growl and wave them off. "Take an hour or two. Have a run if you feel you need it."

They disperse without argument. I snatch up a fallen leaf and murmur a few syllables to it that'll send it on a course back to Hearthshire. When it reaches August, he'll know it's his summons to bring Talia.

He just won't know what he's bringing her to.

The fury I've been shoving down on so forcefully flares despite my best intentions. Claws prick from my fingertips. My jaw aches to stretch.

Hanging onto the last shred of my self-control, I stride into the castle and down the stairs to the roughed-out basement exercise room where sounds are least likely to carry outside. As my heel kicks the door shut with a bang, my wolf explodes out of me.

The animal I've become lashes out in every direction. I lunge at the walls, fully extended claws gouging the wood with a friction that's not remotely satisfying. A strangled howl rips from my throat. My muscles coil and hurl me one way and another, my fangs gnash at the air, and my lungs ache with a chorus of snarls. My awareness narrows down to a rage-hazed blur.

The rage stretches on and on, my body battling to find a release I can't quite reach, until a smooth, quiet voice breaks through my furor.

"Sylas."

My shoulder slams into one of the walls. I spin, panting and paws throbbing, to see Whitt standing by the now-open door. He gazes back at me, his expression mild but his stance uncertain in the way it's been almost always since our confrontation over Isleen's crime against him.

My senses refocus on the room around me. Claw marks scour the walls. The moss padding on the floor lies torn in jagged chunks. The bar mounted at the far end of the room is snapped right through, the broken ends punctured with teeth marks.

Shame trickles through me. I haven't let my most feral emotions take over like this in—possibly ever. Even when Isleen betrayed me, even when we were banished, I stewed and I snapped here or there, but I held onto the steadiness my pack needs from their lord.

I can't help thinking of ages ago when I found August rampaging around a glade in the woods near the castle at Thundervale, taking out his anger toward our father and his grief over his mother's death on every tree and shrub in the vicinity.

He was barely more than a child then. I'm a grown man of over three centuries. I'm a blasted *arch-lord*.

Whitt's posture still looks tense, but his voice comes out typically wry. "As much as I'm sure your honor is compelling you to do so, may I suggest not beating yourself up to anywhere near the same extent that you've demolished this room? The wood can be mended. I'd say we're allotted at least one good blow-up per century, and I suspect you've been stockpiling."

I don't pick up on the slightest hint of judgment in his tone, which is light and calm in its breeziness. Puncturing the tension of the situation by making a joke out of it, like he has in our favor so many times in the past. As I pull in my wolf and straighten up, I'm struck with an odd pang that's almost like homesickness, as if I've missed something about this, something about him, even though he hasn't been elsewhere for more than a day.

I miss the ease with which I used to trust him—and my belief that he trusted me the same way. When I look at him now, I find I don't have any anger left about the past. All that remains is the hollow of mourning within my gut.

But maybe I have some control over whether that hollow is filled back in.

"Thank you," I say to him. "I—" I glance at the room again and flinch inwardly.

"Think nothing of it," Whitt replies as glibly as before, but then his expression darkens. "As much as I'm dreading hearing it, you'd better tell me what put you in this state—and what it has to do with Unseelie oaths."

Not wanting to wallow in the results of my rampage while we discuss the cause of it, I motion him down the hall. My collection of frivolous human movies and August's video games haven't been moved here from Hearthshire yet, but the soon-to-be entertainment room does have a sofa. I sink down at one end of it. Whitt hesitates by the other end before flopping down next to me.

There's no point in beating around the bush, especially with my older brother. "The Unseelie arch-lords have threatened to attack our domains by the Heart if we don't deliver Talia to her soul-twined mate. My colleagues are concerned that the Heart might sway in their favor and allow them free passage. They want us to send her to him for long enough that it's clear she's making her own decision when she leaves."

If she leaves. That possible phrasing sticks in the bottom of my throat. I know firsthand how intense and compelling the intimacy of a soul-twined bond can be. As much as I hate to admit it, that wretched raven has a more valid claim over Talia than any of us do.

She may not want to return after all.

If he truly has been working against his own people to protect us, he might not even be the villain I'd like to see him as. Letting her go to him may be in the best interests of not only my Seelie brethren but Talia as well. If the Heart has blessed her with such a connection to a lord who turns out to be deserving, how can I deny her that?

Whitt paints the air with a colorful string of curse words and then slumps back in the sofa. For a second, I'm half-afraid that he'll shame me for even considering their proposal even though he didn't for my rage.

But he's my spymaster and strategist for a reason. His swift mind probably worked through the factors faster than mine did.

"We'll bind that mangy bird brain in so many oaths he can barely breathe without double-checking," he says. "We'll make sure she comes back. She *will* come back—you know that."

I do. "She'll come back because she feels she owes it to us. Because she wouldn't abandon us to the curse." I know how much honor Talia contains in that slip of a body. The real question is whether she stays or returns to the winter realm once her sense of obligation has been fulfilled.

Whitt looks steadily back at me, the pained set of his mouth revealing that he's making the same considerations. That they wrench at him just as deeply as they do me.

In that moment, the transgressions of a century past feel as substanceless as the visions of my deadened eye. Right here, right now, we are two men united in our love for one startlingly magnificent woman, and I trust that my brother will work as tirelessly toward ensuring her safety and happiness as I will—regardless of where she finds that happiness once every part of this unexpected situation has all played out.

Whitt pushes himself straighter again, clapping his hands together on his lap. "Well, then. Let me tell you the few new tidbits I've gleaned about oaths relative to the winter fae, and we'll see if we can't come up with a plan so air tight it could suffocate a raven."

CHAPTER SEVEN

Talia

Harper stares up at the towering obsidian castle that once belonged to Arch-Lord Ambrose. Her expression tenses as if she's half-afraid he'll come storming out to berate her, even though we both know the vicious schemer who attempted to steal me away from my pack is dead. Then a fiercer spark lights in her eyes, and she makes an obscene gesture at the walls before turning her back on them to look instead at the castle that will be our new home.

"I hope they smash it to dust when our castle is ready," she says, hugging herself.

I have no doubt that she means that whole-heartedly. Weeks ago, Ambrose's pack-kin managed to coerce the young fae woman into helping them with their plot. She made a dress for me with enchanted embellishments that would have recorded my private conversations with my lovers, which Ambrose would have exploited any way he could. Sylas was furious when he found out, but I asked that we give her a second chance rather than banishing her. She used to be my closest friend in the pack.

Since that incident, she hasn't wavered from her efforts to prove how much my friendship and her place in the pack mean to her. Pink lines mark her slim forearm from the slashing claws of one of Ambrose's guards. Harper and I and two of our other pack-kin managed to delay those guards while Sylas was protecting Donovan from Ambrose's murder attempt. She's hardly a warrior, but she threw herself into the skirmish—and between me and those claws that I'm even less equipped to fend off than she is—without a second's hesitation.

Talking with her doesn't feel as comfortable as it did before, back when we bonded over a mutual desire to see more of the world, but the sting of her betrayal is fading. I know she didn't *want* to hurt me. She fell for a horrible trick and didn't know how to get herself out of the mess. I don't know if I'd have made better decisions if our positions were reversed.

I gaze up at the ominous castle too. "I wonder what-all Ambrose had in there. Sylas let his pack-kin take all their belongings from their homes, but he didn't let anyone in the castle."

Since our lord was the one who ended Ambrose's life in fair combat, by fae law the arch-lord's possessions immediately became his own. I suspect he was concerned that if any of Ambrose's pack-kin had vengeful thoughts, they might find ammunition against those Ambrose hated somewhere within those walls.

Harper shudders. "I don't ever want to go back in there to find out."

"Me neither," I have to admit. The black stone is intimidating enough looking at it from the outside; standing in the inner halls, it's suffocating. "Well, I guess there'll be lots of other interesting parts of this domain to explore. There's more magic here near the Heart than anywhere else in the Mists, isn't there?"

"There is." My former friend offers me a shy smile, tucking her sleek flaxen hair behind her lightly pointed ears. "Maybe—if you want to, and you'd want *me* for company—we could still do some of that exploring together."

The tangled sensation that rises in my chest has little to do with her past betrayal and much more with the fact that I don't know when I'll have that kind of freedom again. Instinctively, I summon more light into the glowing barrier inside me. "I hope we'll have a chance. For now we should probably get on with the gardening we told August we'd help with."

Gardening isn't Harper's specialty. Her greatest talent is in designing and sewing gorgeous clothes, a talent with which she'd intended to win her invitations to domains all across the summer realm. But when she heard August was bringing me back to our pack's new domain, she immediately volunteered to come along and help however she could.

As soon as we arrived, August hustled into the partly sculpted castle of trees to speak with Sylas and Whitt, leaving Astrid watching over me from a short distance. She follows the two of us over to the growing cluster of smaller houses that'll become the new pack village.

A man already there points us to some roots that need planting, and we spend the next several minutes digging them into the earth and covering them over. The warm late-afternoon sun, the rich scent of the soil, and the rhythmic movements soothe my spirit a little. It all feels so normal, as if nothing all that major has really changed.

"I guess you'll have no shortage of balls to attend and higher fae to show off your dresses to now," I say to Harper. "Everyone wants to mingle with the arch-lords' packs."

I meant it as a casual remark to make conversation, but she looks up at me, her over-large eyes growing even wider with a vehemence that's echoed in her voice. "I don't care what any of the other packs think about me or what I've made. I'm just glad I didn't ruin my chances of staying with *this* pack." She bites her lip. "I haven't done much sewing since… since everything. Every time I do I remember adding those beads to that dress… The fact that *you're* still okay is so much more important to me than any reward those traitors would have given me."

Her declaration and the guilt etched all over her face bring a pang into my chest. I don't know what to say. The best I can manage is, "I still think your creations are beautiful. I wouldn't want you to stop." I pause, and allow a careful smile to curve my mouth. "Who else is going to make me look like I belong next to an arch-lord and his cadre?"

Harper stares at me for a second as if she can't believe I'd trust her to make anything else for me, and then a grin splits her face. "For you, I'll always do my best work. Even if I'm not making anything for anyone else." Her grin turns a bit sly. "First I obviously need to design you some adventuring clothes, since we won't be able to have nearly enough fun roaming around this domain wrapped up in regular dresses."

An unexpected laugh tumbles out of me. It feels good—until I glance up and see August coming over, obviously to get me. His face, once so often cheerful, is as serious as I've ever seen it. Any good humor in me condenses into a stone that sinks to the bottom of my stomach.

I've already wiped my hands on the grass next to the garden plot and gotten to my feet when he reaches us. He tilts his head toward the castle. "We need to speak with you."

"Of course."

Harper watches us curiously but doesn't pry. No one in the pack other than my men and Astrid know about the soul-twined bond. As far as I know, Sylas has kept it secret from everyone other than his fellow arch-lords.

As we walk to the rough castle, August rests his hand on my back. "It'll be okay. We'll make sure of it."

The statement doesn't exactly reassure me. He'd only say it if he knows what I'm about to hear won't sound okay at all.

Sylas and Whitt are waiting in Sylas's new office with its still-sparse furnishings. If I thought August looked serious, it's nothing compared to the dour atmosphere that closes around me as soon as I step into the room.

August shuts the door behind us. I reach inside myself to pour even more light into the inner barrier, shoring it up with everything I have in me, and then I plant myself in front of the fae lord, my chin high. I'm so tired of having this sense of doom hanging over me. Whatever's going on, I need to know before the awful anticipation kills me all on its own.

"Just tell me what's happened. It's obviously bad. I'm going to have to hear it one way or another."

Whitt lets out a choked guffaw, a glint of admiration shining in his eyes.

Sylas exhales sharply. "You have a choice. You can say no. I'm not going to force you into doing anything."

I can tell from his expression that he's already sure of my response anyway. "A choice about *what*?"

To his credit, he doesn't delay any longer. "The Unseelie arch-lords are threatening to storm our domains here by the Heart if we don't hand you over to your soul-twined mate. It's possible the Heart will let them through without the vow to do no harm because we're defying its intentions by keeping you here. My colleagues have suggested—and I can see the merits of the suggestion—that we allow you to spend a short amount of time with Arch-Lord Corwin so that you can decline him completely of your own free will, without any hint of persuasion from us."

My stomach plummets right to my toes. "You want me to go to the winter realm?"

Sylas's lips draw back with a flash of bared teeth. "I don't *want* you to go anywhere, Talia. If I had my way—" He cuts himself off and shakes his head. "You don't *have* to go. If you say no, even though we're giving you the clearest avenue there that we can, the Heart has to recognize that."

The strain in his voice implies he's not really sure of that statement. I could refuse and spark a battle far more catastrophic than anything the summer fae have faced so far.

I swallow hard, resisting the urge to hug myself. "The Unseelie arch-lords threatened us? *Corwin* threatened us?" After all his talk about peace and building bridges last night...

Anger flares in my chest. Before Sylas can answer, I spin around, putting my back to him and closing my eyes. Whitt inhales as if to speak, but I hold up my hand for silence.

Carefully but quickly, I peel back the mass of glowing energy that's sealed over the open space inside me. Not completely, only paring it back enough so that I can send my thoughts through that ephemeral channel.

Corwin!

I don't know if he had his end of the connection totally unguarded or if my irritation propels the name with enough force to break through. His voice carries back to me an instant later, hasty but with a sense of distraction. *Talia. I'm here.*

It's the first time I've ever reached out to him. The first time we'll have a conversation I initiated consciously. The realization sends a wobble through my gut, but I press on so that our talk can also be *over* as quickly as possible. *Did you tell the Seelie arch-lords your people would go to war over me?*

I get the impression that he's attempting to muffle his emotions, but some slip through anyway: a jab of frustration, a ripple of horror. Enough that I believe him when he says, *No. I'm trying to talk my colleagues* out *of that course of action right now. I meant what I said last night. Unfortunately, what I said about only being one vote is also true.*

Fragments of other sensations slip through: a glimpse of a cavernous, pale room and a long marble table in the middle of it, four figures sitting around that table, a woman talking in brittle tones. —*can't let these tender feelings prevent us from—*

"I'm talking to her right now," Corwin breaks in—aloud, to the other arch-lords. The woman's mouth snaps shut. He turns away from them, closing his eyes so I'm left with darkness and silence until his voice returns. *I promise you, I had no hand in this decision. I should be able to at least delay them taking further action.*

Resignation and resolve have already coiled together around my heart. *All right. I'll reach out again when I have more to say.* Dragging in a breath, I summon another swell of light until no hint of his presence reaches me.

When I turn back to my lovers, they're watching me with varying expressions of anguish. They know what I was just doing—that I was communicating with another man on a level of intimacy I'll never be able to with any of them.

"He didn't have anything to do with the threat to go to war," I say. "He's trying to get the other arch-lords to back down right now, but it doesn't sound like he'll be able to."

August stirs on his feet. "But maybe if we give him time—"

I interrupt him before he can fully express that thought, that hope.

"I don't think we should count on that, and it doesn't seem worth the risk." Swallowing hard, I meet Sylas's mismatched eyes. "You'd be able to make sure I could come home?"

The fae lord inclines his head. "We've already been working out the exact wording of the oaths we'd ask him to take to ensure your safe return and the security of our realm. You'd be back before the next full moon. He wouldn't be able to harm you while you're there or compel you to return afterward if you refused to."

"But I'd have to go alone."

Whitt answers for him, smooth as ever but gentle. "None of us would be able to join you. I don't imagine they'd allow any Seelie warriors as part of the bargain either. If you had someone else in mind you wanted for company, I can see ways we could make a case for a single unmenacing companion."

"And I wouldn't be committing to anything just by agreeing to stay with him for a while, would I? He couldn't… force the issue?" The man I've spoken to didn't sound like he would, but he is Unseelie and therefore one of our enemies, no matter what else he's done. I barely know him at all.

Sylas growls. "You can be sure *that* would be an essential part of the oaths we'd require."

For a few minutes, I stand in silence, sorting through my thoughts. To spend a week or two in Corwin's domain, to share his home with him—but without any obligations… I've survived nine years in a cage, starved and beaten down, without knowing there was anyone left in the world who'd care what was happening to me. Compared to that, this plan is nothing.

Except I'd be treading into a totally unfamiliar realm, surrounded by unfamiliar fae who've been slaughtering my own every chance they get.

My mind travels back to weeks ago when Sylas took me to the domain of his former mate's family to pay our respects over the death of Isleen's half-brother. He was a man who despised me and attempted to mutilate me. His family is one that sneers at humans and considers us to be worth no more than dung.

But witnessing their mourning, speaking with them afterward, I couldn't see them as just villains any longer. They were simply people —people with some awful attitudes, but also devotion to their family and grief over those they'd lost, who were willing to offer me respect when I showed I respected them.

I don't know if I'll see the same in the Unseelie, but I can believe Corwin has good in him. I can stand up for my people and maybe even discover something that could put an end to the fighting forever. How can I say no to that just to protect myself from the unknown?

My men have kept their own councils while I've debated with myself. The emotions roiling behind their gazes are obvious, but they give me the space to think. They don't try to argue or persuade me.

Because they know me well enough to have guessed what I would decide before I even set foot in this room, and they're not going to take that choice away from me.

That realization is what solidifies my resolve. I square my shoulders and look around at the three men, reveling in the depth of faith and understanding that's formed between us. We're bound together too, in ways I won't let any twist of fate shake. We'll get through this—we just have to.

"I'm going," I say. "Tell me what I need to tell Corwin so we can get all the details settled."

CHAPTER EIGHT

Talia

By the time we're done hashing out an agreement, with me passing on Sylas and Whitt's instructions through the soul-twined bond and relaying Corwin's replies, the conviction that carried me through the decision and the conversation that followed is dwindling. As I wearily reconstruct the wall of light inside me, all I can feel is the ache around my heart.

No matter what effort I put into this shield, tomorrow it won't matter. Tomorrow I'll be stepping into Corwin's domain—I won't be able to avoid him.

I'll be leaving behind the three men I've come to love so much.

Beyond the study's window, the sky has darkened. August tucks his arm around me, and we all head down to the unfinished kitchen. Rather than bothering with the equally unfinished dining room, we find places around one of the islands and put together a makeshift dinner out of the sparse assortment of ingredients August has on hand. He shoots more than one offended look at the spot where the not-yet-molded oven will be.

I force down as much of the smoked pheasant sandwich as I can.

None of us says much. Maybe we're all talked out after the extended negotiation. But when we've done a quick clean-up and we all move toward the stairs, something in me balks so hard I stop in my tracks.

August sets his hand on my shoulder. I reach out to grasp Whitt's hand and Sylas's wrist.

The fae lord turns with a frown of concern. "What's wrong, Talia?"

I feel weak saying it. I made this choice. I want to go forward full of boldness and resolution. But the ache in my chest is spreading all through my limbs and up my throat. My voice comes out hoarse.

"I don't want to lose you. Any of you."

"Oh, mite." Whitt leans in to press a kiss to my hair. "We're not going anywhere."

August rumbles low in his chest. "If those stinking ravens try to keep you from coming back to us, we'll slaughter every one of their pompous arch-lords."

Sylas twines his fingers with mine and raises his other hand to caress my cheek. "We're yours, no matter how much distance lies between us. But right now, we're here. What do you need?"

I need this soul-twined bond to disappear as if it'd never formed. I need the certainty that no one will threaten my place among the Seelie and this pack ever again. But since there's no way I'm getting either of those things, I let the longing growing inside me take the lead and ask for one thing I'm pretty sure I can have.

"I want to be as close as I can get to all of you tonight. Together. If —if that's okay. If it isn't some kind of horrible offense against the Heart and the bond."

The heat that kindles in all three of the gazes fixed on me sears across my skin and brings a flush to my cheeks. I can feel it even from August behind me, in the slide of his hand to my waist where it burns like the most delicious of brands.

"You've made no commitment to Arch-Lord Corwin," Whitt says. "Even if you did, the decision about how much mates might seek companionship elsewhere is a matter of negotiation and personal preference, not dictated by the Heart. Enough lords seek other lovers to add to their chances of heirs. If you want this—"

"I do," I say determinedly before he has to go on.

Sylas strokes my cheek again, letting his knuckles trail down the side of my neck this time, and my body sways toward him of its own accord. "Then you'll have it. The tryst room here isn't furnished yet. My pack-kin did insist on ensuring *I* had a well-constructed bed while I work from this castle. If that's acceptable."

My tongue darts across my lips, the longing expanding into a more urgent swell of desire. My body already feels as if it's melting. I find I don't care all that much about where we do this as long as we do it soon, before I burn up from this mix of embarrassment and wanting. "I'm fine with making an exception."

This time it's Sylas who lets out a rumble. As Whitt chuckles, the fae lord scoops me into his arms. He claims a kiss right there in the hallway, tender but scorching. "Let's see how satisfied the three of us can make our mate-to-be, then."

Hearing him call me that, knowing taking me as his mate is still his intention, brings back the ache in my heart. But as we head up the stairs with his arms around me, Whitt's fingers teasing through my hair, and August's thumb tracing the arch of my foot, they conjure enough giddy anticipation for me to ignore the pang.

I'm theirs and they're mine, and not even the bond that tore me open from within can change that. Tonight, we'll prove that not just with words but with our bodies, merging as deeply as any beings can.

Sylas's new bedroom is unfurnished other than the bed, but along with being "well-constructed" it's also even more massive than the one he has back in Hearthshire. I wonder if he requested a larger frame when his pack-kin went to work on it, anticipating that it'd be shared on a regular basis in one way or another.

Then he drapes me across the covers, looming over me with all that passionate devotion in his gaze, and my capacity for any kind of thought goes out the window.

The fae lord holds his body above me, only touching me where he's bent his head to capture my mouth. But I'm hardly neglected in physical contact. As Sylas's tongue coaxes my lips apart and I welcome it with mine, Whitt and August sprawl out on either side of us. August nuzzles my ear and claims the side of my neck. Whitt lifts my hand and begins kissing a path from my wrist toward my shoulder.

I've been with Sylas and August at the same time, and just having two men utterly focused on me was a dizzying experience. To be enveloped by all three sets my skin alight in all sorts of places they haven't even touched yet. I trace my fingers along Sylas's jaw, tangle them in August's hair, reach to embrace Whitt when he comes to my shoulder and brushes his lips ever so gently to my cheek.

I kiss Sylas once more, so hard a thrum of approval resonates from his chest, and then turn my head to seek out Whitt's mouth. As Whitt cups my jaw to draw me even closer, Sylas takes the opportunity to ease down my body and remove my boots. He kisses each foot and then my calf and my knee just below the hem of my dress, sending a flare of heat straight between my legs.

August strokes his hand down my torso and back up to fondle my breast. The swivel of his thumb brings my nipple to a hardened peak with a jolt of pleasure that leaves me gasping into Whitt's mouth. The spymaster chuckles and devours me with a searing press of his lips, his hand skimming across my waist and up to caress the other side of my chest.

When Sylas slides my dress up to kiss the inside of my thigh, I can't help squirming with the sharpening hunger building in my core. The fae lord brushes his mouth to a spot just a little higher and gazes up at me as Whitt releases my mouth to nibble my jaw.

"Shall we get this off of you?" Sylas asks in a low voice, letting the fabric tease across my thighs.

Eager anticipation shivers through me. "Yes, please. But I'd better not be the only one getting undressed."

Whitt smirks and sits up to strip off his shirt without any further prompting. I only get a few seconds to ogle the planes of tattooed muscle before Sylas is tugging up the skirt of my dress. I lift my hips to give him access, my sex tingling when he leans so close between my legs. As I sit up so he can lift it over my head, the warm air settles against my skin.

August has already shucked his shirt off too. I reach for Sylas's, my grip on the ties by the collar wobbling when the other two men return their attentions to my now-bared breasts. August tucks himself close to me, his broad chest against my back, and it's a wonder I remember what I meant to do well enough to yank Sylas's tunic upward.

He tosses it aside and lowers his head to reclaim my mouth. Searing hot skin surrounds me on all sides. Everywhere I reach, my hand slides over hardened muscle taut with desire.

How lucky I am to be in bed with even one of these extraordinary men, let alone three. I don't know what lies ahead of us, but I'm going to make every moment of this night count. I'm going to hold onto these memories when I'm far away from them, knowing that if I'm careful, if I stand firm, I'll have more of this to come back to.

I tip my head to kiss August next. Whitt eases lower to suck the tip of my breast into his mouth. Then Sylas trails his fingers down my belly to the hottest part of me, and my whimper turns into a moan.

The fae lord growls at the dampness of my panties. With a jerk, he snaps those off me and strokes me skin to slickening skin. My hips arch toward him again, another moan slipping from my lips as he delves a skillful finger right inside me. Bliss burns through me from the rocking of his hand, from Whitt's tongue flicking over my nipple, from August kissing me deeper than ever as if we could meld into one.

Sylas rests the heel of his hand against my most sensitive spot while he slips a second finger inside me. I clutch Whitt's hair, August's neck, riding the wave of pleasure they're summoning together.

It breaks over me far too soon, shocking a gasp from my throat. Electric tingles race through every muscle. My men let me sag back into the pillows, but I'm still burning for more. My fingers snag on August's trousers, my other hand gesturing roughly toward the others, and that's all the cue they need to kick off the rest of their clothes.

Suddenly I'm surrounded by three powerful, predatory, and utterly naked men. Maybe I should be nervous, but the emotions radiating through my chest are nothing but a heady mixture of love and carnal longing. The only question is how exactly we're going to make this work from here.

Whitt moves first—to kiss me on the mouth so tenderly it wakes up the ache in my heart and then withdrawing as if it'd never occur to him that he'd play more than a supporting role in what happens next. Sylas watches his spymaster with an expression I can't read.

As August captures my mouth next, the fae lord teases his fingers through the dampness of my release, stoking my hunger. He nudges my legs farther apart and leans in to swipe his tongue over my slit and across the sensitive nub above, just once.

A keening sound that's more demand than plea breaks from my lips, and Sylas grins. Then he moves from between my legs, dappling kisses across my belly as he goes, and meets my eyes with a smolder in both of his.

"I believe my strategist could conspire to bring even more of those lovely sounds from your beautiful throat, if you'll have him."

My gaze darts to Whitt. The spymaster stares at his lord, so startled it takes him a moment to rein in his shock. At the small but warm smile that crosses his lips, something blooms inside me that's deeper than lust, deeper maybe even than the love I've felt before.

They'd agreed to share me—they already were sharing. But Sylas's statement is an olive branch, an expression of trust and affection, and a dismissal of all the pains of the past to focus on what we have between us right now.

I want nothing more than to be a part of the mending of the ties between them—and it's hardly a sacrifice. I know from experience just how good Whitt *can* make me feel.

I extend my hand to him beckoningly. When Sylas smiles back at him, Whitt bends over me, his eyes alight with passion. He steals a kiss, tucking his hand beneath my back and sliding it down my spine until he reaches my rear.

The head of his erection glides over my arousal-drenched opening so slickly he groans. I wriggle to meet him, and he lets out another low chuckle. "We'll get you there, mighty one. Over and over again."

I just about combust at that promise, and then he's pushing into me, filling me with the hard, hot length of him. I let out a growl of my own.

Sylas has moved to my other side, caressing my breast and giving my earlobe a gentle tug between his teeth. August hums happily and kisses my cheek, then my mouth when I tilt my face toward him.

I grasp the back of Whitt's neck with one hand, rising to meet his rhythm, wanting every movement he makes to flow through my body.

The other hand I trail down August's chest until my fingers graze the straining, solid heat of his own erection. I grip him, reveling in his stutter of breath, in the pleasure expanding through my core with every thrust, in this sense of total unity as the four of us join together in the most intimate way we can.

Whitt shifts his angle, plunging deeper. His body presses against my outer nub, and I start to spiral away all over again. As Sylas tweaks my nipple, August runs his tongue along my jaw. I rock my hips faster, urging Whitt on, and he matches my urgency with a blissful groan.

His head bows, the fringe of his hair tickling my cheek. "You're so perfect, Talia. Come all the way with me. Let's see you soar."

A very undignified whine creeps up my throat. "Only—if you come—too."

He mutters a curse, my ragged request sending him over the edge. He clutches my thigh and thrusts into me so hard I do soar, up and away on a tsunami of sensation that sets every nerve blazing. As Whitt slows, both of us drifting down from the high of release, I sink boneless and giddy into the covers.

"Mmm," he says, a sly glint dancing in his eyes. "Don't think we're done with you yet."

A sound slips out of me that's equal parts disbelief and encouragement. With a low laugh, he eases out of me, his hands still on my hips. He tugs them. "There are so many more angles we can explore. I'm sure my lord can take you even higher."

As I flip onto my hands and knees at his urging, I glance at Sylas. If his invitation to Whitt was an olive branch, I guess this is Whitt returning the gesture. Saying in his own way how much it means to him to be part of this union.

The twitch of the fae lord's mouth hints at amusement, but the rest of his expression is all hunger. "It would be my pleasure in every possible way to take up that challenge, if our lady so desires."

Is he kidding me? I wet my lips, holding his gaze. "I want to feel all of you."

Somehow the smolder in his mismatched gaze burns even hotter at that statement. He kisses my shoulder blade, the curve of my waist, and the side of my hip before positioning himself behind me.

I've only had one of the men enter me from behind once before, in the pool at Hearthshire when August and I were both upright. Bent over like this, the stretch of Sylas's shaft penetrating me sends an even stronger jolt through my nerves. I gasp, unable to stop myself from pressing back into him.

But I didn't just mean that I wanted all of him. As my head tips back with the bliss of Sylas's first stroke, I direct the rest of my attention to August, who's lying patiently next to me, skimming his fingertips over my arm and my chest. I'm not done with *him* yet.

I can't get him off with my hands when I'm braced in this position, though. As I waver, caught up in the pleasure Sylas's measured thrusts are propelling through my body and a momentary uncertainty, Whitt provides a spark of inspiration—by sliding his head beneath me so he can lap his tongue over one of my breasts and then down to the sensitive point just above where I'm joined with Sylas.

A cry escapes me. Whitt works over that bundle of nerves with his skillful tongue with enthusiasm, following the swaying of my hips with Sylas's thrusts, and I'm struck with the impulse to do a little tasting of my own.

Not letting myself second-guess my instincts, I jerk my head toward August. "Come closer? I want to—" My cheeks flare, and the words catch in my throat for a second before I gasp them out. "I want to use my mouth on you. If you'd like it…"

My shaky voice falters completely at the surprise that flashes across his face—followed by a look so heated that his golden eyes may as well be liquid metal. "I'd never say no to you when you ask that way, Sweetness," he says roughly, moving to the top of the bed. "And definitely not when you're offering something like *that*."

He stretches out so his erection is just inches from my face. I stare at it, never having looked at this part of my lovers quite this close up before. It juts so rigidly, but I know the veined thickness is covered in velvety soft skin. August's natural scent reaches my nose, manly musk with trace of his own sweetness, as if he brings the essence of his baking with him wherever he goes.

Cautiously, I flick my tongue over the head as the sway of my body brings me right up to him. August groans, and a bead of liquid forms at the tip. I lick that up, and his shaft outright twitches. The effect I'm having with just these small gestures is tantalizingly irresistible.

August reaches to trace his fingers over my cheek, into my hair, and back again. Building my confidence, I open my mouth enough to close it around his length. He makes a strangled sound that's all bliss. Whitt swirls his tongue over me, adding an extra jolt to the flood of tingling heat racing through my body, and I decide I'm going to offer August every bit of the same delight that I can.

Bobbing slightly with the motion of Sylas's thrusts, I take as much of August's shaft into my mouth as I can. When I tighten my lips around him, he lets out another groan. "That's it. Just like that. Heart help me, Talia, you're amazing."

I begin to work my mouth up and down, exploring him with my tongue at the same time. August's voice fractures into wordless murmurs of encouragement and appreciation, his fingers tangling in the waves spilling down my face.

As I find my pace, Sylas picks up his own, faster and deeper, as if urging me on while spurring me toward my third peak of the night. Even more pleasure shudders through my body. My arms start to wobble.

I suck hard on August's shaft, Whitt grazes his teeth against my nub, and Sylas plunges into me at just the right angle that I break into a million shimmering particles of joy. I gasp and then tighten my mouth around August again, echoing the clenching of my sex as I ride out the glittering wave.

Sylas bows over me, kissing my back. His hips hitch, and his heat gushes into me.

With a curse, August gently lifts my head. He grips himself. With a few swift strokes, a jet of pale liquid spurts across his abdomen. Then he sits up and kisses me so passionately he must taste himself all through my mouth, but he doesn't show any sign of caring.

Whitt scoots out from under me and props himself up on one elbow with a grin more pleased and relaxed than I've seen him in weeks. As I let myself ease down on the bed, rolling onto my back, my men form a ring of bodily heat around me. Sylas kisses my thigh. August strokes my hair. Whitt tucks his arm around mine.

It reminds me of the first time I brought them out of their curse, when Sylas called me their lady and I watched their wolves shepherding the rest of the pack—when they curled up around me in Oakmeet's entrance room afterward and I fell asleep nestled between them. It was the first time I felt like I truly belonged in this world, with these men.

I lean into all their caresses, absorbing every bit of warmth and affection I can, and try to forget for just a little longer that tomorrow I'll be walking away from all of this.

CHAPTER NINE

Corwin

As distracted by the day's events as I am, a quiver of awe still passes through me when I soar into view of the glinting landscape of Heart's Cadence.

The spires of my palace appear ready to pierce the sky itself. The vibrant reds and purples of the sunset seep down them, reflecting all across the crystalline walls. The same hues paint over the frozen waterfall that tumbles from the foot of the palace over the curved cliff edge to the mirrored pool far below. Little eddies of twirling snow tease around the regal trees, the pale icicles that dangle from their branches contrasting with the dark gray bark.

But what speaks of *home* the most is the softly sibilant melody that carries on the wind as it ripples across the palace walls and through those branches—the sound that makes my domain's name all the more fitting. A cool gust catches beneath my wings, and I let myself soar higher for a moment.

This splendor is mine.

It isn't long, though, before my thoughts return to all that isn't mine yet. To the uncomfortable hollow running from my chest to my gut, where my soul-twined mate has shut me off yet again.

Tomorrow, I remind myself as I swoop toward the broad terrace that stretches along the eastern side of the palace. Tomorrow I'll see her again face to face, in reality rather than a dream. And for more than a startled second before she's slipping away from me. She's going to stay with me, live with me, for ten days before I have to let her return to the summer realm if she wishes it.

My stomach knots at that thought in a way I don't care for at all. I drop toward the terrace, shifting out of my raven form just in time for my boot-clad feet to hit the polished crystal tiles. Before heading inside, I take in the gleaming splendor of the outer walls for a few moments until my emotions are just as still and cool.

We are soul-twined mates. Even if she's Seelie, even if neither of us could have expected this, the Heart has chosen us for each other. Once we've spent some time together, she'll have to see that accepting the bond is the only reasonable course of action—not just for us but for both our peoples too.

She seems quite loyal to them. There was so much fierceness in her when she challenged me about the harms done or threatened to the summer realm. I allow myself a flicker of admiration at the memory, which seems a fair reaction.

She'll want to do what's best for them. The typical Seelie temper and attitudes might make it difficult for her to understand how important it is for me to do the same for mine… but despite that fierceness, she didn't come across as especially hotheaded or savage when I spoke with her.

We might not get along so badly. Understanding will grow between us as we ease into the bond. If I'm not sure I can expect the depths of love I've seen play out in other couples, well, I've also seen the consequences of such matches. I wouldn't ask for more than a caring ally.

I won't *want* more. It'll be a pleasant enough change simply to have some company in the vast, sparkling halls of my family's long-time home.

As I step into one of those hallways, my footsteps ring out, the sound bouncing off the high ceiling where enchanted domes of topaz glow at intervals along the diamond surface. Of course, I'm hardly *alone* here. The signal of my return brings one of the servants hustling out of a side room with a practiced bow. "We were just finishing making dinner. Did you want to eat right away?"

The girl is human—a young child by fae accounting but somewhere in her adolescence by the mortal lifespan. I like that she waits for my answer without shying from my gaze, looking totally at ease in her role. I suppose she should, given that she was born here.

Some of my colleagues would have muttered about the fact that I let my equally human chef take a partner among the cleaning staff and make a family with her. But then, they'd probably also mutter about having a human prepare my meal over one of fae skill, yet I've never heard any of them complain about the offerings when they've dined here. If you're going to have human servants, I can't see how one born into our ways wouldn't be preferable to those who often have to be drugged or enchanted out of their fears.

"Set it out, covered, on the table," I say. "I'll come when I'm ready."

She bobs her head and scurries back to her father. Charles may not approach his cooking with the same finesse a fae from my flock might, but I can have fae-styled cooking in any other domain on any day I happen to drop in. My father, Heart keep his soul, cajoled the man into returning here with him after a jaunt into the human world where he ate at the man's restaurant, and continued enjoying his work enough to stem his aging. Charles has been with us for over a century now, a fixture in my life since shortly after I reached my adulthood.

In some ways, as absurd as it sounds, he's the closest thing to family I have left.

I stalk through the halls to my private sitting room before any further gloom can descend over me. Though it's getting late, I'm not close to hungry yet. The brief visit to one of the domains that flanks mine barely took the edge off the tensions coiled inside me.

I sink into my preferred chair, willing some of that tension to seep out of me. Everything is in order—as much order as I could manage.

It will play out however it will. There's nothing to be gained by dwelling on events still in the future, beyond my grasp.

And yet my mind keeps attempting to leap forward to tomorrow morning when that pink-haired Seelie woman will step across the border with me.

I've reined my thoughts in for the dozenth time and am just straightening up with the intention of going to dinner now—because although I still don't feel particularly hungry, at least it'll give me something else to focus on—when a trace of sensation trickles through the empty space inside me. I freeze at the edge of the chair and then reach out tentatively. *Talia?*

She doesn't respond. I'm definitely not experiencing the rush of twined experience I did the few times her connection has gone unguarded before. She must have whatever walls she's put in place against me still up.

But they aren't perfectly solid at the moment, and whatever *she's* experiencing is intense enough to seep through. Another tendril of it reaches me—a whiff of pleasure that teases through my abdomen right to my groin as if drawn by the lightest of fingertips. Then a whisper of a sigh released from hitching lungs, a deeper jolt of carnal bliss—

Even as my own breath catches, my throat constricts with sudden understanding. In our shared dream, she mentioned another man, a prospective mate, that she hesitated to leave. She's with him now. *He's* touching her, summoning pleasure in her, so much that it's filtering through her defenses.

My hands clench at my sides. A maelstrom of emotion surges inside me: fury that any other being is enjoying that much intimacy with the woman who is *my* soul-twined mate, pain that she's turning to him even after agreeing to come to me, and tangled through it all, a sharp twinge of arousal that has my cock half-hard where I'm sitting braced in the chair.

I should be the one drawing those sighs out of her, sparking those pleasures in her. And oh, how it would feel to come together as we're meant to, to drink those shaky breaths from her lips, to feel her around me and know every flare of passion and delight is thanks to me—

I shut my eyes and set my jaw, resisting the flood of feeling. Throwing into place a crystalline wall within me like the one I used to shut *her* out during the conversations with my colleagues it was best she wasn't privy to.

Even the faint impressions of her ecstasy fall away. There's only blankness within now, echoing with the thud of my heart and the throb of my cock.

It doesn't matter. Tomorrow she will be with me and leave this intruder to our bond behind. Why shouldn't I want her to get him out of her system as much as she can? Better she does that than come to me regretting that she didn't get one last chance, isn't it?

Yes—yes, it is.

I stand up, perfectly steady, and grimace at the brush of my trousers against my still aching groin. The impulse flickers through me to head to my bedchamber to release it, but I'm no wolf to be led by my basest desires. I inhale and exhale slowly, once and again and three times, and the flow of blood slows. The pressure recedes.

There. It need not mean anything at all. I am master over myself.

I'm even less enthusiastic about dinner now than when I first meant to go, but starving myself certainly won't help matters. Keeping my steps light, I make my way to the smaller dining room where I eat when I don't have visitors. The silver dome covering the plate is still warm to the touch. I haven't let it sit too long.

I get to enjoy the meal, however much I can, for two bites of curried fish and one of braised frost kale. Then there's a knock on the door, and one of the servants from my flock peers around it at my answer.

The stout fae man dips into a quick bow. "I'm sorry, my lord. Arch-Lord Terisse has arrived to speak with you. I can tell her you'll be with her shortly?"

Well, there goes what little appetite I recovered. I nudge my chair back. "That's all right, Oswald. I'll come now. Thank you."

I'd expected this. Perhaps some part of me hoped that when one of my colleagues responded to the brief message I sent reporting that my soul-twined mate would be joining me, it'd be while I was away from home. But I do have to speak to them about it eventually.

It could have been worse. I'd appreciate Laoni's questioning even less—although naturally the self-styled leader of our quintet of arch-lords would see making such a visit as beneath her. If she'd felt that she needed to handle the matter directly, she'd have demanded *I* come to her.

Terisse is waiting in the entrance room just off the terrace, which tells me she flew here—and it appears she did so alone. I'm not sure how much of this unusual situation my colleagues have shared with their coteries so far.

When I enter the room, she turns toward me. Only faint lines on her otherwise smooth, coppery face show she's well into middle-age. The tufts of dark, greenish hair that fan out around her head like shadowed shards of emerald contain no traces of gray yet. She considers me with no hint of approval or concern revealed in the even line of her prim lips.

I dip my head slightly in acknowledgement, no subservience due between equals. "Welcome to Heart's Cadence, Terisse. What brought about this visit?"

She offers a small bob in return. "I apologize for the abrupt arrival. I'll keep this quick so as not to interrupt your night any more than I already have. We simply wanted to get a more extensive report on the new development with your soul-twined mate."

We, because naturally my colleagues conferred before deciding she'd be the one to approach me. I'm speaking not with her but all three of the others through her as soon as she reports back, no doubt.

I snuff out my momentary irritation and nod. "Of course. Everything is settled. I'll go across the border shortly before noon tomorrow with the shielding spell to ensure my security, although my mate honestly believes her pack intends me no harm. I'll take an oath to ensure *her* security in the winter realm and bring her back with me. She's agreed to a trial stay of ten days, but I expect once she's had time to adjust to the bond, all will be well."

"Have you considered that the visit might be a gambit to allow her to commit some treachery against us while she's here?"

"Of course." Of all the things my colleagues might accuse me of, carelessness is certainly not one of them. "Besides the fact that she could hardly lie while so close to the Heart, I have her thoughts from right inside her head. I've sensed no ill intentions from her."

Talia is wary and perhaps even frightened, defensive of her people and the violence that's been committed against them, but I couldn't expect anything less. I didn't glean the smallest bit of vengefulness from her.

"You'll want to keep a close eye on her nonetheless, knowing how... unpredictable the wolves can be." Terisse sucks in a breath just shy of a sigh, and I can't help wondering if my colleagues would have preferred it if the Seelie had refused to hand over my mate after all. If they were bargaining on getting to wage war with that point of leverage.

It wouldn't surprise me. I'd be more startled to learn they gave a feather about my marital success. Other than how that success might suit their ends, now that their first goal is no longer viable.

"See if you can't win her over quickly, then," Terisse goes on with a flick of her hand. "Derive whatever you can about their plans and defenses through your bond. We can't waste this opportunity."

My hackles rise for the fleeting instant before I shake off the instinctive reaction to how callously she's speaking of my mate. Her perspective is a logical way to look at the situation. No doubt I'd be thinking of it exactly the same way if I agreed with my colleagues' larger goals.

I can't ignore her point completely, though. Even if I'd rather we didn't find ourselves at war, we do need *some* kind of a solution. My loyalty to my flock and my people has to come before any devotion to an uncertain mate.

"You can be sure I'll be alert for any information that could aid us in our difficulties," I reply. "I do ask that the rest of you give us our privacy during her visit. If you wish to speak to me, I'll come to the rest of you. It may be stressful enough for her adjusting to the thought of living here without the pressure of more watchful eyes." And Heart only knows what skeptical remarks they might make in front of her, regarding both her and me.

"We can respect the complexities of your uncertain bond." Terisse turns as if to go, but pauses in mid-swivel to glance back at me. "But do keep a close eye on your own heart, Corwin. We wouldn't want *her* to be the one to win *you*. I'd imagine you'd agree that one such catastrophe in your family line is more than enough."

I fix my mouth into a stiff smile, biting back the cutting remark that leapt to my tongue. None of my colleagues would have resisted getting in that jab to drive their disdain home. "Naturally. You have nothing at all to fear there."

She makes a short sound that's barely agreement and steps toward the doors. A moment later, the dark shape of her raven launches into the air from my terrace.

She's gone, but they'll be watching me these ten days—far more closely than they have ever before.

And the worst of it is, I can't even blame them.

CHAPTER TEN

Talia

I hesitate just outside the partly constructed castle, looking toward the temporary pack village. The early morning sunlight paints the landscape with soft golden tones and shimmers off the haze of the border beyond the eastern forest. Just looking at it makes my gut knot tighter.

I probably should have done this sooner, given her more time to decide—but the plan fell into place so quickly, and *I* hadn't quite decided I was going to make this request until I woke up this morning.

Maybe I still haven't totally made it. I waver on my feet before pressing onward to the house I know Harper is staying in.

The summer fae tend to be early risers unless there was a revel the night before. My friend answers my knock already alert and dressed—in a relatively simple gown by her standards. She looks me over, her initial smile faltering. "What's wrong? Has there been more trouble from the ravens?"

I guess that's one way of describing the situation, but it's not at all what she means. I shake my head. "No attacks or anything. I wanted to talk with you about something. Can I come in?"

"Of course." Harper steps back, her brow still knit with worry. I'm not totally sure she *shouldn't* be worried.

The temporary homes the pack-kin are using while the full castle and village are being built contain just one large, circular room with a few basic wooden furnishings. The table in the corner has only one chair. Harper perches on the edge of the narrow bed, and I grab the chair, turning it to face her.

Once I've sat down, it takes a moment for me to find my words. We've been keeping my connection to the Unseelie as quiet as possible—Sylas is hoping to have my visit there stay essentially secret—and talking about it still unnerves me.

I clasp my hands together on my lap and drag in a breath. "Something happened the night of the coronation celebration. When the Unseelie arch-lords came to talk to ours. I—I've formed a soul-twined bond with one of their arch-lords."

Harper's eyes grow so wide there seems to be a real risk they'll fall out of her head. "*What?* But… you're not even fae." Her pale cheeks flush red. "I mean—"

I let out a choked sort of laugh. "It's okay. I know I'm not, and I know how crazy it sounds because of that. But obviously whatever tied my blood to the curse connected me to the world in other ways we didn't expect too." I'm hoping this is the last of those surprises, but at this point, I'm not counting on it.

"So what are you going to do?" She bites her lip, and I assume she's thinking of what my absence would mean for the Seelie and their curse, but I've misjudged her. "I suppose you have to go to him? I'll… I'll miss having you around. We won't be able to see more of this domain together after all."

The fact that she's more bothered by losing my company than my blood reassures me of my choice. I manage a crooked smile. "I'm not committing to anything yet. There are a lot of things and people I'd miss here. And I don't know how much we can trust any of the Unseelie. But I've agreed to stay with him for ten days just to get to know him a little, so that if"—*when*—"I decide to come back, the Heart will know I gave it a try."

Harper nods slowly. "That makes sense. I wouldn't trust them either, after all those attacks. Are you going today, then? You came to say good-bye?"

"Kind of." I rub my mouth. "I was actually wondering… how would you like to explore an Unseelie arch-lord's domain instead?"

She blinks at me, and I swear her eyes nearly do fall out this time. "You—you want me to come *with* you?"

My fingers curl into the skirt of my dress. "I know it's a big ask. It could be dangerous. The Unseelie arch-lord has agreed that I can bring one companion with me, but we had to promise it wouldn't be anyone with much warrior training or experience. It'd be nice to have someone I know that I can talk to while I'm there, someone who can be a second set of eyes in case the winter fae have any ulterior motives… It's okay if it's too much. I won't be upset if you say no."

Not with her, at least. The thought of crossing the border into totally unfamiliar territory with no one I can count on to support me over my Unseelie hosts makes my skin crawl.

Harper is simply staring at me now. "And you'd trust *me* to be that person?" she says in a small voice.

"There isn't anyone else I'd want to ask." With my men and Astrid out of the equation, Harper is the only member of the pack I've talked much with, shared anything personal with. Being in Corwin's home with a companion I barely know might feel even worse than being alone.

She made an awful mistake, but she's done everything she can to make up for it. If she's willing to brave the winter realm to support me there, then that's really all the proof I need that she deserves my trust again.

Her hands twitch at her sides. The idea obviously scares her.

I get up. "You can take some time to think about it. This is coming together quickly—I'm supposed to leave in a few hours—but you don't have to decide this exact moment."

"No." Her chin lifts. "I can decide now. I'll come with you. I'm glad you asked. You need someone there with you, and I won't be happy without my friend here, so it works out for both of us." A hint of a smile crosses her lips. "And it might be a little exciting seeing the winter realm. As long as the ravens don't try to peck us to death or anything."

"I'm pretty sure Sylas is going to make that one of the conditions of the visit," I say dryly, and then a giggle that's as much anxiety as amusement tumbles out of me. Harper laughs too. Right then, I have no doubts at all.

She folds her arms over her chest and gives me a once-over. "You're not meeting your soul-twined arch-lord mate in *that* dress, are you?"

I'm not surprised that would be where her attention goes next. I'm wearing a simple blue knee-length smock like the type most of the female pack-kin wear for their day-to-day lives, airy but plain. "I don't have anything fancy here. I wasn't sure I should make a big deal of it..."

Harper's huff tells me how much she disagrees. She jumps up and grabs the small trunk she brought with her. "You need to make a statement—that you're someone just as special as any bird-brain arch-lord. It's a good thing I came prepared just in case. Let's see... Yes, this one should do it. Just give me a little while to adjust it so it'll fit you properly. I'll have it ready in an hour."

"You really don't have to—" I start to protest, but she tuts at me and shoos me out so she can get to work.

"Go have one of August's breakfasts," she calls after me. "You're getting too skinny again; I'll have to adjust all your other dresses too if you keep that up."

I've actually already eaten, but it's true that my appetite hasn't been great the past few days. I make a silent commitment to eating decent portions of whatever Corwin's going to serve us, because I can't let myself get weak while I'm on Unseelie territory, and head back to the castle to await whatever gorgeous gown Harper is getting ready for me.

I reach the door just as Whitt comes striding out at a much more urgent pace than I'd expect from him first thing in the morning. My pulse stutters with the thought that we're facing yet another calamity, but the moment his eyes land on me, his expression relaxes. "There you are, mite."

"I just went to talk to Harper," I say. "She agreed to come."

He hums to himself. "An interesting choice after what she almost put you through, but I know better than to argue with your judgment. She's shown a fair bit of grit in the past couple of weeks, I'll give her that." He brushes his hand over my hair, careful not to make it too much of a caress while the pack-kin who only know of my more intimate involvement with August might be looking on. "Take a short walk with me?"

Maybe there is unfortunate news after all. I limp alongside him past the temporary village, across the broad field of twinkling flowers beyond, and into this domain's forest. It's less ominous than the thick brush and towering trees of Hearthshire. The trees are more stout than looming, with only small patches of flowers and ferns here and there where the sunlight streams through the canopy. The pulsing energy of the Heart tickles over my skin.

As we walk, Whitt scans our surroundings. Before we've gone far enough for my warped foot to start to ache, he stops at a massive log in a small glade. As he sits, he tugs me into his lap, enveloping me within his arms and beneath his chin as if he never means to let me go.

His breath tickles over my forehead with his voice. "I'd give anything to be the one to go with you, you know. And not just to get a direct eyeful of what those blasted birds are up to. It doesn't matter how mighty you are—you shouldn't have to take this on."

The vehemence in his words brings a fresh ache into my heart. I lean into his warmth and his scent, summery as a sun-baked beach. Whitt doesn't often let much deeper emotion show, even when we're alone. Knowing more about his past, I can see why—and I treasure every moment of open affection he offers me.

Especially when I know it'll be over a week before I'll feel his embrace again.

"I survived nine years in Aerik's cage," I remind him as well as myself. "The next ten days *can't* be worse than that."

"If I thought there was any chance they'd come close, I'd be fighting tooth and claw to keep you here," Whitt mutters.

I reach up to touch his gorgeous face, and he takes the opening to steal a kiss. It lingers on, so tender the ache spreads through my whole chest. Then he nuzzles my cheek. When he speaks again, his voice is raw. "You have been *so*… I was such an idiot to think your presence would hurt us somehow. I wish I could do as much for you as you have for us. For *me*. The thing that kills me the most is that you'll be just across the border but completely beyond my reach."

I swallow hard. "You can't help that. And you *have* been here for me, in so many ways… I hate how much trouble I've brought—"

He catches my cheek before I can go on, dropping his forehead to mine. "Don't. None of that was your doing. From the moment I came after you in the woods that night after I told you off, I've never once regretted having you with us. This doesn't mean much yet, but…"

He lets that sentence hang for long enough that I start to think he's changed his mind about whatever he was going to say. Then he dips his head farther to murmur by my ear. "Wye."

I peer up at him, confused. "Why what?"

His mouth pulls into a slanted grin. "Not the question. It's the first syllable in my true name."

His words knock the breath from my lungs. "But—you're telling *me*? You said—"

Whitt draws me close again, his voice still low. "I've never given it to anyone. It still doesn't do you any good, just having a piece. I can't risk the whole thing now when we don't know what that wretched raven arch-lord might try to ferret out from your mind—it's not just my own security but the entire pack, and Sylas as arch-lord… But I want you to have it as my promise that if there comes a time when that connection doesn't threaten us, I'll give you the rest. Even if we can't be bonded the same way you are to him, you'll be able to reach me somehow or other wherever I am, whenever you need me."

My throat squeezes tight. Having his true name would give me as much power over him as I can summon with my magic—the ability not just to delve into his mind and project my thoughts to him but to order him around if I wanted to do that. I probably *don't* have enough power to overcome his will if he resists, and from what I've heard whatever connection I could form would be only a pale shade of the innate, vivid shared awareness that binds me to Corwin, but still, it's an immense show of trust.

"If you still *want* that connection with me after all of this," Whitt adds. When I start to protest, he quiets me with a quick peck. "I know you would now. But you can't be sure—I've been alive for more than four centuries, and *I* can barely comprehend the power of a soul-twined bond."

He pulls back far enough to hold my gaze. "You need to know that we'd understand if something happens between you and him. The Heart gave you this bond. If you end up feeling more than you expect to and you want to act on those feelings, none of us—Sylas or August or me—will blame you, I promise you that. We all realize it's a possibility. We're prepared for it. I'll consider us *lucky* if what you feel for us overcomes even the Heart's blessing."

I blink back the tears forming in my eyes. My voice comes out thinner than I'd like. "I can't imagine wanting anyone other than the three of you. Thank you—for the beginning of your true name. For wanting to give it to me."

I don't know what else to say, so I settle for kissing him, hard, pouring all my love into our embrace in the hopes that he can sense it all even though no magic ties us together yet.

"It'd be for me as much as for you," Whitt says roughly, tucking me against him again. "Anything that will keep you close in whatever way, I'm all for." He pauses, and his voice drops. "I love you, Talia."

Joy quivers through me, bright and giddying. Maybe I should have assumed by now, after all the devotion he's offered me, after his brothers had made their own declarations, but Whitt's never said it out loud before.

I throw my arms around his neck, and he squeezes me tight. "I love you too," I say, choking up. "So much."

But in a few short hours I'm going to have to leave him and the other men I love behind.

CHAPTER ELEVEN

Talia

As I walk onto the field around the Heart, the dress Harper fixed up for me whispers against my legs. The soft, ivory fabric with its pearly sheen covers my arms from wrists to shoulders and flows down, gently hugging my chest and hips, to my ankles. Panes of lace show peeks of my collarbone and my calves. The intricate patterns shine like frost against my skin.

I look every bit a winter princess, and I'm not sure how I feel about that.

I could see the same hesitation in my lovers' eyes when they took me in, mingled with their appreciation. Harper knows what she's doing—I look *good*, at least. Like a woman who can stand on her two feet, even if one of those feet is a bit wonky, and who won't be cowed by whatever the Unseelie throw at me.

Here's hoping that's actually true.

When we stop several feet shy of the border's shimmering gray haze, Sylas positions himself next to me. Whitt and August flank us, August holding a trunk with some changes of clothes and a few other belongings I quickly packed. Harper stands off to the side, still in her casual dress from this morning so she doesn't upstage me but with her own trunk clutched in her hands.

I want to spin around and claim one last kiss from all my men, but Corwin is due to step across the border any moment now. I might have mentioned my heart's other commitments to him, but starting off this trial run with him seeing me in another man's arms seems like a disaster waiting to happen. So I stand still and straight, my arms at my sides, my heart thudding so loud I suspect all my fae companions can hear it.

My wall of light is still glowing inside me, shored up a few minutes ago. I don't want Corwin seeing just how nervous I am. I don't want to risk him catching glimpses of other, dangerous thoughts that might slip through my mind while I *am* so nervous.

The other arch-lords asked to be present as well, but Sylas managed to dissuade them. I guess it'd be pretty obvious that something big is going on if they were all here. What would the rest of the Seelie think if they knew the cure to their curse was about to cross enemy lines?

I inhale slowly, squaring my shoulders and steadying myself, and the mass of haze quivers. A figure comes into focus through the fog just before he steps out onto the grass on our side.

Corwin is dressed in the formal jacket and slacks I remember from the night of the coronation, though he hasn't brought out his wings. A thin circlet crown gleams silver amid his blue-black curls. His dark gaze shoots straight to me, and my heart stutters harder despite my best efforts at staying calm.

Looking at him, I can't read his emotions at all. His expression is even more impenetrable than Sylas's can be.

At least he seems relatively relaxed about the whole situation, though he stays within a couple of feet of the border as if he thinks he might need to dive back through to the winter side at any moment. He nods to me, his gaze flicking down over me for an instant before returning to my face. His voice comes out cool and even. "Talia. You look lovely. You're ready?"

"Yes." I motion to Harper. "This is my friend Harper. She's the one who'll be joining me. The dress is thanks to her."

He nods to my friend as well. "It's exquisite work." He turns his attention to Sylas, and his frame, equal to the other arch-lord's in height if slimmer, draws just a little straighter. "I'm sure you can understand that I'd prefer not to linger in your realm any longer than necessary. I'm prepared to take the oaths we discussed."

It's really happening. In just a few minutes, I'll be walking with him through that haze into the total unknown. Even Sylas and his cadre don't have much idea how the winter arch-lords live.

My pulse kicks up another notch, and my hand twitches to my hair before I can catch the nervous gesture. As I tuck the stray waves behind my ear, Corwin's gaze slides back to me—and his posture goes totally rigid.

I freeze with my hand still by my face, startled by his reaction and the sudden bewilderment that's crossed his previously implacable face. A flicker of hostility breaches the glowing barrier inside me. What have I done?

Corwin strides forward abruptly. I stiffen, my nerves jangling with alarm. He stops just a few feet away from me with a flare of his nostrils and a widening of his eyes. "You…"

"Arch-Lord Corwin?" Sylas says with a hint of a growl.

Corwin spins to face him. "What's the meaning of this?" he demands, his voice gone flat and outright cold. "You thought you'd pass off an imposter as my soul-twined mate? If you put some magic on her that you thought would disguise her nature, it's failed. She's obviously human."

Oh. Oh, no. A ball of ice forms in my stomach. He didn't realize. He was startled before only because he thought I was a Seelie woman—a *true-blooded* Seelie woman. Of course. It never occurred to him just how unlikely this bond was even beyond that. I didn't make a point of mentioning what I am because I assumed he'd simply know, and he's never gotten that close a look at me before.

"Corwin," I say quickly. "There's no trick. I'm Talia. I—I don't know how it happened; none of us do. It's just—"

My words are only deepening the offended curve of his mouth. I stop talking and do the only thing I can think of that could possibly convince him beyond a doubt: I let the wall inside me drop.

Emotions flood through the space between us: anger and betrayal and a jab of fear, so sharp-edged and swift I flinch. But a second later, all those sensations retreat behind a chilly wave of shock. Corwin stares at me, and I see myself through his eyes in the back of my mind, tense but standing firm.

I'm sorry, I think at him, hoping he can pick up on the honest regret I'm feeling. *I would have told you—I thought you'd already realized.*

For a moment, we all stand there in taut silence, my lovers braced, Harper hugging herself. Corwin's jaw works, but I can't imagine there's any magic that could create an illusion of a soul-twined bond where there wasn't one. He has to know it's true.

"Is there a problem?" Sylas asks, his low baritone unusually terse. "You wanted the chance to meet your soul-twined mate. Here she is. If *you're* rejecting her—"

"*No,*" Corwin interrupts, before I can feel more than a dash of relief at the thought that this bizarre situation could be put to rest that easily. He tugs at the base of his jacket and seems to gather himself. As the glimpses of his emotions filtering to me settle, I get the impression of confusion and curiosity, but no more sense of anger.

"No," he says more smoothly. "I was only surprised. It is… rather irregular."

Whitt snorts. "Yes, we're quite aware of that."

August folds his arms over his chest in a subtle but implicit threat. "It shouldn't mean you treat her any differently than if she was the truest of true-blooded fae."

Corwin takes him in, and I catch wisps of recognition and defensiveness—and a renewed quiver of anger. Then it all fades away as he must reconstruct whatever wall he's used to keep me out of his awareness before.

Can he tell that August is one of my lovers? How much does he care that there may be less of a place for him in my heart rather than seeing me as a possession that's been stolen?

The Unseelie arch-lord raises his chin at a haughty angle. "She's my soul-twined mate. That puts her above any other being in my consideration automatically."

"Then we can proceed with the oaths?" Sylas asks pointedly.

Corwin glances at me. His bronze face has become an unreadable mask again, but I think there's still something puzzled in his gaze. Well, why wouldn't there be? I've known how impossible this bond is from the start, and I'm still unsettled by it.

But I agreed to give it a try anyway, so the least he can do is not be a jerk about it. I raise my chin too, gazing back at him.

The corners of his lips curl upward with the faintest hint of a smile. Enough to melt a little of the icy panic that's been trickling through my veins since he figured out what I am.

Maybe this will be okay. Ten days. I can manage that. I've already seen that he isn't only the cold, impenetrable front he's presenting.

"Yes," Corwin says, still watching me. "Proceed with the oaths."

As Sylas lays out the phrasing previously agreed on, the thrum of the Heart's magic rises, lacing through his words. It resonates through Corwin's voice repeating the oaths. He swears that I will be free to return in ten days' time, that he will do everything in his power to ensure my and Harper's safety from any type of harm, and that he'll keep secret anything he learns from me that relates to the Seelie. He doesn't halt or hesitate once.

Then it's done. Corwin takes my trunk from August. I force myself not to look at my lovers. If I do, I'm afraid I won't be able to hold back the sob prickling at the back of my throat.

My soul-twined mate holds out his hand to me. "Shall we go, then?"

My arm balks at my side, the memory racing through my mind of his touch and the electric impact it had even in a dream. Before I can decide whether to face that intensity or risk offending him, he turns the gesture into a simple beckoning. As I step forward, he lets his hand drop without complaint.

Harper moves to join me. We have to make our own vows to cross the border so close to the Heart.

"By the Heart, I swear to do no harm to the fae beyond this boundary. May I pass in peace and amity," I say. A tingle shoots through my chest straight to my toes, its energy wriggling through my nerves. Harper makes the same declaration.

Then, with Corwin leading the way, we walk into the haze toward the lands of the winter fae.

CHAPTER TWELVE

Talia

It only takes a few steps into the border area before a chill seeps through the hazy air. The whisper of grass beneath my boots hardens into the crinkle of frost and then the crunch of a thin layer of snow. My dress may cover most of my body, but the silky fabric is so thin that the cold licks right through it. I shiver, and Harper grabs my hand, leaning close to me for both reassurance and warmth.

I stay focused on Corwin's tall, lean form just ahead of us, his pale clothes blending into the fog but his dark hair clearly visible. It's only a couple more strides before the border's haze falls away. I suck in a breath, staring at the landscape around us.

The winter realm couldn't look more different from the warmth and rich colors of the summer lands. We're standing on an icy plain which glints with the sharp sunlight falling from the clear blue sky. To our right, near where the Heart keeps up its rhythmic pulsing, looms an immense ivory tower with turrets jutting from its sides like tusks. I guess that's the Unseelie arch-lords' equivalent to our Bastion. Beyond it, I can make out one other building in the distance: a castle of gleaming silver.

That's not where we're heading, though. Just a little to our left, across the vast plain, rises another palace that seems to not so much reflect the sunlight off its translucent stone walls but absorb it and bounce it around in a boundless twinkling. The spires towering high above the main rooftop have the shape of crystal growths, dappled with facets. I can tell from the satisfaction that crosses Corwin's face, taking it in, that it's his home.

There are forests here too—ice-laden, leafless trees in a cluster farther to our left. And at a vast distance, craggy snow-capped mountains stretch toward the sky.

It's all beautiful in a cold, impervious sort of way. Corwin glances back at us and catches my next shiver, partly awe but partly the chill that's biting deeper into my skin. His eyes flicker with concern.

"My apologies. I didn't think—I'm unaccustomed to Seelie guests. Here, we all have warming enchantments woven into our clothes. I can put one in place for both of you quickly… if that's all right?"

My nerves twitch at the thought of him casting any kind of magic on me, but I'm not keen on freezing to death either. "Just that, no other magic?" I say quickly, afraid my teeth with start chattering if I open my mouth for too long.

"Only the warming charm," Corwin promises, and I nod.

He murmurs a few syllables with a brisk gesture of his hand, and heat unfurls over my body, chasing away the chill not just where my dress brushes against my skin but up over my face as well. I restrain another shiver that has nothing to do with the cold this time. The wash of warmth felt too close to being touched in a way much more intimate than I'm comfortable with from my theoretical mate.

At least I'm no longer on the verge of frostbite. Corwin casts the same spell on Harper's clothing, and she lets out a sigh of relief. He motions for us to follow him to the sparkling crystal palace. "I'll have one of the folk of my flock see that the rest of your clothes are similarly prepared."

"Flock?" I say, and then wince at myself. Of course raven shifters wouldn't refer to their people as a "pack." "Never mind." I wave toward the palace. "So that's yours? What did you call your domain—Heart's Cadence?"

His lips form a slight smile as if the fact that I remembered pleases him, but not so much that he's going to make too big a deal of it. He's kept our bond closed off—I can't read his emotions through it. Obviously trust is going to take a while on both sides.

"Yes, this is where you'll be staying," he says. "If you listen closely, you'll already be able to hear how the palace honors its name."

I don't understand what he means until I tune out the rasp of our feet over the icy terrain. Another sound slips through the air, soft and quavering but forming a clear melody once I've latched onto it.

Harper, with the extensive experience with music she has thanks to her parents, must pick the tune up even faster. Her thin eyebrows rise. "That's coming from the palace?"

Corwin inclines his head. "The crystals were sculpted so that they'd resonate when the wind passes over them to form a sort of song. You're never far from music in Heart's Cadence."

The line sounds rehearsed, but the pride in his voice is unmistakeable. I study the palace, thinking about how lords design their homes back in the summer realm. "Are you especially strong in magic to do with crystals, then?"

"Stone of all sorts. Although I can't take credit for more than a few minor renovations to the palace. It's been standing for well over a thousand years. My great-grandmother chose diamond for the hardiness as well as its beauty."

That whole building is made out of *diamond*? I manage to snap my jaw shut before I'm outright gaping. It mustn't be that big a deal when you can summon as much as you want just by saying a true name, but still. The kings and queens still in existence back in the human world would faint over that kind of riches.

And that's where I'm going to be living for the next ten days.

Harper grasps my hand again, but there's a spring in her step now. The flush in her cheeks looks more excited than nervous. I'm sure it's easier to see this as a fantastic adventure when you're not wondering whether you can trust a total stranger whose soul has inexplicably merged with yours.

Corwin is watching me. My sense of the connection between us shifts as he lowers his own barrier, allowing a few impressions to filter through. He's evaluating my reaction, hopeful but cautious. "What do you think?"

I instinctively summoned my own inner wall when I noticed his relaxing, but the tickle of hope sets me more at ease. I let my gaze rove over the palace, the forest, and the mountains beyond again, doing my best to take them in as if I was a traveler simply here to explore with no other pressures on me. Another wave of awe ripples through me, and I don't mind if he feels it. "It's very different from the parts of the fae world I'm used to, but it is beautiful."

Will I get to see much more of this place, or will Corwin want to keep me shut away in his home until he's sure of my loyalties and affections? I don't know how to ask that without it coming out badly, so I push the question away for now.

I expected more of a welcoming party, but only a couple of fae emerge from the palace to greet us. Both are dressed in well-constructed but simple tunics and trousers that make me suspect they're staff rather than anyone in a position of power.

Does Corwin have a cadre like all the Seelie lords do? Don't they want to meet his supposed mate? For that matter, where's the rest of his flock? I don't see any smaller buildings around. Surely they don't all live in the palace with him?

I don't vocalize any of my confusion even mentally, but Corwin must pick up on some of it through our bond. He points to a sheer edge several feet beyond the farthest reach of the palace where the land appears to fall away completely. "My flock has their homes along the cliffside on either side of the falls. There's something to be said for a view that gives you the impression of soaring even when you have your feet on the ground."

If you're used to having full control over any "soaring" you do, I'd bet there is.

When we reach the grand entrance with its onion-dome-topped arch, the two fae who came out to meet us usher us inside. "The rooms are ready, my lord," one says to Corwin. The other offers his hands to take Harper's trunk.

She hesitates and then hands it over. "Thank you."

The interior of the palace sparkles nearly as much as the exterior. Muted sunlight radiates through the high ceilings and the walls, which are thick enough to hide any view of the objects or figures that lie beyond them. Sleek blue-gray rugs cover the floors and muffle our footsteps. The faint melody continues rising and falling around us, easier to make out now that we're right within the palace.

After a couple of turns, the staff stop. Corwin opens a door to a vast bedroom with a pale, marble-framed canopy bed and matching furnishings. "This will be your room, for the time being," he says to me, bringing the prickling awareness that I'd be expected to eventually share *his* room with him. "And your companion will be staying right across the hall."

The man with Harper's trunk has already carried it into the room opposite. Harper walks in after him, gasping as she looks around.

Leaving my door open, Corwin sets my trunk at the foot of the bed and pauses. "I'd appreciate—could I have a few moments to speak to you alone? I feel it might be easier to settle into getting to know each other if we at least begin without an audience."

He might be right, and I don't get any sense of ill intent through the bond, only an honest desire to understand more about me. I have plenty of questions I want to ask him too, and it makes sense that he wouldn't necessarily open up as much with Harper there.

"All right," I say. "But—not in here." Having a private conversation with my soul-twined mate in a room that features a bed seems like it'd raise expectations I'd rather not have on the table. "Is there somewhere else we could talk?"

"Yes, of course."

Harper has overheard the whole exchange. "I'll be fine," she calls from the other room. "Just come get me if you need me."

Corwin steps back into the hall. "You both can venture anywhere you'd like in the palace that's available to you—and most of it is, other than a few rooms that require more discretion. I'd recommend you don't leave the palace without me until I've had a chance to introduce you to the full flock, so I can be sure of their reactions." He stops, maybe not totally sure of his *own* reactions yet, and then motions for me to follow him.

The halls we walk through feel even more empty without the company. I don't spot any other fae or any human servants, if he keeps them. The palace is vast and breathtaking in its spectacle, but somehow that only makes the emptiness feel lonelier.

He doesn't have a mate, of course, but neither does Sylas, and there was always a bustle of energy in and around *his* castle, especially once we were back at Hearthshire.

Corwin leads me into a sitting room with tall windows that look out over a wide diamond terrace with an even more epic view of the mountains. For all the glinting hardness of the palace itself, the sofas and chairs look comfortable enough, their marble seats, backs, and arms set with leather cushions. I sink down onto one end of a sofa, tucking my legs up beside me, and Corwin takes an armchair that he pulls over so he's facing me.

"Why don't you start?" he says mildly. "I can't imagine how many questions you must have that you hesitated to ask through the bond."

I have plenty, but I don't know which might get me into trouble. I go with the most immediate. "Do you have a cadre? Relatives or friends who are like… advisors, and the main people you turn to when you're guiding your—your flock?"

"Cadre is a Seelie term. We refer to our close associates as our coterie."

"So, you do have one then?" I glance around. "Do they live here in the palace too?" *Where* are *they, and why aren't they here for something like this?* I think to myself behind the partial wall I'm still holding against the full force of our connection.

Corwin's mouth twitches as if that idea is amusing. "No, they have their own homes—by the top of the cliff so they're close at hand when I need to call on them. You'll meet at least a couple of them while you're here, but they're mostly off conducting business and handling other matters for me throughout the realm."

Whitt and August often leave on Sylas's instructions, but rarely for more than a day or two, and they spend at least as much time with him. I restrain a frown, sucking my lower lip under my teeth instead as

I decide whether I want to push farther. "I guess you don't… socialize with them all that much, then?"'

"No. I suppose the wolves do?" His tone suggests he finds that amusing as well. My hackles rise automatically, but Corwin goes on without noticing. "I trust my coterie, and they're a great help to me, but our association is strictly professional. Nothing good comes from blurring the lines between colleague and friend."

That's definitely a very different attitude from the Seelie's. After spending so long in the company of my men, witnessing how well they support each other in both personal and official ways, I have trouble believing he's right and that the way he lives doesn't get lonely. But I guess he's never known anything else.

"What about—do you have family?"

A flare of uneasy emotion passes into me and then fades away. No outward sign of distress shows on Corwin's face. "I am an only child, and sadly my parents have met dire fates before their times."

"Oh. I'm sorry." A lump forms in my throat. I extend my sympathy to him through our bond so he'll know I mean that. "I lost my family too."

"Yes." He cocks his head, a thin furrow creasing his brow. "How did you come to be among the Seelie? You weren't working for Arch-Lord Sylas as a servant."

"No. I—" I want to say it's complicated and leave it at that, but I probably owe him more of an explanation, especially when he wasn't expecting a human mate in the first place.

I brace myself, narrowing it down to the facts and avoiding the panic-provoking memories as well as I can. "When I was twelve, my family was attacked by Seelie roaming in the human world as wolves. They killed my parents and brother and brought me back to the fae world with them. That lord kept me in a cage for nine years, until Sylas happened to find me and rescued me. He's allowed me to become a full member of his pack—well, as much as I can be."

The disbelief in Corwin's expression sends another prickle of irritation through me. He might have been willing to roll with the idea of a human as his mate, but he clearly has trouble imagining me as an equal to the fae. Or else has trouble imagining that any summer fae could accept me as one, which isn't much better.

"That first lord," he says. "He treated you quite badly?"

Isn't telling him I was in a cage enough to establish that fact?

Despite my best efforts, a shudder runs through me, dredging shreds of the past with it. The glow I was holding in place thins even more. Corwin must catch glimpses of the hard floor, the filthy blanket, the jabs of my captors' bodies shoving mine, and the snap of my foot. The best I can do is keep my breaths even though shallow.

"Yes," I manage in a rough voice. "It was horrible."

The arch-lord's eyes flash darker and his jaw clenches. If he were Seelie, I suspect his fangs would be coming out. Disgust flows from him back into me. "And this is how the summer fae see fit to treat other beings?"

Why does he have to make this about all Seelie kind rather than those specific monsters? Am I supposed to believe that all *Unseelie* handle humans with kindness and respect after what I've heard about how they treat other fae?

I outright bristle, sitting up straighter. "No. Not all of them. Sylas and his pack have welcomed me as their own."

Even as I say that, my errant mind summons a memory of my first couple of weeks with Sylas, of his former cadre-chosen Kellan who insulted and pushed me around, of my fears that even Sylas wouldn't let me be more than a prisoner. Corwin's mouth flattens. "I see even that isn't completely true."

"It wasn't—he dealt with Kellan—there was so much at stake—" I cut myself off before anything I don't want to reveal spills out, but I don't have as much control over my thoughts. Something in the jumble of recollections makes Corwin stiffen in his chair.

Oh, crap.

"What?" I say, crossing my arms over my chest, dreading the answer.

He stares at me. "Their curse. The savagery their wolves descend into under the full moon. *You* can heal it in them?"

I bite back several choice swear words. This was the thing we least wanted him to find out, and he's pulled it out of me less than an hour after I got here. “You can’t tell the other Unseelie, *any* of them. That was part of your oath.”

“I know.” Corwin blinks, but he can’t quite manage to break out of his stare. “Your position among the wolves makes more sense now. Perhaps even why the Heart might have blessed you so. But… for Arch-Lord Sylas to let you come here when all the Seelie are relying on you—what on earth was he thinking agreeing to this arrangement?”

As if the man in front of me hadn’t been pleading to have me here. “Your people were threatening full-out war, in case you’ve forgotten.”

Corwin shakes his head. “I’d have thought a boon like what you offer would be worth going to war over. Although I suppose thinking straight isn’t exactly the wolves’ specialty…”

A jolt of anger spurs me onto my feet. I’m not going to sit here and listen to him disparage the people who saved me and protected me any longer.

“There isn’t any problem with Sylas’s thinking,” I snap. “He agreed to have me come here because he’s so honorable he does whatever seems to be the most right even if his own people might suffer in the meantime, and that’s exactly why I fell in love with him.”

I know those last words were a mistake the instant Corwin’s face hardens. Without waiting to hear his response, I spin on my heel and stalk out of the room as quickly as my uneven steps will take me.

CHAPTER THIRTEEN

Talia

I'm not sure how long I've been lying on my bed—which is annoyingly cozy, as much as right now I want to hate everything in the winter realm—when a knock sounds on the bedroom door. Corwin's voice carries through, low and a little stiff.

"Talia, dinner is being served, if you would accompany me."

My stomach, the traitor, chooses that moment to rumble. Corwin probably heard the sound with this sharp fae ears. I close my eyes, summoning another swell of the glow inside me that feels more like a shield than a simple wall now.

I promised to give him a chance. I'm stuck here for ten days either way. It's not as if I can starve myself for the entire time—and being that defiant would reflect pretty badly on my pack back home too, wouldn't it?

Besides, I have more questions that I haven't gotten answers to yet that could benefit all the Seelie back home. Like why the heck the raven shifters have been so intent on stealing territory from them. Even if Corwin is kind of a jerk, I can tolerate his attitude if it means I find out something that could stop all the fighting.

I am going to lay down a new ground rule, though.

I push myself off the bed and go to open the door, staying inside the room while I study the Unseelie arch-lord. The slight stiffness in his tone is echoed in his posture, but he manages a small smile that doesn't look too forced.

"I apologize for earlier," he says. "It's a poor host that disparages his guest's associates. I hope we can put that misstep behind us?"

I'm sure he hopes I can put the whole falling in love with Sylas thing behind me too. I give him the steeliest look I can manage. "While I'm here, I don't want to hear any more insults about my pack-kin or the Seelie in general. There's a whole lot I could say about the winter fae if I wasn't trying to make the best of this, you know."

He dips his head, his lips twitching into a brief grimace. "That's fair. I will… reserve judgment for now."

Or at least he won't say those judgments out loud, but I guess that's as much as I can ask for.

I step out, and his arm moves as if to offer me his hand. He catches it before he completes the gesture, maybe remembering my reluctance when he did the same thing before we crossed the border.

As I walk beside him, my limp steadied but not completely erased by the brace built into my right boot, his gaze falls to my legs. "You favor your right foot," he says cautiously. "That was—I caught a glimpse of something when you spoke of your… captivity…"

I brace myself, holding the memories at as much of a distance as I can. "One of that lord's cadre-chosen broke it as 'punishment.' They let the bones heal wrong, so the injury is permanent now. But I get along all right anyway."

His hint of a smile comes back. "Yes, you do."

I glance over my shoulder. "What about Harper?"

"Oh, I had one of the servants escort her already. I thought it would be better if I spoke to you one-to-one."

Corwin says that, and then he lapses into a silence that stretches until we reach the dining room, so he mustn't have had all that much to say after all. He doesn't mention my declaration about Sylas, and *I'm* not going to bring up the other men I love if he'd prefer to sweep the subject under the rug for now.

We arrive at a smaller room than I was expecting with a table of mottled white-and-gray marble that couldn't seat more than eight. Harper is the only one already there. As we come in, she beams at me. I sit across from her, and Corwin takes the head of the table.

It's apparent from the crystal goblets and polished clay plates laid out in front of us that this dinner will be for only us three. Presumably Corwin's business-only coterie eats in their own homes. Do they have families or are their lives totally dedicated to their lord despite the distance between them?

I've already asked so much about Corwin's companions, though, and that's not even what's most important. For a little while, I let myself get diverted by the dishes brought out by the kitchen staff: a middle-aged man and a girl who looks a few years younger than I am, with similar enough bushy pale hair and snub noses for me to assume they're related. I don't know if they're the ones doing the cooking as well, but the creamy soup and delicately spiced steak would have August demanding the recipes.

A twinge of homesickness runs through my gut at the thought of him. Maybe a trace of that feeling seeps through my wall, because Corwin's gaze snaps to me.

I shore up the glowing barrier again and refocus on the present. Despite my best efforts, complimenting Corwin on the meal he's arranged and answering a few careful inquiries he makes about Seelie cuisine, the conversation stays stilted. He doesn't seem to know what to say any more than I do.

The plentiful food only makes me more certain that the Unseelie aren't facing some huge catastrophe, though. Corwin's domain has appeared nothing but peaceful since we arrived, and he's given no indication of any troubles here. But surely his people haven't been attacking and killing mine just for the fun of it?

I try to figure out a way of getting at that subject without asking him point blank why the Unseelie have been so awful, since that approach seems unlikely to go over well. "What sorts of things keep you busy on a usual day?" I ask. Presumably he cleared whatever would normally be on his schedule to make way for my arrival.

Corwin cuts off another slice of his steak with brisk efficiency.

"There are always small matters to attend to in the running of the domain, of course, and regular meetings with my fellow arch-lords. When I can, I visit the farther domains to ensure everything is well across the realm. I like to stay aware of any significant happenings."

"Your coterie wouldn't handle that for you?" I say automatically, thinking of Whitt and his network of contacts.

"They keep me well-informed, but I like the other lords to see that I'm taking an active interest. And I trust my eyes and ears before anyone else's." He pauses. "It's possible I'll need to be away while you're here—never for more than half a day or so."

"That's all right. I wouldn't expect you to ignore your responsibilities." I pause, thinking of the wide variety of landscapes I've encountered in the summer realm, from dense forests to open prairie, swampland to towering hills. "Is most of the winter realm pretty rocky, like here and the mountains? Do all the flocks have their homes on cliffsides and places like that?"

Corwin's eyes light up a bit as if he's pleased that I'm taking any interest in his realm. "Not at all. Every lord and his subjects have their own preferences, and the winter realm is vast. You haven't even seen all Heart's Cadence has to offer yet. If you'd like, I'll make sure you get the chance to take in the falls and the lake beneath it—the spring that also feeds into it makes the water warm enough to swim—as well as some of the other unique features of this place."

I find I can smile back at him without too much trouble. "I *would* like that." It'd certainly beat staying cooped up in the palace all day. I had enough of staying homebound back in Oakmeet in the first month after Sylas brought me there, when my presence had to remain secret. "I'm sure Harper would love to see the sights too."

There's that twitch in Corwin's jaw, a subtle marker of his disappointment. He was picturing more alone time on these excursions, was he? Even though he doesn't say anything against having my friend join us, the fact that he just assumes I'd already feel safe on my own with him annoys me all over again.

Before I can think better of it, the one question sure to remind him of why I *can't* trust anyone here all that much tumbles out of me.

"How about you also walk me through the reasons your people keep attacking mine?"

Corwin's fingers tense around his fork. "I told you, I don't agree with how that situation has been handled."

That's not an answer. I jab at a piece of steak with maybe a bit more force than is necessary. "*What* situation? Why did the other Unseelie arch-lords suddenly decide invading the summer realm is a good idea?"

A whiff of his own frustration trickles into me. "I don't think this is the time to get into such a complicated matter."

I raise my eyebrows at him. "So you're going to explain later, then? When should I expect that conversation to happen?"

The muscle in his jaw ticks two times in a row before he clenches it. His tone flattens. "I feel it would be most sensible to focus on our potential relationship with each other and how we're going to handle the mate-bond before getting into larger political issues."

"That sounds to me like you're saying you won't trust me enough to tell me what's going on unless I agree to accept the bond. What if I can't trust *you* enough to accept it until I understand?"

"Then I suppose we'll have to negotiate some sort of compromise. I'm sure that can be managed."

The strain creeping into his voice suggests he's not so sure after all. He can't really expect me to dive into life with the Unseelie without even knowing why they've been murdering all kinds of summer fae, can he?

"Are you even sure you *want* me to accept the bond?" I can't help saying. "You're perfectly happy to be tied to a mere human, especially one who's spent so much time surrounded by wolves?"

"Every soul-twined bond is a gift, however unexpected. I trust the Heart had its reasons, and that we will uncover them. It isn't as if the connection between us will go away whether we want it or not." His cool dark gaze holds mine. "*I* have been attempting to reach an understanding with you from the beginning. There was no running away on my side."

I glower back at him. "And you're being *oh* so open helping me 'understand' your side now."

Harper's gaze darts back and forth between us, her fork frozen in mid-air. The tension is broken by a figure appearing at the dining room doorway. It's one of the staff who prepared our bedrooms for us. He bows with an apologetic grimace.

"My lord, Verik has arrived with news. He wishes to speak to you with some urgency."

I'd swear Corwin looks relieved to have an excuse to leave the table. As he pushes back his chair, he gives me one last glance. "Verik is part of my coterie. This may take some time. Please, finish the meal and occupy yourself however you'd like within the palace until you wish to turn in for the night."

He stalks out of the room. I watch him go, chewing my last morsel of steak so furiously I can't enjoy the tenderness of the meat at all. Then I stand up, leaving behind my half-eaten roll and a few chunks of spicy carrot-like vegetable.

Harper scrambles to her feet too. "Where are you going?"

"I want to see what's so urgent."

I slip out into the hall, the dense rug swallowing all but a whisper of even my uneven footsteps. My instincts take me in the direction I think leads to the back of the palace with its vast terrace. It looked like an ideal place for landing or taking off—and it seems more likely that news from Corwin's coterie would come from farther abroad rather than from the other direction, within the Heart's domains.

Harper hustles after me, setting her feet carefully too. After a few turns and a bit of back-tracking when we nearly end up in the kitchen, I catch sight of a view of the mountains through a tall window up ahead.

As I hurry closer, I spot Corwin out on the terrace with an older man who has his wings out. They stand a few feet apart, the man I assume is Verik speaking with a few quick gestures, Corwin nodding and frowning. Their attention is fixed on each other, but I don't sense any of the comfortable companionship that Sylas shares with his cadre most of the time. Like Corwin said, they're all business.

Whatever news the coterie man brought, I don't get a chance to hear it. As I venture closer, they wrap up their conversation—and in a blink and a sudden contracting, two ravens large enough that their wingspan could rival the reach of my arms are launching into the sky.

My shoulders sag. Harper comes up next to me, watching the dark forms soar into the distance. "Well," she says, "it's definitely… different here."

I choke on a laugh. "That's one way of putting it." I pull my gaze away from the sky. "Should we do some exploring in the palace?" Anything Corwin would want to keep secret, he's probably hidden well, but that doesn't mean it's impossible we'll stumble on something useful.

And having something to do definitely cheers Harper up. She grins. "Let's see exactly how an Unseelie arch-lord lives."

The proposal sounds like it could lead to some excitement, but the truth is, as we meander through the sprawling first floor of the palace and then climb a sweeping staircase to the second, I'm more and more convinced that an Unseelie arch-lord's life is pretty boring. Or at least *this* Unseelie arch-lord's is.

Every room is neat and clean with the same sorts of pale furniture and few objects that look remotely personal. Even Corwin's bedroom—what I assume is his bedroom anyway, since it's set apart from the hall of guest bedrooms where we're staying, even larger and with fancier furnishings—doesn't show much sign of a real life. I don't feel comfortable venturing into the inner rooms beyond the bedroom, though, and we do come across a couple of locked doors. Maybe he's simply very careful what pieces of himself he leaves in view.

We've meandered around part of the second floor when Harper stops with a jerk. Her head swivels as the rest of her stays perfectly still.

"What?" I murmur after a moment.

"I thought I heard— There it is again." She goes silent, watching me expectantly, but my human ears don't pick up anything. She turns again. "I think it's coming from… this way."

She heads down a narrower side hall, halting every few steps to listen again. "Yes. It's getting louder. What *is* that?" She shudders.

As we reach an alcove at the end of the hall, I understand her reaction. I can faintly make out the odd noises now—a thumping and then a grating sound like something jagged dragged against a smooth surface, so distant I can't tell whether it's coming from around us or overhead. And then the faintest of squeals, barely audible but so high-pitched I flinch.

I reach for the metal knob of the nearest door and twist, but it jars against my fingers. Locked. Harper tries the neighboring one, but it only opens to a linen closet, nothing disturbing there.

Meeting my friend's gaze, I see the same anxious question now running through my head reflected in her eyes. Just how big *are* the secrets Corwin is keeping hidden in this place?

CHAPTER FOURTEEN

August

I force an enthusiasm I don't really feel into my voice. "All right, pack. Let's see all those moves together now!"

The small group of my pack-kin living in our newly established Hearth-by-the-Heart run through the series of fighting techniques I've given them one after the other, lunging and wheeling, slashing out with their claws. Some are more hesitant than others, and none of them are on the same level as our official warriors, but a flicker of pride lights inside me despite my otherwise rotten mood.

If the Unseelie do come for us here, every one of my people will be prepared to defend us however they can.

When they're finished, panting but smiling, I give them a quick round of applause. "Perfect. I think you deserve a break. We'll pick things up tomorrow at the same time." Unless more urgent trouble rears its head, but I'd rather not think about that, let alone say it.

They disperse, and I drag the warm, mid-day air into my lungs. The air is lightly damp after last night's rainfall, but with the sky now mostly clear and the breeze rippling over me, it's refreshing rather than unpleasant. The weather is rarely less than ideal this close to the Heart.

I wish I was in a state to enjoy it.

I prowl around the temporary village as if I'm likely to find anything useful to do. I could make the trip back to Hearthshire to continue working with the pack-kin there and helping prepare for the move, but the thought of traveling even farther away from the border, of not being right here if something goes wrong in the winter realm and Talia manages to reach out to us, makes my gut contract into an uncomfortable lump.

She's over there with our enemies, risking everything that mattered to her here in an attempt to end the warring. The least I can do is be ready in case she needs me.

I've circled the new castle as well and am considering making a patrol of the border despite the sentries already on the job when Whitt finds me. He takes one look at my face and offers me a crooked grin. "It doesn't matter how many imaginary Unseelie you battle in your head, whelp, you won't get her back any faster that way."

I've bared my teeth before I can catch my instinctive reaction. My older brother doesn't take offense. As I shut my mouth, getting a grip on my temper, he bumps his shoulder against mine playfully, like he might have when I really was just a whelp.

"It's only been one day. All I'm saying is pace yourself." He glances toward the border, and the dry humor fades from his voice. "I'm worried about her too."

Somehow having the acknowledgment that I'm not alone in my agitation makes it a little easier to bear. "I still think it's ridiculous that she had to go at all."

"Of course it is. But we all know the alternatives were worse." A glint comes back into his eyes. "I have faith that she won't pick some bird-brain over what's waiting for her at home."

"*That's* not what I'm worried about," I growl.

He cocks a skeptical eyebrow at me, which is fair, because it might not be the *only* or even the main thing I'm worried about, but I definitely don't like the idea of how her bond with this feathered arch-lord might be developing and what feelings could grow alongside it. But honestly… if she decides she'll be happier with him, as hard as I find that to believe, I'll have to live with it. I just need her to be happy. And not torn to bits by raven talons.

That thought must bring the storminess back into my expression, because Whitt gives me another nudge, this one gentler. "She's proven to be far stronger than any of us would have imagined to begin with. Let's not forget to give her credit for that."

"I know." I shoulder him in return and realize it's not just our shared fears that have soothed my spirits. Even though he's clearly concerned about Talia, there's an easy companionableness to his demeanor that was once familiar but hasn't seemed to come so easily to him for the past few weeks.

Our lover had to leave us, but maybe she left us more whole than we were before.

I shouldn't discuss the private frictions between lord and pack where our kin might overhear, but I allow myself a vague, "You're doing all right otherwise?"

As I expected, Whitt is sharp enough to pick up on what I'm referring to. His grin gets both wider and more crooked, but he sounds as if he means it when he says, "I think the past is laid to rest."

"Good." Sylas hasn't filled me in on the details, and I'm not sure I want to know exactly what went on a century ago between Whitt and Isleen. The one thing our lord made completely clear was that the fault in the betrayal was all Isleen's.

I don't have enough words to express how glad I am to have *that* woman out of our lives. Heart save Talia from a soul-twined mate so selfish and ruthless.

Whitt swipes his hands together. "Well, I'm off to oversee some negotiations with our new neighbors down the hill. I'll see you at dinner."

He lopes off, leaping forward into wolfish form after his first few strides. As I watch him go, my gaze trails from his tawny form disappearing down the slope over to the obsidian walls of Ambrose's former palace—and lands on a hesitant-looking figure who's just emerging between the standing stones of the wall I expect we'll soon dismantle.

One of our sentries comes up behind the newcomer, urging the man along. Her dagger is still in its sheath, but her mouth is set in a wary line, her muscles tensed defensively.

A prickle of alarm runs down my spine. I hurry over to meet them, reaching them just as they come up on the palace.

As soon as I'm closer, I recognize the newcomer. He's one of Ambrose's pack-kin, the healer who helped Donovan recover from his poisoning and testified during the hearing to confirm the justice of Ambrose's death. Even so, the sight of him sets my teeth on edge. He might have acted and spoken against his lord in the late arch-lord's death, but as far as we know, he stayed loyal to the man until then.

What can he be doing here now? The last thing we need is another problem.

The sentry tugs the healer to a halt and bobs her head to me. "I found this one skulking around by the standing stones, August."

"I wasn't *skulking*," the healer protests, and fixes his gaze on me. "I came on an urgent matter to speak to Arch-Lord Sylas."

Sylas is off in a meeting with the arch-lords that I balk at interrupting. "The arch-lord is otherwise occupied at the moment. I'd prefer he stayed that way until I know you actually have something useful to put to him. So you'll just have to take a cadre-chosen instead."

The healer cuts a nervous glance toward the sentry. From the looks of his slim frame, I could beat him in a fight in either form in five seconds flat. The back-up is hardly necessary.

I motion her off with a gesture of thanks. As she trots away, I study the healer. "*What?*"

He rubs his mouth, his gaze twitching around us again. "Could we step inside the palace? Ambrose's—the one that was his? I'll need to show you, and I'd rather no one overheard this."

I look him over once more, but I can't see any signs of threat. By all appearances, he's a lot more scared of me than I am of him. It isn't really his fault I'm so on edge.

I sigh and wave him toward the door. We step inside, our footsteps ringing out on the obsidian floor. The healer doesn't appear to be any more comfortable in here than he was outside. He crosses his arms over his chest with a shudder.

Before I have to press for answers, he heaves a ragged breath. "You know that my lord was aiming to go to war against the Unseelie. He spent much of the past two decades gathering weapons, many of them enchanted and highly dangerous, that he expected to use in that crusade. Some of them aren't even acceptable by fae law. He has a vault of them hidden in the lower levels of the palace. I didn't know about them until I overheard some of my pack-kin talking about it a few days ago."

A stash of horrible and illegal weaponry? Yeah, that sounds like the Ambrose I knew. But I still have to ask—"Why are you telling *us*?" And why with such urgency? We'd have discovered it when we demolished this palace anyway.

His mouth twists. "Many of us accepted Lord Tristan's offer to take us on after Ambrose's passing. The cadre-chosen who knew about the weapons told him—he's planning to come while your full pack isn't yet here to claim them for himself."

Of course he is. Just what we need. I swallow a growl and resist the urge to narrow my eyes at the healer.

He came to us over his new pack. He obviously isn't all that loyal to Tristan. And I know Sylas would say that right now in this period of transition and escalating tensions with the winter fae, we can use all the allies we can get.

Wouldn't it be nice for Talia to come home to a fuller pack than before, all the more ready to defend her from enemies both around us and across the border?

I rein in that hope along with my initial defensiveness and jerk my chin toward the healer. "Can you show me where this vault is and how to open it?"

"I know where the entrance is—I'm not sure I have the magic to unseal it quickly."

"Good enough for now. Lead the way."

As he heads along a side hall and down a narrow flight of stairs at the far end of it, I keep a close watch on his movements. I may not be a master of subtle observation like Whitt, but I know how to evaluate an enemy in combat. The healer has gotten more relaxed since he spilled the secret to me, as if he's relieved to have it off his chest. I don't see any indication that he's gathering his nerve to launch any kind of assault.

After everything that's happened, I guess it isn't all that hard to see that he's better off being on Sylas's side than Tristan's, powerful illicit weaponry or not.

In the passage below, the man slows, scanning the walls as he walks. We pass a dusty tapestry that I have to suspect might hide some other secret space and stop where a shallow crack mars the smoothness of the dark obsidian. He taps that spot.

"The entrance is here. There's a locking spell on it, tied to the castle. I don't have much skill for stone work."

"That's all right. We'll get it open." Stone is far from my specialty either, but both Sylas and Whitt are fairly adept in that area. If we need someone who's mastered the true name for obsidian, which I'm not sure either of them has, there'll be someone among our and the other arch-lords' packs.

I turn to the healer. "Thank you for this. You've done us a great service. Do you expect to go back to Lord Tristan now?"

He makes a face. "I… I was hoping that I could trade this information for the opportunity to pledge myself to Arch-Lord Sylas. My former lord rarely consulted me in his plans, and I'd certainly have advised against them if he'd ever asked. I'd be happy to do whatever—"

I hold up my hand to stop him. "You can make your appeal to my lord. I'm sure he'd be willing to listen and consider your case—and that of any others who are uneasy in their current situation under Tristan."

"Oh, there are a few more of those," the healer mutters, and then flushes as if he wishes he hadn't said that out loud.

I chuckle and wave him back toward the stairs. "Arch-Lord Sylas expects loyalty and commitment, but you'll find he's more agreeable to be around than either of your masters so far. He should be finished with his business before much longer, and then we'll get all of this sorted out."

We emerge from the palace to find Sylas already striding across the fields toward us. My pulse hiccups at the severity of his expression. I grip the healer's forearm, bracing myself for the news that I misjudged him, that he's brought some disaster down on us while distracting me, but my lord barely glances at the man.

"There you are," he says. "There's been news from Copperweld—the Murk have made a fatal nuisance of themselves."

CHAPTER FIFTEEN

Talia

By my second dinner in Corwin's home, I've figured out that the middle-aged man and the girl who serve us our meals aren't faded fae but human. When the man burns his hand on the steam as he takes the lid off a pot of still-bubbling curry, Corwin tends to the injury with a quick murmur of magic that's clearly beyond the man's powers. His daughter watches with the eager delight of someone who doesn't expect to ever wield powers like that herself.

Corwin hasn't spoken to them any differently from his other staff, but then, he's pretty distant with all of them, so it's not like he's friendly either. I smile at the girl in thanks when she pours juice into my glass—I've been clear that I don't want anything alcoholic or otherwise inebriating—and study Corwin as he ladles some of the creamy curry onto his plate.

"Do you have many human servants?" I ask after they've left the room.

He blinks as if that's a question he never expected and then gives a subtle shrug. "Those two, a couple of the housekeeping staff, and one in the stables. I inherited them from my parents or took them on from colleagues. I don't make a habit of stealing away citizens of the human world, if that's what you're concerned about."

"They don't have the opportunity to go home if they wanted to, though."

His dark gaze lingers on me for a long moment, and I get the sense he's testing the wall I'm still holding up between us, wanting to gauge my emotional state. "I treat them well—well enough that there's no need to drug them or physically confine them as some of my brethren might. I've gotten no indication that they'd *want* to leave. As you've clearly discovered, the faerie world can hold much appeal even to those not born here."

That's a fair point. I nibble at my lip and then decide I don't really have any basis to be annoyed about it. Even Sylas has acknowledged that he used to have human servants before Kellan came into his domain.

And I can't say I'm not enjoying the food those two make either. The curry has a delicate spicing that mixes perfectly with the creamy texture, the bits of meat perfectly tender. Corwin is definitely keeping us well fed, at the very least.

When we get up from the meal, Corwin glances from Harper to me and asks in a careful voice, "Would it be possible to have some time to ourselves, just the two of us? I thought I might show you my favorite part of the palace."

I start to balk, but Harper is already ducking her head. "I'll be fine," she says. "I don't want to get in the way. You *are* supposed to have a chance to get to know each other."

We are, and I guess I don't need to be nervous about my own safety with Corwin after all the oaths he took. I nod, but the memory of the unnerving sounds we heard yesterday sticks with me as I join him walking down the hall.

Maybe he'd be more inclined to tell the truth about them when it's just me, no extra company.

I hesitate, but Corwin glances down at me, reading something in my mood or an impression that's slipped through our connection despite my best efforts. "If something is on your mind, you can speak it, Talia. I'd rather know than not."

I open my mouth, close it again, and gather my nerve. "Harper and I wandered around the palace for a while yesterday after you left with the man from your coterie. There's a locked door in an alcove on the second floor—we heard some odd sounds that seemed to be coming from somewhere beyond it. Like something moving around up there."

Corwin's lips purse with a slight grimace. "Ah. That was—Let's just say that sometimes restless spirits linger on in this world as they do in the human world as well. I believe you'd talk about ghosts? Better not to disturb them, as they can be unpredictable."

Oh. He's got a ghost in his attic? I'd find that funny if I hadn't experienced how creepy it was even at a distance. "It can't pass through the locked door?"

"No need to worry about that. The problem is contained." He motions to a door we've come up on, murmuring a quick word that must unlock it. "This is where I enjoy spending time on the relatively rare occasions when I don't have any duties to attend to."

I step past him into a room that's small by the palace's standards, but brightly lit even in the evening from glowing yellow sections in the crystalline ceiling. As seems to be Corwin's preferred style, the furnishings are spartan: only a tall marble cabinet against one wall, a cushioned settee across from it, and a massive, elegant harp standing in the middle of the room between them.

The harp's frame looks as if it's made of pure ivory, the strings gleaming with a silvery sheen. It rivals the apparently famous instrument Arch-Lord Donovan showed off during a banquet at his castle. I don't know anything about harps, but even I can tell this is an exquisitely crafted one.

A softness I've never seen before comes into Corwin's face as he looks at the instrument. "My family has always loved having music in our lives in every way we can. There's a particular pleasure in creating it from my own hands. Perhaps I could play for you?"

The suggestion feels like a peace offering, a tentative gift. I'm not sure I'm ready to accept it. I cock my head at him. "Is this supposed to distract me from finding out why your people have been pushing mine to the brink of war?"

I get a full grimace for that question, but Corwin doesn't stiffen up like yesterday. He swipes his hand across his narrow jaw. "I suppose I deserve that jab for my reaction yesterday. I hadn't expected—I clearly should have—" He lets out a quick breath. "What I ought to have told you is that discussing those matters is more complicated than simply answering whatever questions you ask. I have oaths I've taken to my office and my colleagues as well, that restrict what I can say about our political dealings and when."

Oh. That does make sense. "If you'd said so in the first place, I wouldn't have been as frustrated."

"I realize that. I was startled, and then Verik came—" He shakes his head. "I'll be able to tell you more when our situation is more certain, which may take time."

"Okay." I pause, and then, because the disappointment creeping into his expression tugs at my heart more than it should, I move to sit on the settee. "I *would* like to hear you play in the meantime."

He smiles then, reserved like Sylas's but bright enough that I know it's genuine. I relax the barrier of light within me enough to get a taste of his happiness as he sits down on the stool by the harp.

That joy only grows, coursing between us, as he sets his slender fingers against the strings. They move with seeming effortlessness, stirring a stream of notes into the air that reminds me of the sparkling spring tumbling down the rocky waterfall in Whitt's favorite glen.

The music tingles over my skin and into my lungs. As the melody swells, Corwin's hands flitting faster, the vivid tones meld together into a blissful harmony. It's nice seeing him so relaxed, doing something purely for the sake of enjoyment. If it hadn't been for this demonstration, I might have thought he never did anything that didn't have some constructive purpose.

He has his own pleasures. He wanted to share this one with me. A smile crosses my lips, and I close my eyes. I don't think Corwin has cast any magic, but the sound is enough to sweep me away—into more memories of my own happiness in the realm I've left behind.

Golden sun beaming through bright green leaves. The softness of the grass and the warm breeze twining around me. August laughing with me as we assemble pastries together in the kitchen, then sweeping me into his solid arms. Whitt carrying me on his back through the forest to his glen, the rhythm of his wolfish muscles echoing his trust into me. Sylas, standing within the glinting walls of the Bastion as he received the crown he deserved so much.

A pang of longing and loneliness shoots through me. Tears prickle behind my eyes—and the music falls away.

I look up and find Corwin's gaze fixed on me. His mouth is tight. Abruptly, I register the new current of emotion carrying through our connection: an anguished mix of pain and jealousy.

He manages to keep his voice even, but a thread of frustration runs through it. "Even now, you're thinking of them. There are *three* you'd prefer over me?"

Did he think it was only Sylas? I tense on my seat, not sure how to respond. I told him how I felt when we first talked in that dream. Can he really expect things to have changed so quickly?

I curl my fingers around the edge of the cushion. "I hardly know you. They've been there for me from the first moment they rescued me. Did you think I'd simply fall out of love the second I stepped into your palace?"

He drops his hands to his sides, the knuckles flexing. "Our souls are *bound*. You're meant for me as I'm meant for you. The Heart has decided so."

I frown. "Well, I think I should get a little say too."

"That's not how this works."

"Maybe it should be." The good will his playing stirred in me fades away. I raise my chin. "I know you said you only care about what the Heart intends, but having me as your mate doesn't make any sense. I can't give you true-blooded heirs. I bet none of your colleagues would ever respect me—they probably hate me enough just thinking I'm Seelie."

"The Heart has willed it—none of my colleagues can argue with that. The bond wouldn't have formed if we couldn't overcome whatever problems might arise."

"I don't know why you're so sure of that. I've heard about some pretty horrible soul-twined pairings." I motion vaguely toward the world beyond the palace. "Wouldn't it be better for all of us if we could find some way to break the bond so we can get on with our lives the way we want to live them? Most fae never have anything more than a regular mate. You could find some true-blooded Unseelie lady who I'm sure would be happy to have you."

Corwin's eyes flash. "This may not be what I anticipated, but it *is* what I want. I have waited centuries to encounter the one my soul would call to. I can be patient as we navigate whatever difficulties our unusual partnering brings. It'll be worth it to have a mate who's joined with me more truly than any 'true-blooded' fae now could be."

A lump rises in my throat. "What about me? Doesn't it matter what *I* want?"

I catch a twinge of sympathy from him then. "You only want the others because you never knew you might find a deeper bond. You allowed your affections to grow that much without realizing how much pain you were setting yourself up for. I wish the Heart had been kinder to you. But if you can start to let them go—"

I stand up with a jerk and a lurch of my pulse. "You've clearly never loved anyone in your life if you think it'd be that easy. I shouldn't *have* to let them go. I didn't ask for any of this."

"It'll only be more pain if you cling to what you thought you'd have instead of accepting where you've found yourself."

"And if I don't know how I'll ever accept it? If I'm not sure I even can?"

A brief shimmer of anguish slips into me—and then Corwin closes off the connection on his side. His face forms that cool mask I've seen so often, all the joy of the music gone. He gets to his feet too.

"I'm certain the Heart would not have shone on us like this if it were impossible," he says, his voice so calm it sets my teeth on edge. "We simply have to find our path, and I'll help you in every way I can."

I don't want his help, but I'm tired of arguing. I'm just plain tired, really. I rub my eyes, my shoulders slumping. "I'm sorry. I didn't mean to turn this into a fight. I liked hearing you play—thank you for inviting me here. Let's just leave it for now."

We have eight more days to get through. I'd rather they weren't any more agonizing than they need to be.

Corwin seems to agree. He gestures toward the door, not even attempting to offer me his hand. "I'll see you to your room. Tomorrow will be a new day."

We walk through the halls in silence. When we reach my bedroom, I consider going across to Harper's and venting to her, but what would I even say? She probably wishes she'd have the chance to make a soul-twined match. I'd sound like a jerk complaining that I have *four* highly eligible fae men who want me for a mate, even if one is Unseelie. Also, she doesn't even know about two of those men.

Instead, I go into my room and flop down on the bed. I can't work up any enthusiasm for the books I brought with me. After a while, as exhaustion creeps over me, I change into my nightclothes and crawl under the covers, hoping tomorrow's new day will bring a little less pain for both me and Corwin.

How can I make him understand?

With that question running through my head, my mind drifts into sleep. I'm lying on soft grass under a clear blue sky, a dreamy haziness surrounding me, and a soft voice murmurs from somewhere beyond my view in words I don't understand.

A quiver passes through my mind, and then I tumble deeper still to where even dreams won't follow.

CHAPTER SIXTEEN

Talia

When I open my eyes to my bedroom in Corwin's palace, the space feels somehow different. I sit up, peering around me, but I can't pick out anything that's changed. There's a faint mugginess in my head as if I haven't completely shaken off sleep just yet, or maybe it's because of our argument…

What did we argue about? I remember snapping at him, frustration twisting through me, but the exact words we spoke, the things I was upset about, escape me.

Obviously it wasn't anything that important. I've just been on edge since we got here.

As I clamber out of bed and get ready for the day, the mugginess doesn't totally fade. I rub my eyes and go to the window in the hopes that the sunlight will wake me up more. Beams of it streak through the fluffy clouds, tiny snowflakes dancing between the streams of light. It reflects off the snow and the icy plain below toward me, but my head doesn't feel that much clearer.

My gaze slides to the hazy border. Flickers of images pass through my mind—greenery and golden light, and something… something I left behind.

My pack. Always there for me. I'll be back to them soon. If I can bring them news that the Unseelie are backing off on their attacks, even better.

Corwin is moving through the palace, a tentative but steady presence in my awareness. The barrier inside me has faded overnight, and I find I don't feel the need to rebuild it just yet. The thought of him sensing me the same way I'm aware of him provokes a quiver of anxiety, but only for a moment.

We have to learn to trust each other. That's why I'm here, isn't it? That's what will be best for everyone. He's figured out the secret of my blood and the Seelie's curse—what else do I have to hide?

He's giving the kitchen staff instructions for breakfast. I catch the gist of his intention but not the exact words. He must be able to tell I'm paying attention, because a moment later his voice travels through the connection between us, gentle and even.

The food should be ready shortly—it won't be anything elaborate. Shall I walk you to the dining room?

My first instinct is to balk, but why? He's trying to be hospitable, to show me how much he appreciates my being here.

He's my soul-twined mate. I should be giving *him* a real chance too, shouldn't I?

Something about that thought nibbles at my gut, but I can't figure out why. *Thank you*, I say in return. *I'll see if Harper's up.*

I remember belatedly that Corwin hasn't been enthusiastic about my friend's company, but maybe he's gotten over that frustration. I don't sense any discomfort from him over it now. If anything, he sounds pleased. *I'll come and collect you both, then.*

Something about our argument last night or the talks before then must have gotten through to him. He's trying his best too. I have to smile as I head across the hall to knock on Harper's door.

Harper answers with a yawn but somehow not remotely sleep-rumpled. I'm not sure her hair is capable of falling in any way except silkily straight across her shoulders. She stretches her neck and peers into the hall. "Breakfast time? Has the arch-lord stopped insisting on escorting you?"

"He's on his way."

She takes in my smile and offers one in return. "Everything's okay? I heard you coming back to your room last night—you were walking fast, and you closed the door pretty hard. I would have gone over to see if you needed anything, but I..."

She's still not sure how much I really *trust* her. My heart twinges, and I grasp her forearm with a quick squeeze. "I think everything's okay now, and I'll come to you if there's a real problem. But I wouldn't mind you checking in on me either."

"Okay." Her smile widens. She darts a look up and down the hall and lowers her voice conspiratorially. "I'm glad Arch-Lord Corwin hasn't done anything too horrible. August would make him regret it if he really upset you, that's for sure."

As she giggles, I blink at her in momentary confusion. Well, August is very protective of the whole pack—he's our head warrior, isn't he? And... I think he's been particularly quick to come to my defense.

Wasn't there—I have a vague sense of his brawny frame stepping in front of me to shield me, of wolves tumbling together in combat... The memories are foggy and distant, though, as if they happened a long time ago rather than just in the past few months.

I rub my forehead, and Corwin's voice reaches me again. *Is everything all right? You seem a bit unsettled.*

I think maybe I just didn't sleep all that well. I'll probably feel better once I've gotten some food into me.

Well, we can see to that right now.

The last words filter through the bond just as he rounds the corner at the other end of the hall. His lips are curved in the same soft smile I saw when he played the harp last night—*that* memory has stuck with me perfectly clearly.

Have I ever really noticed before what a striking face he has in general? Maybe he seemed too cold before for me to appreciate it. But now, as he walks up to us with those traces of affection in his smile and his eyes, his tall lean frame so measured in its obvious strength, my heart skips a beat. I find myself thinking back to that moment when we dreamed together and he touched my arm. To the thrilling sensation that passed through me.

It scared me at the time. Because… it was unexpected. And—there was something else, wasn't there? I have a sense of waking, of being comforted, but not why I needed the comfort.

Corwin has reached us, his warmth starting to dim behind the same concern he showed earlier. I shake off my confusion and aim my smile at him. "Let's go get that breakfast."

The Unseelie arch-lord might have asked for a simple meal, but the spread is still extensive, and everything from the fried eggs to the berry salad tastes as delicious as everything his chefs prepare. I wonder if he always eats this well or if he's going to special lengths to pamper me. He doesn't seem to linger over the food that much himself, mostly watching my reactions. I catch traces of satisfaction as he observes my own enjoyment both with his eyes and through our connection.

"I'll make sure we have those every morning for the rest of the time you're here," he says when I practically swoon over a pastry so buttery the flaky dough melts in my mouth. I'm starting to think the whole bond thing might not be so bad after all.

I scratch my arm absently, pulling the long sleeve of my winter-appropriate dress higher over my forearm, and a flicker of dismay passes into me from Corwin. He's studying the pale scar along the inside of my forearm. "What happened there?"

A shiver passes through me, thinking back. "A tuskcat. I don't know if you have those here in the winter realm, but they're like big cats with a boar's head. Our enemies cast a spell on one to make it attack me, but one of the pack warriors killed it before it could do more damage than this."

Harper's jaw tightens for a second, probably remembering that those enemies were the ones she briefly made plans with. As if meaning to offset that tension, she lets out a little laugh and says, "Lord Sylas and August looked so furious running to help that I'd be surprised if there are any tuskcats left in our domain after that."

Sylas and August… running to help. Those words don't *sound* wrong, but I can't quite fit them into the version of the scene in my head. It must have been August who healed the wound, right? Because… he's the main healer in the pack too. I'm pretty sure he looked after me other times. And Sylas has always watched over me—he knows how valuable I am.

Why does my head feel so fuzzy when I try to think of anything after Astrid stabbed the beast? I managed to dismiss the weirdness before, but I've been awake for a while now, and at this point I can't blame my fogginess on hunger either.

A chill passes through me. I glance at Corwin, swallowing hard. *He* swore not to harm me, but what if one of his fellow arch-lords managed to cast mind-altering magic on me somehow?

"I think something's wrong. I can't seem to focus on certain memories, like parts of them are blurry or just missing… I only just started feeling like this when I woke up. Could someone have come into the palace and done something to me last night?"

Corwin tenses—just slightly to my eyes, but I can feel it through the bond too, along with a jolt of… guilt? Then it's all gone, shut away like the slamming of a door. He's closed himself off.

"I'm sure no one could have entered without my permission," he says firmly. "It could be that the difference in environment is catching up with you? Perhaps you could use some more rest if you didn't sleep well, and I could have my healer speak to you."

I study him, more apprehension prickling through me. He's hiding something—why else would he shut me out? But *he* couldn't hurt me. He shouldn't even be able to order someone else to. That was part of—the oaths—we talked about—

My memories of those discussions have gone all muddled too. My heart thumps faster, panic swelling inside me. What's wrong with me? Why is so much—

It's all things to do with the three men I know I had those discussions with. Sylas and August and… and Whitt. When Harper mentioned the new arch-lord and August just now, and August before. The argument last night in the music room that I still can't focus on either—was that about them too?

My gaze darts to Harper. "Why did you say what you did earlier about August? Why would he be so worried specifically about me?"

She stares at me and then looks at Corwin, her shoulders stiffening. Corwin makes a brusque gesture as if he can dismiss the question. "I think it's best if we don't exacerbate whatever—"

"No," I say, my voice shaking. "I need to know."

"You've—you've been with August since you came to the pack," Harper says quickly, bracing herself as if she expects Corwin to attack *her* for mentioning it. "I mean, as… as lovers. He'd never let anything happen to you if he could help it."

What? How can that sound so obvious and yet—and yet when I try to even picture August's face—

Horror claws up through me. It's gone. Something *precious* has been warped in my head, and I don't know how to get it back.

"Talia," Corwin is saying, and I see the way he's gripping his fork, the whitening of his knuckles. I remember the flash of guilt. Understanding rushes through me.

"*You* did this." I spring to my feet, wobbling as I set my bad foot wrong, my fingers clamping around the edge of the table to hold me steady.

Corwin leaps up to help me, but he stops in the face of my glare. I hurl the full force of my anger and distress at the bond between us, willing at least a little of it to crack through his wall. "You changed my memories. Blurred them. You wanted me to forget—forget that I was with someone else? How could you—you swore—"

The undertone of Corwin's bronze skin has gone a faint, queasy green. "I think you should go," he says to Harper.

I smack one hand on the tabletop, rattling the dishes. "No. She's the only one here who actually cares about what *I* want. Whatever you did, you're not hiding it from her either."

Harper stands, but she stays there across from me with her back straight and her jaw tight. Corwin frowns at her and lets out a huff of breath as he turns back to me.

"I swore not to harm you, and I didn't. I was trying to *help*. I could feel how it was hurting you, being apart from them, having your loyalties divided, when you never should have been put in that position. So I… attempted to set things right, as if you never had been."

He falters in the face of the pained fury I have no doubt he can sense now, even if only because my eyes must be shooting daggers at him. I didn't think I trusted him, but I did enough that this violation feels like the worst betrayal.

"That wasn't your choice to make," I snap. "I am who I am, and my life is what it is. Were you going to try to make me forget that I'm human next? Or how my foot got broken? Or why the Seelie need me, in the hopes that it'd be easier to convince me to stay? Messing with someone's head like that is—it's *sick*. The only people who've ever done that to me before were the monsters who left me in a cage for nine years, and even they only did it temporarily with fairy fruit."

Corwin winces. "Talia, I swear, I was only trying to spare you—"

"I don't want to hear you try to justify it." Maybe it's true, maybe the oaths ensured he'd only have been able to work his magic on my mind if he meant well, but the fact that it didn't occur to him that I had a right to my memories is almost worse. "Can you fix it? Can you get the fog out of my head? I want to remember everything the way I should."

He nods. "I apologize. I didn't realize it would cause you so much distress. I promise you my intentions were only the opposite. Will you —will you come here?"

I'm so keyed up I flinch at the suggestion, and Corwin's stance turns even more rigid. I force myself to step toward him. "Do it quickly." I don't want to be in his presence any longer than I have to be.

He raises his hands to either side of my head, hovering an inch from my hair, and murmurs several unfamiliar syllables. A rush of tingling energy washes through my mind—and everything is clear again.

I inhale sharply and choke on a sob. August and Sylas and Whitt. All the devotion they've shown me. All the love I've felt for them. Every moment of affection and desire—the warmth of *that* bond wraps around me like an embrace and fills my chest with an ache so poignant my eyes flood with tears.

The man in front of me tried to take all that joy away from me.

I shove myself away from Corwin and march unsteadily to the doorway. "Stay away from me," I say without looking back. "I don't want to see you or talk to you or *anything* with you until it's time for me to go home."

CHAPTER SEVENTEEN

Talia

A tapping sound outside my bedroom door tells me that Corwin has brought my dinner. He's set the tray down on the floor in the hall outside so I can retrieve it after he's gone.

He doesn't just leave, though. Even with all the light I can summon into my body shored up against our connection, I can sense him standing there, watching the door as if he can see me through it.

"Talia, please," he says quietly. "What can I do? What do you need from me? Tell me, and I'll make it happen."

I need for him not to have worked magic on my mind, to have tried to bend me to his idea of how I should be and what I should feel. But he can't give me that, so I say nothing. He's already apologized a few dozen times since yesterday morning. He's offered to swear a new oath before the other arch-lords to cast no magic at all on me so I know it won't happen again.

He even suggested he'd let me in through the bond so I can see that he honestly thought it would help and only regrets it now, and anything else I might need to know to trust him, although I'm pretty sure he'd be able to wall off his thoughts about things like the war with the Seelie out of professional discretion.

None of it feels like enough. None of it has eased the ache still clenched around my gut. I just want to go home and forget all of this ever happened, but he hasn't offered me *that.* I don't know if he even can.

"All right," he says finally. "I don't want your dinner to get cold. I'll keep coming back, but if you're ready to speak to me sooner, reach out through the bond. I'll stay open to you."

I wait until I'm sure he'll be out of sight, and then I open the door to collect my meal. As I bend down to pick up the silver tray with its covered plate and goblet of juice, I freeze.

A sprig of flowers lies next to the plate, bright blue petals around a pinkish center, the leaves a vibrant green. As I touch it tentatively, a faintly sweet perfume reaches my nose.

I've seen flowers like this before, but not on the chilly terrain around this palace. These are summer flowers.

Did Corwin risk going across the border again just to get these for me?

To bring me a little piece of the home I'm missing.

It still isn't enough, but it's the first thing he's offered that feels like he might really understand why I'm so hurt. Unexpected tears well up, and I have to swipe at my eyes a few times before I'm collected enough to pick up the tray.

I don't want to open myself up to Corwin from the inside, but tomorrow—tomorrow, when he brings breakfast, I'll at least thank him. That doesn't mean I'm going to *forgive* him, though.

As I straighten up, Harper opens the door across from me. She's holding a similar tray—she's been refusing to eat in the dining room out of solidarity. "Do you want some company?" she asks, looking meek, as if she thinks she's somehow been tarnished by simply being there when I realized what Corwin did.

I hesitate, but I've done so much wallowing in my frustration and hurt over the past two days that I'm honestly tired of it. And Harper *hasn't* done anything wrong. If it wasn't for her comments, I don't know how long it'd have taken me to figure out what I was missing.

I give her a weak but genuine smile. "Yeah, that'd be nice. Come on over."

There's a small table in my bedroom, but it only has one matching chair. "If people can do breakfast in bed, why not dinner too?" I announce, and set my tray on the blanket before hopping up to prop myself against my pillows. Harper's lips twitch with amusement. She tucks herself against one of the posts at the foot of the bed and crosses her legs so she can balance her tray on them.

Thankfully the kitchen staff haven't prepared anything too messy. There's a tart leafy vegetable that's been sautéed and some kind of fried meat in thin strips that look almost like bacon but have a smokier flavor. Back in Hearthshire, I'd probably have known exactly what these things are and how they were prepared because chances were I'd have been in the kitchen helping August make them.

That thought comes with a fresh pang of longing that tightens my stomach. I force down a few more bites, but despite the deliciousness of the food, I've lost my enthusiasm.

"Maybe we should take over the kitchen sometime and show Corwin just how much *you* can do," Harper says with a glint of mischief in her eyes. "I'm not that handy, but I'm sure you've learned enough from August that you could boss me around."

I have to smile imagining it, even though the idea also sharpens my homesickness. I wave my fork at her. "I'm not doing any cooking for him anytime soon."

"True. He definitely doesn't deserve it after that awful trick he pulled. We'll have to sneak in and make midnight snacks just for us or something." She pauses. "Midnight snacks are a thing, right? I think I read that in a book someone brought from your world."

From the human world, she means, as distant as that place feels to me now after nearly a decade away from it. But I can confidently say, "Midnight snacks are *totally* a thing. My mom was always hassling my dad about leaving crumbs on the counter when he'd go down to sneak a cookie or a piece of toast in the middle of the night."

The pang that comes with that memory is duller but also deeper. I swallow hard, remembering Mom's teasing voice and the wag of her finger, Dad catching her hand and pressing a quick kiss to the tip of that finger as he apologized with a grin. They were so happy. *We* were so happy, as a family. Yeah, we squabbled and sometimes Jamie got on my nerves, but that's what little brothers are for, right?

No matter how much happiness I'm able to find here among the fae, I am *never* going to forgive Aerik and his cadre for destroying all those lives before.

When I come back to the present, Harper is watching me with concern in her overwide eyes. "It made you sad, thinking about that. I'm sorry."

I shake my head. "It's okay. I'd rather remember my family and be sad than forget. It just hardly feels real sometimes, like they should still be back there, even though I know they're not. The attack happened so fast, and then everything was so horrible after for such a long time… I couldn't really grieve when I had to focus on surviving and staying sane, and now I'm not sure how to."

Her mouth tightens with sympathy. "Well, I'm still sorry. Sometimes—sometimes I forget how much you went through before you came to our pack."

"That's not your fault. I don't talk about it much." I didn't even tell her or any of my other pack-kin the truth when Sylas first introduced me to them, because he was still hiding me from Aerik then.

Harper glances away for a second and then looks back at me. "I *should* remember. It's not fair to you if I don't. I…" She jabs at a stray bit of meat but doesn't raise her fork. "Pretty much my whole life, I've felt like I was useless to the pack, you know? I didn't take to music like my parents do, no matter what they named me, so I couldn't help them entertain during the revels, and I don't have much of a knack with gardening or animals or anything else that would really help."

"But you're *brilliant* with the clothes you make," I protest.

She shrugs. "Pretty dresses didn't do anyone any good while we were in exile. My parents never complained, but I know some of our other pack-kin thought I was frivolous. And it was hard for me to relate to everyone else anyway. They all had the weight of the banishment and the memory of losing Hearthshire hanging over them, and I couldn't fully understand it since I'd never known anything else."

It must have been awfully lonely for her as the only child born into the pack after their banishment. I grope for the right thing to say. "At least that's behind all of us now. And I bet a lot of folk in the pack will want those dresses now that we're having balls and banquets and all kinds of celebrations."

"Yes." A sliver of a smile crosses her face and vanishes just as quickly. "But it was— When you first came, I thought you'd be like me. You didn't share all that history, just like I didn't. And since you were human… obviously you wouldn't contribute the same way as everyone else. But then—"

She bites her lip, looking so agonized I can't be even a little offended by her words. I set my tray aside and lean toward her. "I get it. *I* don't even feel like I can contribute on the same level as the rest of you. At least you were nice to me from the start."

"But that's the problem. I mean, *my* problem, not yours." Harper drags in a breath and meets my eyes again. "You made a place for yourself in the pack so quickly. You showed how much you *can* do and how hard you'd try to help out, and soon no one really cared that you aren't even fae, and I—I was a little jealous. I think that's why those girls who came to visit from Ambrose's pack managed to pull me into their scheme. They talked as if I was *more* special than everyone else in the pack who focused on everyday things, and they said things about you…"

She winces. "There was nothing nice about that, or about me going along with it, even if I didn't know just how bad it was going to get."

Maybe I should be upset with her for what she's just admitted, but instead all I feel is a weird sort of relief. It makes more sense now why she backed off from me and got caught up with Ambrose's pack-kin. They spotted a weakness in her, a resentment she hadn't meant to act on, and figured out how to exploit it.

"I know," I say. "I wouldn't have asked you to come with me here if I believed you ever wanted to see me get hurt."

"And I'm so glad for that. When I realized what I could have helped happen—that Ambrose might have been able to take you away because of me—and maybe he'd have been even worse to you than the lord that had you before Sylas—" She shudders. "I hated myself. You and I—we're *not* the same. You've had it so much harder than I have, had so much stolen from you and so many people hurt you. But you keep trying and making a place for yourself anyway. I'm *proud* to be your friend. And if that bird-brain arch-lord doesn't figure out how well you deserve to be treated, then you're better off without him."

She says the last bit so firmly, her eyes flashing with the Unseelie insult, that it melts some of the pain I've been holding inside. She can't fix what Corwin broke, but it helps a lot to know that I'm definitely not alone here, not in a practical sense or in being angry about what he did.

I scoot over to sit right next to her. "Thank you. Maybe it's silly, but it means a lot to hear someone else say that, especially someone who's fae. Hard to know whether my human expectations would seem reasonable."

Harper lets out a huff. "More than reasonable. Trying to make you forget all the good things Sylas and August did for you? That's so selfish of him."

I don't think she's caught on that those "good" things involved Whitt too, or that they were romantic with anyone other than August. I might feel comfortable letting her in on that secret someday… if it even still matters after all this is over.

I rub my forehead. "I just don't know what happens if I do decide I'm better off without Corwin. Where do we go from there? The soul-twined bond won't just disappear because I don't like it." If it would, it'd have been gone days ago.

Harper frowns. "I wish I knew what to do about that. I'm sure Sylas is working on figuring it out right now. In the meantime… do you want to sneak over to the kitchen with me and see if we can grab a little dessert?"

I have to laugh at her conspiratorial tone, my spirits lightening more than they've been since I uncovered Corwin's betrayal. "Let's do it. Sugar makes everything at least a little bit better."

The rest I'll figure out when I have to.

CHAPTER EIGHTEEN

Corwin

Talia's bedroom door has appeared more impenetrable to me every time I've stood before it over the past two days. Looking at it now, I yet again grapple with the conflicting impulses inside me.

My soul-twined mate is on the other side of that door. Even with the bond between us dulled by her resistance, it tugs at my heart. The knowledge of how angry she is, how much I damaged her trust in me, has been searing into me like a burning blade from the moment she berated me in the dining room. If I let go of the tight grip I'm holding over my emotions, I might go as mad as those wolves she cares for so much do under the full moon.

It was a misstep, not a purposeful act of betrayal. I *couldn't* have harmed her with intent. She knows that, and yet reasoning it out, offering whatever is in my power to give her, hasn't been enough to bring her back.

Maybe that's fair. The Heart doesn't work through reason, does it? What kind of madness is it already for me to be bound to a human woman who's already devoted herself to not one but three Seelie?

A soul-twined bond isn't meant to be a business partnership. It's about the deepest affection and intimacy. I didn't really think I'd be able to hold back as much as I do in every other area of my life. I just never expected it to turn out like this, with so many complexities and obstacles…

I close my eyes, my hands clenching at my sides. Every nerve in my body balks at the display I came here planning to make. I'm well aware of what comes with unchecked passions and how thoroughly they can ruin everything else around them.

But Talia needs to know how much this bond matters to me. How much *she* matters to me. She's come all this way, left behind everything she knew and cared about, to give me a chance. How can I say I deserve her if I won't compromise anything of myself?

These past two days knowing she's here and being unable to even see her have hollowed out my chest in a way I haven't felt since—Well, I'd rather not think of that. And truthfully, this is even worse.

The dining room where I once ate on my own at leisure now blares her absence. I can't sit at my harp without remembering her poised on the settee listening to me play for that brief, beautiful moment when we were utterly at peace with each other. When I try to sleep, her voice rings through my mind, sharp with the pain she showed when she discovered my uninvited spell.

This isn't how these ten days were supposed to go. And with every passing hour, she's slipping farther away from me.

If I want to bring her back before she's too far for me to ever reach, I have to give her everything I can.

Girding myself, I sink to my knees and rest my forearms on the floor. I bow so low my forehead touches my clasped hands. The pose sends a prickle of shame through me, but I ignore the sensation. I ease back the tight lid I've been keeping on the turmoil inside me—not all the way, but enough that a rush of the grief and horror floods through me.

She has to feel it, at least a little.

"Talia," I say, loud enough to be sure my voice will carry through the door, "I've wounded you in an unconscionable way, and all I can think to do is humble myself before your rightful anger. I will remain here at your mercy until you see fit to speak to me, however long it might take. Nothing in my domain or elsewhere can come before making amends with you."

It's possible the security of not just my heart and soul but my entire realm as well rest on proving my commitment to her. Her tie to the Seelie's curse raises possibilities I'd never considered… but I can't use that information to persuade my fellow arch-lords while the oath I swore holds my tongue, and I can't speak to Talia about it while she's still so loyal to the fae who consider us their enemies.

So I stay as I am, prostrate before her door, not allowing myself to consider how it will look if one of the servants or even my coterie come by. I shamed myself by stealing into Talia's mind. Why shouldn't they witness the results of that? I have only myself to blame.

My back twinges, my wings itching to spring free and shelter me. I will away the urge. My remorse swells through me, but I get nothing back from the other end of the bond.

Then my ears pick up the faintest of sounds from beyond the door—the whisper of her feet brushing across the floor with her uneven steps. The thought of the beasts that shattered her foot summons a protective fury within me, but I shove that down too. This isn't the time for it.

But when my mate is fully mine, I will carve every wolf who hurt her into pieces with pleasure.

The violence in that idea unnerves me—*this is what comes of unleashing one's emotions*—but then the door is easing open and I can't focus on anything except the woman peering down at me.

My head is still bowed, but I hear the soft hitch of Talia's breath and the rustle of her dress as she leans far enough to glance down the hall. As if *she's* worried about who might witness my demonstration of regret.

"What are you *doing*?" she says, her voice shocked and possibly even horrified.

My throat tightens around the words, but I can't say they feel wrong coming out. "I kneel at your feet to beseech your forgiveness. I overstepped my authority so far—I failed to honor you as you deserve—it was not my place to alter your history or decide which parts of it should be valuable to you. I offer no excuses. I only mean to show I understand how horribly I erred."

Talia swallows audibly. "Don't you care if someone sees you? What kind of fae arch-lord grovels in front of a human?"

I let myself look up at her then, as well as I can while keeping my back bowed over. Her mouth is pressed in a taut line, her eyes wide and starkly bright with uncertain emotion. She grips the doorframe, looking as if she might retreat and slam the door in my face at any moment—but she hasn't yet.

She's here. She's listening.

"Your being human matters no more than if you were fae," I say. "Even if you were simply my guest under the care of my household, my conduct would have been appalling. But you aren't simply a guest. You're my soul-twined mate."

"You didn't choose me any more than I chose you. And don't say you'll go along with it because of the Heart and all that."

I hold her gaze despite the awkward angle, hoping she can feel the truth of this statement as I say it. "I choose you now. Not only because of the Heart's will but my own as well. You're an intelligent, determined woman who I can see has earned every bit of respect your Seelie pack offered you. It will be my honor to have you stand beside me as my equal, and it sickens me that I have threatened that future with my actions."

Her lips part, but she hesitates, still deliberating. Still on the verge of walking away.

I was too distracted by all the surprises that came with her arrival and all the politics surrounding it to recognize her strength at first. She's endured so much—she's enduring so much now—and instead of appreciating the steely will and nobility it took for her to come here despite the love she feels for those other men, I treated her as if she were a broken thing I needed to fix.

What does it matter if she's mortal? I could imagine her standing up to every one of my colleagues in ways I've never dared. Removing those other lovers from her mind would be no more than a cheap ploy. If I'm going to earn her love or at least her dedication as well, I have to prove I can match them.

I have to prove I can accept them and what they mean to her.

I brace myself against the additional discomfort that comes with the offer I know I need to make. "You don't have to forgive me yet. I would only ask—will you share with me what I was unthinking enough to try to steal from you? I want to hear about the men you love and how they came to mean so much to you, so I can understand. So I can know you and everything about how *you* came to be as you are. They're important to you, so they're important to me too."

The barrier in our bond wobbles then. It softens, and a trace of her emotions drifts through to me: a tangled mix of pain and anger and the recognition of how hard that request was for me to make.

Talia wets her lips. Then she says, quietly but clearly, "All right. You can come in. Take the chair by the table. I'll think about where to start."

Relief rushes through me, so sharp it's almost painful in itself. I ease upright and follow her into the room, respectful of the distance she's keeping between us. As I take the chair she indicated, she perches tentatively on the edge of the bed across from me.

"How much do you want me to tell you?" she says, with astonishing tenderness considering how badly I hurt her and how fresh that wound still is. "I know it makes you uncomfortable hearing about it—about them."

A pang shoots through my chest, poignant and undeniable. This woman's resilience and will would make her a worthy partner for any arch-lord, but her compassion… That makes her exactly the partner *I* would want.

I could fall in love with her if I let myself. I know that beyond a doubt now.

I lean back in the chair, trying to appear relaxed so as not to concern her. "Everything. Anything you want to tell me. Anything you're willing to show me through the bond. You can leave out information you think they'd want to keep secret for the sake of their people, of course, but I want to know you as well as I can. That's the only way I can be the mate you deserve."

"Okay." She twines her fingers and rests her hands on her lap. Her gaze goes distant, a fond light glowing in her eyes that sparks a flicker of jealousy I can't totally suppress. "It was August I really fell for first. He's in Sylas's cadre, the head of the pack's warriors. But he's only ever been gentle with me. Right from the start, he went out of his way to make me feel like I could belong..."

As she goes on, talking about the first few weeks she spent with Arch-Lord Sylas's pack, more vivid impressions filter through the connection between us. She's lowering her defenses. Each jolt of joy and quiver of remembered pleasure pricks at me like a series of thorns, but I hold myself steady and still, taking it all in.

It *does* hurt, listening to her speak so affectionately of these men who won her heart before I ever knew she was meant to be mine. But I have to welcome every part of her and everything she's been through.

It's the only chance I have of winning my own place in that heart, for my own happiness—and perhaps the very survival of my people.

CHAPTER NINETEEN

Sylas

"Well," Whitt says, surveying the ruined bins lying in disarray in the small storage hut, "the Murk couldn't have happened to a worse bunch of fae. And by that, I mean I fully approve of their choice of target."

August lets out a huff that sounds like agreement. I grimace, my fangs pressing against the inside of my mouth. As soon as I spotted the rodent footprints dappled in the earth around the hut and smelled their unmistakeable vermin stink inside, I couldn't hold them back.

"Better the Murk didn't harass any of our kin, even those we'd consider enemies," I mutter. "And regardless of what we think of their lord and cadre, the rest of the pack doesn't necessarily deserve our ire, including the poor fellow who met his end over this mischief."

It is difficult, though, to be in the presence of that bone-white castle without thinking of the last time we were here, in the dimming evening light, carrying Talia away from her filthy prison. My fangs might be out even if the Murk hadn't worked their spite on Copperweld at all.

If it wasn't for the murder of the one pack-kin who must have happened upon the rat shifters at the wrong time, this mess would appear to be merely mischief. I wouldn't blame Aerik for wanting an arch-lord's attention on the matter regardless. Any overt activity from the Murk needs a careful eye, no matter how seemingly innocuous. They might mainly stick to aggravating us in minor ways, but I know with the twinge that creeps through my deadened eye just how vicious the rat shifters can be. That eye catches a ghostly flicker of scurrying forms cavorting amid the wreckage, there and then gone.

The Murk like nothing more than to bring us as low as they possibly can. I'm sure they wish they could drag us all the way down to their own wretched level. They certainly didn't show any respect to the man they left bleeding out under a sprinkling of dirt behind this small storage building.

Speaking of wretched figures… Aerik's shadow crosses the doorway. His arms are folded over his chest. I suspect he's no more pleased that I'm the arch-lord who took up this investigation than I am to be here. "Well, what do you make of it?" he demands.

Whitt replies for me. "It looks like their typical approach. Sneak in, wreak a little havoc, sneak out again." He glances around at the baskets of mushrooms gone black and mushy with rot and wrinkles his nose. "As much as your pack might have valued these delicacies, their loss is hardly catastrophic. My regrets to the family of your pack-kin who crossed their paths so unfortunately, though. If we catch them, you can be sure the mangy rats will pay for that."

"I don't like that they were so bold about it in general," I add. "Slipping into a building so close to the castle and the village. Did no one else see any sign of them?"

Aerik stiffens as if I've outright accused him of poorly protecting his domain. I'm more concerned because I assume he *has* been vigilant. He's probably been on guard against *us* ever since we brought him and his cadre to yield on Talia's behalf.

But perhaps his sentries were keeping watch against wolves and not taking enough care against rats. The mangy vermin are so small it isn't that difficult for them to lurk throughout our territory without being caught.

One of Aerik's cadre-chosen appears at his side. It's Cole, who I think frightens Talia even more than his lord, which means the sight of him brings my claws prickling to the base of my fingers. "They were as tricky about it as the pests always are," he says. "The rest of the pack didn't realize until one of the kitchen staff came to gather a few mushrooms for our breakfast."

Aerik appears rather mournful as he takes in his ruined stores, as if the loss of them bothers him more than that of his pack-kin. It *was* quite the collection of fungi, many rare species his pack must have gathered over time. I'm not above taking a minor satisfaction that he's being denied the delicacies I'm sure would have mainly been consumed by him and his cadre rather than the rest of their pack.

I step forward, and he draws back to let me pass, leaving a careful distance that I know isn't just out of respect to my station. One wrong move, and I'd happily snap the monster's neck as I wish he'd given me provocation to do the other afternoon.

The warmth of the midday sun barely penetrates my skin. I study the tiny paw marks in the dirt around the building again and then consider the pale castle. There is no "wrong" magic in the world, but nonetheless, Aerik's affinity for bone and his use of it in his home send a quiver of revulsion through my gut. "This was the only resource they destroyed?"

Aerik nods. "That we're aware of, but as soon as we discovered this intrusion, I had my pack scour the domain. There's no further trace of them. No indication of how they made their way into or out of our territory either. The only signs of their presence are what you can see and smell around this building—and of course the wounds they left on my fallen guard."

They covered their tracks everywhere else. That's even more indication that the Murk didn't leave those signs out of negligence but because they were taunting us with the fact that they could pull off this trick so blatantly. August lets out a growl and scans the landscape around us as if he thinks he might spot one of the perpetrators right now and take a chomp out of them.

I restrain a sigh. "It doesn't appear there's anything else we can do at the moment, but I'll report their boldness to my fellow arch-lords and put out the word across the realm for all our brethren to be particularly wary. If you need any assistance setting down appropriate protections—"

"No," Aerik bites out in a tone that's just shy of insubordination. "I can look after my people perfectly well as I am."

I give him a steady look and watch him not quite hide a flinch. I overpowered him when we were on equal footing as lords. He knows how steep the consequences are for betraying an arch-lord. Even Ambrose couldn't get away with that kind of treachery.

"We'll be on our way then," I say. "Do inform the domains of the Heart at once if you find any further information about the culprits."

We've only just left the Copperweld's castle behind in our carriage when August gives a brisk shudder as if shedding the atmosphere of the place. "I can't be angry at his entire pack—none of them knew about what he was doing to Talia—but there's nothing I'd like more than to see that place razed to the ground."

I tip my head toward him. "I suspect you'd like even more to see Talia stepping back across the border to meet us."

A smile much smaller and sadder than is usual for my younger brother crosses his face. "Well, yes, there is that." He drags in a breath and squares his shoulders. "Nearly halfway there."

Assuming all goes well. Assuming Talia is still all right even now. I've never much cared about the separation between the summer and winter realms before, but now that what's happening on the other side of the border matters to me very much, the perpetual silence itches at my skin.

"No wars declared, no further skirmishes," Whitt points out. "All in all, it can't be going too horribly." But his gaze is pensive as he gazes off across the terrain around us.

There are an awful lot of outcomes we'd hate to see that wouldn't involve outright war. But it doesn't do me any good to worry about those or whether the woman I love will even still be *mine* when she returns. I have duties to my entire realm to carry out.

When we reach the new Hearth-by-the-Heart, I take a little satisfaction in seeing the growing walls of our new castle, looking closer to its finished form by the day. Most of the pack will spend their first full moon since my coronation back in Hearthshire, but soon after we'll be able to bring them all here and be completely united again. I don't like having them at such a distance any more than I do Talia.

"I'll go check on the construction progress in the village and any new discoveries regarding Ambrose's weapons stash," August says, hopping out.

Whitt springs after him. "I'm expecting a couple of our sentries to check in. If they have word of Unseelie or Murk activity, I'll bring it to you immediately."

And just like that, I'm on my own. It doesn't take all that many responsibilities to divide me from even my cadre on a regular basis.

I can't join either of them, as I'm meant to report to my arch-lord colleagues on my observations in Copperweld. I stretch my limbs to work out the stiffness from the carriage ride and magic a quick message to travel to Celia and Donovan. Then I head toward the Bastion, where they'll meet me.

Before I've quite left the castle behind, Astrid catches up with me, moving at an impressively athletic lope considering her age. However many centuries she has behind her, it'll be a long time yet before she really slows down, I think.

She falls into stride beside me. "I just got in with the new group of workers from Hearthshire to handle the additional aspects of construction. The original crew are already giving them instructions and getting them started. Is there anything else you wish me to see to now, my lord, or should I take up my usual patrol?"

I pause, and Astrid stops next to me, her eyes darkening with immediate concern. This woman has known me since I was an infant, and she picks up on my moods faster than anyone outside my cadre. By this point, I doubt my own father knows me as well as she does.

But the thought that just struck me isn't a worrisome one. At least, I don't believe it would be.

I've been treating Astrid as almost like part of my cadre already, haven't I? When Whitt and August aren't available, she's the one I've instinctively turned to. I entrusted her with Talia's safety when we couldn't be there, and she saw that duty through without fail. I can't think of any task I wouldn't feel comfortable putting in her capable hands.

I've simply grown so used to relying only on myself and my brothers for our most fraught matters that I hadn't seen what was right in front of me. I *do* need more pack-kin by my side if I'm to rule as arch-lord effectively. If I have any secrets Astrid would think ill of me for, then no doubt I'd deserve it.

It seems like a bit much to spring on her out of the blue when she was asking for nothing more than basic orders. I grapple for a way to broach the subject—to make sure she wouldn't find the offer more of a burden than an honor. "Astrid, you've served me and my family before me for a long time."

Her eyebrows lift slightly. "I have, my lord."

"Have you ever felt you might want to step back from service to enjoy the rest of your life at more leisure?"

They rise even higher. "If you're suggesting that I haven't been performing adequately and it's time I put these old bones to rest, then I hope you'd speak to me more plainly than that. But I feel perfectly capable, and I'd enjoy continuing to know I'm of use a great deal more than sitting around getting mossy."

Her response is so unsurprising it seems absurd that I even asked her. The corner of my mouth curves upward. "So you wouldn't object to being of even more use than you already are, then?"

Astrid fixes me with a wry look. "I wouldn't chide an arch-lord, my lord, but you'll get an exact answer sooner if you say exactly what you're thinking. I can certainly take on more if you need me to. Honestly, having work to carry out on behalf of the pack is what keeps me feeling fully alive. With my mate's passing, my family got both smaller and larger. I consider all of Hearthshire to be it now."

Her words bring warmth into my chest. I couldn't have hoped for a better perspective, and now I'm completely certain of my choice.

"In that case, how would you feel about joining my cadre?"

Whatever Astrid might have imagined I was going to say, it clearly wasn't that. She stares at me for several seconds before she recovers her tongue. "I—your cadre—are you *sure*, my lord?"

I can't help chuckling. When was the last time I saw her startled enough to lose her composure? Possibly never. "I'm certain I wouldn't be asking unless I was sure."

"Of course. I only—" She shakes her head as if to clear it and smiles at me, crookedly but obviously pleased. "I never expected to receive such a lofty invitation. Or maybe I assumed if I was going to find myself in a cadre, it would have happened sooner."

"Well, if I've learned anything, it's that life rarely follows the patterns we'd expect." I expected to have my soul-twined mate's cadre to join with my own. I expected to rule over Hearthshire and not the entire summer realm. But here we are, and I can't say I'm sorry for it on the balance. "An arch-lord has much more to attend to than the mere lord of Hearthshire. I've realized it's time I expanded my inner circle. Only if you're willing, of course—"

"Yes, yes, that shouldn't be any question." She smiles more broadly, and I could kick myself for waiting so long to make this invitation. However many years she has left with us, she deserved more of them in a position that offered her all the respect she was due.

She pauses, and a soft twinkle enters her eyes. "There is one point I should probably clarify first, though."

"What would that be?"

"As far as certain, ah, arrangements exist between yourself and the current members of your cadre, I feel I should make clear that I have no desire to take on any further mates and am perfectly happy to leave all of that business to the three of you."

A laugh tumbles out of me. We've been careful, but there's only so careful one can be, especially with the one we asked to watch over Talia closely. "I'd imagine neither we nor Talia will expect anything other than a professional relationship from you."

"Excellent." She laughs herself and then lifts her chin. "Well, then —when do I start, my lord?"

CHAPTER TWENTY

Talia

"That's done with," Corwin says, stepping back from the crystalline stable building he just finished adding a few feet to with his magic. "I'm sorry—I'm sure that wasn't the most exciting work to watch."

"I'm not complaining." I hesitate and then ease back my inner wall a little more than I already had so he can feel more of my genuine appreciation of his skill. I may have gotten somewhat used to fae companions casting magic around me, but witnessing any of them bend the world to their commands still fills me with a sense of awe.

And it was kind of nice seeing the intensity of Corwin's concentration stripping away that coolly composed mask he puts on so often. The determined smolder in his eyes and the power ringing through his measured true words might have made my pulse stutter in a way that wasn't totally unpleasant. I'd rather he hadn't picked up on *that* subtle reaction, though.

If he did, he doesn't show it, only gives me one of his restrained smiles. "You'll have to come and meet the new steed once it arrives. I understand it's a rather impressive one."

I raise an eyebrow at him. "I'm still trying to figure out why you need any kind of steed when you've got wings."

The Unseelie arch-lord lets out a brief chuckle that seems to surprise him as much as it does me. His mouth twitches with a flicker of embarrassment, but his emotions settle quickly enough, his tone relaxed when he answers. "With multiple types of terrain, we need many options for optimal traveling. Neither wings nor conjured vehicles can navigate forests as well as our mounts do, should we need to attend to what's within the trees rather than simply soaring above them."

"Fair enough." I glance across the short span of icy fields to his towering palace. The sun is starting to sink, the deepening purple of the sky seeping across the diamond spires. Thanks to the warming spell on my clothes, the chill in the breeze barely touches me before it's whisked away, but the wintry area around Corwin's home feels even lonelier than inside its halls. "Where to next?"

"Now I'd typically consult with my kitchen staff about the dinner preparations. If you'd like, you can determine for yourself that Charles and his daughter are perfectly happy here among the fae."

Is there a hint of teasing to that suggestion? I study Corwin, but as usual his expression doesn't give away much, although I might sense a smidgeon of amusement through our bond. "All right. To the kitchen it is."

I don't know if I could say that I'm enjoying myself, but the silence between us as we walk back to the palace does feel more comfortable than I'd have expected a couple of days ago. Since his desperate plea outside my bedroom yesterday morning, Corwin has been on his best behavior.

We spent all of yesterday talking about my history among the summer fae—well, mostly *me* talking and Corwin listening, taking in the memories I let him experience through me, even though I could feel his hackles rising here and there. But I can't blame him for his instinctive reactions. Something about the soul-twined bond gives *me* a jab of guilt thinking about men other than him, even though I know I haven't done anything wrong.

He didn't let any animosity out, didn't say one word against my lovers or the Seelie in general. I don't think he could have faked the gratitude I caught from him when he told me how glad he was that Sylas and the others have protected me so adamantly.

With every moment we spent together discussing the love I've already experienced, any fear I had that he might try to take it away again dwindled until that concern disappeared completely. So when he offered that today I could join him for some of his duties around the palace and get to know the servants a little better, I accepted. So far he hasn't given me any reason to shut myself back in my bedroom to wait out the rest of my time here, but I'm still wary.

The kitchen Harper and I snuck into two nights ago looks even vaster fully lit. The fading sunlight combined with the yellowish glow of the extra lamps make the diamond counters and the silvery shapes of the ovens shine.

The human girl is just taking a fresh loaf of bread out of an oven, its crisp doughy scent lacing the air. Her father—Charles—is talking with a fae woman who appears to have brought in some vegetables. He turns to Corwin as soon as we enter.

"My lord," he says with a much broader and warmer smile than the Unseelie fae typically produce. "We've got quite the bounty today. Is there anything in particular you have a craving for?"

Corwin nods to me. "Perhaps my guest should have some say about tonight's dinner. Talia, the meals we've enjoyed so far were all thanks to Charles and Beth's impressive talents. Anything you'd like, I'd imagine they could find a way to whip up."

Beth comes over, rubbing her hands together. "Absolutely. A challenge just makes it more fun."

Okay, these human servants definitely appear to be totally at ease with their jobs here. I think over the meals we've had so far, all of them delicious, trying to decide which of my favorite parts I could ask them to replicate. "Do you ever cook fish with that reddish sauce we had on the quail? And I really liked the braised vegetables that looked kind of like asparagus that we had at lunch yesterday."

Charles gives his daughter a playful nudge with his elbow. "She's got good taste, doesn't she? That sounds like a perfect combination. Why don't you go and fetch a couple of trout?"

As Beth hustles off to the cold room, Corwin thanks his chef and moves as if to leave. Something deep within me balks. The arch-lord stops before I've said anything, picking up on my mood. "Is everything all right, Talia?"

"Yes. I just—" Will this request sound like a total imposition? Or simply ridiculous? I grapple with the impulse for a moment before spitting it out. "I used to help out in the kitchen a lot back… back home. Would it be okay if I pitched in with dinner?"

Corwin blinks, definitely startled, but he glances at Charles in question rather than denying me. The human man shrugs, his bright eyes twinkling. "Never hurts to have an extra pair of hands, especially if they know what they're doing. Do you think you can manage trimming the moss-shoots?"

I smile back at him, an unexpected lightness washing over me. "Show me with one and I'll remember for the rest. I'm a fast learner."

The moss-shoots turn out to be the asparagus-like vegetable I asked for. Charles demonstrates the preferred cuts, and then I get to work, carving the knife methodically through the pile while he prepares the sauce for the fish. Corwin watches from a short distance, our roles reversed for the first time today. A faint glow of satisfaction washes over me through our connection.

He likes seeing me find a place for myself here, even if it's among the servants for now—and I like it too. The rhythm of the work and the familiar bustle and clatter of kitchen activity around me settle my nerves more than anything else I've experienced since I came to the winter realm.

When I finish with the shoots, Charles hands me a mortar, pestle, and a small bowl of spice seeds, trusting I'll know what to do with them. I drop a handful of seeds into the mortar and put my shoulder into the grinding, my mouth watering at the tart tang that rises up. The scent reminds me of the cloves August used in some of his cooking…

A wave of homesickness sweeps through me, too fast for me to suppress it. A week ago, I'd have been perched like this next to August's brawny form, warmed by his smile and his encouraging words. Assembling a meal together in the perfect harmony produced by months of mutual experience—and love.

A pang of pain and jealousy prickles into me from Corwin, and my first instinct is to shove down those memories as quickly as I can. But… wasn't the point of yesterday to prove that he could handle me and my emotions as they are? That he could accept the commitments I've already made, the joy I've felt with the lovers I already found?

If there's going to be any chance of trust between us, I need to know that acceptance wasn't just a one-day thing.

I've barely come to that conclusion before Corwin has gotten his own reaction under control. The prickling discomfort subsides. He extends a tendril of apology and then, his inner voice cautious, says, *If you wanted to bring some ingredients and recipes back to share with him, I wouldn't mind. If* he *wouldn't mind attempting Unseelie-style cooking, that is.*

I glance at him with a jolt of surprise and unexpected affection. *I think he'd enjoy expanding his repertoire. Thank you.*

There's definitely amusement in Corwin's tone now, understated as it is. *I should be thanking you. You're the one preparing our dinner.* He pauses. *And I should thank him as well, for giving you a place you could feel at home among the fae, no matter whose home you're in. Will he still be spending so much time in the kitchen, even now that he's cadre to an arch-lord?*

I laugh out loud. *Maybe not quite as much, but I don't think you could keep August out of a kitchen for long unless the Heart itself commanded it.*

I suppose his pack can be happy for that.

We lapse into silence between us as Charles and Beth bicker amicably about the exact size the trout filets should be, but in that moment, I do feel at home. As at home as I *can* be when my real home is out of bounds.

Then another fae servant slips into the room carrying a tray of empty dishes. He draws up short at the sight of his lord—and my awareness of Corwin becomes abruptly dulled, as if he's shored up his own walls against our bond.

"It's fine," Corwin says with a brisk motion toward the far end of the counter. "You're not interrupting. I trust everything is in order."

"Yes, my lord. As well as it ever is."

There's a stiffness to both their voices. The servant darts to the corner, sets down the tray, and bobs up with his hand reaching into one of the cabinets, but I don't see him take anything out. Odd. I give Corwin a questioning look, and the barrier between us fades again.

My apologies. An instinctive reaction to an unexpected arrival. I should have remembered not everyone in the palace eats on the same schedule.

Is he embarrassed that I'm seeing a reminder of his separation from his servants? That answer doesn't totally sit right with me, but I don't know what to ask. The fae man heads back out again without a sign of concern, so maybe I shouldn't make all that much out of it. Corwin and I are both still finding our footing with each other, after all.

Beth comes over to rub the spices into the fillets alongside me, and then Charles has me sampling the sauce, and in no time at all the meal is ready. Corwin sends a servant to summon Harper while the cooks portion out the meal across several plates, including two for themselves and a few I assume are for other staff.

Corwin, Harper, and I gather in the small dining room like so many times before—only this time, I'm not just a recipient of the meal but a participant in its creation as well. Somehow that knowledge brings a more vivid flavor to the combination of flaky fish and savory sauce. I bite into the moss-shoots I trimmed with a weird sense of ownership, even though Charles did the actual braising.

Harper finishes her last bite with an approving hum. "The food here is always delicious, but I think this was the best dinner yet."

Corwin's smile comes out. "It was Talia's choice—and she had a hand in making it as well."

My friend grins at me. "That explains it, then."

The arch-lord considers both of us with a contemplative vibe and then asks, "Would the two of you like to accompany me to my music room? Perhaps I should make use of my own meager skills at entertainment for my guests."

My gaze darts to him. He's balked at including Harper in our activities before, but I don't catch any sign of resentment in his expression or through our bond. I send a whiff of gratitude his way. "I'd like that." I turn to my friend. "He's very good on the harp. I think even your parents would be impressed."

"Well, I can't miss a performance with a recommendation like that," she says. "Especially when it's the instrument that's my namesake."

I'm a little afraid I might have oversold Corwin's abilities, since I'm no musical expert, but it only takes a few notes pealing from the strings before Harper is beaming. She sways a little with the melody he produces, a more buoyant one than he played before. It brings images of the dancers at Whitt's revels into my mind.

Do the winter fae even have parties, or is that too wild for them?

We have plenty of ways of celebrating what we value, Corwin says, picking up on the gist of my curious thoughts. *Perhaps not quite so… boisterous.* He stops at the end of the song and swipes his hands over his thighs. *The Seelie who led those festivities—you showed me that he took you once to a spot you quite admired. Perhaps I can give you a similar gift.*

Before I can ask him what he means, he switches to speaking out loud. "I thought I might pay a call on a domain a couple of hours from here tomorrow. It has some impressive sights. If the two of you would like to make the trip with me, I'd be pleased to share one of the winter realm's greatest wonders with you."

For a second, I tense up at the thought of leaving the relative familiarity of this palace and venturing farther beyond with this man I've only just found myself capable of forgiving. But he's gazing at us so earnestly. No trace of jealousy came through in his reference to Whitt, nothing but…

Nothing but hope.

I did want to see more of this realm before I left. I think I might even enjoy seeing it with the relaxed, generous version of Corwin he's letting me get to know.

For the first time since I got here, I can truly believe that some kind of peace between my people and his is within reach.

Harper is watching me, waiting for me to answer first. I know she'd love to get out of the palace. So I smile, my own hopes lifting just a little. "Let's do it."

CHAPTER TWENTY-ONE

Talia

For all the differences between the winter and summer fae, when the Unseelie want to get somewhere without using their wings, they use methods pretty similar to the Seelie. The vehicle Corwin conjured for this trip looks like a wider and shallower version of a summer fae carriage, though with a clear crystalline wedge jutting from the bow to cut down on the cold sweep of the wind and no canopy to stop the bright sun from warming us. A darker wood than the juniper I'm used to forms the carriage's body, and the unpadded seats stand down the middle rather than against the walls.

Since this is my first time seeing the winter realm beyond Corwin's domain, I've spent most of the journey standing by the side of the carriage rather than sitting on those seats, peering at the passing terrain. A lot of it has been snowy or rocky or both, but I guess I can't complain about that when most of the summer realm is either forests or grassy plains. We did pass a vast field of twinkling flowers that spun at random intervals and a landscape where several rivers cutting through each other created a patchwork of islands.

Corwin glances over at me from where he's poised at the bow, and the warmth of his smile travels through our bond as well as showing in his expression. *I'm confident you'll like what I'm going to show you more than anything you've seen so far.*

You're setting high expectations, I can't resist teasing. *Tempting disappointment.*

The corners of his lips quirk a little higher. *If you aren't impressed by this, I don't deserve to be an arch-lord.*

Sitting on the bench near me, Harper nudges me with the toe of her boot and raises her eyebrows at me as if she can tell we've been having a silent conversation without her. Her own sly smile suggests she doesn't mind. She might have been willing to kick Corwin to the curb over how he treated me, but she's happy that we're getting along now.

And… we actually are getting along, aren't we? Over the past couple of days, we've reached our own kind of peace. He knows where I stand, and he hasn't made me regret my growing openness once since that horrible offense that he was willing to prostrate himself to make up for.

I haven't let him completely in. I'm still avoiding letting him see anything to do with my unexpected ability to wield true names, which his oaths wouldn't require him to keep secret from his colleagues. As accepting as he's become of my Seelie lovers, there are intimate moments I'd prefer to keep to myself because they're too personal to share.

He hasn't pushed for everything, though. I'm sure he's keeping plenty to himself as well. He still hasn't told me what's behind all the Unseelie attacks on the border, after all, although if he's made other oaths to keep information like that secret, it's not his fault. In every way I can think of, he's been showing how important it is to him to make up for our rough start.

I can't imagine giving up the men I left behind. A pang of longing still runs through me when I think of home. But it *is* a relief to relax more, to not feel like I'm up against an enemy. Corwin approaches things in a different way from the summer fae and from any human I can remember, but… I'm even starting to like being around him. Maybe we would have been friends if we'd met in some other way without all these pressures on us.

Looking over at him again, at the sunlight bringing out the sapphire blue in his black hair and the bronze tones in his handsome face, I might have to revise that thought. When he offers me one of his rare wider smiles that reach his eyes, it makes my heart skip a beat.

My appreciation of him isn't *only* friendly. But the soul-twined bond is at least partly to blame for that.

I still don't know what I'm going to do about that problem. I'm hoping that by spending more time together, the answer will come to me, even if it's hard to figure out what solution there could possibly be that won't break my heart or his.

Corwin must sense the lurch of tangled emotion that worry brings. A waft of soothing reassurance flows through our connection. *You don't have to make any decisions yet. You don't have to decide anything at all before you go back to the Seelie. I just want whatever decisions you make to be based on a full and accurate picture about what your life here could be like.*

So this excursion is only for the interests of accuracy and not to prove that you can also arrange a fantastic day trip? I ask with a hint of amusement, remembering how he mentioned my memory of Whitt taking me out to his favorite glen when making the invitation.

I'm allowed to have multiple motivations, aren't I? You're clearly an explorer at heart, and far be it for me to deny you the opportunity. He pauses, pulling his gaze away for a second before returning it to meet my eyes. *And it gives me great pleasure to see you happy.*

The affection that wraps around those words and flows through my chest makes my pulse stutter again. This time, *I* look away. I can still sense myself through his sight, his admiration of the way the sunlight brings out the vibrance in my own hair and lights up my face, his awareness of my eagerness and awe at getting to travel so far.

If he had qualms about my being human at first, I haven't caught anything that would make me think they've lingered. The fae put so much trust in the Heart and what it creates.

It'd be easier if I just accepted whatever blessing it's supposedly given us too, wouldn't it?

A castle of pale gray stone comes into view up ahead, and the carriage slows. I pull myself straighter, grateful to be distracted from the direction my thoughts were heading in. As Corwin directs the carriage to land on the outskirts of the sprawl of stone houses that arcs around the castle, Harper stands up to join me.

A few fae come over to greet us. Corwin hovers his hand just over my shoulder, careful as he always is not to touch me. "I've brought a couple of guests to see the painted forest. They've never gotten to experience it before."

The woman at the front of the small group beams. "I hope you enjoy our work, then. I'll let our lord know you've come by in case he wants to join you, Arch-Lord Corwin."

They all dip into a bow and head back. Corwin motions for us to follow him toward a stretch of small, pale trees farther across the icy ground. I can't see anything about them that looks painted or particularly impressive.

Patience. We're not quite there yet, Corwin says with a fondness that feels almost like a caress.

A narrow path has been cleared amid the trees and the frost-tinged bushes. A delicate scent, like what candied pine needles might smell like, tickles my nose. We walk for about five minutes, Harper sticking close by my side. Then the smaller trees thin and disappear completely to make room for a stretch of taller ones that extend their high, spindly branches toward the sky.

The trunks of those trees hold a riot of color. As I step closer, my breath catches, understanding now why this is called the painted forest —and why the woman mentioned their "work."

From the roots to where the branches sprout high above my head, paint covers every inch of the smooth bark with a vast assortment of scenes. One tree shows some kind of festival taking place all across a castle's grounds. Another depicts fae battling magical beasts while others tend to the wounded. I stop at one on which the winter fae have taken to the skies, some in raven form, some men and women with only their wings extended, soaring here and there amid the clouds and other flying creatures. The strokes of paint nearly bring the movement to life.

"Wow!" Harper murmurs, gaping at a neighboring tree. "This pa—I mean, this flock, they painted all of this?"

"It's been a tradition going back centuries," Corwin said. "They consider it an honor when the flock decides someone is ready to claim their tree. But you haven't seen the best of it yet."

I cock my head at him. "What do you mean?" *It's spectacular already*, I add silently. *Thank you for showing me this.*

He flashes what might be the first full grin I've seen from him. "All we need is the wind to rise—you'll see." *And you'll thank me even more then, I promise.*

I step back, peering up at the branches, and just then a breeze ripples through them. A glinting dust, fine and pale as sugar crystals, shimmers down from the branches. I follow its fall—and lose my breath all over away beneath a rush of wonder.

The paintings *really* move. As the powder blown from the branches glides past the images, the figures come to life. The flying birds and fae swoop past each other, spin, and glide. I even make out faces shifting with exhilaration and laughter. On the next tree over, fae children scramble along a mountainside, leaping and sliding.

I glance from one trunk to the next, my jaw gone slack, my chest full of amazement. The impulse rises in me to jump and whirl alongside the painted figures, as if I can join in their magic. As if I wouldn't stumble after a few steps if I attempted to be so graceful on my warped foot.

That's all right. It's enough just to watch.

Corwin's voice travels into my mind laced with unmistakable delight. *That's the reaction I was hoping for.*

The powder wisps away. The air has gone still again. I step back to take in more of the trees. "How often does that happen?"

"The breeze is never totally still for long. Take your fill."

When the air stirs the branches again, I drift between the trees, wanting to glimpse every scene in the extensive collection. I'm not sure I've seen even half of the wonders this place holds when footsteps rasp along the path toward us.

"Arch-Lord Corwin?" a fae man says, dipping low. "My lord wishes to speak with you on a somewhat grave matter. There's been—"

Glancing back at Corwin, I watch him raise his hand to cut off the rest of the man's sentence. The happiness in his expression is already fading, an uneasy chill rippling from him into me. A second later, my sense of him falls away. He's put up a partial wall, muting almost all of my awareness of his inner state.

"I understand," he says to the man. As I tense, he catches my gaze with an apologetic grimace. "I'm sorry. Matters of politics. You'll be safe here. You can continue exploring until I can return, or make your way back to the castle when you're ready and the flock will ensure you're comfortable."

"If there's any way I can help..." I have to offer.

He shakes his head. "With luck, I won't be gone too long. Don't let this ruin your enjoyment of the forest."

His closing off and his departure kind of does, though. Harper and I meander among the trees through a few more dust-falls, and each painted scene provokes a fresh wave of awe, but my stomach stays knotted.

What was the man going to say that Corwin didn't want me to hear? What's going on inside the Unseelie arch-lord that he's decided to keep me shut out after all his work to gain my trust?

I shouldn't be wandering around gaping at pretty pictures, no matter how magical, if something important is happening here.

Harper is alert enough to pick up on my mood. "Time to go back?"

"Yeah. I want to know what this 'somewhat grave matter' is."

I'd have considered sneaking into the castle if I thought I'd have much of a chance at eavesdropping on whatever is so secret. But when we've reached the edge of the village, I spot Corwin just emerging, an older fae man in fine clothes who I'm guessing is the local lord walking beside him, his posture downcast.

I slip between the buildings as stealthily as my limp allows, Harper trailing behind me.

"I just didn't expect—it's the second one this year," the lord is saying in a rough voice. "Has there been any progress at all?"

"We at the Heart are doing everything we can," Corwin says, and then, to my frustration, the fae woman who greeted us comes bustling over to escort me the rest of the way to him.

As soon as the arch-lord sees Harper and me, the conversation dies. He turns to the lord, his mouth slanting at a painful angle. I might not have much sense of him through our bond right now, but his sadness at whatever the situation is rings through every word. “You have my promise I’ll pursue every avenue until we come to a solution.”

I hold my tongue until we’ve clambered back onto the carriage. “A solution to what?”

Corwin looks at me, the sadness I heard before etched all over his face. “It’s a private matter. If there *is* anything you can do at any point, I will let you know.”

“Okay,” I say, believing him, but that’s not enough to stop the lump from rising in my throat.

We’re bound as tightly as any two souls can be, and yet there’s still so much distance between us.

CHAPTER TWENTY-TWO

Talia

At first, I'm not sure what's woken me. I jolt into consciousness tangled in the sheets on my bed with a vague sense of dread creeping through me but no memory of any dream that stirred it up.

I'm no stranger to night wakings. It's been weeks since my last nightmare of my time in Aerik's cage, but those haunted my sleep for a long time after Sylas and his cadre rescued me.

My first thought is that the old torments have followed me here in a vaguer form. I try to shake off the uneasiness and press my head back into the pillow, but the dread gets stronger instead, swelling inside me into a sharper horror.

As I sit up, hugging my knees, my mind wakes up enough for me to realize the impressions aren't my own. The disturbed emotions are washing into me through the soul-twined bond. Corwin is the one feeling that dread and horror.

Images dart through my head, washed up by his anguish: figures I don't recognize, their skin pale and eyes staring glassily, their mouths contorted in obvious pain. My stomach lurches. The faces—the corpses?—fade in and out of a darkness that winds suffocating around both them and the awareness seeping into me from Corwin. No conscious thought comes with the images, no understanding that I'm seeing this too.

Corwin? I think at him. *Are you all right?*

He doesn't answer. The horror takes on a deeper chill even as the images waver. *He* must be dreaming—dreaming some gruesome nightmare that he isn't waking up from.

Corwin! I shout at him inwardly as "loudly" as I can pitch my inner voice, but nothing changes.

I shiver, gathering my imagined light to rebuild the barrier between us. As the images dull, guilt fills my chest instead. I've pushed the horrors away, but my efforts have done nothing for him. He's caught up in all that awfulness—how long will the dream go on?

All those times Sylas came to break me out of nightmares… He offered me that kindness before we were really anything to each other. Am I going to ignore my soul-twined mate's distress? I don't like the idea of Corwin tossing and turning while those horrible images haunt him.

I hesitate for a few moments longer and then shove myself out of bed.

I don't remember exactly which doorway leads to Corwin's bedroom, but when I let the wall of light thin, it's easy to follow our connection to him. My sense of him tugs at me, leading me down the hall and to a door. I knock on it, and then, when there's no answer, twist the knob. It opens easily.

The room on the other side is dark. The sound of Corwin's breath reaches me, soft but ragged. The blankets shift with a jerk of his limbs. A jab of agony shoots through our bond despite my glowing barrier, and my own breath catches in my throat.

"Corwin," I say out loud. "Wake up."

He's wrapped so deeply in the nightmare that my voice isn't enough to shatter its spell. I limp barefoot across the floor to the bed. He's right by the edge of the mattress closest to me. The scent of him, cool and piney as a snowy forest night, fills my lungs.

Bracing myself in case he startles, I grasp his shoulder through the blanket. "*Corwin.*"

The arch-lord flinches. My vision has adjusted enough to the darkness for me to see his eyes pop open. He stares at me, another raspy breath hitching through him. His voice comes out hoarse. "Talia?"

"You were having a nightmare," I say quickly. "I didn't—I didn't want to leave you in it."

A mix of relief, shame, and gratitude hit me in the instant before he resurrects his own walls. He sits up gingerly, the covers falling to his waist. I can only make out the faintest shapes of the true name tattoos that mark his dark skin all across his chest and arms. His tone turns stiff. "Thank you. I'm sorry I disturbed your sleep."

"It's all right. I know what it's like—getting caught up in nightmares." I hesitate, biting my lip, part of me wanting to flee back to my bedroom and the rest caught in a tangle of concern and curiosity. "You were dreaming about people… who died? Did that really happen?"

I think they were Unseelie. From what I remember of the fleeting glimpses, they all had at least somewhat pointed ears, so they were definitely fae, and I can't imagine Corwin being brought to nightmares over the deaths of the Seelie, even if he isn't exactly in favor of the attacks on them either. There wasn't any blood or obvious injuries in the dream, though. If those images were based on memories, what *did* happen to them?

Corwin swipes his hand across his face. "You know from your Arch-Lord Sylas that sometimes one has to make decisions where there is no happy answer. Some of my regrets come to me in human form. It's nothing you should trouble yourself with."

I think he's implying that the people in his dream weren't real, only representations of his emotions, but he's using that tricksy fae phrasing that avoids the subject without saying anything direct enough to be a lie. Whatever the nightmare was about, he clearly doesn't want to talk to me about it.

I pull back instinctively, meaning to go, but with the same movement my gaze falls to his hand. It's clenched against the pale blanket—his whole arm is tensed, the lean muscles taut from wrist to shoulder, tightly enough that it's obvious even in the darkness.

He may not want to tell me about the nightmare, but it's still troubling him—a lot.

Without any conscious thought, driven by the pang of compassion that rings through me and the impression of closeness that hasn't totally faded even with our bond now walled off, I reach for him. My fingers graze his forearm—and sensations explode through my entire being.

It's ten times as intense as when he touched me in our shared dream. In that first instant, all barriers between us are blasted away. I see myself through Corwin's eyes, standing before the faint line of light around the ajar door, as clearly as I see his form on the bed through mine. I feel the lurch of his pulse, somehow both ecstatic and panicked at the abrupt intimacy, the claws of anguish still gripping his lungs tightly, the tension wound all through his body as he fights the conflicting urges to either bury all that emotion as deep as he can or to offer it up to me.

There's awe in him too, swelling through me as it expands in his chest—that I risked this physical contact after avoiding it for so long—that I risked it out of concern for him. It wells up inside me so swiftly and completely I almost choke on it.

I don't know what to do with that much emotion from him. I don't know how to answer it—

He reins it in. The effort it takes washes through me, but as it does the sensations dwindle. They're not gone completely, but it's as if the volume has been turned from blaring to a murmur.

I'm stripped bare, every nerve trembling. I can't seem to summon one particle of light to shore up my own defenses.

How much did he see in *me*? Have I given away—no, I can't think about anything I wouldn't want him to know—is he still seeing—?

My hand has slid to his wrist. I'm clutching him, and maybe it's our physical connection that's stopped the soul bond from being sealed completely. I can't quite will my fingers to loosen, though. Beneath the cacophony of all the impressions and emotions still whirling through me, a note peals out as clear as one plucked from the strings of Corwin's harp.

We're meant to be twined like this. The Heart bound our souls together, and as confusing as the experience is, something about it is perfectly *right.*

I close my eyes, mentally shaking that thought away. I only feel like that *because* of the bond. It's still my choice—the Heart doesn't get to dictate my life without any say from me.

Carefully, Corwin rests his hand over mine. When I look at him, his dark irises stand out against the whites of his eyes, intent on me. "Thank you," he says again, and this time his gratitude sweeps through me with the words. "I know it's been hard, trying to navigate the bond. I had no idea exactly how it would feel either. Perhaps I've kept you at more of a distance than I should have when I've wanted you to open up to me. Given my position…"

He trails off as if he isn't sure how to finish that sentence. But I understand. He's keeping things from me for the exact same reason I'm keeping things from him—because of our other alliances, because of conflicts we have no way of settling on our own, no matter how generous we are with each other.

Whether or not we accept this bond is our choice, but the tensions between his people and mine go far beyond that.

I'm pretty sure I already know the answer, but I find I need to hear it from his own lips, when I know he won't lie and when the connection between us hums so powerfully I'll even feel the truth of it within me. "You want me to accept the bond, to stay with you—is it only because you don't want to defy the Heart and you think it'll help stop the fighting? For the greater good?"

His gaze doesn't leave my face. The affection that emanated from him during our trip tingles through my chest, along with the unfurling of a more potent longing. Ever so tentatively, his thumb traces a line across my knuckles, sparking a quiver of sensation I'm afraid to focus too closely on.

"No," he says. "I have plenty of more selfish reasons too. You are… nothing I would have expected from any partner, and many things I wouldn't have let myself want. Things I'd like to have in my life." He swallows audibly. "I think I've managed to put aside any resentment toward your Seelie men, but I won't deny I still envy the bonds they've been able to build with you. I don't know how I can offer you what they have when our situation is so complex. But I will try, as long as you'll let me. I think I could be a good partner to you too."

That should be all I need to hear. To know he values me as a person, that he wants to build that kind of trust and devotion between us—and maybe it *would* be enough if I didn't have those other men in my life.

But I do have them, and as much as my heart thumps with the urge to embrace Corwin and throw myself into this fate I didn't ask for, it also aches from going without the love I already found.

I don't have to say any of that. Corwin must pick up on my inner turmoil through the bond.

He raises his hand to graze my cheek. "I don't blame you for being uncertain. I won't blame you if you choose them. The fact that you care for them so much is part of what I admire about you. I handled some things very badly when you first arrived here, and I still regret all of that. I am… honored that nevertheless my well-being matters enough to you that you came to help me tonight, that you haven't rejected me outright."

The hope that comes with those words ripples between my ribs into a blossoming of warmth. How can I *not* care when he speaks to me like that?

His fingertips linger against my skin so softly his touch feels like a breath, and I taste the impulse he's reining in, to lean across the short distance between us and kiss me. Heat spreads through my lips. The bond winds through me, tugging at my heart even more urgently.

Corwin simply watches me. If I went to leave now, he'd let me go.

I don't want to leave.

Whitt's reassurances rise up in the back of my head. He expected me to find out what I can make of this bond—all three of my Seelie men did. They knew how powerful it would be, how many urges it would provoke. How can I decide what's best when I'm holding myself back from experiencing so much of it?

I step closer and tip my head to bring my mouth to Corwin's.

It's only the lightest of kisses, a brushing of our lips, but the electric shock of the intimacy surges right through to my bones. The firm heat of his mouth melds with his awareness of the softness and sweetness of mine. Joy and pleasure crackle between us as if on a constant circuit.

Before I'm even aware of my intention, I'm pressing my lips even harder against his, absorbing the rush of sensation. Every part of me is lighting up with the sizzle of desire that only seems to grow as it races between us. I want—I want—If a simple *kiss* can feel this good—

The hunger dizzies me, overwhelms me—frightens me. All at once, I'm drowning in this wave rather than being carried aloft on it.

I wrench myself backward with a gasp, my skin still scorching, my body trembling. Corwin looks rather unsteady himself.

"I—I can't," I manage to stammer. "It's too much."

"I know," he says raggedly. "It's okay." The bliss he felt in the moment thrums into me, but his inner voice is tender carried with it. *Take whatever time and space you need. Just know that I'm in this with you, whatever you need from me. We'll find the path that's right.*

I want to believe that, but it's hard to even breathe with the memory of that kiss blaring through my mind. I take another step back, my wall of light coming to me easier now that I'm not touching him at all anymore. "I think—I should get some more sleep."

He nods without any hint of frustration, but as I flee into the hall, I can't shake the feeling that I'm somehow betraying him *and* my lovers back in the summer realm—and maybe even myself as well.

CHAPTER TWENTY-THREE

Talia

Breakfast is a relatively simple affair: hardboiled eggs and fresh-baked rolls, fluffier and fatter than August usually makes them, with cream, peach-like jam, and honey straight off the comb to spread on them. Corwin notices how much I'm loving the honey and offers another chunk of comb to me, and I find myself blushing as I hold out my plate to accept it.

I felt settled enough when I woke up this morning, but just being in his presence, being aware of him through the only partly walled-off bond, has put me off-balance all over again. My gaze keeps snagging on his lips with a tingling through mine when I remember our kiss.

He doesn't show any sign that he's noticed what I'm thinking about, but I can't believe he hasn't picked up on it at least a little. Every now and then a similarly eager warmth filters from him into me.

Like right now, as I bite into the roll I've just drizzled honey on.

My cheeks heat again, but I'm distracted from my embarrassment by Harper shifting on her chair. When she notices my attention on her, she shoots me a quick smile, but a moment later she's winding a few strands of her hair around her finger. She's not usually this fidgety.

It reminds me of how she acted when Ambrose's pack-kin were cajoling and intimidating her.

One of the servants appears in the doorway just then. "My lord, Olander has arrived and is asking to speak with you when you're able to."

Corwin wipes his fingers on his napkin and looks at his empty plate. "That's all right. I'm done here—I'll come now." He glances at me. "Olander's from my coterie, but it may not take long. You can wait for me here—I'll let you know my plans as soon as I find out what this is about."

I nod, and he leaves. Harper tears the rest of her current bun into little chunks. Watching her, I swallow my current mouthful and ask, "Not all that hungry this morning?"

She gives a little twitch as if shaking herself. "Sorry. I just—I didn't sleep all that well."

She hesitates, and I give her a closer look. "If there's something else bothering you, please tell me."

"I just don't want to make it sound like something's wrong when things have started to go well for you." She rubs her mouth, her gaze darting around nervously.

I summon more of my inner light to make sure Corwin won't accidentally overhear what Harper has to say. "Go ahead. I can't make a real decision if there are things I don't know."

"Okay." She drops her voice lower. "I—I woke up early this morning and couldn't get back to sleep. It's just so different from back home. Anyway, I went out and wandered a little, and I ended up back by that spot where we heard the strange noises before, the alcove where the door was locked. At first it was quiet, but then as I started to walk away, I thought I heard an actual *voice* from up there. Like a person's. Mumbling something—I couldn't make out the words—but it definitely sounded almost like talking. I've never heard of a spirit that could hold a conversation. It's usually just, like, a ball of energy, bumping against things."

She looks at me as if worried I'll be upset that she's mentioned it despite my reassurances. I don't know what to say. She's obviously unnerved by the experience, but—

"I haven't gotten the sense that Corwin would want to harm anyone," I say slowly. "Or that he has prisoners here, or anything like that. We haven't opened up to each other completely, but I don't think he could completely hide it if he was the kind of person who'd shut people away in so much pain they'd make sounds like the ones we heard before. Maybe someone went up there to try to settle down the spirit or… whatever you normally do when you have one that's restless?"

"I don't know. It was earlier than I've seen servants up before. Whoever it was sounded pretty miserable and out-of-sorts. And I waited a while afterward, and no one came out through the door." Harper shivers. "But it was only for a moment. Then everything went quiet again. Maybe I made it into something bigger in my memory."

That seems possible too when she's said she hadn't gotten enough sleep and was uneasy here in the winter realm in general. I don't want to discount her distress completely, though. She has a lot less reason to lie to me about anything upsetting going on here than Corwin does. I can't remember his exact wording when he talked about spirits, but it might have been vague enough to avoid giving the full story.

"I'll pay even closer attention when I'm talking with Corwin, watch for any sign that there's something we should be worried about going on. Maybe once we're more comfortable with each other, I can convince him to introduce us to this spirit, and we can see for ourselves what's in there."

"All right." Harper laughs softly. "I'd actually be interested to see one. I've only ever heard stories."

A prodding sensation inside me tells me Corwin is reaching out. I let the glow inside me thin. *Sorry, I'm listening now.*

I'm afraid I need to go down to the village to consult with my flock-folk on some matters today, he says in an apologetic tone. *I'm not sure exactly how long it'll take—at this point I'd imagine I'll be returning by lunch.*

That's okay. I know I'm not your only responsibility. Far from it. I hesitate, sucking my lower lip under my teeth, and then venture, *Could I come along? I'm finished with breakfast, and I'd like to see the village and meet more of your flock. I won't interfere with whatever business you need to do, just hang back and watch.*

There's a pause. My awareness of him dulls again as he must close off our connection to consult with his coterie man. My heart sinks with the assumption that he'll brush me off like he has every other time I've tried to find out more about his actual work as arch-lord, but when his voice returns, it's cautious but not resistant. *That's a reasonable request. I've sent my people to get everything ready for the meeting. Can you join me on the terrace so I can escort you down?*

A smile springs to my lips. *Yes, I'll be right there.* I don't imagine this will unravel any of Harper's mystery, but maybe today I'll learn a thing or two that'll help me understand the conflict between summer and winter.

Harper sends me off with a wave, looking more relaxed now that she's shared her anxieties, and I find Corwin waiting on the terrace as promised. A light snow is falling, glinting here and there when the thin sunlight catches it. The flakes brush my cheeks with a chill before the warming spell in my clothes rises up to melt them away.

The Unseelie arch-lord turns to meet me, and his wings unfurl from his back in the same moment. I halt in my tracks, a strange mix of awe and uncertainty spreading through my chest at the sight of him.

I'm only just getting used to appreciating the dark curls of his hair and those burgundy-brown eyes I've now seen soften just for me. The black feathered expanses stretching out on either side of him give his tall frame a grandeur I haven't witnessed since back when I considered him an enemy.

It's… it's kind of magnificent. And kind of scary, how hard it is not to gape in wonder.

I manage to regain control of my tongue. "I—do we need to fly down?"

Corwin's mouth tightens with a hint of apology. "There are paths along the cliff, but they'd take much longer. I can carry you so that our skin doesn't touch, if you want to avoid the intensity physical contact brings to the bond."

The intensity I embraced for at least a little while last night. But I don't want to end up too distracted by our connection to focus on the actual business he's going to be attending to—and being carried by him in flight is bound to be plenty distracting on its own.

I step closer, taking a deep breath. "That sounds like a plan."

He picks me up carefully, one arm around my back and the other beneath my thighs, and gives me time to adjust myself against him so I'm comfortable. If comfortable is even the right word for it. Even without skin-to-skin contact, every inch of me hums at his nearness, the heat of his body washing over me from his arms and his chest where I'm leaning against him. His wintry forest scent wraps around me.

I swallow hard, keeping my gaze low, nervous of looking into his eyes when our faces are so close together. "I'm ready."

We sway with the first swish of Corwin's wings lifting us off the ground. My pulse hitches, and I grasp his padded tunic. But with a few more flaps, the steadiness of the rhythm eases my nerves. It's only a gentle rocking as he picks up speed and then totally smooth as he soars down over the edge of the cliff toward the homes clinging to its face on either side of a glittering frozen waterfall.

The houses we glide past look almost like ice themselves, formed out of crystal just like Corwin's palace, though many in different hues from his colorless diamond. They all have a small terrace of their own jutting out where it'd be easy for anyone arriving by air to land. A few of the members of Corwin's flock raise their hand to him as we pass.

He lands lightly on a terrace about halfway down, right next to the torrent of ice. The frozen waterfall looks perfectly solid, but a faint trickling sound tells me at least a little actual water is tumbling down the cliffside behind that mass.

Corwin sets me down at once and studies me as I straighten my dress as if checking for signs of distress. I'm simply gathering my composure. When I look up, my balance sufficiently regained, I smile at him. "That was kind of fun."

One of the rare, warmer smiles I can't help treasuring crosses his lips. He retracts his wings and beckons for me to follow him into the house.

Two men and a woman are waiting in the room inside, the woman and one of the men sitting on stools of pale wood, the other man standing across from them. Aside from a few other chairs set against the walls, the circular space holds no other furniture. It must mainly be used for meetings like this.

As we step inside, Corwin's expression reforms into his usual solemn mask. He motions for me to take one of the chairs by the wall and introduces me with the same gesture. "This is Talia, a guest of mine of some importance. Talia, meet Olander and Zelpha of my coterie, and Mithron, one of my flock's most dedicated sentries. He's been stationed to travel along the fringe domains of our realm."

The three all dip their heads, more out of respect for their lord than for me, I'm sure. I wonder if anyone in his coterie knows why I'm really here, but I can't help being grateful that he isn't revealing my real role. I can't imagine what kind of stares I'd get over being introduced as his soul-twined mate. If I end up deciding to see the bond through, then I'll be willing to deal with whatever chaos ensues.

As I sit down, Corwin folds his arms over his chest, focusing on Mithron, a slight, sinewy-looking man with a jutting chin that could almost be a beak in itself. "As I understand it, you've come to report an increasing presence of hostile beasts in those fringe domains."

Mithron nods sharply. "Yes, my lord, and other domains as well. At first it was just a few extra reports of maulings and other attacks in the villages nearest to the edge of the Mists, but there've been more every week for the past month, and what prompted me to come immediately was several in the past few days from domains closer inward where the creatures never used to venture at all."

"What sort of beasts exactly are we talking about?"

"It hasn't been just one but a few different sorts. The most deaths have been from chimeras and searmaws, as you'd probably expect."

Corwin frowns. "And *those* have ventured farther inward as well?"

"Yes, my lord." The sentry grimaces. "The warriors of those flocks have been culling their numbers as well as they can, but with—with the reduced situation nearly every domain is finding itself in… it's more difficult to keep the beasts under control than it used to be."

His eyes dart to me for an instant. A prickle runs over my skin. Reduced situation—fewer warriors because of those who've died fighting the Seelie? It's hard for me to summon a lot of sympathy when they'd never have been "reduced" if they hadn't attacked my people in the first place.

"The lords I spoke to asked me to come to the arch-lords for guidance and any other aid they can offer," Mithron adds. "I thought it best to speak to you first."

"And I appreciate that." Corwin glances at his coterie members. "What have we heard from the rest of the realm?"

The man on his feet—Olander—is stouter than the sentry but with a robust sort of grace. He doesn't answer, pacing slowly from one end of the room to the other, his pale eyes distant with concentration.

The woman—Zelpha—leans her muscular frame back in her chair, her chestnut-brown face drawn with concern. "Similar reports have come back from other areas along the fringes, although not so urgent that anyone brought it to an arch-lord's attention yet. My best estimation would be that they're struggling more than they've admitted, not wanting to add to the troubles already keeping us busy."

Olander hums. "I looked through the records ahead of reaching out to you. There hasn't been an incursion of beasts like this since several centuries ago, and even then it wasn't on this scale. They were quickly driven back after their sudden arrival."

Corwin exhales slowly. "All right. Let's go over the strategies the affected flocks are already implementing and what we might add to those."

While they hash out the details, I simply sit and listen like I promised I would. I can't follow everything they mention, terms I'm not familiar with popping up here and there, but I get the gist of it. Now and then, one of the three shoots a glance my way with a pause in a sentence or the overall conversation. Wondering why I'm even here if all I'm going to do is gawk at them, no doubt.

What do I know about vicious faerie beasts anyway? My thoughts slip back to the tuskcat that attacked me. Astrid killed it with a sharpened stick—Corwin has already discussed the weaponry the winter fae are using.

But the tuskcat had strayed beyond its usual territory too. In that case, it'd come because Ambrose's pack-kin had drawn it into Sylas's domain through magic. I doubt this huge influx of creatures into all sorts of domains would be happening on purpose, but maybe…

I open my mouth and then balk, not sure how to insert myself into the conversation. Instead, I tentatively reach out to Corwin through our bond. *Would it be okay if I mentioned something?*

At the next natural pause, he turns to me, as if it was his idea—since the others don't know I could have spoken to him silently. "Do you have anything you can make of this matter that we haven't already covered, Talia?"

I send a tendril of gratitude his way. "Yes. I—are there any fae who've mastered the true names for those creatures? If those people are spread out across the domains now, maybe bringing them together and having them tackle one area at a time would be helpful so there are enough to get the beasts under control. If there's no way to simply discourage the creatures, they could draw them into a trap or at least a situation where it'd be easier to hunt them…"

My throat closes up with the pressure of four sets of fae eyes now trained on me. "I mean, probably you've already considered all that."

"No," Corwin says. "It's a good point, making more of a combined force out of those efforts. Olander, find out who remains with the appropriate true names for one or another. They *have* always played a role we took for granted in maintaining the borderlands, but their numbers may well have dwindled. We might want to take a longer-term approach, see about training more fae to master those names." He runs his hand along his jaw.

From the rest of the conversation that follows, it doesn't sound as if I've come anywhere close to solving their problem, but then, I didn't expect to. I get the impression that I might have made some small difference, at least. Better than sitting here like a lump the entire time, not contributing anything.

Flying back up to Corwin's palace is easier, now that I know what to expect. I still don't look into his face while he's carrying me, but he gives me a chance to take in the view across the winter realm from an angle I've never seen before. The mountains look even more sublime when I'm viewing them from mid-air.

It seems a little too soon that we're landing on his terrace. The snow is starting to thicken, but I'm not quite ready to go inside. I brush the cold flakes from my hair and offer Corwin a hopeful smile. "It wasn't so bad having me along, was it? I didn't cramp your style?"

He chuckles. "No. I—I rather liked it." His eyes catch mine with a sudden intensity. His voice softens. "I'd like to think there could be many more meetings like that, with you playing an even larger role as you come to know my people better."

If I accepted him as my mate. Picturing it sends a giddy quiver through my chest, but memories stir at the same time: the happiness I felt when Sylas let me in on his discussions with his cadre for the first time. The plans we built together, the challenges we've overcome.

I can't say anymore that I don't want anything to do with this place. But I know down to the depths of my being that I can't give up the men I've come to love so much. This situation is just… impossible.

A spark lights in my head with an even giddier rush of sensation. Unless—

Corwin cocks his head. "What's made you look so pleased with yourself?"

"I just—" I almost falter and then gather my courage. I'm only here for a few more days. I *have* to say it sometime. Better if he has more of a chance to let the idea sink in.

"I just was thinking, maybe I could have that with you… without having to lose everything else. I don't know exactly how it'd work, and I'm not even saying for sure I'd want to go through with the bond yet —I'm not ready to decide that—but if I did… A lord like Sylas wouldn't normally have gotten involved with a woman who has other lovers as well, but he was able to adjust to the idea, even to appreciate what it meant. If he and his cadre would agree, and you'd agree—maybe I wouldn't have to give up on *anyone*."

Corwin stares at me. A flicker of shock and something pained passes into me and then fades quickly as he walls off his emotions. The warmth that filled his expression a moment ago vanishes. "A lord sharing with his most trusted advisors is hardly on par with some sort of arrangement between fae of different realms—arch-lords no less—*my* soul-twined mate no less."

The wind whips over me, tossing my hair, but I don't let myself look away from him. "If there's no arrangement, then you might not end up with any soul-twined mate at all. I don't care what the Heart thinks it's doing. I was theirs first."

His voice goes even flatter. "It isn't even about me. *They* would never agree to it. They were barely willing to allow you out of their sight to come to me as it is."

"That's different. They had no idea what you're like. They were protecting me." I set my hands on my hips. "You won't know unless you ask them about it."

"I assure you, I don't need to." Corwin spins toward the door to the palace with a jerk. "Consider the matter put to rest. No good can come out of discussing it, only more distress for both of us."

CHAPTER TWENTY-FOUR

Corwin

I can tell from the moment I step into the Hall of the Heart that I'm not going to enjoy this discussion with my fellow arch-lords. Of course, I was already fairly certain of that from the moment they summoned me out of my chambers before I'd even had a chance to *think* about breakfast. Especially considering we only just spoke yesterday afternoon concerning the growing issues with roaming beasts coming in from the fringelands.

None of my colleagues have bothered to sit. Laoni, Terisse, and Uzziah all eye me with chilly expressions as I take my spot at the polished marble table. Only Neve looks unperturbed, but these days the frail elderly fae woman occasionally seems not totally aware of what's going on around her, so that's no guarantee she's on my side. If her hazy periods start to overtake her lucid ones, I expect her son will demand she let him take over her post.

I might not have been prepared when this position was first thrust upon *me*, but I've had plenty of time to hone my approach since then. The best way to hold my own among my colleagues, who are all centuries older and more established than I am, is to maintain the coldest and most impenetrable of fronts myself.

I fold my arms over my chest and draw my spine as straight as it'll go, which brings me a couple of inches taller than even Laoni with her ample brawn. "What is so urgent we had to gather so soon after our last meeting? Has some catastrophe occurred?"

"I'd say so," Laoni bites out with a toss of her turquoise hair. She considers herself the highest authority of us all on the grounds that she's held her position the longest, although that's not so much due to an excess of competence as the fact that her father had her late in life and passed when she was not much older than I was at my own coronation. That fact hasn't given her any sympathy for my situation, though. If anything, it's the opposite.

She continues in a brittle voice. "It's come to our attention that the Seelie woman you brought to your palace, the one you claim is your soul-twined mate, isn't Seelie at all. She's *human*."

Ah. I hadn't seen any need to inform my colleagues of that development until I was sure Talia would be remaining among us for a longer period. Mainly because I expected the news would be received with exactly the reaction I'm facing right now. One of the fae who observed us on our brief travels must have been gossipy enough for the fact to make it back to another arch-lord.

"I didn't consider the information immediately relevant," I reply, reining in a flicker of annoyance and keeping my own voice perfectly even. "Either way, she has ties to the Seelie. Either way, the Heart's choice is unexpected."

Uzziah sputters, sending a ripple through the doughy flesh of his dour face, which sags as if gravity weighs on it harder than it does the average fae. "Unexpected? It's a travesty. It must be some mad trick of the wolves, making you hallucinate a connection. The Heart would never—"

"It has," I cut in. "I'm not some fledgling who'd be distracted by shiny tokens. I've been inside her mind and she in mine. We shared dreams before we even spoke in person. Do you know of any possible spell that could create such a bond?"

He doesn't, clearly, because all he does is glower at me in answer.

Laoni shakes her head. "It doesn't matter whether it's a true bond or not. You can't accept it. If it had been a true-blooded Seelie, we might have used that for leverage. Even a mostly dilute fae wouldn't do us much good, let alone some human who was likely no more than a servant as it was."

As if the only possible use of me having a soul-twined mate is to help us negotiate for our ends. Anger stirs in the pit of my chest. I have reason to believe that Talia could be the solution to our people's hardships beyond anything we'd even dared to hope for—but my oaths prevent me from saying anything about that to the four around me. I still haven't even risked saying anything to *Talia* for fear of the consequences if she tells her Seelie arch-lord what we've faced.

My mate wouldn't use our vulnerabilities against us. I've seen enough to know she's far too honorable for that. But the Seelie—no matter how much *she* trusts them, no matter how kind they've been to her—it's not for nothing that they shift into wolves. They can be as vicious as the beasts we need to push back to the edges of the Mists. And I can't see any reason that their hearts would soften for any of us in the winter realm.

I inhale slowly to steady my temper. "I can hardly dismiss her and ask the Heart for a different mate. She's the one it's seen fit to give me."

Terisse scoffs. "Better a regular mate than to be soul-twined to a dust-destined mortal. You can't seriously be considering binding yourself to that flimsy thing permanently, bringing it into your confidence—"

"*She* is a perfectly capable being in her own right." I cast my gaze around the table, more anger rising. "How thorough a vetting did each of you give *your* soul-twined mates before accepting them? What tests did they have to pass to prove themselves worthy? Or did you simply follow the bond because clearly it was what the Heart offered you?"

"When it's one of our own kind, there's no reason to be so concerned," Uzziah retorts. "It's hardly the same situation."

"I think it is. The question is what the Heart wills, and the Heart wills that I should be bound to this woman." I wave my hand in the direction of the glowing mass that sends its thrumming energy over us even as I speak. "Would you defy the very source of all our power?"

Laoni hums to herself with a patronizing air that sets all my nerves on edge. "The Heart's first will is that we serve our people as well as we can. But perhaps you are letting sentimentality dictate your thoughts rather than logic. From the looks of it, you've already grown attached to this human girl. Taking her on romantic trips across the realm? Hiding her true nature from the rest of us?"

As well as I can, I resist the urge to bristle, which becomes even harder when Terisse makes a tsking sound. "It wouldn't be the first time in your family that emotions led one astray from one's duties to—"

"I'm fully aware of my duties," I interrupt, not quite a snap but with enough of an edge that I wince inwardly. The three who've been berating me look at me almost pityingly, as if I've proven their point and myself incompetent with that minor lapse. Even Neve studies me with a vaguely sad slant to her mouth.

And into that moment, Talia's voice reaches me. It's barely more than a whisper through the imagined crystalline wall I've conjured inside me to shield her from this discussion, but she's compelling her voice forcefully enough for it to filter through. *Corwin, is everything all right? You feel… upset.*

Dust and doom. I can't imagine how much more than "upset" the emotions she sensed must have been for them to have reached her at all and for her to feel she needed to reach out. I clench my jaw, about to tell her everything is fine, but the gazes still fixed on me with their accusations and their disdain make me hesitate.

Whatever they say, she isn't fragile. Not so fragile that hearing them talk about her as if she is would damage her. If she's going to make an honest choice about her future, she deserves to know at least this much of what she's walking into, doesn't she?

She deserves a mate who'll treat her like she has a real place here.

My fellow arch-lords have discovered that you're not quite the Seelie lady they assumed, I say, letting my inner wall drop. *I'm failing to appreciate their advice on the matter.* Then, squaring my shoulders, I address the figures before me. "My soul-twined mate is witnessing this meeting through me now. If you're going to disrespect the bond the Heart gifted us with, you may as well do it in the face of that bond."

Talia stays silent, but I can sense her awareness within me, taking in the room through my eyes with a prickle of irritation I know is directed at my colleagues rather than me. Terisse has stiffened.

Laoni's face goes absolutely rigid, as does her voice. "Allowing any other party access to the private meetings of this quintet is highly irregular."

"Challenging a soul-twined bond is highly irregular," I reply. "Can any of you honestly claim before the Heart that you've never shared aspects of our conversations here with your own mates?"

The silence that follows is answer enough. "That's hardly the same either," Uzziah begins.

I fix my sternest look on him. "It's *exactly* the same. She is my soul-twined mate as determined by the Heart, and no words you throw around can diminish that fact."

Laoni aims an icy scowl at me and steps back from the table. "You've heard our opinion on the matter. I expect you to think it over—and consider what is truly best for the people you've sworn to serve."

Oh, I already have. She hasn't the faintest idea.

The other arch-lords stride away from the table without so much as a farewell. I turn too, an odd rush of exhilaration sweeping through me even though beneath it my gut has tightened.

I've given them more ammunition for their stockpile against me, their justifications for never taking my views into as full an account as each other's. But I find I can't regret that. What I said needed to be said, or I might as well roll over in a much larger and more permanent way.

If I lose Talia, it'll be because *she* refused me, not because I let those sneering bastards dictate the terms of my life.

Talia's voice carries to me with a wry but tentative question. *I guess I broke up the party?*

Not your fault. They had a little taste of their own hypocrisy and found it unpalatable. I apologize for disturbing you.

No, it was fine. I… I like it better when you let me see what's going on with you. She pauses, and through my impressions of her I gather she's leaving her bedroom, already dressed. The emotions that seep through our bond are such a twisted mix of contrasting shades that I have trouble picking any one apart from the mass. *Are you coming back now? It smells like breakfast is just about ready.*

Yes. I'll see you in the dining room.

It doesn't occur to me to pay attention to her making her way there. I'm focused enough on my own surroundings, crossing the snow-clad plain between the Hall of the Heart and my palace, that I'm taken completely by surprise when I stalk past the front door and find Talia in the entrance room waiting for me.

I stop in my tracks. She smiles a little shyly, and the hints of affection that shimmer through our bond make me even more uncertain on my feet. For a moment, all I can think of is the kiss we shared two nights ago, the delicate warmth of her breath and the subtle strength wound all through her body, the pleasure I managed to summon in her alongside my own—

As she steps toward me, I tamp down on those thoughts, hard as it is with that luminous face and those bright green eyes before me. She's chosen the same pale-pearl dress she wore when she arrived here, and though she looked a tad uncomfortable in it then, now she moves amid the folds of gleaming fabric as if it's a part of her. The only detail stopping her from looking like the loveliest of Unseelie ladies is the rounded tops of her ears, mostly hidden by the fall of her vibrant hair.

In that moment, I truly don't care about that detail one bit. This is my mate. And she *is* lovely, in much more than just her appearance.

She ducks her head. "I know they're giving you a hard time because of me. I—I just wanted to say thank you. For what you told them. For standing up for me."

As if she should be grateful rather than expecting it. I summon whatever reassurance I can gather to offer through the bond. "Of course. It had to be said. I may very well need to say it again many times."

"Thank you in advance for all those times too, then." She takes another step, bringing her close enough that she can slip her arms around me and lean her head against my chest.

My heart stutters, and the rest of me freezes up. I want *so much*—it's dizzying, like dropping into a freefall and finding you can't flex your wings. My colleagues' insinuations are still ringing in my head, and the memories of sobs and wails, and—

I close my eyes, and other memories that aren't mine drift through our connection: Talia's arms embracing other men who hugged her back with enthusiastic tenderness. Who didn't stand there rigid as a boulder the way I'm doing right now.

A stab of panic—that I'm failing, falling short—splits through all the other turmoil inside me, and I force myself to move. To relax into her hold. To ease my own arms around her and pull her just a little closer to me.

Talia squeezes me tighter, with a pang of affection that seems to match what's echoing through her memories. For all the envy in me that those men feature so large in her life, it's also an honor to find I might have a spot alongside them, however precarious it might be.

I don't know how to say any of that aloud, so I let as much of the feeling as I can coherently convey pass from me to her.

Is this sentimentality? Am I proving my fellow arch-lords right that I'm following my heart over my mind?

All I know is that this moment feels perfectly right. *Talia* is right, for me and for the people I serve.

Heart help me manage to convince her of that too.

CHAPTER TWENTY-FIVE

Talia

I've just gotten out of the bath. The room around me is hazy with steam, and what I can see of it doesn't make much sense. These vibrant tiles on the floor belong to the sauna back in Hearthshire, but the crystalline walls are all Heart's Cadence.

I reach for my towel, and somehow Corwin is there, handing it to me. Looking at me, standing naked in front of him. A flare of heat courses through our bond and sparks something sharp and dizzying in me.

He's nearly naked too, a towel of his own wrapped around his lean hips, so much sleek, sculpted muscle on display above and below it. His eyes smolder as they meet mine.

Desire ricochets between us, winding through my chest, summoning a throbbing between my legs. Every pulse of it tugs me toward him. *Mine. Mine. My mate.* The call of it clangs so loudly I can hardly think.

"Talia," Corwin rasps, looking just as overwhelmed, a wildness in his expression I've never seen before. My pulse hitches harder, as if propelling me into him—and then our mouths have collided, his hard and hot against mine. His fingers tangle in my damp hair, his other hand tracing the curve of my waist and yanking me against him.

Yes. Every particle in my body cries out in eager relief, as if I've been waiting for this moment for years. His skin sears against mine, but it doesn't feel like enough. I ache to melt right into him, to merge with him bodily as thoroughly as our souls are twined. A matching longing careens from him into me.

I kiss him with all that pent-up hunger, and he groans against my lips. *Talia,* he murmurs through the bond. *Talia.* As if there's no room left in his mind for anything but me. He tips my head to kiss me even more deeply, cupping my breast at the same time. The swivel of his thumb over my nipple sends a jolt of pleasure through me that leaves me whimpering.

My hips grind against him with a mind of their own. That heated friction does nothing but intensify the ache in my core. I *need* him, need to be joined with him, to carry out our bond in every possible way—

Yes, he mutters, his tongue delving between my lips to stroke over mine. *Yes, all of you, now. Mine.* The words are barely coherent, but the same thoughts whirl in my head.

His hand slides to my bottom and he hefts me up against him, bracing me against a wall that's suddenly right behind me. The bulge beneath the towel presses between my legs, and I almost sob with the demand for release. I grasp at him, kissing him frantically, running my fingers over every inch of taut muscle they can reach, pulling him closer. My hips rock against him in a motion that's nothing short of begging.

The towel drops. The inferno of longing and lust spiraling between us burns hotter as his rigid length rubs against my most sensitive spot. I gasp, clutching him. With a groan, he lines himself up and plunges in to meet the place where I need him the most—

And I jerk awake, my heart racing, the sheet that's twisted around me damp with sweat. I'm in my bedroom, enveloped in darkness.

It was a dream. Just a dream.

But the feelings weren't imaginary, not entirely anyway. I squirm, and my hardened nipples graze the fabric over them with blissful quivers. My skin still feels hot enough to scorch my nightgown, and a torturous pang reverberates up from my core.

Not just from *my* core either. The heat that's flooding me tastes of Corwin too.

As my mind wakes up more, I sense him on the other end of our connection in his own bed, his body aflame with unfulfilled desire, his rigid erection pressing against the covers.

I can't help remembering what it felt like to have that length filling me for the instant before I woke up. Another peal of need quakes through me. Corwin's stutter of breath reaches me from the inside out —and then his hand dives beneath the blanket to curl around his hardness.

Oh. A real gasp falls from my lips at the surge of pleasure that gesture brings him—and me through him. He slides his hand up and down his length, spreading the liquid that's already formed at the tip, and the spot between my own legs grows even slicker than it already was from the dream.

Spurred on by my response, he picks up his pace, imagining the tight wet heat he thrust into in that imaginary sauna of the dream. The taste of my skin. The feel of my body against him and around him.

A breath shudders out of me. So much tension swells through me I think I'm going to explode. I shove my arm under the sheets and curl my fingers against my sex.

That first touch comes with a shock of relief and headier hunger—and a bolt of urgent lust that shoots straight to my core from Corwin. Clamping my teeth against a moan, grateful that the diamond walls in this palace are solid enough to dull any sounds that might escape me, I rock the heel of my hand against the tender nub that's aching for contact.

Oh, God, it feels so good. The blazing pleasure builds with each stroke of Corwin's hand over his hardness. I echo that bliss with the rhythm of my fingers now pushing right inside me.

It isn't enough, I'm not nearly filled, but I match his pace as closely as I can. My hips arch up, my whole body straining toward its peak.

The ecstasy flowing between us flares hotter and brighter with every electric jolt flowing between us. Corwin grips himself harder, and I work my hand against my sex faster.

With one final flare, we shatter together into giddying burst of sensation. A rush of shooting stars whites out my vision behind my closed eyelids and crashes through the rest of me, leaving me boneless.

I slump into the mattress, my fingers wet with my spent arousal and my nerves still tingling. My sense of Corwin dims. In the wake of our release, exhaustion rolls over me, and I tumble back into a sleep that's deep and dreamless.

When I wake up to morning sunlight, it takes me a moment to remember why my fingers are faintly sticky. A flush burns my cheeks. I scramble out of bed and clean up as quickly as I can at the wash basin.

As I get dressed, a twinge of guilt settles in my gut. I didn't *actually* do anything with Corwin. I had no control over the dream, and afterward… I'm not sure I could have fought the pull of desire through our bond no matter how hard I tried. Not once in there did I really touch him.

But the act we shared still feels incredibly intimate. Farther than I'd ever have wanted to take our relationship when I'm not even sure how much of a relationship we're going to have.

My men back home wouldn't blame me. I know they were prepared that our connection might be so strong I'd literally have sex with Corwin—consummate the bond, leave them behind for good. They wouldn't say I've betrayed them. But I can't quite shake the guilt.

Squashing it down as far as it'll go, I test my current sense of the Unseelie arch-lord. I'm vaguely aware of his existence—I think he's still here in the palace—but nothing comes through quite strongly enough for me to be sure of exactly where or what he's doing. I don't pick up anything particularly intense in his mood, so maybe he's taken this whole thing in stride? He might even have expected something like that to happen.

Is he going to want to *discuss* what we did? Even more heat floods my face. I swipe my hands across my cheeks and take my time lacing my braced boot around my warped foot, waiting for my emotions to even out.

By the time I step out into the hall, I don't think anything odd is showing on my face. Harper emerges at the click of my door, and she doesn't react to my expression. Of course, she looks kind of distracted herself.

"One more day," she murmurs, rubbing her arms as we head down the hall toward the small dining room. "I can't wait…" She trails off as if realizing I might not be feeling the same way she is about our impending return and glances at me more carefully. "Do you know what you're going to do?"

That's the big question, isn't it? I grimace, my stomach clenching for a totally different reason. "No. It's so complicated. And there's so much I still don't know." How can I decide when I'm not even sure why the Unseelie have been attacking the summer realm, whether Corwin agrees with that conflict or not? I have to convince him that he can trust me, to open up to me—there must be *something* more he can tell me that wouldn't betray his other loyalties.

But I can understand why he has to be cautious with that kind of information. He knows *my* loyalties are still mainly with the Seelie. Argh, it's such a mess.

"I'm not definitely refusing the bond," I add. "It seems like that would be kind of dangerous anyway. But I'm not ready to stay here either, and everyone back home still needs me to help with the curse. I guess I'll see how I feel once I'm back in the summer realm." Maybe I just need to spend more time going back and forth, getting to know Corwin as quickly as he'll let me.

I study Harper. "It's okay that you're looking forward to getting home, though. I think if I make another trip here, I'd be comfortable enough to come alone."

She shivers, but her jaw clenches defiantly. "No, I wouldn't want you to be stuck here with just the ravens around. I still don't know if even this palace is safe." She hesitates. "I went back to that alcove by the locked door again, earlier in the morning. I didn't hear any noises, but I did see a servant coming out with a meal tray. With a proper plate and goblet and everything—dirty like they'd been used. A spirit *definitely* wouldn't be eating regular meals."

A quiver of uneasiness winds around my lungs. "No. That does sound odd." And there was that time when I helped in the kitchen making dinner—Corwin got a bit awkward when a servant came in carrying a tray. Maybe it wasn't just because he was startled that he put up his guard, but something to do with who had eaten that meal. I frown. "I'll ask Corwin about it and see if I can figure anything out."

When we step into the dining room, the arch-lord is already there. He's holding a couple of empty goblets and appears to be debating the exact configuration he wants to set them in as if it's a complex puzzle. At the sight of us, he startles just slightly. Maybe he expected me to wait in my room until he came to escort us.

A wavering flash of heat rushes from Corwin into me, and I think I catch a hint of ruddiness beneath the bronze skin of his face. Then his composure snaps back into place, and he's the coolly dispassionate winter arch-lord I'm used to again.

Well, coolly dispassionate and a tad awkward. He fumbles with the goblets for a second before putting them down where I suspect they already were and seems to grope for his words before managing a basic, "Good morning."

I'm definitely not the only one uncertain about where we stand after last night, then. Somehow that sets me a little more at ease, even though my nerves squirm in my belly. "Good morning."

Harper gives me a more considering look then, so I quickly take my seat and fix my gaze on the platters the kitchen staff are bringing out. Corwin sits down too, his posture even more rigid than usual. I haven't quite decided how to bring up the issue of the locked door upstairs when a different servant hustles into the room.

She dips her head low. "Apologies for the interruption, my lord. You've been summoned to the Hall of the Heart at once."

Corwin exhales audibly and gets back to his feet. "Tell my colleagues I'll be there in a moment." He glances at me. "I'll try to settle matters with my fellow arch-lords as swiftly as I can, but don't wait for me."

Are they going to harass him about my presence in his life again?

As he heads out of the room, I send a thread of sympathy and reassurance his way—only to slam into a wall between us so solid my head spins for a second. He's shut me off again, so completely I can't sense even a hint of him.

Whatever he thinks the arch-lords want to talk about this time, he doesn't want me hearing it.

CHAPTER TWENTY-SIX

Talia

I eat my breakfast on autopilot, barely tasting the buttery eggs or the crumbly pastry. Corwin let me hear what the other arch-lords said about me during that last meeting. What secrets does he think they might reveal now that it's so important to him to keep hidden?

Does he believe they're going to talk about the war with the Seelie?

The fact that I still don't know the reason for the attacks gnaws at me. But I don't see any way of convincing Corwin to share much more when he's restricted by his duties to the other arch-lords, who obviously aren't fans of mine. A restless urge tugs at me harder the longer we sit without his return, nothing but blankness where our connection should be.

There is something else I can do at least a little about. I catch Harper's eyes from across the table, where she's just setting down her now-empty goblet. "Since I can't *ask* Corwin about what's behind that locked door right now… what do you say we go take a closer look ourselves?"

Harper's overlarge eyes light up with a gleam that's both eager and nervous. "All right."

Now that she's been to that part of the palace multiple times, she leads the way back to the spot easily, only stopping once to consider a branch in the hall. The alcove with the locked door is empty and, for the moment, silent.

I study that door, deepest into the alcove. Stepping close, I lean my ear against the thin gap by the doorframe. Harper waits quietly as I listen.

At first, there's nothing except the thump of my pulse. The seconds slip by. I'm about to pull away when a faint noise reaches my ears. A whimper and then a distressed-sounding mumbling. My body stiffens.

It's so muffled I can't tell whether the voice isn't saying any actual words at all or I just can't make them out, but it definitely has the quality of a person, one I'd assume was living.

I strain to make out more. The mumbling fades. There's a choked sort of sob, and then a ragged shout that's just loud enough for me to catch one bit of sense in it. "—Heart take me—"

My own heart lurches. I pull back, staring at Harper. "There's definitely someone up there. Are you sure spirits can't talk like people?"

She nods, wringing her hands. "My father loves getting any account he can about spirits and things like that. He's always said the reason they act out so much is out of the frustration that they barely even remember what they used to be and can't do any of the things they could before. 'Just a tangle of energy you wouldn't even know was there unless it collides with something.'"

"Well, whoever I just heard, they sound like they're upset or hurt." What the hell is going on? Why would Corwin have someone locked away—why would he have dodged the question rather than telling me the truth if he has a good reason? Unless the winter realm has spirits that *can* talk… Of course, that wouldn't explain the servant with the meal tray.

Harper hugs herself. "What should we do?"

Corwin is still keeping me shut out—and I'm not sure I trust him to give me any real answers anyway. I worry at my lower lip. "The servant you saw—how did they lock the door after they came out?"

"She had a couple of keys on a ring. I thought it was strange that they were using physical locks instead of magic. But maybe whoever's up there is fae and might be able to magic their way out otherwise."

Which means we couldn't magic our way in, even if we knew the right words. I hesitate, and another faint cry seeps past the door, pained enough to send a streak of ice down my spine.

"Let's go to the kitchen," I say. "If that's the main reason servants are going up there, maybe we can find the key and see for ourselves what's going on."

Harper looks even more anxious than before, but she hurries alongside me on the way downstairs. We peek into the kitchen.

It looks like Charles and Beth have already finished washing our few breakfast dishes—if this place is anything like August's kitchen, Corwin's arranged for them to have that special faerie water that does most of the cleaning work for them. The gleaming space, all crystal and silvery metal, appears to be vacant now.

We steal farther inside, scanning the counters and the walls. Harper starts opening the drawers, shuffling through various utensils and cloths. I scan the room, thinking back to the other evening when the servant came in with the tray. He set it down at the far end of the counter—and reached up into the cabinet there.

But he came away empty-handed. If he wasn't taking something out… maybe he was putting something inside it.

It's too high for me to easily reach. I beckon Harper over. "Can you check inside that cabinet?"

She opens it and bobs up on her toes to peer inside. A triumphant smile curls her lips. Carefully, she reaches in and retrieves a silver ring with two keys that was tucked away next to the goblets. "Good guess! I'm almost sure this is the key ring I saw. I wonder why they keep it in there?" Her brow knits. "The goblets on that shelf—they're different from the ones we've been using. I think it was one with that pattern that was on the tray the servant brought out."

I peer past her at a row of crystal goblets with a pattern that looks like blooming flowers rather than pointed icicles. They might be styled differently, but they're equally fancy. Why would this prisoner get their drinks in special goblets as elegant as the ones the arch-lord himself uses?

None of this makes much sense.

I motion for us to leave before the staff can catch us—and before I lose my nerve. "Come on."

We hustle back to the alcove, Harper keeping the keys hidden in her hand. When we pass a servant who's murmuring a cleaning spell over the floors, her posture tenses, but the man doesn't give us a second glance.

The alcove is still empty. Whoever's upstairs has fallen silent again. Harper and I exchange a glance, her mouth set in a pale line. "What if the person up there is dangerous?" she asks. "The arch-lord might have a good reason for keeping them locked up."

That worry has already been running through my mind. I give her the same answer I came up with for myself. "They're not right on the other side of the door. We can barely hear them. They must be farther away, in another room or something quite a bit farther back. That's why there'd be two keys, right? We don't have to get too close." And if Corwin had a *really* good reason, he'd have told me the truth to begin with.

Harper nods, more daring returning to her expression. As she tries one key in the lock, I watch the hallway, alert for anyone coming this way. The first key doesn't fit, but the second slides in and turns with a soft click.

Anticipation prickles over my skin. Harper sucks in a breath, making a quiet sound as if preparing a spell to defend us. I smile at her, a little scared but abruptly so very grateful that she's here with me, that I'm not facing the possible horrors of the Unseelie realm alone.

She nudges the door open. On the other side, a narrow spiral staircase winds out of view. Only a thin wash of sunlight penetrates the thick diamond walls.

We close the door gently behind us so it won't attract attention and creep up the stairs. We've only made it to the level of the first window when a low moan reverberates down to us, much louder now that we're inside.

"There must have been a quieting spell on the doorway to swallow the worst of the sounds," Harper says under her breath. She hesitates and then presses onward.

I keep pace beside her, shuddering inwardly at the rattling sigh that reaches us next. A mournful voice—definitely female, I can tell now—undulates down the stairs. "Oh, my heart, my heart." Then a string of syllables I don't recognize, true names maybe.

We keep walking until it feels as if we've traveled upward at least three more floors. This must be one of the palace's spires—one I wouldn't even have realized contained any rooms.

My warped foot is starting to twinge. I pause for a second to give it a rest, and Harper peeks around the next bend.

"I see the next door," she whispers. "What do we do now?"

I push myself onward with her to a small landing several steps farther up. It's barely large enough for the two of us to stand comfortably side by side. A single, solid door stands before us. A sputtering sound and a thump carry through it.

Corwin's prisoner is right on the other side.

We risked enough coming up here. I'm not reckless enough to throw open this door and face whatever might be waiting beyond it.

I inhale slowly and pitch my voice to travel through the door. "Hello? Is someone in there? Do you need help?"

There's a hitch of breath and a brief silence. Then a scrabbling sound that's almost animalistic, like claws against stone. But the voice that follows is undeniably a person's. "Oh, please. Oh, please. I can't stand it any longer. I must get out. I must follow him."

Follow who? Corwin? My heart squeezes at the anguish that colors the words. "We'll do what we can. Who are you? How did you—"

The prisoner cuts me off, becoming more frantic by the second. "Please! It's been so long, so long I've— Oh, it's so wrong." Her voice rises to a wail. "I can't bear— You must let me go! Now!"

By the end of that broken tirade, my eardrums are ringing. Fists pound against the door, followed by the scratching of fingernails, and her voice careens even higher into a shrill scream. I stumble against the wall, my pulse stuttering—and footsteps pound up the stairs from below.

I spin around just as Corwin rounds the last bend. He stares at me, his bronze skin grayed, his eyes wide, looking so much more out of sorts than even at breakfast this morning. "Talia," he says in a tight voice. "You…" He doesn't seem to know what else to say.

"What's going on?" I demand as the scream trails off into a series of sobs. "Who *is* that? What have you done to her?"

A tremor runs through my body with the knowledge that if Corwin wants to cover up what we've found, neither Harper nor I have anywhere near enough power to fight him. He swore not to hurt us, but who knows if he might have some devious way to get around that. Harper steps up shoulder-to-shoulder with me all the same, her chin raised defiantly.

The Unseelie arch-lord stands there, his handsome face becoming increasingly pained by the second. He closes his eyes and seems to gather himself. "I suppose you'd have to know eventually. I'll introduce you to her."

He eases around us to the door, pulling a key of his own from one of his pockets. As he speaks a few words that thrum with potent magic, the sobs on the other side dwindle. There's a sigh that sounds more resigned than agonized.

"I calm her as much as I can, but it never has more than a brief effect, no matter what I try," Corwin says with obvious regret. "She should be subdued for a few minutes, at least." He unlocks the door and motions for us to step in just ahead of him.

I venture into a small round room that holds bookshelves—mostly empty—as well as a table and chair and various small objects strewn around, including a few of the books that must have been on those shelves at some point. At the far end of the room, another doorway shows more stairs leading to further rooms above.

The chair is tipped on its side. Crouched on the floor next to it, leaning a nearly skeletal arm on the wooden back, is an emaciated woman.

Her black hair, streaked with gray, hangs nearly to her waist, strewn wildly across her shoulders and back. Dark eyes burn into us from within her pinched brown face. Her hunched body trembles with her breath. Her fingers curl where her hands are braced against the floor. A ragged dress hangs off her emaciated frame—the fabric looks clean enough, but it's been ripped all along the hems.

Corwin shuts the door and comes to stand beside me. He keeps his tone measured and gentle. "Hello, Mother. Talia and Harper have come to meet you."

Mother? My gaze jerks to him, and an ache of confirmation passes through our bond, which he's allowed to open just a little.

The woman just glowers at us. Then she presses her hands to her face with a quiet sniffling sound. She shakes her head as if refusing us, the room at large, maybe the entire world.

"It's all right," Corwin says in the same even voice, but I can hear the sadness wound through it. "It was good to see you."

I keep my mouth shut until he's ushered us out and locked the door again. My questions come out more tentatively than the first round. "What happened to her? Why do you keep her locked up like that?"

Corwin holds out his hand to Harper, who gives him the keys from the kitchen with a guilty twitch of her mouth. He looks at the key ring rather than me as he replies. "My father—the arch-lord before me—died rather suddenly in his prime about five decades ago. The death of a soul-twined mate is always hard on the surviving partner, but my mother was particularly… overcome with grief. At first she simply refused to leave her regular rooms and sank deep into mourning, but after a time she became obsessed with joining him in death."

Harper winces. I don't fully understand the magnitude of his statement until he explains for my benefit. "Fae don't die easily under normal circumstances, even when they wish to. Our innate instincts to preserve our own lives are nearly impossible to completely override. She made a few attempts that fell short of the mark, only causing her great pain and distressing our flock-folk who witnessed her. If she's allowed to roam freely, she'll continue to harm herself. I keep her confined with only what objects have proven or been enchanted to stay reasonably safe and do my best to alleviate her distress."

The pang that echoes from him into me speaks of how much he feels he's failed at that goal. My throat constricts. I have the impulse to hug him like I did the other day after his previous meeting with the arch-lords, but he's holding himself so tensed I'm not sure he'd appreciate the gesture. Most of his emotions are still muted.

"I'm sorry," Harper says quietly. I'm not sure if she's apologizing for stealing the keys or for what happened to his mother or possibly both.

"We heard her again—Harper saw someone bringing down a meal tray—it seemed obvious it wasn't just a spirit." I pause. Do I really need to ask why he avoided the subject? It's obviously painful for him to talk about. But still…

"You came here to understand what being my mate would mean," Corwin says without any trace of anger. "Perhaps I should have been more open from the start. It's only—" He stops short with a flare of emotion that's oddly both frustrated and shamed for reasons I can't grasp. His wall slams back into place, cutting off that too. "Well, you know now. Let's leave her to whatever peace she can find."

We descend the spiral staircase without another word. When we come out into the hall, Corwin halts to lock the second door behind him. I waver on my feet. "Are you going to finish your breakfast?"

"It's been brought to my study. I have a few things to look over there." He nods to me, polite but distant—a distance that feels strained after the closeness we've shared both intentionally and otherwise.

The motion feels like a dismissal, but I don't like it, not after what we just saw. As he walks off, my legs balk for a moment. I glance at Harper. She's frowning, but she waves for me to go after him.

I hurry after Corwin as fast as my limp allows, and I think he slows just enough that he doesn't leave me behind, but he doesn't acknowledge me either, not until he reaches his study. With one hand on the doorframe, he glances at me.

When I first met him, I'd have taken the impenetrable mask of an expression he's wearing right now and the unyielding set of his shoulders as cold indifference. Now, even without the benefit of our connection, I can see how much effort it's taking for him to keep up that front. How much of a front it is.

Does he put up those walls because he doesn't want to show the rest of us what's going on inside him or because even *he* doesn't want to deal with it?

"Yes?" he says, a single syllable that somehow holds so much understated emotion. I can't tell whether he'd rather I leave or push on, but it's not only up to him.

My hands twitch with the urge to fidget. I tuck them under my elbows. "What you just told me—it's obviously a big deal. You almost said more about it. I don't know why—you could have told me more of the truth, at least, when I asked you before. That she was sick or something. If there's something else… I *do* want to understand what it'd mean to be your mate. But I can't if you shut me out about things that are so important to you."

Corwin's shoulders sag, just slightly. He opens the door and waits for me to walk past him inside.

His study is formed out of the same gleaming diamond as the rest of the palace, but the furniture in here is pale wood like the chair in his mother's room rather than marble. Everything on the sleek desk and the shelves carved into the walls is perfectly tidy, with a blatant sense of personal order. Even his breakfast tray is laid out with precision. I doubt there's one thing in the place that Corwin couldn't find instantly if he needed it.

Rather than sit behind his desk, the Unseelie arch-lord sinks onto one of the thinly padded chairs that encircle a low table at the other end of the room. Maybe he sometimes has meetings with his coterie there. I follow him, settling onto one of the other chairs.

He peers at the shelves in a detached sort of way, but at the same time he opens his end of our bond. Not all the way—just enough for a stream of tangled grief and shame to wash over me. His hands flex against the arms of the chair.

"You're right. There was no legitimate reason for me to keep this from you. It has no bearing on matters of politics and it offers no threat to my flock or the rest of my people." He sighs and drags his gaze to me. "It was selfish. I didn't want you to think less of me."

I blink at him. "Why would I think less of you for something awful that your mother has gone through? It isn't your fault. It must be awful for you too." Losing his father so suddenly, having to take over the arch-lord position sooner than he'd ever have expected, trying to help his mother or at least keep her from hurting herself at the same time...

Sympathy wells up inside me, and I convey it to him as well as I can through the connection between us.

Corwin's mouth twists. "I suppose it makes sense that you'd see it that way. I'm more accustomed to... My fellow Unseelie, and my colleagues in particular, consider the state my mother has fallen into to be a flaw in her nature. A rather serious one. And they're particularly concerned about that flaw having been passed on to me."

Flickers of memories that aren't mine dart through my head: the faces I saw around the table in his Hall of the Heart chilly with condemnation, fragments of sentences in sneering voices. *Over-sentimentality. Emotions out of control. Instability. How can we trust...?*

"She lost her mate," I protest, my hackles rising at the remembered specters of those haughty fae. "Isn't it normal for her to struggle after that?"

"It's always painful, and there's always a grieving process, but we of winter pride ourselves on our self-control." Corwin swipes his hand over his face, rumpling the glossy curls along his forehead. "To be completely incapable of functioning, especially when you have other responsibilities—to get to the point of wishing to cast yourself to the Heart before your time... I don't know whether that might be more typical among the Seelie, but it's rather unusual here. Enough to draw plenty of remarks."

"But there's no reason for them to assume it has anything to do with *you*."

He shrugs. "I was quite young when my father's responsibilities were passed on to me, and I couldn't let us lose the domain as well. I made a few of my earlier decisions hastily, misplaced my trust... let my temper get the better of me at least once." His pause speaks of even more pain. "If you and I are to fulfill our bond, I'll tell you more about that another day. Suffice to say, my colleagues found ample excuse to question my fitness for the position. I'm lucky I found my footing soon enough to avoid an outright challenge."

So many things he hasn't outright said hang heavily in the air, but I can put together enough of the pieces to see the full picture of the fae man in front of me as I never did so clearly before. I already knew he wasn't anywhere near as cool and emotionless as he likes to present himself. In that dream last night, he showed a passion that could match any of my lovers back home.

I thought he was holding back and keeping me at a distance because he didn't trust me yet, but it's so much more than that, isn't it? He doesn't even trust *himself.*

He doesn't believe he should have much in the way of feelings in the first place. He's *ashamed* of the fact that he cares as much as he does. His father died something like fifty years ago… How long has Corwin been training himself to suppress every feeling he has that goes beyond mild interest or annoyance?

How hard has it been for him to open up as much as he has at my coaxing?

A sharper appreciation rushes through me for the tender words he's managed to offer me, the declarations he's made on my behalf, even that hug he hesitated before returning the other day. I mean enough to him that he's willing to risk his fellow arch-lords' opinions of him—his own opinion of himself—to earn my devotion.

I get up and cross the short distance to his chair. Corwin watches me, wary but with a hint of welcome in the reactions trickling through our bond. I don't let myself hesitate as I extend my hand to graze my fingers across his high cheekbone.

Sensation jolts between us, but I'm better prepared for it this time. I *want* him to feel how much I mean this.

"I think it must have taken incredible strength to have held your flock together as well as you have, considering everything. Anyone who complains that you weren't absolutely perfect is a judgmental idiot. If I don't accept the bond, it won't have anything to do with expecting you to be impervious. If I do accept it, it'll be because you let yourself be more than diamond and ice with me."

Corwin's lips curve into the faintest of smiles. Something that was strung taut amid all his other emotions dissipates with my words. He takes my hand and presses a soft kiss to the inside of my wrist, and somehow that small token of affection ripples through me with twice as much heat as anything we did in our shared dream last night.

"So you are making me see," he says in a low voice. He turns my hand to kiss it again, on the knuckles this time, and releases my fingers. And it occurs to me that what I just said—what *he* just said—may be exactly why the rest of the Unseelie arch-lords would rather see me gone from their realm forever than united with this man.

CHAPTER TWENTY-SEVEN

Talia

I didn't bring much with me to the winter realm, and it should all come back with me for now, but the morning of my return to summer, I find myself pawing through the contents of the trunk, unable to decide on what to wear. I've left my clothes to wash and to tug at my hair in front of the mirror and finally to pace around the room aimlessly several times when there's a knock on the door. I sense before he speaks that it's Corwin.

"Talia, I… have something for you."

The words come with a whiff of hope and nerves. I look down at myself and decide it doesn't matter that I'm only wearing my nightgown. He's seen me in it before anyway.

He's seen me in much less, if we're counting dreams.

With the heat of that memory chasing at my heels, I open the door. Corwin stands a little stiffly on the other side, but my line of thinking has brought a hint of a smolder into his burgundy-brown eyes. I resist the urge to shore up my inner wall so he won't feel the tingle of attraction that races through me.

I'll only be with him for a few more hours. The least I can do is stay at least partly receptive to our bond for that time.

Because he's Corwin, he doesn't remark on either of our reactions. His gaze veers from my face to my shoulder, and his forehead furrows with a flare of concern. "You were wounded."

My dresses have hidden the scars from Aerik's jaws. It was so dark and he was so caught up in the aftermath of his nightmare the other night that he mustn't have noticed them then. I wonder if they even showed up in that other dream—we were both awfully caught up in other emotions during that one.

I brush my fingers over the hardened ridges of darker flesh. "A long time ago. When the fae who captured me attacked my family. It doesn't hurt anymore. It just… isn't pretty."

Consternation flashes across Corwin's face. "There is *nothing* that could stop you from being absolutely lovely," he says, meeting my eyes again. Anger trickles through the bond. "If I get the chance to venture farther into the summer realm, I'll happily return that pain to the monster who dealt it a hundred times over."

My mouth twitches, his vehemence dulling whatever pain does linger from the memory. "I know at least three Seelie who'd be happy to join you."

"Yes. Well." He looks down at the folded bundle of fabric he's holding, abruptly awkward, and offers it to me. "This isn't as intricate as the work your friend does, but I had the craftsman who produces most of my own clothes create something for you. If you're willing to wear it. I wanted to give you something of the winter realm to bring back with you."

I can tell how much my response means to him. I accept the bundle, the cloth downy soft against my hands. He has solved one of my problems, assuming there's nothing objectionable about the outfit. "Thank you," I say. "I'll put it on now."

He gives me one of those tiny smiles. "I look forward to seeing you in it."

Before I can think better of it, an offering of my own tumbles out. "Wait right there. You can be the first person I show it to."

I shut the door—because I'm not at the point of taking *off* my nightgown in front of him, no matter what ideas get into my dreams —and change quickly. The dress Corwin gave me slips over my slim frame with a cozy warmth that makes me want to curl up and just snuggle it. But the gown still manages to be sleek and elegant. When I take it in, turning on my feet in front of the full-length mirror, a bittersweet pang forms in my chest.

The dress is designed in the Unseelie style I've seen various flock-folk wearing: more structured than the typical flowing Seelie dresses, with separate panels around the waist and across the bodice. The trimmer skirt hugs the line of my thighs almost to my knees and then expands with a subtle flare of fabric.

But Corwin has commissioned it in a color I haven't seen any of the winter fae wearing. They all tend toward muted, grayish tones, whether pale or dark. My dress beams a vibrant green, almost the same shade as my eyes.

He's given me a winter dress in summer colors. Like the reverse of the airy, snow-pale gown I arrived to meet him in.

A little of the tension balled in my stomach releases. Maybe… maybe everything will be okay after all.

Uncertain anticipation seeps through me from the man waiting outside. I open the door again and then step back to let him in, not sure I want to put on some kind of fashion show in the hall where the staff might pass by.

Corwin steps inside tentatively. His uncertainty falls away with a flare of appreciation that ripples through me and gleams in his eyes, even though he doesn't let it touch the rest of his expression. "It fits you well."

"It does. I like how it feels, too." I smooth my hands over the skirt and glance up at him. "It's perfect. Thank you."

He lets his smile widen then, with a rush of relief that's tinged with sadness.

Because I'm leaving. Because he doesn't know when I'll be back—*if* I'll even be back.

But if I'd had any doubts about that still lingering, this gift has banished them. I don't know how we'll make our way through this tangled mess of interconnected lives and loves, but I'm not willing to give up on any part of that mess yet.

I rest my hand on his chest, the padded doublet he's wearing as soft as my dress, and hold his gaze. "I have to go to them. They need me, and—and I love them too much to let them go. But I'll come back. We'll figure out some kind of compromise for me to travel back and forth until we can decide on a more permanent solution."

The sorrow doesn't leave him, but a glow of happiness warms our bond in spite of it. "I hope your Seelie men will be as generous as you are."

I make a dismissive sound. "It'll be my choice. They don't rule me." If there's one thing I know for sure, it's that Sylas would never try to cage me in any way.

That thought brings up other concerns I can't totally avoid, as much as I might like to. I pause and force myself to say, "You know how I feel about them. How close I've been with them. I—I'm still going to be *with* them while I can. I'll close off the bond as much as possible so you don't have to—"

Corwin touches my arm, stopping me. His jaw clenches for a second, but I don't sense anything worse than a tremor of discomfort.

"Close yourself off from me if you feel *you* need to," he says quietly. "I can understand there may be moments you'd rather keep between yourselves. But anything you don't need to hide for your own comfort, don't shut me off for my sake. They're part of your life, and I want to experience as much of your life as you'll allow me to. I won't know just how much I can compromise if I'm pretending away the full truth of our situation."

Imagining him being aware of some of the particularly intimate moments I've shared with my lovers in the past brings a flush into my cheeks—and makes my gut twist guiltily. "Are you sure? Wanting them in my life doesn't mean I want to hurt *you*."

"I can take care of my own reactions. If it bothers me too much in the moment, I'll step back on my end." His thumb grazes my skin with a gentle sweep over the fabric of the dress. "I don't blame you for having trouble deciding, but I want you to know that I'm completely committed to you and whatever having you as my mate brings."

The determination in his voice makes me choke up a bit. I let instinct propel me onto my toes, my hand sliding up his chest to grip his neck.

Corwin bends to meet my kiss with a swell of emotion that's all delight. As our mouths meld together, that delight sweeps through me, leaving every nerve humming with it.

It isn't fair that I should be so deeply connected to a man who's so far apart from the others I love. Just this brief embrace brings out a tug of longing to join as completely as the bond demands, with a spark of heat shooting low in my belly.

I pull back before that spark can burn hotter, lowering my head and closing my eyes as I will down the crackle of desire. Of *need.* We might not have done anything outside of that dream, but it's made my body and soul so much more aware of the possibilities.

Corwin reins in his own flash of lust. When he speaks again, his voice is low and rough. "You know—I didn't direct that dream in any way—I found myself in it as unexpectedly as I'd imagine you must have. The bond draws us together automatically. I wouldn't have tried to force anything you weren't ready for."

"I know." But suddenly it's very hard to think about anything other than the heated presence of the man in front of me, the connection intent on pulling me toward him, and the bed that's just a few steps away. "Maybe we should go get breakfast now."

He laughs with a bit of strain. "I'd be pleased to escort you to the dining room."

Harper meets us in the hall and exclaims over my dress. She beams even brighter when Corwin says it hardly compares to her skills with cloth and thread. For a little while during breakfast, I focus on nothing but the food and the easier conversation we've been able to fall into with most of the secrets between us stripped away.

But it isn't long before my eagerness for my return bubbles to the surface too forcefully for anything to distract me. It's been ten days since I last saw Sylas, August, and Whitt. I have no idea what's been going on in the Seelie realm during that time. Our greatest enemies on the summer side have already been dealt with, and I haven't seen any sign that the Unseelie have launched further hostilities while I've been here, but still…

It's been too long since I felt their arms around me, welcomed their caresses, heard their voices murmuring words of affection in my ear. Since I got to tell them how much I love *them*. Even if everything's been perfectly peaceful over there, they have no idea how *I've* been. Whether I might return only to say that other than giving my blood once a month, I'm devoting myself completely to my soul-twined mate.

Maybe sensing my growing urgency—and the twinges of guilt I can't suppress, knowing that he's sensing it—Corwin leaves me to Harper's company for the rest of the morning until it's time for me to leave. He lifts my trunk without a word, and the three of us walk across the chilly plain to the glinting haze of the border.

After eyeing the sun to judge the time, Corwin intones the words of the vow that will let him cross so close to the Heart unhindered. "By the Heart, I swear to do no harm to the fae beyond this boundary. May I pass in peace and amity."

My pulse hiccups at the thought of the risk he's taking, the trust he's putting in my people. "You don't have to come with me if you'd rather not take the chance. I can go through with just Harper."

The Unseelie arch-lord shakes his head. "I won't cower in the safety of my domain when it comes to my soul-twined mate. And I'd prefer to discuss the details of your next visit to the winter realm, should he agree to it, with Arch-Lord Sylas directly. I'm not unprotected. I'll cast the spell that will retaliate against any who cast the first blow."

I watch him as he murmurs the spell-casting words, the thrum of energy that carries from the glowing Heart rising alongside them. A faint glimmer settles over his clothes and sinks into him. He lifts his gaze to meet mine again. "Are you ready?"

I nod, my chest full to bursting with a weird mix of impatience and a little sadness of my own. I can't wait to be home, but I can already tell I'll miss Corwin's presence after I leave. The bond between us isn't going to let me forget I've walked away from him.

He offers me his hand, and I take it, not shying now from the sharper rush of sensation that comes with the contact. Mixing in with the sorrow and affection wound through him, I pick up on a trace of pride as well.

He's told me plenty of times before that he wants to make this work despite who and what I am, but until this moment I'm not sure I ever totally believed he was *happy* about the Heart's choice rather than simply accepting it.

Harper grasps my other hand, and we step into the haze of the border together. The chill in the air falls away with each step. The summery scents of fresh grass and sun-warmed earth reach my nose before I can see more than a faint impression of them. My homesickness overwhelms every other sensation in me, speeding up my uneven pace.

We step free of the haze onto the field where I left. My three Seelie men stand in a row several feet from the border, their stances tense but relief crossing all their faces at the sight of me.

Seeing them, my heart flips over with an even deeper jolt of longing. It feels like it's been a hundred years since I looked into Sylas's mismatched eyes, watched Whitt's mouth curve into that fond smirk, basked in the warmth of August's beaming face.

No power in the world could stop me from dropping the hands I was holding and darting forward. I barely even notice the wobble of my warped foot. Since I don't know who else might be watching from farther away, I can't fling myself at all of my lovers whole-heartedly, but I hurtle straight into August's arms.

His chuckle comes out a little choked as he sweeps me off my feet. I tuck my head into the crook of his neck as if it belongs nowhere else and hug him back with everything I have in me. His musky scent with its hint of sweetness envelops me, and in that moment I'm nothing but joy.

I still have them. They're all here and fine—they came for me.

As the initial burst of happiness evens out, my sense of Corwin seeps back into my awareness: a prickle of discomfort, an urge to wrench me back. But there's also an unexpected thread of tenderness weaving through the rest.

August eases me to the ground, and I glance at Sylas and Whitt with a smile I hope conveys how happy I am to be here with them too, even if I can't express it as fully. "You can see I'm fine. Corwin kept his word. He was a very good host, even with everything being so... complicated."

Sylas inclines his head to the Unseelie arch-lord. "I appreciate your willingness to compromise on this matter."

"She's worth it," Corwin says from where he's hung back by the border. He speaks simply and quietly, but there's a power to the words that wraps around my heart as much as August's arms just encircled my body.

I reach for Sylas's hand and twine my fingers with his, deciding I can be allowed at least that much intimacy. His firm grip in response steadies me. "I still consider this my home," I say. "But... I'm not ready to reject the bond either. I don't know exactly how this is going to work in the long run, but I want to go back to the winter realm sometime after the full moon for another stay. There's still a lot we need to figure out."

Any fear I had about Sylas's reaction vanishes with his nod, though he squeezes my fingers a little tighter as if he'd rather not let me go ever again. "Of course there is." He pauses and then returns his attention to Corwin. "I'd imagine you might prefer to discuss the details of her next journey to your realm now, while we can speak face to face."

"Yes, I'd like that." Corwin ventures a few strides closer, his shoulders relaxing a tad from their previously rigid position. "I realize Talia has more of a commitment here than just the matter of the curse. Perhaps we could—"

Before he can finish that sentence, several fae bolt across the field from the sparse trees that frame it.

By the time a startled yelp has broken from my throat, they're already on Corwin. He heaves backward, jerking his arms up around his face as if bracing for his protective spell to blast them away—but they don't strike any blows. As most of them hurtle into a ring around him, the man who reached him first snaps two pieces of metal around his neck like a collar.

Corwin gasps raggedly, a jolt of shocked distress shooting through our connection. A stinging pain radiates from the collar all through his body, dulling his sense of the Heart's energy.

"What are you doing?" I cry, limping forward.

The other fae close tighter around Corwin, much less careful with him now. One whips a vine around his wrists to tie them. Another shoves him to his knees. And he can't fight back because of the vow he took.

The agony of his helplessness peals from him louder than the pain of their mistreatment. The spell he cast to defend himself mustn't be working.

"What is the meaning of this?" Sylas demands as he strides over to join me, his aura of authority radiating controlled fury. "This man is here on our invitation, and—"

"They're carrying out my orders, Sylas." A tall, stately figure steps out from the trees, her shimmering ivory hair rippling over her dark shoulders as if on its own breeze and her heavy-lidded eyes stern.

Arch-Lord Celia considers Corwin with a disdainful glance and then turns to us. "I'm afraid there's been a small difference of opinion in our approach to the Unseelie. He came on your invitation; now he's my prisoner."

CHAPTER TWENTY-EIGHT

Talia

My feet won't stay still, even though the warped one is beginning to ache. I pace from one side of Sylas's new office to the other in a restless if wobbly circuit. "How could she do it? To go behind your back like this…"

Sylas's mouth has been set in a frown since his conversation with Celia less than an hour ago. She insisted that he step aside with her to discuss the situation, Donovan coming out to join them, but I refused to leave the field even though there was nothing I could do to stop her warriors from hauling Corwin away to—to wherever she's taken him.

Our bond has been quiet since that first blare of pain and panic during the attack. Is he shutting me out because he doesn't want me to feel what they're doing to him *now*? Or because he thinks I was in on this plan?

Both possibilities make my stomach churn.

"She and Donovan decided it was too good an 'opportunity' to let it pass them by," Sylas says, his voice rough with barely veiled frustration. "I suspect it was almost entirely Celia's idea and she simply convinced Donovan to go along with it. Two arch-lords carry the trio

—they didn't need my permission to go forward, although she acknowledged that it was 'unfortunate' that she blindsided me."

"You didn't even get a chance to say how you felt about it! They should have at least told you beforehand."

He sighs. "I haven't held the position for even a month yet, so they don't quite consider me their equal yet, I'd imagine. And they see my input as biased because of my connection to you."

Celia probably realized that not only would Sylas have argued against the plan, he'd have interfered when they insisted on going through with it anyway. But Corwin doesn't know that. Whatever he thinks about my involvement, I'm sure he assumes my Seelie men were partly responsible for his capture.

August steps closer to me, catching me before I can continue my pacing and hugging me tightly. I can't quite relax, but I slump a little into his embrace, leaning my head against his chest. "What do they think they're going to get out of this? Isn't holding an arch-lord hostage even *more* likely to start a war?"

"She didn't want to get into the details of her strategy with so many witnesses around," Whitt says, the caustic note in *his* voice not at all veiled. "We're to meet in the Bastion to discuss the matter more formally as soon as we get word."

A chill ripples through me. "They aren't going to kill him, are they?"

August strokes his hand over my hair. "I can't see how that would benefit the Seelie in any way." He glances toward his brothers.

Sylas shakes his head. "At this point, the most I've gathered is that she wants to use him, not destroy him. Her men treated him more roughly than I'd prefer, though. I don't understand how they were able to subdue his magic in the first place."

"It was one of the artifacts from Ambrose's secret stash," Astrid pipes up from where she's been observing the meeting near the door. When we headed to the palace, Sylas mentioned to me that he was taking her into his cadre, though they haven't had a chance to carry out the formal ceremony yet. "I got one of her people who helped sort through them talking. Apparently the band they fixed around his neck has an iron core. When the ring is closed, the iron shatters any magic the prisoner would try to cast—and any already cast on them, I'd imagine."

August winces. "That's against our laws of warfare—it should have been destroyed. I can't imagine even *making* something like that."

"Apparently Celia sees eye to eye with Ambrose in a few areas, one of them being illicit weaponry," Whitt says.

I turn in August's arms to look at the others. "What stash? What does this have to do with Ambrose?"

Sylas's frown shifts into an outright grimace. "One of Ambrose's former pack-kin defected from Tristan's pack to ours. He came with information about a storeroom full of weaponry—much of it in defiance of our standards of morality—that Ambrose maintained in his palace. I informed Celia and Donovan, naturally, and their packs have had a hand in sorting through what we found. I assumed everything we'd consider unnaturally cruel was being disposed of."

Whitt lets out a curt huff. "Ambrose was stockpiling for his intended assault on the winter realm. We know Celia balked more at instigating a full-out massacre than getting retribution in general. She simply made use of the tools he left behind for her own approach."

A leaf whips through the window, veering toward Sylas so purposefully I know it's enchanted before he says anything. He snatches it out of the air. "There's our summons. Whitt, come with me to the meeting—we can go over every possible argument against keeping Arch-Lord Corwin prisoner on the way. Astrid, survey the grounds around the Heart and alert me if you notice any other concerning developments. August, you stay with Talia."

Normally, the ease with which he commands his cadre reassures me. Now, it only reminds me of how serious this situation is.

I raise my head. "I want to come to the meeting too. I'm the only one here who knows Corwin. I can speak up for him."

"I'm sorry, Talia," Sylas says grimly. "There's no way Celia would allow that. She's aware that anything we say you could pass on to him through your soul-twined bond. But I know enough to defend him—and even if he *were* a villain, this isn't any way to go about resolving our issues with the Unseelie. I'll come straight to you as soon as the discussion is over."

As he, Whitt, and Astrid stride out of the room, I sink deeper into August's arms. "I feel like I should be doing *something* to help, but I have no idea what."

He rubs my back. "Sylas will argue Corwin's case in every way he can. Donovan's trusted his advice before—hopefully we can sway him if not Celia."

Right. Because if two is enough, then Sylas and Donovan could overrule Celia. I cling to that speck of hope. "I guess there's no chance they'd let me see him?"

"Celia wouldn't even let *Sylas* talk to Corwin. Can't you reach out to him through your bond?"

"I can't sense anything from him right now. Maybe that steel collar thing is interfering with our connection too."

August hums thoughtfully. "I wouldn't think so. A soul-twined bond isn't constructed magic, it's pure Heart energy. Nothing should be able to interfere with that. But I could believe him wanting to shield you from what he's going through." He ducks his head to nuzzle my temple. "You've come to like him."

It's a statement, not a question, but he says it without a hint of accusation. I swallow thickly. "Yes. He's—he's a good person, even if he thinks about some things differently than you would. We *didn't* get along all that well at first, but when I stood up to him, he listened, and he really tried to make me feel at home. And he's the only one out of the Unseelie arch-lords who I think wants peace with the summer realm. I don't see how holding him hostage is going to do anything except make things worse."

"Celia has contributed a lot to fending off the attacks—she's lost plenty of her own pack-kin to the winter fae. It's possible she's not being all that rational about this plan. But if that's the case, then Sylas should have no problem showing it." August scoops me right off the floor. "Let's go to the kitchen. I know you're worried, but you haven't had lunch yet. You'll feel even worse if you're starving."

"Always looking for a chance to put food into me," I mutter, but I don't complain about him carrying me down. At the moment, I'll take all the comfort I can get.

We're in the kitchen, August slicing a fresh-baked loaf of bread to create sandwiches, when the first flash of sensation I've felt from Corwin in ages shivers through my nerves. I freeze on my stool, focusing on the impressions that reach me as closely as I can.

There's a stinging pain, mild but radiating all through his body. A sense of a hard floor beneath him where he's sitting. I can't see anything—I think his eyes might be closed. The weight of the iron collar presses against his throat.

My hands clench with a mix of anguish and anger. I propel my inner voice with as much force as I can give it. *Corwin? Can you hear me?*

Talia. His response sounds weary but at least not accusing. *I didn't even realize I'd shut you out at first. I was so out-of-sorts…*

It's all right. I'm just worried about you. I'm so sorry. I had no idea anything like this would happen.

It's not your crime to apologize for. I could feel how upset you were—I know you weren't involved.

I shift forward on my stool, bracing my elbows on the kitchen island. August glances at me but stays quiet, probably able to tell how hard I'm concentrating and guessing why.

Sylas didn't know either—it was the other arch-lords acting without consulting him. He's trying to negotiate your release right now.

Corwin's first, wordless reply is a wash of doubtful resignation. *He wouldn't tell you anything else, would he? Having me out of the way would certainly solve plenty of problems for him.*

This isn't *how he solves his problems. And he respected our bond enough to let me go to you in the first place.* I stop, shaking myself. I don't want to argue right now. My distress over Corwin's capture swallows up everything else inside me. *Are you okay, other than that collar thing that's stopping your magic? They aren't hurting you?*

They haven't been what I'd call considerate, but they haven't roughed me up particularly. So far. He pauses with a quiver of emotion I can't identify. His tone goes wry but quiet. *I'd have thought* you *might be relieved if the Seelie happened to dispatch me. It would make your situation so much simpler.*

There's no holding back the surge of horror that floods me at the idea of him being "dispatched"—of losing him to some violent act.

Tears spring up so quickly they trickle out even when I squeeze my eyes shut against them.

Of course not. I don't care how complicated things are—I don't want you gone. I… My mind trips back to the morning when he prostrated himself in front of my bedroom door in his palace, to the way he looked at me as he explained why he was willing to humble himself before a mere human, as if it shouldn't need any explanation at all. The words slip into my inner voice as easily as if I've said them a thousand times before. *You're my mate.*

And he is, in the most important way that matters to the fae and others besides. Even as I sit next to the first man I've ever loved, I know that with a fierceness that winds through my chest and quivers through my bones. I don't understand why the Heart chose us for each other or what will come of it, but Corwin is *mine.*

Corwin startles, but his shock fades into a swell of happiness that seems totally out of place with his current situation. *Yes, I am,* he says, with a tendril of intention as if he's grazed my cheek with his fingertips.

We'll keep doing everything possible to get you out of there quickly, I tell him. *There isn't much—*I *don't have any real authority there—but it's only a few days until the full moon. I have power there even if I don't anywhere else.*

I can survive this. I don't want you doing anything that'll put you at odds with your pack, Talia.

I won't be. If Sylas can't settle things by talking it out, he might even suggest that tactic.

Corwin doesn't answer with words, but I can taste his skepticism. He might have held back his less-than-complimentary thoughts about the summer fae after I argued with him about it and accepted my affection for my three wolfish lovers, but he still doesn't trust the Seelie.

Maybe I can't sway the arch-lords' opinions, but I can do something about *that* problem, can't I?

Exhilaration trickles through me at the possibility of having something concrete I can put my mind to. August nudges my sandwich toward me, studying my expression. "You were talking with Corwin? Have you figured something out?"

"Not—not exactly." I dig into the hearty bread, butter and smoked meat mingling with its flavor into a delicious combination I can now appreciate at least a little. As I chew, I mull over my options. I'm not going to be able to pull this off on my own—that much seems obvious.

August polishes his own sandwich off in less than a minute. I glance over at him as he drops his plate into the sink of wash water. Is he going to be offended that I'd ask this?

I gulp down my last mouthful. "August, I want to hear what's happening at that meeting in the Bastion. I know Sylas said Celia won't allow it. Is there… any way you could get me in there without them realizing? Just to watch?"

Through our connection, I feel Corwin stir with renewed attention, but he doesn't comment on my request. I let the bond remain fully open. I'm doing this *because* I want him to see how all my men will stand up for him.

August rubs his mouth, considering. He looks me up and down. "You're not quite the tiny thing you were when we first found you, but you're still small enough that I do have a trick I think could work."

He hasn't balked or tried to talk me out of it, even for a second. I beam at him. "Then let's try that. As long as you don't think you'll get into trouble."

He grins back at me. "I don't plan on getting caught, but if we are, we'll just say the Heart compelled you and I felt a duty to respect that."

August ducks out of the kitchen and returns with a sheet of thick cloth. Once he's motioned for me to stand, he drapes the cloth around me and then scoops me up in his arms like he did to carry me downstairs, except tucking me into a tighter ball with my knees close to my chest. I nestle against him, closing my eyes in the darkness beneath the fabric. "Won't they realize what you're carrying even if I'm covered?"

August chuckles. "I know a spell or two that can help me shift the look of a thing. The guards should see me bringing a sack of 'evidence.' I can't see them turning away one of the arch-lords' cadre-chosen."

I stay crouched and motionless in his hold as he heads out of the castle. Only a faint whiff of the fresh outside air seeps through the cloth, but it smells familiar, like the wood that all Sylas's homes have been constructed out of. I focus on that and the solid strength of August's arms, tuning out my nerves as well as I can.

Whatever you hear, I'm not going to resent him for it, Corwin says. *I tried to wipe them out of your very mind, as much as I regret that now. I can't blame Sylas if he'd want to be rid of me.*

I convey my certainty through the bond. *I'm not at all worried about that. You'll see.*

I only know we've reached the Bastion when August comes to a halt and speaks. "My lord expects that any useful new evidence in the Unseelie matter will be brought to him."

It's a perfect lie that's not really a lie—Sylas *would* expect that, but August never said that what he's carrying *is* that evidence.

The guard at the entrance must wave him in. His footsteps thud louder on the stone floor inside. He turns, and we ascend a staircase.

August murmurs a few more words under his breath—other spells or true names to help conceal us? Finally, he stops again and carefully lowers me to the ground.

He eases the folds of the sheet aside so that only my face is uncovered. We're huddled in an alcove with a narrow opening that overlooks the main room of the bastion below. "I don't know that anyone will look this way," August whispers. "But keep any movements slow just in case. We'll just have to make sure to leave before the meeting's over."

I nod, squeezing his hand gratefully, and tip forward just enough to make out the figures on the floor below.

I've missed quite a bit of the discussion, but the arch-lords are still at it. Celia is sitting on her throne, her posture regal. Sylas and Donovan stand in front of her, Sylas looking from one to the other as he speaks. "—past weeks since the soul-twined bond was formed have been our most peaceful yet. Threatening one of their leaders seems much more likely to turn those attitudes back to blatant hostility than to end the conflict."

"It's been nearly thirty years of constant attacks and raids," Celia retorts. "Finally we have some real leverage to force their cooperation. How many more of our brethren would you have die instead?"

"I don't believe those are our only choices." Sylas turns to Donovan. "You've seen how far I'll go to protect our people. But this isn't the right way. How can we stoop to the depths Ambrose was willing to plumb? We win this fight by keeping our honor even if the Unseelie haven't, not by throwing it away."

Donovan's expression is pained. "I don't know, Sylas. Celia's arguments are sound. We *haven't* been able to end the attacks in all that time, for all the higher ground we've kept."

Celia sniffs. "What would *you* have us do with the feathered villain then?"

"What we should have done in the first place," Sylas says. "Let him return to his home and continue to foster whatever understanding we can between the winter and summer peoples now that one of their leaders is invested in one of our own. *That's* an opportunity we've never had before—"

"And what makes you so sure you can call that human girl 'one of our own'?" Celia cuts in, so sharply I flinch inwardly. "She owes no real loyalty to us, and now that by some strange act her soul is twined with one of them, no doubt it's only a matter of time before she's completely devoted to the Unseelie. I'm not waiting around to watch that happen."

Sylas doesn't bristle visibly, but I can hear the growl in his voice. "Talia has more than proven herself a loyal member of my pack."

"And that's precisely why I can't indulge your thoughts on this subject for very long, Sylas." Celia stands up, as haughty as any of the winter fae arch-lords. Funny, she'd probably get along well with them if they hadn't been battling the past three decades. "You're fond of the dust-destined girl, and I don't fault you for that, but you have to see it's clouding your judgment."

"Celia, we're hardly done discussing—"

"I say we are." She strides off, and August lets out a soft curse. While he bundles me back up in the cloth, the last voice I catch is Donovan's, apologetic but unyielding. "I'm sorry, Sylas. I have to think of what's best for all our people. The Unseelie have already threatened outright war. If this is what it takes to ensure a fair negotiation… then I have to side with her." His footsteps rap against the floor as he too walks away.

As August hefts me up, my heart sinks. I got what I thought I wanted—Corwin saw that my men will fight for his freedom. But now I'm even less certain that the fight they can offer will be enough to win that battle.

CHAPTER TWENTY-NINE

Whitt

As we come up on Donovan's glazed clay castle in the dwindling daylight, Sylas lets out a rough sound. "I'd rather we were coming invited than turning up unexpectedly."

I make a face at the smooth brown walls, one I'd never aim directly at their owner. "Oh, I'm sure he expects a visit like this sooner or later, and most likely sooner. He knows he's the deciding vote, especially when Celia's gone rigid as a slate-tree. He's probably waiting for us to turn up and put on a song and dance for his entertainment."

Sylas still has enough good humor somewhere under the day's grimness to raise an eyebrow at me. "How much dancing are you planning on doing tonight? Should I have brought our musicians?"

I snort and elbow him—lightly, because he is still my lord, after all. But with our brief banter, a renewed sense of certainty settles over me.

We still have a potential disaster to untangle ourselves from, and a great many things hang in the balance, but the fissure between the two of us seems to have sealed. I'm not sure we've ever understood each other quite so well as we do now. The resentments I tried to bury extended much farther back than Isleen's entrance into our lives. They don't prick at me at all now.

Perhaps there was even a tiny bit of good amid all the havoc Sylas's mate wreaked, forcing those fault lines into the light where we had to address them. Not that I intend on giving her credit for anything.

While I assumed Donovan anticipated our visit, I'm surprised to have him greet us as we reach the castle's main door. One of his servants must have alerted him to our approach. His youthful face looks weary, the wayward strands of his fiery hair arranged in an even more erratic configuration than usual. I don't think he's taking his opposition to Sylas lightly.

And well he shouldn't. He wouldn't be *alive* if it weren't for Sylas putting his own life on the line.

"I'm not sure there's anything you can say that'll change my opinion on the matter," he says without preamble, "but I'll listen."

Sylas nods with infinitely more patience than I have with that statement. "That's a start."

Donovan leads us through the warmly lit halls to his study, the contents of which have a haphazard quality similar to his hair. He sinks into the chair behind his desk, and Sylas and I take seats in the armchairs opposite, as if we're going to have a perfectly civil conversation about holding a fellow arch-lord hostage.

Wisely, Sylas begins with the main reason this whelp should be glad my brother *is* talking civilly and not cuffing him on his ears. "You trusted my judgment enough to take me into your confidence when Ambrose posed a threat, and to put me forward as arch-lord afterward. I don't believe I've done anything to damage that trust. And I can assure you that even if Arch-Lord Corwin weren't the soul-twined mate of one of my pack-kin, I'd disagree with this tactic."

Donovan's mouth twists. "You can't say that for sure, because he is. You wouldn't know his name or anything about him if it weren't for his connection to the human woman. I know you value her—and she's given much to the Seelie—but how can her accounts of his intentions be anything but skewed? She *is* his soul-twined mate; she's compelled by the Heart to see the best in him."

"He was willing to risk himself by coming to us and showing how much the cooperation between our realms meant to him," Sylas says. "He fulfilled his oaths and returned Talia and her companion as agreed with no harm done to either. He has stated clearly that he was the one who warned us about the impending attack two moons past—he couldn't have gotten away with a lie that bald so close to the Heart. Those are all objective facts."

"Even so, he hasn't been able to stop the attacks so far, has he?"

I lean back in my chair, studying the other arch-lord through narrowed eyes. "I'd say that's more of a point *against* this plan. His colleagues haven't valued his opinion enough to cater to it. Why would they back down simply because his life is under threat? It seems much more likely to me that they'll use this offense as a new excuse to come at us even harder. There's no pretending that the kidnapping of one of their rulers isn't an act of war. If you don't care about that, what did you have to argue with Ambrose about?"

Donovan glowers back at me. "Ambrose wanted to stage a full-out assault—as much manpower as possible, with undoubtedly hundreds if not thousands of lives lost on both sides. We simply wish to force a cease-fire."

"But my strategist is right," Sylas says. "Holding Arch-Lord Corwin gives us no power if the other Unseelie arch-lords would be willing to sacrifice him for the sake of carrying out their war. We're lucky they haven't already noted his absence and stormed across the border right into our domains."

Donovan shifts his weight, clearly uncomfortable with that thought. "We've already summoned warriors from the nearby packs. We didn't take this step unprepared. But surely even those feather-brains value their oaths to the Heart enough not to choose bloodshed when we're perfectly willing to return their colleague to them for a simple promise of peace."

I shrug. "It'd be nice to think that. You may even be right. But it hardly seems worth the gamble when they've already proven themselves bloodthirsty many times over. And what kind of peace would we really receive if it's agreed to under duress rather than through a real truce? They'll begrudge us this violation until they find some way to pay us back. Whatever agreement we reach, they'll be brainstorming ways to circumvent it the moment it's set."

"Then we ensure there is no circumventing it," Donovan says stubbornly.

Sylas shakes his head. "The greatest minds have never managed to strike a bargain neither party could wriggle their way out of. If we free Corwin and atone for this transgression now, he may yet speak up for the peace you want. We'll prove we can be reasonable, even if our baser instincts got the better of some of us today. But that window of opportunity is closing. If we're going to change anything, we have to do so before Celia alerts the winter realm tomorrow."

The younger arch-lord's gaze slides away from us, his eyes hazing with thought. A furrow creases his forehead. When he returns his attention to us, I can tell from the strain in his voice that we've gotten as far as we can with him.

"Perhaps I should have consulted with you before we proceeded with this course of action. I can see I might have decided differently then. On the other hand, when we had to make the decision, we didn't yet know how the human's return would play out."

"I still would have said—"

"I understand your position," Donovan cuts in, quiet but firm. "Please understand this: I can't become dependent on your judgment while I'm arch-lord in my own right. I was convinced by the points Celia laid out… and now I feel we've come too far to truly backtrack. What peace could our prisoner want with us no matter how we proceed? If we set him free, we'll suffer all the negative consequences of the attempt and none of the good. I'm sorry, Sylas."

Sylas inclines his head, accepting the impasse. "Let us hope we can avoid the worst of those possible consequences, then."

We remain silent for most of the long walk back to the new castle. My limbs itch to free my wolf, to run through the forest so swiftly the world narrows down to the thunder of my paws against the earth and the panting of my breath. But Sylas doesn't shift, so I remain beside him, waiting for him to indicate he's ready to start planning our next moves.

"Do we have any grounds for delaying Celia's overture to the

Unseelie tomorrow?" he asks as the castle comes into view, a few windows still glowing with amber light.

"I'm sure I could stitch together an excuse that sounds halfway plausible, but I'm not sure she'd accept anything less than undeniable."

"That's true." He exhales slowly. "What are my options here, Whitt? I have an even greater responsibility to uphold the decisions of the arch-lords now that I *am* one. I can't imagine what chaos would result if I made a move against Celia and Donovan. But this plan of hers—I can't picture any way it ends well."

I appreciate his faith in me. If only I had more helpful advice to give. "I can't either, but your hands *are* rather tied. Perhaps there is some way Talia could press the advantage of her blood's boon with the full moon so close?"

Sylas makes a dismissive sound. "Celia doesn't care much for her beyond her blood. She'd order it taken by force if Talia attempted to put any conditions on her contribution. Then we'd have a different sort of war between the arch-lords."

I roll my shoulders, soaking in the warmth of the breeze before we head into the castle. I foresee a sleepless night ahead of me. "I'll dig through every record I can get my hands on. If there's a viable solution, you'll have it from me as soon as I've come across it."

As we cross the entrance room, Talia herself appears in the archway at the other end, luminous as always with her vibrant hair falling around her pale, pretty face and that new green dress following her lithe curves. The hope in her expression fades at the sight of us. "He wouldn't change his mind?"

The frustration in Sylas's expression deepens. "He didn't deny the points we raised, but he's afraid that even if we altered course now, the Unseelie will be so affronted that we'll have war on our hands either way."

She frowns, folding her arms over her chest. "They don't even know he's been captured yet, do they?"

"I expect someone will have wondered at his absence by now, but Celia won't be making a formal proclamation until tomorrow." Sylas grimaces. "I supposed we should be glad she granted us that much amnesty to make our own case, as poorly as it's gone. Donovan assumes that even if she doesn't get the chance to reveal her plot, Corwin won't hesitate to after how she's treated him."

"He doesn't want war either. No matter what happened today."

"I know. But I can understand why my colleagues would find it hard to believe."

Sylas walks over to Talia, checking that none of our pack-kin are nearby, and enfolds her in an embrace. Any jealousy I might have felt watching her hug him back so tightly is long gone now. I only wish we had better news to comfort her with.

The three of us will stand together around her, whether she's bound in soul to that blighted bird shifter arch-lord or not.

"We haven't given up," Sylas assures her as he releases her. "There's still a little time."

Talia turns her bright, worried gaze on me. "You're going to look for answers—some policy or precedent that might convince Donovan or stop Celia? Can I help?"

I think of the boxes of parchment records recently carted over from Hearthshire that clutter my new office. I'm not sure she'd be able to make much of even the archaic fae handwriting many of our ancestors and peers documented their thoughts in. But the need to do *something* practically vibrates off of her. I don't know how to deny this sweet, fierce spirit I've come to love so much that it's been a constant ache inside me these last ten days.

It might do *me* some good, having her by my side for what little time she can stay there.

I beckon her over. "More eyes on the task can't hurt anything."

She falls into step beside me as we climb the stairs, slipping her hand into mine as easily as if she never left. As if she doesn't technically belong to another man in a way I can never hope to match. I squeeze her fingers, and she tightens her grip in return.

"So," I find myself saying lightly, "your wintery arch-lord didn't turn out to be quite as horrifying as we feared?"

"No, not at all. Just… different. It took a while for us to understand each other properly. And we still have a ways to go." Talia looks up at me. "That hasn't changed anything. I don't—I don't love you, or Sylas or August, any less than I did before."

I can't stop a smile from spreading across my lips. "And he doesn't mind knowing that?"

"I think he can't help minding a little. He didn't seem to think that we could compromise. But he's willing to be patient while I figure things out."

"Perhaps less patient now that our kind have collared him like a mongrel." Celia's scheme may have damaged not just our chances of real peace with the Unseelie but any hope of Talia's soul-twined mate accepting our place in her life as well, damn her. I resist the urge to grit my teeth.

"He knows that's not your fault," Talia says with so much confidence I envy her. She touches my face and draws me to her, and Heart help me, even if that soul-twined mate of hers is aware of this through her bond, I can't bring myself to care. I'm not going to deny her one bit of the passion I'm longing to pour into our kiss.

Talia's fingers curl against the back of my neck. I revel in the soft heat of her mouth, coaxing a whimper from her with a flick of my tongue. She's his, but for now, she's also *mine*.

And I'd be hers in every possible way I could be if so much wasn't at stake. She eases back down, her hand lingering by my neck and her head tipped close to mine. "It's not safe for me to know your true name yet, but I still hope someday it will be. If you still want to offer it by then."

I press another kiss to her temple. "I'll never not want you, mighty one." The desire to show her just how much I want her winds through me in a scorching current, but I rein it in. Our chances of ever reaching that day depend a great deal on us occupying ourselves in more productive ways tonight. "Come, let's see if we can't divert tomorrow's catastrophe."

"We'll figure something out," Talia says as we continue up the stairs. "There has to be something." But she sounds as if she's trying to convince herself as much as me.

CHAPTER THIRTY

Talia

When I step outside, the darkness closes in around me with the cooling night air. Only one window still shines with light overhead—the one in Whitt's study. It didn't take long for me to figure out that most of the fae records were more likely to give me a headache than let me solve our current problems, but I got the impression Whitt planned to stay up through the night if that's what it took.

I told him to let me know if he found anything that could help Corwin, even if he had to wake me up. But after I left the study, I discovered I was too restless to go to bed yet. I came downstairs instead, hoping the fresh air and the stillness of the night would help put my nerves a little more at ease.

Corwin has managed to drift off himself, as far as I can tell from the definite but formless sense of his presence on the other end of our bond. At least he's getting some rest. My heart squeezes at the thought of him slumped in the stone-walled prison room I caught glimpses of through his awareness. Celia isn't treating him with any more dignity than a basic criminal.

Of course, for all I know she'd be even worse with any fae who *wasn't* an arch-lord.

A slim figure emerges from one of the pack village houses, which my pack-kin have started to expand to their full size. Harper pauses when she sees me and then walks over to join me, her mouth tightening. "No news about Corwin?"

I shake my head. "Not so far." And tomorrow morning, Celia will be informing the Unseelie arch-lords of his imprisonment and her demands. Once she does that, I don't know how there'll be any coming back.

I rub my arms, chilled from within, and Harper sidles closer. "It isn't right, what she did. I know she's an arch-lord, and I don't love the ravens or anything—but I don't think she's being fair to him at all."

"The trouble is getting *her* to see that." I sigh. "The Seelie and Unseelie have never really gotten along, right? And it's been almost thirty years of attacks from the winter side. It makes sense that she's fed up. I have no idea how you can change someone's mind in a situation like that."

Harper drops her gaze and then looks at me again. "I did something horrible to you, and you've been able to forgive me. If that's possible… there's got to be some way to make her see he's not a bad person."

"Or at least make Donovan see it. But Sylas and Whitt already talked to him and couldn't convince him. They know fae politics—if *they* couldn't get through to him…"

My friend offers me a soft smile. "Was it politics that convinced you to give me another chance? From what I've seen, you've been able to convince a lot of fae to change their minds about how much they should respect *you*. Maybe you can do that for your soul-twined mate too."

An ache comes into my chest. I wish it were that easy. "Yeah." Exhaustion rolls up over me, and I rub my eyes. "I guess I'll hope that sleeping on it will give me some answers."

"I'll see you tomorrow." Harper gives my forearm a comforting squeeze, and I shoot her a quick smile in return before heading back inside.

But once I've burrowed under the covers on my bed, I don't fall asleep right away. Harper's words keep running through my mind.

It's true—I *didn't* forgive her because it made sense to or out of some political strategy. It wasn't even her proving over and over how dedicated she was to making up for her mistake, although that made it easier to trust her.

No, when I really started thinking about her as my friend again—it was that evening in Corwin's palace when she sat with me and admitted how she'd envied me and how much she admired me. When we really talked like two people who wanted to understand each other, and it felt like we were more the same than the differences of being fae or human could come between us.

Has Donovan even talked to Corwin? Does he have any idea who the enemy he's condemning really is? Before I got to know the Unseelie arch-lord, *I* saw all of the winter fae as cruel villains.

Maybe there is something I can bring to Donovan that my men couldn't. I can make it personal instead of political.

That thought chases me into an uneasy sleep. I wake up with the dawn, my nerves prickling.

There isn't much more time. If I'm going to talk to the youngest arch-lord, I have to do it now.

I dress and wash quickly, debating asking one of my men to accompany me. But if they haven't come to tell me they've found a fix, then they're still working on the problem or getting much-needed rest of their own.

Besides, I want Donovan to know that I'm speaking totally for myself, not acting as a mouthpiece for Sylas. I've never really talked with him before. He has to see me as a person in my own right, a person with valid viewpoints he might not have considered.

As I head out of the castle, my heart thumps faster. The daylight is still thin, the sun not yet risen to where it's visible in the sky. I'm not sure Donovan will even be awake himself yet.

Oh well. I can't wait for him to have a leisurely morning. I'll drag him out of bed to hear me out if I have to.

I've never walked from our new domain to Donovan's before. Even with the castles set fairly close to the central Bastion, it's a bit of a hike.

By the time the glossy clay walls come into sight up ahead, my warped foot is throbbing in the braced boot, my limp becoming more pronounced.

My jaw clenches, and I force myself onward as quickly and steadily as I can. I don't need him thinking of me as weak.

Corwin's voice travels to me from within. *What are you doing, Talia?* The words come with a sense of resignation and fatigue, as if the sleep didn't do him much good.

Whatever I can to get you free, I reply firmly. *I'm not giving up without trying everything.*

A flicker of fear licks through me. *Don't put yourself in any danger on my account.*

I don't think this will be dangerous. The worse that'll happen is I'll embarrass myself. At least, I think so. Sylas has always said Donovan has the kindest views toward humans out of all the original arch-lords, and I'm still the source of their cure. He's not likely to allow me to get hurt even if he's annoyed by the intrusion, right?

Although even if I thought he might, I'd still be doing this.

The aches of Corwin's body from lying on the hard floor echo into me. He must catch my flare of anger on his behalf. *I'll survive this. I've been through worse.*

I'd like to aim for something a little higher than you simply surviving, I say.

As I wobble the last few steps to the castle door, uncomfortably conscious of the sun rising ever higher, a couple of guards materialize on the front steps. I raise my chin to stare at one and then the other. "I need to talk to Arch-Lord Donovan."

They eye me with some skepticism. My pink hair combined with my human attributes must make me immediately identifiable, but to most of the fae I'm still more a blood dispenser than a being with my own will. They wouldn't be expecting me to come calling on their lord by myself.

"On what matter?" one asks.

"That's for me to discuss with him." I frown at her. "You know I'm with Arch-Lord Sylas's pack. You know there's no way I could be a threat to any fae, let alone an arch-lord, anyway." I hold up my hands in a gesture of helplessness. I didn't even put on my belt with my dagger and my pouch of salt. Better that they see me as harmless.

The guards step closer together to mutter to each other, and I resist the urge to shift impatiently on my feet. Finally, the woman beckons me to follow her inside. "Come with me. I'll check whether he's willing to see you."

I hustle after her through the halls, past the ballroom where we gathered for a banquet what feels like years ago, into a tighter network of passages. The guard motions for me to stop at one bend and marches off alone. I stand there, hugging myself and tuning out the pain in my foot as well as I can.

If she comes back and tries to send me away, I'll have to make a scene. Yell at the top of my lungs, hope Donovan hears me and that I can say something that'll catch his attention. What would do that?

Thankfully, I don't need to find out. A minute later, the guard reappears and gestures for me to follow her with a jerk of her hand. The set of her mouth suggests that she's not pleased with the situation. She leads me around another corner to a door that's slightly ajar.

"She's here," she announces through the gap.

"Send her in," Donovan says in his warm tenor.

I slip past the door and find myself in a room that's clearly his office, though a lot messier than Sylas's, let alone Corwin's. Donovan is leaning rather casually against the front of his desk, but he watches me enter with wary attention as well as curiosity. His light brown eyes gleam with alertness, nearly as bright as his flame-like hair. At least it doesn't look as if my visit called him out of bed.

"You've come alone?" he says, even though the guard must have told him that. There's a click as she shuts the study door for us.

I'd like to sit down to rest my foot, but while he's standing, I draw myself up as straight as I can instead. "You've already talked to Sylas and Whitt. I'm here to make my own case. Would having someone fae with me make you more likely to listen?"

Donovan blinks at me as if he's startled that I've drawn attention so directly to my humanity and the prejudices that come with it. It takes him a moment to recover. "No. I'm willing to hear what you've come to say, although I must tell you it's unlikely you'll change my mind."

"Maybe you should wait until you've actually heard me before you decide that," I say with more tartness than I'd usually allow myself. But I'm getting tired of constantly having fae assume I'm not just harmless but hopeless as well, and at least my boldness brings a sharper intentness into Donovan's gaze.

He flicks his hand toward me. "By all means, begin."

I inhale deeply, my pulse kicking up another notch. Corwin's presence in the back of my mind both bolsters my resolve and justifies it. "I've come to speak for my soul-twined mate. To ask you to side with Sylas and insist that Celia let him go rather than continuing with her plan."

"And that's what Sylas and I have already spoken about. I was clear in my feelings on the matter. Nothing you say could change the facts of the situation."

"I don't want to change the facts. I just think there are a lot of them that you don't know and probably haven't considered. You don't believe that Corwin will forgive what Celia's done to him. I *know* he will. I know that if he's released, he'll still work to stop the attacks on the Seelie."

Donovan's expression takes on a pitying cast that I don't like at all. "I can understand you feel close to him given your bond, but of course he'd portray himself in that light if he thinks it'll get him out of the prison."

I have to restrain a glare. "Do you think I can't tell the difference between a direct statement and the way fae like to talk around a subject so they don't have to lie? The problem isn't that I don't know what to believe—it's that you assume there's no way you can trust him. But you have a lot more in common with him than you've bothered to find out. I bet you're more like him than you're like Celia."

The arch-lord coughs a guffaw at that idea. "I hardly think one of the Unseelie and I—"

I cut in, with a quick whiff of apology to Corwin for revealing any of his history myself. "Did you know he found himself in the arch-lord position unexpectedly because his father died before his time? Like what happened with your mother. He's had to prove himself and deal with older colleagues who think they know better than him just as you have."

Donovan's face darkens. "Don't bring my mother into this."

"I'm not. I'm only saying that you've experienced a lot of the same struggles." I grope for a less fraught example. "You love music, don't you? You have that famous harp that everyone wanted to see during your banquet. Corwin's family named their domain after the music the castle they built creates. Heart's Cadence. He has a gorgeous harp—he plays it well too."

"I don't see what any of this has to do with the potential of war between our peoples."

Oh, for God's sake. I glower at him. "Do *you* want there to be full-out war? Even after all the attacks and the deaths that've already happened?"

"Of course not," Donovan says. "But it isn't my decision. As soon as word gets back to the Unseelie arch-lords about what we've done, they'll be even more up in arms. That's why we need some leverage."

"No, that's why you need to let Corwin go before Celia tells them. That's the only way they won't find out."

"You expect me to believe that after being captured and imprisoned—"

"Yes," I snap. "If you can get over thirty years of raids and killings and still want to find a way to make peace, then you should be able to imagine that he could get over one night in a prison cell. Maybe even for the exact same reasons it matters to you."

I flinch afterward even though Donovan hasn't moved, aware of how hostile my tone sounded. That's definitely not how anyone is supposed to speak to an arch-lord.

Donovan stares at me. My obvious fear of his reaction might even make him stop and think a little longer.

"Please," I say, willing my tone to soften. "I thought the winter fae must all be horrible too. I don't know why they've been attacking the Seelie, but I know they're still *fae*, not mindless monsters. I promise you, I can tell the difference there too. The worst fae I've dealt with so far were right here in the realm of summer."

The corners of the arch-lord's mouth twitch downward—and so does his gaze, to my warped foot. To the way I'm standing with my weight mostly on the other to offset the ache. "You should sit down," he says abruptly.

"I'm fine. *I'm* not the one you need to be concerned about right now."

He lifts his head to meet my gaze, his stance less tense now but his gaze penetrating. "And what will *you* do if we release your mate? Will you go back to the winter realm and make a home for yourself with those fae?"

"Are you worried that I'll forget about helping with your curse?" I let out a short laugh. "I've met the worst fae here, but also the best. The summer realm has my loyalty first."

"For now."

The idea comes to me with a prickling sensation that starts in my gut. But once it's occurred to me, I can't shake it. Maybe I'll regret this, but I need him to trust *me* before he's ever going to trust Corwin.

"I'll swear to it. That I'll never spend more than a week at a time with the Unseelie and that I'll always return for the full moon, as long as the curse still exists. You and the other arch-lords can decide on the exact wording of the vow and the consequences of breaking it, and I'll take it. This morning, if that's what you need. Then you'll have that guarantee. Anything that hurts me will hurt Corwin too. You'll still have your leverage if anyone tries to break my promise."

My stomach twists, but Corwin reaches out to me like a squeeze of my hand. *It's all right. If they need that commitment, I don't resent you making it. I already knew you weren't going to be mine alone.*

Donovan considers me for several seconds longer. Then he lets out a rough chuckle. "I'm starting to see how you've won so much of Sylas's respect. I appreciate your dedication and that you were brave enough to speak up. But it still comes down to this Unseelie arch-lord who's all but an unknown quantity and a soul-twined bond proves very little about his loyalties. I'm sure you believe what you're saying, but his truth is the only one that matters."

I swallow hard. *Corwin, I'm not sure you're going to like this, but it might be our only way out. Can* you *trust me?*

He replies without hesitation. *What do you need from me, Talia?*

I answer him and Donovan at the same time. "Then speak to Corwin. Let's go talk to him right now. He can tell you how much the peace matters to him, straight from his own mouth."

At least, I hope he can lower those walls of his enough to show Donovan how much he means it—before it's too late to make a difference.

CHAPTER THIRTY-ONE

Corwin

I brace myself against the stone walls of my prison cell, holding in the urge to tug at the ridiculous collar that chafes my neck. The searing sensation of the iron within it has dwindled to a dull burning, but it still spreads all through my body with every movement.

That's not what I'm bracing myself for, though. I'm preparing for the interrogation about to commence.

Talia has kept her side of our bond open since we arrived here. I can follow her now as she and the red-haired Seelie arch-lord stride up to the entrance of the same limestone castle I was escorted into yesterday. Her determination cuts through her anxiety, but she *is* nervous. She's afraid her gambit won't play out in our favor.

I'm not certain it will either, although I'll give it my best.

Before her eyes, the elderly Seelie arch-lord in charge of the warriors who took me into custody appears. She and the other arch-lord exchange stern words back and forth. Talia watches it all with a knot in her stomach. I try to extend reassurance toward her, but it may not be all that convincing. My own gut has tightened into a ball.

What will this young arch-lord whose past is strikingly similar to mine want to ask me? How much will I even be able to answer? I still have my duty to my own people to consider. It doesn't do me any good getting released from this prison if I put all the winter fae at a disadvantage with what I reveal.

At least he seems reasonably well-spoken. When he points out to my captor that she has no reason to stop him from speaking to me, that if what I say would change his mind about her plan then it's all the more important that he has the chance to hear it, she sighs but backs down. With a tentative rush of relief, Talia follows him into the castle.

Her foot is hurting her. A twinge shoots from her to me with each limping step. My hands clench at my sides with the wish that I was in a position to sweep her right off those feet—the way that one of her men, August, did when she first rushed to them on our arrival.

The memory doesn't raise my hackles as it might have once. So much joy flowed through her just at seeing them. When I accept that those three are intertwined with her life nearly as much as I am—more, in some ways—and set the jealousy aside… that joy is mine too. I can accept it from her and make it my own.

I can't remember the last time I felt anywhere near the level of happiness that she shared with me in those first few moments before the warriors descended on me.

There's very little to rejoice at this particular moment. My awareness through Talia and of the outer world start to merge with the tapping of footsteps my own ears can pick up from farther down the dim hall. Talia's nose wrinkles at the damp, muddy scent that my senses adjusted to many hours ago. Another jolt of anger races through her knowing this is where I've been locked away.

So fierce is my soul-twined mate. It seems absurd that in my first realizing what she was, I balked at the idea of her human failings. If anyone called her weak within my hearing now, I'd laugh in their face.

Even in this precarious situation with so much resting on the conversation ahead, the knowledge that her ferocity has come out on my behalf wraps warmth around my heart.

Then the door to the cell swings open, and I'm seeing her before me—my mate and the red-haired arch-lord beside her. In that first second, it's hard to focus on anything but her: her gaze taking in the dried blood from a blow to my temple that I haven't had the magic to seal, the bindings that truss my wrists and ankles to ensure I can't put up a physical fight much easier than a magical one. Even more anger flares behind her delicate features.

"Who hurt him?" she demands of the guard who must have unlocked the door.

The Seelie warrior's expression turns carefully blank, but he speaks with an audible growl. "The occasional wound is unavoidable when ensuring a prisoner is secured. No magic can touch him to heal it while the iron-cored collar is on him."

"I can see to it," says the arch-lord—Donovan, I've heard him called in Talia's presence. He shoos the guard away before returning his wary gaze to me. "If you'll let me."

"It isn't bothering me so much that I'd trouble you," I say evenly. "But if it's important to you, I wouldn't argue about it."

He crouches down near me, confident enough in his strength and my bindings to show no fear of attack. "Whatever you might think of us right now, we aren't brutes."

I could argue that I didn't need this one incident to think of the hotheaded, wolf-shifting summer fae as brutes, but my predicament and the memory of Talia's chiding hold my tongue. It is true that in the past few decades, we Unseelie have played that role toward the Seelie much more than vice versa. Certainly most of the glimpses I've had of Talia's pack through her eyes have been unexpectedly civilized, even if she's faced plenty of viciousness elsewhere in this realm.

Donovan pulls a square of cloth from one pocket and a small flask from another, and pours a little liquid on to the cloth. When he dabs at the scrape, my skin stings, and Talia tenses.

Donovan straightens up and draws back a step. "That's the best I can do for now. It's at least clean."

Talia remains near the door, a longing radiating from her to come to me and offer whatever comfort she can with her embrace. She doesn't want to interfere with the conversation, though, or to emphasize my current helplessness. I extend a current of affection through our bond.

"Your soul-twined mate has spoken valiantly on your behalf," Donovan says, as if I wasn't privy to that conversation too. Perhaps he doesn't realize. "I'd like to hear from your own mouth, with the Heart watching over us, your current feelings on relations between our peoples."

I'm well-practiced at speaking under pressure, at stripping away any emotions nagging at me to present the sort of crystalline practicality expected of an arch-lord. I aim for the words that'll express my thoughts most directly, without room for debate.

"I believe, as I have from the beginning, that the violence the Unseelie have perpetrated along the summer border was unnecessary, and that we would have been better served by reaching out to address our concerns peacefully. My current situation hasn't altered that opinion."

"What would your intentions be if you were freed without repercussions?"

"I would return to my domain and make no mention of this misstep to my colleagues. And I would continue to press them to open a dialogue with you and the other Seelie arch-lords, even more emphatically now that I have a stake in the lives of those in the summer realm." My gaze slides to Talia for a moment before returning to Donovan.

The Seelie arch-lord eyes me as if he's trying to work out some way my words can be a lie. Well, that likely *is* what he's thinking—that I'm twisting my statements to hide my true intent. But I'm not sure I could have been more baldly honest.

I'm almost starting to relax when he crosses his arms and shoots his next question at me. "And what can you tell us about your people's reasons for launching all those assaults on us in the first place?"

My breath catches at the base of my throat. I haven't even spoken to Talia about this. As she well knows. My noble mate leaps in before I have to say anything at all. "He can't talk about that without permission from the other Unseelie arch-lords."

That's true, but not quite as thoroughly as I let her believe. I smother my awareness of that fact and force a tight smile at Donovan. "All I can say is that while I highly disagree with their methods, I understand why they felt the need to take some kind of action. It wasn't out of malice."

I can't blame him for looking skeptical. "Then why do you disagree with them?" he asks. "Why not support them in their aggression against us, if you don't see it as unjustified?"

I roll my answer around in my mouth, every part of me balking at having to answer at all. There's no easy way to talk about this without giving away more than I trust this man who belongs to summer to know.

His eyes narrow with each passing second before I speak. I push myself to get on with it. "I can believe there's an urgent need for *some* sort of action without agreeing with the specific methods. I was willing to think better of the Seelie than my colleagues. I felt we should be able to reach a compromise that didn't require any violence. They were unwilling to take the risk of a true parlay."

Donovan scoffs, anger flashing in his eyes. "You talk about compromise and thinking better of us, and yet you won't even tell us why your people have been *murdering* ours for tens of years. How am I supposed to believe you're being fully honest? Why should you care what happens to any of us in the summer realm, especially after how you've been treated in the past day?"

I don't know how to answer that at all. My chest constricts, and a flicker of panic washes from Talia into me. She bites her lip, and I know she can tell as well as I can that the Seelie arch-lord is moments from walking away and leaving me here.

What does he want from me? I've told him what I can as plainly as I can. What more is there—

Talia's voice breaks through my thoughts, taut with worry. *He doesn't see how much it matters to you. He can't* feel *how you feel about it the way I can. He isn't going to think less of you if you show him you do care, I promise you. They're not like the Unseelie that way.*

No, they're not. As I gaze back at Donovan, meeting his glare, understanding hits me like a smack of fiery heat.

That's exactly what we've always scorned about the summer fae, isn't it? Their tempers and passions that they let overrun logic and good sense. But the Seelie arch-lord isn't seeing earnest practicality in my words any more than Talia did when I tried to wipe her longing for her lovers from her mind.

My colleagues would have applauded my self-control—if they were feeling generous—but to him I must sound cold. Unfeeling. And the matter to him is clearly one of intense emotion.

Why *should* he believe that I'm dedicated to peace if I only talk about it so dispassionately?

I open my mouth, and the constricting sensation crawls up to my throat. In the back of my mind, the memories rise up of my mother's sobs wrenching from her bedroom, of her scream as she stabbed a knife into her chest just shy of a fatal blood. The horrified faces of my flock-folk. Other faces, frozen in deathly agony. My colleagues' sneering voices.

Shameful, the way we carried on. All that emotion whipping us this way and that. A crack of instability running straight through the family line…

Bad enough that my own people saw it. To let what I'm feeling show through now, to admit my hopes and fears, I might as well be tearing off my clothes in front of this man who's both a stranger and, at the moment, my enemy.

A flare of my own anger rises up. If he'd just listen to reason—if he didn't insist on doubting everything I say—

But then, wouldn't I be furious if the Seelie had been slaughtering the fae of my flock without any explanation, no matter how I might try to suppress that rage? Haven't I distrusted Talia's companions every step of the way?

I close my eyes against the clash of impulses inside me.

I spoke of compromise. Donovan's coming to me, asking me these questions, is his version of practicality. No doubt his emotions would dictate that he toss me to whatever fate his harsher colleague has in mind without concern for the larger consequences.

All Talia is asking is that I meet him halfway.

I can do this. I can let my guard down for her, for my people, for the future I've been arguing for all these years. If it backfires, if I go too far or reveal too much, then at least I tried instead of hiding away behind borders and walls both inside and out like the other winter arch-lords have insisted on for so long.

Inhaling sharply, I meet Donovan's eyes again. "I apologize. I've been speaking to you as an arch-lord, as I've spent decades teaching myself to act to fill that role. But you deserve an answer from one man to another. I've seen too much death in this lifetime to welcome it regardless of which sort of fae are meeting it. I've felt sick to my stomach with each new assault—and horrified with myself that I haven't been able to convince my colleagues of another approach. We've treated you horribly, and I can't tell you how sorry I am for that."

The strain of admitting so much to him and of the fraught emotions themselves brings a rasp into my voice. The Seelie arch-lord blinks, surprise softening the hostility in his face. "But in the end, you'll side with your kind ahead of ours as you have before," he says. "Has all that much really changed? If your soul-twined mate joins you in the winter realm—"

"She's already offered to swear to return here regularly," I break in, not seeing any point in pretending I wasn't watching when she made that promise. "And besides that…" I look at Talia again, an unmistakable swell of longing and affection squeezing around my lungs. Sensing it, she offers me a small but encouraging smile that just about kills me.

This isn't how I'd have wanted her to hear these words first, but if I don't give the conversation everything I have, I might not get a chance to do it properly. And all the ways she's defended me in the past day have only made me certain of how true they are, after only suspecting it before.

I drag my gaze back to Donovan. "I love her. More than I knew I could love anyone. But her soul is tied to the Seelie in ways even the Heart's will can't sever—and having seen her here among you, I wouldn't wish it to. Your people matter to her, and so they'll always matter to me as well."

Corwin… Talia's inner voice sounds both shaken and moved. She doesn't seem to know what else to say. I keep my gaze fixed on

Donovan's, but I send all the warmth I have in me her way. I don't expect her to be able to match my devotion just yet. It'll be an honor to earn it in as much time as it takes me. Simply remembering her calling me her mate lights me up inside all over again and bolsters my next words.

"Give me the chance to take up the cause myself," I tell the Seelie arch-lord, "and I promise I won't rest until I've gotten my fellow arch-lords' agreement to have a proper negotiation with you so we can resolve this conflict peacefully. Before, I didn't know anything about the people we were attacking. Now I do, and that makes all the difference."

A tremor runs through me as I finish. It's been a long, hard day, and I've let loose more emotion in the past few minutes than I have for years before.

It's drained me, but in a strange way there's a relief to that fatigue. The constant swallowing down and bottling up left a weight in my gut that's been partially lifted.

It takes a little while before Donovan recovers his own voice. He dips his head with more respect than he showed me on his arrival. "All right," he says. "I apologize for misjudging you and assuming all the Unseelie saw the situation the same way. Let me talk to my colleagues before it's too late to change course, and I'll see that you get out of here."

CHAPTER THIRTY-TWO

Talia

"I'm glad that we can say our farewells on friendlier terms than appeared possible earlier, and hopefully for only a short time," Sylas says, with the slightest of bows to Corwin as he holds out his hand.

The Unseelie arch-lord offers a hesitant smile and a firm shake in return. "As am I." His gaze slips from Sylas to Whitt and August flanking him. "I look forward to getting to know you all better face to face as much as I have through Talia."

There's no suppressing the giddy rush of seeing all of my men—and Corwin *is* mine, I can't deny it now—accepting each other and taking these first steps toward some kind of alliance.

Even more affection sweeps through my chest when Sylas steps back with a nod toward me. "We'll give you your privacy to say your goodbyes to your mate."

I shoot him a quick smile in thanks. The three of them draw back to where Astrid was watching from the outskirts of the field, and together they meander into the sparse stretch of trees between here and the open area around the new castle.

I turn back to Corwin where he's standing just a few steps shy of the border's haze, almost the exact same spot as when he brought me back here yesterday.

The iron-cored collar has left a reddish ring around his neck that Sylas's healer couldn't completely erase. The sight of it sends a jab of distress through me. I go to him, rising up on my toes to gently touch that spot.

Corwin shows no pain from the contact through the sharper awareness that snaps into place with the brush of my skin to his, only a flicker of eager heat. "I'll just have to wear shirts with high collars for a few days until it fully heals," he says, with a trace of amusement as if he'll enjoy pulling one over on his colleagues. Considering what jerks they've been to him, maybe he will.

I let my hand drop to his chest. "You don't think the other arch-lords will suspect something went wrong here?"

He shakes his head. "I'll tell my staff that I was… encouraged to stay the night in honor of our bond. It's true enough in a way. If any of my colleagues have bothered to notice I was gone longer than expected, they'll hear the same."

"How long do you think it'll take to persuade them to agree to a proper meeting with the summer arch-lords?"

"I don't know, but I'm not going to be put off this time. They were already vaguely considering other options when we arrived for Sylas's coronation. The idea was to test out the Seelie's hostility to us and the success of the retaliatory spell… Our soul-twined bond complicated matters."

I remember the hostile faces I saw through his eyes around the marble table in their Hall of the Heart. "They're even less happy about that than they were before."

"They'll come to terms with it. I can tell them now that the Seelie arch-lords have vowed to allow us peaceful entrance into their space to speak with them, and that they're also willing to take the vows to cross the border and meet us on our territory if we'll swear the same. It'll be easier to persuade them." Corwin's mouth twists. "After that last battle during the full moon, I think it became undeniably clear that our current approach wasn't accomplishing our goals."

As long as the Unseelie don't decide to try some approach that's even more aggressive, I guess any kind of meeting will be a win. "You'll let me know as soon as anything's settled?"

"Of course." He strokes a careful hand over my hair, his expression its usual cool mask but a gleam of fondness in his eyes. "Perhaps it'll give me the chance to see you again sooner than your next visit."

I give him a crooked smile. "It's not as if I'll ever be completely out of reach."

"No. But I won't intrude on your time here. I know you wouldn't have rejoined me right away regardless."

That's true, and not just because of the Seelie curse and the three other men I've been apart from for too long. The only way we could convince Celia to agree to the terms of assembling with the Unseelie arch-lords was for me to take the oath I suggested to Donovan.

As long as the full-moon curse exists, I'm now bound to stay in the summer realm for the week around the full moon, and not to remain in the winter realm for more than a week at any other time without at least a day here in between. But Corwin hasn't shown any animosity over that promise. If anything, he's seemed almost pleased that I've solidified my loyalties to the Seelie.

I still don't know how we'll balance my conflicting affections in the long run, but we've reached a tentative, temporary understanding. I'll be mates in all but name to my Seelie men while I'm here, and continue to see how I might settle into the role of soul-twined mate to Corwin while I'm with him, with no resentment on either side. For now I think they're all just glad that I still want each of *them* in my life as well as the others.

I lean my head against Corwin's chest, and after a moment's hesitation, his arms rise to wrap around me. His embrace floods me with the tender joy that came with his words to Donovan this morning.

I love her.

Will I be able to say that in return sometime in the future? Everything still feels so precarious. But I'll miss him, even though he'll still be with me no matter how far apart we are. I want to know him better so I can find out just how deep my feelings for him will run.

You can take all the time you need, he says quietly through the bond, hugging me tighter. *I've waited centuries to meet my soul-twined mate. Patience is not a problem.*

My smile turns bittersweet. That line of thinking has stirred up one difficult subject I have to touch on before he goes.

I ease back so I can gaze up at him. "Corwin—I know there are restrictions around what you can say about the Unseelie's political decisions and the rest. But I'm going to need to understand why all that fighting happened. Why you thought it was justified enough that you didn't interfere with the other arch-lords' plans. I get that you can't talk about it right now; I just—"

He quiets me with a graze of his fingers along my jaw. His dark eyes go intent and yet distant, as if he's focused on something a long way from here. Through the quiver of physical contact, I pick up on a tumultuous whirl of emotions he's sorting through. So much goes on inside this man, hidden beneath his cool exterior.

"I can tell you the basics of it now," he says in a low voice. "I just ask that you don't share it with any of the Seelie, that you let us bring the matter to them. My responsibilities allow me to speak up when I trust that it'll help my people more than harm them. If you say you can hold to that, I'll trust that you mean it."

My pulse hiccups. "It isn't anything that could hurt the Seelie, is it?"

"No, I can't see that it affects them in any way other than how we've reacted in the past. If my efforts fail and my colleagues strike out with more violence, then I won't fault you for betraying the secret."

"Okay." I drag in a breath. "Unless it comes to that, I can keep it to myself."

He's silent for a moment as he seems to gather his words. Then he lifts his other hand to my face, cupping it gently between his palms.

"A different curse is spreading across the winter realm. One that has stolen too many lives already, including my father's. And I can't help but think that whatever it is in you that heals the Seelie's curse may give us the answer to ours as well."

ROYAL MATE - BONUS SCENE

How did Corwin feel when he first discovered Talia as his soul-twined mate? Get the tumultuous moment when the bond formed from his point of view!

Corwin

As usual, I'm not all that pleased with the plan Laoni has proposed and Uzziah and Terisse have agreed to. Also as usual, none of them gives much consideration to my objections, and Neve barely seems to register what we're talking about. So even though the plan strikes me as being an unnecessary provocation of our enemies, I find myself standing alongside my colleagues with wings unfurled, ready to step through the border by the Heart to examine the Seelie's new arch-lord.

Of course, Laoni made it obvious that's not her main motivation. After our recent failure to take advantage of the wolves' curse, she's looking for any possible means to intimidate them. I have no doubt our abrupt arrival will accomplish that. I'm just not convinced intimidation is what we should be striving for.

But not even all the losses we endured that night have convinced my fellow arch-lords that we should attempt some approach other than direct violence. My stomach roils at the memory of the savaged bodies.

It's my fault, partly. I didn't want to see us take such an underhanded approach against any foe, but somehow I also believed the Seelie wouldn't react quite so brutally. But that's what the summer fae are known for, isn't it? Hot tempers supported by fierce fangs and claws.

I gird myself against the memory and raise my chin. Laoni and Terisse's voices wind together in the incantation of true names they've worked out that will deflect any attacks the Seelie launch at us, since we have to take our vow of non-aggression to pass over the border this close to the Heart. They've tested the spell out with their coteries multiple times to ensure it'll buy us enough time to escape if the wolves launch an offensive.

The magic tingles over my skin. Then Laoni waves us toward the border. We walk forward in a steady line, her in the middle, me at one of the ends. I resist the urge to adjust the silver crown on my head like a nervous fledgling to make sure it's perfectly straight.

The haze of the border washes over us, lit by the pulsing glow of the Heart just steps away from us. On the other side, we emerge into a rush of warmth and music.

The summer fae are dancing and exchanging toasts and generally making merry all across the broad, grassy plain on their side of the Heart. At least, they are in the first brief seconds before our arrival is noticed.

Several figures spin and stare. The music cuts out abruptly as the players lower their instruments. Human forms morph into wolves that approach us with snarls and bared teeth.

"We come in peace," Laoni calls out, pitching her voice to carry. "We come to parley. But if you attack us during this gesture, there's magic on us that will punish you for the attempt. Do not try us."

A strident female voice rings out through anxious murmurs of the crowd. "Back away, everyone. We'll deal with this."

As the other summer fae follow the command, clearing the area around us and then standing there in a tense semi-circle, two Seelie march out in front of us. Their bearing is so regal I have no doubt that they're arch-lords even before I spot the golden crowns atop their heads, a summery echo of our silver adornments.

The female arch-lord is older, with near-black skin and hair a contrasting white with a shimmer not unlike the diamonds that form my palace. Her heavy-lidded eyes are narrowed, her tall, lean frame poised for battle. The other looks younger than even me, with hair like fire.

"What's the meaning of this?" the woman demands, staring us down. "What kind of parley are you seeking?"

Uzziah cocks his head. "We got word that you have a new arch-lord among your ranks. There are three of you, aren't there? We would prefer to have you all where we can see you."

The woman glances around and appears to make eye contact with someone who must understand her silent request. She turns back to us. "Our newest colleague will join us shortly. Stay where you are until then if you refuse to speak further."

Then the young man before us isn't the new arch-lord our furtive attempts at espionage have caught wind of. Is the third of their number even greener?

My heart pounds as the seconds slip past us, but it can't be more than a couple of minutes before another crowned figure strides through the crowd, which parts for him without hesitation. To my surprise, this one is younger than the Seelie woman but certainly older than his more established colleague. He's a giant of a man, both tall and broad, with a purple sheen to his dark hair and a pale scar that cuts through one of his eyes across his tan skin. An air of authority rolls off of him. I suppose I can see why he might have been chosen to stand beside these other two.

As he comes to a stop beside his colleagues, the woman tilts her head at a haughty angle. "The three of us are before you now. What is the meaning of this visit?"

Laoni flicks her hair back from her face as if there's nothing all that momentous about the occasion. "We heard there's been a changing of the guard in the lands of summer. Is it so strange that we'd want to see the new line of authority on the other side of the Heart?"

"Here I am," the newcomer says in a low, even voice, his unscarred eye studying us intently.

I hold his gaze when it skims over me, but as soon as his attention veers back toward Laoni, I make my own scan of not just the arch-lords but the larger crowd. The highest summer fae will have the supporters they call their cadres with them, won't they? Protective spell or not, we should be wary of a potential attack.

My attention sweeps over the crowd, catching a glint of vividly pink hair at the corner of my vision. There's a young woman, presumably true-blooded given that unusual hue, standing at the far edges of the crowd where it's thinner. My eyes veer toward her, drawn by that striking color—and our gazes crash into each other.

The invisible impact of the sudden connection slams into me. My heart lurches. Energy blazes through my body too swiftly and sharply for me to raise any defenses. It frays my nerves and strips me open, and a flood of impressions race in to fill the sudden void within.

I see the woman—and I see myself echoed back at me as my lips part in shock. I feel the faint ache of a sore foot and horrified shock rippling through a slim frame.

Understanding shivers through my chest alongside my own bewilderment. I know what this feeling means. I just never expected…

My inner voice carries through the bond I was utterly unprepared for without my realizing I'm going to speak. *How can— It's you. My soul-twined mate.*

Somehow the emotions radiating from the Seelie woman become even more panicked. She stumbles backward, pulling away into the crowd. I can't stop myself from taking a step toward her, heedless of the voices of the other arch-lords that are continuing beside me. A silent protest erupts from my mind. *Where are you going? We have to— We must speak.*

I don't know why this is happening, but I can't deny that it is. That woman is my mate—the mate I've been waiting so long for. No matter how bizarre the circumstances, we can't *flee* from it.

But she's trying to. She gives no direct response to my plea other than a frantic *No, no, no, no* that reverberates through my core and brings unbidden tears to my eyes at the anguish in it. She is mine; she's meant for me—I know that's true no matter what kind of fae she is. How can she not feel the rightness of the bond as much as I do? How can she run?

Please come back. I know you must be startled too, but—

She spins right around, into the arms of an older woman with the build of a warrior. They're vanishing from view. I take another step toward her, vaguely aware of Laoni's head swinging my way, and cast my voice toward her as emphatically as I can. *You must— Wait. We can talk about this like reasonable—*

No! My mate's voice peals into my head with much more force than her previous mumbled denial. *No, go away, stop, get out of me.*

Her refusal hits me like a stab to the gut. My stomach knots around the pain. I move to rush after her, the bond and my wavering hopes yanking me toward my mate, but a hand catches my elbow.

Uzziah is glowering at me. "What in the realms are you *doing*, Corwin?" he grates out under his breath.

All of the arch-lords are staring at me—the summer ones included. I'm not sure if I should tell *them* what just happened, not yet, not while we're here in such a vulnerable position. I don't know what to do.

"Just—wait," I say to him. "There's something—" My mind is too scrambled with the flashes of fear and distress from my mate for me to get a coherent sentence out.

Terisse scowls at the Seelie arch-lords. "Have you cast some mind-muddling magic on our colleague?"

No, it's not that at all. I don't want this to turn into an excuse for more fighting.

Come back, I shout at my mate across the distance, as if the fact that I can't see her matters when our minds are so closely entwined, but I get no response at all.

Suddenly, Laoni is in front of me. "Corwin?" she says, sounding more irritated than concerned.

I can't deal with all of this at once. I can't undermine us in front of the Seelie arch-lords. So I do the only thing I can think of to gather myself momentarily—I clamp down on the bond as well as I can, shutting off the flow of impressions from my mate, even though the act sends another piercing ache through my abdomen.

"We should leave," I manage to say. "There's something I must discuss with you, *now*."

Laoni shoots an icy glance toward the Seelie arch-lords and nudges me toward the border. We all march back through, keeping as much dignity as we can summon in our hasty departure.

As soon as we're back on the frozen plane on our side of the border, Laoni whirls on me. "What *was* that, Corwin? I know you disagreed with the parley, but to throw some kind of—"

"My soul-twined mate," I interrupt, still holding the connection as tightly closed as I can while my emotions whirl inside me. I need to get a grip on them—need to stay in control. I can't let them overwhelm me, no matter the situation. "She was—I felt the connection with one of the Seelie in the crowd."

Uzziah's eyes nearly bug out of his skull. "A *Seelie*?"

"I'm as confused as you clearly are," I say with an edge in my voice I can't restrain. "But I know what I felt. It's not exactly difficult to mistake, as I'm sure you all know, having experienced it yourselves. I could see through her eyes. Feel what she felt."

A flicker of those emotions shoots past my attempt at a barrier, just as Laoni spits out, "You can't *seriously* be saying that the Heart has bound you to one of those mangy wolves."

I shore up my defenses as quickly as I can, simultaneously agreeing with Laoni's revulsion and hating the thought of my mate hearing it. My next words come out perfectly firm. "Yes, I am. She's back there. She ran, she was so bewildered." And frightened, and horrified, which I decide not to mention.

"The Heart works in mysterious ways," Neve murmurs, as if that's any help. Although she does have a point in this particular case.

Laoni mutters a curse and jerks her hand for us to follow her to the Hall of the Heart. The cold wind gusts over us as we step inside. She stops by the silver side table and fixes her gaze on me. "We'll get to the bottom of this. I trust you know better than to let her see *anything* that goes on over here?"

"Of course," I say, my mouth going dry. I hadn't even had time to think about that—about all the secrets I could inadvertently expose to our enemies.

All the more reason we need to bring my mate here. To keep her with me. She doesn't belong with the wolves anymore. She's *mine*.

And I know as surely as I'm aware that Laoni is going to argue about it every step of the way that I'm not backing down until the woman with the vibrant pink hair is standing by my side.

SECRETS OF WINTER

BOUND TO THE FAE #5

CHAPTER ONE

Talia

I adjust my position in the armchair in Sylas's study, the soft padding not so comfortable at the moment. The attention focused on me from the four figures around me is only supportive, but a prickling of pressure runs down my back regardless. Maybe because I've failed at my goal several times already.

I tune out my awareness of the Seelie arch-lord and his cadre as well as I can and stare at my cupped hands. In the back of my mind, I summon other impressions of these men I adore: smiles and wry remarks and tender caresses.

The joy of those memories blooms around my heart. I push as much of that emotion as I can into my voice. "*Sole-un-straw.*"

A glowing golden light flickers into being above my palms. I will it to expand and brighten, but just like in my earlier attempts, it wavers for a second and then fades away. I can't help letting out a huff of frustration.

August lowers himself onto the arm of my chair so he can slide his brawny arm around my shoulders, leaning in to press a kiss to my temple at the same time. "It's all right, Sweetness. Magic is hardly an exact process. Easier to bake a hundred perfect rolls than to get the same effect from a true name twice in a row."

I guess I should take comfort from his lack of concern. The pack's lead warrior is the one who's acted as my unofficial tutor when it comes to my fledgling skills in fae magic. If he thought something was wrong, he'd probably be blaming himself for messing up his teachings.

Astrid clears her throat where she's leaning against the polished wood wall near the door. "I'm plenty impressed just by that. How long have you been working true names again?"

This is the first time the wizened fae soldier who's the newest member of Sylas's cadre has witnessed my abilities, which we've kept secret from the rest of the pack, since a human isn't *supposed* to be able to draw on true names at all. My other unexpected abilities have made me enough of an object of fascination to the summer fae without adding another complication into the mix.

"I learned the true name for bronze from Aerik," I say, restraining a cringe at even a brief reference to the fae lord who imprisoned and tortured me for years. "He didn't mean for me to—I just heard him say it every time he opened my cage. I didn't know what it was then, only that it could be the key to escaping..."

Even months after Sylas and his cadre stole me away from Aerik's domain and gave me a real home, I can't completely tamp down on the flashes of memory from that time or the shudder that comes with them. August's arm tightens around me. I focus on that steady warmth, real and here in the present.

"You're quite the mystery, aren't you?" Astrid says quickly, clearly sensing that it's better not to pry farther on that specific subject. "Have you gotten the marks?"

I shake my head, and Whitt speaks up from where he's propped against Sylas's broad desk. "We're assuming it's some difference in a human using them, or else that she hasn't mastered them quite solidly enough yet, impressive though it is that she can wield them at all." The spymaster shoots me a fond but slightly crooked grin.

Seated behind his desk, Sylas leans his elbows onto its top, his hands clasped. He considers me with his mismatched eyes—both the whole dark one and the ghostly white one, which is split through with a savage scar that cuts through his brown skin from forehead to cheekbone. "You're consistently able to produce at least *some* effect at this point. Can you think of anything that might help you generate a stronger effect, Talia?"

I swallow hard. I can, but it's nothing they can give me. Mentioning it will only add to the tension that's already woven through the room despite the summery warmth of the night and the comforting scents of cedar and oak. Some of it I can't mention at all.

Tomorrow I go back to the winter realm to spend a week with the Unseelie arch-lord who's somehow my soul-twined mate, even though humans aren't supposed to have *those* either. During the first ten days I spent with Corwin and the periodic conversations we've had through our bond since I returned here, I've come to trust and even like him quite a bit… but there's still so much I'm unsure of. Not least of which is how I'm going to navigate my magical connection with him without losing the bonds of love I've already formed with the three men around me now.

My magic has always seemed to be tied to my feelings. I can only use the true name for bronze effectively when I'm scared—or remembering times when I was scared before. Air requires the sensation of swift, free movement. And light… light needs joy.

It's hard to feel nothing but joy when I'm all too aware that my heart is being pulled in two directions. As much as I could, I've spent the past week with my Seelie pack thinking only of the present, enjoying the moments I had with them as if nothing could threaten that happiness. I want to treasure this last short time with my wolfish lovers, but it's a lot harder to ignore the lingering questions about the future on the eve of my leaving.

And on top of that… Right before Corwin and I said our goodbyes last week, he shared a secret I've sworn to keep for him. Just as the summer fae have been suffering from a curse for several decades now, apparently the Unseelie have faced a curse of their own, one deadly enough to have killed many of the winter fae.

My blood has worked as a temporary cure for the savagery that comes over the Seelie under the full moon, so it makes sense that Corwin is hoping something in me might help his people as well. But

I still don't know the full details of their curse, let alone what I might do for it.

He said it'd be better if he can show me the rest once I'm with him rather than trying to explain with only words. And he doesn't want the Seelie knowing about the winter realm's weakness until he's sure his fellow arch-lords will negotiate with Sylas and his colleagues rather than continue their attacks along the border between the realms.

I push that knowledge aside and refocus on the room around me as well as I can. "No," I say to Sylas. "I think my concentration just isn't all there."

He nods. "That makes sense. And you'll have put quite a bit of energy into your inner wall."

He's right about that. At the start of this practice session, I summoned a barrier of imagined light inside me to seal off my connection to Corwin. I haven't told him about my use of true names yet. So many secrets I'm keeping from one side or the other.

I've held a partial wall up the whole time I've been apart from Corwin just so that I know I'm not projecting *every* thought and emotion that passes through my mind his way—and so I can quickly yank it full into place if some sensitive issue comes up. But I haven't often shut him off completely. If he's noticed, he probably assumes I'm engaging in much more intimate activities than this with my Seelie lovers.

That thought sends an uncomfortable pang through me. I refused to give up the men who won my heart before I ever knew Corwin existed, but I know it can't be easy for him to sense my affection and desire for them. The soul-twined bond stirs up plenty of guilt in *me* even though I made the decision myself. Those pangs have also gotten stronger with the knowledge that I'll be seeing him again tomorrow.

August nuzzles my hair. "Don't worry yourself. You've got a good enough handle on the true names you know that you can count on them to help a little if you should need them."

Despite his reassuring words, there's a tautness in his voice. He's been encouraging me to practice when I can so that I have every possible advantage among the winter fae. Even if I don't believe

Corwin would ever hurt me purposefully, his colleagues are another story.

Maybe *all* of the Unseelie are potential threats. I haven't spent much time with any of them except my mate. They have been killing summer fae unprovoked for nearly three decades.

But I also agreed to the additional practice for other reasons of my own. Who knows whether these skills might help against the Unseelie's curse? No matter why they've been fighting the Seelie, I'm not going to stand by and watch them die if there's something I can do to fix things.

"I suppose I'll have to tell Corwin about my magic sooner or later," I say, sinking back into August's embrace. "With the bond, it's likely to slip out eventually whether I want it to or not… Better to explain things upfront."

"That may be wise," Whitt says. "But I wouldn't rush to confess if it isn't necessary."

Sylas's expression turns more serious, but he gives me another nod. "I can't help worrying about your security, but you know him best. It's your decision when you're ready to share that aspect of yourself with him, when you feel you trust him enough to be certain of his reaction."

Astrid straightens up with the alertness that made her an excellent sentry. "Are you sure you want to head back there alone? Your friend—Harper—she seemed unfazed by the last visit. Surely she'd go with you again?"

I hesitate. It was comforting having my closest summer-fae friend with me on my first visit to the winter realm when I had no idea what to expect at all. But Harper has a life here, big dreams of taking on clients from other packs with her dress-making skills and getting to visit domains all across the realm… She hasn't had much of a chance to even get settled in our new home here by the Heart, now that Sylas has been named an arch-lord.

"I can't ask anyone else to split their time between the realms like I need to," I say. "Especially when the whole pack is dealing with another move so soon after getting back to Hearthshire. Now that I know Corwin better, I think it'll be okay. I should start seeing what life would really be like over there, right? She wouldn't follow me around forever."

The shadow that passes over all of my men's faces makes my gut twist. I didn't mean those comments as if I'm thinking of moving to the winter realm permanently and leaving them behind, but we all know that's the outcome most would expect from a soul-twined bond.

None of them expresses any of their concerns, though. They've been trying so hard not to pressure me when they know how difficult the situation already is.

August strokes his thumb over my shoulder, and Sylas gives me one of his reserved smiles that still manages to convey the warmth he feels for me. "If experiencing the winter realm on your own helps you make a more informed decision, I won't object. But if you find you miss having the company, we can always arrange an escort of your choice on your next visit."

For however many trips I make back and forth before I figure out what I'm actually doing with myself and my heart. I glance down at my hands, a surge of emotion that's a weird mix of grief and hope sweeping over me.

Astrid sketches a quick bow. She's not quite in the habit of seeing herself on the same level as the rest of Sylas's cadre yet. "I'll take my leave now, if it pleases you, my lord."

Maybe she realizes we might want some alone time before I go. She's the only one other than the men in this room and Corwin who knows about my joint relationship. The rest of the pack and Sylas's fellow arch-lords believe I'm only involved with August.

Sylas aims his smile at her. "Thank you for your able service today. I continue to be glad I brought you into my cadre."

Astrid flashes a quick smile in return and retreats, shutting the door in her wake.

I curl into August's embrace, and he lets out an encouraging rumble, trailing his fingers along my jaw. But too much tension is knotted inside me for my usual desires to run free. I grasp his free hand and look at my other two lovers, who are watching me with careful but heated gazes.

"I don't—I don't want to be alone tonight," I say, "but I'd just like to have you with me while we sleep. If that's all right."

Sylas stands with a sound that dismisses any uncertainty I might have felt. "I'm sure we will all take immense delight in your presence without needing to make any greater demands."

Whitt chuckles. "Not all trysts need to be of the carnal sort. We'll be here for you however you need us, mighty one. Never doubt that."

I don't, not after everything we've been through. The only thing I doubt is whether I can make a choice that won't break more than one heart, including mine.

CHAPTER TWO

Whitt

One could say it's my job as spymaster to be constantly on the alert. Even when I'm technically at leisure, dancing or feasting or sleeping, I've trained my senses to pick up any hint of disturbance or concern around me.

So although I'm not particularly inclined to emerge from my doze in the early hours of the morning before Talia leaves us again, the stirring of her body near mine tugs me out of my dreams. After some negotiation over exact arrangements in the bed last night, I ended up sprawled at her right, my head tipped by her shoulder. The bed is wide enough for Sylas to have stretched himself out by the headboard, where he stroked her hair until she drifted off. August lies opposite me, his arm tucked against her back and his chest rising and falling with a faint snore.

Gingerly, Talia sits up in the midst of our ring of bodies and swipes her hand over her hair. I haven't opened my eyes yet, but I can sense the tension in her pose without even looking at her. Something has been bothering her since last night… perhaps for her entire week with us, only coming to a head now that she's about to return to the winter realm.

Whatever it is, I suspect it's what's roused her from slumber at this early hour. The dawn light streaming from above is still so thin it barely penetrates my eyelids.

I wait to see what she'll do, resisting the urge to wrap my arms around her and pull her into an embrace, as if I could cuddle every worry she has out of her. I can't anyway, and I want to see what she does with the space I'm giving her.

After a minute, she must decide there's no point in trying to sleep more. She eases out from under the blanket and manages to slip over August's prone form without provoking more than a slightly stuttered breath from the whelp. Her feet patter softly across the floor with their uneven rhythm, more pronounced without the help of her brace. There's a rustle of her nightgown, and then she's slipped out the door.

I lie there for a few minutes longer, debating whether to give her even more space or go after her and see what she might say when it's just the two of us. My brothers will wake up before too much longer, and neither of them is going to want to be far from her during our last few hours with our lover.

The thought of her crossing the border again, moving so far beyond our reach, makes my own chest constrict.

That soul-twined mate of hers has proven decently honorable so far, but I still can't put that much trust in him, let alone the rest of his kind. Who knows what plans they may have for our lady of the castle? If it wasn't for that uncertainty, I'd give her my true name in an instant just to know she could call out to me from anywhere in the world as long as she concentrated hard enough.

But I can't compromise the lord and brother I'm sworn to serve. Giving her that much access to my mind might compromise the safety of my entire people.

Which is the same reason that after my deliberations, I climb out of the bed with equal care and head out after her. If something's bothering her about her trip to the winter realm, I need to know for our sake as well as hers.

I pause at my bedroom to change into clothes that aren't sleep-rumpled and splash some water on my face from the basin. Running my damp fingers through the erratic tufts of my hair, I set off to locate the mite.

She isn't in her own bedroom, though from the traces of scent around it, I can tell she stopped in there briefly. I follow the woodsy sweet smell of her down the stairs to the kitchen, which isn't a surprise. Thanks to August's encouragement, she seems to feel as at home in that room as the one dedicated to her use.

I find her perched on one of the stools by the larger island, wearing the structured green dress her Unseelie arch-lord gifted her with before she came back to us and the boots Harper made for her that encompass a brace for her misshapen foot. That leg is swinging casually, but her elbows are rigid against the countertop, her hands clasped a little too tightly in front of her, her pretty face drawn.

If I could ensure she never has any cause to look that serious ever again, I'd do just about anything to accomplish it. She's had far too much weighing on her over the past few months—the past several *years*, to be honest. It's more strain than any one being should have to bear.

When I allow my steps to fall louder as I walk through the doorway, her swinging leg stills and her head jerks up. I can see how determinedly she forms the smile she gives me, as if it's a feat of strength. The clenching in my chest intensifies.

What is haunting this precious woman who's already taken so much onto her shoulders?

I grab a duskapple from a basket on the counter and toss it in my hand as I amble over to sit across from her. "Restless morning?"

She shrugs, still smiling her determined little smile that practically stabs me through the heart. I will my claws from the fingertips of my right hand and neatly cut a slice out of the apple. It occurs to me when I'm partway through the process that the gesture that came so automatically to me might disturb her, but when I glance over at her, she's watching without any hint of distress.

Well, she's ridden on my back in wolf form. If she had any qualms about the beast inside me at first, they must have been gone by then. I don't imagine her traumatic recollections involving wolfish fangs and claws had anything to do with snack time.

I pop the slice into my mouth, the tart flavor grounding me, and carve out another to offer to Talia. She takes it with a murmur of thanks but doesn't eat, only turning it in her hands, frowning at it as if I've handed her a new problem rather than a piece of fruit.

I cluck my tongue at her. "Come on now, there's obviously been something eating at you. Whatever it is, you can let it out. You may be mighty, but you should know by now that being strong doesn't mean you have to tackle the world on your own."

Talia drags in a breath, and a shiver travels through her body. My stance tenses, watching her, abruptly certain that whatever's on her mind is even worse than anything I'd have guessed.

I set down the apple. "Talia, if something went badly in the winter realm that you haven't told us—if you have some reason to be *afraid* of going back there—"

"No," she interrupts, with an almost panicked urgency that's hardly convincing. "I—I'm not afraid to go back. There's just so much going on, so many things I'm still not sure of that matter so much…"

I study her, more skepticism coursing through me. I've spent a lot of time around this woman since she came into our lives, and her response doesn't look like her typical pensiveness to me. "You might be able to lie in ways we fae can't, but I'd prefer if you didn't, even if you think it'll spare us some unrest. There's something specific on your mind beyond the general muddle things are in, isn't there?"

I thought I'd spoken calmly and evenly, but Talia pales, her fingers curling into her palms. "I'm sorry," she says, her voice even more fraught than before. "I shouldn't have—I gave him my promise—it's nothing that could hurt anyone here. Or me."

My hackles rise instinctively. The bird-brained interloper has insisted she keep something from us—something that's troubling her. Perhaps he isn't so honorable after all. Preventing her from even talking to us properly when he can reach straight into her very thoughts…

I fight to keep the edge out of my voice. "If he'd have you go without help when you need it—"

Talia shakes her head so vehemently I stop. "It's nothing like that.

Really. And I'm sure you'll find out about it soon. He just needs to get the other Unseelie arch-lords to agree to have a proper discussion with Sylas and the others." She inhales shakily with a hint of a sob. "I don't *like* keeping secrets from you. He only mentioned it at all in order to reassure me rather than leaving me totally in the dark."

My heart wrenches with guilt. I'm off my seat and by her side in an instant, tucking her close to me with a careful embrace, chiding myself for pushing her as far as I have. "Hey, now, I'm not angry. I didn't mean to upset you. If you're sure it's nothing that threatens your safety or happiness or our pack's, then it's nothing for me to pry into. I apologize. I should have trusted that you know what needs to be said or not and let it be."

She leans her head against my shoulder, but her slim frame is still rigid within my arms. "It's all right. I know it's your job to figure out everything that's going on, especially about anyone who could be an enemy."

"*You* will never be our enemy," I say firmly. "No matter how many blasted raven shifters you find yourself tied to. I can promise you that."

To my relief, my declaration manages to get a sliver of a laugh out of her. "Let's hope it's just the one. I think I've defied the laws of the faerie world enough without taking on a horde of soul-twined mates."

I give an exaggerated shudder and tip her face up so I can claim a swift but sweet kiss. "I'd like to think the Heart will be kinder to you than that."

She hums to herself, snuggling against me in a much more relaxed pose that makes me ridiculously giddy, as if *I'm* a whelp in the grips of feckless puppy love.

I suppose for all my years, in some ways I am. I haven't loved a woman like I love this one before. There's never been any being I've wanted to defend so wholeheartedly with everything I have. And that includes even my lord. Other than… other than that one misstep with Isleen I'd rather not give any more space in my head, I've never faltered in my duty to Sylas, but I can't deny there were moments I resented carrying it out.

"I wonder if the Heart would think it's actually being generous," Talia says, her warm breath grazing my neck. "I mean, I already had the three of you. I didn't *need* a soul-twined mate. So why not throw in a few more while it's already on a roll?"

Her tone is wry but not entirely joking. I chuckle. "Most things about you are only unusual because you're human, not for fae as well. And I've yet to hear of even the truest of true-blooded fae finding themselves tangled in more than one soul-twined bond. I feel reasonably confident in saying you're safe from that."

"Safe," she mutters, as if she doesn't put much stock in that word. I can't say I blame her.

"Look at it this way," I say, tugging her closer to enjoy this nearness for as long as I can before she's gone. "You've earned the devotion of not one but two arch-lords. A highly impressive feat! It's only unfortunate they're on opposite sides of the border."

She makes a dismissive sound. "It's not only Sylas and Corwin I'm taking into account."

"Ah, I wouldn't be offended if you put slightly more stock in their part in this melodrama than my own or August's," I tease, but the truth is that a twinge shoots through me as I say the words.

It may very well come down to that—to what kind of arrangement she can make between the two men with a claim who have the real authority in this world. All August and I can do is watch from the sidelines.

I shove that discomfort aside and steal another kiss, this one long and lingering. I've half a mind to see if she'll let me give her a very potent reminder of the delights we of Hearth-by-the-Heart can offer to take with her when she goes, but my ears catch the thump of the front door as some of the servants arrive for the day. Instead, I reluctantly draw back.

I can't resist giving Talia's hair an affectionate ruffle before I pull away completely. "You've proven yourself to be awfully resourceful during your time among us, mighty one. I'm sure you'll settle on the best solution that's within the realm of possibility, whatever that may be."

And Heart willing, there'll still be a place for me in her life when she makes that final choice.

CHAPTER THREE

Talia

Like the first time, Corwin crosses the stretch of glinting fog that marks the border so he can escort me to the winter realm. The last time he made the passage, one of the other Seelie arch-lords ambushed him with her men and threw him into her dungeon, so I wouldn't blame him for being hesitant. But although he glances around him with a faint air of wariness, by far the strongest emotion I sense from him is joy at seeing me again.

It feels strange, seeing *him*. Having him standing there in front of me in the flesh, tall and lean with those dark eyes watching me with their usual intentness, the blue-black curls of his hair falling around his striking face. We've spent all week in nearly constant contact during our waking hours, if often only an awareness of each other's presence rather than actual conversation, but our bond thrums so much more powerfully when he's actually near me.

In many ways, as much as we've shared, he's still a stranger. The emotions that rise in my chest are a bewildering mix of happiness, relief, and anxiety. How can I feel so close to him and yet so uncertain at the same time?

His voice travels through our bond, as cool and even as it usually is when he's speaking out loud. *It's all right. We're still finding our footing with each other. I'm just glad I'm getting more of a chance to do that. Do you need to say any further good-byes?*

He'll have noticed the good-byes I already said, hugging each of my Seelie men tightly and indulging in a few final kisses before we left the privacy of the castle. A twinge of guilt runs through me at how he might have felt about that, but he doesn't show any jealousy. I made it *very* clear during our first ten days together that if he wanted me to give him a chance, he had to accept the other sorts of bonds my heart has formed.

I guess this week will have given him a lot of practice in exercising his tolerance, even though I raised my inner walls every time things took a particularly heated turn.

I glance back at Sylas and his cadre—and Harper, who's come along to see me off too. She brought over three new dresses this morning, as if I didn't already have plenty of finery to wear around Corwin's palace. I told her more than once that I didn't mind going on my own, but I think she still feels she owes me something.

There's nothing really left to say. I raise my hand. "I'll be back in a week, right before noon."

"We'll be waiting for you," August says with a warm if bittersweet smile.

Corwin lifts the trunk with my clothes and other belongings. I step forward to join him, saying the words of the vow the Heart requires of anyone who crosses the border so close to its glowing, pulsing energy. "By the Heart, I swear to do no harm to the fae beyond this boundary. May I pass in peace and amity."

We step into the haze. It doesn't totally sit right with me, walking alongside Corwin but keeping this distance between us like awkward acquaintances. I waffle for a second and then sidle closer to slip my hand around his elbow.

The physical contact doesn't provoke the usual electric quiver and the deepening of the bond I'd feel if I were touching his bronze skin rather than only the soft fabric of his jacket, but contentment unfurls through our bond all the same. *It's a pleasure to see you wearing that dress,* Corwin says.

I brush my other hand over the light green skirt, a color I know he chose to match my eyes. He had the dress made for me shortly before I left last time, a combination of Unseelie styling and Seelie vibrance. *It seemed fitting. And I knew it already has a very good warming spell in it.*

Definitely important, he agrees with a hint of amusement, but it's also true. With each step, the temperature in the air cools until a chill tickles over my skin in brief wafts before the enchantment cast on the dress wisps the worst of it away. As we emerge onto the vast icy plain on the winter side, the breeze licks over my head.

Corwin glances down at me. "I like your hair this way."

I touch the loose waves self-consciously. Months ago, August dyed them a rich pink for me. It was a way to reclaim my identity and self-control after the years I spent in imprisonment. But over the past week, that color started to feel a little childish. It was based on my preteen tastes, after all. And I've come a long way since even those first few days in Sylas's old keep.

I'm a lady of winter as well as summer now. So when August touched up the dye this morning, I asked him to mix the pink with strands of a deeper, cooler purple.

Corwin may have picked up on some of the reasoning from my mind, but I say it out loud anyway. "That seemed fitting too. Like the dress—summer and winter together."

I can read a certain hesitation in Corwin's thoughts that he doesn't express outright. He might have made peace with Sylas and accepted the role the Seelie arch-lord and his two cadre-chosen play in my love life, but there are still immense frictions between the realms.

A lump rises in my throat. I don't want us to end up arguing so soon after I've arrived, but I can't wait much longer to understand.

We come up on the shining diamond fortress that Corwin calls home, an innate melody humming off its crystalline forms with the movement of the wind. I let it lift my spirits as I summon some of the boldness that's gradually becoming more natural to me.

I don't want to talk about the curse out loud while we're so close to the other Unseelie arch-lords' domains. I don't think they'd be happy if they found out Corwin shared their secret with me, however vaguely. So I take our conversation inward. *The curse you mentioned—have you convinced your colleagues to talk to the Seelie about it?*

I get the impression of an inner sigh. *I'm still working on them. They're essentially agreed that it would be a logical step now that we have some connection established across the border, but they're dragging their heels on deciding exactly how to best broach the subject. Caution has served us well many times before… I don't entirely blame them for being wary, as impatient as I might be to see this problem dealt with.*

I catch a flash of a memory: the iron-core collar burning around Corwin's neck when Arch-Lord Celia held him captive for that excruciating day. Maybe we're lucky Corwin himself wants to negotiate rather than go back to war.

If you're right, and my blood can act as a cure in your case as well as the Seelie's, I venture, *I suppose that might make the situation less tense?*

It may. You shouldn't feel it's your obligation, though—I may have many hopes, but I wouldn't force your assistance.

I squeezed his arm. *You don't have to. I want to help if I can. And as soon as I can. Now that I'm here, will you tell me more about the curse?*

The current of emotion that ripples through our bond contains a little regret that our reconciliation is focused on such a serious matter, but also the recognition of how deeply that matter has been weighing on me for the past week.

I'm sorry, Corwin says as he smiles at the servant who opens the palace door for us. *I thought having a partial understanding might ease your worries more than stir up new ones. Perhaps I miscalculated. I didn't intend to leave you fretting over it.*

It's okay. I might have fretted more over not having any idea at all why the Unseelie have been attacking the summer realm and whether they might again. I just want to know what I'm dealing with, now that I can *know. You said when I was back here, you could show me…?*

Yes, of course. I'm only sorry that I must begin your visit with such a horrible story and such an immense request all in one.

Since my arrival, Corwin has kept his own partial wall up against our bond to stem the flow of his emotions through our bond. I'm not sure he'd want me to notice the glimpses that waver through to me now of more pleasant activities he wishes we could have shared: him playing his harp while I listen, us chatting in the dining room over one of his human chef's delicious meals. A little ache forms in my heart.

I know Corwin loves me. He admitted it to Donovan, the third of the Seelie arch-lords, in his efforts to prove he'd support a truce between the realms, and I felt the truth of the words. But he hasn't said it to me directly, maybe not wanting to pressure me when he can probably tell I'm not ready to make any declarations that intense in return. But he's been waiting a long time to find his soul-twined mate, and even though I'm not what he could have expected, he's still welcomed me.

I might not feel outright love for him yet, but I do care about him beyond the tug of our bond. I didn't just come back to see about the curse, and he shouldn't think I did.

When we've stepped into my room—the same bedroom I used during my first stay—Corwin sets my trunk against the wall. He turns as if to direct me right back out, but I stop him with my hand. At his questioning look, I ease closer to him and slide my arms around him in a tentative embrace.

With the softest hitch of breath and a jolt of delight he can't contain, Corwin hugs me back, tucking his chin over my head. I relax into his embrace, his cool woody scent like snowy forest nights washing over me, and open my end of the bond completely so he can feel just how much *I* welcome the chance to explore our connection.

Even if I'm not willing to give up my Seelie men, I'm coming to recognize how the bond the Heart forced on me may be a gift after all.

"I missed you," he says quietly. "It may sound odd when I've lived within these walls for hundreds of years without you and only spent ten days with you here, but I felt your absence every day."

The ache in my heart expands. "I missed you too," I admit. Just as I'll miss my men of summer while I'm here. For a second, the vastness of my romantic predicament threatens to overwhelm me.

As if deciding that it's best to distract me with a change of subject, even if the topic is an unpleasant one, Corwin lowers his arms and grasps my hand. "Come. I shouldn't make you wait any longer. I've just gotten word that the curse has befallen a woman in a domain about an hour's journey from here. I'll explain everything I can on the way, and then you can see the effects for yourself—and determine whether there's anything obvious you can do for her."

There's a small carriage waiting for us outside. Corwin must have assumed we'd make this journey soon if not right away.

I hold my tongue until I've settled onto the wooden bench and the vehicle has lifted off into the air on its magical propulsion. "I guess… start from the beginning? What is this curse? How did it start? When did it start?" If it struck just one woman today, then it obviously isn't tied to the full moon like the Seelie curse, and it doesn't affect all the winter fae at once.

Corwin leans against the prow of the carriage by the crystalline windshield that blocks all but wisps of the cool breeze. He rakes his slender fingers back through his hair, his mouth momentarily twisting in a rare overt display of discomfort. "We first started seeing the signs several decades ago, but it took some time before the ailment became truly serious. My father was one of the first to die from it."

That was about five decades ago, he told me before. Leaving his mother so ravaged by grief she couldn't stand to even live. "That's a similar timeline to the Seelie curse, from what I've heard. But—how do you know it isn't a regular illness?"

"No practitioner of any health-related art has been able to determine a cause," Corwin says. "Or any way of alleviating the symptoms, let alone cure them. It seems to come out of nowhere, striking down fae at random. We haven't been able to determine any pattern to who succumbs to it, and it doesn't spread in the typical fashion of a disease. Most of the time, the victims have had no contact with any other victim, and no one close to them contracts it at the same time."

As he speaks, the hairs on the back of my arms rise. How horrible to have no way of protecting themselves or predicting where this sort of disease might appear. I swallow hard. "Does everyone who gets it die?"

He nods. "Since my father's time, yes. The last victim I'm aware of who survived was taken by the curse not long after my father was and was left with permanent weakness. And more and more of my people have been claimed by the curse as time has gone on. Back then, it might have taken only a half a dozen in one year. Now, we've already lost five across the realm in just this month."

For beings who expect to live thousands of years if all goes well, that many fatalities must be nothing short of catastrophic.

"The Seelie curse has been getting worse too," I say. "It's strange that the curses seem to be connected somehow in timing and in patterns like that, but very different in the way they affect you."

"Perhaps it is the same curse, gripping us according to our natures." Corwin's mouth flattens into a grim line. "It drives the summer fae even wilder than they already were, beyond any hope of control, bringing out their inner beasts. And for us…" He lets that sentence hang.

"What does the illness do?" I prod.

He inhales raggedly. "It's as if the victim is freezing to death, but no source of heat can warm them. Their skin turns blue and cold, their limbs become increasingly rigid until they're paralyzed, and in the end their organs shut down completely, all within the course of a few days. When our doctors have examined victims to try to understand the ailment, they've found even the food remaining in their stomachs has turned to ice."

My own stomach turns at the image. A wintry curse indeed. I could say something about it amplifying the Unseelie's rigid natures as well, but I'm not sure Corwin would appreciate the observation right now.

"You'll see when you meet this woman," Corwin says. "She should still be mobile and able to speak at this early stage, though she may appear somewhat disturbing." He pauses. "With the Seelie, the way you've brought them out of their curse is to allow them to consume your blood, I believe?"

Instinctively, I rub my forearm where Aerik's men used to drain me. "Yes. They only need a little bit—we mix it with other ingredients so it's easier to distribute as a sort of tonic. But—it only prevents the curse for that specific night. That's why I have to keep going back if I'm going to help them. I don't know… Even if my blood heals someone under your curse in the moment, the effect might not last."

"Even a stop-gap solution would be better than none at all. But of course—I wouldn't want to see you stretch yourself thin—"

I offer him a tight smile before cutting in. "I know. Let's just see if I'm any use at all before worrying about that."

Corwin stares at me for a moment before returning my smile with more warmth—and a glow of admiration that seeps through me from the inside. Just like that, our bond tugs me toward him.

Even with the images his words painted lingering in my head, the urge rises up to escape them in the giddy thrill I know his kiss can bring. Desire flares low in my belly.

The Heart won't be satisfied until we've consummated that bond in every conceivable way.

I close my eyes for a second as if that will shut out the emotions I don't want to deal with in this moment. As I open them again, Corwin gestures to the landscape beyond the carriage, speaking in a tone that tells me he's doing his best to distract me from the turmoil within. "I can take the opportunity to introduce you to a little more of our lands. You can see the frostfire forest in the distance there—the ice forms on the trees like licks of flame, cold until you break one off and then the center melts into a steaming beverage that's quite enjoyable."

He talks on for the rest of the journey, answering my questions and pointing out other features of his world. Making no mention of my brief hunger for him or how I rejected it. I might criticize the winter fae for being rigid, but I do appreciate their patience—or at least his.

The carriage slows by a keep and a sprawling village of wooden buildings—though not the same kind of wood as Sylas and his pack conjure into their homes. This is birch-pale with a weathered texture like driftwood.

The fae woman who must rule over this flock strides out of the keep with a few underlings at her heels. She bows her head in greeting. "Arch-Lord Corwin, I am honored by your visit. I didn't expect…" She trails off, her gaze landing on me with unmistakable confusion.

Corwin rests his hand on my shoulder. "I've come to see the one of your flock who's been struck by the curse. This is Talia, a guest of mine who may be of some assistance."

Those remarks don't appear to resolve the fae lady's confusion, since from what Corwin's told me, *nothing* has "assisted" against the curse so far, but she doesn't argue with her ruler. "She's at the healer's house," she says with a beckoning gesture, a thread of hopelessness wound through her voice.

The man who answers her knock at one of the nearby houses looks equally despondent. He steps back with an even deeper bow for Corwin.

The curse's latest victim draws my gaze in an instant. She's sitting hunched in a plump armchair near the healer's crackling hearth, her legs drawn up to her chest and her chin braced against her knees. Her skin, which must have been a deep tan before, has taken on a bluish shade that's turned it almost purple. Streaks of frost cling to her ruddy hair. She shivers, hugging her legs tighter.

"I would speak with her alone," Corwin says with an air of absolute authority I haven't often seen him bring out. The lady and the healer leave immediately. I guess he doesn't want to get their hopes up about my possible curative powers.

He comes to a stop in front of the woman and crouches down so their faces are level. I'd recognize the pain etched in his expression even if it wasn't coursing into me through our bond at the same time. He feels so desperately, searingly helpless in the face of this inexplicable threat.

His tone now is nothing but gentle. "I have a draught I would give you to see if it might warm you some. Would you be willing to try it?"

The woman nods with a stiffness that suggests her joints are already starting to freeze in place. Nausea churns inside me. I've never seen a corpse dead long enough to cool, but my instincts are telling me that this is what death looks like. She's nearly a zombie.

Even if I *can* cure her, how much damage has this bizarre disease already done to her?

That doesn't matter unless we can rid her of the curse to begin with. Corwin turns away from her and pulls a small flask from within his jacket. He reaches out to me, and reading his intention, I give him my hand.

With a murmured word that must be a true name, he splits open a small cut on my index finger. It barely stings. He lets a few drops of my blood fall into the flask to mix with whatever liquid it already contains and then seals my skin just as quickly as he broke it.

When he returns to the cursed woman, I struggle to keep breathing. He brings the flask to her lips, and she manages to tip her head enough to accept the drink. Then he steps back, and we wait.

A shudder runs through the woman's body. My heart leaps with the thought that she might be shaking off the effects of the curse—but then she wraps her arms tighter around her legs, and I'd swear her skin takes on an even chillier tone. After a few minutes, my gut has completely knotted, and there's no sign of any change.

It didn't work. My blood can cure the Seelie's curse, but not the winter realm's. Or if it can, it doesn't work the same way.

We tried, Corwin says silently. *It isn't your fault. It could be it'll just take more time for the effect to take hold.* But his anguish at the probable failure rings all through his inner voice.

CHAPTER FOUR

Talia

Dinner back at Heart's Cadence is a desolate meal. The food is as delicious as always, the tender meat melting on my tongue with a delicately sweet flavor, but Corwin shows no sign of enjoying it. He says little, the connection between us mostly closed off, what I can sense from him a turmoil of uneasy emotions.

We stayed in the town with the cursed woman for a couple of hours, just in case she started to recover gradually. Corwin talked business with the lady of the flock, and I listened on the sidelines, figuring it was better to absorb all the information I can for now rather than intrude. I gathered that this isn't the first time the curse has stuck that particular flock. Over the past few decades, they've lost two others to it. As Corwin said, there's nothing tying the current woman to either of the others.

By the time we left, she'd only gotten worse. The doctor had just been moving her to a bed as her limbs had stiffened so much he was afraid she'd end up stuck in her hunched pose.

I have to think the illness *is* a curse, like Corwin and his colleagues assume, not just because of all the aspects that don't fit any regular disease but also the fact that it emerged and escalated alongside the Seelie's curse. But I don't *know* anything about undoing curses. I have no idea why my blood brings the summer fae out of their wolfish rages.

I poke at my last few slices of a turnip-like vegetable and venture a question. "Is it normal for a curse—any curse, not even necessarily one this big—to come out of nowhere? Or if there's a curse, does that mean someone must have cast it on you?" Memories of creepy Halloween stories flit through my mind, although those were human fables made up for kids.

Corwin stirs out of his melancholy reverie. "Both are possible. You've seen how much magic these lands themselves can hold of their own accord. That magic can twist into malignant shapes, though we've never faced anything anywhere near this immense. And fae can work malicious magic on each other, of course, although a spell that's afflicted our entire realm for so long… That would take an incredible effort. I don't believe one or even a few of the most powerful among us could accomplish it."

And why would anyone have wanted to anyway? I nibble at my lower lip thoughtfully. "I still don't understand why I'm tied to the Seelie curse at all, or why I would be only to that one and not yours. Unless it's because the trace of fae heritage in my background is Seelie? But that'd be the same for my brother and my mom too, and their blood didn't affect the fae who took me the same way."

"It is obviously a tangled conundrum," Corwin acknowledges. "I trust your Seelie arch-lord has taken many steps to unearth the answers."

I nod. "We haven't found out anything very specific. I wish I knew more about how fae magic and the rest work in general so I had more of a chance of figuring it out."

Corwin lowers his inner wall enough to send a tendril of affection and reassurance my way. "We can't expect you to decipher the causes of our malady when none of us who are so much better versed in magic can ourselves. But… you may yet turn out to be tied to our curse as well—if it even is a separate curse and not the same one with different expressions. Perhaps just as our curse affects us differently, the way *you* could affect it would also be different."

My spirits lift just slightly at the idea that there might be something I can do after all. "How would we figure out what that is?"

"I'm not sure. I suppose we could try as many possibilities as we can come up with—that won't make you or the cursed victim uncomfortable..." Corwin sets down his fork on his now-empty plate. "This is the sort of thing I'd prefer to consult with my coterie on rather than relying on my wits—and yours—alone. I trust that anything we discuss with them wouldn't leave that circle. But I realize not all the secrets we'd have to reveal are mine to make that decision about."

My chest clenches at the thought of admitting my role in the Seelie's curse to any other winter fae. But I've wanted to get to know the men and women Corwin works most closely with for a while. I know how careful he is. If he trusts them to be discreet, then I'd imagine I can trust them too. And they'll definitely have more insights than I can offer when I haven't spent even two weeks in Unseelie territory yet.

"How do they feel about the attacks against the Seelie?" I have to ask.

Corwin smiles grimly. "I'd say at least a couple of them are even more eager for peace than I am. None of them have argued with me about my resistance to the aggressive approach preferred by my colleagues. I wouldn't ask you to speak to them if I believed you had anything to fear."

Of course he wouldn't. His faith in them carries through our bond.

I inhale deeply. "All right, then. I'd like to meet them."

Corwin stands. "You'll only be meeting three of them—two are away seeing to more distant business—and of those here, you spoke with Olander and Zelpha briefly during your last stay. It shouldn't be too overwhelming. If you start to feel hesitant, you can always decide you've said enough."

"Okay. That's fair." The coterie members I met several days ago weren't exactly full of warmth and sunshine, but this is the winter realm, so maybe around here friendliness is simply not giving someone the cold shoulder.

"I'll call them in now and determine where we can best meet. I'll be back when everything is arranged."

As Corwin moves to go, his chef's daughter hustles into the room carrying a platter of pastries with jellied centers. "There's still dessert," she says, taking in his stance.

"I'm afraid I'll have to skip that tonight," Corwin says apologetically. "If my portion will keep, I'll have it later on."

Beth sets the platter on the table and places her hands on her hips. "Last time we made these, you regretted leaving them to get stale. I seem to remember."

I've never seen any of Corwin's fae servants talk to him that boldly, but Corwin just chuckles. "You know, I remember that as well. I suppose I can carry one with me. Thank you."

He scoops it up and takes a bite as he heads out of the room. Beth nudges the platter closer to me so I can grab as many as I'd like. I lift one that contains a yellow jelly with a citrusy scent and give the girl a closer look.

I don't think she could be more than fourteen or fifteen, still with a bit of youthful gangliness in her body as if she hasn't quite grown into all her features yet. For her kitchen work, her fawn-brown hair is pulled back in a bun, but I can tell from the curly sprigs along her forehead that it'd be pretty wild otherwise. Corwin mentioned once that she was born here in the fae realm.

"You're not worried about talking back to him," I say.

She cocks her head with a teasing smile. "Should I be?"

I find myself smiling back. "No, I don't think so. But most of the fae are pretty deferential to Corwin. I mean, he is an arch-lord and all."

Beth shrugs with a casualness that I don't think would look out of place in a mall or school cafeteria back in the human world, even if she's never set foot there. "He doesn't 'lord' it over us that much. Even if you all have all kinds of powers we don't, I don't think I could stand to go around feeling scared about it all the time. My mom always says we might as well act the way we want and ask for what we need, or what's the point in being alive at all?"

I can't argue with that philosophy—actually, I kind of admire it. But I realize I need to correct one assumption. "I'm not one of them—

not fae." I touch my hair. "This is dyed. I was… taken from the human world when I was a kid."

For all her supposed nonchalance, Beth stiffens at that revelation, blinking at me. Her freckled cheeks flush. "Oh, I—I can't really tell, you know. I wouldn't have thought— Never mind." Her blush deepens, and she hurries out as if she thinks she's made some horrible faux pas. As if I don't already know how odd it is that I'm here dining with a fae arch-lord.

I wish she hadn't left. It's more enjoyable to eat with company. I still polish off the tartly sweet pastry and lick the powdered sugar from my fingers, wondering what it'd be like to have parents here, to not have the constant awareness of a whole world that used to be mine that I've lost.

Someday when everything in the fae world has settled down, I'd like to go back to the human lands just to see how the reality compares to my memories, even if I can't imagine trying to make a new life for myself there.

Just as I'm starting to get restless, Corwin returns. He stops in the doorway. "They're joining us here in the palace, where I can be most sure of our privacy. Would you come with me to my study?"

"Of course." I get up and, on an impulse, take his elbow like I did when we were walking to the palace earlier today. As we step into the hall, a pleased warmth travels from Corwin into me.

A question that has nothing to do with the curse occurs to me. *Do your coterie know who I am to you—that I'm your soul-twined mate? And that I'm human as well?*

I explained all that they need to know about our bond while you were in the summer realm, he replies. *They wouldn't have been dismissive of any guest of mine, but I did want to ensure they treated you with the full proper respect.*

I catch a hint of pride with that statement, which I find it hard to wrap my head around. That he would be *proud* to declare me his mate, when I'm so far from being the true-blooded Unseelie fae everyone would have expected to take that role…

Corwin must pick up on that twinge of emotion. *You may not have the bloodline I expected, but in every way that matters, you're everything I could have wanted in a mate.*

I grip his arm tighter, wishing in that moment that I could say the same back just as wholeheartedly—that my heart wasn't so divided. Then he ushers me into his study, and those more personal concerns fall away as I'm faced with three members of the arch-lord's professional inner circle.

I've actually seen all three of them before, although Corwin couldn't have known that. The older man with streaks of gray in his dark hair, who's sitting in one of the study's armchairs, came to speak to Corwin right after I arrived during my first visit. I snuck over to try to listen in on their conversation but was too late.

The other two, who discussed the problem of roving beasts with Corwin while I mostly observed, have remained on their feet. The stout but agile man with the ice-pale eyes would be Olander, and the muscular woman whose chestnut hair is pulled back in a loose braid is Zelpha.

It occurs to me now as the details of our earlier conversation come back to me that they were talking around the curse the whole time. That's the reason the Unseelie have been struggling to push back the savage creatures along the fringes of the Mists—because they've lost so many people to that freezing sickness.

All three of the coterie members eye me as I limp into the room. This is the first time any of them are seeing me as not just an unusual guest of their lord's but his especially unusual soul-twined mate. My skin twitches under their scrutiny, but I keep my back straight and my head up despite my urge to retreat.

Corwin moves to the chair behind his desk, sticking to formalities even in this company—but I notice he's set up another chair next to his. He beckons me over, and I take that seat, feeling a weird mix of relief at having the buffer of the desk between me and our audience and anxiety over taking a position that marks me as almost an equal to the arch-lord.

"You know Olander and Zelpha," Corwin says. "This is Verik, the longest-serving member of coteries in Heart's Cadence—one of the first to serve my father before me. And now I can introduce you to them properly as my mate."

I rest my hands on the arms of the chair, as much as I'd like to hug myself, and manage a hesitant smile. "Hello."

They all incline their heads in acknowledgement, but their gazes stay just as intent. "It is an honor to have you among us," Zelpha says, in a tone I don't *think* is mocking, although I can't quite believe she totally means it.

Olander turns to his lord. "You said we may have a new strategy for tackling the curse. How did that happen—and how quickly can we get started on it?"

"The how should become clear shortly. As to the other details, we're meeting in order to determine them." Corwin glances at me. "Would you like to provide the initial explanation, as much as you feel is necessary for context?"

He's letting me take the lead to make sure I'm totally okay with everything these Unseelie find out about the summer realm. I nod, appreciating the gesture as much as taking charge in any way in this setting unnerves me. His coterie members are studying me even more penetratingly now.

"You know that the Seelie have been suffering from a curse too," I begin, gathering my words. "One that forces them to shift into their wolf forms and turns them savage on the nights of the full moon? It turns out that somehow I'm connected to that curse..."

As succinctly as I can, I lay out the story of my capture by Aerik and my rescue by Sylas, and the way the Seelie have continued to benefit from my blood to stave off their curse. As I go, my nerves gradually settle.

The only real danger in telling them all this is in the possibility that one of them would see me as too valuable to allow me to return to the summer realm, but the oath I took to the Seelie arch-lords would hurt their own lord through me if they tried to hold me back. And I can see a light of hope coming into at least Zelpha's eyes as she must understand where we're going with this.

I finish by spelling our own hopes out. "Since it seems like the two curses have some connection to each other, we're thinking that I might be able to do something to help with yours too. We just aren't sure what."

Corwin picks up the thread when I pause. "I took her out to see the latest victim today. A draught with a few drops of her blood had no discernable effect, and the woman's condition continued to worsen. So whatever Talia might contribute, it clearly isn't the same as what she offers the Seelie. I'd like us to compile a list of the reasonable possibilities."

Verik gives a soft cough. "This whole situation is—well, I'd say it's preposterous if I didn't know you'd never say all this without clear verification, my lord. But for a human girl, soul-twined mate or not… I hardly think *relying* on such a person—"

"Oh, lay off with the bluster," Zelpha says dryly. "I say we rely on whatever in the lands we can, which is better than the dung-all we've got right now. Anyway, Talia showed she has a good head on her when we were hashing out the issue of the roving beasts."

Verik frowns at her but doesn't say anything further. Corwin watches their minor spat with a calm that soothes my own nerves. He doesn't see anything odd about it; to him, it's all part of the close-knit dynamic that allows them to work together so well.

He might not be best friends with his coterie, but the bonds of trust and cooperation between them hum through the air.

Olander starts to pace, apparently willing to accept the story of my powers and dive right in. "It could be *anything*, couldn't it? Not necessarily giving of her body, but some action or words or—the possibilities are nearly endless."

"Perhaps," Corwin says. "But for the start of our list, we should focus on what we can attempt without causing Talia or the victims significant distress. Or being too overt in what we're attempting at all. If word gets out that we're experimenting with possible cures, I hate to think how tensions will rise unless we're immediately successful, which seems unlikely."

Zelpha drums her fingers against her hip. "A taste of blood seems fitting to the Seelie curse, doesn't it? They go wild, looking to draw blood, and this particular blood cools the urge. What would create a similar association for our troubles?"

That's a good point. My first thought is that I could warm the victims somehow—but I don't tame the Seelie, I give them what they theoretically want. What does the Unseelie's curse drive them to do?

Nothing, really. It locks them in place, preventing them from even moving soon enough. I frown. "Maybe I could try some kind of embrace, like hugging them, if that wouldn't upset them? I guess that sounds silly, but it would be sort of holding them in place like the curse does… I don't think there's any part of me that would work like cooling them off."

"I think that would be worth a try." Corwin scrawls a note on a piece of paper he's set on his desk.

Verik speaks up in a slightly stiff but clear voice. "We should consider other bodily materials regardless of whether we can see a clear association. Skin and hair are easy enough, perhaps muscle and bone which can be derived relatively painlessly with the right magic." He considers me as if expecting me to object.

"I'll try it," I say. "If it could save so many people from dying—there isn't much I wouldn't try."

Olander draws to a halt and swivels to face the desk. "*What* we try isn't our only consideration, is it? My lord, if we go around to every fae the curse strikes with new draughts and a human girl offering embraces and whatever else, word will get around soon that *something* odd is going on. It won't escape the other arch-lords' awareness."

Corwin sighs. "Yes, I've been considering that. We'll have to come up with a suitable story, but they'll have plenty of questions regardless." He turns to me. "I can leave you out of it as much as possible. Claim it's solutions you've suggested from your experiences among the Seelie rather than anything directly *from* you."

His voice carries through our bond at the same time. *I won't let them lay one finger on you, you can be certain of that.*

My own fingers curl toward my palms, but I catch them just before my hands outright clench. Of course I can't expect to try to solve the greatest problem the Unseelie have ever faced without their other arch-lords having any clue.

"All right," I say. "Just… tell them as little as you can get away with."

Because when it comes to his warmongering colleagues, I don't trust *them* to care what happens to me or Corwin if it gets in the way of their goals.

CHAPTER FIVE

Corwin

Mother is never truly calm. Even when I cast the most soothing of spells to saturate her rooms, when I enter I find her huddled in a corner or crouched by the shelter of the table. All even my extensive magical ability can accomplish is to ease the violence of her distress, and that only for perhaps an hour at a time.

Apart from a few grave missteps early on, I believe I've stepped up to the role of arch-lord rather well, especially considering how abrupt, unexpected, and chaotic the transition was. But faced with my mother, I always feel like an utter failure.

Today, she's tucked herself into the nook between the bookshelves and the wall. Her wary eyes track my movements through the strands of her stringy hair. I'm not completely sure she recognizes me at this point. Decades of desperation seem to have worn down her mind to only a few basic impulses, the greatest of which is self-destruction.

I feel like even more of a failure at the thought that passes through my head: perhaps the Heart is wrong about this one thing. Perhaps it would be kinder to let her abandon this life. She hardly seems to be taking any enjoyment from it.

But every fae life is so hard-won and long in coming, who can decide it's right to make such a sacrifice? We may yet end the curse. For all I know, it's played a part in addling her mind, and she could recover if given the chance. It would be a grave crime to steal that opportunity from her.

I tip the chair she's knocked over right side up and sit on it, keeping every motion slow and fluid so I don't startle her nerves. I will my voice to stay perfectly steady as well, holding back the anguish that's collected at the base of my throat at the sight of her. "My soul-twined mate has returned. You met her that one time. I think you'd have liked her when you were well."

Mother offers no response, only a single blink. I continue anyway. "There's a chance she might be able to stem the tide of the curse. We may soon be able to protect so many from the grief you had to experience. I only regret it's taken so long to uncover that possibility. If I could have saved Father…"

The curse moved less swiftly in those days. At first he simply complained of being mildly chilled. Once his limbs began to stiffen, he took to bed for a week before the seeping cold overcame all of his body's functions.

I remember his pose beneath the heaped covers—his face blue and rigid, his arms and legs unnaturally straight—with uncomfortable vividness. He couldn't answer me either, the last few times I spoke to him, not so much as a croak.

Mother shows no sign of caring about my news, but it's impossible to say what might be going on inside her head. It may give her some small comfort even if she isn't fully conscious of the fact.

I take the glazed chocolate truffles I brought for her from my pocket and set them on the table. "I thought you might like a treat. Charles whipped them up this morning. I'd bring some to my meeting in the Hall, but somehow I don't think my colleagues will be swayed by sweets."

I chuckle without much humor. Mother remains still and wary. I may be causing her more distress by staying than I'm comforting her with my company.

Standing, I dip my head to her. "May the Heart shine warmly on you." Then I head out, my own heart heavier than when I came in.

Perhaps it's for the best that I approach the coming discussion carrying a somber weight within me. One wrong step here, and I could jeopardize both my mate's safety and our budding alliance with the Seelie.

As I leave the palace and set off across the plain toward the Hall, Talia must pick up on my growing apprehension from where she's joined Charles and Beth working in the kitchen. She sends a current of fondness my way alongside her soft voice. *You're meeting the other arch-lords now?*

Yes. It may take a while to hash this out. I'll find you when it's done.

Let me know if there's any way I can help. If they want to speak to me directly… I *can lie.*

My lips twitch with an unexpected smile. *Not a skill I ever imagined I'd appreciate, but here we are. I'll spare you their comments for the time being, unless it seems absolutely necessary.* With that, I raise my inner wall of imagined crystal against our connection.

I'm the first to arrive at the meeting room in the Hall of the Heart, but only by a small margin. I'm not often the one to call the meetings here. My colleagues' inquisitiveness over the request grows as each enters the room with the marble table, until the space thrums with unspoken questions as well as the pulse of the Heart's energy.

Neve shuffles in last, even her pale eyes alert with interest rather than clouded by their frequent haze. As the oldest of us reaches her spot at the table, Laoni clears her throat before I can begin, flicking her turquoise hair back from her brawny shoulders. "What's this about, Corwin?"

I tamp down my irritation at her insistence at always being in charge, even though in theory we're all equals. "I have no definite information yet, but there is a matter I felt I should notify you of before I put it into action. There are some new strategies I intend to attempt to defuse the curse."

I hadn't seen any point in beating around the bush. In an instant, all four of my colleagues are staring at me even more piercingly than before.

Laoni's eyebrows rise. "What new strategies are these, and how have you developed them?"

Uzziah lets out a huff, the planes of his doughy face turning even more dour than usual. "And why is this the first we're hearing about them?"

"I only just had the opportunity to consider them myself," I say, picking my words carefully so I'm being truthful without revealing too much. *Only just* is hardly an exact length of time. "We're all aware now that the Seelie have been dealing with a curse of their own. My soul-twined mate has witnessed efforts they've undertaken that have temporarily alleviated its effects."

Terisse makes a derisive sound, folding her coppery arms over her chest. "Why would any solution those wild ones have come up with apply to us?"

"They may not," I say quickly. "But when we haven't yet found any method that works at all, it seemed to me only reasonable that we set aside our pride and try whatever we can. Our people's lives are at stake, after all."

They can hardly argue with that point—as Laoni well knows, from her frustrated grimace. "How do we know these attempts won't make the situation *worse*? Not only are they strategies borrowed from the summer fae, you're gathering them from your *human* companion, who may not have a full understanding of what she's seen."

I resist the urge to bristle on my mate's behalf, glad I blocked our connection off so she wouldn't need to hear this conversation. It's not likely to get kinder.

"Whatever her heritage, she *is* my soul-twined mate," I say evenly. "I've seen her memories; I can confirm her observations and reconsider her interpretations as need be. We certainly know that the Seelie do have an effective cure, given that they were able to shake off the curse in order to push us back during that battle three moons ago."

"There's no disputing that," Uzziah says. "It's simply a matter of caution when dealing with our enemies."

I fix a firm stare on him. "They weren't our enemies until *we* made them that by striking out at them. And my mate is eager to help us in any way she can—I can read how genuine her intentions are through our bond too."

Laoni scoffs. "The mongrels have probably addled her mind. I still don't see why you'd put up with a mate so feeble and—"

I cut her off, letting an edge creep into my voice. "Mind what you say about the partner the Heart chose for me. If you believe the source of all our power could be misguided, I'm not the one you should take that concern up with."

I motion in the direction of the Heart itself just as a fresh pulse of energy washes over us. Laoni's mouth tightens. She'd happily tell *me* that I should defy the Heart's choice, but she wouldn't take action contrary to it herself.

Neve stirs on her feet, speaking up in her reedy voice for the first time. "If this newcomer to our realm can offer a cure to our curse, then I would have to say the Heart has chosen exceedingly well."

At least I have a little support, even if it's from the most frail of my colleagues. I glance around at the others. "I'm simply informing you of my plans as a courtesy so you won't be taken by surprise if you hear reports of my visits with the next victims in the coming days. I require no further involvement unless I find a strategy that does offer concrete benefits."

Terisse cocks her head. "Do you mean to go off and carry out your experiments without even sharing with us what you mean to do?"

"My mate prefers to share her knowledge with no one other than me and my coterie, as she has legitimate reason to worry that other parties among the Unseelie might use it to the Seelie's detriment. She may want to help us, but she still has friends among the summer fae."

Laoni's eyes flash. "Then you would take a dust-destined imbecile's word on—"

I set my hands on the table just forcefully enough to cut her off with the sound. "We're *all* dust-destined if we don't solve this curse. You all have continued to hesitate to reach out to the Seelie directly and make use of what knowledge or resources they might share with us if we explained ourselves. I've found an approach that doesn't require their involvement—you should be glad of that, not fighting it. I've been arch-lord for just past fifty years now; I have the authority to act on my own under conditions such as these."

There's a moment of tense silence. Then Uzziah speaks in a reluctant tone. "I suppose you do have a point there. If we're going to make use of Unseelie strategies, perhaps it's better if we can do so without them even knowing."

That's not the message I wanted them to take away from my proposal, but it may be the best I can get. I incline my head. "Exactly. I won't attempt anything that I can imagine doing the victims any harm. And frankly, the curse steals them away so quickly there's little we could do that would worsen their condition, is there?"

Laoni speaks up again, her voice taut but quiet. "You can't blame us for being concerned, Corwin, given the emotional feebleness that's appeared in your own family line. Perhaps this dung-body has managed to lead you astray through the power of your bond."

My jaw clenches, even though I could have predicted her taking that tactic. The memory of my mother as I left her less than an hour ago swims up through my mind. May none of the figures before me ever have to lose their own mates as horribly as she did.

I will myself calm before I answer. "Do you have any recent evidence that would suggest my capacity for reason is insufficient?"

"You have been awfully keen to make peace with the wolves, even before this mate of yours appeared," Terisse puts in.

"For reasons I've laid out with clear logic," I reply. "I could say that *your* reasons for attacking them rather than negotiating are far from logical, driven by distrust and fear rather than rationality."

Silence stretches again. Laoni rolls her shoulders with a dip of her head as she might ruffle her feathers in raven form. "Your behavior hasn't raised any significant concerns so far. But let us be clear on this: Should it appear your loyalties have been compromised, we won't hesitate to take every necessary action to diffuse that threat."

"Understood," I say, my throat tightening. "I would expect nothing less."

I know without any of them saying it that at this point, it wouldn't take much. One shred of evidence that they can spin into proving I'm no longer fit for this position, and they'll strip me of my title in the blink of an eye.

CHAPTER SIX

Talia

The next curse victim I meet is part of an Unseelie lord's household staff. The lord has set him up in a guest room in one of the turrets of his coral-like castle on the verge of a gray sea.

"Balem is our flock's best metal-worker," the lord says to Corwin in a hushed tone before we go in. "To lose him… He knows true names no one else here has gained."

"We'll do what we can for him," Corwin says. "And if you have a need of assistance later, you only need to send word, and I'll see that someone capable attends to the matter."

The lord bobs his head in gratitude and pushes open the door. As Corwin, Zelpha, and I step into the room, he gives me a curious but not hostile look. All the fae can tell I'm human once they're close enough, of course. Whatever he makes of my presence, he must assume the arch-lord knows what he's doing, because he doesn't question Corwin about it.

No one is attending to Balem at the moment. He's sitting on the bed with his skinny legs stretched out as if bending them would cause him pain, a book propped open on his lap. A glowing yellow ball of magic wafts ineffectual heat from where it hovers next to him.

His head turns jerkily to take us in. When he closes the book with one hand, I notice three of his fingers stay rigidly straight. Only a faint bluish cast colors his pale skin, but the paralysis is already setting in.

His ears show a point nearly as sharp as Corwin's—he must be close to true-blooded. Not that the fae-ness of his heritage matters to the curse. It took Corwin's father, after all.

His voice comes out a bit creaky. "I didn't—I wasn't expecting visitors." He squints as if that's necessary to properly see us, and I notice a frost-like sheen hazing his eyes. His back goes even more rigid than it already was as he recognizes Corwin. "My lord. I—it's an honor."

"I hear you're quite the metal-worker," Corwin says in a calm but warm voice. If I didn't already know how much he cares about his people's well-being, the comfort he's trying to offer in that friendly praise would say it all.

Balem brightens a little despite his chilly pallor. "I do my best. Is there—is there something I can help you with, my lord?"

"Actually, there is." Corwin walks to the side of the bed, beckoning Zelpha and me with him. "I'm sure you must be in grave discomfort, and I'd like to attempt some new methods that might ease your suffering. If you would allow us to? Some of them are rather… unusual, but I'm committed to exploring every possibility, no matter how remote. None of them should do you any further harm."

The man's eyes widen a little. "Yes—yes, of course. I put myself in your hands."

"I only need you to confirm that our attempts will stay between us until I say you may speak of them elsewhere. In such a fraught situation, I want to be sure I have a handle on how the information is spread."

Without a second's hesitation, Balem speaks up in a magic-laced tone. "I swear I will not speak of what you and your companions do in this room without your express permission, my lord."

I'm not sure whether he trusts his ruler that emphatically or he's simply that desperate for a cure. He's definitely going to be a lot more puzzled once we're finished here.

But if anything we try works, nothing else will matter.

We already agreed that I'd attempt the strategies that involve me in action first, mostly because if one of those has an effect, then Zelpha will need to whisk me off to the woman I met yesterday to see if I can help her in her precarious state as well. Verik and Olander went to see her while we came to Balem, bringing the draughts Corwin made this morning using every bodily material I could reasonably offer.

Corwin nods to me. "Talia will tend to you first. Please relax as well as you can and simply accept what she offers."

That sounds more ominous than I hope is accurate. I bring to mind the list of actions we agreed I'd take and limp forward. Balem blinks at me. "It'll just be for a moment," I say awkwardly. Then I wrap my arms around his cool torso, at first gingerly before hugging him a little tighter.

The warmth of my body seems to absorb right into him and vanish, leaving my own skin chilled. I step back, resisting the urge to rub heat back into my arms.

"Tell me about the work you're most proud of," Corwin suggests, drawing the man's attention toward a happier subject while we wait to see if there's any delayed effect. If we try more than one possibility too close together, we won't know which attempt did the trick.

The arch-lord keeps Balem talking for several minutes with no sign of any change. Bracing myself for the man's cold touch, I approach the bed again and reach for just his hand, wrapping my fingers around his. Corwin keeps talking and encouraging Balem's answers as if nothing at all odd is happening.

After a minute, I pry my fingers away. Corwin said the curse isn't contagious like a typical illness, but my joints ache from just that temporary exposure.

I still don't see any difference in the man. I swallow hard, waiting out the passing minutes until Corwin signals me again. Then I start to sing.

I'm not a major talent by any means. It's just one more idea we came up with when brainstorming—to sing a lullaby, fond and soothing. Whether the sentiment would do the trick or the idea of going to sleep would align with the gradual freezing, we have no idea.

As my voice wavers with the lilting words my mother used to sing to me when I was little, I remember a phrase she used to throw around too. *Throwing spaghetti at the wall to see what sticks.* I can't think of any better way to describe what we're doing here.

The rest of the next hour is more of the same: I offer some gesture, Corwin keeps up an amicable conversation with Balem, my heart sinks farther when we get no indication we've affected the curse in the slightest. Zelpha watches the proceedings in silence, but I can't help imagining that the hardened woman must be getting impatient. From the looks of her, she's more a warrior than anything else, like August is for Sylas. Not being able to fight the curse in any clear way must frustrate her.

Finally, I reach the end of our brainstormed list. Corwin thanks me without letting any trace of disappointment show outwardly, but I can feel his sorrow from within. He brings the first draught out from his pockets and hands it to Balem. "Now I have a few potions I'd like you to drink. They should only take one or two swallows to get down."

As the other man tips back the first, Corwin turns to me. "There's no need for you to linger here while I see through the rest of the course. Zelpha, you could take Talia to get some fresh air outside and appreciate the local scenery. You've never visited the sea before."

I open my mouth to protest and then hesitate. Part of me feels like I should stick out the entire process, that I owe it to Balem somehow. But my being here won't change whether or not the draughts work—and maybe he'll be more relaxed with just the arch-lord present and not two other strangers studying his reactions.

Plus, my spirits are so low that I doubt I'm hiding my own disappointment as well as Corwin is. Balem shouldn't have to shoulder my burden on top of his own.

Zelpha grasps my sleeve, tugging me toward the door. "Come on then. There's nothing as bracing as the winter sea atmosphere."

Let me know the moment anything seems to work, I tell Corwin silently.

Of course. You've been wonderful—don't let our lack of progress discourage you.

I don't see how wonderful I could have been if the curse hasn't budged at all. But I follow Zelpha down the spiral staircase and along a hall to one of the palace's outer doors.

The wind rising off the frothing waters is invigorating, brisk and salty and oddly not all that damp against my cheeks. Zelpha motions for me to follow her along the rocky shoreline that stands several feet above the water.

"If you watch closely, you can sometimes spot a siren-sculler in the waves," she says.

I peer more closely at the gray water. "A siren—like a mermaid?"

"Ah, no, they're just fish, nothing more. But they have a captivating twinkling of color to their scales—it's said that they can lure sailors just like the supposed sirens could with their voices."

"So there *aren't* really sirens?"

Zelpha cocks her head as we head down a path jutting from the cliffside, closer to the water. "I suppose there might be. Not in this world. Not *all* your human fables are true, you know."

I find myself raising my eyebrows at her teasing tone. "It's a little hard to be sure when I've found out faeries and werewolves and all kinds of other supposedly imaginary beings are real."

She laughs. "Fair. Well, even if we don't spot a siren-sculler, I'm sure I remember… Here we are! I knew there was *something* I liked about this dreary place."

We come to a stop on a wider ledge, seawater flecking my face. As I walk up beside the coterie woman, my jaw goes slack.

At the end of the path, the cliff falls away into a shallow hollow. The gray stone there has become so polished by the waves that it shines like silver. But that's not what's most striking about the spot. The silvery stone has become worn down in grooves, leaving columns jutting here and there, and as the sunlight bounces between all those shiny surfaces, it splashes images across them that must come from much deeper within the sea.

Brightly colored fish dart by. Luminescent seaweed wavers in and out of view. Glittering currents weave back and forth across the undulating wall. Staring into the hollow, it's as if I've become submerged far down in the ocean where I'd never be able to venture otherwise.

My voice comes out breathless. "Wow. I've never seen anything like that."

"Not bad for a hole in the wall," Zelpha says wryly, propping herself against the duller stone next to us.

She gives me a while to absorb all the wonders of the reflective hollow, watching it not quite as avidly as I am. Once I've taken my fill, my attention slides to her. She seems like the youngest of the coterie members I've met so far—not that any of the adult fae are "young" by human standards—but she's less formal with Corwin than the other two, as if she's more comfortable in his presence.

"How long have you been serving on Corwin's coterie?" I ask.

"Oh, not all that long, but I've been working with him one way or another since close to the beginning of his reign. My… family had become quite close to his, so we got to know each other, and I did everything I could to support him in the early years when he had, well, a lot to deal with."

Was there more beyond his father's death and his mother's grief right at the start? I guess his mother's condition deteriorated somewhat gradually. And he's indicated that the other arch-lords have never been all that keen on having him join their ranks. But Zelpha sounds like she might mean something more than that.

I don't know how to ask without sounding overly prying. And then I don't get a chance, because Zelpha rubs her hand across her mouth and gives me an evaluating look. "You're not sure of him yet. Of any of us."

My head snaps around with a jump of my nerves, but her tone wasn't accusing, at least. "I… I never said that."

She shrugs. "You don't have to. It's obvious with this arrangement you have to go back to the Seelie. You don't need to be there next week when the moon is new, but you want to be. I'm not saying I don't understand. All right, I don't understand how *all* this came to be when you're human—it'd be bizarre even for one of us to randomly contain a cure for the curse. But clearly you couldn't have been expecting the soul-twined bond, and you already have some ties to the wolfish ones. And I suppose they don't speak too kindly about us."

"You haven't given them much reason to lately," I can't help saying.

"I haven't taken part in any of the raids." She sighs. "Anyway, I only wanted to say—he's a good one. Corwin. I'm sure he comes across a bit awkward and all. He's out of practice with the whole romance thing, and after the number that's been done on him— But I can tell how much he likes you already. And I'm seeing why. You've really stepped up. I've no doubt he'll be incredibly devoted to you if you let him be. You won't find a better mate in this realm."

She can't speak to the summer realm the same way, but I hold my tongue about that. The affection in her tone stirs a twinge of curiosity in me. If she's that fond of him…

Zelpha catches my look and chuckles. "No need to speculate. I've never wanted to stake that kind of claim myself. Certainly my own mate would have a lot to say about that, Heart shine on her."

My cheeks flush at the speculation she picked up on, but in the same moment, Zelpha's laughter fades, her gaze shifting to a point behind me.

I turn to see Corwin approaching, his mouth set in a tight line. He's walled his emotions off from me, but I don't need our bond to tell how downcast his mood is. Before he even speaks, I know what he's going to say.

He inhales sharply. "Nothing worked, at least not yet. Come, we'd best be getting home."

CHAPTER SEVEN

Talia

When the news comes that Balem has passed away, all I want to do is burrow into my bed as if I can escape the final confirmation of our failure there. I've been moping in my room for a couple of hours when Corwin reaches out to me through our bond.

We tried everything we could think of—and we'll think of more. After all these years, it'd be surprising if we stumbled on the answer on the first or second try.

I know, I reply, flipping over on the bed and scowling at the ceiling. *It just seems so easy with the Seelie curse. I don't like that there might be something I can do that could stop people from* dying, *and I'm missing it.*

Perhaps more ideas will come to us if we give our minds a break from stewing over it. The unconscious can sometimes piece together problems better without our focused interference. Corwin pauses, and I sense that he's come to a stop in the hall outside my room. *We haven't had much chance to simply enjoy each other's company. Would you join me for a small outing including lunch?*

I don't feel particularly hungry, but he has a point about taking a break from brainstorming. And lying on my bed in a cloud of gloom isn't helping anyone. I shove aside the blankets and reach for my boots. *All right. I'm just not sure whether my company will be all that enjoyable right now.*

A hint of a smile travels through our connection. *I never fail to find you delightful.*

I could point out that there were at least a few times he found me less than delightful when we were first getting to know each other, like when I told him off for criticizing the Seelie or for messing with my memories of my other lovers, but he has taken those criticisms to heart with more grace than I'd have expected. Why bring up past troubles that don't matter anymore when we have plenty to deal with right here in the present?

Corwin stands just beyond my doorway, the handle of a silver basket slung over his lean forearm. "I thought you might like to get a closer look at the frostfire forest," he says. "There's a spot there I'm rather fond of. Since it isn't very far… we could fly."

I'm about to say that we were flying the last time we passed it—in the carriage—when I catch a flicker of a thought that tells me he means by his own power, using his wings. A weird shivery tingle races over my skin. He's only taken me on a short flight that way before, down into the flock village along the cliffside. It was a little scary, but also exhilarating.

And the bond immediately urges me toward him, seeking out that closeness.

I rein in the urge, but I nod at the same time. I *am* supposed to be figuring out my relationship with him as well as attempting to cure the curse while I'm here. "All right. As long as it won't tire you out too much."

He smiles, one of the rare wider ones that warms me to the core. "I'm certain I'm up to the task."

He escorts me out into the broad diamond terrace at the back of his palace, overlooking the cliff that holds his flock's village and the vast landscape beyond it. With a rustle of feathers and a warble of the wind, his wings spring into being, the black shapes fanning out on either side of him.

An even giddier tingle passes through me at the sight. Corwin never looks quite so much in his element as when he shows his raven side.

After pushing the basket all the way to his elbow, he holds out his arms to me. I step closer and let him scoop me up to his chest. My forehead comes to rest against the side of his neck, the meeting of skin against skin deepening our connection with a sudden thrum of emotion—and desire.

I do my best to ignore the more intimate sorts of heat flowing through me and brace myself for the takeoff. Corwin flaps his wings, there's a slight hitch as we leave the ground behind, and then we're soaring over the edge of the cliff.

I turn my head so I can take in the view and watch the snow-and-ice-covered terrain around us whip by. Corwin swoops in a gentle arc with a shift in the breeze, veering toward the glittering forest he pointed out to me a few days ago. I don't let myself think about the journey we were on then or how it ended.

It does occur to me that while I've been distracted by trying to tackle the curse, there are other problems I haven't really gotten answers to. Maybe having Corwin totally alone will make for a good time to ask those questions.

Corwin glides lower over the forest and falls into a loose spiral with easy flaps of his wings. We descend into a small glade amid the trees. Their dark branches, nearly the same blue-black shade as his hair, hold dozens of icicles, but rather than jutting down like I'd expect, these point upward. They waver as if they're not quite solid at all—as if they're cool blue-white flames.

"I can see how this place got its name," I say as Corwin sets me down.

He glances around us. "It can seem eerie, but I find it peaceful. And this clearing offers one of the best views with the sun streaming in and the stone providing a seat."

He motions to the large slab of mica-laced granite that fills the middle of the glade, at least ten feet long and nearly as wide. Setting the basket down at the edge, he pulls out a thin span of pale fabric. When he unfurls it, warmth wafts through the air against my face. It's got a spell on it just like our clothes.

I climb onto the rock and settle onto the blanket. As Corwin lays out the lunch he must have had Charles and Beth pack for us, I gaze around at the forest some more. The beaming sunlight really does amplify the effect, making the icicles it catches on appear to outright dance. The breeze whispers through them with a faint melodic hum I suspect Corwin appreciates as well.

"I was digging around in our store rooms while you were gone," the arch-lord says, bringing my attention back to him. He holds up a pair of bronze spoons. "I found these—I think they must have been a gift or from a trade back when relations between the summer and winter realms were more cordial. You might have noticed we tend to favor silver here."

I hadn't really thought about it until he mentioned it just now. As I take one of the spoons from him, the true-name for bronze runs through my mind. I shove it aside with a hitch of my pulse. I haven't decided for sure when or how to tell Corwin about my other abilities.

"I don't mind the silver," I tell him.

He shrugs with a small but relaxed smile. "I thought it was fitting to bring them out while we're trying to make strides toward renewed peace."

He doles out soup from a small sealed tureen into two bowls and slides one toward me, alongside a platter heaped with dumplings I know on sight are stuffed full of spiced meats and vegetables. My mouth starts to water despite my earlier hesitation about eating. Then he breaks off two of the icicles, tipping them over into a sort of cups and offering one to me.

Like he mentioned when he pointed the forest out to me, the center of the ice is already melting with a thin wisp of steam. I bring it to my lips and take a tentative sip. The liquid that seeps across my tongue has a startling tangy, spicy flavor that reminds me of hot apple cider.

I alternate between the strange drink and the soup, the peppery broth warming me up even more from the inside. Corwin watches me as he eats, his happiness at seeing my enjoyment radiating into me. I'm finished faster than I expected. Picking up one of the dumplings, I decide I'd better get on with the potentially awkward part of the conversation.

"Corwin… You told me the curse had something to do with why your people have been attacking the Seelie. But I haven't seen anything yet that explains the raids. Why would this strange freezing illness make anyone think barging into the summer realm was a good idea?"

Corwin grimaces. "I'm sorry. I should have thought to explain all of it right away. I keep hoping my colleagues will see reason…" He rubs the heel of his hand against his forehead. "It will probably sound somewhat ridiculous that we've carried on for so long, but I think once the idea took root and we were foiled in our attempts to test it, many of the arch-lords and lesser lords dug in their heels and became increasingly adamant about it."

"About *what*?" I ask.

He picks up a dumpling of his own but doesn't bring it to his mouth. "You have to remember that until recently, we didn't know the Seelie were suffering from a curse as well. Many Unseelie assumed the summer fae were responsible for our malady—that it was an attempt at weakening us for some later assault. So Unseelie feelings toward the wolves were… not particularly friendly in general."

"Why would the Seelie want to hurt you anyway? It's not like you have anything they need, do you?"

Corwin spreads his hands. "I don't know, but we could have possessed something they desired without knowing it. In any case, resentment and hostility had been growing for some time, and then around three decades ago, a couple of my colleagues hit upon the idea that the summer realm might hold the cure to the curse as well as the cause. Since the condition involves extreme cold, they thought that victims brought to the summer realm might recover there—or else that living in the summer realm might prevent the curse from striking in the first place."

The pieces are starting to fall into place in my head. "But no one wanted to *ask* the Seelie if you could intrude on their territory when you suspected they might have been out to weaken you to begin with."

"Exactly. So a small party including one victim of the curse made to cross over and set up a temporary camp just beyond the border, far enough from the Heart for the vow not to be necessary. From what I understand, Seelie sentries came upon them sooner than expected, harsh words were exchanged, and the encounter ended with blood spilled on both sides."

Which the Unseelie probably took as proof of the Seelie's animosity, while the Seelie would simply have known that they'd been defending against apparently aggressive intruders. I shake my head. "Let me guess—after that they decided they had to go in fighting right off the bat."

"Essentially." Corwin dabs the dumpling in the remains of his soup. "The plan evolved into the idea that we needed to capture a decent section of summer territory to claim as our own and hold off the Seelie while we determined whether living there alleviated the curse. But we never managed to hold onto any ground for long enough to judge, and frustrations on our side—and the Seelie's, no doubt—only increased with each failure."

"You could have just asked," I said quietly. "In the beginning, before any of the fighting. I'm sure they'd have agreed to let you set up some kind of temporary settlement then."

"You may be right. But we didn't know that, and so much has happened since then…" He exhales sharply. "But now at least we seem to have reached an agreement that the fighting is only resulting in more lives lost without gaining us anything. My fellow arch-lords remain hesitant about admitting our weakness to the Seelie, though, even knowing the summer realm lies under its own curse."

His gaze has drifted away from me. Now it slides back. He considers me for a moment before saying, "I've started to wonder whether the Heart isn't responsible for inflicting this curse on all of us—as a punishment for letting our opposing sides drift so far apart in temperament and understanding and as a way of ultimately uniting us as allies once again. Perhaps that's why it brought you to us as well."

There's a rightness to that idea that grips me. "But do you really think the Heart would be that cruel to you?"

"Perhaps it wasn't totally in control once the die was cast, and our own mistakes following that are to blame for how the situation has worsened. The Heart is the power of the natural world, and nature can be harsh. Rot and raging storms serve as much of a purpose as anything of beauty."

"I guess that's true." I take a bite of my dumpling and chew it slowly, mulling that idea over. I don't want to be a bullet point in some lesson the Heart is trying to teach the fae, but there are worse purposes to have. At least I can hope that possibility would mean the solution isn't too far beyond our reach.

"The other arch-lords *have* to talk to the Seelie about this," I say. "The sooner they can actually test out their theory about the summer realm, the closer we'll be to ending the curse."

Corwin nods. "I'm doing my best. But wariness is deeply ingrained in our natures. I think it's only a matter of time. They can't avoid seeing that it's the only reasonable approach."

"I'd like to go back to Sylas with good news about confirming the peace."

Corwin's smile comes back, bittersweet this time. "And I'd like to give you that news."

We finish the meal in contemplative silence. Then Corwin reaches tentatively across the blanket to rest his hand over mine. His touch sparks a jolt of heat. "Beyond all the concerns about the curse, how have you been feeling about this visit, my mate? Have you been lonely without your friend around?"

There's so much affection in his words and flowing through our bond that a lump fills my throat. "No, I think I'm fine without her now. We've been so busy anyway—and I'm glad that I can spend some time just with you without worrying about *her* being lonely."

"If there's anything else I can offer that you might want…"

"I know." I turn my hand to twine my fingers with his. "I have enough." If anything, the problem is having too *much*, not too little.

But right now with our hands clasped together, I can't deny the urge to get closer to him. I scoot across the blanket and tuck myself next to him, snuggling in even more when he puts his arm around me. His air of total contentment and his foresty scent envelop me.

Our embrace doesn't quite satisfy the tug inside me. With his scent comes the awareness of how close the bare skin of his neck is to my lips. Would it taste the same way he smells?

The question and the longing it rides on stir up a twinge of guilt with the memory of my other lovers, but only for a moment. I got way closer than this with my Seelie men while Corwin waited for me on the other side of the border. Sylas, Whitt, and August all expect that I'll become closer with him.

If I indulge that longing just a little, I'm not doing anything wrong. I don't have to go any farther than I'm comfortable with.

I twist in Corwin's arms, tipping my head so my mouth grazes the base of his throat. A wave of desire sweeps through me, both my own and his through the bond.

Corwin holds perfectly still, letting me press another gentle kiss and then a more determined one against the warm column of his neck. The rush of physical connection aligning with our emotional bond leaves me giddy.

Talia, Corwin says with a hint of a groan that sends heat spiking low in my belly. Do I really want to stop at all?

I aim the next kiss higher, brushing the corner of his jaw. His arm tightens around me—and a savage shriek splits through the peaceful forest.

I jerk back just in time to see a gray, wrinkled creature that looks like some kind of panther-rhinoceros hybrid lunging through the trees toward us. It opens its maw to let out another shriek, revealing jagged teeth that glint like glass.

Corwin whips around, spitting out a spell that slams into the beast. His magic tosses it to the side just a few feet from our granite seat. The creature stumbles but whirls around as if it's barely fazed. When Corwin hurls another spell at it, it appears to leap out of the way and launches itself toward me instead.

My pulse hiccups, and my body reacts on instinct. My hand shoots out to grasp one of the bronze spoons. The syllables I've hidden for so long stick in the back of my mouth for a split-second, but I'd rather reveal the secret than risk either of us getting hurt. Which maybe is all I need to know.

"*Fee-doom-ace-own!*" I shout, brandishing the spoon. The true name sends a flare of power through my fingers, and the utensil jerks and lengthens into a thin bronze spear. I jab it toward the beast's chest, my other hand braced against the stone beneath me.

The flash of the metal sends the creature veering to the side again, just as Corwin snaps out another magically-charged word of his own. This time, his spell hits the mark. Rather than battering the creature, it freezes the beast in mid-lunge.

The thing wobbles and then topples over onto its side. Corwin sucks in a breath with a muttered curse. "A searmaw, all the way out here…" He trails off, his gaze dropping to my spoon-turned-spear and then locking with my eyes. The punch of shock as he processes what I did echoes into me. "You—you used a true name."

My face flushes. "I was nervous about telling you. I don't have very much power, and I've only managed to learn a few. I don't have the marks or anything. We haven't been able to figure out why."

Our bond is open; he must be able to tell I'm being truthful. He keeps staring at me. Then he lets out a soft chuckle. "And you continue to surprise me, Talia. The Heart definitely looks kindly on you." He hesitates. "I want to hear all about it, but… I think it's best we don't let the rest of my people find out about *that* irregularity just yet. It'll be one more element for my colleagues to be suspicious about."

I nod, torn between relief that he's only startled, not upset, and a sinking sensation at his last remarks. I already knew my unusual powers might cause more controversy. Now, I can't help thinking that I could tear apart the emerging peace just as easily as strengthen it.

CHAPTER EIGHT

Talia

Corwin's fingers dance across the harp's shimmering strings. The vibrant music reverberates through the air, seeming to seep right through my flesh into my bones. I can't help swaying with it on the bench I'm watching from, a smile touching my lips.

The instrument is enchanted, but I'm not sure any other musician could produce notes quite so sweet from it. The Unseelie arch-lord becomes totally absorbed in his playing, adjusting his stance as if he's conjuring the melody with his entire body. Music is one of the few things Corwin appears to enjoy without any bittersweet or outright tragic overtones weighing it down.

Which is why I suggested we come to the music room. After I explained and showed everything I could about my experience with true names so far, he had me demonstrate—but I struggled to will any light into being. My spirit was still too heavy from our failures over the curse. Yesterday he asked what might bring me enough happiness that I could manage it, and we ended up in here.

It worked then, and it works again now. The delight of the

moment has lit a sort of glow inside me. As Corwin lowers his arms, the last notes fading from the air, I raise my own hands and murmur to the space between them. "*Sole-un-straw.*"

A soft, golden light forms between my palms. I hold it out to him as if I could give it as a gift. From Corwin's expression and the satisfaction that trickles through our bond, it's enough of a gift just watching me do it—knowing that he can make me happy enough to create this minor magic.

"Perhaps there are more true names I'd be able to teach you, so you can continue your studies during the weeks when you're here," he says. "I appreciate you having some additional means of defense in this world that can be so dangerous even for fae, let alone a human."

Even more joy swells inside me at his offer. It was enough that he wasn't upset about me hiding my small talent from him or disturbed that I have it. For him to want to support my emerging skills in any way he can is more than I'd dared to hope.

"I'd like that," I say. "I know I'll never be on equal footing with an actual fae, but it is nice knowing I have ways of protecting myself that fit this world. Thank you."

He beams at me, and a different sort of delight flickers through me with an edge of desire. Catching it, Corwin rises and comes to sit next to me on the bench. When he traces his lithe fingers along my jaw, I tip my head instinctively to receive his kiss.

It's still overwhelming, the demanding rush of pleasure and longing that crashes through me whenever our mouths meet. After our brief intimate interlude in the frostfire forest, I've indulged the urging of the bond—and my own attraction to my soul-twined mate—a couple of times, feeling it out, deciding how much I want, and hoping my mind and body might adjust to the headiness of it so that the flood of heat doesn't carry me away quite so much. But I can't say it's become any less intense with practice.

Maybe it won't until we've joined in every possible way.

Maybe it won't *ever*. This might be one more reason why the fae treasure their soul-twined mates so much.

And it's not exactly surprising the way the heat builds, flaring hotter with each shift of my lips against his, each careful caress he offers. I'm drinking in not just my own reactions to this intimacy but his as well. I can feel him reveling in the softness of my mouth and skin, taking glee in the stutter of breath he provokes when he teases his fingertips into my hair.

I sense without him saying anything, without us even breaking the kiss, his desire to see how much more pleasure he can stroke into being. I lean into his touch without thinking, seeking what he's offering.

He hesitates for a second as if confirming my reaction and then trails his fingers down the side of my face, over my neck and shoulder, to cup my breast. At the sweep of his thumb over its peak and the giddy jolt that comes with the caress, a hungry sound escapes me. Even more heat courses through me, pooling between my legs with an urgency that still unnerves me.

Corwin feels the bond's pull just as much as I do. I can sense how much passion he's holding back so that I can set the pace. I want all of it, and yet—thinking of my Seelie lovers and all the uncertainty about my place in the realms—will it become too hard to walk away once I've given in to our connection that much?

Picking up on my conflicted emotions, Corwin eases back. He presses a gentler kiss to my temple with a sniff of my skin. "We don't have to do anything more. I will say, though—you were fertile two days ago but no longer, so there wouldn't be any lasting consequences. Consummating the desire won't bind you to me any more than we're already connected. It's the confirmation ceremony that solidifies the soul-twined bond."

I let out a shaky laugh. "Well, that's good to know." I'm still not sure my own emotional state is up to navigating that kind of closeness with him before I've decided whether I want our overall closeness to last for the rest of my life.

Corwin shows no sign of impatience. I guess for a nearly immortal fae, waiting a few weeks is like a few hours for a human. I tip my head against his shoulder, still enjoying his warmth and the feel of his lean muscles.

A different thread of tension winds through my gut. He *will* have to wait at least another week. Tomorrow my seven days here are up, and I return to the summer realm—with a few more answers but barely anything accomplished. I'm not any closer to figuring out how to handle my personal affections, and while we've discussed additional strategies for dealing with the curse, there haven't been any new victims to attempt to cure.

"When are you meeting with the other arch-lords again?" I have to ask, even though I know that subject will ruin the contented mood of the moment.

"In a couple of hours, after dinner. We need to discuss the growing incursion of hostile beasts into the domains, but I'll push the idea of opening negotiations with the Seelie again. Unfortunately, I've already put forward all the arguments I can. I suspect at this point it's simply a matter of waiting them out while I wear down their sense of caution."

Waiting them out for how long while most of my wolfish companions see the ravens as the enemy, while more winter fae die of the curse who might not have to? I itch with impatience. *I've* been doing everything I can as a frail mortal so many fae like to sneer at, and what are the other arch-lords contributing other than standing around making snarky remarks about Corwin's judgment?

I pause, my thoughts circling back. *Have* I done everything I possibly can?

Corwin runs his thumb over the peak of my shoulder. "What are you thinking, my mate? I can sense the gears turning in your head."

My mouth twitches with a smile. "I just—" I balk for a second, and then Beth's words from an earlier evening come back to me. *We might as well act the way we want and ask for what we need, or what's the point in being alive at all?*

I sit up straighter, raising my chin. "What if—what if I came with you? To the meeting? I can speak on behalf of the Seelie. I can vouch that their arch-lords would work with you all to find a solution to the curse, not exploit it."

Corwin stiffens. "I—It would be highly unusual to include you. We rarely have even our coterie members join us at the meetings."

"But you'd bring in another fae if they had something important to contribute, wouldn't you? And it's not as if the meetings are totally secret from soul-twined mates even if I'm not in the room with you."

"While that is true, I don't imagine my colleagues would see the matter as being quite so simple."

His arm tightens around me with a protective vibe, but that's not the only emotion that carries through our bond. I taste a quiver of anxiety not just about how the other arch-lords will respond to me but also how… how *he* will act in my presence.

I frown up at him. "What are you worried will happen if I'm there? I won't do anything to embarrass you. I've been around fae enough to know how to be properly polite and whatever."

Corwin's mouth opens and closes before he pulls together an answer. "It's not you. It's how I feel about you. I can keep a calm, controlled front with the other arch-lords when we're apart, but if you're right there, if I have to witness them insulting you…"

Images and bits of speech flicker to me from his memories: his colleagues criticizing his attachment to me, accusing him of being unstable, rubbing his family's history in his face. My hackles rise on his behalf. "Caring about me doesn't make you *weak*. Don't they care about their mates?"

Corwin rubs his face. "They do, but none of their mates are humans who'd face so much additional scrutiny and be less equipped to fend it off themselves."

I let out a huff, squeezing his hand. "I can fend for myself just fine. Maybe that's where your problem is. You're assuming you'd need to get upset on my behalf. I know what kinds of things a lot of the fae think about me. I've heard worse than I'm sure the arch-lords would stoop to in front of you. They're not going to throw magic at me or challenge me to a sword fight, are they?"

"No," Corwin admits, his tone going a bit dry. "As much as a couple of them might like the idea of doing so."

"Then I can handle it, and you need to give me the chance to show I can. If I can't survive four fae sneering at me, then I don't deserve to be your mate anyway."

Corwin blinks at me and then lets out a rough chuckle. I can tell he's still nervous, but he dips his head. "All right. If you can be as convincing with them as you just were with me, you might have a real chance."

When we step into the meeting room in the building Corwin calls the Hall of the Heart, I don't need any kind of soul connection to gauge his colleagues' reaction. All four of the imposing figures standing around the large marble table go rigid. The thrum of the Heart's energy, so close by, raises the hairs on my arms and the back of my neck.

"What is the meaning of this?" snaps the burly woman with the turquoise hair, glowering at us so menacingly that Corwin stops in his tracks, halting me with him. I remember her from the night the Unseelie appeared at Sylas's coronation—the night I discovered my soul-twined bond to Corwin. She acted as if she was the leader of the group. It appears that's the case even without a larger audience.

Corwin grasps my shoulder. His voice comes out steady, but tension winds through it. "My mate has an appeal to make on behalf of both our people and the Seelie in regard to the curse. I believe it's worth hearing her out."

A depressed-looking man with bags under his eyes shakes his head. "We already granted you some leniency in attempting your treatments for the curse on her suggestion, Corwin, for all the good it's done. Our generosity can only extend so—"

I clear my throat, cutting him off. Corwin's grip tightens, but he doesn't move to stop me from speaking.

"You all have had around seventy years to find a way to reverse the curse, and so far you haven't succeeded," I say, as evenly as I can manage with my stomach twisted into one huge knot of nerves. "Isn't it a little much to call my efforts pointless after just one week?"

The woman's gaze sharpens into a glare. "This is a sacred space, no place for your kind."

I stare right back at her, refusing to cower the way she'd clearly like. "The Heart has decided to give me a soul-twined mate from among the highest of the Unseelie, so I don't think it objects to me.

What exactly would hearing me speak hurt? You have thousands of years to live. All I'm asking is that you spare a few minutes to listen to what I have to say, since I'm the only person in a long time who's become familiar with fae on both sides of the border."

They think they're so high and mighty with all their talk of logic and reason—let's hear them give one logical argument to that.

The man stirs on his feet uneasily. Another woman, with tufts of dark green hair framing her copper-brown face, works her jaw but can't seem to think of how to respond.

And the fifth arch-lord, a thin, pale woman who looks like she could have been constructed out of peach fuzz and dandelion fluff, taps her wizened hand against the tabletop. Her voice is barely a wisp but still firm. "I say we let her speak."

The burly woman's jaw clenches, but apparently she can't think of any way listening to me would harm them either. "All right. Let's have it quickly, then," she says, sounding as if she's restraining a sigh.

Corwin releases my shoulder, and we walk up to the table together, slowly so my limp doesn't become too pronounced. He bobs his head. "I appreciate your open minds."

Ha. I manage not to roll my eyes and rest my hands on the cool marble. Pulling myself as tall as I can, I glance around the table, not shying from any of the gazes fixed on me, however hostile. "Tomorrow I return to the summer realm for a week. I'd like to come to the Seelie arch-lords with the news that you'll be arranging a parlay to open negotiations—so that you can determine whether spending time in the summer realm cures the curse or prevents it from taking hold."

The burly woman's expression darkens with a scowl. "Of course you'd suggest that we reveal our most fraught weakness to them. Anything to benefit your keepers."

I focus on her. "How could finding out about your curse possibly benefit the Seelie? They already know you've lost some of your population through the battles *you've* instigated. They can't predict where or who the curse will strike any better than you can. And even though it should be obvious to you by now that they weren't behind the curse since they're dealing with their own, if they *were*, then they'd already know about it. They've only become your enemies because you treated them like that instead of having a conversation in the first place."

The somber man shifts his weight again. "You can't possibly know all the means by which other fae could exploit the information."

My heart is pounding, but I fold my arms over my chest. "No, maybe I can't. But unless you can mention one of those ways, one that sounds plausible, I'm going to keep saying that you're risking more by avoiding reaching out than by finally doing it. Just in the week I've been here, two of your people have *died*. If you'd talked to the Seelie already, maybe those two people could have lived. How many of the Unseelie you're supposed to be serving are you going to let down out of this paranoia?"

Giving their caution such an irrational label makes the three main figures around the table bristle. The elderly woman is gazing off into space as if she's listening to a song only she can hear, but I'll take that over more skepticism.

"The impertinence," the man sputters.

"Did you come here to discuss the subject or to insult us?" the burly woman demands.

I gaze back at her, my muscles tensed to hold back a shiver at the power she emanates. "I didn't mean it as an insult. I'm using the word by its standard definition, based on the information I have. You're worried that the Seelie would strike out against you somehow. Why would they now when they've refused to go on the offensive after all the years you've been attacking *them*?"

The copper-skinned woman frowns. "Why *wouldn't* they want to retaliate?"

I resist the urge to grit my teeth in frustration. "They've been avoiding that specifically to hold onto the higher ground before the Heart. They don't want anything you have—they only want the violence you're committing to stop. Finding out about your curse isn't going to change that."

If only they could see how much they're like the Seelie despite all the lines they try to draw between the realms. Celia and Donovan acted on similar motivations when they took Corwin captive. But I managed to convince Donovan that peace was still possible. What will it take for these fae to recognize the same thing?

From the look the burly woman is giving me, it'll take more than I can provide. The sneer I was expecting colors her tone. "We certainly aren't going to share our suspicions and strategies with you right before you return to the rampaging wolves."

I drag in a slow breath. I'm not sure there's anything else I can say anyway, but I can't drop my case without making one more appeal to the rationality they claim to prize so highly.

"Fine. You don't have to. All I can say is that from all my observations and conversations among the Seelie, which I've had many of considering I'm in an arch-lord's pack and he respects my opinion, the summer fae have no interest in hurting you or taking anything from you. I have every reason to believe they'd let you set up a small community in the summer realm to test out your theory. Corwin can attest to my honesty on everything I've said."

Beside me, my mate nods. "I've seen it through the bond and in conversation with her arch-lord with my own eyes." The strain of staying silent during the rest of this conversation trickles through to me, but he gives me the space to go on.

I send a tendril of thanks his way and lift my voice once more. "I've told you everything you should need to know to realize you can take this opportunity to try to help your people. Either you can decide not to listen to me, because I'm a human and you judge me as unworthy simply because of that, or you can recognize how much sense I've made and act like the level-headed rulers you're supposed to be. That's up to you."

I step back from the table, my chest constricting even though I'm done. The Unseelie arch-lords are staring at me again, even the elderly one this time. She speaks first, in a slightly louder voice. "Regardless of her heritage, the girl's words ring true. The Heart did choose her for our own."

The burly woman's mouth twists, and she opens it as if she's about to protest, but the copper-skinned woman twitches anxiously and beats her to it. "I think we should attempt the parlay. As soon as possible. We can't let our people continue dying over vague, unproven fears."

"Terisse," the burly woman hisses, but even the man is starting to nod. I don't know if they need a full consensus to make the final decision, but my heart starts to lift.

Corwin brushes his knuckles against the back of my hand. *It may take more discussion, but—I believe you have them, my mate.*

CHAPTER NINE

August

There's nothing quite like the moment when Talia emerges from the haze of the border to meet us. I always find her beautiful, but something about spending days missing her presence amplifies the joy of seeing her again to the point that my heart swells close to bursting.

She limps over to us with a brilliant smile, accepting my hug with a tight embrace of her own, but her happiness isn't as unrestrained as the first time she returned to us. A worry line has formed in the middle of her brow. As she nestles against me, she turns in my arms to look back the way she came.

Corwin followed her out, carrying her trunk. As Whitt strides over to accept it from him, the Unseelie arch-lord catches Sylas's eye. "Arch-Lord Sylas, if I could speak with you and your fellow arch-lords briefly… I'd like to see about arranging a formal parlay between all of you and the arch-lords of winter."

The Unseelie rulers are ready to have a proper meeting with ours? Sylas's eyebrows rise, but he strides over with a dip of his head. "Of course. Astrid, would you see about summoning Arch-Lords Donovan and Celia to the Bastion of the Heart? I'll meet them there." He turns back to Corwin. "Perhaps you and I should go over the gist of the situation just the two of us before bringing it to a larger audience."

Corwin smiles grimly. "I can see that might be advisable." His gaze slides past Sylas to Talia, still in my arms. I tense instinctively, bracing for hostility from her soul-twined mate at the sight of her so close to another man, but he simply shoots her a softer smile. She nods to him. I get the sense of unspoken communication passing between them before he turns to walk with Sylas.

I know how lucky I am to have this woman in my arms at all when the Heart has bound her to another, but the knowledge that I'll never have as much closeness with her as *he* does niggles at me anyway.

Whitt cocks his head toward her. "Managed to convince them to have a civilized sit-down, did you?"

Talia slips from my embrace but takes my hand as we set off toward the castle. "Corwin didn't take any convincing. He's been wanting a parlay like this for ages before I was in the picture. But… I think I might have been a major factor in swaying the others."

My brother chuckles. "I'd expect nothing less from our mighty one. Woe betide any who underestimate you."

I can't summon as much good humor as he can about the situation, but then, Whitt can find humor in just about anything.

The Unseelie are going to speak with us—good. But what are they going to say? What if they only make demands and threats that'll make us wish they'd stuck to skirmishes along the border?

Whitt sidles up to Talia as we reach the castle's doorway and nudges her with his elbow. "I don't suppose you have more details on what this parlay will involve."

She elbows him back fondly. "I do, actually, but I thought it'd be better to discuss them somewhere more private."

"Hmm. Let us take this conversation to my office, then."

We stop at Talia's bedroom to drop off her trunk and make our way into Whitt's new office. He's moved all his belongings over from the old castle at Hearthshire now, managing to make the larger space here look full. I wonder if he's actually read all the books lining his built-in shelves and whether he really has any idea what half of the curiosities placed among them are meant to do.

His office back in Oakmeet always held a faint tang of alcohol. I find I'm relieved that his new space smells only of leather bindings and wood. I haven't seen him partaking from his flask much in recent weeks other than during his periodic revels. Talia's position here may have become more uncertain, but my brothers have found their footing with each other—and perhaps themselves—in a way I appreciate seeing.

Talia immediately drops into one of the armchairs, curling up her legs and leaning back as if she needs the support. Whitt props himself against the edge of his desk as expected, and I stay by the door I've just closed.

Talia rubs her mouth, the furrow in her brow deepening. "I guess I should jump right in. Corwin said it was okay for me to tell you this, since he'll be telling Sylas anyway, but it's better if his colleagues get to be the ones to tell the other arch-lords."

"Understood," Whitt says. "Our lips will remain sealed."

He glances at me, and I nod. Who would I tell?

"All right." Talia's hands clasp together and then release as she gathers her words. "The main thing is, the Unseelie have been facing a curse too—one that seems to have started and gotten worse on pretty much the same timeline as yours."

"What?" I burst out. Of all the news she could have shared, I'd never have expected that, even if it doesn't sound so odd once I have a moment to think about it.

The corner of Talia's mouth curves up at a wry angle. "I had no idea either until Corwin told me. They've hidden it well. And it's not as if there's been much conversation across the border anyway, right?"

Whitt has drawn himself up straighter with increased alertness. "And has it turned out you're tied to this second curse as well?"

My gut lurches as that line of reasoning catches up with me. It might not even be a different curse but the same one. If the Unseelie have that kind of claim on Talia as well as the mate bond, they might insist on having her in their realm for even more of the time.

Talia curls deeper into her chair as if under the weight of a heavy burden. "We haven't figured that out yet, but it seems likely. Let me explain everything we know so far."

As she tells us about the freezing illness that's struck the Unseelie and her attempts with Corwin and his coterie to cure it, her shoulders tense and a hint of strain creeps into her voice. She *is* carrying a heavy burden—the thought of all the deaths she couldn't prevent, the uncertainty of whether she can stop more in the future. It's dimmed her usual hopeful light just a little.

Even though I can't blame Corwin for accepting her help when so much is at stake—even though I know Talia would have insisted on it if he'd tried to stop her, which for all I know he did—I kind of want to strangle him. Not that doing so would make *her* feel any better. I settle for flexing my hands at my sides.

Whitt asks a few questions that are clearly based on some historical or cultural understanding he probably picked up from all the books around us, and Talia answers as well as she can. She tucks a stray strand of hair behind her ear and gives us another tight smile. "I'm sure I don't know everything the Unseelie have done to investigate the curse, but you all haven't been able to figure out much about yours either, so it's not really surprising that they've struggled too."

That's true. I step forward, about to reassure her that she's clearly gone above and beyond in trying to help the blasted ravens, when the door swings open. Sylas strides in, looking even more regal than usual. "Ah ha, here you all are." His gaze fixes on Talia. "I take it you've been filling in my cadre? Astrid learned of the new developments during our brief meeting in the Bastion with Corwin."

Talia springs to her feet with a swish of her vibrant hair, her eyes wide and anxious. "Did Donovan and Celia agree to the parlay? How soon will it be happening?"

Sylas goes to her as I meant to, setting a gentle hand on her shoulder. "Everything has been arranged. We'll meet in the clearing by the Heart, where I had my coronation celebration, with the three of us taking oaths that we'll do or order no harm as the Unseelie have requested. They should be arriving tomorrow."

"All right." Talia bites her lip. "Maybe I should talk with all three of you—see if there's anything I can tell you about what to expect that

Corwin might not have covered. I'm sure he's been truthful, but he won't have wanted to paint his colleagues in a bad light..."

From her tone, clearly there are bad things *she* could say about them. I bristle inwardly again.

I can tell Sylas would like to keep her out of the thick of this conflict too, but there isn't much either of us can do when she's already so entwined. He has to think of what's best for all of us.

"That might be a wise idea," he says. "Come with me, then. We were already planning on having a longer meeting after we'd consulted with our cadres."

Whitt gathers himself, since obviously as the strategist among us, his input will be useful. I waver on my feet. "What would you have me do, my lord?" The entire point of this negotiation is to *avoid* any further warfare, so it's not exactly my specialty.

"Speak to our warriors," Sylas says. "We'll want them on guard both against violence from the Unseelie toward us and hostility from our own people toward the ravens while they're here."

"We don't want to make it too obvious that we're prepared to fight," Talia says quickly. "If the Unseelie arch-lords get any sense of a threat... They were worried enough about coming to you as it is. I don't think it'd take much to scare them off." She makes a face.

"Noted. Make sure our people take that concern into account." Sylas raises a hand in farewell, and the three of them leave together.

So I'm to prepare our guards to defend us but without being intimidating about it. That's not a job I'd have signed up for, but it's what I've got.

I gather the warriors of our pack, Astrid joining me soon after. We get a number of protests about the idea that we'd need to ensure the safety of the winter fae as well as our own, but I think I manage to emphasize how very important it is that the Unseelie feel comfortable in our domain. "We're acting as hosts," I remind them. "We'll just have to impress the socks off them with our immense hospitality."

There isn't much to discuss beyond that. Our people are well-trained, and they'll do as their lord asks regardless of their personal qualms.

After I've returned to the castle, Talia, Sylas, and Whitt send word back that they'd be eating in the Bastion during the meeting. I pace around the kitchen, wishing I could at least apply myself to making a meal as some kind of contribution. Finally, I whip up a quick dessert that Talia usually loves. But when I finally see her again, trudging in with the others, she looks so weary I can tell she isn't in the mood for sweets.

"I'm still not sure how they'll react to that arrangement," she's saying to Sylas.

"We'll approach it tentatively," he reassures her.

She stops and can't seem to think of anything else to comment on just then. I take the moment to swoop in and scoop her up.

"Hey!" she says with amused if exhausted defiance.

I nuzzle her hair. "You've been working all day. I declare it time for a rest. You're coming with me."

She sighs and lets me carry her to my bedroom, where I tuck her carefully against me on top of the covers. The tremor that runs through her body as she nestles closer brings a lump into my throat.

"They aren't your responsibility, you know," I have to say. "You didn't *have* to help us with our curse, and there's no reason you have to help the ravens either."

She tips her head against my chest. "I know. But if there's something I *can* do… I can't just let people die."

Of course she can't. I grope for an argument she'll accept. "I'm just suggesting that it'd be better if you don't run yourself ragged in the process. We've been dealing with this problem for decades. It isn't your fault if you can't solve it all in a few days—or months, or whatever."

Talia is silent for a moment. Her voice comes out thick with emotion. "The Heart chose me for a reason, right? It gave me powers no human is supposed to have; it tied me to Corwin. I might have a chance to end all the fighting and the damage the curse has done… I have to give it everything I can."

I wouldn't expect the woman I love to say anything else, but hearing it pains me anyway. I hug her closer and try to will away the ache in my heart.

What if curing everything that's wrong with this world drains her too much? It might not be the Unseelie I lose her to but the Heart itself.

And I can't think of a single way I could stop that from happening.

CHAPTER TEN

Talia

I'd imagine there's been some occasion in the history of the world when a group of people looked *more* awkward than the summer and winter arch-lords attempting their parlay, but it's hard to picture what that could have been.

The Unseelie arch-lords have staked themselves out in a shallow semi-circle just a few steps from the border with their backs to that wall of glinting fog. All of them except Corwin are poised as if ready to leap back toward the winter realm the second anyone on the summer side so much as blinks funny.

The three Seelie arch-lords face them from several feet away—because the winter fae didn't want them getting any closer. Celia stands rigidly straight, her expression sour. Donovan has his arms crossed tight over his chest. Even Sylas has an air of apprehension around him.

I tried to suggest a table and chairs, maybe some refreshments, anything to make the meeting more comfortable and friendly. One or the other side wasn't having any of it. I'm lucky they're having *me* anywhere in the vicinity. The burly woman who likes to think she's boss of the Unseelie side—Laoni, I've learned her name is—kicked up a fuss about my presence.

Sylas pointed out that with my experience on both sides of the border, I may be able to contribute something the rest of them can't, and Corwin took his colleagues aside for a brief conference. In the end, I stayed, but not without several glowers—mostly from Laoni, but a few here and there from the gloomy man whose name is Uzziah and the copper-skinned woman whose name is Terisse. The elderly woman who's spoken up in my favor—Neve—has mostly just gazed off into the distance. I'm not sure she'll be much of an ally.

"And why exactly should we *help* you now, after you've spent so long trying to take what you wanted from us by force?" Celia asks, her voice so sharp I wince inwardly. After a couple of hours, the Unseelie have finally spit out what's going on and what they're hoping to get from the Seelie, but she clearly isn't in a generous mood. "Do you have any idea how many summer fae died during your attacks?"

Laoni draws herself straighter and stiffer, as if she's in a competition with the most senior Seelie arch-lord for who can do the best impression of a lamp post. "Many died on our side too. We have paid for our imposition."

Celia sniffs. "I don't think you have. Before we *offer* you anything, I'd like to see real reparations made to our people."

It's not an unreasonable request, I think to Corwin. Donovan is nodding along, and I'm not sure even Sylas would argue against it. *Do you think they'll ever agree?*

His inner voice travels to me with a grim edge. *We'll see how much the Seelie ask for.*

I did tell Sylas and his colleagues that the less they demanded, the more likely the Unseelie would negotiate a solid peace agreement, but I guess I can't blame Celia for not accepting peace out of hand after everything her people have been put through. I still wish she'd be a *little* less cutting in her remarks.

Uzziah's mouth twists. "That is something we can discuss. We can admit… we were at least partly at fault for going on the offensive—"

"Partly?" Donovan breaks in with a short laugh of disbelief.

Terisse raises her chin. "Our initial party into your territory disturbed no one until they were set upon by your warriors."

"We have only each side's word for how that encounter escalated," Celia says, dry but still sharp. "However, I can't think of anything our warriors could have done that was so odious it'd justify nearly thirty more years of raids."

The Unseelie stir restlessly. Laoni scowls. "We were under duress from our curse and acting in what we felt were our people's best interests. But reparations are possible—*if* you're willing to consider allowing a small settlement of Unseelie to live on your lands at least long enough to see how that affects the occurrence of the curse."

Celia exchanges a glance with the other two summer arch-lords. "Our willingness will depend on many factors, including the exact location, the size of the settlement, how long they anticipate staying, and what restrictions we may place on their activities. However, it is 'possible.' I'd like to discuss the possibilities of our reparations before we make any guarantees on that matter."

"Fine." Laoni turns away. "We'll deliberate amongst ourselves on that subject and present you with a proposal within a few hours. You may anticipate our return at the sun's peak."

I'll do my best to ensure they're generous with their offer, Corwin says as the five of them stride back toward their realm.

As soon as they've disappeared amid the haze, Celia exhales roughly. "Wretched featherbrains."

I swallow thickly. Corwin might be going to try his best, but I suspect "generous" by the Unseelie's evaluation is barely going to be adequate by hers. If her accusatory attitude hasn't made them balk completely, that is. But *me* talking to her isn't likely to do any good when she hasn't taken much of what I said earlier to heart.

As I push to my feet, planning to stretch my legs, Sylas leaves his colleagues to join me. After a glance toward the border as if to confirm the Unseelie aren't returning already, he walks with me as I amble in my uneven way toward the nearest stretch of trees.

"What do you make of their response so far?" he asks. "Has Corwin offered any insight?"

My soul-twined mate has dulled our connection—all I can sense from him right now is a vague impression of frustration that doesn't seem promising. "He said he'd try to encourage them to be generous as far as the whole reparations thing goes. I don't know how successful he'll be."

Sylas nods. When we come to a stop in the shade of the nearest tree, he touches my arm to turn me toward him. His dark eye studies me intently. "And what of your own insights? Is there any way you feel we should adjust our approach to get through to them better?"

A flicker of warmth washes through me at the question and the attentiveness with which he's waiting for my response. I've insisted on sharing my opinions on various political matters during the time I've been in Sylas's pack, but for him to turn to me of his own accord as an arch-lord—for him to value my advice that much… It sets off a glow of happiness inside me that's close to magic without any true names necessary.

I pause, figuring out how to give my advice effectively. "I think you all need to remember how much the Unseelie are focused on logic and practicalities," I say carefully, mostly meaning Celia when I say *you all*. "Seeing that you're angry about the attacks or passionate about doing right by your people isn't going to convince them of much—if anything, they'll use any show of intense emotion as an excuse to write you off as 'savage wolves.' If you can make it sound like the reparations you'd want are totally reasonable—"

"Of course they're reasonable," Celia interrupts, halting beside Sylas with Donovan coming up behind her. "The ravens struck at us without provocation again and again, and now they think they can dodge responsibility?" She frowns at Sylas rather than me. "Why are you discussing this situation with the human rather than us? We've heard what she has to say, but these matters are far beyond her purview."

Sylas keeps his tone even. "I'd say they're well within her purview, considering she's had far more experience with the ravens in the past month than any of us has in our lifetimes."

Donovan clears his throat. He seems a bit hesitant, but he speaks up for me anyway. "I've found Talia's contributions to be sound and well-thought-out. What reason do we have to ignore them?"

Celia glares at both of them. It's almost funny seeing her act so much like Laoni, trying to exert authority over the colleagues who should be her equals, when she dislikes the Unseelie arch-lords so much. At least Celia has a fair claim on being an authority when she's held her position for centuries longer than either Donovan or Sylas. But that doesn't mean she's always right.

"What *reason*?" she says. "How about the fact that she's bound to one of those feathered fiends and owes them more loyalty than she does to us now?"

My hackles come up at her insinuation. Sylas starts to speak, but I stop him with a raise of my hand. I can fight some of my own battles. "I still consider myself part of Hearth-by-the-Heart's pack and see that domain as my home. And I'll remind you that I've saved *you* and all the Seelie a lot of suffering by volunteering my blood, which I didn't have to do—the last time just a couple of weeks ago."

Celia stares down at me haughtily. "That proves very little."

"What about the fact that I've managed to keep my involvement in your curse a secret from all of the Unseelie except my mate? You can tell they don't know, can't you? Or they'd be trying to negotiate some control over *me*, not just your lands."

Her jaw tightens. She has no argument for that.

"I say we follow the suggestions Talia gave us earlier and that she's repeating now after witnessing the parlay," Sylas says. "We must *all* give every appearance of level-headedness and rationality, and spell out our terms from that standpoint. If we're not happy with the outcome of that approach, then we can try a different tactic."

Celia sounds as if she's restraining a growl. "If you expect me to let off the ravens for their crimes rather than taking them to task—"

"That's not what it means," Donovan breaks in, looking a little shocked at himself that he's dared to cut her off. "I agree with Sylas. We have a chance now to determine what specifically we expect and how to respond to the Unseelie when they return with their offer, not to mention the limits we'd place on their request for a settlement. We should lay it out in the most logical terms possible and stick to that approach throughout the next section of the parlay. We can still insist that they're paying heavily for the harm they've done."

Celia grimaces. "They deserve to know the pain they've caused."

"They won't care," I say quietly. "Maybe they will later on, if you can manage to form more of a truce with them as allies and your well-being starts to matter to them, but for now… It won't make them any more likely to give you what you want."

Sylas gives the other woman a firm but compassionate smile. "I understand your fury. I feel it myself. But what's more important: berating the ravens for the past or ensuring a peaceful future for our people?"

"Not only that," Donovan says. "Sylas and I are in agreement. We carry the majority. If you go against us, it'll be just as much treason as Ambrose planning his war behind our backs. I know you wouldn't stoop so low, Celia."

The oldest Seelie arch-lord closes her eyes for a second and then sighs. "All right. I hear you. As long as we're agreed that we must see progress *today* or we'll revise our strategy."

Sylas inclines his head. "We can reconvene tonight and hash out whatever we need to then."

Celia hasn't looked at me since her accusation about my loyalty, but I pipe up anyway. "Thank you. *I* want peace for the Seelie too."

She only acknowledges my words with a hint of a shrug, her attention staying focused on her colleagues. "The rest of this discussion I wish to have just the three of us."

Her brush-off stings, but the relief of knowing she's listened at least a little stops me from minding. I just hope Corwin has at least as much luck with his Unseelie companions.

CHAPTER ELEVEN

Talia

"What about deliveries of provisions?" Terisse asks. "Our people may not be satisfied with the crops and game on your side of the border. Surely one more can join them temporarily to bring supplies from the winter realm?"

"That's easily dealt with," Celia replies with studied evenness. "Arrange a specific time frame in which regular deliveries will arrive, and members of your settlement can accept them at the border with no need for those bringing them to linger."

They eye each other across the wooden table the arch-lords finally agreed to sit down at—after Sylas and his colleagues conjured it—yesterday morning. From my seat at the edge of the gathering, I watch the Unseelie side carefully, braced for another argument. But those have been coming fewer and fewer across the two days these negotiations have stretched over. After a moment, Terisse and Laoni incline their heads.

"That is reasonable," Laoni says, managing to keep a pompous tone even when she's giving in.

Corwin speaks through our bond with a hint of amusement. *Wonders never cease.*

The corners of my mouth twitch upward. *Hey, I'm just happy you all have managed to make some kind of agreement instead of stomping back to the winter realm.*

It does look promising, but I'm not holding my breath for a quick finish. I'm sure my colleagues have approximately a thousand more details they'll want to nitpick apart before they're satisfied.

The final negotiations haven't been the most exciting spectacle ever. I lean back on the stump-like stool, soaking in the early afternoon sun, and footsteps rustle across the grass behind me.

"There's our mite." Whitt comes up beside me and gives my hair an affectionate ruffle. "Still enjoying the show? Sylas said there wasn't much left to discuss."

I suppress a yawn. "It seems like there's a lot, but it's minor details now." Everything we hoped for is actually going to happen: the settlement, the experiment to see if the winter curse can be cured by the two realms sharing resources. A little thrill races through me at that thought.

Then my stomach gurgles. Whitt chuckles. "And that's why I've come to get you. Celia's people are preparing a meal for the arch-lords, but August wanted me to convey you back to the palace so you can have a break from all the politicking. Your reward will be whatever elaborate feast he's whipping up right now for the three of us."

I'd protest that I intended to see the negotiations through to the end, but my mouth immediately starts watering at the thought of August's cooking—and it isn't as if I've had anything to contribute so far today anyway.

We've kept our voices low, but of course Corwin doesn't need to use his ears to pick up on our conversation. He gives me a mental nudge. *Go on. I'll let you know if any disaster looms that requires your attention.*

It seems like the most likely disaster you'll have to deal with is a plague of boredom, I reply, and he swipes his hand across his mouth, hiding a flash of a grin.

I push myself off the stump and shake out my legs before limping after Whitt back to Sylas's castle. Sweet floral scents lace the warm summer breeze, a few birds are twittering in the trees—the atmosphere couldn't feel more peaceful. I'll take that as a good sign.

We step into the palace to even more appealing scents: fresh-baked bread and some kind of spiced meat that involves cloves. When we walk into the kitchen, August is just finishing slicing up a melon as a fruit accompaniment. He's already laid out three plates on thin wooden trays.

He beams at the sight of me. "Good, Whitt managed to tear you away."

"I don't think I'm missing much. They've finished the major deliberations." I bob up on my toes to give him a quick hug and am struck by the sense of how normal this moment feels—like how my life was in the brief periods of peace before I became entangled with the Unseelie. There are plenty of issues that are still up in the air right now, but there's nothing wrong with pretending for a little while that it's just an ordinary, cozy day with two of the men I love, is there?

Whitt cocks his head toward the counter. "What's with the trays? Are we going somewhere?"

August's grin widens. "I thought since this one has been running herself ragged"—he bends to kiss my temple—"we should get in as much relaxation time as possible while we've got her. We can bring the food down to the entertainment room. Sylas's whole collection has been moved over now. You can pick whichever movie you want, Sweetness."

Suddenly, nothing could sound better than vegging out with delicious food in front of the TV. A smile springs to my own lips. "Perfect."

It takes me a few minutes of pawing through the human-world movies Sylas has accumulated before I settle on one. He's mostly collected comedies for his own relaxation, but I suspect Whitt, at least, won't be too impressed by anything full of slapstick antics or bathroom humor. I do want them to enjoy our time together too. In the end, I settle on a British film that appears to be more clever than silly.

We all hunker down on the sofa while we eat. Seeing my two men laughing along at the early jokes warms me as much as my own laughter does.

When we're all finished with our lunches, August stacks the trays off to the side and scoots closer to me. I end up tucked between him and Whitt, my legs over August's lap and my head tipped against Whitt's shoulder. Whitt strokes his thumb over the back of my hand while August massages my bare calf with gentle pressure.

We haven't gotten to enjoy each other in more intimate ways much since I've returned, I've been so wrapped up in either thinking about or monitoring the negotiations. A deeper warmth blooms inside me, pooling between my legs. By the time the movie's over, every inch of my skin is tingling in anticipation.

"Imagine getting into that much trouble over a serving dish," August says with a laugh, and nuzzles my hair. "It did make me think, though—you've gotten pretty solid with bronze. Maybe I should teach you the true name for silver next. You mentioned that's in more common usage on the winter side, didn't you?"

"It is." I pause, considering. "Corwin said he'd start teaching me true names as well as he can while I'm there. Maybe it'd be better if he handled anything that's more of a winter fae specialty."

"Ah." August sounds a bit startled, and his muscles tense for just a second where I'm resting against him. "That would make sense. And an arch-lord would have a better grasp of the magic anyway."

"You've taught me just fine," I say, nudging him with my heel, but his smile in return doesn't look quite as bright as before. I find myself remembering that comment Whitt made before my last trip to the winter realm—something about how he wouldn't be offended if I cared more about Sylas and Corwin than him and August, just because the other two are arch-lords. Whitt and August don't really think the other two men matter more to me than they do, do they?

For the first time, I wish I had *more* soul-twined bonds instead of fewer. It's so much simpler to let Corwin know how I feel about him when all I need to do is offer my affection through our bond. I can say and do all kinds of things to try to show my devotion to my Seelie men, but I'll never be able to express it quite as plainly and undeniably as I can to the Unseelie arch-lord.

And maybe it's not surprising that they might both feel a bit pushed aside when I've spent most of my first few days back in the summer realm focusing on the arch-lords' parlay.

An ache forms around my heart, and more desire flickers low in my belly. I do love them—and want them—just as much as I always have. And maybe I can't offer up a direct line inside my mind, but there are other ways we can connect that should make my interest *very* clear.

A discomforted twinge travels to me from the bond I do have, but before more than a brief prickle of guilt can hit me, Corwin's voice follows. *It's all right. They've earned their place in your heart—I'm not going to dispute it. I'll just keep my own walls up until you need me again so I'm not distracted from the parlay.*

I send him a rush of appreciation before summoning my own inner barrier of light. Then I focus on August, curling my fingers into the fabric of his shirt. "Thank you for all of this. I definitely needed the break. But there's something else I need." I glance over my shoulder at Whitt. "From both of you."

Whitt hums and leans closer. "And what would that be, mighty one?" he asks in a suggestive tone that floods me with heat.

I reach up to graze my fingers along his jaw and look at August again. "I need you to let me show you how much you matter to me. How much I enjoy being with you in every possible way."

August's eyes light up with an eager flare. His voice comes out husky. "I think we can manage that. Do you want to go upstairs to the tryst room?"

I shake my head. "I don't want to wait even that long. It's been too long already."

I tug him to me, and he captures my mouth without a moment's hesitation. Whitt teases my hair to the side and kisses the back of my neck. Just like that, we come together in a mass of shared adoration.

How could the Heart ask me to give this up when I feel so much like I belong here?

But maybe that isn't what the Heart wants at all. Maybe I'm meant to unite summer and winter in my heart as well as in political negotiation. To accept love from both sides and create a different sort of truce.

If only I could figure out how exactly to make that more personal truce work in practice.

I don't want to think about that right now, though. I want to celebrate what I have and these amazing men who've cherished me every bit as much as I cherish them. We've come so far, and I've overcome so much. I have to believe I can find a way through this dilemma too.

Kissing August hard, I swivel to straddle his lap. Whitt eases closer, marking a trail down my neck and across my shoulder with his skillful mouth and a hot wash of his breath.

As August's tongue coaxes my lips apart, he cups my breast, provoking an eager whimper from me. Whitt reaches to the other side of my chest, drawing my nipple to a stiffened peak with a flick of his fingernail across it. A jolt of pleasure ripples through me and stirs up an unexpected impulse.

I pull back from August just a bit, touching his face and then Whitt's as I gaze into their eyes. "I love every part of you, the wolfish parts as well. I want… I want to enjoy those parts of you too. What happened in the past shouldn't stop me from appreciating your fierceness. I'm stronger than that."

Whitt's expression turns so tender it makes my throat constrict. He brushes his thumb over my cheek. "Being affected by the horrible events of your past doesn't make you weak, mighty one. Not in the slightest. We all have our scars."

I froze up once before with him when he nipped me with just his regular teeth. But I know how exhilarating it is to be swept up in the full power of a fae man. That one day when Sylas took me with the wild passion of a lover refusing to accept it might be our last time… I want to experience that intensity again and again, as many times as I can.

"You wouldn't hold back your fangs and claws with a Seelie woman, would you?" I say. "I'm not afraid of them; I'm not afraid of anything about you."

August ducks his head to press his lips to my neck. He electrifies the skin there with a swipe of his tongue and a heated murmur. "I'll give you everything you ask for, Sweetness. You just say the word if it's too much."

His teeth graze the sensitive skin with the sharpened points I know are his wolfish fangs. He traces them across my skin so gently the panic I was worried I'd have to conquer never rises up, only a quiver of giddiness.

I know these men would never hurt me. What made my former tormentors monsters wasn't the wolf in their nature.

The tips of claws glide across my upper back. Whitt gives my shoulder the lightest nip and then drags his claws downward. They neatly sever the fabric of my simple dress. The rasp of the splitting cloth and the feel of it falling away across my skin sends a thrill straight to my sex.

With increasing urgency, I seek out August's mouth with mine. He kisses me back with equal furor, his fangs just barely nicking my lips. Moving around behind me, Whitt teases both of my nipples between the cool edges of his claws. A moan tumbles out of me.

The spymaster works me over until I can't help grinding against the bulge forming in August's slacks. Then, testing his teeth against my shoulder, Whitt slits the fabric of my panties as well.

I arch up to let the cloth fall away, and Whitt retracts his claws to delve his fingers between my legs. As they slide across my clit, I gasp.

August takes the opportunity to capture the tip of my breast between his lips. He suckles me with alternating flicks of his tongue and grazes of his fangs. Whitt tips my head so he can claim my mouth for himself, still fingering me. A possessive growl reverberates from his throat, but I know it's not aimed at August, only the thought of any intruders on our shared love.

I rock between them, bliss building in my sex and lighting up my skin. Just when I think I might die of frustration, August wrenches down his trousers and frees his erection. He pulls me down over him, filling me with the ecstatic burn I've come to appreciate so much.

He grips my thighs, his claws forming little pinpoints of pain. When I whimper, he jerks his hands back, but I grab his wrists and bring them back.

"No," I mumble between kisses. "It was good." Like a hint of sour bringing out a deeper sweetness in a candy.

Whitt trails his own claws down my spine, sparking a path of giddy shivers in their wake. When he reaches my bottom, his touch stops, the claws vanishing again. His lips move against my shoulder, his voice low and sultry. "If you're in an experimenting mood, dearest, there is a way you could have both of us at once."

My breath hitches at both the new, adoring nickname and the implication in his words. "What's that?" I ask, already suspecting it before he skims his fingertips across my behind to the opening there.

I've never given that part of my body much thought in terms of sex, but the delicate stroke he gives it brings a flicker of pleasure and another whimper to my lips. "I'd be careful with you," he says, repeating the gesture. "I'd like to see what heights we could take you to working in tandem."

August lets out a rough encouraging noise. I can't see any reason to deny any of us that experience. I nod. "Yes, please."

Whitt chuckles. As I sway over August, taking him deeper, the spymaster continues to massage my other opening, gradually adding pressure and a slickness formed with a whispered word of magic.

It feels strange but so good I can't help shifting my posture to open up to him. Then he slips a finger right inside me there, and my breath shudders out of me with the pulse of pleasure.

"Good?" he asks, pumping in and out with a little more pressure to warm up the muscles. "Would you like more of me there, mighty one?"

I manage an inarticulate sound of agreement. So much ecstasy is swelling through me now that I can barely think, let alone speak.

He adds a second finger, and then a third, with a surge of bliss so strong I cry out. "Oh, I think you're ready now," Whitt purrs, more cat than wolf now.

There's a rustle of his slacks as he drops them and kneels, and then the hard length of his cock brushes against me. I go still over August as the other man carefully eases into me.

It's a different sort of burning, tighter but headier because it's so new. I find myself panting, overwhelmed with the sensation of being doubly filled.

I'm Talia McCarty, a human who survived the fae and now stands beside some of the most powerful in the realm, and I will take every delight my men can offer me.

I start to move again, slowly and then gaining speed as the three of us find our joint rhythm. August brings my mouth back to his, our kisses shaky with broken breath. Whitt groans, embracing me from behind. Their rigid shafts plunge into me in unison, and the incredible sensation expands all through my body. I grip August's shoulder, Whitt's arm where it's tucked around my torso, my breath breaking into giddy pants.

With so much stimulation, it doesn't take long before the wave cresting inside me crashes over its peak. I shudder and clench, coming with a cracking of bliss so intense it blanks my mind.

August's grip on my thighs tightens as he bucks up and follows me over the edge. Whitt thrusts inside me a little longer, tossing me straight into another orgasm with a renewed blaze of pleasure, before he stiffens against me with a choked sound he muffles against my back.

For a few minutes, we linger in our combined embrace, our bodies coming down from the high of the encounter. Then we untangle ourselves slowly, Whitt moving back to the couch in time for me to collapse half cuddled by both of my lovers. I wrap an arm around one of each of theirs.

"You're mine," I say with a little wolfish fierceness of my own. "And you're staying mine."

August kisses my sweat-damp forehead, his smile back at its usual brightness. "No argument at all from either of us, Sweetness."

Too bad solving all the fae's problems isn't this simple.

CHAPTER TWELVE

Talia

"So which place is your favorite?" Harper asks me a little breathlessly, swinging her legs where she's perched on her crafting table. I've been hanging out with her in her new house here by the Heart—where she's living on her own now rather than with her parents—telling her about the sights I saw on my second visit to the winter realm.

I tip my head to the side, considering. It's a little hard to focus with the awareness that just a short distance away, the negotiations between the arch-lords are finally wrapping up. Corwin told me he expects they'll be finished within the hour. After three days of hashing things out, the Unseelie arch-lords have finally become at ease enough to be willing to let the Seelie host them in the Bastion, where both sides will swear oaths when the agreement is totally worked out.

"I think the painted forest is still the most impressive out of everything," I say. "So I'm glad you got to see that."

"The frostfire trees sound pretty amazing too. And that cave by the ocean!" Harper gives a gleeful shiver. "It has been good getting some time to settle in here, but eventually you'll have to give me more of a tour."

The corners of my lips twitch upward. "I guess once I've seen all the best sights, I can make sure I take you to the highlights." Assuming I still have a place in the winter realm by that point—assuming a summer fae would be welcome as a visitor…

I can't fully sink into the conversation with all the uncertainties and secrets hanging over me. I'm not sure I've been a great friend this morning. The things happening in Harper's life right now are so distant from what I'm going through, and she doesn't know the half of it to even try to understand.

I get up from the armchair I was sitting in. "I think I'm going to see if they've finished with the negotiations." That's not totally true—I know they're not, because Corwin would have told me otherwise—but it's a reasonable excuse to leave that won't hurt Harper's feelings.

She bobs her head with a smile that shows she isn't offended. "You're here for another couple of days, right? I'm going to make you another dress for your next trip across the border."

A twinge of guilt hits me. "You really don't have to. Your work is absolutely gorgeous, but the winter fae seem to care mostly about practicality… No matter how friendly the realms end up getting, I'm not sure you'll pick up many new clients over there."

Harper shrugs. "It's not for me. I like knowing you're over there looking like a real lady. Put anyone who'd think less of you in their place."

I won't argue with that motivation. "Well, thank you," I say, wishing I could give her more than travel stories in return. I should ask Corwin if there are any special kinds of fabric or embellishments used in the winter realm that I could bring back for her to experiment with.

Outside, the air is crisper against my skin than it was yesterday, with a hint of coolness in the summer warmth that suggests a light rain might fall tonight. It doesn't seem to ever rain during the day near the Heart.

I set off through the scattered trees around the pack village, drawn by the rhythmic pulsing of that glowing spot that determines so much of what goes on in the entire faerie world. The Heart's energy tickles over my body more noticeably as I emerge from the trees and cross the vast field toward it. The table from the earlier negotiations has been removed. There's no sign it ever existed amid the pale pink and blue flowers bobbing with the breeze.

I limp right up to the vast glowing area in the border, its power rising to a thrum. When I'm standing just a few feet away, the mass of the Heart stands at least twice as tall as me and far wider than I could ever reach, its light pulsing in time with its energy. Staring into its golden depths, I have to catch my breath.

What do you want from me? I think at it. *What am I supposed to do here?* Questions I don't dare ask out loud, in case some passing fae overhears. And also, *Why me?*

If it chose me for some special purpose, shouldn't it give me more of an explanation? I have no idea what role it expects me to fulfill—whether I should be focusing completely on uniting the summer and winter fae, whether I'm meant to be paying more attention to the curse itself. Whether it even has a purpose for me at all or its effect on me is actually simple random chance.

As many good things as I've discovered in the faerie world, I'd hesitate to call that chance "luck."

The Heart doesn't give any indication it's heard me. It just pulses steadily on, the thrum starting to make my bones ache while I'm standing so close. It overwhelms my senses to the point that I don't hear footsteps approaching until Astrid comes to a stop beside me.

"You look like a woman thinking deep thoughts," the old warrior says in a gently wry tone.

I let out a huff of breath. "I just… I don't understand why I've ended up so connected to this place. It seems like the Heart must have something to do with it." But I got straighter answers from the tree-bound sage we visited, in all his vague rambling.

Astrid's mouth twists into a slanted smile. "The Heart's ways are difficult to discern even for those of us who've drawn on its magic for over a thousand years. I tend to think of it as something like the sun rather than some sort of conscious entity. Its power fuels our lives and strength, but it simply *is*. Any patterns that arise are merely the natural order of things."

I can't hold back a snort. "I don't think there's anything natural about a human with curse-healing blood and a soul-twined mate."

Astrid raises an eyebrow. "Maybe it's just a natural order too complex for us lesser beings to fully comprehend." She turns to the Heart, tipping her head back to soak in its glow, which seems to smooth the wrinkled planes of her aged face. "I find it's easiest not to worry about what those patterns might be. I trust that my intentions were shaped by the same power, so therefore what I decide to do with myself should fit in with any grand plans one way or another."

I wish I had the same faith. But then, there isn't much I *can* do other than keep going the way that seems best to me, is there?

"Thank you," I say, because it is a little comfort to know that even a fae woman with centuries upon centuries of life behind her finds the Heart as mysterious as I do.

Corwin lets down his inner wall a little more, giving me a clearer glimpse of the circular meeting room in the center of the Bastion and the voices carrying around him—filled with relief and satisfaction. The oath-taking must be over. The truce and the agreement for the Unseelie settlement are confirmed. At least that one thing has wrapped up smoothly.

Smiling, I set off toward the Bastion, Astrid ambling alongside me. I'm halfway across the field when Corwin and his colleagues emerge.

I feel the second that Laoni lays eyes on me. Her gaze sends a chilly prickle down my spine, but she pitches her voice low enough that I only hear it through Corwin's ears. "I still say your mate is too close for comfort with that one Seelie pack."

"She does seem to spend a great deal of time with them and to look to them for guidance," Terisse agrees.

Laoni's gaze travels past me toward Sylas's castle, even though she won't be able to make it out from that angle. "Especially those *men*. Are you so sure of her loyalties?"

I bristle and shudder inwardly at the same time. Have I given away more about my relationship with Sylas and his two cadre-chosen than I'd have wanted to?

All I sense from Corwin is irritation and defiance, though. "Her association with Arch-Lord Sylas played a large role in ensuring the success of this parlay. I'd prefer that to her being the sort of woman who'd drop her loyalty to those who've earned it the second the wind changes course."

Without waiting to hear his colleagues' response, he breaks away from the others to stride to meet me. *Don't mind them. The Seelie arch-lords could have offered us half the summer realm, and they'd still find something to grouse about.*

Astrid makes a gesture of farewell and leaves me to my mate. The other Unseelie arch-lords hustle on past us toward the border, apparently eager to return home and stay there this time. I can't say I'll miss them.

Corwin on the other hand… "I guess you need to get back to Heart's Cadence," I say as he reaches me.

"I have been somewhat neglecting all my duties there over the past few days." He takes my hands in his. "I didn't want to leave without a proper good-bye, though, even if you'll be rejoining me in a short while."

There's no more judgment in those words than in his retort to Laoni, but I can taste the bittersweet undertone. He can't help wishing I was coming back with him now.

The wind whips across the field, sending a burst of bright petals spiraling. Suddenly it seems absurd that he's spent all this time in the realm that was my first home among the fae while barely seeing any of it.

I squeeze his fingers. "Can you hold off on those duties for another hour or two? You've shown me some of your favorite spots in the winter realm—I could show you some of the summer realm's magic."

I brace instinctively for him to dismiss the idea, but instead one of his rare brilliant smiles crosses his lips. "I'd like that very much."

I glance down at my boots. "It'll go faster if you fly us. It's a little bit of a hike from here. If you don't mind bringing your wings out around the Seelie, that is."

"I should be asking you whether you wouldn't be shunned if you're seen with one of us ravens," he replies with a hint of dry humor.

"It'll be fine. Just don't go waving any swords around."

He unfurls his wings, stretching them to their full span before folding them closer to his body again. In the summer sunlight, the black feathers shine with a faint iridescent gleam I never noticed before. I let him scoop me up and give him directions that take us over Donovan's domain.

Like on the winter side, the area around the Heart here is a broad plateau. Most of the way around that hill, the climb to its broad peak is a relatively easy slope—not that I'd enjoy trekking up it very far with my warped foot. But in one spot in Donovan's territory, one Whitt told me about back when we still lived in Oakmeet and showed off to me a couple of weeks ago, the land falls away in a narrow, sheer cliff with an equally narrow waterfall.

I have Corwin set us down on the grassy bank near the bottom of the falls where the thin river winds away into forestland. He gazes up at the waterfall. It isn't as expansive or fierce as the falls in his domain, but the cascading water glitters with an effervescence that puts even his diamond palace to shame. I swear you can see every color in existence, including some I've never known existed, twinkling off the torrent.

"They call it the Shimmering Falls," I tell Corwin, sitting down and running my fingers through the silky grass. It gleams a green as vibrant as an emerald. All of the plant life around the falls has absorbed some of its vividness, the flowers and ferns beaming in a blazing mass of color that would be overwhelming if it didn't feel so harmonious at the same time.

Well, it feels that way to me. Corwin blinks hard, the scenery so intense and so different from what he's used to that I sense his eyes outright stinging for a moment. But as he adjusts, awe sweeps away any discomfort. "It's spectacular."

"I wouldn't want you to think the winter realm had all the best sights," I tease, and lie down on my back. The grass caresses my arms, and the sun grazes my skin, and I feel wrapped in a cocoon of contentment. It's even better getting to share this beautiful spot with someone who's never been here before.

I guess this must be how my fae men have felt showing me so many remarkable sites for the first time. Now I understand why they enjoy playing tour guide so much.

Corwin sinks to the ground next to me and strokes gentle fingers over my hair. The affection traveling from him into me has a tang of sadness to it. I look up at him, about to ask what's wrong, but he beats me to it.

"You love this place very much," he says.

I shrug as well as I can in my current position. "Like you said, it's spectacular. It makes me feel like… like I'm floating on some kind of song made out of color."

I'm not sure that description makes much sense, but Corwin smiles. "Yes." He pauses. "But that's not what I meant. I meant this *entire* place—the summer realm itself."

"Oh." A lump rises in my throat. "Yeah. I mean, I haven't pretended I don't."

"I know. It's simply different experiencing it myself and through you at the same time, seeing you as well as sensing your impressions…" He exhales slowly, and the sadness expands. "I can't take you away from this. I could never—to ever expect you to dedicate yourself completely to the winter realm…"

I sit up abruptly, reaching for his hand. "We found a way around that, for now at least. I don't mind going back and forth."

"It can't continue that way forever. I know you're aware of that as much as I am." The same pensive uncertainty that's dogged me for the past few weeks echoes from him through our bond. "When I go back, I'll have some time before you're with me again. And a lot to think about in that time."

I grasp his hand tightly with a wrench of my heart. "Don't go making any decisions *for* me. I don't want to lose you either—and the rest of the winter realm is growing on me."

Corwin tugs me closer to him and slips his arms around me. "I promise I won't take any action without consulting you first. Let's not worry about that. For now, I'd like to just enjoy this piece of happiness you're sharing with me."

I nestle into his embrace, but my own happiness has taken on a bittersweet tinge. For all the beauty and magic the fae world has to offer, this one thing I want so badly feels as far out of reach as ever.

CHAPTER THIRTEEN

Sylas

It wasn't hard to determine where Arch-Lord Corwin had gone. The Unseelie are a rare enough sight in the summer realm, and especially this close to the Heart, that I had multiple reports back from my sentries of a raven-winged man carrying Talia toward the Shimmering Falls before I even set out to look for him.

I don't have to go very far to find them. As I expected, he brings Talia back close to my castle, tightening his embrace for just a moment before he sets her down on her feet. I pause where I've been waiting in the shadows of the trees along the edge of the field. When he bends to give her a quick kiss, my wolf roars within me, longing to charge at him and tear him away from her.

But he has a much more legitimate claim on her affections than I do. I haven't even been able to admit my interest in her to anyone outside my cadre.

That thought—and the memory of how close I'd been to claiming her as my mate before her soul-twined bond came into being—makes me bristle in a different way. I clench my jaw to hold back a snarl that's not really directed at anyone in particular, only the situation at large.

This Unseelie arch-lord *is* her Heart-given mate, and I have to respect that if I want to maintain any kind of relationship with her. I only wish it was easier to be glad that he's proven himself worthy enough that she hasn't turned her back on him. If he'd been a villain, we'd have so much more turmoil on our hands.

Talia leaves Corwin to head back toward the castle, her gait typically uneven but her windblown hair and flushed cheeks giving her a wild beauty that sends a twang of desire through me. I tamp down on those urges and focus on the winter arch-lord now turning toward the border.

Striding forward across the grass, I catch his attention before I've spoken. He glances at me and stops just a few steps shy of the wall of haze. He's withdrawn his wings, but I can see the raven-ish apprehension in the tilt of his dark head.

"Arch-Lord Corwin," I say evenly. "Before you head home, I was hoping I could speak to you just the two of us."

"Of course." He glances around, perhaps wondering whether the subject I wish to bring up is safe around potential eavesdroppers.

I intone a quick spell to give me a sense of the nearest fae in the area and motion for him to follow me back toward the trees, where our conversation should proceed uninterrupted. As he falls into step beside me, there's a certain reluctance to his movements that I can't help noticing.

He's consulted with me before, but only when it helped his cause. I'm not sure whether he's more unhappy about my presence or uneasy about how I'll respond to his.

In the shelter of the trees, I face him. "I simply wanted to confirm, before she's due to cross the border again, that as far as you've observed Talia is adapting to her time in the winter realm and to the transitions back and forth reasonably well."

Corwin's eyebrows rise slightly. "Isn't that a question you should be asking her?"

I have to respect his response even though it rankles me that he'd think I don't value her own assessment. "I'd imagine you've gotten to know her well enough by now to realize that she's hesitant to admit any worries or weakness if she thinks she can overcome them on her own. She doesn't like coming across as a burden, even though I've never considered her one regardless. It seemed wise to get an impartial perspective. Or at least a perspective less skewed toward keeping up that resilient front of hers."

Corwin's expression stays implacably calm with the coolly detached air all of the Unseelie seem to have. "And if I said she was experiencing any difficulties with the present arrangement, would you use that as justification to suggest she shouldn't continue her visits after all?"

My fangs itch in my gums at the insinuation, but I will them back. "I'd hope that by now you're aware that I wouldn't stoop to such underhanded tactics. I've been fair in my dealings with you, haven't I?"

Corwin offers me a smile—small and tight, but unexpected enough that it diffuses my irritation. "I apologize. You have. Perhaps I've spent too much time in my colleagues' company these past few days, and it's put me too far on the defensive."

Interesting that he'd blame *his* colleagues for that rather than my own, although I have gathered from both him and Talia that he doesn't see eye-to-eye with the other Unseelie arch-lords on a variety of subjects.

"I'm concerned about her well-being, nothing more or less," I say. "If there *is* anything she's been struggling with, I'd want to do what I can to help her while she's with us. And since she wants to continue exploring the soul-twined bond, that would include helping her be at ease in your realm."

Corwin inclines his head. "I think she's been taking to the new environment well. She's clearly very adaptable to have found a place for herself so quickly among your pack in the first place. The greater difficulty may be encouraging everyone *else* to adapt to having a human woman standing by an arch-lord's side, but if they see that she's been instrumental in tackling our curse… those hesitations should be smoothed over without too much trouble."

I consider him. "She's said her blood didn't have any effect on the victims of your curse, nor any of your other attempts. I assume that's why you switched your focus to creating the settlement here. Do you believe there's much chance that the atmosphere of the summer realm will really be all the cure you need?"

The Unseelie arch-lord glances away for a second, his expression darkening. "I don't know. I'd like to have faith in the idea, especially after all the pain we've put your people through striving toward that goal, but… it feels too simple to me. Even Talia's blood hasn't been a full cure for your curse, only a temporary one. I can't shake the sense that there's something more to this, a missing piece we require to get to the heart of the problem."

His sentiments echo my own so well that I find myself unexpectedly reassured even though we're no closer to the answer. "Indeed. At least we're proceeding with the trial, so we'll know more than we did before. And I expect that being able to collaborate to whatever extent between our realms should speed our progress toward a real cure even more."

Corwin's smile comes back, perhaps a little brighter than the first one. "I'm glad we were able to reach that point. And Talia can certainly take a great deal of the credit for it." He lets out a soft chuckle. "She's skilled at seeing the best in any person and situation she encounters—and finding ways to bring it out into full view."

The warm fondness in his tone, so different from his usual cool demeanor, puts me even more at ease than before. Perhaps I was still somewhat concerned about how her theoretical mate valued her. It couldn't be more clear that he appreciates her for much the same reasons I do.

Now it's even more difficult to resent his presence in her life.

"She does," I agree. "One of her many impressive qualities. I'd challenge anyone who claims she can't hold her own among the fae to point to more than a handful of our own kind who've shown as much fortitude and compassion."

Corwin hesitates, and then says, with an awkward twitch of his hands, "I'm also glad she has you. The three of you. It was hard, at first—sometimes it's still hard—but with every day I spend with her, it's easier to understand how she could have won so many hearts and found room in her own to offer so much love in return. I know how much you mean to her. It's not my wish to wrench her from you completely. I simply haven't determined a better arrangement than what we currently have."

A constricting sensation winds through my chest. Both because of the generosity in his words—and the unstated fact that we're nonetheless both aware of, that our current arrangement *can't* be the final one. It's suitable for the short term, but we can hardly jerk Talia back and forth between the realms week by week for the rest of her life.

And I haven't come up with a better proposition yet either. Corwin and I both have our duties to our peoples as arch-lords. We're bound to our sides of the border as much as she's bound to him.

"I appreciate that," I say, hoping he can tell how genuinely I mean the words. "I'll do whatever I can to find a solution that allows us all our happiness." Drawing in a breath, I step back. "Thank you for speaking with me. I won't delay you from your journey home any longer."

I'm not sure whether I feel better or worse for the conversation as we part ways. I definitely feel worse seeing Celia stalking across the field toward me when I emerge from the stand of trees. From her expression, she's gathered that I've been talking with the Unseelie—or one of them, anyway—alone.

She may have toned down her animosity for our negotiations, but she still isn't remotely friendly toward them.

She glances toward Corwin's figure vanishing into the border's haze and comes to a halt abruptly in front of me. "Making some additional negotiations?" she demands with her typical imperious air.

I swallow a sigh. Celia approved of my appointment to arch-lord, but she wasn't as enthusiastic about the prospect as Donovan—and since he and I joined together to overturn her decision to take Corwin prisoner, she's aimed more of her temper at me than usual.

"We didn't discuss the Unseelie settlement or the peace accord at all," I say. "I was merely inquiring about the more personal matter of Talia's visits to their realm, which seemed better dealt with between just the two of us."

My colleague's stance relaxes a little, but her expression stays stern. She eyes me with a penetrating gaze I don't particularly care for. "You're very invested in what goes on with this woman."

"She's the closest thing to a cure we have for our own curse. Why wouldn't I be?"

"It isn't just that, though. The oaths protect us from losing the benefit she provides." She pauses. "Your cadre-chosen who was enamored with her—I still see them showing affection to each other. Does her Unseelie mate know about that?"

I catch myself just shy of gritting my teeth. "Of course he does. It would be difficult for her to hide something like that while they're bonded. Talia has insisted that she not have to give up the other sorts of bonds she's formed, and so far her mate has respected her wishes on the subject. We're waiting to see how that plays out. At the moment, there have been larger issues to focus on."

Celia hums to herself. "And perhaps it also matters to you on a personal level more than it should. You can *like* the creature, but don't forget that the security of your people must come before your concerns for any one individual—especially when that individual is a mortal we've already outlived at least twice over."

Without waiting for my response, she turns on her heel and marches off. I watch her go with a sinking sensation in my gut.

Corwin spoke of his people's acceptance of Talia as his mate. I've been contemplating how to keep her in my life while she's tied to him as well. But I have the problem of my own peers too, don't I? Even if the Unseelie arch-lord and I can reach a happy compromise, how will I explain it to my fellow rulers in a way *they'll* understand?

And what obstacles will they throw in our way if I can't?

CHAPTER FOURTEEN

Talia

After a week in the summer realm, the first day back in the chill of the winter side is always jarring despite the warming spell on my clothes. It doesn't help that within an hour of my arrival, my lunch with Corwin was interrupted by a message that the curse has struck a woman in another domain. Corwin, Zelpha, and I have been riding in one of the Unseelie carriages for what feels like ages.

At the speed my soul-twined mate has pushed the vehicle too, some of the icy wind whips past the crystalline shield meant to protect us from it. A thin haze of cloud has turned the sky gray and dimmed the sun. I've tucked myself as close to the windshield as possible, my knees drawn up and my arms wrapped around myself, trying not to let my nerves overwhelm me.

There are strategies for tackling the curse that we discussed after the last time but haven't had the chance to try yet—mostly attempting more than one of our past ideas in combination. And this is the first time I'll attempt to heal a victim so soon after the curse has hit them. But I can't get rid of the uncomfortable knot in my stomach at the thought of failing yet again. Of knowing that our failure will mean this woman's death.

Corwin has been putting together his "draughts" while we travel, taking the particles of my blood and skin and even my bones so carefully I feel only a faint, split-second stinging with each one. Zelpha studies the landscape beyond the carriage, even her usually nonchalant expression turned serious.

"If this doesn't work," I say, "she could still join the settlement in the summer realm, right? You wanted to see if a stay there could cure the curse as well as whether it can prevent it."

Corwin frowns. "I'm not sure the preparations will be ready in time. They haven't finished constructing all the buildings or ensuring the initial supplies are in place. As you could probably tell from the parlay, neither side was eager to rush into anything."

"I was due to head over and see how things are progressing tomorrow anyway," Zelpha says. "It was meant to be ready within the week. I might be able to hurry things along."

But it'll be easier if something we try today works and the summer settlement doesn't need to factor in at all. I drag in a breath and gird myself for the coming attempt as well as I can.

Corwin sinks onto the bench next to me, slipping his arm tentatively around me. When I lean into his embrace, he hugs me closer to him. Sharing his warmth eases my worries just a little.

Just the fact that you're trying so hard is incredibly admirable, he tells me. *And we might not have the settlement being created at all if it wasn't for you.*

I know. And I want *to help. It seems so much easier, the way I can wake the Seelie out of their curse. I don't know why there isn't something more simple for you.*

His hand glides up my arm to rest on my scarred shoulder. *I wouldn't call what happened to you to make that discovery "easy."*

Fair point. The memory of the attack ripples through me with a shudder I can't quite suppress. Corwin's arm tenses around me, a wordless apology traveling through our bond.

I really hope I don't have to lose as much as I did that night to unravel this side of the fae's curse.

"Here we are," Zelpha says, straightening up.

I twist on my seat to peer through the crystalline windshield. We've dipped into a valley between two sheer cliffs. Like in Corwin's domain, the flock village has been formed along the rocky face—on both sides. The houses here are formed out of the same stone as the valley walls, though, as is the craggy castle that juts up toward the sky near the edge of the cliff on the right.

A man waves to us from a terrace partway down. There isn't anywhere for the carriage to come to rest there, so Corwin draws it up alongside the railing and lets it hover while we clamber out.

"I'm glad you could come so quickly," the man says, his face both flushed and drawn. He looks sick himself, though not in the way of the curse. "I hope—if there's anything you can do for her—"

"We'll try our best," Corwin says. "Will you give us the space to make our attempts in private? We can't be entirely sure how any external factors will affect the situation."

We have no reason to think having another person around would change anything—it's never been a factor when it comes to helping the Seelie curse—but we're still trying to keep it quiet just how involved I am in our "attempts."

Unlike past supporters, this man hesitates, wavering on his feet for a few seconds. His mouth twists as if he wants to argue. Then he ducks his head. "Whatever you think is best, my lord. I just want them to be okay."

Them? I puzzle over that remark as we step through the doorway into the man's home. Either with his fae senses or simple instinct, Corwin passes through what looks like a living room to another doorway beyond.

As soon as we come into the bedroom there, understanding hits me with a lurch of my gut.

The woman sitting in an armchair by a small hearth has her arms cradled around her rounded belly. She strokes it and shivers, her voice lilting in a faint crooning.

She's pregnant. Fairly far along, by the size of her, but maybe not enough that the baby could survive being born just yet.

But if the curse takes her, if it freezes her straight through… the baby will die too.

The knot in my stomach multiplies into a dozen. I swallow hard as Corwin walks to the woman's side. "How are you doing?" he asks, calmly but gently.

Another shiver ripples through her. She looks up at him, barely seeming to register who he is. Grief is already etched throughout her expression.

What agony must she be in, knowing not only is her life on the line but her child's—a child she might have waited hundreds of years to have a chance to bring into the world?

"Cold," she murmurs. "I'm cold, but it's not too sharp yet. I can still move all right. Well, as much as I could before in this state." Her arm tightens around her belly protectively. Then she blinks, some of the distance drawing back from her eyes. "My lord, you think there's something you can do?"

She gazes past him to Zelpha and me, and the hope that darts across her face nearly kills me.

"We're going to try everything we can think of," Corwin reassures her, his own distress radiating through our bond into me. He knows more deeply than I do how treasured children are among the fae, who bear so few. "I've brought a couple of my people with me to assist. Are you comfortable here, or would you like to lie down?"

The woman glances toward the bed where the cover lies neatly across the mattress and shakes her head. "I'll stay here by the fire unless you need me elsewhere."

"Right there should be just fine." He inhales slowly, and I can feel him steadying himself for the task ahead as much as I did on the carriage.

I have no idea how to rein in my nerves now. As Corwin draws out his first draught, one that combines two aspects of my body, I wrack my brain for any tactic we might have missed that I could add to our plans for today. But we've already gone over so many possibilities together. The heavy thumping of my heart only makes it harder to concentrate now.

Zelpha touches my back in a tentative gesture. "If there's a way, we'll find it," she murmurs, and I realize she's attempting to reassure me. My anxiety must be showing. I shove it down as well as I can, not wanting to add to the immense distress the cursed woman must already be experiencing.

Because it would take an awfully long time to go through every possible combination of bodily contributions and actions, we agreed the last time we had a discussion about tackling the curse that we wouldn't worry as much about separating out the effects. If something works, then we can look at all the factors that were in play around the moment the victim seemed to turn the corner and separate those out more later.

What really matters is giving the victim every possible chance of surviving.

So, as soon as the woman has swallowed the first draught, I step up to her and hold out my hand. After a second's hesitation, she takes it. Wrapping her hand in both of mine, I sing the same lullaby I offered up to the victim before her.

A burn starts to creep up behind my eyes. I learned this song from my mother. Maybe she sang it to me before I was even born, like this woman was singing to her child.

Her skin is chilly to the touch. Nothing I'm doing, not even the press of my fingers against hers, seems to warm her. Her other hand shifts over her belly as if she's felt her child moving inside her.

Corwin offers up another draught, and then another and another. My throat gets hoarse from singing that tune and then a few others I throw in, because why not? I give the woman quick but emphatic hugs, hold her hand, and massage her shoulders and then her feet. She gives me a small smile of thanks even though I can tell that whatever comfort I'm offering her isn't fixing the larger problem.

Zelpha brings out some snacks I helped bake back in Corwin's kitchen, quick little sugary treats that didn't require much preparation before we left. The woman straightens up to eat them and flinches with the movement.

I can tell in an instant that her back is stiffening up. She holds her posture awkwardly as she chews, a little more of the color draining from her already grayed face.

Nothing's working. She's only getting worse.

I offer every gesture I can again and finally step back, my heart aching. The woman slumps back in her chair with a wince. The angle of her jaw looks tight now too.

How much longer does she have before she'll barely be able to move at all?

Another mother and another child dead because I couldn't do enough. Because I couldn't act the right way when it mattered.

The burning fills my eyes, and I turn around before she can see the tears that overflow. A sob clogs my throat. I force it down, swiping at my face, but I can't hold back the tears completely. They streak down my cheeks and over my hasty fingers. I manage to stay quiet, but my breath comes out shaky.

Talia? Corwin says, his inner voice taut with concern.

Just focus on her. I'll get myself together as quickly as I can.

I've never cried in front of him before, I realize. He's seen me upset but not like this, not in reality rather than my memories. I can tell from the emotions whirling through him that it's an unusual sight in the winter realm. That's not surprising when the Unseelie value emotional control so highly.

All the more reason I need to get a grip before I freak out the woman I'm supposed to be helping.

Zelpha comes up beside me, her brow knit. "Is there anything I can do?" she asks quietly.

I shake my head and focus on breathing slow and steady. After a minute or two, the burning eases off enough that I can blink the last tears away. I wipe at my cheeks, knowing they must be splotchy and my eyes red-rimmed, but there's not much I can do about that. Maybe I should just go outside until Corwin's finished with the last few steps.

Before I can move to go, the woman's soft voice reaches me. "You're weeping—for me and my baby?"

I turn toward her, not wanting to speak with my back to her but hesitant to let her see how affected I am. "I'm sorry—I just wanted so badly to make things better for you."

She stares at me, but she doesn't look offended, more amazed. "I'm honored that a companion of the arch-lord cares so much."

The tension inside me twists with a bittersweet pang. On an impulse, I step toward her instead, touching her cheek as if I can pass on how much I do care through that contact the same way my emotions can travel to Corwin more easily skin-to-skin.

But of course, I don't have any kind of bond with this woman. I get no sense of inner connection. I'm about to pull back when she grasps my wrist, a gasp spilling from her lips.

And then I feel it. The faint warmth blooming beneath my fingers across her cheek. Her hand is warm where it grips my arm as well. Her eyes widen, the awkwardness of her posture easing.

She takes a big gulp of air. "It's—it's going away. The cold. I can feel—I can feel the fire again. And the warming spell on my clothes."

I clasp her hand, rocked by the surge of joy that rushes from Corwin into me. But my own burst of happiness is tempered by the knowledge that the cures I offer have never been enough to chase away a curse completely.

Maybe we've figured it out. Something I just did tipped the balance. But how long will she have until the cold creeps over this poor woman again?

CHAPTER FIFTEEN

Whitt

I can't say I'd been looking forward to spending the day hanging around a bunch of mangy ravens, but it's certainly interesting seeing how similar and yet how different the Unseelie folk are. They've grouped together to work on the buildings of their new settlement with similar focus, summoning the same sorts of materials our kind can. The voices raised in approval or suggestion around me could have belonged to Seelie just as well.

On the other hand, their gestures have a subtle but noticeable bird-like quality I'd never had much chance to observe before. After ambling along the fringes of the settlement for a couple of hours watching the progress of the construction, I suspect I could have picked out a winter fae in a crowd of Seelie without even being close enough to scent them.

Although it's no trouble scenting them here with so many together. The spot we offered them in between two Seelie domains near the border now stinks of raven.

Stepping back to take in the entire area at once, I have to reflect that it's an odd-looking town for either realm. With mate-pairs from various Unseelie domains coming together and no lord overseeing them, they've all constructed their homes out of the materials they feel most comfortable with. The result is a jumble of wood, stone, metal, and any other material that can be raised or woven into walls.

I don't know how large a typical Unseelie flock is, but this village makes a decent-sized pack. Sylas and his colleagues agreed to allow a hundred of the ravens to make their home here. They've all had to take an oath that they'll do us no harm as long as we don't attack them unprovoked, although there's no telling whether one or another will try to find a loophole.

Of course, as Sylas pointed out, there shouldn't be any reason for them to undermine our rules if the ravens are telling the truth that the only reason for the attacks was to take control over some of our territory in the first place. I suppose we'll just have to see whether it turns out our lands help offset their curse. If living here shields them from that icy death, we may have an invasion on our hands. It's not as if we'll want to trade and take their frozen terrain in return.

For now, the newcomers are eyeing the few of us wolves prowling around the edges of their new home with wariness that I'll admit is understandable. We're here both to make sure they're settling in without issue and to ensure all the requirements we insisted on are being met.

So far, no one I've seen has put a toe—or a talon—out of line. But I can't shake a creeping uneasiness that something about this situation isn't quite right.

It's merely a vague impression. It could be simply the discomfort of having so many of our recent enemies on our soil right in front of me. But my instincts are well-honed, and if something's telling me I'm missing a factor of concern, I'm inclined to trust that sense.

I continue circling, watching several fae performing the magic to allow working pipes into their homes for drinking and washing, and another group getting a garden started with vegetables that may or may not take to our climate. No doubt August will have all sorts of questions and tips for them when it's his turn to check in on the settlement.

When my gaze passes over a woman I recognize as one of the

Unseelie arch-lords—not the loud, arrogant one, but not the friendliest of their number either—I pause. She's swiveling on her heel in the midst of several of the half-formed houses, her head cocked in contemplation. When her eyes catch mine, they narrow. Only for a moment, but enough to know she doesn't like us keeping an eye on them.

Can I blame her for that? Maybe not. That doesn't mean I should completely ignore the understated hostility, though. They're our guests, here by our grace only.

A wry voice pipes up from just behind me. "Don't mind Arch-Lord Terisse. She's mostly annoyed that she got stuck with overseer duty today."

I turn to find a woman almost as beefy as August standing nearby, her deep brown hair tied back in a loose braid. She's a raven—no whiff of wolf breaks through the overall birdish odor that permeates this place—but she's being awfully familiar with me for one. I wouldn't expect even one of my fellow Seelie to speak that casually about one of our arch-lords to me, let alone to a potential opponent.

Possibly she's hoping to catch me out in some sort of insult. If so, she picked the wrong wolf. I smile back as mildly as I'm capable of, keeping my tone equally inoffensive. "I suppose it's understandable that the transition would cause some stress."

The woman rocks on her heels, watching the other Unseelie in their preparations for a moment. Why isn't *she* helping them? How many overseers do they need? From the muted point of her ears, she doesn't have the authority of a true-blooded lady.

"Well, different folk among us have different levels of enthusiasm for our duties," she says, and shoots a much broader smile than mine at me. "I'm Zelpha, by the way. I'm part of Arch-Lord Corwin's coterie. He wanted an update on the progress that's been made here."

That explains why she's here but not why she's talking to me. I continue to study her reactions carefully. "Was there something in particular you needed from me?"

She lets out a bark of a laugh that makes me like her despite myself. "I was talking to one of your wolfish brethren, and he mentioned you're a cadre-chosen of Arch-Lord Sylas's. I figured I might as well come over and introduce myself, seeing as we have a significant mutual friend now."

"Talia," I say, still uncertain of her true intentions.

"That would be the one." The Unseelie woman's smile softens in a way that eases some of my suspicions. "I think she's as anxious to know how things are coming along here as my lord is. I'll be sure to tell her I spoke to you and that we haven't pecked you to death so far."

A snort of amusement escapes me before I can catch it. All right, I'll admit it, I do like her. And if this is the sort of fae Corwin picks for his coterie, perhaps I'll have to like him a little better too.

The thought of Talia sends a bittersweet twinge through my gut. It's only been two days since I last saw her, and she seems to integrate herself into Unseelie society better with every visit—but that isn't exactly a comfort.

"How is she, beyond that anxiety?" I have to ask, still careful with my tone. Corwin might know exactly how much the mite means to me, but Talia's indicated that they've kept it quiet from everyone else in the winter realm as we have here.

"Oh, running around trying to save the whole world with her own two hands like usual," Zelpha says breezily, in what does sound like an accurate summation of Talia's typical approach to any problem. The Unseelie woman tips her head in the opposite direction from the village, lowering her voice. "There's been a development as far as the curse goes as well, but one I'd prefer to discuss with less of a potential audience."

Her tone stays light, but the words themselves are ominous. I don't imagine I have anything to fear immediately from one of Corwin's chosen. If I can take her word on her being one. She does sound pretty familiar with Talia. I'll stay on my guard nonetheless.

I nod, and we meander farther from the village until we're a safe distance from eavesdroppers. It's a particularly hot day, and the breeze that sweeps over us has the feel of a furnace. I soak it in with an appreciative stretch of my neck, but Zelpha shudders. "I don't know how they're all going to get through the next year with it being this blasted *warm* around here all the time."

I chuckle. "I suppose they'll all have to hope you get answers about your curse before a whole year is up, then, won't they?"

Practically speaking, it could take much longer to judge the effectiveness of this tactic. Moving winter fae who are already cursed to the settlement to see if they recover will provide some information, but it could take some time before they can be sure that the curse won't strike anyone already on this side of the border.

If that's the case, would they start going wild under the full moon instead? Part of me wouldn't mind witnessing that chaos just once. Maybe they'd quit their snarking about our savagery if they were brought to it themselves.

"It may be sooner than that," Zelpha says, still quiet. She looks toward the border, her expression tensing a little. "Corwin, Talia, and I went to call on a victim of the curse yesterday, and it seems Talia was able to at least temporarily ward off the curse's effect."

My eyebrows jump up. "Then why is the settlement still being built?"

The Unseelie woman gives me a baleful look. "Because we don't know how temporary the warding off will be. As you've found, it may return—it's possible the summer realm will offer a more permanent solution. And we also haven't had a chance to try to repeat the process. We're not entirely sure how she did it. There were a few different things going on at once, and many we'd tried not long before the obvious turn-around."

"Not very scientific of you," I say.

"Well, we had a lot to get through, and there's no way of knowing how long we'd need to wait to be sure one or another thing *wasn't* going to work. And it's hard on Talia, the longer we're there trying." She lets out a breath, the corner of her mouth curling upward at a wry angle. "She grows on you, doesn't she? I've never talked much with any human before. Maybe that was a failing of mine, not theirs."

I hum to myself while mentally giving her another several points of favor. "Based on my experience, I'd say that Talia is an extraordinary figure in general, all considerations of heritage aside."

"I guess that's why the Heart chose her for... whatever it is her role is supposed to be. Well, hopefully we can figure out the exact element that made the difference quickly so it'll go much faster in the future. Anyway, I thought you'd like to know she's had some success. It's definitely put her somewhat more at ease, though I get the impression she won't rest easy until she's cured the lot of us."

"She does like to take on a lot." I pause, contemplating the woman in front of me. She's given every indication of knowing Talia as well as she says and of being honestly fond of her. I doubt she'd be aware of many of the things she's mentioned to me if she wasn't working closely with Corwin. A touch of hopeful warmth lights in my chest.

If this is the sort of fae we're dealing with on the winter side, at least in some respects, then I might be able to believe that we could reach a more permanent compromise between our realms, even if I can't imagine what that would look like just yet.

I'm not about to let my tongue fly loose without absolute confirmation of this woman's station, but I can extend a little trust of my own. I motion toward the village. "You'll know your people better than I do. While you've been here, have you seen any signs of outright unrest—more than a general discomfort at adjusting to the change in environment?"

Zelpha frowns thoughtfully. "No, I would have noted that. The last thing we need is more fighting. Why, do you have reason to suspect there's a larger conflict brewing?"

"No. Nothing concrete." I study the town again. "It may simply be that it feels too much like an ideal setting for something to go wrong, more so than that something already is. If you do notice anything, you'll pass on word to Arch-Lord Sylas?"

"I can do that." She dips her head with total confidence, but the niggling sensation inside me isn't satisfied by that either.

Whatever may be coming, we'll just have to face it once it's here. At least Talia has one more fae on her side to shelter her from the worst of any impending storms.

CHAPTER SIXTEEN

Talia

"It has to have been the tears, I'd say." Verik rubs his mouth where he's standing near one of the bookcases in Corwin's study. The light filtering through the diamond walls brings out the streaks of gray in his dark hair. "We didn't even consider attempting to use them originally—I can't think of the last time I saw one of our own weeping—"

He pauses with a sidelong glance at me and an awkward tensing of his mouth as if he's concerned I'll take offense. I can't help noticing he's become a little more deferential to me since finding out I've managed to heal one of his people.

I give him a tight smile in return. "I know the Unseelie aren't much for emotions. And *I* didn't think of it either. It's not like tears are a typical bodily material or whatever that're always there."

"But you could encourage yourself to produce them," Corwin says from where he's seated next to me behind his desk. "If you're willing. I realize it'd require bringing up memories of past pain."

You really don't need to put yourself through any more anguish, he adds through our bond.

I shift on the chair he set up for me as before, almost but not quite as if I'm ruling side by side with him. It won't be fun dredging up the thoughts of my family and the torment Aerik put me through to force those emotions to the surface, but… "If the alternative is fae dying, I think I can handle a few minutes of discomfort."

Olander paces the study in his typical restless way. "We can't discount the other factors. The woman *noticed* you crying and was affected by that. And you touched her cheek right when the effect was taking hold. Had you made that exact kind of contact before?"

It's hard to remember every individual gesture I tried during our previous attempt. "I don't think so. It wasn't something we'd specifically discussed. It could definitely have been that."

There's a light knock on the door. "Come in," Corwin calls.

Beth nudges the door open with her shoulder, carrying a tray with glasses of a steaming beverage the winter fae are fond of that tastes like warmed, creamy root beer and fried dumplings. "You said I should bring refreshments," she says with a smile.

Corwin gestures for her to set the bounty on his desk. "Yes, perfect, we may be here a while yet, and it's getting on toward lunch."

Verik turns to me, apparently not fazed by the other human now in our midst. "I'd say we try every possibility at once, all the factors that were present when that woman recovered, just to ensure you *can* cure the curse again. Once we have that certainty, we can worry more about narrowing it down."

I open my mouth to agree, but I'm startled silent by the widening of Beth's eyes as she spins to gape at me. "*You're* curing the curse? That's—I know it's been a problem since before I was born. How did you manage it?"

The fact that I'm directly involved in providing the cure isn't a secret anymore. It would have been pretty much impossible to keep it one after what happened with the pregnant woman two days ago. But this is the first time I've had to say anything about it to the residents of the winter realm, since Corwin has done the other sharing of the news.

My cheeks flush. "I've only done it once. It's hard to explain—I don't even understand it. I seem to be connected to the curse somehow, magically or through the Heart. We're not sure."

She stares at me a few moments longer, maybe re-evaluating me all over again like she did when she found out I was human. Does this weird magical aspect make me even more unsettling than if I were fae?

My stomach twists at the thought, but I don't know what to say to her. I had kind of hoped I might have another friend in the palace once I got to know her better—someone who understood the human aspects of my life. Before I can come up with anything to ease the tension, she's bobbing her head to Corwin and hustling out of the room with an apology for the intrusion.

My mate doesn't show any concern about her reaction. As he picks up his glass, he nods to Verik. "I agree. We'll attempt to recreate the last few minutes before the woman recovered as accurately as possible. I'd also like to attempt a draught with a few tears in it to see if that might have an effect on its own. Then Talia wouldn't need to be present every time someone falls ill."

Which will get awfully inconvenient when the curse strikes while I'm on the summer side. I bite my lip, and another unnerving thought hits me. What if the woman it seems I saved gets sick again while I'm gone, and we lose her and the baby after all?

"She's seemed okay so far, right?" I ask. "The woman I already cured? The curse hasn't come back at all?"

Olander pauses long enough to give me a mildly reassuring look. "All reports seem promising. I realize that the Seelie re-experience their curse every month regardless… I suppose there's no way to know what kind of timeline ours might run on."

"All we can do is wait," Verik says. "And hope we're able to meet whatever new challenges present themselves."

He's partway through that sentence when Zelpha bursts into the room. "I'm not sure what you're talking about, but we've got some kind of challenge right now. A nearby one, at least. A fellow in Uzziah's domain has just caught the chill."

Corwin springs up, his expression darkening, and I don't think just at knowing another of his people is facing the curse. We haven't needed to deal with the arch-lords directly so far.

I push myself out of my chair, my chest constricting. Uzziah will have some idea that I'm providing the cure now, but he's never actually seen me try to work it.

"We'll go right away," Corwin says, and glances at the refreshments we hadn't gotten to yet. "Do you want something, Talia—to shore up your strength…?"

The thought of trying to eat anything before I attempt to repeat my previous success only makes me queasy. "No," I say quickly. "I'm fine. Let's see what we can do right away." What would the other arch-lord think if I turn up nibbling on snacks like I think I'm at a tea party?

"We'll fly." Corwin releases his wings as he steps into the hall. "Zelpha, you join us in case you can think of some factor we forget from last time, and Verik, why don't you come as well to observe. Where exactly is the afflicted man?"

The other two fae unfurl their own wings, Zelpha's a deep brownish black and Verik's speckled with gray like his hair. "Uzziah has already brought him into his castle. I told the messenger to let him know to expect us shortly."

Getting into position for Corwin to lift me up for flying has become a practiced motion. I settle against his chest, taking a little comfort from his solid warmth. The three fae sweep out onto the terrace and spring into the air without hesitation.

Zelpha and Verik contract into full raven form, since they don't have anyone to carry. They swoop ahead of us, dark graceful shapes against the stark blue of the sky. Corwin soars after them, tucking his head close to mine.

We know what we're doing now. We know we can fix this. There's nothing to worry about.

He can say that, but I know his emotions aren't totally settled either. I lean into him. *I'll do my best. I know the arch-lords were already skeptical. Maybe if they see it with one of the folk of their own flock, they won't mind having me around so much.*

They shouldn't have minded in the first place, Corwin says, but a matching hope flows from him into me.

Uzziah's domain lies on the other side of the Heart. His castle is a broad, gloomy fortress of dark metal that reminds me a lot of the solemn man whose family must have created it. The sight doesn't inspire much in the way of uplifting thoughts.

We land just outside the imposing doorway, Zelpha and Verik shifting into human form in mid-flight. A servant opens the door immediately to usher us in.

We find Uzziah with his typically stern expression down a narrow hall deep within the castle. The metallic scent trickling off the walls gives me the unnerving impression of raw meat. As Corwin inclines his head to his colleague and gives his condolences, I have to swallow another surge of queasiness.

"The curse-struck one is in here?" my mate asks, motioning to the door Uzziah was waiting outside of.

The other arch-lord folds his arms over his chest. "Yes. Do you need to make any preparations before you see him?"

"No, we have all we need. We'll work through the process on the spot. Since we've only managed the effect once before, it'll most likely still take a little trial and error." Corwin draws in a breath. "If you'll give us an hour or so, I feel reasonably certain we'll come to you with good news within that timeframe."

Uzziah's eyebrows arch. "Come to me? I'll be with you. I'm not having you work this strange Seelie magic on my people without bearing witness." At the rapping of footsteps from farther away, he glances down the hallway. "When Laoni got word, she said she'd come to observe as well."

Oh, great, the only winter fae who makes me *more* nervous than Uzziah.

Corwin draws himself up straighter as the imposing Unseelie woman comes into view at the end of the hall. *I'm sorry,* he says only to me. *If I try to prevent them from observing, they'll only be more suspicious of what we're doing. I don't have any grounds to outright bar them from the room.*

I gather my nerve. *It's all right. It had to happen sometime, I guess.* At least now I have a halfway decent idea of what I'm doing.

When Laoni reaches us, with a narrow glance and a nod at Corwin and no acknowledgment of me at all, Uzziah leads the way into the room. "We have visitors who may be able to sort you out," he announces.

The man who's sitting cross-legged on the floor near the hearth looks up at us. The curse must be gripping him quickly—a hint of blue already stains his cheeks. He's the youngest of the fae I've tried to help so far, maybe not yet out of the fae equivalent of his teens.

But that's okay. I'm going to stop the curse from leaching any more of life's warmth from his body.

"Let's start with the gestures we can attempt right away, and then move to the more involved possibilities," Corwin says a little stiffly. I can tell from my impressions through our bond that he means we'll hold off on the crying part until it's absolutely necessary.

Uzziah and Laoni take positions beside the hearth where they have a clear view of the proceedings. Ignoring their penetrating stares, I crouch down beside the young man and raise my hand. "I'm going to touch you, only for a moment."

He peers back at me and shivers. "All right."

I brush my fingers tentatively against his cheek and then hold them there more firmly. The chill in his face seeps into my skin. No warmth expands from where I'm touching. Well, it was probably too much to ask that the solution be quite that simple.

I ease back and straighten up. "Now…?" I say, checking Corwin's expression.

He glances at Zelpha. "Was there anything else that happened right before?"

She shakes her head. "We'd tried giving the woman the confections we brought, but that was at least ten minutes before any effect showed. After that, Talia stepped aside. You talked with the woman a bit. I'm not sure how much of a difference that made."

"It can't hurt to include it." Corwin turns back to me. "Prepare yourself, and when you're ready, let him see."

"Okay." I inhale deeply and swivel so my back is to the young man, like I did in the room with the pregnant woman. Maybe it makes a difference for him not to be sure what's happening right away too.

I can't compare this young fae to my mother, but what about—he's about the age, in fae terms, that my brother would have been now if he'd survived, isn't he?

What would Jamie's life have been like if Aerik and his cadre hadn't killed him? What things might he have done? There's so much he missed out on—so much he should have had… And if I can't come through, this fae man will lose so much time he should have had too. He's barely had time to come into his own.

It takes longer than last time for the burn to well up behind my eyes, maybe because of the pressure of multiple gazes watching the proceedings. I tune out my awareness of my spectators' presence as well as I can, focusing on the memory of Jamie's shrieks and the glimpses I caught of his savaged body, on every milestone that was stolen from him, on all the joy he'd been able to express at just eight years old and how much more he could have experienced…

And it was my fault. Maybe not completely, maybe not even mostly, but in some ways, it can't be denied. I led him on that chase into the woods. I teased him into following me.

If I hadn't been playing games, he'd still be alive.

If I can't pull myself together to help the young man right here, *his* death will be on my shoulders too.

A lump creeps up my throat. Moisture forms in the corners of my eyes. The first tears trickle out slowly, but once they've started, more stream out, faster than I can blink them back.

But I don't want to blink or wipe them away. The fae man needs to see them—to see that I'm crying for him.

I turn back around. Corwin is ready, having sensed my emotions. "See how she weeps for you," he says to the young man, gesturing to me. "It pains her to know you're suffering. She cries to think your life might be cut short."

"What is this about?" Laoni breaks in, her voice stiff with what sounds like horror. "How is your human having a meltdown going to cure anything?"

I wince, but I force myself to step closer to the young man anyway.

"Give her a chance," Corwin insists. "This is how it worked the last time."

Uzziah lets out a discontented mumble. The other arch-lords are both scowling now as well as staring. Apprehension prickles down my back. I can't see any change in the young man yet.

With tears still trickling down over my skin, I touch his cheek again, trying to replicate the exact angle and motion as I did with the woman two days ago.

Then, it felt so natural in the moment. Right now I only feel awkward. I will the warmth to chase away the chill in his skin, but nothing happens.

"I'm not seeing any grand effect," Uzziah mutters.

Laoni steps toward us. "This is a ridiculous spectacle. Whatever you're trying to prove, it's clearly misguided."

Panic flickers from Corwin through our bond. "Let me at least try —" He swipes his forefinger across my jaw to collect a few tears and brings them to the young man's lips.

Laoni lets out an indignant sputter and leaps in to yank his arm away. It's too late. I can tell Corwin managed to give the young man a taste of them. I hold my breath, pleading with everything I have in me for the blue to vanish beneath a healthy flush of life, for there to be *some* sign that what we're doing here made a difference.

But nothing comes. Laoni marches Corwin out of the room, motioning for Uzziah to usher me after them. Zelpha and Verik follow, their expressions stormy. They won't speak out of place among the other arch-lords unless Corwin prompts them to, though.

"What in the lands was *that* meant to be?" Laoni snaps once we're out in the hall. "You're likely to sicken him more seeing this dust-destined mortal so overwrought."

"I swear to you, we're only repeating what worked in the previous case," Corwin says emphatically. "Please, if you'd let us continue—there may be some pattern to it we haven't identified—"

"Maybe it was the confections beforehand?" Zelpha ventures.

Laoni ignores her. "What else would you do, exactly?"

Corwin's uncertainty travels into me. We went through all the basics of what worked with the other woman. "Perhaps… Perhaps he needs to have spent more time with Talia first, to feel more comfortable with her…"

"So you want to badger this one of my flock-folk with even more hysterics while he's already suffering?" Uzziah says.

"He's going to suffer anyway," I break in, unable to stay quiet. "We *know* something worked before. Is there really anything that wouldn't be worth trying if it ends the curse?"

The fae around me fall silent. Then Laoni turns to Corwin, her gaze icy. "You will prepare everything you offered to the woman you cured and have it on hand. Then you may return with your 'mate' and make another attempt. But if that one fails too, then I think we must assume the previous recovery was simply a milder case, not a curing. Our people don't deserve to be put through even more torment in their final moments. We'll send him to the summer realm and hope for better luck there."

Corwin dips his head in a jerk of acceptance. "It shouldn't take long. We'll return as soon as we're ready. Come."

He holds out his hand to me, beckoning to his coterie with the other. I grasp his fingers, but a sense of hopelessness too big for me to shake sweeps over me.

They're giving us another chance, sure. But what if we still can't get it right? What if that one moment before *was* some weird fluke, or some specific synergy that formed between me and the pregnant woman for reasons that no longer apply?

If we can't cure this man, the other arch-lords will have even more reason to dismiss everything Corwin suggests for the rest of his reign.

CHAPTER SEVENTEEN

Talia

It's late evening by our second return to the palace from Uzziah's castle. Stars are glinting into sight all across the darkening sky. It should be a beautiful sight, but I can't appreciate it. My eyes are stinging, my heart thumping heavily in my chest.

That's it, isn't it? I say to Corwin, not wanting to discuss our failure—*my* failure—out loud with his coterie members too. *They said they'd give us one more chance. They won't let us see him again.*

If we think of something we missed, they'd have to give us the opportunity to offer it, Corwin says, but his inner voice is as downcast as I feel.

Laoni said they're going to send him to the summer realm settlement right away.

I'll take you there if I think we have a chance.

I don't know why the chances we had today didn't get us anywhere. Maybe my tears were too forced, or I didn't manage to produce enough of them? It isn't like bleeding, where all it takes is a nick of my skin and the fluid springs out. Or was it some aspect of my interactions with the pregnant woman that none of us noticed that drove back the curse?

My blood can snap *all* of the Seelie out of their wildness. Surely whatever I can do for the Unseelie curse wouldn't be restricted to just pregnant women—or women—or people who make me think of my mother—or any other random criteria?

But then, none of the magic that's tying me to the fae makes sense to begin with, so who can say?

Just inside the palace, Corwin turns to Zelpha and Verik, who stayed with us and offered whatever suggestions they could through our second visit with Uzziah's afflicted flock member. The arch-lord dips his head to Zelpha. "If you remember anything else from the other day that might serve us…"

"I'll let you know right away, my lord," she says, her usually energetic voice somber. She manages a stiff little smile, and the two of them head off.

"Are you hungry?" Corwin asks me.

I've had nibbles of things here and there throughout the afternoon—we thought maybe sharing a meal with the cursed young man might help somehow—and my stomach is too tight for the thought of eating more to appeal to me. I shake my head. "Just tired." And frustrated with myself. And horrified for that fae man I haven't been able to save. A stew of unpleasant emotion churns inside me.

If I were back in the place I still think of as my main home, with Sylas, Whitt, and August, right now I'd go to one of them and let them wrap me up in their arms. It wouldn't make all the wrong things about today right, but it'd ease the pain inside me a little. None of them are here, though.

But my mate is. I look at Corwin, taking in the distress etched on his own face and the worries for his people overshadowing every other emotion I sense from him, and nothing in me balks. He *is* my mate. I care about him, and I trust him. Maybe I don't feel exactly the same way about him as I do my Seelie lovers, but his embrace would be a comfort too.

I just feel guilty asking for it when I'm the one who let us both down.

I can't bring myself to put the request into words, but the longing rises up strongly enough that Corwin must catch it anyway. He meets my eyes as if checking to confirm and then holds out his hand to me.

Whether I'm being selfish or not, I can't help myself. I twine my fingers with his, letting the affection he's sending through our bond wash over me, and walk with him back to my bedroom.

On the threshold, he hesitates again, even though the comfort I'm desperate for isn't anything especially intimate. I just want to be held. I squeeze his hand and lead him in, and he follows with a flare of happiness he can't suppress—or maybe he doesn't want to.

At the edge of the bed, he scoops me up much like when he's flying me somewhere and settles us on top of the covers together, my head tucked under his chin, his arms encircling me, our legs folded against each other.

He strokes his hand over my hair. I press my head against his chest, his wintry forest smell filling my nose. Even after all the tears I forced out over the past several hours, new ones prick at my eyes.

I thought his embrace would give me some comfort, but instead I only feel more guilty. He probably has other, more important things he needs to be doing to repair whatever damage I've done to his reputation.

"I'm sorry," I mumble, not totally sure which of the vast array of failings I can think of I'm apologizing for.

Corwin's arms tighten around me. A flood of compassion and tenderness courses through our bond, so intense and undeniable it brings a different sort of tears to my eyes.

"You have nothing to apologize for," he says. "You're giving so much of yourself already. No one could ask for more than that."

"But it hasn't been enough. There must be something I'm missing that made things work with the woman before but not today. And now the other arch-lords are blaming *you* for everything."

Corwin lets out a faint huff. "I'm sure they'd have found something else to blame me for if it wasn't this. You know they were never that fond of me, from well before you ever set foot in our realm."

"They've threatened to remove you from your position if they think your judgment is off," I have to point out. "If you lose Heart's Cadence because of me—"

"No," Corwin cuts in firmly. He pulls back far enough to tip my chin so he can meet my eyes. In the dim twilight of the room, his glint like black diamonds. "They can try, but they won't succeed. And nothing they do is *because* of you. Talia—" A roughness creeps into his voice. "I couldn't be more impressed by your strength and generosity when it comes to my people. You can feel that, can't you? You barely know us, and you've set aside every other thought to contribute whatever you can, no matter how much strain it puts on you."

The truth of his words resonates into me. I swallow hard. "I just don't want to give them excuses to attack you."

"You don't need to worry about that. It's *my* job to defend you from my colleagues. They're for me to deal with."

He brushes a gentle kiss to my forehead before meeting my gaze again. "They think love makes a person weaker, that you have to keep it reined in or it'll break you like it did my mother. I started to believe that too. But you've shown me that it's the opposite. Having you in my life, loving you—it makes me *stronger*. Every challenge is easier to meet. Every setback easier to face. Never doubt that you have made my life better in every possible way."

I stare at him, hardly daring to believe him—but there's no denying the conviction that rings through his words and sings through our bond. It strengthens my own resolve.

This problem is complicated and difficult, and I hate that we haven't solved it yet, but we're not done fighting. And I'm not fighting it alone. I found my footing among the Seelie, but Corwin is helping me uncover new determination and confidence within myself too. While I might not know yet why the Heart tied us together, I'm glad that it did.

Another longing swells inside me, one that might also be unfair since I can't offer the same in return just yet, but I'm not sure I could hide it from my mate when we're this closely entwined anyway. My voice comes out in little more than a whisper. "You've never said it to me."

Corwin blinks. "Said what?"

"That—" My cheeks heat as I fumble with the words. "How you feel about me. I've felt it, and you told Donovan, and you talked about it just now, but you've never…"

"Oh." He caresses my hair again, studying me. "I didn't want to make you feel pressured to return the sentiment. You *shouldn't* feel pressured. And I suppose I'm still not the most adept at expressing my emotions." He drags in a breath. "I love you, Talia, and I will wait however long it takes to earn your love in return. I couldn't have asked for a better mate among the truest of true-blooded fae."

His love shines into me like the glow of the summer sun, so bright and warm it's hard to believe it could have come from a man who normally has a lot in common with the cold, impenetrable lands he grew up in. I want to soak it all up, in every possible way.

I want to offer everything I can back. I might not be ready to say the same thing just yet, but I can't deny that I'm falling for him.

Why should I deny myself any of this?

I run my fingers into his thick curls and bring his mouth to mine. Like always, the kiss sparks a sharper heat right down the center of me. But this time, I don't try to dampen my reaction. I let the flames keep kindling inside me as I meld my lips even more perfectly against his.

A soft groan escapes Corwin. He kisses me back hard, his own desire roaring to life. The sense of how much he wants me fuels my own hunger and sets off a fresh wave of his, on and on in a blazing cycle between us.

It's scared me before—the intensity of our connection. But I know I'm strong enough to revel in it without losing myself. I've got to have at least as much faith in myself as he does.

I roll onto my back, pulling him with me. Corwin follows, his nerves lighting up as his body comes to rest on top of mine with a tingling eagerness that races into me. I want—I *need*—this man so much it's hard to imagine I ever pulled away from him before. His yearning smolders just as hot.

He kisses me on the mouth again before charting a searing path along my jaw and down the side of my neck. When he finds a sensitive spot at the crook of my shoulder, I gasp. My hands fumble with the collar of his shirt, searching for the snaps to loosen it.

His fingers skim up the side of my torso, burning with eagerness. *Talia?* he says without lifting his mouth from my skin. It's both a question and a plea, so much longing in it my skin quivers.

Yes. I want… I want to feel all of you.

He lets out another groan, his lips moving down over my collarbone as he finds the fastenings on my dress. *When this happened, I meant to take it slow. To treasure every moment. To ensure you experienced every pleasure. But I don't know—I've wanted you so much. I'm not sure how well I can hold back.*

Don't. His fingers delve beneath the dress's bodice, and I arch into his touch. *You don't have to hold back or pretend with me. I* like *seeing you as you are.*

With a strained noise in his throat, his mouth crashes down on mine. I manage to peel back his shirt to trace the lean muscles underneath. His thumb swivels over the peak of my breast, sparking a jolt of pleasure.

Everywhere we touch, the flames of desire flare hotter. The rush of pleasure spikes higher with his thrill at my reactions, with the shivers of delight that course through his flesh beneath my hands. We're alight with not just our own pleasure but each other's, or maybe it's all the same, one immense wave of bliss sweeping through both of us in tandem.

With a series of hasty tugs, Corwin unwraps me from my dress and tosses it aside. His mouth roves over my body with gentle nips and avid swipes of his tongue, as if I'm the greatest delicacy he's ever consumed.

When he sucks one nipple between his hot lips, my head tips back with a whimper. As I dig my fingers into his hair, he teases the nub to a stiffer peak with a swirl of his tongue, the graze of his teeth. Giddiness shimmers between us. I can't tell who's enjoying the moment more, only that with every fresh spark of pleasure, it grows on both sides.

I wrench him back up over me, claiming his mouth, exploring his tautly muscled body now that I've managed to strip off his shirt completely. The responses that ripple from him into me tell me exactly which caresses provoke the greatest effect. For a few minutes, I'm content to summon as much heated bliss in him as I can just by running my hands over his chest.

Finally, I dip my fingers right down to the waist of his trousers. The bolt of lust that shoots through our connection has me drenching my panties even though he hasn't touched me that far down yet.

An oversight that can be quickly remedied, Corwin says with fervent amusement. As I grapple with his belt buckle, he slides his hand down between us to cup it between my thighs.

The electric tingling at his touch, at how pleased *he* is to feel my arousal, reverberates through my veins. I can't help pressing into his fingers, chasing the heights they promise. A growl slips from my mouth that pleases him too.

Then I yank his belt away and ease my hand into his trousers, and all conscious thought evaporates from his mind with my grasp around his already hardened erection. The heady sensation searing through him radiates into me. I buck into his hand, melting and soaring at the same time.

Between scorching kisses, he kicks off his trousers and boxers. As I stroke his rigid length up and down, my brain short-circuits at just how much pleasure I never knew this gesture could summon. Corwin keeps his head enough to make short work of my panties.

I raise my knees on either side of his hips, welcoming him. Pure joy races through his body. He lines himself up and plunges into me in one swift stroke.

Oh! It's even more overwhelming than the flood of impressions before—feeling his hardness stretching me, filling me; feeling my slickness clenching eagerly around him. I've never experienced anything like this before, and somehow I'm still spiraling higher and higher.

I pant for air, pressing back into the pillow. Corwin ducks his head next to mine, hot breath and shaky kisses marking my neck.

My love, he says with his inner voice, punctuating each thrust with words radiant with happiness. *My heart. My soul.*

My mate, I answer automatically, my hands gripping his shoulders.

The words somehow set off an even headier surge of need than before. We rock together wildly, spurred on by each other's blaze of passion as we hurtle toward our release, and I can no longer tell where his body begins and mine ends. It's just *us*, twined together, merged into one being of bliss.

The giddy pressure builds and builds—and finally crashes over us in a breathtaking maelstrom. I quake beneath Corwin, and he clutches me to him with a groan—and oh, God, if it could have been like this from the start, why have I been resisting this for so long?

We come to rest still linked together. Corwin kisses my temple and then my cheek, and I taste the salt of my sweat on my skin through his lips. The joyful satisfaction resonating through him echoes my own so well it brings a smile to my face.

More than worth the wait, he tells me, as if he picked up my earlier thought.

My muscles have gone so slack I can barely move. Corwin eases down next to me and nestles me against him like before. I sink into his embrace with a happy sigh. But as I relax there in his warmth, three truths settle over me with a weight I can't shake off.

I'm falling for this man. It may not be long at all before I can say I love him. And I still have no idea how to reconcile that growing devotion with all the love I have in me for my lovers back in the summer realm.

CHAPTER EIGHTEEN

Talia

The atmosphere during breakfast is a strange mix of contentment and somberness. After sleeping next to Corwin all night—and rediscovering just how good our bodies can feel together this morning—a happy glow infuses our bond. Every time I look at him, a flutter passes through my chest, giddier when he happens to be looking back.

But at the same time the knowledge hangs over us that the young man from Uzziah's flock will have been taken to the summer settlement last night. Maybe the warmth and the vibrant surroundings will melt away the curse's grip on him. If they don't, then it'll only be a couple of days before he's dead.

And we have no idea why I couldn't help him.

We don't communicate much other than wordless wisps of fondness through our connection. I suspect neither of us wants to break the spell of our recently shared passion by bringing up any of the many subjects we'll need to get back to discussing. But we don't get to linger in that peace very long anyway.

Just as we're finishing up the last of our meal, a headier warmth filling me as Corwin tracks my tongue licking traces of honey from my thumb, a fae man I recognize as one of Corwin's servants hustles into the room. "My lord," he says with a deep bow. "Apologies for the intrusion. Domhnall sent a messenger who wishes to speak to you as soon as possible."

My mate lets out a noise of concern and gets to his feet, a serious cast coming over his face. "I'll be there at once." He turns to me. "Domhnall is another of my coterie members—he's been traveling the realm on my behalf. If he's reached out without feeling he could return to speak to me himself, it must be a grave matter."

I push back my chair. "Do you think it's to do with the curse?"

"It may."

As I stand, Corwin pauses, and I sense that he didn't expect me to come with him. But he recovers within seconds and gestures for me to follow him. *As my mate, you should be aware of anything critical going on in the realm. I'm simply not used to having the company yet.*

It's all right, I reply. *I know it's still an adjustment.* For me as well as him. But after what we've shared, both between each other and in facing the curse, I can't stand to hang back while he takes this new problem on by himself.

He shoots me a smile. As we walk toward the terrace, he keeps a measured pace to account for my limp.

The messenger stands just inside the door to the terrace, the thin sunlight filtering through the broad windows making her look like some kind of snow nymph with her pale skin and equally pale clothes.

"My lord," she says, with a bow just as deep as the servant's. "Domhnall wishes to have your presence as soon as you're able to reach him. He didn't convey all the details to me, but it's in regard to the incursions of beasts farther in from the borders. He's waiting for you in Lakeshine."

A flicker of discomfort passes through Corwin, there and then stamped out so quickly I'm not sure I didn't imagine it. I glance at him, but his expression has taken on its impervious lordly mask. I feel as if the walls around our bond have risen just slightly.

He shows no outward distress. "Thank you for your haste. I'll set off immediately. Do you require passage back?"

The messenger shakes her head. "I have business in a domain nearby, and I can make my own way easily enough. It was a pleasure to serve my arch-lords."

She slips out onto the terrace, unfurling her wings as she goes. When she fully transforms, her raven is a muted gray that blends into the snowy landscape the moment she soars off over it.

Corwin murmurs a scrap of bark into being with a few words marked on it and sends it off like I've seen my Seelie men do with leaves to send a message. "I'll bring Olander," he tells me. "Better to have too much support than too little."

"And me," I put in. "I should know what's going on, right?"

My mate hesitates again, this time with a deeper twinge of uneasiness that reminds me of his earlier discomfort. "I wouldn't want —if it's a matter to do with the beasts, you'd have trouble defending yourself."

The memory of the searmaw that attacked us in the frostfire forest comes back to me with a shiver, but I hold my ground. "I'll have you and two of your coterie members right there. I promise I won't go wandering off or anything stupid like that. If it's *that* bad, I can just stay in the carriage and you can make it hover ten feet off the ground. Unless some of these beasts fly?"

Corwin's lips twitch with a hint of amusement. "No, the creatures we've been dealing with have been land-based."

"I do want to be a full participant here," I go on. "I need to understand every part of your work as an arch-lord. And maybe there's some other way I can help."

Since I'm struggling so much to help with the curse, I don't need to say. A waft of compassion wraps around me, and Corwin's expression softens. "All right. I know I can't be treating you as if you're so terribly fragile. But do stay close to us while we're there."

"Of course. I don't want to end up as a searmaw's breakfast."

I'm not sure if Corwin and Olander would have flown by their own wings to Lakeshine if I wasn't coming along, but it's too far for him to carry me. We go out onto the icy plain beside the palace, and by the time Olander meets us there, the arch-lord has summoned a small carriage into being.

Olander gives me a slight nod but doesn't say anything to me, which I'm okay with. Hopefully my participating in situations like this will show him that I do have a legitimate place alongside his lord. I tuck myself into my favorite spot near the bow, and Corwin and his coterie member lean against opposite walls of the carriage.

"Domhnall didn't say what specifically he's so concerned about right now?" Olander asks. "We've been having these issues with the beasts for months now."

Corwin shakes his head. "Perhaps it was too sensitive for him to want to pass the information on through a messenger. Lakeshine is pretty far inward from the fringes… Years ago, it'd have been unusual to see any beasts of the most hostile sort in that area. If there's been a particularly large influx, that might have been enough to worry him all on its own."

"But not really worth keeping secret." Olander frowns. "He has a good head on his shoulders—not the type to panic. It must be bad. I don't like this at all."

"Neither do I." Corwin sighs. "Have you continued to work on the true name for chimeras? I know you can handle a searmaw already, and just about anything else we could run into."

"I've been meditating on it, but it's always difficult without direct interaction. And I think chimeras will be a tricky one to master in general. If you can spare me to spend some time on the fringes where I could 'commune' with them more, I'd get there faster."

Corwin hums to himself. "I think our current situation is too precarious for me to want to send you off that far. But if we can get matters relating to the curse more settled, then it might be feasible."

One more thing being delayed by my difficulty with the curse. I suck my lower lip under my teeth but manage to hold myself back from worrying at it.

Are there any simpler true names that could help against the beasts? Maybe we could work on one of those to start on my magic training here, and I could actually get involved in fending them off—

No, Corwin interrupts, gently but firmly. *Your Seelie men have kept your additional powers secret from the rest of their kind for a good reason. If you show them publicly, I have no idea how my colleagues or the rest of my people will react, but I suspect it'll cause more chaos than joy.*

When my spirits sink, he adds in an even softer tone, *But that doesn't mean we can't see where we can get with those true names one on one. I just hesitate to have you use them in a meaningful way in public until your position here is more secure.*

Of course. I understand. Even if I don't like it.

I'm getting tired of having to hide so much of who I am. As if it's my fault the Heart's magic has ended up twined through me in so many unexpected ways. As if it's a problem when you'd think it should be a gift.

But then, how can I be frustrated that the Unseelie may not totally accept me when I haven't even totally accepted my soul-twined mate yet? I haven't let myself really become a part of this world in every way it wants me to.

I chew on that thought for some time, not liking any of the conclusions it leads me to. When the carriage finally starts to slow, I shake off my reverie and stand up to take a good look at the domain we're arriving in.

Unsurprisingly, Lakeshine's castle and village stand by a large, glassy lake. The water lies so still, only the faintest ripple caused by the breeze reveals that its surface isn't frozen solid. The castle and its buildings have been formed out of dark gray stone that sparkles with patches of mica.

As inert as the lake looks, there must be life in it, because the air that meets my nose when I climb out of the carriage has a faint but distinct fishy odor. The breeze is almost warm by winter realm standards, though.

I stick close to Corwin as he strides toward the village. Before we reach the nearest houses, a man hurries over to join us: short and spindly-limbed, with hair so short it's merely a dark sheen on his brown scalp. He bobs his head to Corwin and raises a hand in greeting to Olander, his gaze stopping on me only for a moment with a fleeting trace of curiosity.

"My lord, if you'll come with me. I think you'll understand why I've called you in once you have the whole story."

He sets off around the edges of the village at a swifter pace than I'd expect from someone so delicate-looking. I keep up as well as I can, ignoring the prickling of pain in my warped foot when I push myself faster.

Around the far side of the village where the lake is no longer in view, three large beasts sprawl in pools of blood. A mix of fur and scales covers their massive forms. I step even closer to Corwin, just in case they're not quite as dead as they appear.

The man who must be Domhnall lowers his voice. "It's odd enough to have them coming in this far. But the thing with these three is—scouts spotted them two domains away. They headed straight here, ignoring the other villages closer by that they passed."

Corwin's forehead furrows. "Did no one try to stop them?"

"Of course. But there wasn't anyone with solid enough true names to hold them back, and they were quite determined not to be diverted. Word went out, and I arrived here just as they did. It took a considerable amount of power to tackle them here when they'd rather have ignored me and continued on into town."

"As if they were being driven—or summoned—by magic," Olander says, and I remember the tuskcat some of Ambrose's pack-kin sent after me months ago.

"Who would they have been after?" I ask without thinking.

Domhnall gives me another quizzical glance, but at Corwin's nod, he answers. "I don't know. I've asked around the village—surreptitiously so as not to provoke too much anxiety—and it doesn't sound as if there've been any major conflicts between anyone of this flock and another in recent times. I'm not even entirely sure these three *were* magically compelled. I've checked them over and found no trace of any but their innate magic. I thought possibly with your keener awareness, you might decipher the spell, my lord."

Corwin moves forward and kneels by the first of the creatures. He intones a few words under his breath and stretches his hands out over the monstrous body. They hover over each part of the beast before he draws them back and rubs his mouth. "I don't sense anything in that one. Let me try the others."

As he works, a small crowd of villagers gathers a short distance away. Olander and Domhnall stop them from getting any closer, but the coterie members seem to feel it'd be worse to try to shoo them away completely. The villagers stir restlessly on their feet, looking plenty anxious already.

When he's examined all three, Corwin straightens up with a clouded expression. "If there was magic on them, it's already faded. That could be the case if it was tied to their life's energy. But it's quite an odd tactic regardless. To settle a dispute this way—and so far from the fringes, where the beasts' presence would immediately draw notice—is highly unlikely to have a controlled outcome."

Olander hums. "Beyond the savagery of it, it's not particularly smart, is it?"

"It doesn't appear so. But perhaps I can unravel the mystery more." He turns to our small audience. "Since you're already here, I hope you won't mind if I ask you a few questions."

There's a snort from the back of the bunch. My gaze lands on a stout, middle-aged woman who's crossed her arms over her chest. Several other gazes zero in on her, including Corwin's. A tremor of uneasiness passes from him into me.

"Did you have something to say, Pippa?" he asks in the most carefully even voice I've ever heard from him.

She wets her lips. Something hostile sparks in her eyes and then fades. "I'd only say if it turns out these things *were* sent our way on purpose, I hope you'll make sure the punishment for the crime is just."

She turns and walks off. The other flock-folk focus on Corwin again. He smiles tightly, but his emotions are roiling behind his impassive front.

What was that about? I have to ask.

Nothing to worry yourself about. She won't say more than that.

But why would she want to? It's obviously upset you. It bothered you as soon as you heard we needed to come here. What's—

Corwin's inner voice breaks through mine with unusual sharpness. *Let it* be, *Talia.*

I'm so startled I take a step back, as if he's physically pushed me away. Corwin's gaze jerks to me, his eyes widening. *I'm sorry,* he says quickly. *I—there are things I try not to think about, let alone discuss. But*

I suppose you deserve to know. He draws in a breath and faces the flock again. *We can't talk about it while there are others around. When we get back to the palace, I'll explain, I swear.*

His apology and his promise ring true, but all the same, a lump fills my throat as he steps closer to the flock-folk to ask his questions.

What can my mate have managed to hide from me that he's even more hesitant to share than his family's tragedy?

CHAPTER NINETEEN

Corwin

Talia's impatience trickles through our bond for the entire journey back to Heart's Cadence. I hate that after we've come so far, I'm shutting her out more than I have in days—after she welcomed me into her bed, after we shared the greatest physical intimacy we can. But I don't want her glimpsing too much of the tumultuous emotions inside me either.

I'm annoyed at myself for letting Pippa affect me, for showing any distress at all about going out to Lakeshine. Frustrated that I couldn't come up with any answers to explain why those beasts homed in on that village. Dreading the conversation to come and how Talia might react to me afterward. What if hearing this account chills all the trust I've won from her?

I wouldn't have avoided the subject forever. At some point, this part of my history would have to come up. I'd just hoped it'd be after we were more formally united and solid in our bond.

But perhaps I deserve to have it out in the open now. I'd like to think it doesn't define who I am in the present in any way, that it was a lapse driven by a culmination of circumstances that could never repeat themselves, but that doesn't ease the pang of old guilt that's risen up through my turmoil.

We can't hash it out just yet. Even in the relative privacy of the carriage, I don't want to start the conversation with Olander present. The words exchanged through our bond might be imperceptible to outside eyes, but our reactions to the subjects we touch on aren't. I can't focus completely on Talia when I have to consider how one of my coterie will be noting my behavior as well.

To give her credit, Talia doesn't badger me about it. For all her internal restlessness, she holds her tongue, not saying anything even through our bond until the carriage lands outside the palace. Olander sets off for his home in the village, and my mate glances at me with a question she doesn't need to put into words in her eyes.

"Let's go to my study," I say, wishing my voice hadn't come out hoarse.

She nods, and then after a second's hesitation, reaches to grasp my hand. The simple gesture makes my throat constrict even more. I haven't lost her trust *yet*, in any case.

Whatever it is, you need to let me decide what to make of it, she says, lacing her fingers through mine. *I don't believe it can be anything all that terrible. Maybe I don't know everything about you yet, but I do know* you.

Heart help me, let her be right about that.

We reach my study, and I shut the door firmly behind us. Then I find I have no idea where to start, even though I've had hours to consider it.

Talia settles herself into what appears to have become her favorite armchair in the room, slipping off her boots and pulling her legs up next to her. I stay on my feet. I manage not to pace, but I can't will myself to relax enough to sit down either.

"Something happened with that woman in the past," Talia prompts.

"In a way." I inhale deeply and turn to face her. "I want you to know from the start that I'm ashamed of the decisions I made—they were born out of anger and pain rather than reason and good sense, and while those emotions weren't unjustified, I believe I owed better to those involved."

Talia studies me, her calm expression unwavering. "Okay, I'll keep that in mind."

It's too awkward after all just standing here motionless. I cast about for something to hold onto and finally sink into one of the other chairs, though not the one behind my desk. I don't want any reminders of my authority between us while I explain.

"There's a custom among the Unseelie that the few fae who are blessed with multiple children may send a child to one of the arch-lords' courts to be fostered there," I begin. "When a family already has one or two to carry on their own legacy, it gives the additional child a special opportunity. They generally integrate into the arch-lord's flock and remain there as adults, and frequently they become close enough with the arch-lord to enter the coterie."

"That makes sense," Talia says. "Was someone like that sent to Heart's Cadence?"

"Yes. When I was still a child, my parents took a boy a couple of decades younger than me as a foster. Lazlo."

Even though the moment is more than two centuries distant now, the memory of our tentative first meeting sticks vividly in my mind: that young version of Lazlo ducking his head shyly even as his bright eyes glinted with curiosity. "He lived here in the palace," I go on. "We essentially grew up together. It didn't take long before we were close friends."

Talia's gaze weighs on me. I can feel her putting together the pieces before she speaks. "I haven't met him. He isn't here anymore?"

"No. He— I—" I pause, rubbing my forehead. The words catch at the back of my tongue.

I want to lay it out as dispassionately as I'd need to before my fellow arch-lords, as if it were something that happened millennia ago to someone I never met. But that will only make Talia see me as being as cold and cruel as Pippa no doubt does.

I'm just not sure—I've never really *let* myself grieve. I'm still not certain I even deserve to.

"The world didn't end when you told me about what happened to your parents," Talia says softly. "I don't think it will over this either."

"I know. But this is different. That was something that happened around me—this was something that happened *because* of me. When I was at my worst." I've only just realized how badly I must have let Lazlo down, with Talia showing me that I don't have to stay quite so bottled up to fulfill my role as arch-lord after all. If I'd met her back then—if she'd existed back then—

Of course, if I'd had my soul-twined mate by my side, *everything* would have been very different.

I force myself to continue. "Lazlo did everything he could to support me when my father died. I took on Verik, Domhnall, and Meriol, who you haven't met yet, from my father's coterie, but Lazlo was the first who was solely my choice. But as my mother deteriorated, as I struggled to find my footing among my colleagues and they began to judge me based on her behavior—you know that I've closed myself off."

"You tried to make yourself like ice," Talia says, with a hint of affection. "Or maybe like diamond. Hard and unshakeable."

"And cold. Even with Lazlo. I didn't want to appear partial or to risk our friendship affecting my judgment… so I started holding him at a distance. Speaking to him about little other than the business of the realm. Showing no interest in the rest of his life. He tried to maintain the rapport we once had, but he couldn't do it on his own. Looking back, I can tell I hurt him badly."

I let those memories wash through me, knowing Talia is catching glimpses of them too. The smiles that cooled and faded over time, the laughter dwindling into silence, the overtures he simply stopped making, aware of what my response would be.

I told myself it was for the best. That the loss I felt was a necessary sacrifice. I can't imagine my sense of purpose did anything to ease *his* loss, though.

Talia extends a tendril of sympathy that I'm not sure I'd receive if I'd finished the story. "He ended up leaving?"

"Yes, but not quite as you're thinking." I clasp my hands together in my lap. "There was also—after I'd settled into my responsibilities and found ways to at least… stabilize my mother, I took notice of a fae woman in the flock who was unmated." Just the thought of her sends a sharper jab of guilt through me, as if I've betrayed Talia somehow before she was even born.

"It's okay," Talia says, though I catch a tremor of discomfort through our bond that presumably she can't control either. "I know it's normal for the true-blooded fae to take other lovers when they haven't found their soul-twined mate yet—and even when they have."

I bristle instinctively at her final remark. "You won't need to worry about *that*." Reining in my emotions, I gather myself. "But yes. I wanted that sort of companionship, and I liked Ensley a great deal—and she liked me as well, as far as I could tell—but I always kept her at a careful distance for the same reason I held myself back from Lazlo. I didn't want to become too emotionally entangled, especially after seeing my mother so affected by a broken heart."

"I think that's understandable."

"Perhaps. But it did mean two people very close to me who spent a lot of time in each other's company because of that didn't feel they could count on me or that I cared very much about either of them." I grimace, more at myself than anyone else. "Lazlo and Ensley fell in love and began a relationship in secret. I'm not sure exactly how long it was going on, but—she became pregnant. With his child, she knew because of the timing, but she implied that she'd discovered it sooner than she had to give the impression that it was mine."

Talia stiffens in her chair. "She lied to you about *that*? Or—as close to lying as I guess she could, being fae? That's awful."

I spread my hands, unable to summon any of my anger from back then. It all burned out decades ago, leaving nothing but ash. "They decided together to lead me to false conclusions. Even if the child wouldn't be true-blooded, it would have been better off believed to be an arch-lord's. And they were also afraid of how I'd react if they revealed their relationship at that point. I hadn't given either of them any reason to expect compassion."

Talia's voice goes quiet. "But you obviously found out somehow."

"Yes." I can't sit still any longer. Pushing myself out of the chair, I allow myself to stalk through the room as if the movement will make the rest come out easier. "I was very excited by the thought of a child, as much as I tried to rein my emotions in. I started attending to Ensley more closely and stumbled on the truth. And then…"

I stop at my desk, bowing my head for a moment before swiveling again. "The deception and the realization that the child wasn't my own hurt me—so much more than I'd been prepared for. I think the fact that I'd become so invested without knowing it fueled my anger more than the betrayal itself. Which wasn't fair to them. I should have simply sent them away to seek a home in some other domain. It might not have made much difference, but at least I'd have spared them a little suffering."

"What did you do?" Talia asks, tracking my path across the room.

I force myself to meet her gaze. "There's an area on the fringes where criminals are sometimes sent. The work they're tasked to do there is grueling. I banished them both there. And that might even be why—it seems to strike a little more frequently in the outer domains—a few years later, the curse took them both."

The image that has featured in so many of my nightmares wavers up from the depths of my unconscious: the rigid blue-white faces of my former best friend and my former lover. I hadn't heard until they were already gone, not that I could have saved them at that point anyway.

"It's the only case I know of where two people in close contact fell victim to the curse at the same time," I say roughly. "So I can't help thinking my actions had something to do with it. I never found out what happened to their child—likely they sent him or her off to another domain to have a better life than the fringes would offer. I stole parenthood from them too, for the short time they'd have experienced it."

Talia's tone stays even, but I can taste the trickle of horror that ripples through her. "And how does that woman in Lakeshine fit in?"

"She's Lazlo's mother. She feels, understandably, that I punished him far too harshly. Not that she'd dare spell it out so clearly to my face."

Talia is silent for a long moment. The clash of her emotions carries through our bond and shows in her tensed posture.

I swallow hard. "It's a lot to hear all at once, and it isn't—it isn't how I'd want you to think of me, but I realize you can't simply dismiss it out of hand."

Her hands twist together in front of her. "Have you really forgiven *me* for being with other lovers?"

I'm so startled by that question that I hope she can recognize the truth of my answer. "It wasn't something for me to forgive in the first place. You've been honest with me the entire time. You've never tried to trick me or mislead me. Even if you *did*, I wouldn't let my temper and my fears get the better of me like that again."

"Okay," she says, but there's something different in her expression when she looks at me, a wariness I haven't seen since her first few days here. It sends a lance straight through my heart.

She gets to her feet. "It is a lot. I just—I just need some time to let it sink in, all right? I'm still glad you told me."

I'm not. There wasn't anything else I could have done, but as I watch her leave the room, I can't shake the looming sensation that I've just soured everything good we had together.

CHAPTER TWENTY

Talia

I haven't generally ventured outside Corwin's palace on my own, although he's assured me that his domain is totally safe. But after an uneasy night's sleep and an awkward breakfast, I find myself slipping out the door to walk along the river's bank all the way to the cliff edge where the water tumbles over in the broad torrent of the falls.

There's no wall or any other kind of barrier along the cliff. I guess when most of the beings around here can shift into a bird in an instant, no one has much fear of heights. The roar of the waterfall and the knowledge of the sheer drop just a few steps away jangle my nerves, but after I've stood there for several minutes, gazing out over the spectacular if chilly view, they settle down. There's something reassuring about the fact that despite the chaotic natural phenomenon going on right next to me, I can remain steady on my feet, like I've made it through so much else.

If only I had a better idea what might be waiting for me on the other side of all this confusion.

I don't hear the approaching footsteps over the rush of the water until Zelpha is nearly at my shoulder. She stops next to me, folding her arms over her chest. For a moment, we both stay silent, just taking in the sprawling landscape beyond the cliff: snowy plains, dark forests, icy rivers, and distant mountains.

"So, he told you," she says without preamble.

My gaze jerks to her. Did Corwin say something? Does she even definitely know *what* he told me?

I'm not sure how much I want to say, although presumably she already knows the whole story. She was probably here when it all happened. "I… What do you mean?" I ask.

She looks sideways at me. "It wasn't hard to figure out. I heard you went out to Lakeshine yesterday, and there's been a virtual cloud hanging over the entire palace since you got back. Corwin obviously thinks you're unhappy with him. Are you?"

I open my mouth and then close it again, grappling with my answer. "I don't think unhappy is the right word." It's just that the thought of him being so vengeful—and not really that long ago in fae terms—has shaken me.

For now, he's accepting the Seelie men in my life. For now, he isn't blaming me for being unwilling to completely devote myself to him. But what if he gets impatient? What happens if I fully accept the bond and he starts thinking of me as entirely his?

I've seen so much of him, gotten to know him from the inside out, but he hid that part of his past from me. There could be more I haven't seen. And it isn't as if I've had a shortage of experience with how cruel the fae can be.

"It doesn't fit with how I thought of him before," I continue finally. "I'm having a little trouble wrapping my head around it." That sounds like a polite enough way of putting it when talking to a coterie member who's obviously on his side.

Zelpha nods. "That's fair. I just thought you should know, whatever account he gave you is totally colored by the fact that he's been beating himself up over his decision for more than thirty years. I'd imagine he came across *worse* in his version than he was in reality.

And this is coming from someone who was not only there but had plenty of reason to be pissed off at him over it if his actions hadn't been understandable."

I blink at her. "Why would you have been upset?"

She gives me a crooked little smile. "Ensley was my little sister."

"Oh." My eyes widen. She did say her family had been close to Corwin's. "And you—you thought she deserved to be banished to that awful part of the fringes?"

"I think everyone could have made better decisions, but that Corwin's were the most reasonable of the bunch given his situation. You probably haven't been living here long enough to understand how precious children are to us, especially to the true-bloods like him. To allow him to believe he had a child on the way only to tear that joy away from him, when he'd lost all the other family he had less than two decades before..."

I might not totally understand, but I've heard enough of the fae refer to their feelings about children to know it's an incredibly big deal. "Why would she do it, then?"

Zelpha shakes her head. "She might have been my sister, but I didn't always understand what went through her head. She had to know the truth would come out eventually and hurt him horribly when it did, but she decided to mislead him about it anyway. If they'd told him what was going on as soon as they realized she was pregnant—by the Heart, if she'd broken things off with Corwin to begin with when Lazlo caught her eye—a whole lot of pain could have been spared all around."

"I guess she must have been scared."

"Not of Corwin, I wouldn't think," Zelpha says. "He's never been anything like a tyrant. Ensley did care about him, but she also liked the prestige that came with being attached to an arch-lord. I think she was hesitant to lose her position in case things didn't work out with Lazlo, and she justified it by telling herself Corwin wasn't that invested in their relationship anyway, that she hadn't made any official commitments. Of course, all that went out the window once there was a baby in the mix."

She turns more fully toward me. "I wouldn't have sent them out to the workcamp, no. Simply banishing them in general would have been enough. But they still had opportunities. The camp has a debt system, and if you work hard, you can earn your release. They were together—he didn't insist on separating them. They could have arranged to recover their child once they earned their way out. No one could have predicted that the curse would take them. Corwin certainly had no control over that."

Okay, that doesn't sound quite as dire as Corwin put it. But… "Lazlo's mother seems to blame him."

"Yes, well." Zelpha shrugs. "A lot of people had a lot of thoughts about Corwin in those days. He was young to take over the arch-lord position, and the situation with his mother had noticeably affected him, as well as it being rather unnerving all on its own. Some of our flock-folk muttered about his judgment after the fact. But I wouldn't be surprised if they'd have accused him of being too lenient if he'd picked a gentler punishment. When they saw me speaking up in support of him, as Ensley's sister, that calmed things down pretty quickly. That's actually how I took my first steps toward joining the coterie."

My eyebrows rise. "You haven't been in it for very long, then?"

"No, only about fifteen years. It took a while for him to realize I'd keep having his back, but it's hard to fault him for being skittish after all that went down. It's a hell of a lot of work sometimes, but it's work I enjoy. And… maybe I feel I kind of owe it to him to help keep him on track after my sister's deception threw him so off course."

She turns to me with a crooked grin. "Do you want to come down into the village and get to know more of the flock? Maybe spending some time with them, hearing how they talk about him, will help you get your bearings."

I hesitate, but what else am I going to do? Mope around here or in my bedroom? I'm not going to clear my head that way. And before too long, this flock might be mine nearly as much as it is Corwin's. "All right. Do—do we need to fly?"

"Ah, no, there's a path for walking too if you'd rather go by that route. Just takes a little longer."

"That's okay. I'd like to know how to get there on my own anyway." It still feels a bit odd letting Corwin carry me around. I'm not sure I want to get into the habit of letting his coterie do it too.

Zelpha leads me a short distance along the cliff edge and shows me what looks like just a notch in the rock that turns out to be a flight of stairs when viewed at the right angle. The path *does* have a railing, probably because any raven shifter using it mustn't be confident in their flying. I grip it firmly, following Zelpha down the cool passage toward the village. The roar of the waterfall dulls to a muted rumble.

I can just see the closest terraces up ahead when the path flattens out and veers inward. Glowing crystals on the ceiling light our way into the cliff itself. I'm about to ask Zelpha where we're going now when we emerge into a huge cavern so large it could hold the entire castle at Hearth-by-the-Heart.

As I look around, my breath catches in my throat. Even though we're deep within the cliff, radiant light beams down over us, seemingly reflected by diamond fixtures across the ceiling near small openings that must reach to the surface. An invigorating mineral scent fills my lungs.

Fae from the village move all around the space. At one end, a few are tending to some sort of underground garden. Another group appears to be assembling a large piece of furniture together. A couple of younger-looking fae simply stroll through the place, chatting with each other. What appears to be a small band start a song and then stop to discuss how to best shape the melody from there.

"The village common," Zelpha says. "We like having access to the open air from our homes, but it's hard to gather together to get much done right on the cliff-face, as you can imagine."

"Of course." I bite my lip. "Who should we talk to? Everyone looks pretty busy."

"Oh, I don't think that'll be a problem." Zelpha chuckles. "Here we go."

A couple of the garden workers have noticed us and left the plants to meander over. At first I think they assume Corwin's coterie member must have something important to say, but then I realize their gazes are fixed on me with restrained curiosity.

"You're the arch-lord's human companion," the woman says when they reach us, her hands squeezing shut at her sides. "The one who's been working on a cure for the curse?"

Word has spread quite a bit. I shove down my twinge of discomfort. "Yes. I've been trying."

"That's fantastic. I never would have thought—" She cuts herself off, maybe about to say something not entirely complimentary about humans, and lets out an awkward laugh. "Is there something *we* could help you with? I haven't heard that you've come down here before."

"I just… haven't spent much time in the winter realm in general yet," I say weakly. Maybe I should have insisted on visiting sooner.

I glance around. What can I say that would get me the kind of answers I need? "It must be frustrating waiting so long without knowing how to stop the curse."

"We can endure. We've always known our lord is taking every step he can to ensure our safety."

There's an opening I can use. "I understand it's been a little… difficult for him since he had to take on the arch-lord position so suddenly."

The man stiffens as if I've tossed out a grave insult. "Arch-Lord Corwin may have needed a little time to grow into his role, but he's never neglected us. I doubt any of the other arch-lords come down to speak with their folk directly so often."

"He comes down here a lot, then?"

"Nearly every day," the woman says with a prideful air. "There's rarely any need to trek up to the palace and call on him, because you can always count on him coming by soon enough to see if there are any matters of concern."

I smile in a way that I hope will soothe any ruffled feathers. "I didn't know—he hasn't mentioned it, and like I said, I haven't been here very long."

The man hums to himself. "He keeps his own council, as well one should. But if there's anything required of him, he'll see it through. You never need doubt about that. Better action than empty words any day."

When I ask about their garden, they happily show it off to me, prompting more inquisitive comments from their colleagues. By the time Zelpha and I have made the rounds, I've ended up talking to at least a dozen flock-folk, and I'm at least convinced that everyone here has faith in Corwin's ability to lead reasonably and conscientiously.

"Thank you," I say to Zelpha as we head back up to the top of the cliff. "Talking to them does help put some things into perspective."

"Hey," she says lightly. "You're going to feel what you feel. I can see why hearing that story all of a sudden would put you out of sorts. I just…" She hesitates, and her tone goes more serious. "I'd already found the mate I wanted to be with before Corwin ever became arch-lord. I wouldn't want to see him lose out on the same sort of happiness because he painted himself in too poor a light, that's all. It's been obvious how much you mean to him already."

As if to punctuate that point, Corwin's voice carries through our bond that moment with a whiff of panic. *Talia, where are you?*

Despite my tangled emotions, my automatic response is guilt and concern. *I just went down to the village common with Zelpha. We're coming up now. I'm fine—I'm sorry if I made you worry.*

His tone smooths out immediately. *No, that's all right. It's good for you to see more of the village. I only— Would it be all right if I came out to meet you?*

He's asking me permission to move around his own domain? *Of course. Maybe… maybe we should talk some more.*

A flicker of hope touches me. *Yes, I'd like that.*

When we come out onto the open plain at the top of the cliff, Corwin is already there waiting for us. Zelpha gives him a bit of a bow. "I didn't lead her too far astray, my lord."

Corwin gives her a baleful glance at her teasing and turns to me as she heads off. "What did you think of the village common?"

That wasn't what I expected we'd be talking about. "It was… it was lovely," I say. "It's silly, but it didn't occur to me there had to be somewhere the flock could get together. Everyone was, well, pretty welcoming. I think they all still find my being here a little strange."

"They'll adjust. I'd see that they view you with all due respect." He studies me carefully. "Is there anything else I can tell you? Anything you'd want to know?"

He doesn't mean about the village now, clearly. I waver, but maybe there is.

Can you be totally open with me? I ask silently. *No walls up at all? I don't want to pry; I just want to be sure I'm seeing everything.*

Corwin's stance tenses and then relaxes. He closes his eyes. *Yes. I can do that. I'd want for there to be a time when we're often completely open with each other.*

He holds out his hand, and I grasp it. As the last fragments of his inner barrier fall away, the rush of impressions from him sweeps over me even more forcefully than before.

There's so much emotion inside him that doesn't show on the outside, whirling and rippling this way and that. His worries about the curse, his frustrations and anxieties about his colleagues, his devotion to his flock… and his love for me. It washes over me, pure and unhampered by any resentments or jealousies. I even catch a twinge of *affection* for Sylas and how well he's protected me.

It isn't all exactly positive. I can sense his regret that my Seelie lovers have had more time with me and got to know me before he ever could. He's afraid that I might still choose them over him and shut him out completely. But the emotions tied to that regret have the flavor of loss, not anger.

My fingers tighten around his. Suddenly there's one more thing I want to see. He's shown he'll let *me* see the vulnerabilities he tries so hard to hide, but will he be able to let go of a little of his rigid exterior if I need him to? I don't want him disgracing himself in front of the other arch-lords, but I don't want a mate who can never reveal his fondness for me in public.

I tug him closer and rise up on my toes. There's no one nearby, but we're in view of at least one other castle and anyone who might be flying near the Heart, if they happened to look.

The awareness of those facts and a momentary balking pass through Corwin, and then he dips his head to meet my kiss.

It's short but sweet. When I draw back, my heart feels both lighter and heavier.

If I don't really need to worry about Corwin, if he's learned from his mistakes in the past and grown beyond them… then the only person holding us back from the bond we're meant to have is me with my divided loyalties.

Corwin bows his head to kiss my temple with a wash of tenderness that suggests he caught my uneasy thought. "Come with me," he says. "There's something I should show you."

CHAPTER TWENTY-ONE

Talia

I walk with Corwin past his palace and on toward the border. Curiosity prickles at me, but I stay quiet, knowing he can feel my eagerness and that he'll answer it when he's ready.

We stop several feet from the hazy barrier that separates the winter and summer realms. Corwin glances around, confirming there's no one nearby to overhear. His nervousness seeps through our bond, but it's tinged with hope. He thinks I'll be happy with what he's going to say but doesn't want to assume.

He takes one of my hands and runs his thumb over my knuckles, looking down at it. Then he raises his eyes to meet mine. "I've been thinking about this—well, I've been thinking about possibilities since I first understood your ties to the Seelie. But after spending that time in the summer realm last week, speaking with Sylas, seeing how our peoples can find a compromise if we work at it hard enough, a clearer idea started to form."

"A clearer idea of what?"

"How our future could look—one where you aren't constantly traveling between the realms, constantly going without people you care about no matter where you are. It seemed overly ambitious at first, but I've pored over all the records I can find and tested my magic and meditated with the Heart, and I've come to believe there's a good chance of it working."

"*What?*" I say again, a glimmer of excitement rousing my impatience. Has he really figured out a solution?

"It'll depend on Sylas agreeing and working with me on it," Corwin cautions. "The one thing I'm certain of is that for the magic to come together, it'll require cooperation from both sides. But—I know how much you mean to him and his cadre—it seems there'd be a good chance—" He cuts himself off with a small noise of frustration. "Let me just show you what I'm picturing. That'll be easier than trying to explain with only words."

He releases my hand to step away from me, opening the space between us. In a low, steady voice, he speaks the syllables of a true name—or perhaps more than one.

The sounds form a slow sort of melody, like an echo of the song the wind makes as it winds around his palace, and something glitters in the air. After a moment, I realize it's frost. He's conjuring a shape out of delicate ice—and particles of what looks like stone, fine as sand.

I peer at it as the elements expand and multiply. It's starting to look like... like a building, with an arched doorway and impressions of windows. No, like a castle, drawing higher and broader with each murmur he makes. Turrets rise up, spires glint in the morning sunlight.

But it isn't like any fae palace I've seen before. He's mixing the ice and the bits of stone together in an odd sort of merging. At first I think they're combined fairly evenly, but as the building continues to solidify, it becomes clear that one end is made primarily of ice and the other side of the rock, which as the bits gather is showing a brownish-gray color and a texture almost like bark. It's only in the center of the building that the two materials twine together, forming a swirling pattern on the wall.

When Corwin's voice falls silent, the delicate model he's created stands nearly as tall as me and as wide as my outstretched arms could reach. I step a little closer, taking in every detail but afraid to so much as breathe too near it in case I shatter the thin walls.

"I doubt what we'd come up with would look *exactly* like this," Corwin says. "It's only an approximation to illustrate the basic idea. But I don't see any reason why our strengths shouldn't work in harmony. The trickiest part will be adapting the border magic."

I glance up at him, still not totally following his line of thinking. "The border magic?"

"Yes." He turns toward the wall of shimmering fog. "Sylas's domain is just across from Heart's Cadence. I believe with our combined efforts, we should be able to construct a castle that straddles the border. We'd simply have to bend the spell that requires the vow of nonviolence to encompass a slightly wider section of land, where either end protrudes beyond the typical borderlands. Which would simply mean that anyone setting foot inside the building would have to swear to do no harm at the entrance. You couldn't ask for better protection than that."

It takes me a few seconds to wrap my head around everything he's saying. "You want to build a new castle that's right on top of the border? You and Sylas together? *Oh*."

My gaze jerks back to his model. The rocky part has a bark-like texture and color for a reason. Corwin was trying to give the impression of the wood Sylas and his pack use to construct their castle and homes. And the icy area is a stand-in for Corwin's diamond. It's a castle born from their strengths working in harmony to produce a single structure.

A giddy tingle shoots through me that I'm afraid to focus on too much in case I've misunderstood. "It'd be a *shared* castle?" I clarify. "One for both you and Sylas to use?"

"Yes!" Enthusiasm lights in Corwin's eyes as he must sense my own growing excitement. "As a symbol of commitment to the continuing cooperation between the Seelie and the Unseelie… A space where we can regularly touch base and stay in tune with what's going on in both the realms. We could frame it to the rest of the arch-lords as Sylas and I being ambassadors to each other's people."

I can't help looking back toward the diamond palace that's been in his family for generations. "But—you wouldn't want to completely give up your original home."

"Oh, no, I don't imagine we'd live in the border castle permanently. We could move between it and our usual palaces as need be. But—" He pauses and comes around the model of the castle to touch my face. "*You* could live there. You could see any of us as often as you liked without having to go back and forth. And any time you wanted to go right into either realm, it'd be as simple as stepping through a doorway. I was already picturing—we could make fine quarters for you right in the center of the castle where the two sides most closely merge..."

He skims his fingers up the side of the model. I can almost picture it myself: a bedroom with diamond and wood woven together across the walls, warm light streaming in through the crystalline panes, and at least some of the time, *all* of my men within reach just down a hallway or two.

A smile stretches across my face. "That would—that would be amazing. It'd be *perfect*."

Corwin beams back at me. "I'm so glad you agree. Of course, we can't know whether the Heart will actually accept a structure across the border until we try it... but I'd very much like to try it."

A wave of affection sweeps through me, so immense I can't contain it, can't compress it into words. I throw my arms around Corwin and hug him tightly. He returns the embrace with a sense of such utter joy that I can't doubt anything he's said.

But I still have to ask one thing. I nestle my head against his chest and speak through our bond. *Are you sure you'd want to live like that—with your soul-twined mate* always *having other men around? Won't people ask questions about why I'm living there rather than just with you in Heart's Cadence?*

Corwin presses a kiss to the top of my head. *How much we tell them is up to you. You're my mate, and that will be true no matter how many other men you love. It will be my honor* as *your mate to give you all the happiness I can. If you want to be open about your affections, I'll tell anyone who asks just that. If you'd rather keep that part of your life private, we can simply say you're living there out of respect to your ties to both realms—as far as the curse and the rest goes.*

He sounds totally calm, totally certain. And suddenly I am too. I didn't know before what I needed to hear—I couldn't have predicted this is what would do it—but any doubts that might have been lingering in the back of my mind dissolve.

How can I worry that this man might lash out at me or my Seelie lovers when he's spent the past several days devising exactly how I can still be with them as well as him?

But it's more than just that. A strange, heady burning sensation spreads through my chest, as if something inside me has cracked open to emit a flood of warmth.

I squeeze Corwin tighter, tears that are all joy prickling in the back of my eyes. *I love you. I—Whenever we can arrange it—I'm ready to confirm the bond.*

Corwin exhales sharply with a flicker of surprise. He'd hoped to reassure me about the future, but he obviously hadn't anticipated it'd affect me quite so much.

"Are you sure?" he murmurs, leaning his head close to mine. "It isn't a requirement of putting this plan into motion. If you wanted to wait and make sure Sylas will agree and we can manage to pull it off—"

"No. There'll be less argument from the other arch-lords and whoever else anyway if I'm officially bound to you, right? And..." I breathe in his woodsy scent, still afloat on the swell of emotion filling me. "I know I want to stay in your life, no matter what happens. I can see that even if this plan doesn't work out, we'll figure out something that does. You've offered this to me, and I want to offer you the clearest demonstration of *my* love that I can."

Corwin leans in to kiss me, his adoration rushing in to join mine for him. It's a longer kiss than the one we shared by the cliff, potent and passionate. By the time he draws back, I've practically melted into him.

"It doesn't take long to prepare the ceremony," he says. "A day or two—we could arrange it before your next return to the summer realm. If you don't think that's too quickly."

After the weeks of agonizing uncertainty, part of me wants it settled right now. “I think that would be fine.”

“Then I’ll set things in motion at once, my soul.” He kisses me once more, quickly but tenderly. Then he gives his model of the border castle a regretful look. “As much as I admire my own conjuring, I think I’d better deconstruct it. It’ll raise too many questions if it’s noticed.”

“It was just a practice run for the real thing anyway,” I say.

His smile comes back. “Yes. The real one will be much more spectacular than this, besides.”

With a wave of his hand, the frost and bits of stone disperse. He wraps his fingers around mine, and we head back toward the palace.

We’ve only taken a few steps when a carriage hurtles into view from farther down the border. It races across the snowy terrain and slams to a halt just ahead of us. An Unseelie man leans over the hull, his face strained.

“Arch-Lord Corwin,” he says in a ragged voice. “I came as quickly as I could—the summer settlement has been attacked!”

CHAPTER TWENTY-TWO

Talia

"All right," Corwin says. "Tell me exactly what happened and why you believe the Seelie are responsible."

The young fae man who raised the alarm stiffens where he's sitting on the bench at the opposite side of the carriage. He must have constructed it hastily, because the pale walls and floor vibrate with the speed the vehicle is moving at. Corwin only paused long enough to get the gist of his story and then call his nearest coterie members and a few of the flock's warriors before setting the carriage back toward the Unseelie's summer settlement.

"We were just finishing setting up the last few houses," the young man says. "Almost everyone's already moved in now—we even managed to get some of the plants we wanted growing there—I don't know about those summer crops…" He halts and shakes himself as if to get back on track. "Then there was this shrieking sound like a horrible ice storm descending on us."

Zelpha raises her eyebrows where she's leaning against the side of the carriage a few feet away from me. "An ice storm struck in the summer realm?"

The young man grimaces at her. "No, it just sounded like that. I don't know *what* it was. But the next thing we knew, one house and then another were collapsing like they were being blasted over by some kind of gale, all in a row right along the edge of the new village. A lot of them had people inside—they couldn't get out in time—the man Arch-Lord Uzziah sent who's bad with the curse can barely move as it is, and he was in one of those hit."

Corwin's expression is rigid. "You said before that our people were hurt. Do you know how many—how serious the injuries are? Did we lose anyone?"

"I'm sorry, my lord—I'm not sure." The other man looks down at his hands, which have clenched where they're resting on his knees. "I don't have much magic that'll help for healing. The people who do were rushing in to help—I thought the best thing I could do was hurry back to the Heart for help. You said if I saw anything concerning, I should let you know. You can't get much more concerning than *that*."

"No." Corwin rubs his face. "I can't see why the Seelie would attack the settlement after we came to such a firm agreement, though."

"It was their arch-lords you made the agreement with, wasn't it, my lord?" one of the warriors ventures. "I doubt many of the wolves are eager to have us on their territory, and they're not exactly known for keeping their animosities to themselves."

I tense instinctively at the insult, and Corwin fixes the woman with a measured look. "Neither have we for quite some time, and most of *our* animosity was born out of a misunderstanding. I don't think we should start laying blame until we've had a chance to properly investigate."

His reaction brings down my hackles, but my mind spins back toward something else the man from the settlement mentioned. "The man from Uzziah's flock—the one who was cursed. He hasn't gotten any better since arriving in the summer realm?"

A shadow crosses the young man's eyes. "No," he says. "He was still a little mobile when he was brought in, and the chill has gripped him even more since then. From what I last heard, he was past the point of talking or motion. Unless it turns around very soon, I don't imagine he'll make it through the day." He pauses, and his expression darkens even more. "If he even made it through the attack."

"Are we sure it even was an attack?" Verik asks in his coolly thoughtful way. "We're unfamiliar with the weather patterns and such on the summer side. For all we know, this blast was a natural phenomenon like one of our storms."

"That just happened to strike our settlement in the right spot to destroy a dozen of the homes?" the young man says.

Several pairs of eyes turn to me, presumably recognizing me as the only one in the carriage who has much experience with the Seelie realm.

I spread my hands helplessly. "I've never seen a storm like that, but I haven't been out in the summer realm weather for all that long either. I don't think it's impossible it's just a coincidence."

I don't think it's very likely either, but it seems wiser not to say that in this company.

We'll sort it out, Corwin says through our bond. *The Seelie have had their representatives watching over the settlement too—I'm sure they're already aware and are making their own investigations.* A thread of worry winds through his inner voice, though.

I can't blame him for being uneasy. *I* don't totally trust that the Seelie had nothing to do with it. Arch-Lord Celia took Corwin prisoner unprovoked just a few weeks ago. It's not that difficult to imagine she might have had a change of heart and arranged some kind of sabotage that wouldn't violate the terms of the agreement. Or it could have been other fae who simply objected to the idea of letting the Unseelie use any of their lands.

The tensions between the realms have been building for a long time. It'd be ridiculous to think they could be smoothed over with a few days of conversation.

What will it mean for Corwin's plans of unity if it turns out someone from the Seelie side is behind this act of destruction? It could set off a whole new war.

I restrain a shiver and lean into Corwin just slightly, not wanting to make too big a show of our closeness with so many from his flock right here. He squeezes my hand with a wash of affection and reassurance.

The summer arch-lords didn't want the Unseelie settlement anywhere near their own domains, so the spot they ended up picking is about halfway out to the fringes, far enough from the Heart that no vow is required to cross the border there. But when we cruise through the thick haze, the air warming by the second, we emerge to find a small band of Seelie warriors stationed there.

They bristle at our swift arrival, a few raising swords. "Halt, there. What's your business in the Seelie realm?"

Corwin stands, and I scramble onto my feet beside him. "I'm Arch-Lord Corwin of Heart's Cadence," he says, even but firm. "One of my flock-folk informed me of a destructive incident at our settlement here, and I've come to determine the cause of it and confirm my people's safety. Is that a problem?"

The guards murmur to each other discontentedly, but one steps ahead of the others. I recognize him from Donovan's typical retinue—I think he's one of the arch-lord's cadre-chosen. "Arch-Lord Corwin is our ally," he tells the others. "He's the one who pushed for the peace." His gaze comes back to the carriage. "You appear to have brought a fair bit of company."

I speak up, hoping they'll listen to my words with a little less suspicion than the Unseelie's. "If there's some kind of danger, we need to be ready to defend ourselves and the other villagers. We just want to go to the settlement and find out what's going on."

They hesitate for a moment longer, and then Donovan's man waves us onward. "There are people from the bordering domains keeping an eye on the area. We'd appreciate it if you stuck to the settlement territory and didn't pass farther into our lands."

Corwin nods. "Our only interest is in the situation in the settlement."

"Trying to stop an arch-lord from seeing his own people," one of Corwin's warriors mutters as we glide onward.

Corwin shoots him a sharp look. "They're being cautious, as we would in the same situation. They *did* let us pass. If we want them to assume good intentions on our part, we need to stop assuming the worst of them."

The warrior snaps his mouth shut, chagrinned. Then, as the sparse stretch of trees thins further, the settlement comes into view up ahead.

I don't need any bond to sense the horrified shock that sweeps over our entire party. It was one thing to hear the young man's story and another to see the result. We stare silently at the scene as we draw closer.

A broad swath of rubble runs the length of the village, with chunks of wood, stone, shell, and other building materials scattered all across the grass. Fae are gathered all along it, some tending to others: murmuring over wounds, examining limbs. I can already see splotches of blood on some of the injured people's clothes.

Heart help us, Corwin mutters, rage mixing with his horror. *When we find out who did this…*

Looking at the destruction, I wish I could say that I'm sure none of the Seelie would have shattered the hard-won truce like this. But I really don't know. I've seen the Seelie attack their own, attempt to frame colleagues for crimes and even to murder them… I'd just hoped that all three of the arch-lords were committed to their agreement and that all the other fae would respect their rulers' decision.

"Verik, Frain," Corwin says out loud as he stops the carriage at the edge of the settlement. "You're the strongest healers among us—see if there's anyone who needs more tending to. The rest of you, stay with me."

He helps me out and turns to face the Unseelie settlers. Several of them straighten up, still looking weary and upset but clearly relieved at the sight of one of their arch-lords. Corwin's colleagues might not have a lot of faith in his abilities, but his people recognize and respect his authority.

"Are there any casualties?" he asks, striding forward.

One of the women who's been helping the injured moves to meet him. "Not yet, but we have one who took a bad enough blow to fracture his skull. Thankfully, our main healer wasn't caught in the attack and is doing what he can to repair the damage. He thinks he'll come out all right."

Corwin inclines his head in acknowledgment. "One small mercy. Have you faced any further assaults since the initial blast?"

A man who's rubbing his bruised temple pipes up. "Nothing else, but what they did to begin with is bad enough. Convince us to trust them, to let down our guards on their territory, and then lash out at us at the first opportunity…" He lets out a disgruntled sound.

"From what I understand, we don't know who exactly is responsible," Corwin says, his gaze taking in the two fae who've spoken to him and the others assembled around him. "Has that changed, or are we still only speculating?"

The woman scowls. "It must have been the savage curs. It's been clear enough they aren't *that* happy about us being here."

I don't see any Seelie within the town itself, but a small contingent appears to be stationed in the field a short distance away, simply keeping an eye on things. I nod toward them. "When did that group show up?"

"Not until about an hour after the attack," the woman admits. "But that doesn't mean they didn't know about it."

"Have any of the Seelie approached you to speak with you?" Corwin asks.

"No. They've been keeping their distance." The woman pauses. "Well, one came close enough to ask if we needed healers sent in, but we told them we could look after our own."

"Can't be sure they'd cure us and not kill us," the bruised man mutters.

Corwin walks along the swath of destruction, checking on each of the injured and offering whatever words he can of concern and comfort. I limp along beside him. Nothing jumps out at me as evidence of how this happened or who's caused this ruin.

We've covered most of the line of rubble when Corwin stops with a jolt of alertness. He's caught a sound my human ears can't pick up.

He glances around, and I follow his gaze. A Seelie-style carriage is just coming into view in the distance, flying toward the settlement at a fast clip. Apprehension twists in my gut.

Then a figure stands up by the bow of the vehicle, the sight of him sweeping all my newer worries away. It's August.

The Unseelie around me aren't having the same reaction. "What do the bastards want now?" one of them says in a low voice.

"Probably going to pretend to offer help while gloating over our troubles," another mutters.

I swallow hard. The peace we managed to form was shaky as it was. Whatever the hell happened here, this incident may have been enough to completely shatter it. Are we going to be starting all over from scratch?

Well, they can think whatever they want, but I'm not afraid to show how much faith I have in the Seelie—especially this particular man. "He's here to help," I say, pitching my voice to carry, and set off to meet the carriage without waiting to hear any more grumbling.

CHAPTER TWENTY-THREE

August

I'm not sure what makes my heart sink farther: the ruin of several buildings stretching along the nearest edge of the Unseelie settlement or the unmistakable hostility in most of the gazes that're fixed on me as I bring the carriage to a stop. The report we'd gotten from the Unseelie settlement hadn't been *good*, but I still hadn't expected to see quite so much destruction.

Talia is already limping across the field toward me. She must have come with Corwin, who I spot speaking to a couple of the winter fae before starting after her. I hop out of the carriage, motioning for the two warriors I brought with me to follow but stay at my flanks, and hurry to meet her halfway.

"I wasn't expecting to see you here," I say, resisting the urge to ruffle her bright hair or, even better, pull her into a hug. I'm not sure how our Unseelie audience would react to a show of affection when at least some of them may know by now what she is to their arch-lord. I settle for giving her shoulder a light squeeze.

Talia offers me a tight but relieved smile in return. "We came as soon as we heard. It's awful. No one seems to have any idea how it happened."

"That's what I'm here to try to figure out. I'd imagine Donovan and Celia have their own people making inquiries."

Talia nods. "We ran into some of Donovan's pack-kin when we crossed the border..." Her voice tenses. "They seemed more focused on protecting the summer realm from the Unseelie than protecting the Unseelie from whoever attacked them here."

I'm not totally surprised, but there isn't much I can do about that fact. The only people I have authority over at the moment are the two men with me. I glance past Talia toward the settlement. "I guess I'd better take a closer look and see what I can make of it."

"You might not get the warmest welcome," Corwin says as he reaches us. "My people are convinced the assault was carried out by the summer fae."

I bristle instinctively, even though he spoke with no accusation in his tone and it's a possibility I was already considering. I will my own tone to stay even. "Has anyone found evidence of that?"

"No," Talia says, rubbing her arms. "But it's understandable that they'd assume that, isn't it? The summer and winter fae haven't exactly been friendly in a long time."

Corwin glances back toward the village, his mouth pressed into a tight line. "And unless you'd suggest that my people sabotaged their own efforts—and risked the lives of their companions—who else *could* it have been?"

I'm debating whether I can reasonably say that I wouldn't put it past some of his colleagues to orchestrate something this malicious just so they could frame us for it when Talia goes still. Her gaze jerks to me, her eyes widening. "There is another option, isn't there? You're not the only fae in the world. Wasn't there an attack on Aerik's domain by some of the Murk a little while ago?"

I never would have connected that incident to this one, but Talia wasn't there to see how different they are. She doesn't understand just how feeble the rats' power generally is with their scorning of the Heart.

"That was a petty prank," I say, "only turned murderous because one guard caught them at it. To blast down several buildings... I'm not sure many of those vermin would even have the power to crumble *one*."

Talia raises her chin. "That kind of thinking is how Sylas got his scar. At least a few of the Murk have powerful magic. And if they mostly want to make mischief and cause chaos, wouldn't disrupting our new truce be a perfect way to do that?"

It would, come to think of it. I turn to Corwin. "Have your people had any difficulties of your own with the Murk lately?"

Corwin considers for a moment. "Not that I'm aware of. But—the curse and our dwindling population have made for much more chaotic times in general. It's possible they've been stirring up trouble now and then that we haven't realized they were to blame for."

Talia grasps his arm. "What about those beasts at Lakeshine? No one ever figured out why they'd targeted that town, did they?"

He gives her a crooked smile. "I'm not sure why the rat shifters would want to target it either. But I suppose they wouldn't need a clear reason. They do often delight in simply sowing whatever confusion they can."

"It should be easy enough to determine," I say. "The attack only happened a few hours ago. The culprits will have left at least a small trace of scent. If there were rats around, we'll smell them out." I gesture to my men. "Make a wide circuit of the area around the settlement, noses to the ground, alert for any hint of the Murk."

They leap into wolf form and lope off in opposite directions. Talia hugs herself. "What if they don't find anything? If it *was* some of the Seelie deciding to break the peace, will you be able to figure out who?"

I grimace. "That'll be harder. There are plenty of us around, and we've been coming to and from the settlement to oversee the construction for days. It's one thing to sniff out the essence of the animal and another to narrow it down to a specific individual. But there are other kinds of evidence we might turn up. I'd better join in and see what I can find."

I step back from them and let the shift wash over me, stretching my limbs and bringing my senses to even sharper alertness. As I set off with the warm breeze licking over my fur, the uncertainties that were gripping my gut fall away. Everything feels simpler as a wolf.

The one thing I am still sure of is that I need to get to the bottom of this fast. The fragile peace depends on it—our chances of keeping any kind of relationship with Talia while she's bound to the Unseelie depend on it. I will not let her down, even if it means taking my fellow summer fae to task.

Skirting the settlement, I quickly determine that the spell that blasted through that entire row of buildings must have come from the west. Whoever cast the magic would have needed to remain out of view. I head toward the nearest patch of forest in that direction, about half a mile away, taking whiffs of the grass as I go just in case. Nothing's been trampling this field except Seelie feet.

Once I reach the trees, I slow, both to inhale more deeply and thoroughly and to keep my ears pricked for movement. I'd imagine the perpetrator fled the scene to avoid detection, but that's not a guarantee.

I weave between the trees, drinking in the rich, living scents of the forest. Here and there I catch a wolfish musk, but none of that sharper ratty odor I've come across only a few times in my life. No hint of ravens in this area either.

Was it my own people then, turning against their own arch-lords? My lips curl back from my fangs at the thought.

With the motion, a thicker wave of scent trickles through my senses—and it occurs to me that the forest smells in this exact spot are a little *too* rich. I pause, taking one slow breath and then another, my nerves tingling to high alert.

The scents I'm taking in are the sorts I'd expect, but there's something unnaturally strong about them, as if they've been enhanced or saturated… to cover up a different scent someone didn't want being detected?

I shift back into my man form so that I can intone a few words of my own magic. They resonate against the spell I suspected was lingering in the air. With a couple more syllables and a sweep of my hand, I manage to dispel the enchantment cloaking the space. Then I drop back down on my wolfish feet to take another whiff.

My fur nearly stands on end. There it is. Faint but undeniable now that the villain's efforts at covering their tracks have been dealt with—the prickling tang of the Murk.

Those mangy vermin. I cast about in increasingly wider circles, but I can't tell how many of them were involved or where they might have gone from here. It happened recently enough and they stood in this spot long enough that they couldn't erase all trace of their presence, but it is only the faintest trace.

Curse them. I'm not sure the ravens' noses will even be able to pick up the scent to accept it as proof. It's fading quickly even while I search for more.

But would the Murk really have pulled off this prank and then left the area without waiting to watch any of the chaos they wrought? They like to revel in their mischief the way Whitt revels in dancing and alcohol. Wouldn't they want to know the outcome of this particularly vicious "prank"?

But how in the lands am I supposed to find them if they didn't leave any trail? I could send out more magic to chase after that rodent essence, but unless they're right nearby, they *will* flee the second it touches them.

An idea glimmers in my head. I almost dismiss it because of what it requires, but then I push myself to spin and race back toward the settlement.

If Talia can find a mate in one of the Unseelie, then I can manage to work together with one for a few minutes. And if the arch-lord doesn't like being asked for favors, then he can say so.

Corwin is crouched at the edge of the field examining the spot where the blast must have hit the first house. He tenses a little as I charge up to him in wolf form but holds his ground. Talia hurries over at the sight of me, reaching us just as I've shifted.

"It was the Murk," I say in a low voice. "I caught a tiny bit of their scent in the forest to the west. I'd like to see if we can catch any of them that might have remained in the area to keep an eye on the results of their efforts."

Surprise flashes through the arch-lord's eyes followed by a grim setting of his jaw. "I would very much like to have a few words with the culprit myself. How do you propose we track them down?"

I motion to the landscape around us. "I can send out a searching spell that'll latch onto the presence of any Murk within a few miles. But they'll feel it when it reaches them. I'd suggest that you take to the sky while I cast the spell so that you can watch for the vermin when they make a run for it. I think I can add an element to the magic that'll light them up a bit temporarily when it touches them, to make them easier to spot."

Corwin doesn't even hesitate. "Of course," he says. "Make a sweep of it, from north to south—that way I'll have a smaller area to focus on at a time. Signal me when you're ready?"

I nod, and he springs into the air, transforming into a large blue-black raven in an instant with a flap of powerful wings. I've never thought much of the feathered form before, but I have to admit to myself now that flight is a pretty handy ability.

"I want you to wait here," I tell Talia. "The Murk become vicious when cornered."

She draws back to the shelter of the nearest unharmed building but watches from there. I wait until Corwin is circling against the sky, and then close my eyes, concentrating on the spell I want to perform.

I've never stretched my powers as far as I want to today, but the more ground I can cover, the more chance I'll actually catch the rats.

As Corwin suggested, I propel the energy out to the north first, as far as I can will it to go. With the words I murmur under my breath, I twine my memory of the rats' scent into the magic. *Find it. Make it glow.*

I have only a vague sense of the spell rippling across the terrain. When my chest starts to ache with the strain of being stretched too thin, I tug it to the left, swinging it across the land as steadily as I can. Searching, searching, extending myself even farther as I catch a second wind—

At the same instant that a jolt of success hits me, Corwin lets out a croak loud enough to reach us down below. When my eyes pop open, he's already diving—toward a spot beyond the forest where I caught the scent. I hurtle forward, releasing my wolf in mid-stride.

My paws pound the earth. In my mind's eye, I see exactly where the raven plummeted. I can't let him tackle the fiend alone. This is my lord's realm—this is my responsibility.

My muscles strain just as I strained my magical abilities before. I throw myself forward even faster, the ground falling away beneath my feet. Another ravenish cry rises from up ahead.

I charge through the patch of forest, heedless of the twigs and pebbles scattering under my feet, and burst out the other side. At the far end of a grassy plain stands a cluster of narrow boulders. I catch the flash of dark wings amid them.

I rush across the rest of that distance in time to find Corwin in the form of a winged man, pinning a sinewy, spiky-haired woman to the ground. She hisses through her teeth at him. The stink of rat clogs my nose.

Springing to his side, I shift at the same moment and draw my sword. When I bring it to the woman's throat, she doesn't so much as flinch, but she does stop struggling against Corwin.

"Did you act alone, or do you have companions here?" I ask. "Where are they?"

The Murk woman lets out a ragged laugh. "Ooh, there are so many more of us. Just you wait."

"That's not a real answer. Tell me who was responsible for—"

I don't even get to finish my demand. Corwin must have loosened his hold just slightly seeing my sword in place, and the Murk woman doesn't value her life. She smacks her fingers against her palm—and a current of energy slams through her body, making it spasm.

Her eyes go dull, her lips parting slackly. In a matter of seconds, she's nothing but a limp shell.

Corwin stares down at her. "What—how—"

I bare my teeth. "She had a suicide spell on her. I've heard they defy the Heart that way too—casting it on each other with a trigger they can use if they'd rather die than be trapped."

With a few vicious words snarled under my breath, I shove myself away from her. We know who attacked the Unseelie settlement, but the perpetrator has managed to flee us on her own terms after all.

CHAPTER TWENTY-FOUR

Talia

Normally being back in Hearth-by-the-Heart would comfort me. But even surrounded by all four of my men and Astrid, my frequent protector, in the familiar cozy atmosphere of Sylas's study, my nerves stay on edge.

I thought I had a pretty good idea of all the threats we were up against. Now it turns out there's a major one I never really considered.

"I don't like it," Whitt says from where he's in his typical pose propped against the built-in shelves. "The settlement had barely finished construction. We didn't put out any big announcements. How closely must the Murk have been watching to realize it even existed, let alone was a significant target?"

"It's possible it was just chance," Astrid puts in, shifting her weight near the doorway. "Good luck for them and bad luck for us that one of them stumbled on the new village and figured they could upset a lot of fae by striking at it."

I can't help worrying at my lower lip. "They don't usually pull 'pranks' that big, though, do they? It doesn't feel like a spur-of-the-moment thing."

"I agree." Sylas steeples his fingers where he's sitting behind his desk, a frown darkening his face. He glances at August, who's standing as if on guard by my chair, and then Corwin, who's sitting in the armchair next to mine. "You discerned nothing useful from the rat you caught?"

August shakes his head with an apologetic grimace. "She activated the killing spell too quickly. There was no evidence on her. I don't know if she was even responsible for the spell in any way—she had no true name marks on her. I guess it could have been a different sort of magic, though. Who knows how the Murk might twist the small blessings they scrape from the Heart?"

"The one thing she did say to us was quite ominous, if vague," Corwin says, sounding a little cautious to be giving his input when he's the lone Unseelie in the room. "Perhaps it was an empty threat meant only to unsettle us, but she implied that they had more planned that we wouldn't like."

Astrid lets out a dismissive huff. "I wouldn't trust a word that comes out of those vermin's mouths. If she saw the opportunity to confuse and distract us, she'd have taken it without a single concern to the truth."

"The Murk can lie, then?" I ask.

"Any of us *can* lie, mite," Whitt says. "It's just most of us value our connection to the Heart too much to risk damaging it by doing so. The Murk have fewer qualms on that score. Although it sounds as if the vagueness of this one's remarks might have avoided outright falsehood anyway."

Corwin nods. "She certainly wasn't remotely specific about what we should be waiting *for*."

Even after months in the faerie world—years if you count the time when Aerik held me prisoner and I never saw more of this place than his one room—I barely know anything about the rat-shifting fae. I motion to Astrid. "What was that rhyme you told me humans used to sing about all the different fae?"

Her lips twist into a slanted smile. She recites the words in a faintly wry tone.

"Wolves of summer, winter ravens

Where they dwell find no safe haven.
But most beware the rats of Murk
Sowing spite wherever they lurk."

My stomach knots. "I guess there isn't anything much more spiteful than wrecking the peace we're trying to build." Does that mean the Murk are going to keep trying to ruin our truce?

Sylas rubs his jaw. "They've generally preferred to sow that spite among humans, since the mortals make easier targets. But we've had more significant incidents with the Murk in the past few weeks than for decades before now. Perhaps they've gotten bored of their human victims and decided they needed a larger challenge."

"You don't think—" I feel abruptly ridiculous suggesting this with none of the much more experienced fae around me have, but I can't help going on. "They dislike you, and they want to unsettle you. The curses—"

Whitt snorts, and even Sylas, who's faced the hostility of the Murk directly, shakes his head. "Magic on that scale would be an incredible feat even for a host of Seelie or Unseelie dwelling close to the Heart. It's an order of magnitude thousands of times beyond the destruction in that village, which was a bigger effort than we generally see from the rat shifters in itself. But…" His forehead furrows. "The curse has struck us on both sides of the border. It's possible it has affected the Murk as well."

I see his reasoning immediately, with a chill that wraps around my gut. "It could be what's making them act out more than before, just like the Unseelie's version of the curse was driving their raids along the border."

A tremor of revulsion reaches me from Corwin at the thought of being bound in a curse connected to the rats. The thought leaves my skin crawling too. If that's what's happening, if they find out that I'm involved in curing it, will they try to call on me?

Would I even want to help them? The winter fae had only been attacking the Seelie for a few decades, with millennia of peace before then. The Murk have always been "sowing spite." With every new thing I learn about them, the less I want to have to do with them.

Whitt makes a dismissive gesture. "Somehow I doubt they'd let us in on that knowledge even if it's true. We can only work with what we know."

"Whatever their motives were, they won't disturb the Unseelie settlement again," August says, drawing himself up a little straighter. "We have sentries patrolling all through that area now, watching for any sign of the rats."

"And the repairs to the destroyed buildings?" Sylas asks.

"My people wished to see to those themselves," Corwin says. "I appreciate the help the Seelie offered, but… feelings are still somewhat raw, and even having heard the Murk were to blame, it's hard for them to shake their initial suspicions right away. I'm sure tensions will ease again when the rest of our plans proceed unhindered."

Sylas inclines his head. "I hope that's true, but I understand their wariness. Thank you for coming so quickly and for working together with August to find the perpetrator." He looks toward the window. Outside, the sky is darkening, the purple haze of the sunset fading. "You've lost the better part of the day because we failed to guard our lands well enough. I think it's only fair if I give you leave to extend Talia's visit by a day to make up for the loss, assuming that suits both of you."

I feel the leap of Corwin's spirits through our bond. My own heart skips with a bittersweet sort of happiness. It warms me that Sylas is going out of his way to be generous, that he's honoring Corwin's claim on my company, but at the same time I don't want him to think I'd rather be in the winter realm than with him and my other lovers here.

Why can't that shared castle Corwin talked about be built already? No more negotiating over where I'll be—having a space that can be a home for all of us.

"I appreciate that," Corwin says with a dip of his head in return. *Talia? There should still be time to arrange the ceremony in that case.*

Yes. I want that, I do, but sitting here with my other lovers around me, the thought feels suddenly overwhelming. I can't just come back in a few days and announce that the confirmation of my bond is already finalized. They need to be prepared—and they need to know how generous Corwin's intentions are too.

"That does make sense," I say to Sylas. "Thank you. But I'll still look forward to coming back." Then to Corwin, silently, *And before we go, I think I should tell them I'm going to confirm the bond… Can I share your idea about the joint castle with them too, or do you want to wait until you're more sure it can be done?*

Corwin hesitates, but I sense it's mainly nervousness over whether Sylas will approve, not any reluctance to pursue the idea. *I don't think we'll know what's possible until we put our magic together on it regardless. Perhaps it would be better for you to bring up my proposal first so you can gauge their reaction. I can give you some privacy for that.*

He gets up, reaching to give my hair a brief caress. "I believe there is something my mate wishes to discuss with you before we go." He meets my eyes. "I'll be appreciating this domain's natural wonders. Let me know when you're ready to leave."

As he steps out, Astrid glances around at the rest of us. "Somehow I get the feeling this is going to be a discussion that doesn't require the full cadre."

My lips twitch with an unexpected smile. "It doesn't."

"Perhaps you could watch over our honored guest and make sure my colleagues don't act out any hostile inclinations on the spur of the moment," Sylas says dryly.

Astrid gives him a little bow and heads out, and all three of my Seelie men fix their attention on me.

"What's going on, Talia?" Whitt asks, his blue eyes intent, his tone gentle. I'm suddenly sure he's already guessed—the first part of my news, at least.

They're all too far away from me. I stand up, reaching out beckoningly, and they move to encircle me without question. I lean into August's touch on the small of my back, grasp Whitt's hand, and slip my other arm around Sylas's, tugging them even closer. The heat of their bodies and their combined, wild scents wrap around me.

I have to simply spit it out. "I'm going to confirm the soul-twined bond with Corwin."

There's no mistaking the tension that grips the men gathered around me. I hurry onward. "It doesn't mean I don't still want all of you, or to be part of the summer realm, or—or anything like that. I just don't think it's helping anyone leaving it up in the air, and I'm sure of Corwin now—I definitely don't want to put either of us through whatever *breaking* the bond would do to us... And I think having an official position among the Unseelie will make finding a compromise easier."

"How's that, my love?" Sylas asks, his voice only a little gruffer than usual. He strokes his fingers down my cheek, no sign of resentment or anger in the gesture.

"Corwin thinks we may be able to set things up so that I could be with all four of you pretty much always. It sounds like the magic side of it will be a little tricky, but he's done some research—I'm sure he can explain the details better if you agree to give it a chance." I drag in a breath and go over everything my mate told me about his plan for the shared castle—how it would be constructed and where, how they'd explain it to their respective colleagues.

My Seelie men listen quietly and thoughtfully. When I'm finished, they stay silent for several seconds. Nervous impatience itches at me. "What do you think?" I can't help prodding.

August looks at Sylas over my head. "Could it really work?" The hopeful note in his voice melts some of my anxiety.

Sylas cocks his head, but a small smile touches his lips. "I haven't looked into it myself, but Corwin seems a conscientious man. I doubt he'd have brought it up unless all the evidence he found indicated it was possible. I can't think of any reason it definitely *wouldn't* be."

A giddy bubbling sensation rises in my chest. "Then—you'd be willing to try it? I know it's a lot to ask—"

Sylas grasps my shoulder. "It isn't, Talia. Not after everything you've done for us. Not when you mean so much to us. It *would* be beneficial to both our peoples to have regular contact between the realms, so it'd hardly be selfish besides. It's hard to know how such an arrangement might work out in the long run with the tensions that have existed between us, but I'd say it's more than worth the attempt."

He glances at the other two. Whitt lowers his head to kiss my temple. "If your soul-twined mate came up with this scheme, then it only convinces me he's worthy of you—and worthy of us offering our own trust and cooperation. He didn't have to make such an offer."

"You know if there's a way to stay by your side, I'll take it,

Sweetness," August murmurs. "I only—" He cuts himself off with a shake of his head. "We'll make it work. Wolves and ravens may have been at odds for a short time, and we may never have been great friends, but that can change."

He sounds as if he's trying to convince himself more than speaking from certainty, but maybe that's the best I could hope for. *They like your idea*, I tell Corwin as I tug each of my other men to me in turn, giving them a quick kiss farewell. *They're willing to give it a try. Do you want to talk to them about it now?*

His reply comes with a rush of relief and gratitude. *I think we've had enough on our minds today, and it may be best to let them think the contributing factors through some before we get down to the decision-making. But you can tell them we'll discuss it further when I return you here at the end of your stay. I'll meet you in front of the castle.*

I pass on his words to Sylas, who gives my jaw one last lingering caress before waving me off. I make my way downstairs, buoyed by more lightness than I've felt all day, and nearly bump into Harper coming out of the kitchen just beyond the stairs.

"Talia!" she says, her over-large eyes opening even wider than usual, and throws her arms around me before I can respond. "You're all right. I heard there was an attack at the Unseelie settlement, and someone said you were there with Corwin, and that the Murk were making trouble…"

With a startled laugh, I hug her back. "I didn't even see any of the Murk. We came a couple of hours after the attack happened. It was pretty awful, but I'm perfectly okay."

"Oh! I didn't really get the clearest details." Harper pulls back with a bashful smile. "Well, I'm still glad you're okay. Are you staying here now, or…?"

She looks so eager that my answer comes with a pinch of guilt. "No, actually, we just stopped by to discuss the situation with Sylas and now I'm heading back to the winter realm. Corwin's waiting for me." A spark of inspiration propels more words from my mouth. "But —I'm going to accept the bond—there'll be a confirmation ceremony in a few days. Maybe you'd like to come back to the winter realm to see it?"

I nudge Corwin through our connection as I ask, hoping I'm not breaking some rule I didn't know about, and he reacts with surprise but fond enthusiasm. *It's a moment of celebration. Any guests you'd like to have are welcome.*

Harper claps her hands together. "Really? I— Yes, of course. You should have someone from our pack there, shouldn't you? And I've never seen any confirmation ceremony before, let alone an Unseelie one."

She's so obviously excited at the prospect that I find myself beaming at her. "Great. When I know exactly where and when it's happening, I'll send a message back." Maybe I should invite my Seelie men as well—or would that be awkward? Would they even be able to leave the summer realm on a trip like that when Sylas has so many responsibilities?

I guess it can't hurt to ask them once I know what'll be involved. I say my good-byes to Harper and hurry out to meet Corwin so he can get on with making those arrangements.

As we walk to the border, the Unseelie arch-lord takes my hand to twine his fingers with mine. *I'm glad that this incident hasn't dampened your eagerness for our union.*

Not at all, I say. *If anything, seeing you and August taking on the Murk together made me think of how much I'm looking forward to seeing you all collaborate more often once we've worked out all the official stuff.*

He chuckles out loud and teases his thumb over my knuckles in a way that lights up the skin all up my arm.

I don't get to enjoy it for very long, though. When we pass through the border into the chilly air on the winter side, a sentry is waiting for us beneath the glinting starlight.

"Arch-Lord Corwin," he says without even looking at me. "Your fellow arch-lords request your presence in the Hall of the Heart for an urgent meeting about the Seelie catastrophe."

Corwin peers at him. "There was no 'Seelie' catastrophe. My people should have made it back here hours ago. Didn't they explain that the Murk were behind the attack on our settlement?"

The sentry keeps his posture rigid. "It may be so, but we can't be sure the Seelie didn't put them up to it to get around their oaths, my lord. At least, that's the sort of speculation I've heard among the flocks, if you don't mind me saying."

Corwin's mouth tightens, and my heart plummets. *I* know none of the wolves would ever associate with the fae they consider vermin. Are the Unseelie, even the other arch-lords, really going to blame the summer fae for a crime they had nothing to do with?

CHAPTER TWENTY-FIVE

Talia

"No one's outright insisting the Seelie were behind it," Corwin tells me over breakfast the next morning, looking weary. "They're just unwilling to assume they definitely *weren't* involved. I've gone over everything we saw and discovered, and explained that I have every indication that the summer fae would never associate with the Murk, but… you've seen how stubborn my colleagues can be."

I nudge the scrambled eggs on my plate half-heartedly, not able to summon much appetite despite the creamy smell of them filling my nose. "Do you think it'd do any good for me to talk to them? I know just how unfriendly the Seelie are to the Murk. They've had their issues with the winter realm, but they still recognize you as equals. The Murk they barely see as fae at all." And considering the way the Murk behave, it's easy to understand why.

Corwin shakes his head with an apologetic pursing of his lips. "I already suggested they speak with you, but they've banned you from the Hall on the basis of your connections to the summer realm. I even told them we're going to be confirming the bond so that you'll officially be lady of Heart's Cadence… Maybe once the ceremony has happened, they'll recognize your loyalty."

Or if I could finally figure out a way to consistently stop the curse. No wonder the other Unseelie arch-lords are skeptical of me when I cure all the Seelie once a month but can't seem to bring more than one of the winter fae out from their icy illness.

I rub my forehead. "Has the curse struck anyone while we've been dealing with this? If I could manage to heal someone else…"

"Not that I've heard," Corwin says. "And I'm sure I'd be notified immediately if there had been." He sighs. "I'm meant to consult with my colleagues again this morning. I think I can at least talk them down from demanding a full contingent of our warriors be stationed at the settlement. I'd imagine the Seelie will allow at least a few guards given the circumstances."

His gaze goes distant in thought. He pokes at the last few bits of food on his own plate and glances up at me with a flow of warmth through our bond like an inward embrace. "I'll let you know as soon as their tempers are more settled. We have more to discuss about the ceremony, after all—and I would like to spend a *little* more of your time here on matters that have nothing to do with politics."

I offer him a small smile. "Keeping the peace and looking after your people have to come first. If we can solidify the truce between the realms, then we'll have a lot more time just for enjoying ourselves in the future, right? I just wish there was more *I* could do."

Corwin makes a humming sound. "You push yourself too hard. There are a *few* things that aren't your responsibility. You should take some time while I'm gone to think about happier things—perhaps come up with some ideas of what you'd like to see in our joint castle, which I'm still determined we'll build whether the rest of the fae like it or not."

The defiance in his voice makes my smile widen a little, but after he's left, I find I can't concentrate on anything that far in the future. How can I get excited about sharing a home with my men of both realms when I'm not even sure their peoples won't be inciting war against each other in the next few days?

Corwin has closed off our connection while he meets with the other arch-lords, so I have no idea how their discussion is going. I wander through the palace, searching for inspiration in the halls and rooms that are becoming increasingly familiar. After a while, I end up in the alcove where the locked door leads up to Corwin's mother's room.

I stop there, eyeing it, considering grabbing the key that'll take me to the entrance to her rooms. I don't know how to do the calming spell Corwin cast over her so that he could talk to her without her becoming violent, but I could try to speak to her through the door up there. She should be able to hear me.

I'm just not sure what I'd say to her. Is she aware enough to care what happens to her son anymore? To take any joy in the knowledge that he's found his own soul-twined mate? Maybe hearing that would only make her more upset over her loss.

As if answering my unspoken questions, a scratching sound and a low moan reach me from up the stairs. Knowing who's making them doesn't make them sound any less unnerving. I hug myself, rubbing my arms, and turn at the tapping of soft footsteps.

Zelpha comes around the bend. She cocks her head when she sees me. "What are you doing over here?" she asks mildly.

I don't know how to explain it in a way that'll make sense to her. It doesn't even make sense to me. I look back toward the door. "I guess I was just thinking about all the people the curse has hurt... Wondering if there's anything I can do to make *any* of it better." I pause. "Maybe it goes against the Heart to say this, but it kind of seems wrong to me that she has to keep living if she's in so much pain and doesn't want to. The Murk..."

The Murk offer each other a way out if they feel it's better to end their life than continue it. August told me that's how the woman they caught was able to avoid questioning. Maybe working a spell like that means they have less magic to draw on in general because of the Heart's disapproval... but I can't help feeling like your own life *should* be something you have control over.

Zelpha shudders. "You don't want to be taking any cues from how the Murk handle their problems. If we offered her a way out, then there'd be no chance of helping her if we got the opportunity later.

Once we have a handle on the curse, maybe it'll be easier to cure her grief too."

"I know that's possible. It makes sense. I just—" I think back to a moment months ago when I stood in front of the former Arch-Lord Ambrose holding a knife at my own throat. "There was once a time when I'd rather have died than let our enemies get their hands on me. I used that fact to save myself. I wouldn't want anyone taking *that* opportunity away from me either. I've already been through enough to know there are things worse than dying."

If I was ever wrenched away from my men and my friends, if I knew they were lost to me and there was nothing but pain up ahead—or that my captor would use me to cause all kinds of pain for others—While I hope to the Heart I never find myself in that position, I wouldn't want to go on living if I did.

But the Unseelie are too rigid to consider that point of view—as rigid in their opinions as their bodies become in the grips of the curse. The answer must have something to do with that strictness, but I still don't see how I fit in. With the Seelie's curse, I don't stand up to their savagery or prevent it, I let them indulge it, and *that's* when they snap out of their rage.

My head hurts just trying to think the problem through.

Zelpha gives my back a light pat. "The way we see it, it's true that some things can't be fixed. But when that's the case, we must make the best of them in their broken state. There can be beauty even in what's damaged."

Is that how they'll think about relations between the summer and winter realms if they can't resolve all their conflicts and suspicions?

My chin comes up at the thought. "Well, I think there are a lot of things we can still fix." The arch-lords don't want to hear from me, but what about all the other Unseelie? What are *they* saying about the attack on the settlement now? From what the sentry who summoned Corwin yesterday said, everyone's been speculating about the Seelie's involvement.

I turn to Zelpha. "I want to go down to the village common again and speak with the flock."

Zelpha raises her eyebrows. "Did Corwin give that plan the okay?"

"I hadn't come up with it the last time I talked with him, and he's busy with his meeting now. He didn't mind you taking me down there before, did he?"

She looks uncertain, maybe because last time she was bringing me to see the flock for her own purposes and now she's unsure of mine. "They know you have ties to the summer realm. They might not be as friendly today."

"Well, that's exactly why I should see them. So they can realize that the summer fae had nothing to do with what happened and there's no reason to be unfriendly about it." I study her. "I know where the path is now. I can go on my own."

"Now hold on—"

I hold her gaze steadily. "Would you be telling me whether I should take a walk down to the village if I were fae? I might limp, but I'm not an invalid. In a few days, I'm going to be standing by Corwin as his confirmed mate. I hope you wouldn't think of treating me like I'm a servant who can be ordered around then."

Zelpha winces. "All right, all right, you know how to drive a point home." She gives me a considering glance up and down. "Are you sure you don't have a sizeable portion of fae blood in you after all?"

I have the ridiculous urge to stick out my tongue at her. "Humans have minds of their own too."

"Clearly." A laugh sputters out of her. "I still think you'd be better off with a coterie member along for backup. Just in case."

"Come on then."

I head through the palace and out to the cliff overlooking the village. It isn't hard to find the path again now that I know what I'm looking for. I march down it without waiting to confirm Zelpha is following, hearing the rasp of her boots trailing behind me. My heart is thumping faster both at the thought of what I might face in the village and from the argument with her, but all of Corwin's coterie need to see me as more than some frail human girl who somehow stumbled into their lives and might have a cure to the curse accidentally up her sleeve.

When I reach the village common, it's busier than last time. Many of the winter fae are standing around in clusters, talking with each other in terse voices. Those tending to the garden are frowning, barely seeming to notice what they're doing with their hands.

Several of the fae's gazes turn my way as I walk out under the reflected light that streams from the diamond fixtures overhead. I stop in the middle of the space, steadying myself against the smooth stone of the floor, and look around me.

"If anyone has any questions about the Seelie or what happened in the summer realm yesterday, you can ask me," I say, raising my voice slightly. "I visited the settlement with Arch-Lord Corwin. And I've lived among the Seelie for a long time. I know them."

The conversations fall off. Most of the Unseelie drift toward me, their expressions hesitant. The wariness in their stances unsettles me. Has the attack made them so suspicious that they see even me as a potential threat?

"We don't need anyone to tell us that most of the wolves would like to tear us to bits," one of them says.

"No one should tell you that, because it isn't true. They never attacked you even when you were launching raids on their territory, did they? All they wanted was for *your* attacks to stop."

"Or maybe they were just scared to step into our lands," another Unseelie pipes up. "As soon as we set foot in the summer realm in an attempt at peace, our people are getting blasted and battered. That doesn't seem like a coincidence."

"Your own arch-lord caught one of the Murk who was responsible," I remind them. "You don't think *he* would lie about that, do you?"

They murmur discontentedly. "The Seelie could have hidden an alliance with the Murk," the first man says. "From Arch-Lord Corwin and from you. Who knows how much they might be hiding?"

As far as I've seen, the Seelie aren't anywhere near as in the habit of hiding things as the winter fae are, but I don't think it'll help relations for me to point that out. "I've been around a lot of different Seelie during my time there, and I've never heard any of them show anything but hostility toward the Murk," I say. "I promise you, they think of the rat shifters as the enemy and are just as eager to catch them and stop them from hurting you again as you are."

A woman near the back of the bunch steps forward, her eyes narrowed. "Maybe *you're* in on it with them. You're a human—you could lie for them if they wanted you to."

Zelpha moves closer to my side. "I hope you're not making accusations of our lord's honored guest."

The other fae stiffen a little at her intervention. I raise my hand to Zelpha, motioning her back. I have to show I can handle this confrontation myself.

I turn back to the gathered fae. "I don't want to see you hurt either. That's why I'm here—why I've been trying everything I can to cure your curse."

"How can we be sure of that?" another fae man demands. "All these offers of help could be just a way to set us up for some greater trick. Have you really cured anyone?"

A voice rises from off to one side. "I heard you pushed for the arch-lords to agree to the settlement in the first place."

"You came from the summer realm," a woman says. "You've been part of one of their packs. You don't even really belong here."

I swallow hard, groping for the right words, and it hits me. *I've* been hiding too, and maybe it's time I stop. Not in every way—I remember Corwin's warnings about revealing my magic too well—but it can't hurt for me to admit the main reason I've come here, can it? In a couple of days, we'll be announcing it to everyone anyway.

I suspect Corwin would have preferred to be here to tell his flock himself, but he's not. And this is my truth as much as his. I've accepted it—his people will have to too.

My heart pounds even harder, but I pull my spine straight and speak as steadily as I can. "I do belong here. I belong here in this domain alongside Corwin, because I'm his soul-twined mate. That's why I came in the first place—that's why I've kept coming back."

The fae around me gape at me. Someone sputters a laugh. Zelpha's face has tensed, but she sets a hand on my shoulder and glowers at the crowd. "I can verify it. I've heard it from our lord myself."

"Then why hasn't the bond been confirmed?" a woman demands.

I can be honest about that too. "Because I wasn't totally sure I wanted to confirm it. I *do* have loyalties to the Seelie as well—to summer fae who've supported me and looked out for me. Being bound to Arch-Lord Corwin doesn't change that. But that's why it means so much to me that you and the Seelie can make peace with each other. I belong to *both* realms, and I want to see them united, not fighting each other. Especially when it looks like you're both facing another enemy you could tackle more easily together."

Restless talk echoes through the cavern, blending together in a mishmash of voices I have trouble picking apart. Zelpha's stance remains on guard. No one is speaking to me now, only their fellow fae.

My stomach sinks. Did they not believe me? Or they believe but don't approve?

But even if that's the case, I don't regret having the truth out in the open.

Maybe I should let them stew on the situation for a while rather than expecting them to embrace me as their ruler's partner right away. I ease back, lifting my voice to make one more promise. "When I'm the lady of Heart's Cadence, I'm going to do everything I can for this flock, just like Corwin does. But part of that will be making sure you can see the Seelie for who they really are, just as I know them. I promise you, they aren't villains any more than you are."

"I suppose that depends on which specific fae we're talking about," Zelpha mutters as we hustle back up the path.

I can't summon a smile at her attempt at humor. If the Heart wants me to bring the realms together, I can't help thinking we've still got an awfully long way to go.

We cross the plain in silence. As we reach the terrace wall, a servant comes darting out of the palace to meet us, his eyes wide.

"Zelpha," he says with a bob of his head and a flick of his eyes my way that suggests he's not sure whether he needs to address me or how. "I didn't know what to do—Arch-Lord Corwin hasn't returned from the Hall of the Heart yet—"

"What's the matter?" Zelpha says evenly, drawing to a halt.

"Well..." The man wrings his hand. "We have a visitor. From the summer realm. It's one of their arch-lords—he says his name is Sylas."

CHAPTER TWENTY-SIX

Talia

For all the times I've wished that the men I love weren't so separate from each other, I've never actually imagined what it'd be like to have Sylas sitting here in one of the armchairs in Corwin's study. It's weirdly thrilling and unsettling at the same time.

Corwin doesn't appear to know exactly how to handle the unexpected visit either. At first, he sat behind his desk as if it were a professional meeting, but now he's gotten up again, standing beside it instead. He eyes the Seelie arch-lord, opening his mouth and closing it again before he finally speaks beyond initially ushering us in here.

"I could ask my kitchen staff to bring refreshments, if there's anything you'd like. I wouldn't want you thinking ill of me as a host."

"I'm fine as I am," Sylas says, although the massive fae man looks a little awkward too surrounded by the diamond walls and pale furniture. Like he's a little worried he might break something if he moves too quickly. "I simply hoped that we could talk, and I believed it was only fair that I come to you this time after you've made the journey to the summer realm on multiple occasions. But if this is a bad time for you, you certainly don't need to drop everything for us to have this conversation now. I wasn't sure how to arrange it in advance."

"No, it's all right." Corwin's hand flexes, and I can feel he's suppressed the urge to rub it over his face. He's doing his best to keep a cool composure despite his agitation underneath.

I reach out through our bond with the equivalent of a squeeze of his hand. *I'm sure he isn't going to make any problems for the confirmation ceremony. It's a pretty big show of trust, him coming into Unseelie territory on his own like this.*

It is, Corwin agrees, and his stance relaxes enough that he lets himself sink against the front of his desk, using it as a temporary seat. "I'd just finished speaking with my colleagues when you arrived. They're still quite disturbed by the attack on our settlement. If you wanted to check in about our response, I expect we'll be putting forward a couple of new requests within the next day, but I've managed to keep those within reason. They still want the experiment to continue in case it proves to be our best hope of avoiding the curse."

"I'm glad the Murk haven't managed to disrupt our truce completely despite their efforts," Sylas says, matching Corwin's even tone. "But I actually came to address a more personal matter."

He pauses, his mismatched eyes focusing on me for a second where I've settled into one of the other armchairs, a hint of a fond smile touching his lips. Then he returns his attention to Corwin. "I'd imagine you know that Talia conveyed your idea of a joint castle straddling the border to me and my cadre."

Corwin draws his posture a little straighter. "Yes. She said you were open to the possibility. I've been looking forward to discussing it with you directly. First I'd like to say just how much I truly do hope we can work together to continue the peace between our realms."

Sylas nods. "As do we. And also to see that our lady receives all the adoration the four of us can offer in combination—that's your intention as well, unless I'm mistaken?"

A muscle ticks in Corwin's jaw hearing Sylas state it so openly, but he inclines his head. "Yes. I—I do understand how important you are to her and she to you, and this is the best way I could think of to honor your connection. Regardless of the bond the Heart has blessed us with, I can't see how it could be its will that I shatter the happiness she's already found. The more love she has in her life, the better."

I can sense the traces of discomfort that statement still provokes in him, even though I know he means it. Sylas must catch some of it with his own senses as well, or maybe it's easy enough to guess. He knows what the attachment of a soul-twined bond is like.

"I agree," he says. "But I'm also aware of how difficult it can be to go against one's instincts to claim and possess, especially with so strong a connection of your own… I wasn't sure I could accept sharing her affections when she first made it clear she wasn't willing to pick me over my cadre-chosen, and I didn't have the same depth of bond stirring up my emotions."

"I've given it plenty of thought," Corwin says a bit stiffly. "I wouldn't suggest it if I wasn't committed to seeing it through."

Sylas holds up his hands. "I don't mean to question your commitment. I'm only being… practical, as I understand you ravens appreciate. Thinking about a thing and actually seeing it through are very different propositions. Before we go forward and provoke all the chaos we're likely to create by asking to build this castle between the realms, I thought we should make sure you really can tolerate that kind of sharing of affections in practice."

A giddy tingle washes over my skin as I guess what he's getting at. Corwin studies him, his stance tensing even more. "What do you mean?"

"Consider this a sort of experiment in itself," Sylas says. "It's perfectly all right if you find you can't accept it after all. Say the word, and I'll withdraw. I won't blame you either. We've been prepared that compromising might not actually be possible since the soul-twined bond first took hold. I simply think it's best that we determine that up front… It'll be much more complicated to discover it's unbearable for you once we've already proceeded with your plan."

The Seelie arch-lord extends his arm toward me beckoningly. My heart skips a beat.

Corwin has frozen against his desk, a conflicted tangle of emotion reaching me through our connection. He's seen glimpses of my intimate moments with my other men through my memories, fragmentary impressions that I couldn't totally shield him from when I've been with them, but he's never had to watch anything happen right in front of him.

Sylas is right, though. We should know exactly how far we can take this compromise before we try to put it in motion. I'm not sure it'd change anything about what I do in the next few days, but *I'd* like to know just where my mate really stands when it comes to my relationships with my other lovers before I make the ultimate commitment to him.

I have to at least go forward with my eyes fully open.

I get up and walk to Sylas. When I'm close enough, he reaches to trail his fingers down my arm from the elbow-length sleeve of my dress to my bare wrist. Heat sparks in the wake of his touch. I gaze into his mismatched eyes, sharply aware of both how much desire this man can stir in me with a simple touch and how much turmoil is rippling through my mate witnessing it.

Corwin? I say tentatively. If he asks me to stop this, I will. I don't want to hurt him. But then I'll know where we really stand.

He grapples with his answer for a moment before he voices it. *Go ahead. I swore I'd let you have this. If he can bear to see you in other men's arms, then I have to manage to tolerate it too.*

I'd like us to get to some point beyond mere tolerance, but that'd probably be asking too much right now.

I step closer to Sylas, touching his cheek. He loops his arm around my waist and tugs me right into his lap. One of his hands comes to rest on my thigh, tracing delicate circles there. The other tips my head to the side so he can press a quick kiss to the side of my neck.

The brief heat of his mouth sends a heady jolt through my body, one that travels into Corwin as well. A flicker of his own desire rises up in response. He may not be overly enthusiastic about watching another man bring me pleasure, but that pleasure still affects him.

His voice comes out a bit ragged. "You want me to simply watch, while you and she…"

Sylas looks at him over my shoulder, pausing to nuzzle my hair. "That's up to you. You can stick to watching if that's all you're comfortable with. But I'd hoped we could make this our first collaboration, if you're willing."

A collaboration. The image flits through my mind of both my arch-lords skimming their hands over my body, grazing their mouths against my skin, and a deeper heat swells inside me. I meet Corwin's eyes, wanting to encourage him without pushing him beyond what he's ready for.

Holding my gaze, he wets his lips. My excitement has stirred more of his own, and an ache is running through his chest to please me any way he can, to show he can handle everything he proposed. But the sight of Sylas caressing me has set off a flare of possessiveness he hasn't quite mastered.

He clenches his hands against the edge of the desk. Sylas dips his head to nibble at the crook of my shoulder, and I can't help tipping my head back to welcome the teasing kisses. *It feels good, but it'd feel even better if you were with me too.*

Corwin lets out a rough sound, and then he's moving, crossing the space between us in a few quick strides and tangling his fingers in my hair. He claims my mouth with a determined kiss. Sylas nips my shoulder, and hungry flames surge all through my body.

I'm caught between two of the most powerful men in the fae realms, and I can't imagine wanting to be anywhere else.

Corwin deepens his kiss, his tongue delving between my lips. I whimper encouragingly. When I arch toward him, my body quivering with the need for more contact, he drops his hand down my side. He strokes his fingers from collarbone to hip over my dress and then cups my breast.

Sylas lets out a low growl, tasting my eager reaction. His hand slides over my leg to caress the even more sensitive flesh of my inner thigh, close but not quite reaching the spot where I'm already burning hottest.

Corwin sucks in a breath, and another pang of hesitation reverberates through him. Feeling my arousal has already made him hard, but it unsettles him how much of our shared desire is being conjured by another man.

Don't think of him as an outsider, I suggest, with as much coherence as I can summon in the moment. *He's adding to the experience, not taking anything away from you. We* both *get to feel more.*

Corwin kisses me again, even harder than before. He swivels the heel of his hand against my breast, sending blissful shivers through the stiffening peak. Then a sudden sense of resolve comes over him. He pulls back, brushing his lips to my cheek and my temple, and looks at Sylas behind me.

"Touch her sex," he says with a husky note I've never heard from him before. "She's aching for it."

An approving rumble emanates from Sylas's chest. He dips his fingers right between my legs, tucking the fabric of my dress with them, and a gasp slips from my throat. I press into his hand, seeking more of the pleasure that floods me with the contact, and satisfaction echoes through me from my mate.

I grasp Corwin's shirt, tugging his mouth back to mine. Sylas brands the side of my neck again, his fingers working against me through my dress as Corwin massages my other breast, and it's hard to imagine we could ever have thought this was anything but a fantastic idea.

I love you, I think at Corwin, running my hand down his lean chest, gripping Sylas's arm with my other hand. *I love you.*

I love you too, he replies, his inner voice full of tenderness and hunger. *You deserve all the love this world can offer.*

"Her dress," he rasps out loud. "It needs to be off."

Sylas gives no objection to the command, dragging the fabric up over my hips as Corwin opens the fastenings that tighten the bodice. As I adjust my position on Sylas's lap, the rigid length of his erection rubs my bottom. Corwin senses it and the flare of lust it provokes through me. As soon as they've tossed my dress aside, he grips my thighs and settles me right against that hardness.

I can't help squirming, and Sylas's breath catches. He delves his fingers between my legs again, humming happily at the feel of my soaked panties. I tip back against him, and Corwin leans over me, his hand braced against the arm of the chair, his head dropping so he can suck the nub of my breast into his mouth.

The swipe of his tongue and the rocking of Sylas's hand take me from burning to scorching. I grasp Corwin's hair, bowing my back to offer myself up to him, swaying with Sylas's touch. It's all so good I don't know how to ask for anything else and yet I want more, everything, the rush of release I can already taste the edges of.

Corwin teases my nipple between his teeth, my urgency egging on his own. He rises to rest his forehead against mine, both our skin damp with sweat. Desire resonates through me, through our bond.

"She needs to be filled," he says, the invitation clear in his tone. "Let's take her as high as she deserves."

Sylas loosens his slacks and frees himself from his drawers while I shimmy out of my panties. As I sink down over Sylas's length, Corwin keeps his hand against my face, his thumb stroking over my cheekbone, drinking in the giddying stretch and the heated fullness that brings a moan to my lips.

Sylas adjusts his position under me to drive in even deeper and holds me there, pressing a kiss to my shoulder blade. "Have you ever taken your soul-twined mate into your mouth?" he murmurs.

The suggestiveness of the question sends an eager quiver through me. I push back against him, reveling in the fullness where he's entered me, and gaze up at Corwin. My mate's eyes gleam darkly with a longing he can't suppress.

He shouldn't need to suppress it. "No," I say, nudging him to straighten up. "But I'd like to."

I slip my fingers over the front of Corwin's trousers and the bulge straining beneath them, and he can't hold back a groan. He helps me open the ties, caressing my hair with a gentleness that sends tingles over my scalp. I dip forward, still taking Sylas in as I angle myself to flick my tongue over the head of Corwin's stiff erection.

There's something so intoxicating about the effect of that simple gesture. Awed bliss washes through Corwin's body. His fingers tighten in my hair, not so much pulling me to him as holding on for the ride. *So good, my soul—it feels so good.*

I know, because I'm feeling every bit of that delight flooding into me as well. I take him right into my mouth, absorbing the woodsy flavor of him, reveling in every twitch and stuttered breath brought by the pleasure I'm giving him. Even more giddy heat flows through me from where I'm locked in Sylas's embrace as well.

The Seelie arch-lord grips my thigh and rocks into me with increasing force. I let his rhythm carry me up and down over Corwin's shaft. Sylas reaches his other hand to fondle my breast, and Corwin gives my hair just the slightest tug that toes the line between pain and pleasure. Dear God, if every collaboration between summer and winter worked out this spectacularly, I can't imagine anyone would be complaining.

Talia, Corwin says with a tremor of concern, the force of his release ready to burst inside him.

I only suck him down harder. *I want you. I want all of you.*

He comes with a salty spurt in my mouth and a thrill that sings through his veins and mind, so ecstatic it throws me over my own peak. Sylas thrusts inside me, and I clench around him with a cry. The Seelie arch-lord mutters a curse as he pumps into me a few more times before spilling over inside me.

I lift my head, seeking out Corwin's lips. He bends to meet me, no hesitation over his flavor on my mouth, only a fresh wave of fervent appreciation. I turn, slipping off Sylas's shaft, to kiss the other man as well. The Seelie arch-lord hugs me to him with affection I don't need any magical connection to feel. "My love."

"My love," I whisper back.

I turn in his arms and hold my hand out to Corwin. A momentary awkwardness settles over us as the impact of what we've just done sinks in. My mate wavers, and then steps in to squeeze my fingers and brush his lips to my temple, sharing the embrace.

"Have I proven myself acceptably adept at compromise, Arch-Lord Sylas?" he asks with a trace of wryness.

Sylas offers him one of the rare wide grins that turns his fearsome face absolutely stunning. "I think our lady will be well taken care of. It will be an honor to stand with you by her side."

Corwin bends to offer me my dress, and we all get our clothes back into proper order. Then the Unseelie arch-lord draws in a careful breath. "I'm not sure if you would want to witness it or be able to attend, but it would please me—both of us—if you and your cadre could attend the confirmation ceremony. It'll be the start of a step forward for all of us, I hope, and you should be a part of it."

I grasp Sylas's arm. "Yes—I'd like for you and August and Whitt to be there, if you can. And maybe, if the joint castle works out and we can keep the peace, we could have a ceremony of our own, even if it's not quite the same."

Sylas watches Corwin's reaction, but my mate only nods at the suggestion. A softer smile touches the brawnier man's lips. He sets his hand over mine. "I'll speak with the others, but I expect their answer will be the same—nothing would make us happier than to be a part of your life in every way we can."

I beam back at him and then at Corwin, able to tune out the tension in my gut for just a few more minutes in their presence.

Now if only the rest of the fae world would accept the cooperation between our peoples just as willingly.

CHAPTER TWENTY-SEVEN

Sylas

I purposefully called the meeting at the Bastion for a time a little later than I intended to arrive myself so that I could have several minutes to wander that glowing space and reflect in the presence of the Heart. The veins of gold pulse with the thrum of energy, their warmth washing over me. I take in the flow of magic, searching it for any sign that my decision is misguided.

But the images that stir in my mind are of my interlude with Talia and Corwin yesterday. The passionate heat generated between our bodies. The way the Unseelie arch-lord's defenses dropped and he gave himself over to the sharing of pleasures.

I hadn't been sure when I'd arrived how he'd react to my proposal. I'd been prepared for him to delay seeing it through or outright reject the suggestion, as would have been his right. He means well and he wants Talia to be happy, but putting a plan into action is a very different thing from merely imagining it. It was too easy to picture catastrophe if he didn't have to face the reality of not just a joint castle but a joint relationship until we'd already invested in bringing it into being.

But he didn't just face it—he was an active participant. I think we even started to find our footing with each other, a give and take of power and commands with Talia as our focus, without balking too much at giving one another due room. How that might play out once all four of us are in the mix, I can't predict, but I feel certain now that we can navigate those waters without veering into disaster.

And how wonderful was it seeing the glow in Talia's face as *she* discovered just how well we could cooperate given the chance?

I know what she wants, I know what my cadre-chosen and I want, and now I know that Corwin will meet us halfway as promised. I wish those were the only concerns I needed to consider. But I don't believe I can explain our dedication to a castle within the borderlands without finally acknowledging our dedication to *Talia* to my colleagues—not without skirting closer to outright lying than I'm comfortable with.

I meant to claim her as my own in their eyes weeks ago. The only difference now is that there's one more mate who owns a piece of her heart. The rest of the Seelie would consider our relationship odd regardless. I was prepared for this.

I don't need them to celebrate our romantic commitments, only to agree not to get in the way. Whether that's too much to ask remains to be seen. Celia has already expressed some reservations about my interest in Talia.

The Heart doesn't give any indication that it disagrees with my purpose here. If anything, the rhythm of its pulsing soothes my nerves. My connection to Talia is born out of love, as is that of my cadre-chosen. When she welcomes that love, it can't be wrong. It certainly doesn't hurt anyone. I haven't let it interfere with my duties to my people. And if we were still living on the fringes in banishment, it wouldn't be anyone's business at all.

As if roused by that thought, an image forms before my deadened eye. I see a filmy figure of myself standing in the middle of the Bastion's main room, surrounded by three arch-lords sitting on their thrones: Celia, Donovan, and Ambrose.

A snarl twists Ambrose's mouth as he says something with a swipe of his hand cutting through the air. My past self's jaw is clenched, but the turmoil of emotions that was roiling inside me echoes into me now while I watch.

The vision fades away as quickly as it appeared. I shake the lingering uneasiness it brought off as well as I can. It was showing the day my pack's banishment to the fringes was proclaimed.

Is it an ill omen that my eye focused on that moment in my history? Or perhaps I should take it as an attempt at reassurance. Who would have thought I'd have come so far from that moment to now own one of these thrones myself?

No matter what troubles we face, we'll find a way to rise above them.

Celia's arrival prevents me from dwelling on the matter any further. I recognize her elegant, poised stride from the soft tapping of her shoes across the stone floor before she comes into view.

As I requested, she's come alone. Before long, word of our relationship with Talia will spread through the entire summer realm, but I'd like a little privacy for the initial announcement.

"Sylas," she says with an acknowledging tip of her head, and crosses the room to her throne, though she doesn't sit in it, only positions herself in front of it. That's fine. If she'll feel more secure standing by the symbol of her authority, perhaps she'll find less to argue about in my news.

"I trust your pack-kin have picked up no further activity from the Murk?" I say. She should have passed on the word if they had, but if there's a particularly recent development, it might not have reached me yet.

Celia shakes her head, her pale hair hissing over her ebony shoulders. "Other than the one you caught with Arch-Lord Corwin, there's been no sign of them. They do have a knack for vanishing into the shadows." Her lip curls with distaste. "I don't like how quickly they're increasing in boldness. They take too much delight out of startling us."

"I agree. Perhaps, once we're sure of relations with the Unseelie, we could pull many of the troops who've been stationed along the border to seek out whatever communities the Murk have been forming within the realm or along the edges of it."

Celia frowns, but she doesn't reject the idea. "I suppose that will depend on the ravens."

Donovan approaches with a brisker rapping of footsteps. He strides across the central room to meet the two of us, a faint furrow in his brow but his tone upbeat. "It's good to see you both looking well. I hope that will continue after we hear what you have to say, Sylas."

I give him a mild smile at his gentle teasing. Between my two colleagues, I have less idea how he'll react. Celia, at least, has had the experience of taking mates of her own, both soul-twined and not, even if she might hesitate over my specific choice. As far as I know, Donovan has yet to commit himself to anyone. He's been on my side more than once in recent months, but I have no sense of his views on more intimate relationships.

"I don't think what I wanted to speak to you about *should* cause any distress, if you take it in the spirit I mean it," I say. "It shouldn't take very long for me to explain either. This matter has simply been a long time brewing, and it appears that I'll be taking some action in regards to it soon, so I felt you should know."

Celia cocks her head. "And what exactly is this matter?"

I inhale slowly, girding myself. "It involves Talia. You know that she's confirming her soul-twined bond with Arch-Lord Corwin tomorrow."

Both of my colleagues nod. "But the oath she swore to return here regularly is still in place, is it not?" Donovan asks. "We have no need to worry when it comes to the curse."

"We don't. Corwin has expressed the intention of letting her offer her aid as she always has before for as long as she wishes to—and I know Talia is determined to continue helping us in every way she can."

Celia is studying me with a knowing gaze. "I suppose that will be difficult for your cadre-chosen August. He became quite attached to her."

Well, she's given me the perfect opening. "That's a factor in what I need to tell you. There are actually two aspects you should be aware of. The first is that it isn't only August who's formed a more personal attachment to Talia. I don't expect you to understand because you don't know her as we do, but she is quite a remarkable woman regardless of her heritage, and both Whitt of my cadre and I myself are quite devoted to her as well."

Donovan's eyebrows leap up. "What are you saying, Sylas?"

I keep my tone as even as possible. "I'm saying that before the unexpected soul-twined bond appeared, the three of us had intended to bond with her in our own way in a shared mating of the sort that isn't unheard of among cadres."

Celia lets out a startled cough. "It's highly unusual for a lord to join in such an arrangement, let alone an *arch-lord*."

"Perhaps, but she's a highly unusual lady. It is both her preference and our own not to force any limitations on her affections. We have managed to balance our fondness for her without issue for months now; I don't think it should affect anything beyond the walls of our home."

"Other than she's about to be bound to another man—an Unseelie, of all things," Donovan points out, still staring at me.

"Yes, well, that is the second part." I meet his gaze and then Celia's with all the calm authority I can summon, even though my wolf stretches inside me with the urge to roar out that we will have her as we wish regardless of their hesitation. "Talia hasn't hidden her pre-existing ties from her soul-twined mate. To do so would have been quite difficult. And he has come to accept the role we play in her life even if it isn't quite as close a bond as theirs."

Celia's lips part with a slackening of her jaw. "You're not really saying— How could he possibly agree to give up his own soul-twined mate, and to his enemies, no less?"

I give her a sharp look. "We aren't enemies anymore. I should hope we all expect the truce to last if we stay faithful to it. And he wouldn't be giving her up. In the interests of both cherishing this very special woman who's sacrificed so much to stem the tide of our own curse and allowing an ongoing dialogue between the summer and winter realms, we are going to attempt to create a single home for her that we and Corwin would share, if the Heart will allow it."

"You're going to construct a dwelling *within* the border," Celia says, catching on quickly. She rubs her temple. "Sylas, this is all without precedent. Are you sure you've considered the full implications—she may have done a lot for us, but she is still a mere human woman—"

"*Can* they even do it?" Donovan breaks in. "With the spell on the border—unless you mean to build it farther from the Heart—but you have your responsibilities here—"

I hold up my hands to halt both sets of questions and protests. "My domain by the Heart and Corwin's in the winter realm lie across the border from each other. We would attempt to work with the required vows to create this new castle there. And neither of us would treat it as a permanent residence. It would primarily be Talia's home—a place where she could be safe, as no one could enter without the proper vows taken, and where either side could call on her if we would request further help with our curse or any other concern."

Celia gives only a sputter of a laugh, still looking bowled over by the entire situation.

"Nothing is finalized yet," I go on. "Corwin needs to put the matter to his own colleagues, and we'll have to see what flexibility the Heart's magic will offer us. But the Heart has blessed Talia with both the means to subdue our curse and a soul-twined mate, so I believe we have reason to expect it to accommodate our attempt at collaboration. And it will be good for both of the realms to have two arch-lords in regular contact with one another—with all necessary discretion, of course."

"Discretion," Celia mutters. "When you're sharing a lover."

"I'm certain we can manage not to spill political secrets while enjoying our mate's company," I say dryly.

"You sound like you've made up your mind," Donovan says. "There isn't any way we could persuade you not to attempt it?"

I turn to him. "Would you try to persuade me? If you have worries about the end result, I'll do my best to address them."

He opens his mouth and hesitates. "I don't actually know. I'm just so surprised—it seems as if there must be a dozen ways it *could* go wrong."

"You've trusted my judgment in the past," I say quietly. "*Both* of you have, if not always at the same time. The very fact that neither of you realized the depth of my connection to Talia shows that I'm capable of staying discreet. But you are my colleagues, and together we have the highest responsibility in the realm to our people. My association with Corwin will affect that responsibility, I believe for the better. I felt you deserved to know my intentions before I began carrying them out."

"I appreciate that," Donovan says, but his expression is still tense. Celia looks no less uneasy. I don't know what else I can say to ease their fears when I suspect neither of them can fully justify those fears to begin with.

"We still need to be careful of the ravens," Celia says finally. "You must stay wary of this Corwin—and watch what you say around Talia, regardless of your feelings for her, since he can glean whatever he wants from her mind."

I inclined my head. "I will not jeopardize the safety of my people for anything. You have my word on that. If you can point to a moment when she's distracted me from fulfilling my duties in any way thus far, please do."

She lets out a huff. "Your point is taken. I can't say I approve, but I can't say I have grounds to fight you on this either, Sylas. In the end, it is your personal decision. But I will be keeping a close eye on your associations with the Unseelie and this proposed building on the border. If I see any hint that your judgment or our security is being compromised..."

My stomach twists, but I can't argue against her need for caution. "I understand. You *should* be monitoring these developments, as we all monitor each other to ensure our realm is ruled with the highest standards of accountability and loyalty. Heart willing, we can usher in a new era that benefits all the fae who deserve it."

Celia gives me a skeptical look as if she assumes my intentions are mainly to do with keeping Talia in my bed. I suppose I can't blame her for such speculations.

We'll simply have to prove to my colleagues just what a good thing this step can be for all of us—and before they stumble on any reason to cut our efforts short.

CHAPTER TWENTY-EIGHT

Talia

It seems strange that an hour before I officially swear myself to Corwin for the rest of my life, I'm only just meeting his entire coterie for the first time. Zelpha, Olander, and Verik have been around all week, of course, and Domhnall joined us at Heart's Cadence last night for the largest dinner I've had in the winter realm. But it was only this morning that the fifth member turned up to help with the final preparations.

Meriol reminds me of a hummingbird flitting around the temporary cabin constructed at the base of the cliff. The bright green and mauve streaks in her fluttering hair must be magically dyed like my pink and purple shade, because her ears are nearly as smoothly round as mine are, so she's definitely not true-blooded. She looks me over with small but bright eyes, like dark pebbles in her pale face.

"Well," she says in her high, sweet voice. "They definitely won't be able to say you're not fine enough to be our lord's lady."

She and Zelpha have been overseeing the two flock-folk who've been fiddling with my hair and my dress for the past hour. I guess the male members of the coterie are fussing over Corwin in the cabin's other room. I'm just trying not to think about the large stage that's been formed out of diamond just beyond the thin walls around us, where I'm going to confirm him as my mate for a large crowd of his people to see.

Not just his own flock, either. Corwin felt that making as large a spectacle of the ceremony as possible would help the rest of the Unseelie recognize me as one of their own, as much as I am by association with him. Give them lots of positive associations to go with the sight of me attaching myself to one of their arch-lords.

Musicians are playing on the stage right now to entertain the hundreds of fae who've already shown up to watch, many from the other arch-lords' domains but quite a few from farther abroad as well. I caught a glimpse of rows of carriages lined up across the icy plain when Corwin flew me down to the cabin. The swelling melody carries to my ears, cajoling me to sway with it, but my nerves are jumping too much for me to get totally wrapped up in it.

My Seelie lovers and my closest friend have arrived too. A buzz ran through the crowd when Sylas and the others arrived. Corwin assigned several of his warriors to "accompany" them, by which I suspect he means to provide a barrier between them and the winter fae in case anyone's hostile feelings toward the summer realm spill over.

I hope he's not second-guessing his decision to invite my other men to begin with. The last thing we need is a skirmish in the middle of the ceremony. But I know that even if the Unseelie try to provoke my men, they'll do whatever they can to keep the situation peaceful. They'd leave before they let blood be shed during this special moment.

I'd just rather it didn't come to that. Having them here is helping keep my uncertainties at bay, reminding me that I'm not losing them by accepting Corwin.

Zelpha nudges me toward the full-length mirror at one end of the room. The woman who's been working on my hair trails after us, her hands twisted together in front of her, looking oddly nervous about a mere human's opinion. But then, as soon as I'm officially Corwin's lady, I *won't* be just a human anymore. I'll be an Unseelie arch-lord's closest companion, with a certain amount of authority granted just by my connection to him.

Not that I want to go lording it over the fae in any significant way.

And my attendant has nothing to worry about when it comes to my opinion anyway. At my first sight of myself, my jaw drops. I stare at myself for several seconds before I can form words. "Wow. I—this is wonderful. Thank you."

I touch the tendrils of hair streaming over my shoulders tentatively, afraid of breaking the spell. Because it does feel like some kind of magic has been draped over me, elevating me from my regular human self into a much more ethereal figure.

The dress is one that Harper brought especially for this occasion, following the same theme as the first gown she made me for the winter realm. The spider-weave fabric overlaid with the most delicate of glittering lace hugs my slim frame from shoulders to hips and then flares out to drift like a gust of snow around my legs down to my ankles. Swirls of pale, iridescent blue, gray, and ivory mingle together, seeming to flow across the silky cloth with every move I make.

And my attendants must have added some kind of literal spell to the dress as well, because the lace no longer just glitters faintly but twinkles as if embedded with tiny stars.

My hair has undergone an unearthly transformation too. Swept back from my face, the top section has been braided into an elaborate crown atop my head, woven with diamonds and delicate ice-blue flowers. The rest streams down to the bodice of my dress in perfect waves that mimic the waterfall outside. I swear I can see them rippling as if with a current even when I'm standing still.

I notice with a grateful pang that for all the work they've done, my flock-folk haven't hidden the tips of my ears with their human curves or attempted to disguise my boots with the brace for my warped foot. I still am who I am—just a more fantastical version of that woman.

Zelpha grins. "Corwin's going to trip over his feet the second he sees you. Maybe we should make sure he gets a good look before you go out on that stage so he doesn't melt down out of admiration in front of the audience."

Meriol snorts and swats her colleague. "I'm sure he can hold himself together in front of a beautiful lady, soul-twined mate or not. The hard part is getting him to loosen up, not keep himself in check."

"True, true."

I sense the rest of my coterie is gossiping about me, Corwin says through our bond in a dry tone, but I pick up on his own jitters of nerves and eagerness underneath. *Are you faring all right?*

Better than all right, I reply, and focus on my reflection in the mirror again, encouraging him to see me through my own eyes.

The waft of awe that rushes through me tells me Zelpha wasn't totally off base about his reaction. His voice wraps around me like he wishes his arms could in this moment. *I already knew it, but I'm undoubtedly the luckiest man in the realms.*

I suspect most people watching will think it's the other way around.

They don't know you as I do. But they'll come to see just how honored we should be to have you among us, starting today.

Meriol sets her hands on her hips. "Ask him if he's ready to get started, because you definitely are."

My cheeks flush, realizing she must have been able to tell I was communicating with Corwin, but she only looks amused. *Did you hear that?* I ask him.

I think we can begin now. Verik says the other arch-lords have arrived. They'd have been annoyed if we started without them.

"He says yes," I tell Meriol for simplicity's sake.

She grins and then snaps her fingers with a brief darkening of her expression. "I almost forgot. Something to be prepared for—the curse struck in one of the more distant domains last night. I heard that the lord and the victim's mate have brought him here in the hopes that you might try to heal him, but they won't want to interrupt the ceremony. Just keep an eye out for them when it's complete."

My pulse hitches, but I nod. I may be proving myself Corwin's partner today, but I'm still a long way from showing I can help the Unseelie in all the ways I'd like to. What if I fail again? We still don't know why all our efforts last time went nowhere.

Don't dwell on that right now, Corwin says. *We'll give it our best attempt when it's time. The moment ahead is about celebrating the bond the Heart blessed us with.*

I nod, knowing he can feel my agreement through our connection.

Maybe solidifying that bond will make all the difference anyway. I can tell I'm so close to breaking through the curse's grip…

After. I'll focus on that after the ceremony is over. I have plenty of other things to be nervous about already.

The attendants from the flock hustle over to the door to hold it open for me. Zelpha and Meriol escort me out into the cool wintry air and then up the shining steps to the diamond stage. Corwin is just mounting the platform at the other end, his other three coterie members at his flanks.

He hasn't gotten quite the same beautification treatment I have, but he's stunning all the same. The brilliant sunlight beaming down on us brings out the blue highlights in his glossy black hair, and tiny diamonds gleam all through the silver thread that embroiders his formal padded jacket over the dusky violet fabric. He's wearing his silver crown for the first time I've seen it since he and his fellow arch-lords appeared before the Seelie months ago, nestled amid his curls.

But as we walk toward each other, the coterie hanging back at the sides of the stage, it's his eyes my gaze is drawn to. They're the same deep burgundy as ever, intent and thoughtful, but with a pleased glint dancing in them that matches the happiness thrumming through our bond.

We meet in the center of the stage. Corwin holds out his hand, and I take it. Then we turn to face our audience, the fae faces forming a sea so expansive I lose my breath. There must be thousands of people here to witness us confirming our bond.

I've heard that there hasn't been a confirmation ceremony for an arch-lord in over a century. And after everything these people have been through in the past few decades, I'm not surprised they'd jump at an excuse to celebrate such an occasion.

My attention leaps to my Seelie guests in their little cluster by the left side of the stage. Zelpha and Meriol have already stepped a little closer to them, scanning the crowd warily. I shoot a quick smile at my lovers and Harper. The warmth in the eyes of those men gazing back at me steadies me on my feet.

I have so much love to offer and so much given back to me. This ceremony is just one more way of recognizing that love.

Corwin draws in a breath, readying to speak—and another figure steps onto the stage.

Staggers is more like it. It takes me a moment to recognize Terisse, she's so hunched over, her normally copper-brown face grayed to a sickly tan. Laoni hurries after her, grasping her arm to help her balance. She looks out over the crowd and pitches her voice to carry.

"We hate to interrupt this honored ceremony, but it appears that the curse has taken one of our own arch-lords. With time of the essence, we're sure Arch-Lord Corwin's new mate wouldn't want to delay in helping her with her supposed skills."

A murmur carries through the audience, and my back stiffens. They're staring at me even more avidly now. News and rumors about my attempts to cure fae of the curse will have spread all over the realm by now. I thought I was going to make my next attempt in private, afterward…

My gaze darts to Meriol. Her mouth has slanted into a tight frown, her brow knit with confusion. No, this isn't the curse victim she mentioned would be here. She said it was someone from a distant domain—someone who traveled with their lord, not an arch-lord themselves. Has the curse hit *two* fae in less than a day's time?

Corwin and I step back to make room for the two approaching arch-lords. My gut twists into a tighter knot. *Did you have any idea she was sick?*

No, Corwin replies with a mental shake of his head. *It must have just struck her. I'm sorry—if I'd known, I would have prepared you.*

It's not your fault. I'll just—I'll have to do whatever I can. I glance in the direction of the Heart for just a second, sending out a plea to it to show me what to do.

If I fail to cure one of the arch-lords in front of all these people who count on them, they won't see any cause for celebration here today.

And Laoni doesn't expect me to be able to help. I can tell that the moment she reaches us, her cold eyes fixing on me for just a second before she turns back to the crowd. The way she spoke about me: "her supposed skills."

She *wants* me to disappoint everyone. So she can use my failure as proof that Corwin's judgment is shaky? Would she be able to prevent us from confirming the bond?

I can't let any of that happen. I *have* to make this work. Too much depends on it.

Terisse comes to a stop in front of me by the edge of the stage. She sits down on the diamond surface, her head drooping, even her dark, green-tinted hair looking wilted. The sickness is taking her so quickly.

If I *can't* heal her, who will take her place among the arch-lords? What will it mean for the truce?

There's a lot more at stake than just my bond with Corwin.

I swallow thickly and walk up to her. My anxiety has already brought tears prickling to the back of my eyes, so at least I don't need to fight to force them out. I think back to the pregnant woman I healed, to the warmth that seemed to flow from my touch right through her skin. I wanted so badly to cure her, and something in me or in her responded.

I need Terisse to be well. I need her to stand with Corwin and the others at the table in their Hall of the Heart, to make decisions for the good of all her people. I need the Unseelie to stay strong and united so that they can stand up to whatever enemies threaten both them and the summer fae.

A few tears trickle from my eyes. A hush falls over the audience as they watch. I kneel next to Terisse and bring my hand to her cheek.

She simply shivers. A chill seeps from her face into my fingers. I dab at the tears streaking cool over my skin and touch her again with damp fingertips. I reach my other hand to squeeze hers.

Please. Please, let me send this curse away. Let me fend it off. If I'm not doing it right, show me how.

No bolt of inspiration comes to me. Terisse's pallor doesn't budge. Should I try singing to her or hugging her or— But none of those things worked before, and I have the weight of thousands of stares pinning me in place. What if it looks as if I've made her *worse*?

Corwin moves to join me, maybe to offer to create one of his draughts in case that will help, but Laoni draws herself up to her full height in front of him, her chin raised.

"It is as I thought. This human woman our colleague means to join himself to is proving to be a traitor who only pretended to hold some sort of cure to our curse. She's cured all the Seelie with her blood dozens of times over—why can't she do the same for even one of us when asked? Clearly all her loyalty is with the vicious wolves."

A chill rushes through me that has nothing to do with the curse. "No," I say, but I can already see the victorious edge to her smile. She doesn't want to be proven wrong. She set this up to make me look feeble or unwilling, either because she honestly believes that I'm too dedicated to the Seelie or that I've been lying, or she simply—

She set this up.

That one fragment of thought sticks in my head. The crowd shifts restlessly, a few voices calling out harsh words, but my attention narrows in on the woman beside me. On Terisse with her faded skin and crumpled pose.

What are the chances that the curse *would* strike two fae so close together, and that one of them would just happen to be an arch-lord? Right at the perfect time to interrupt our ceremony too?

The certainty tingles over me that what I'm seeing isn't a curse but some kind of illusion. There's magic on Terisse, but it came from herself or one of her colleagues, making her *look* sick when she isn't really. Laoni even phrased it that way, saying she "appeared" to be cursed, not that she was. To avoid a lie?

If that's the case, there's no way I could have cured her when she isn't suffering from the curse to begin with. It's all part of their plan to discredit me.

Even as the understanding rises up inside me, I realize what I need to do. I need to shine a light through this deception and prove that I'm more than an ineffectual human.

Talia, Corwin says, but I can tell he doesn't have a solid argument to stop what he can read of my intentions. If I don't do something, in a matter of moments the crowd before us will turn on me.

I'm tired of hiding so much. Let them see everything that I am, just as the men I love have.

I can dispel whatever magic is on her, Corwin offers.

No. Laoni could just claim that your magic was the illusion, trying to hide that she's still sick. That you're protecting me. They need to know what I can do. They need to see what I stand for.

I glance at him, feeling him braced to leap to my defense and awash with adoration even though I'm being used as a tool against him. Then I look toward my Seelie men, who are watching with taut expressions. Sylas, who would whisk me away from here the second I seemed to be in clear danger. August, who'd fight off the entire crowd to save me if he had to. Whitt, who looks ready to spring onto the stage and proclaim my goodness to the realm.

How could I possibly cherish them more? No matter what challenges we've faced, I've never been happier than when I'm with them.

Love swells inside me and fills me like a glow. I open my mouth and let that glow spill out of me. "*Sole-un-straw!*"

Light flares from my hands and washes over the woman I'm kneeling by. With a shudder that ripples over my skin, it burns through the illusion that dulled her skin and weakened her stance.

Terisse jerks away from me, startled, as the copper tones of her true skin shine through. The appearance of stiffness melts from her limbs. She stares at me and then down at herself. "You—"

I raise my voice. "The Heart has given me some of its magic as well as a soul-twined bond, and the light I call on shows what is real. There is no curse here."

CHAPTER TWENTY-NINE

Talia

The audience stares at the cluster of figures on the stage in stunned silence. Laoni recovers first, jabbing a finger at me. "It's impossible—unnatural—"

My hands clench at my sides. "What's unnatural is pretending someone's sick who isn't to try to hurt me and my soul-twined mate. Whatever magic I have must have come from the Heart, mustn't it? It's let me push back the curse, find a bond with one of your own arch-lords, and understand some of the true names, so it must want all of that from me."

She strides toward me. "You still haven't proven you can cure *any* of us. If this power comes from the Heart, if you're as devoted to us as you are to the curs across the border, why haven't you given us the same benefit you offer them?"

She holds herself tall and defiant, her muscles flexing all through her body, but up close, I catch a tiny tremor that runs through her body. Is she *scared*? Of *me*?

Maybe that isn't so hard to believe. I came from the summer realm, and she doesn't trust the Seelie at all. She doesn't understand what I am or how I can be so entwined with the fae—even more so now that I've shown just how much magic I can wield. She doesn't understand, and so I'm a threat to her.

But she'd never admit that. No, that's the real curse the Unseelie suffer from: this insistence on hiding so much away, of pretending they have no emotions about anything…

The idea hits me so hard a gasp slips from my lips. Laoni stares at me, but I spin toward the crowd, ignoring her.

"I've tried," I say. "I did heal one woman, but I didn't know what I'd done right. There's still a lot about the powers I have that's unclear to me. But I think—I think I know what made the difference now. I heard there really is someone here who's in the grip of the curse, who wanted to ask for my help after the ceremony. If that person is here, I'll try to help them now. You can all watch. And if I fail, then maybe I don't deserve to stay among you after all."

Talia, don't say that, Corwin protests, coming up behind me. He rests his hands on my shoulders, and I reach to set my hand over his.

It'll be okay. I see how it is now. I hadn't worked it all out before—but the cure has to come from the same place as the curse, I think. Whenever I give blood to the Seelie, it's through violence, even if I accept that violence. They cut me with a knife or magic or their teeth… we've never tried magicking blood straight out of me without any wound.

But we don't need violence. That isn't our curse.

No, your curse is locking you up inside your own body. Freezing out all your emotions so you feel nothing but cold. I was trying to skip straight to warming people up again without recognizing what's gone wrong first.

At least, I hope that makes sense when I act it out. It *feels* right, deep inside me, with a headier pulse of energy that seems to hum straight from the Heart.

The crowd is parting, three fae moving through the gathered bodies toward the stage: a man partly supported by an older man and a young woman gripping his elbows. His skin has an icy pallor that hasn't been faked.

Laoni's jaw works, but the voices carrying through the crowd are eager with anticipation. Her people won't want her stopping the demonstration I offered. She can at least tell when she's lost, even if she doesn't intend to stay defeated.

She motions to Terisse, who backs away with her. They both stay on the stage to watch, their cold gazes watching for any hint that I've faltered and given them another opening to dismiss me.

If I do, maybe I deserve to be dismissed. Because if this last try doesn't work, then I really might be useless to the Unseelie.

I can't believe that's true, though. I must be here—I must have the powers I've been given—for a reason. I won't stop believing that until it's proven otherwise.

Rather than make him come around to the steps leading onto the stage, several of the other fae lift the man up right in front of me. The woman who I guess is his mate scrambles up to help him catch his balance on the diamond surface.

The cursed man gazes up at me, his eyes hazed with growing frost. His voice comes out in a croak. "You think you can take away the cold? There's still—there's still so much left I want to do. I don't want to leave this world yet."

Of course he doesn't. I choke up, emotion burning behind my eyes. So many fae have had centuries of their lives cut short because of this awful curse. There are so many that I wasn't here in time to save—or didn't see the answer in time to. But now, now I can make a difference.

Not tears offered freely. Tears hidden away just as the Unseelie would try to disguise their own grief.

In some ways, that answer is harder to get at than what I give the Seelie. The bodily pain the summer fae's curse demands is immediate and innate. With this emotional pain, my impulse is to show it for all the fae before me to see—to prove how much I care. It never even occurred to me to hide it once I thought my distress could heal them.

That's what's so tricky about the curse. It twists the Unseelie to mimic the strictest part of their nature and requires a cure from me that goes against my own instincts.

I force myself to turn away from the cursed man even though his anguish tears at my heart, even though I can feel the entire audience watching and thinking I'm rejecting him. I blink back the tears until

I'm facing the back of the stage and the cliff beyond it, where they can't see them. But that isn't enough. I turned away from the man from Uzziah's flock too.

Then, I was only repeating that one motion. I let my tears fall freely, let him see them as soon as I'd summoned them. This time, I have to scrub them away. Pretend I'm not experiencing this sorrow.

Drawing in a shaky breath, I wipe the tears from my cheeks and rub my eyes like I did when I tried to stop my sadness from upsetting the pregnant woman all those days ago.

My grief *is* weakness, in a way. And I don't really want the fae to see me weak any more than they want to show their own weaknesses to each other. But that weakness can become a strength when I pass it from me to them.

"Please," the man rasps.

Surely I've held back for long enough? I allow myself to swivel toward him, still blinking hard. In time with the thudding of my heart, I walk up to him and crouch down. The faintest tingle of dampness remains on my fingers when I bring them to his face.

"I don't want you to leave either," I tell him. I might not know anything about him other than what he's said in the last five minutes, but I mean it all the same.

The man stares back at me, and my chest starts to constrict. Was I wrong? Has it still not worked?

But then, with a flare of joy right through the middle of me, I catch a whisper of warmth spreading over his skin.

The man's eyes widen. A blush of color blooms across his cheek, and the woman with him gasps. She touches the other side of his face and then spins toward the crowd.

"She's done it! The chill is leaving him. He feels—he looks—he's turning back to normal, as he was before."

More gasps and startled murmurs rise up from the crowd. Many of the figures push in for a closer look.

I step back, and the man sways to his feet. He looks down at himself, testing his increasingly limber joints, running his hand over his face, and letting out a startled but delighted laugh.

He turns toward me with a smile that's almost nervous. Even after all that, it doesn't come easily to him to show any emotion to me, to make himself vulnerable.

That's all right. That's how the Unseelie are—how my mate is too. I can't expect them to change completely.

"Thank you," the cursed man says, his voice emphatic even if his expression isn't. "You—I don't know how to thank you enough."

"I'm just glad you're okay." Relief rushes through my limbs as I realize that's true. I've done it again—I've repeated my cure. We know what the curse needs now.

Corwin steps up next to me on the stage like he did when we first arrived and clasps my hand. He raises it with his into the air. "You've seen how much my soul-twined mate cares for our people and the gift she can offer us against our curse. Will you all support us in confirming our bond and making her a full part of the winter realm?"

His voice rings out across the plain, and a chorus of responses rises up like a cheer, all of them eager and approving. Next to us, Laoni's expression tightens. Terisse has ducked her head, her mouth twisted with what looks like shame, but the self-named leader of the arch-lords strides to the front of the stage.

I stiffen, but she's clearly recognized that there's no turning the tide against us after what I've just done. She brushes her fingers across my shoulder, ruffling my hair with the faintest pinch of my scalp that vanishes an instant later. Before I can react, she's rested her hand on the cursed man's head.

"It gives me great happiness to see you well again," she says to him. "Any ruler can only claim to be an authority if they're willing to admit when they're wrong. I apologize for misjudging my colleague's mate and hope we can all celebrate the boon her presence brings to our people."

She says all that looking out at the audience without so much as glancing at me, which provokes a jab of consternation in Corwin, but I find that I don't care. Let her save face with her people, as long as she's giving me credit at the same time. Today, thousands of fae saw that I can cast away the curse. There's no way she can deny it ever again.

Terisse speaks up too, her voice more strained. "I only wished to ensure none of us were misled. Our test has brought out the best in this woman, and for that I am grateful."

Sure she is, Corwin mutters silently, and I squeeze his hand. Somehow I suspect he's going to have significantly less patience for his colleagues' dismissiveness going forward.

He shifts his attention to me with a flicker of affection like a caress down the middle of me. *Shall we continue with our confirmation as intended?*

I smile up at him. *Yes, I think it's about time.*

Corwin lifts his other hand, and the crowd quiets. "I am pleased to acknowledge and welcome my soul-twined mate before all of you, and to ask you all to welcome her too. I know she will be a shining light of truth in all things, not just today. Before my people and the Heart, I confirm my commitment to my soul-twined mate, Talia of Hearth-by-the-Heart. May our souls be ever twined."

Magic resonates through his last two sentences, the official vows of the ceremony. I drag in a breath, nearly overwhelmed with a giddy sort of nervousness, as if something more might go wrong. But nothing stops me from following his voice with my own.

"I'm so happy to have found a home here with my soul-twined mate and all of you, and I look forward to doing all I can to serve you alongside him. Before the Unseelie gathered here and the Heart, I confirm my commitment to my soul-twined mate, Corwin of Heart's Cadence. May our souls be ever twined."

With the final syllable, a shock of magic hits me, the connection between Corwin and me flaring brighter with a deeper sense of each other's presence and consciousness than I've ever experienced before.

A flash of surprise lights in Corwin's eyes and through our bond. Then, all thought of the watching crowd melting away, he leans in to kiss me, propriety be damned.

Another cheer goes up, even louder than the first. Joy flows between us like a whirling star. I have my mate, and the bond between us couldn't be firmer.

As Corwin eases back and signals for the musicians to return, I look toward my Seelie men in the crowd, half-afraid I'll see consternation on their faces now that the ceremony is complete. But

August is beaming at me, Sylas's expression is full of pleased relief, and Whitt's eyes are alight with sly affection. I extend my hand to them just for a moment, like a promise. Someday, before much longer, we'll confirm our own bonds in our own way.

Then the music washes over us. Corwin tugs me into his arms for the first dance, and there's nothing left to do but rejoice.

CHAPTER THIRTY

Talia

Harper ambles over and plops down next to me on the soft grass where I'm watching the early stages of construction at the border. She cocks her head, following my gaze. "It'll be an interesting building, that's for sure. No one will ever be able to see the whole thing at once, will they, with all that fog in the way?"

My mouth twitches with a smile. Of course the dressmaker would be most concerned about the visual impact of the building. "I guess that's true. I'm interested to see whether the fog insists on sticking around inside the castle or if it'll be content to flow over it."

So far no one's gone inside the fledgling castle at all. I can only just make out Sylas and his cadre's forms and the trunks of the trees they're slowly urging out of the earth within the border haze. The summer side of our shared home will look a lot like the main castle of Hearth-by-the-Heart, just as I expect the diamond side Corwin is erecting will look a lot like Heart's Cadence.

My mate's excitement tingles through to me from where he's working alongside a few of his coterie members across the border. This is the first time he's created a castle that's all his own. The main palace of Heart's Cadence was constructed centuries ago by his ancestors, and he's only needed to do minor repairs and adjustments in his decades as arch-lord.

I'm glad that the first home you're bringing into being yourself is something we can enjoy together, I say through our bond.

He sends the impression of a smile in response. *As am I.*

Harper wiggles her bare feet in the grass and leans back on her hands with a happy sigh. "So, you're going to be living in that place most of the time after it's fully built? You won't really belong to either realm."

"I'd like to think of it as belonging to both," I say. "And you'll be able to come by and visit whenever you want, no matter which side I'm paying the most attention to right then. All you'll have to do is make your border vow at the summer-side door and you'll be able to enter."

"Hmm. I don't think I should drop by unexpectedly *too* often, considering you'll have plenty of things—and people—to keep you busy." She raises her eyebrows mischievously at me.

My cheeks flush. When Sylas announced to the Seelie around the Heart that he and Corwin were collaborating on this joint castle so that they could act as ambassadors to each other's realms, he also expressed his intention to formally recognize me as his mate—in a ceremony that'll recognize August and Whitt as well. After all the chaos of the past few months, most of his pack-kin seem to have taken it in stride, although at larger gatherings, I've gotten some odd looks from the fae of the other nearby packs.

The memory sends a prickle of discomfort over my skin despite the summer warmth. "I'm not sure everyone is totally happy about that part."

Harper lets out a dismissive huff. "They're just frustrated to have three very prominent bachelors taken off the market, I'd bet. But they've got a whole new arch-lord's pack to get to know." A dreamy smile crosses her lips. "Maybe I'll find a mate of my own in one of the other domains by the Heart. Besides, with you being human—"

She cuts herself off with a pained expression. I glance at her, and understanding clicks. With me being human, I shouldn't be competition for my lovers' attention for very long by fae lifespans.

I grimace. "It's okay. We all know I'm not going to live centuries upon centuries like you do. I'm just… glad to have what I do while I can have it."

"Yes. Exactly. Maybe it makes sense that you should get to have extra loving while you're here since you don't get as much time to enjoy it."

A laugh tumbles out of me. "You'll have to put it that way to the other fae and see if they buy that explanation."

I think it's a perfectly good one, Corwin remarks, and a broader smile crosses my lips.

Harper glances up, her fae ears picking up some sound mine couldn't. A shadow crosses her previously peaceful face. "I think that's one of Arch-Lord Celia's sentries lurking around again."

I follow her gaze just as the woman she noticed ducks out of view between the trees at the other side of the field. I didn't get a chance to recognize her, but I wouldn't be surprised if Harper's right. The other arch-lords on both sides of the border have remained uncertain about the continuing alliance between the realms—and about my role in that alliance.

I turn back to Harper. "I guess it can't hurt for them to be keeping an eye on things. Then they can see for themselves that nothing so horrible is going to come out of us working together."

The Unseelie have decided to keep their summer-side settlement for the time being, just to see if it has any more permanent effect on who the curse strikes. I've managed to lift the cursed chill off two more winter fae in the past week, but we're still not sure how long my "cure" will last. I can't believe it'll be permanent when my blood doesn't offer that kind of benefit to the Seelie.

A quaver of uneasiness and confusion passes to me from Corwin. I sit up a little straighter, my senses going on the alert.

A few moments later, his voice reaches me through our connection. *Talia, can you come across the border? Have Sylas or one of his cadre escort you if you'd like. Laoni and Uzziah have come to speak to me—they say there's something you should hear.*

That sounds ominous. I shake off my own unsettled nerves and get to my feet.

Corwin must have communicated the situation to my Seelie men, because as I step toward the border, August emerges from the fog to meet me. "Do you have any idea what this could be about?" he asks, offering his hand.

I slip my fingers around his, my pulse thumping faster. "No. Considering how they've treated me so far, I'm guessing it isn't going to be a house-warming party."

"Well, let's see what they're up to now. Sylas, Whitt, and Astrid are at the ready if we need them."

I'd like to say I'm sure Corwin's colleagues would never attack me outright, but then, I'd never have thought they'd fake the curse to try to prove me a liar and a traitor during our confirmation ceremony.

Holding my head high, I walk with August into the cooler atmosphere of the winter realm. We pass the looming diamond walls of Corwin's side of the castle and come out to find him, Verik, and Meriol facing the two other arch-lords.

"Here's my mate," Corwin says, beckoning both me and August over. He takes my other hand without a hint of rancor that I'm still holding onto one of my other lovers as well. "What is it you have to say about her?"

Laoni looks at me, her cool eyes hardening even as she puts on a thin smile. Uzziah stirs on his feet next to her, placing his hand on his stout belly as if he's got indigestion.

"We took a small sample of Talia's flesh some days ago," Laoni says evenly. "It seemed only reasonable to investigate her exact origins."

A small sample of my flesh? My mind darts to the moment she touched my shoulder during the confirmation ceremony, the momentary pinching I felt. She must have pulled out a hair by the root and smoothed over the pain with magic.

My back stiffens, and anger trickles through my bond with Corwin. Before my mate can speak up, August shakes his head. "My lord has already tested her essence in every way we can think of. You already knew as much as we do about her connection to the Heart."

Laoni aims her icy gaze at him. "You'll forgive us if we'd want to make our own tests, but that isn't what I meant. We wanted to discover more about her history in the human world."

Despite my uneasiness, a tremor of excitement runs through me. Have they found out something about the trace of fae ancestry in my family? "And you did discover something?" I ask.

Laoni motions to Uzziah, who clears his throat. "A few of my people did their best to trace your bloodline—and one of them uncovered a direct, living connection we can't help suspecting may have his own ties to the Heart if your own were born through your family line."

My stomach sinks. "Like a distant cousin or something?"

Ambrose already tried to push for the Seelie to gather any relatives of mine they could find, however distant, to use in whatever ways they could. Sylas managed to dismiss that idea, but if the Unseelie have taken it up too…

Uzziah's next words knock those suddenly minor concerns out of my mind in an instant.

"No," he says, gazing at me with what might even be a tiny bit of sympathy. "It seems the wolves didn't slaughter all of your immediate family after all. We believe we found your brother, alive and well."

SECRETS OF WINTER - BONUS SCENE

What prompted Sylas to make his unexpected appearance in the winter realm to see if Corwin would "collaborate" with him to please Talia? Find out in this bonus scene from his point of view!

Sylas

I watch Talia leave my office with a fraught mix of emotions tangling in my chest. There's a lot of hope in the mix, more than I've felt since that blasted soul-twined bond first established its hold on her, but wariness and uncertainty as well. When I look at my brothers, a similar turmoil shows in their eyes.

"The magical side of the raven's plan may be sound," Whitt says in a measured tone. "But how sure can we be of *him*? I respect that he's made the offer—and thought it through as well as he already has—but I haven't gotten the impression that it's easy for him even letting her come back to us where he doesn't have to see what we get up to. I wonder how he'll actually react to having us in the same building as him. Sharing the same bed with her."

August frowns and glances at me. "You're the only one of us who's experienced a soul-twined bond before. How easily do you think he'd be able to overcome the innate possessiveness? There are a lot of other soul-twined mates who take other lovers."

I grimaced. "Usually only temporarily and mainly for the purpose of heirs rather than a full-blown love affair. I know there are some who tolerate a longer-standing secondary relationship… I have no idea how comfortable it is for them. Even a brief affair jarred too much against my bond for me to want to consider it."

And they know the result of my mate's dalliance. For Whitt's sake as well as my own, I'd rather not bring up the explicit details.

"Somehow I don't think your fellow arch-lords are going to be all that 'comfortable' with the situation either," Whitt mutters. "Well, Donovan has a more open mind, but Celia will have plenty to say about it, little of it good, I'm sure. And Heart only knows how Corwin's frigid colleagues are going to react to his proposal."

"We can work around their concerns," I say. "Those are matters of politics and debate. Matters of the heart are much more difficult to negotiate."

August rubs his mouth, his expression unusually pensive. "There isn't anything to do but go ahead with it and see what happens, is there?"

I gaze off in the direction of the border, unseen beyond my walls but ever-present. As the thrum of the great Heart's energy washes over me, the beginnings of an idea unfurl in my head.

It will be risky… but Corwin has already put himself at plenty of risk crossing the border to us so often. I can meet him halfway, as it were. And see just how far he'll be willing to go to meet us in every way.

"I think I may go have a word with the raven on his home territory," I say. "Tomorrow, after they've had some time to sort out the aftermath of the Murk's attack on their settlement."

Whitt pulls himself straighter. "I can be ready to accompany you, with maybe a few of our—"

I raise my hand to cut him off. "I'll go alone, as he has come to us. I don't want it to look like an attempt at intimidation."

August bristles. "On your own, into the midst of those featherbrained menaces? *Corwin* might be all right, but most of them were still waging war on us a few weeks ago."

I shoot him a baleful look. "I'll stick to his territory, and I think you know I'm fully capable of defending myself as need be. He's forgiven us for throwing him in a dungeon. I believe I can extend a little trust in return."

Whitt's mouth has slanted at a pained angle, but he doesn't argue. "If you feel that's best. Far be it from me to argue with an arch-lord." He says the last bit with enough wryness to take any possible resentment out of the statement.

"I'll let you know when I'm leaving," I assure him. "And when you can expect my return. With full permission to bring our warriors to bear if it appears I've gotten in over my head. But I don't imagine it'll come to that."

A day later, standing at the edge of Hearth-by-the-Heart in front of the shimmering border haze, my earlier certainty momentarily wavers. Should I send some sort of message ahead, get the winter arch-lord's permission for this visit?

But I'm not even sure how to ensure such a message got to Corwin, and besides, if we'll be sharing a home of sorts, he won't have prior notifications of our comings and goings, of when he might encounter Talia's other mates. So showing up unannounced is its own sort of test. If he can't handle my mere presence without prior preparation, that doesn't bode well for the success of this joint castle.

With every inch of me on guard, I square my shoulders, speak my vow, and stride across the border. The nip of cold on the icy terrain I find myself walking onto makes my skin twitch with discomfort. How any fae can stand to live in this awful chill rather than the bountiful warmth of the summer side, I can't conceive.

My arrival hasn't gone unnoticed. A sentry swoops down from the sky and lands a few feet away from me, his hand on the sword at his hip. "What business do you have here, wolf?"

He's stern but not outright hostile. I raise my hands in a pacifying gesture. "I'm Arch-Lord Sylas of Hearth-by-the-Heart, the pack your Arch-Lord Corwin's soul-twined mate hails from. I wish to speak with them. I've taken my vow and intend no harm to anyone here."

The sentry frowns at me, but his eyes widened a little when I announced my title. After a moment's wavering, he motions me toward the tall, glittering palace that's closest by—the one Talia's told me about. Heart's Cadence, Corwin's home.

My face is prickling with the cold by the time we reach the front door. The sentry escorts me in and motions a servant over. "This is Arch-Lord Sylas, here to meet with our lord."

He's gone again before the servant can even answer. The smaller man peers up at me with a nervous twitch. "I—er, Arch-Lord Corwin has gone to the Hall of the Heart to consult with the other arch-lords."

"I can wait," I say amicably. "Wherever you direct me to. Is Talia here—his mate?"

The servant shakes his head. "She left a little while ago too. I'm not sure where she's gone."

Well, I can wait for both of them, then. "It's my fault for coming unannounced. I can be patient."

He leads me into a sitting room with a broad window that overlooks the edge of the plateau the castle is perched on. A vast view of the winter realm stretches out beyond that, and even I can admit there's beauty in its icy expanse. The sun beams over the frozen surfaces, making them shine as if they're made of the same diamond as Corwin's palace.

I stroll along the width of the window, settling in for a potentially long wait, but it can't be more than half an hour before multiple sets of footsteps rap against the floor outside.

Talia pokes her head in first with one of Corwin's coterie members poised behind her. My love's face brightens at the sight of me and then tenses with worry. She hustles over as I move to meet her. "Sylas! What's going on? I didn't know you were coming. Is everything okay?"

"Everything's fine," I assure her, resting my hand on her shoulder. I'm not sure how Corwin's flock would react to seeing his soul-twined mate fully embraced by another man. Their reactions will be his to deal with if we see his plan through. "I had something I wanted to talk about with you and your mate."

Talia pauses, and her eyes go momentarily distant in the way that tells me she's communicating with Corwin through their bond. She nods, her smile coming back. "His meeting with the other arch-lords is just finishing. He'll be here soon."

When Corwin arrives, indeed quite shortly, he stops in the doorway with a briefly flustered expression before his usual impervious calm snaps into place. I'm sure Talia will have told him I was here, but perhaps the momentousness of the visit didn't sink in until he saw me for himself.

"Arch-Lord Sylas," he says. "This is a surprise. You have something to discuss?"

I nodded. "A matter best discussed in private."

"Come to my office, then."

He leads me down the glittering halls with Talia following and ushers me into a painstakingly neat room that makes me wonder how much his opinion of me would lower if he caught sight of the moderate disarray in mine.

The pale furniture looks both austere and somehow delicate. I lower myself into one of the armchairs facing the gleaming desk with more care than I'd usually take. Talia sits in the neighboring chair, a couple of feet distant, and Corwin takes the seat behind the desk. But he only lingers there for a moment before getting up again and moving around the desk to stand in front of it, taking an uneasy breath.

"I could ask my kitchen staff to bring refreshments, if there's anything you'd like. I wouldn't want you thinking ill of me as a host."

So concerned with propriety to the last. Another reason for my own concern about his ability to carry out his proposal.

"I'm fine as I am," I say. "I simply hoped that we could talk, and I believed it was only fair that I come to you this time after you've made the journey to the summer realm on multiple occasions. But if this is a bad time for you, you certainly don't need to drop everything for us to have this conversation now. I wasn't sure how to arrange it in advance."

"No, it's all right," he says, with a stiffness to his tone that tells me it isn't entirely. This isn't a man who enjoys being surprised.

But after a moment he relaxes a little, propping himself against the front of his desk rather than standing up straight. "I'd just finished speaking with my colleagues when you arrived. They're still quite disturbed by the attack on our settlement. If you wanted to check in about our response, I expect we'll be putting forward a couple of new requests within the next day, but I've managed to keep those within reason. They still want the experiment to continue in case it proves to be our best hope of avoiding the curse."

None of that information is startling. And it makes sense that he'd assume I'm here about our people's relations. Better to set him straight right away.

"I'm glad the Murk haven't managed to disrupt our truce completely despite their efforts. But I actually came to address a more personal matter." I glance toward Talia, unable to restrain a quick smile before focusing on Corwin again. "I'd imagine you know that Talia conveyed your idea of a joint castle straddling the border to me and my cadre."

A little of his earlier stiffness comes back into the raven's stance. "Yes. She said you were open to the possibility. I've been looking forward to discussing it with you directly. First, I'd like to say just how much I truly do hope we can work together to continue the peace between our realms."

"As do my cadre-chosen and I. And also to see that our lady receives all the adoration the four of us can offer in combination—that's your intention as well, unless I'm mistaken?"

Corwin's jaw clenches for an instant, but he tips his head in acknowledgment. "Yes. I—I do understand how important you are to her and she to you, and this is the best way I could think of to honor your connection. Regardless of the bond the Heart has blessed us with, I can't see how it could be its will that I shatter the happiness she's already found. The more love she has in her life, the better."

A sentiment I fully approve of. The real question is whether he can act on it as well as he speaks.

I study him carefully. "I agree. But I'm also aware of how difficult it can be to go against one's instincts to claim and possess, especially with so strong a connection of your own… I wasn't sure I could accept sharing her affections when she first made it clear she wasn't willing to pick me over my cadre-chosen, and I didn't have the same depth of bond stirring up my emotions."

Corwin's posture turns even more rigid. "I've given it plenty of thought. I wouldn't suggest it if I wasn't committed to seeing it through."

I raise my hands in an apologetic gesture. "I don't mean to question your commitment. I'm only being… practical, as I understand you ravens appreciate. Thinking about a thing and actually seeing it through are very different propositions. Before we go forward and provoke all the chaos we're likely to create by asking to build this castle between the realms, I thought we should make sure you really can tolerate that kind of sharing of affections in practice."

At this point, the Unseelie arch-lord may as well be carved out of diamond himself. It takes him a moment to speak. "What do you mean?"

Oh, from how much he's tensed up, I think he understands the implications perfectly fine. But I'll spell it out if he prefers.

"Consider this a sort of experiment in itself. It's perfectly all right if you find you can't accept it after all. Say the word, and I'll withdraw. I won't blame you either. We've been prepared that compromising might not actually be possible since the soul-twined bond first took hold. I simply think it's best that we determine that up front… It'll be much more complicated to discover it's unbearable for you once we've already proceeded with your plan."

With that, I hold my hand out to Talia. She blinks at me, a hint of a blush coloring her cheeks, but I recognize the spark of desire in her eyes as well. She hesitates for a second, her gaze sliding to her mate, presumably judging his response both inside and out. But when he doesn't speak, only holds in place as still as a statue, she stands and walks over to me.

I'll start slow. I don't want to push Corwin too far in one go if there's going to be a moment that breaks his resolve.

I brush my fingers down Talia's forearm, watching the heat in her eyes flare brighter. She wets her lips, wavers, and then steps close enough to touch my cheek.

I don't know what silent communication she might be carrying on with her mate, but he still hasn't leapt in to stop us. I grasp my love's waist and ease her down onto my lap. My other hand rises to tease over her thigh through my dress. I tip her head to the side and give her neck a quick kiss that provokes a ghost of a sigh.

Finally, the raven speaks, his voice rough. "You want me to simply watch, while you and she…"

I glance at him over Talia's shoulder. He should realize I don't intend to be selfish in this encounter. I only want to know how far he'll go.

"That's up to you. You can stick to watching if that's all you're comfortable with. But I'd hoped we could make this our first collaboration, if you're willing."

Corwin's tongue flicks over his lips, but his hands tighten around the edge of the desk a moment later. He's still grappling with his impulses. Well, I'm not going to just sit here and wait for him.

I lower my head to chart a trail of delicate kisses over the crook of Talia's neck. With an encouraging sound, she tips her head back to allow me greater access. And then, just as I reach her shoulder, a ragged sound bursts from Corwin's throat.

Before I can worry that he's about to tear us apart, he pushes forward and delves his fingers into Talia's hair while pressing his mouth to hers. Suppressing a smile, I test my teeth against her shoulder.

She whimpers, arching between us. Her obvious delight must embolden her mate, because he slides one of his hands down her chest to cup her breast.

The hungry flush of her skin turns my cock so hard I can't restrain a growl. I stroke my fingers higher up her leg, almost to the apex of her thighs, wanting to give her everything but also to stretch out her enjoyment of this encounter. And to give Corwin time to find his pace.

The winter arch-lord pauses, his gaze dropping to the movements of my hand. His shaky inhalation has me braced for a rebuff. But then he claims Talia's mouth with even more passion, caressing her breast.

I keep teasing the sensitive skin of her inner thigh as he draws back an inch with a soft kiss to her temple. His eyes seek out mine.

"Touch her sex," he commands, his voice rough in a very different way from before. "She's aching for it."

I don't try to hold back my grin, a rumble of approval reverberating through me at the same time. It hadn't quite occurred to me just how effective a partner in this collaboration the raven could be when he knows exactly what Talia desires most at any given moment. And he's offering up that knowledge to me rather than making use of it himself, welcoming me as an equal contributor to our shared tryst.

I delve my fingers between Talia's legs as Corwin requested, any tension I'd still been holding in washing away. Nothing matters but the woman between us and the pleasure we can conjure in her together—and I'm sure now that her mate believes that in practice as well as principle.

She is ours, and we'll bring her to the heights she deserves, now and always.

FATED CROWN

BOUND TO THE FAE #6

CHAPTER ONE

Talia

I stop at the edge of the park in the shade of an oak, several feet from the busy city street. The sight of the cars whizzing by and the roar of their engines sets my nerves jangling. My chest tightens up, only loosening as I take a few slow, deep breaths.

This place is technically my real home. I was born into it and lived in it for the first twelve years of my life. But it's been nearly a decade since I last set foot in the human world. My memories and Sylas's collection of Hollywood comedies haven't prepared me for the vivid reality of returning.

Does every part of the human world *smell* this bad? I've gotten used to the ever-fresh air of the fae world, warm and sweetly floral on the summer side and crisply cool on the winter side. Here, each breath brings a tang of burned gasoline and other chemical scents I can't identify prickling into my lungs.

Beside me, Corwin rests his hand on my shoulder and squeezes. He can read my uneasiness through our soul-twined bond—and I can pick up on his own distaste for certain elements of our current surroundings. His nose wrinkles as he inhales the same odors, and the rush of traffic makes his eyes skitter trying to follow it.

"There are other parts of your world that are much more pleasant than this," he says. "Humans have left some wilderness relatively untouched, and even the smaller villages can be reasonably peaceful."

The other member of our party, a broad-shouldered woman from Arch-Lord Uzziah's coterie, snorts and raises her pointed chin toward the road. "You couldn't give me enough treasure to convince me to live this far from the Heart and among these creatures, that's for sure."

Her gaze flicks to me, but she shows no obvious concern about the insulting way she just referred to people like me. She motions for us to follow her. "From my observations, he should be in that building across the way. Around this time we may catch them rambling around in the courtyard."

"Okay." I rub my arms, catching a tingle of the magic that's wrapped around us. Before we emerged from the Mists into the human world, Corwin cast a spell around us to make us invisible to human eyes. A Golden Retriever we passed in the park sniffed in our direction and offered a few brisk barks, but the man holding his leash looked straight through us, so the illusion appears to be working on its intended targets.

Of course, I'm pretty sure one of those cars could still splatter me all over the road, invisible or not.

We walk to the nearest corner, where the streetlights gleam red and then green. The act of crossing on the walk signal feels so mundane and yet so foreign at the same time that my chest starts to clench up all over again. When one of the cars honks at the vehicle in front of it, I jump half a foot in the air and wobble on my warped foot.

Corwin grasps my elbow to steady me. He keeps his fingers curled loosely around my arm the rest of the way across. Apprehension is coiled in his stomach, much like the tension wound through me beneath my more visible jitters.

We haven't even gotten to the reason for our visit yet. I'm not sure what I *want* to happen, only that no matter what does, it's going to be hard.

Uzziah's woman leads us across a grassy field lined with some kind of sports markings toward a two-story brick building that stretches the length of the block. Teenagers lounge on the front steps outside the double doors of the main entrance. We slip past them unseen and around to the other side of the building, where two wings jut out around a large cobblestone courtyard that holds several metal picnic-style tables. More teens are sitting around the tables or in clusters on the cobblestones, eating their lunches and chattering with each other.

"There he is," Uzziah's coterie woman says, pointing to the edge of the courtyard by the end of the wing opposite us. My stance tensing, I follow her gesture with my gaze.

The boy she pointed out is sitting at a table with his back to us, nothing showing but burnished brown hair that curls around his ears and a lean frame in a black long-sleeved tee and baggy jeans. I can't tell anything for sure from that. My heart thumps harder as we circle the courtyard to consider him from a better angle.

With each detail of his face that comes into view—the angle of his jaw, the slope of his nose, the glint in his wide-set eyes—an ache swells around my heart. It *is* him, isn't it? My little brother, Jamie, who'll be seventeen now if he survived the attack by the monstrous wolf-shifting fae who attacked my family, which I've always believed he didn't.

Then he turns his head, revealing the other side of his face, and my heart just about stops. Any remaining doubts flee.

He must have had reconstructive surgery to deal with the worst of the scarring, but it didn't remove the effects of the attack completely. Pale pink marks across his left cheek and jaw, running down to his neck and probably across his chest as well, show where the wolf's vicious fangs carved open his skin.

Oh, Jamie. My pulse lurches, propelling me toward him, but my legs lock at the same time.

He has no idea *I'm* alive. He definitely can't have imagined I've spent the better part of the last decade among faerie beings he'd never have believed existed. I can't just march up to him and launch a sudden family reunion. Even if a pang is ringing through me to wrap my arms around him, to tell him how sorry I am for… for everything.

For teasing him into chasing me into the woods so long ago. For not knowing he'd survived until just now. For leaving him alone all this time.

A burn of tears forms in my eyes. I blink hard, grasping for Corwin's hand.

It wasn't your fault, he says gently through our bond. *You couldn't have known what you were leading him toward, and you had no opportunity to find out what had become of him while you were caged all those years.*

I know, I reply. *But even after I got out, it never occurred to me to confirm what happened to him and my parents. I just assumed that I'd seen right, even though it was dark and I was terrified.*

I rub my face, the ache inside me expanding even farther. Wouldn't it be wonderful if Mom and Dad had survived too, if they'd had each other to get through the trauma and my disappearance? But this is the only direct blood relative the winter fae turned up with their extensive search, at least among those that interest them.

The fae sage indicated that my connection to their kind came from my mother. It seems my maternal grandparents passed on in the last nine years—losing their only child in such a horrible way can't have helped. Jamie has been living with my aunt and uncle on my father's side and our two young cousins here in this city, a few hundred miles distant from the town where we lived before.

It was far enough distant that we didn't see them very often back then. At eight years old, recovering from a savage mauling, my brother had to move in with people who were only one step above strangers, even if they were family on paper. I don't wish the fae that stole me away had taken him too, because what I went through was more than I'd wish on anyone, but he hasn't had it easy by any means.

As if to illustrate that thought, a trio of guys saunters by the table where Jamie is eating alone. One of them does an exaggerated double-take at Jamie's face and clutches at his chest in mock-horror. "Oh my God! It's the creature from the Black Lagoon."

The other two guys burst into laughter. Jamie's shoulders tense, but he keeps his gaze fixed on his sandwich. My hands ball into fists at my sides.

The bullies aren't done yet. The guy who made the first remark sits down on the table next to Jamie's tray and swats at his container of fries, sending half of them skittering onto the cobblestones. "I don't think the Swamp Thing should be getting food from our cafeteria. This isn't a school for monsters."

At the sneer in his voice and his cruel smile, I can't hold myself back. I march over, fury flaring up through my throat onto my tongue. "The only monsters are the ones who did that to him—and *you*, as far as I can tell."

But none of them react, because of course they can't see or hear me.

Talia, Corwin says softly, coming up beside me. I turn to him, debating asking him to take the magic off me right now so I can give these jerks a piece of my mind for real, but Jamie is getting up.

He gives the guys a bored look, picking up the rest of his fries so they're out of reach. "If they serve you, I guess anything goes."

The first guy's expression goes from amused to pissed off in an instant. He springs off the table. "What the hell did you say, McCarty?"

He steps forward as if to grab my brother, but just then a teacher ambles by. She gives the guys a questioning look. "Is everything all right here, boys?"

The main guy puts on an ingratiating smile. "Completely fine, Mrs. Green. Right, Jamie?"

Jamie shrugs and walks off before the teacher leaves.

With a heavy heart, I watch him head into the school. He not only got torn from our family and horribly wounded, but the scars the fae left on him are making him a target for the villains of the human world.

If he could know he's not really alone—if he could have me to turn to again…

Corwin's arms come around me in a careful embrace. A hint of discomfort travels into me—he isn't totally at ease showing even this much affection in front of our unfriendly spectator from Uzziah's flock—but he offers that affection all the same, because it matters more to him how I feel. I rest my arms over his and hug them to me, abruptly aware of the deeper inner turmoil he's trying to suppress.

If I returned to the human world on even a semi-permanent basis, it'd mean leaving my soul-twined mate behind—and my other lovers too. Corwin doesn't want to interfere with my decision, but the thought of having me so far away for any length of time wrenches at him.

I don't know what to say to him. I don't know what I want to do. I owe so much to so many people… But how can I abandon my brother all over again when he's been on his own for so many years already?

I managed to find a balance between my loyalties to the summer and winter fae. Is there some way I can bridge this gap as well, even though it's so much wider?

Uzziah's coterie woman must be thinking along similar lines, although with very different motivations. She clears her throat and turns away from the courtyard to face me. "That was him, wasn't it?"

"Yes." The magic they used to trace my genetic line will have already confirmed it, but I guess she wanted to hear it from my own mouth too.

"Excellent." She rolls back her shoulders. "If he's as useful as you are, this will solve all our problems and simplify the cure completely."

I blink at her, dread trickling through my stomach. Corwin's body tenses against me at the same time. The other winter arch-lords didn't say anything about Jamie "solving problems" before we set off on our journey here. It was supposed to be just a chance for me to check that their story was true and see how Jamie is doing now. But I'm familiar enough with the fae way of thinking to guess what she's getting at.

"What do you mean?" I ask.

A satisfied smile curves the woman's lips. "Two cures for two realms. You can stick with the winter realm alongside your mate, and the Seelie can make use of your brother. We couldn't have asked for an easier solution."

CHAPTER TWO

Talia

The new castle that my summer and winter lovers have collaborated on, which straddles the border between their realms, contains just a few rooms right in the center. On the second floor, there are a string of chambers dedicated to my personal use. Below them lies a large ballroom we might host parties in if the two realms ever become that friendly, and a smaller meeting room beside it. The outer areas of the castle aren't finished yet, but the middle portion is complete enough for us to make use of it.

Both the table there and the floor, walls, and ceiling show the merging of the two materials that form the castle. Sylas's polished wood twines with Corwin's glittering diamond right down the center of the space. The mix of warmth and coolness usually appeals to me, a sense of harmony amplified by the soft pulse of the Heart's energy that flows through the space, but the company we have in this room today has left me uncomfortably chilled.

All eight of the arch-lords from both sides of the border are sitting around the table, the three from summer on one side and four of those from winter on the other. Assorted members of their cadres and coteries stand along the walls behind them, including my other two lovers: Sylas's half-brothers, August and Whitt.

Corwin had me sit at the head of the table while he took the foot. I appreciate having him across from me whenever I need the reassurance of catching his eyes, but my position feels like a lot of pressure. But then, we are here to talk about a situation that concerns me more than anyone else.

None of the arch-lords look particularly happy about that—or the building they're in. The six of them who didn't have a hand in designing this space are glancing around with expressions that range from wariness to outright revulsion. Laoni, the winter arch-lord who's been most hostile toward me and Corwin, has even wrinkled her nose.

But even though the outer rooms aren't finished yet, this central space seemed like the best setting for a joint meeting. To enter the structure immersed in the border so close to the Heart, everyone had to take the vow to do no harm.

I wish I could take a little more comfort from that fact. The real problem is the harm they want to do to someone who isn't even here, who doesn't even know they exist yet. And I'm increasingly convinced I'd like it to stay that way.

"The situation with the curse is too urgent for personal feelings to come into it," Laoni is saying now. "We must bring the boy here and determine whether he has a similar connection to the curse."

The edge of distaste in her voice suggests that the personal feelings of a human like me matter even less than if I were fae. There's a new glimmer of hostility in her gaze along with the usual disdain. I'm not sure how much of it's because I'm now officially Corwin's mate or because of the minor but unexpected magical power I displayed during our confirmation ceremony.

If I thought wielding a little of the same powers the fae have might bring me more respect, I was wrong. If anything, I've gotten the impression the other winter arch-lords object to my presence even more now that I've shown I'm less helpless than they'd assumed.

Celia, the strictest of the summer arch-lords, gives her counterpart a narrow glance. But she agrees, if grudgingly. "If the powers Talia possesses come from their family line, it stands to reason that her brother would have them as well."

"You can't just tear him away from his life like that," I protest, my hands clenched in my lap beneath the table where they can't see them. "The fae have already destroyed his family and left him scarred. He's had a chance to recover from that, and now you want to rip him away from everything he knows—to use him against his will?"

Terisse, a winter arch-lord who often sides with Laoni, frowns at me. "I thought you were dedicated to healing us of this ailment. Didn't you give your loyalty to the fae when you swore to stand with Arch-Lord Corwin as his mate?"

"*Talia* dedicated herself," Corwin puts in. "That doesn't mean she's required to approve of her brother being forced to make a similar sacrifice unknowing."

Sylas shifts in his seat where he's poised close by at my right. "I believe Talia's generosity of herself should earn her some consideration on this matter. She *has* sacrificed a lot for us. If we're going to ask more of her and hers, we should allow it to be on her terms."

"And what terms would those be?" Laoni sneers. "As far as I can tell, she wants us to forget the idea and what we've discovered—she'd rather we'd never found out her brother was living at all. Perhaps she's already imagining leaving us herself to join him in the world she belongs to."

Her words hit close enough to the truth that my stomach twists. I will my voice to stay steady. "No matter what happens, I swear I'll continue helping you hold back the curse however I can. But you can't reasonably ask me not to care about anything else. You all have more than one responsibility you have to balance in your lives. Why can't I look out for the fae *and* my family?"

"Corwin and his flock should be your family now," Uzziah says coldly.

Sylas makes a disbelieving sound. "Come on now. Do you expect us to believe that all of you required *your* mates never concern themselves with the packs or flocks they came from after they confirmed their bond to you?"

Laoni glowers at him. "If a member of my mate's former flock turned out to be instrumental in fighting this curse, I'd absolutely expect him to prioritize that over a little discomfort."

I can't stop the protest from bursting out of me. "A little discomfort?" But when all the gazes around the table turn toward me, I'm not sure how to follow that up without insulting all the fae here.

August takes a step toward me and then catches himself. The arch-lords are aware of his and Whitt's relationship with me now, but the news is very fresh in their minds, and I know they all have qualms about that unusual arrangement too. It probably wouldn't look good for him to offer any gestures of affection in front of them, especially when the winter fae look down on any displays of emotion at all.

To my surprise, it's Donovan who speaks up next. The youngest arch-lord often lets his colleagues guide his judgment, but he's the only one other than Sylas and Corwin who's ever supported my right to make my own decisions.

He keeps his tone mild. "What exactly are your concerns about bringing your brother here, Talia? If we can understand where you see the harm, we may be able to offset it."

I drag in a breath and resist the urge to drop my gaze.

It's all right, Corwin says through our bond, his gaze intent on me. He knows what I've been through at the hands of the fae better than anyone else, even the three men who rescued me from captivity, because he's been able to experience the memories directly from my mind. *You're simply stating facts. If they question any, I can vouch for the truth of them, as can Sylas in many cases.*

That's true. I do have people on my side here.

I look around at the other arch-lords' faces, trying to show confidence on my own. "I've made a home for myself here, but I didn't come because I wanted to. I suffered for nine years at the hands of the Seelie lord who took me and his cadre. And even since Sylas took me in and I've been able to help with the curse with much more freedom, I've been insulted and treated like a tool rather than a person more times than I can count. I've been attacked and had some of the highest fae scheming to take my freedom away."

"We did settle that matter," Celia says, her stance tensing.

"One of them," I say, meeting her gaze straight on. "The fae who killed my parents, stole me from my home, and tormented me for years haven't been punished at all. A lot of you don't see doing that to a human as a crime at all. Right here at this table, talking about my own brother, I'm being treated as if I'm less than the rest of you."

The fae around the table stir uncomfortably, but none of them attempt to deny that accusation before I go on. "Jamie has already suffered so much because of the fae. Why would I want him brought somewhere he'll have no one he knows except me—if you even let us see each other more than occasionally—and where nearly everyone around him won't care how he thinks or feels about anything that's happening to him?"

There's a momentary silence. Corwin extends a tendril of his love to wrap around me like a gentle embrace.

Terisse speaks first, sounding slightly chagrinned. "You can't blame us for putting our own needs first when it's a matter of the survival of all our people. It isn't simply about fae compared to humans, but thousands of fae lives compared to that of one human."

"You already have one human," I retort. "Me. And you're not listening to me. Have you even thought this through properly? You're so quick to assume that Jamie could help you, that it's worth dragging him into the fae world and upending everything he believes in to see how he might benefit you—but obviously he didn't have any effect on the curse back when I was taken, or Aerik and his cadre would have noticed and brought him too."

"Of course we've taken that into account," Laoni snaps. "We've also taken into account that your ages were rather different, and powers can take time to emerge—often triggered by factors such as puberty. Given what the Seelie have reported of their sage's words about your family line, it's a logical assumption that whatever connection to the fae exists in you, it'll exist in him as well."

Celia leans forward, her gaze fixed on me. "We could certainly make sure he's comfortable and treated well. And what if it wouldn't need to be a permanent relocation? We have two curses or a curse with two aspects… Couldn't it be that if the two of you offer your unusual healing abilities together, you might eliminate the problem completely?"

Oh. I have to admit that in my worries about what would happen to Jamie and my struggle about what I owe him, that possibility hadn't occurred to me.

I don't trust most of the fae around me to know what treating a human "well" actually looks like, but—if that were possible—if it would only be a short while and then Jamie could go home—how selfish would I be to stand in the way of it?

Every part of my body still balks at the idea. I swallow thickly. "*Would* you let him simply go back to his old life after he's seen your world?"

"I don't see why not," Uzziah says. "We can wipe his memory of the experience with magic so he won't remember we exist."

Of course they can. I rub my forehead. It still feels wrong to put my brother through whatever he'd face here even for a short time, even if he won't remember it. And it's easy for them to say now that they'd send him back. Somehow I suspect they'll be more hesitant if it turns out he can cure them like I can. They'll want to keep him here in case they need him again. No matter what, most of them see him—and me—as only a resource they want to keep control over.

We don't even know yet if your brother will provide any sort of cure at all, Corwin reminds me. *It may be as simple as a few tests and then dismissing him as unnecessary.*

Coming here even for a day would still mess with his head, I reply, but then a spark of inspiration lights in my head, bringing so much relief my breath catches.

Sylas has started to speak. "We've dealt with our curse for decades now. I'm sure we can wait at least a few more days to give Talia time to—"

"No," I break in. "I have an idea right now. It'll be the full moon in less than a week. That's the perfect test right there—and my brother doesn't even need to be in the fae realm to carry it out. The day of the full moon, send someone to the human world to collect a little of his blood without him realizing it. I know you have enough magic to manage that. Then test it on a few of the Seelie to see whether it stops them from going wild. If it doesn't, then we already have our answer."

If it does cure them… I don't want to think about that. I'll have until the full moon to decide what I'd do then.

Donovan skims his hands across the table as if clearing the problem from it. "There you go. A simple, unobtrusive solution, at least to the initial question. I don't see why we couldn't begin that way."

Laoni scowls at him, but she obviously doesn't have any good argument against my proposal. "The Seelie won't handle it alone," she says. "One of us will need to oversee the process as well. This woman has had quite the effect on more than one of you, and I don't want personal biases skewing the results you report."

Celia bristles but keeps her voice flat. "Having one of you present to observe would not be a problem, though I assure you we wouldn't resort to deception, especially on such a vital matter."

"It's settled, then," Corwin says, shooting a quick smile down the table toward me.

I smile back, but my stomach is still churning with uneasiness. Have I just saved Jamie from a bunch of misery—or set him up for even more?

CHAPTER THREE

Whitt

I was the obvious choice for this particular mission. As Sylas's spymaster, my skills are naturally inclined toward stealth and subtlety. And while others might have the same qualifications, I wouldn't trust anyone outside our inner circle to treat Talia's brother with the necessary care.

Like, for example, the lug of a winter fae arch-lord who has insisted on coming along to "supervise" my methods.

Arch-Lord Uzziah, whose dour-sounding name fits his appearance and his personality to a T, hasn't stopped frowning since he met me near the border to travel to the fringelands. He seems to be taking his part in this venture as a personal affront, even though he and his colleagues were the ones who insisted on him joining me. About half a dozen times already, I've bitten my tongue against reminding him that if it were up to *me*, I'd be here alone.

As we come up on the house we've determined Jamie lives in, cloaked in both our magic and the shadows of very early morning, Uzziah's frown pulls into a deeper grimace. He draws in a snort of a breath and shakes his head. "How these creatures can live with all this filth around them, I'll never know. Dulled minds, the lot of them."

And this man works alongside Talia's soul-twined mate. I restrain a shudder provoked much more by him than our surroundings and manage to speak politically if not totally politely. "And yet the Heart deigned to bless at least one of these 'creatures' with the power to heal all our kind. It's almost as if *it* thinks they're owed some respect."

Uzziah shuts up, but his glower holds plenty of words he simply isn't saying out loud, none of them particularly polite either. When we come to a stop in front of the bungalow, rather charming as human structures go with its blue-trimmed white walls and darker roof, he sighs. "So then, what's your plan from here?"

"Your people identified the specific bedroom the boy uses." I amble across the lawn to the side of the house, dodging a coiled hose, and stop by a window near the back. It's closed, a hum in the air suggesting some sort of mechanical cooling system is running inside to take the edge off the late spring heat, but that isn't a problem. "I can manipulate the glass and go in that way. Then it'll be a simple matter of drawing a bit of blood. I'll only need a few minutes."

The winter arch-lord's bushy eyebrows draw together. "I'll be coming in with you."

I barely stop myself from rolling my eyes. "You'll be able to see just fine through the window. The room itself is rather small."

He studies me as if he assumes I'm making excuses to hide some nefarious plot rather than pointing out a simple practicality. "I'd prefer to have as clear a view as possible of the proceedings."

"Fine. Just stay well back and give me plenty of space to work."

I roll the true name for glass off my tongue, focusing on the pane in front of me. At my urging, the material melts away, leaving an empty frame large enough for me to clamber through. Uzziah follows, huffing a bit as if it's a strain. Thank the Heart our spells cover all the sounds we make as well as hiding us from sight.

The boy's room *is* small, just a narrow bed in one corner, a tiny side table next to its headboard and a compact desk tucked up against its foot. There isn't enough space to place any furniture against the opposite wall, which has pictures and posters tacked all over it. The closet door next to the window hangs ajar, a few rumpled shirts poking out from a heap on the floor inside. The artificially cool air trickles past us toward the now-open window.

The boy himself is lying on the bed, the sheet tangled around his slim frame. His face is buried in the crook of his arm against his pillow, but I can make out enough of it to note bits of family resemblance between him and Talia. I'm familiar enough with her to taste a hint of their connection in the human scent lacing the room too.

Ignoring my instructions, Uzziah stays right next to me. I motion him back toward the closet, but instead he steps around me to stand by the side table. Well, at least he's a little more out of the way there.

I slide a vial—bronze rather than glass, to avoid concerns of breakage—from my pocket and crouch next to the bed. Jamie's nearest arm sprawls across the mattress almost to the edge of the bed. I whisper a few words to encourage his mind into a deeper sleep and ease his hand just a little farther so it extends out into the air.

Holding the vial beneath his wrist, I compel my magic to open a tiny cut to the vein closest to the surface. A trickle of blood spills into the vial. When I've gathered a couple of teaspoons' worth, enough to cure an entire pack of the full moon curse, I direct the flesh and skin to close again.

My efforts will leave a faint mark, but one so slight he's unlikely to notice it. If he does, he shouldn't think it anything more than a small blemish of the sort humans seem to produce at random.

I nudge his hand back onto the mattress and straighten up. Once I've stoppered the vial, I tuck it away. Uzziah stays where he is with his arms crossed, scrutinizing my every move. I raise my eyebrows at him. "Any concerns?"

He waves his hand dismissively, but he only takes one step toward me before he pauses, looking at the boy again. "It's a pity our own cure can't be harvested so easily."

"You have Talia at your beck and call whenever your curse strikes another victim," I point out. "We Seelie all face ours at the exact same time."

He doesn't respond to that. His gaze hasn't shifted from Jamie.

Something in his expression has changed, a calculating glint breaking through the dour gloom.

Apprehension ripples through me. I've already tensed before he even speaks.

He gestures to the boy and then finally meets my gaze. "We're here now. It's hardly a full test unless we can try it on both sides of the border. We may as well just take him and be done with it."

Somehow I had enough faith, however slim, in the bird-brained Unseelie to be surprised by his proposal. "We gave our word to Talia that we'd make this first attempt without disturbing her brother," I say, not bothering to smooth out the sharpness that's crept into my voice.

"What of it? It wasn't an official vow—there'll be no harm done in changing our minds now that we've seen how simple the prospect would be."

No harm done? After all the mite's done for his people and the way the Heart bound her to one of his closest colleagues, that's how much respect he has for Talia? The casualness of his tone sets my teeth on edge.

But before I can come up with a suitable retort, he's already stepping closer to the bed, ready to scoop the boy right up over his shoulder from the looks of things. With a jolt through my nerves, I push in front of him, blocking his way. "We follow the plan agreed to on between all the arch-lords. If you want to argue for a change of course, do it in front of them."

Uzziah glares at me. His tone turns biting. "I think you're forgetting the difference between our stations, mongrel. You don't give orders to an arch-lord."

I glare right back at him. "No, but I follow the orders I got from my own. And Arch-Lord Sylas expects me to return with only this sample of blood, not the whole boy."

"I'm not sure his colleagues would have the same issue. You all are too wrapped up in that dust-destined woman's apparent charms to think clearly." His lip curls with a sneer, and he motions for me to move aside. "Get out of my way. I have the authority here, and I say we bring him before there's any more need for debate."

I stand my ground, my legs locking. "I say *no*. We got what we came for. The day is on the verge of breaking. Let's leave as we were meant to, and I'll see no need to mention to anyone that you attempted to deviate from our agreement."

It isn't a lie. I might not deem it strictly necessary, but naturally that doesn't mean I won't tell Sylas anyway.

Whether Uzziah detects the subterfuge in my statement or simply doesn't care, he attempts to shove me aside. Uneasiness twangs through me at the thought of scuffling with an arch-lord we've so recently negotiated a hard-won peace with, but I will not let down both my lord and my love in one swoop for this mangy raven's self-interest. He needs to see this attempt is getting him nowhere.

Without hesitation, I shove him back, as hard as I can. His shoulders thump into the wall, the sound muffled by the spell on us but not totally muted. On the bed, Jamie stirs.

The winter arch-lord's hostile gaze shoots daggers at me, as if it's *my* fault we might have woken him.

"Attempt to touch him again," I warn in a low, menacing voice, "and I won't hesitate to throw you right through the wall. Just try me."

Fury twists the other man's features, but I'm taller and stronger than he is, and he doesn't want this coming to a full fight besides. The temptation was all in making an easy theft of the boy. He doesn't want to leave traces of our presence here any more than I do, though I'm willing to risk it to ensure Talia's brother stays where he belongs.

Never before have I been so glad of the castle we're constructing with Corwin. Imagine if Talia had to keep living fully on the winter side for weeks at a time, subjected to pricks like this.

"I'm going to remember your insolence," Uzziah hisses at me.

I curl back my lips, letting my wolfish fangs emerge. "I'm counting on that." It's only because he's an arch-lord that I don't add "you feather-headed asshole" on the end.

I stay between him and the bed as we head to the window. The dawn light is just touching the sky, turning it from deep blue to hazy gray. Outside, Uzziah mutters to himself as I seal the glass. His words are inaudible, but his tone is deeply peeved.

He's lucky I care enough about him and his colleagues keeping a somewhat favorable opinion of my lord that I don't show him just how peeved *I* am.

We make our way back to the spot in the nearby park that connects to the Mists. Uzziah doesn't speak the entire journey back in the swift carriage. I'm content to listen to the warble of the passing wind, but my stomach rests heavy in my abdomen.

I can't think of any better way I could have handled that situation, but I'm not convinced the way I did was actually *good* either.

When we reach Hearth-by-the-Heart, it's mid-afternoon by our time, though only a few hours have passed since we left the human world. Our days rarely match up with the world beyond the Mists. One of Uzziah's coterie members along with a couple sent by the other Unseelie arch-lords are waiting outside the castle to oversee the actual administration of Jamie's blood. Uzziah himself marches off across the border without more than a brusque nod toward Sylas, who came out to meet us.

I hand the vial over to August, and he hurries off to the kitchen where he's been preparing the usual tonic from Talia's blood for the many summer fae we won't be experimenting on tonight. Astrid goes with him, keeping a wary eye on the winter fae who are following too. I want nothing more than to flop onto a comfortable sofa or perhaps throw back a gulp of good absinthe, but I know Sylas deserves a full reporting first.

He takes in my expression and motions for us to go inside as well—up to his study. Once the door is closed and he's taken his chair behind his desk, he fixes his impervious gaze on me. It used to sometimes irritate me how unshakeable he always seems, but lately I've found myself increasingly appreciating that quality of his.

"What happened?" he asks.

I pace the length of the room, my claws itching in my fingertips at the memory. "The blasted raven arch-lord tried to steal the entire boy away after all. He wasn't satisfied with taking a little blood. Figured his people should get to make their own experiment."

Sylas's eyes flash. A growl comes into his voice. "But clearly you prevented him."

"Yes. I had to get rather… forceful about it. He wasn't pleased." I turn to face my brother, grimacing. "I may have created more trouble for our relations with the winter realm."

"I'll deal with that trouble if it comes up," Sylas replies. "I wouldn't have had you do anything else. They'd better not interfere with our test tonight."

A small smile crosses my lips. "I suspect between August and Astrid, the feathered fae down there don't stand a chance."

"Indeed. But we'll want to remain on guard." Sylas rubs his jaw, his expression going momentarily pensive, and then focuses on me again. "In all other respects, the task went smoothly?"

I nod. "We didn't disturb Jamie or anyone else around. He should have no idea he was ever visited or that any part of him was taken." As long as we don't have to go back and retrieve the entire young man after all. My mouth sours at the thought.

But if it turns out Talia's brother could be the final piece in the puzzle of solving the curse, how could we refuse to protect our people?

I can see the same inner struggle playing out in Sylas. Before he can say anything else, Talia bursts into the room, her expression pinched. I avert my eyes from the marks on her arm, as gentle as I know August is in his blood-taking.

"Did it go all right?" she asked. "Is Jamie okay?"

"Everything's fine, mighty one," I say, moving to her and ruffling the waves of her hair with its new mix of purple and pink. "Your brother slept through the entire thing."

I slip my arm around her slim shoulders, wishing I could sweep her up in an embrace so complete it'd shield her from all the horrible decisions that might lie ahead of us. "We've got hours left before nightfall. Why don't we get in a few rounds of that driving video game August is so fond of to see if one or the other of us can't get good enough to beat him next time."

I'll do whatever I can to distract both of us from the looming question about to be answered—and all the others that'll arise afterward, regardless of the result.

CHAPTER FOUR

Talia

The drinking of the blood tonic has never been such a spectacle, at least not at any of the times I was around to watch. Pack-kin from domains all across the Seelie realm have already come by to pick up their vials. Now a bunch of us are gathered in the clearing in front of the Heart to see what will happen with Jamie's.

Ten fae from the three arch-lords' packs volunteered to take the untested tonic. The arch-lords wanted enough test subjects to be sure no effects we see are a fluke but few enough that it won't be too difficult for the rest of their pack-kin to contain them if they succumb to the curse. The ten are standing in the center of our ring, speaking to each other in uneasy conversation as we wait for night to fully descend.

At least a hundred other fae watch and wait around them, including Laoni, Uzziah, and several winter fae folk they've brought with them. A couple I recognize from their coteries, but others appear to be simply guards, there to protect them from the "savagery" of the wolf shifters, I guess.

Corwin has come as well, of course. He and Sylas have insisted on staying close to me and keeping me at the back of the ring, near where the Unseelie are standing. Sylas summoned a tree trunk he shaped into a sort of pedestal-slash-stool for me to sit on, both to keep me even farther out of reach from slashing claws and teeth and to give me a clear view over the heads of the much taller fae.

The wooden seat is smooth and warm against my skin, but I'm finding it hard not to squirm. What happens tonight could protect Jamie from the fae or confirm him as a target. But it's hard not to feel guilty about hoping his blood *won't* help when I know how many of the people around me must be wishing for a fuller cure than I've been able to offer.

I want that too… just not at the expense of my little brother.

I sink deeper into the seat, which is wide enough for me to sit cross-legged, and lean against the arched back, taking a few deep breaths. If the tonic doesn't work and the ten fae who volunteered transform into raging wolves, I need to be ready. I've conquered a lot of the fears that've gripped me ever since that fatal night when Aerik and his cadre attacked my family, but I haven't had to face a Seelie in the grips of the curse in months. I don't want to lose myself to the panic even for a minute while Laoni can see my reaction.

I'll be right here with you no matter what happens, Corwin assures me, picking up on my anxiety. He reaches up to brush his fingers over my arm, which is currently level with his shoulder. *Sylas won't leave your side either. The summer fae know exactly what they're dealing with, and they have your version of the tonic ready to dose these ten if necessary.*

I know, I reply, but that doesn't stop my nerves from jittering. Even knowing I only lost two members of my family all those years ago, not three, hasn't dulled the horror of my memories of the attack as much as I'd like. I'm not sure I'll ever escape the terror they provoke completely.

The sky has deepened from blue to indigo. Stars are starting to twinkle into view. The moment of transformation can't be more than a few minutes away. I can't feel it myself, but the Seelie will know as soon as the possibility has passed us by.

My gaze strays to the other Unseelie arch-lords. Laoni is stirring restlessly on her feet. Maybe she shouldn't have insisted on coming an hour early if she didn't have the patience for the wait.

One of the Unseelie guards standing by her glances her way. He must have quite a bit of human heritage, because his ears are rounded like August's and no hint of unusual color shows in his dark brown hair, which is tied back in a short ponytail. The only way I know for sure he's fae—other than the fact that I can't imagine Laoni bringing an actual human to protect her—is the dark wings he's keeping folded close to his back for now.

"Is there anything that would make you more comfortable, my lady?" he asks Laoni, seeming both careful and hopeful with the question.

Laoni's attention snaps to him, and her chin rises haughtily. Her voice comes out flatly cutting. "Certainly nothing *you* could provide. Mind your duties."

His head jerks back toward the clearing, his mouth tightening, and I wince inwardly on his behalf. She's always been sneering toward me, but I've never seen her treat any of her flock-folk with that much hostility.

I haven't seen her around her flock all that much, though, so maybe her response isn't that unusual.

How does Laoni keep the respect of her flock if she speaks to them like that? I ask Corwin.

He frowns, following my gaze to the guard with the dark brown ponytail. *She isn't normally so severe with them, from my observations. I believe I've seen her speak harshly to that specific one before. Perhaps he's overstepped sometime in the past, and she feels the need to keep him particularly in his place.*

Odd that she'd keep him on her staff at all if that's the case, but what do I know about how that woman's mind works?

The other fae around us adjust their weight on their feet, the sense of their restlessness creeping over my skin. Then the full moon gleams a little brighter—and all ten of the Seelie in the center of the ring flinch and shudder.

The full moon transformation is nowhere near as seamless and graceful as the purposeful one I've seen many Seelie enact by now. The fae who took Jamie's tonic lurch onto their hands and knees, their shoulders hunching, their limbs spasming. Fur sprouts from their skin in bursts. My fingers tighten around the edge of my chair, the ridged bark there digging into my palms.

The prepared pack-kin, August among them, rush forward before any have shifted very far—a jaw jutting into a muzzle here, a tail unfurling there. They already have the vials with my tonic in their hands.

The cursed fae snarl and gnash their teeth even in their only partly transformed state, but with two kin to each of them, it isn't long before the proper tonic has been splashed into their mouths. One manages to wrench away from the helpers and lunges toward the rest of the crowd, but two more fae leap in to restrain him. In less than a minute since the transformation began, they're all standing on wobbly but fully human-like legs, their faces flushed with a mix of exertion and embarrassment.

I release my grip on the chair, dragging in a breath that's only a little shaky. The sight of their initial wildness sent a jolt through my pulse, but not much more than that. Part of me is relieved. Jamie's blood didn't cure them at all.

But another part dreads whatever's going to come next, now that the arch-lords who put so much stake in this possibility will be disappointed.

The expression on Laoni's face looks like total disgust. For all she's criticized the Seelie for their violent nature, she's never actually seen a cursed transformation before. Even Corwin feels a little shaken.

I didn't realize it took them quite so… brutally, he says through our bond. *It's certainly clear the curse is gripping them, bending them to its will, rather than letting loose something they enjoy freeing. Even if my colleagues might want to think otherwise.*

Maybe this demonstration will set them a little straight then, and they won't complain about the Seelie wildness so much, I say, but my stomach stays knotted. What now?

Sylas, Celia, and Donovan have stepped into the ring from their positions among their own packs. "Thank you for your service tonight," Celia says to the ten volunteers. "Even if the experiment was a failure, it was important that we determine as much. Please, make your way home and get some rest now that you're well again."

"And if you experience any ill-effects that you haven't encountered before, let us know immediately," Sylas adds, though I don't think any of us believes there's much chance that Jamie's blood will turn out to harm the fae if it doesn't help them.

"Well," Laoni says in a disgruntled tone as Corwin helps me off the seat, "we're back to just the one cure, then."

Her guard turns away from the scattering crowd of Seelie. "I suppose that does keep things simple, at least."

Laoni glares at him. "If I want your opinion, I'll ask for it. Not that it's ever likely to come to that." She swivels away from him with an imperious air and fixes her gaze on Sylas, who's striding back to rejoin me and Corwin. "You'll be returning the human woman to her soul-twined mate on our side of the border while that misshapen castle of yours is still under construction?"

Despite the words, she almost sounds as if she wishes he'd say no. She really can't decide whether to welcome me for what I can offer her people or shun me as the weak but unpredictable mortal I know she still sees me as, can she?

"Talia will return tomorrow," Sylas says evenly, setting a protective hand on my shoulder. "We'd like to keep her close by for the night in case anything unusual arises from this experiment."

"Yes, yes, of course." Laoni spins on her heel, the other Unseelie following her as if they can't get across the border fast enough. Corwin lingers long enough to give us an apologetic grimace and bends to press a quick kiss to my lips. The flare of heat that comes with his touch sears even hotter with Sylas looking on, reminding me of the day not that long ago when my two arch-lords showed me how much pleasure they could bring me together.

A hint of heated amusement passes to me from Corwin even as he draws back. *I might have been uncertain of proceeding with that collaboration at first, but I can say I'm now looking forward to bringing you to such heights again.*

I can't hold back a mischievous smile. *Well, once the border castle is finished, we'll definitely need to celebrate.*

The look he gives me then is hot enough to make me spontaneously combust, but he pulls himself away with a wordless promise of delights to come.

Whitt and August have joined us during that silent conversation. Whitt watches Corwin slip into the border haze and then raises his eyebrows at me. "Somehow I get the impression you two were having a *very* interesting conversation, mite."

My cheeks flush. They can all probably smell my arousal. But it's already fading, tempered by the uncertainties still twisting through me.

I take in the emptying clearing, feeling weirdly adrift. I spent so much time carving out a real place for myself among the fae, and now everything about my situation has turned precarious all over again.

August nuzzles my hair. I can tell he's sensed my mood, the gesture more soothing than provocative. "It's been a long night already. Should we go home?"

I nod. "But first we should talk about what happens next, right?"

"We'll have time in the morning if you're tired now," Sylas begins, but I touch his arm to stop him.

"I don't think I'll be able to sleep until I have a better idea where we go from here. But we'd better talk back at Hearth-by-the-Heart."

"I can help with that," August announces, and scoops me up against his broad chest as he's become very fond of doing. I give him a mock-glower, but the truth is, there's nothing quite like being nestled in his brawny arms.

"Fine." I lean against him and let him carry me back to Sylas's main castle. I've been on my feet a lot today anyway, and my warped one is starting to ache even with the brace.

My men hold their own councils until we make it to Sylas's office. As August drops into an armchair with me on his lap, Whitt leans against the edge of Sylas's desk and studies my face.

"I'd think the immediate matter is pretty much settled," he says. "Your brother's blood had no effect on our curse, so he clearly doesn't hold the same powers you do. We have no cause to interfere any further in his life. But there's clearly something else on your mind."

I hesitate. I don't often wall off my bond with Corwin these days, but if I'm going to talk about this subject with him, I'd rather it's later, face to face like I am with my Seelie men right now.

I summon an impression of a seal of light over our connection before I speak. Then I look down at my hands, feeling abruptly awkward in August's arms. "I *hope* we can leave him alone now. I don't know if the Unseelie will try to insist on testing specifically their curse, even though it's so much more complicated. But, even if we can… *I* can't forget about Jamie just like that now that I know he's alive."

"Of course you can't, Sweetness," August says, kissing the back of my head.

I swallow hard. "I just don't know how to be there for him and not mess up the balance we've finally managed to find between here and the winter realm… It was hard enough figuring out a compromise that didn't mean constantly traveling back and forth, and the human world is a lot farther away."

The men are silent for a moment. Then Sylas speaks, low and firm. "If you feel you need to reconnect with your brother and be part of his life again, I'll do whatever I can to ensure you get the opportunity. Even if it means less time by our sides. From what I've seen of your soul-twined mate, he'll understand too. You never should have been stolen from your world to begin with, Talia, and we'd be little better than Aerik if we tried to deny you your family after all this time."

"I doubt the other arch-lords will feel the same way," I mutter, remembering Laoni's comment about only having one cure. "Now it's even more obvious how dependent both realms are on me to hold back the curse. I don't think everyone's happy about that."

"We shouldn't be. I've always said it shouldn't be your responsibility." Sylas frowns. "We still need to determine a larger cure to end it completely."

"Has there been any news from the Unseelie's summer settlement?" August asks.

Sylas shakes his head. "No one there has been struck by the curse, but it's only been a short time. Having that group of them living among us won't prove whether they can escape their curse that way for several months, perhaps years. I'd like to seek a faster solution if I can."

"But in the meantime, whatever you need, we'll figure out a way to make it work," Whitt says to me. "Strategy is my speciality, after all."

They're being so supportive that my stomach clenches up. I swipe my hand over my face and admit the thing that's been gnawing at me most of all. "I want to see Jamie again, talk to him, make up for all the time I've been gone. But I also don't want to leave all of you for however long that takes. It's not about responsibilities, just… I hate being apart from you. I've been looking forward to the border castle being done so I don't have to leave any of you behind even a little, and now…"

Is it awful that I feel that way? My brother's had no one for years, and I'm selfishly worrying about losing a little time with my lovers. But the human world isn't mine anymore, and I barely know Jamie after missing more than half of his life. It's all such a muddle.

Whitt pushes off the desk and comes to stand next to August, wrapping his hand around mine. "You've had to make so many difficult decisions since we found you, mighty one. If I could take this one on for you I would. But I'm sure there's no rush on how long we spend coming up with the best course of action. You have time to sort out your feelings—and we can all put our minds to brainstorming solutions."

I give him and then Sylas a tight but genuine smile. "You're right. I don't have to decide anything yet."

But how long can I really leave Jamie the way I saw him a few days ago, alone and harassed by his classmates, before *I'm* the villain here?

CHAPTER FIVE

Talia

The breeze that streams around the crystalline windshield of Corwin's flying carriage is nippy enough to keep me focused on the present. The snowy landscape around us whips by. We're soaring over the terrain as quickly as Corwin feels is safe.

A woman in a flock a few hours from his domain came down with the freezing curse in the middle of the night, and the messenger who summoned us reported that she appears to be deteriorating quickly. Corwin asked me to come back from the summer realm early this morning and had the carriage already waiting.

This woman will be the first winter fae I've healed since the man during our bond confirmation ceremony—and *he* was only the second Unseelie I've ever healed. My nerves are prickling with the worry that I haven't figured the process out as well as I think, that I'll stumble again and fail.

So many lives are depending on me. No matter what I choose when it comes to Jamie, I'll feel like I'm being selfish, either in abandoning him or abandoning all these fae.

Corwin sinks down on the bench next to me and slips his arm

around me. I lean into the warmth of his body, breathing in his wintry forest scent.

I'm sure it'll be fine, he says through our bond so as not to have to compete with the warbling of the wind. *I saw how you looked when you cured that man. You had the answer, and you put it into action. Once we've reached the village and you're fulfilling that purpose again, you'll feel how right it is.*

I inhale deeply and nod. *I hope so.* The shame of remembering the fae I couldn't cure before who've now died lingers in the back of my mind. *We still don't know how long even the cures that worked will last.*

What is it humans like to say? We'll cross that bridge when we come to it? I think that applies here.

That's fair. Unfortunately I seem to be faced with multiple other bridges already, and I'm not even sure which to cross.

I shove those thoughts away and gaze over the side of the carriage at the looming mountains we're approaching. These jut twice as high into the sky as the tall plateau that holds the domains around the Heart. Their peaks gleam like spears of icy snow.

From a distance, I thought they were made of a mottled rock with patches of pink and yellow amid the gray. Now that we're closer, I can see that those are actually patches of vegetation: delicate golden trees clinging to the lower crags, stretches of pale peachy flowers dappling the steep slopes higher up. And just coming into view around the side of the nearest mountain are a series of Unseelie dwellings.

The outer parts of the homes built into the mountainside appear to be made out of the same golden wood as the local trees. They all have terraces to land on for entry into the rooms carved right into the mountain, as with Corwin's folk village. The lord's palace shimmers in the sunlight, rising several narrow stories from a jutting ledge, with curved branches fanning out along its rooftop.

I wonder what Sylas would make of this kind of tree-built castle, so different and yet oddly similar to his.

"That's our destination," Corwin says out loud, rising to direct the carriage's final course.

As we glide closer, I realize many of the terraces I noticed are occupied. Anywhere from one to a whole family of fae stand on them, their faces turned toward us, apparently tracking our arrival.

A nervous shiver runs through me, and I hug myself, rubbing my arms. The woman who's sick must be a major figure in the flock to draw this much interest in her hopeful recovery. Which means so much potential anguish if I can't make that recovery happen.

Corwin brings the carriage to a stop at a nook for that purpose in the larger terrace outside the palace. As he helps me out, a true-blooded fae man with a lilac tint to his silvery hair hustles out to meet us, two staff—maybe members of his coterie—hurrying behind him.

"I'm incredibly grateful you could make it here so quickly, Arch-Lord Corwin—and Lady Talia," he says, with a bob of his head that appears to encompass both of us. I blink, a little startled by the formality he's offered me. But I guess that's how any lord's official mate would be referred to. I've just spent too much time among the other arch-lords who probably cringe at the thought of calling me a lady like one of their own.

"Of course," Corwin says.

I dip my head in return, unsure of the proper formalities. "I'll do whatever I can for your flock member."

The lord's gaze lingers on me for a moment, but not with any doubt or hostility, more simple curiosity. "It's a wonderful gift the Heart has given you. Come. We've brought the afflicted one to the village common so there'll be plenty of room."

Corwin pauses, his eyebrows drawing together. "We don't need a particularly large space."

"Oh, yes, it's not that." The lord laughs, a hint of embarrassment flushing his cheeks. "A few of my flock-folk were able to travel to your confirmation ceremony—I wish I could have come myself. They've been talking about how amazing it was to watch Lady Talia heal the curse. Several have already told me they'd like to see the process for themselves. If that would be all right?"

He wants me to perform for an audience? Is *that* why all those fae were watching our carriage arrive?

My back tenses instinctively at the thought, but… I healed that man on a stage in front of over a thousand gathered fae. It isn't as if I haven't faced this kind of situation before. It only makes the possibility of failure even more uncomfortable.

Corwin glances at me. *It's up to you. Whatever you're comfortable with. If we say you'll have more chance of success without any distractions, I'm sure they'll understand and comply.*

I waver on my feet, debating. I don't want all those eyes fixed on me while I'm trying to work the magic I'm still not fully confident in, but will refusing stir up doubt and suspicion? We're already facing enough of that from the arch-lords—we can use all the supporters we can get.

It's actually kind of nice, when I let my anxiety settle, to know the fae here have been talking about me so effusively, even if it's mostly because of what I can do for them.

"We can try that," I say to the lord, hedging my bets. "But it might turn out I need more privacy to totally concentrate."

He offers another small bow, this one just for me. "Naturally, we wouldn't want to interfere with the cure. Just say the word. I'll have a room ready in case it comes to that. Here, I'll escort you down myself."

He makes a quick gesture to the two fae with him, who leap into the air with their wings whipping out and soar down to the buildings below, presumably to prepare that room… and maybe to spread the word that the show is starting? Apprehension raises the hairs on the back of my neck, but I will myself to stay as calm as possible as the lord leads the way into his palace.

Somehow in this wintry realm even the golden shade of the wood has a cool feel to it. The sharp smell of sap hangs in the air inside. The lord strides to a spiral staircase deeper inside the building, which winds down into the rock.

The wooden steps give way to stone after the first couple dozen. The air turns cooler but lies still against my skin. Veins of glowing quartz run through the pale gray rock, lighting our passage. I grip the banister tightly and set my warped foot down as steadily as I can.

Finally, we reach a short hall that opens into the village common. Other than the different shade of the stone, the space looks a lot like the common for Corwin's flock, if a bit smaller. Patches of winter crops and projects in the middle of construction stand around the edges of the space, but they're quickly becoming hidden by the fae streaming in to gather around the center with its high, domed ceiling.

A padded chair has been set up under that dome, with two fae standing by the chair and a woman seated in it. The balls of magical fire hovering around her only emphasize her cursed state. Streaks of frost ripple through her dark hair, and her skin has already paled to a deep grayish blue color like a lake viewed through thin ice.

Her shoulders have hunched, her head jutting stiffly forward at an awkward angle. The curse's grip has altered her so much I can't tell whether she was young or old before it caught her.

My chest constricts. I walk over to where she's sitting, Corwin and the flock's lord following only part of the way. For the last few steps, I'm on my own. Even the fae who were watching over the woman back up a short distance. But while they're giving me plenty of room here in the middle of the common, dozens of gazes are fixed on me from the crowd all around. The whole flock must have turned up.

Silence falls throughout the huge room. I drag in a breath and focus on the cursed woman. She peers back at me with frost-hazed eyes, her mouth twisted into an even more pained shape than it formed before.

"I'm going to do my best to bring you out of the cold," I tell her. Someone in the crowd gasps, and someone else shushes them. I do my best to tune out my awareness of the spectators as I add, "I'm so sorry this happened to you. No one deserves it."

Now that I've done it purposefully before, it's easier to summon the thoughts that'll bring tears to my eyes. This woman might have children she'll be torn from like my mother was from me and Jamie. Those children might be watching right now, just as August had to witness his mother's death. The cold is turning her as helpless as I felt when I was locked up in Aerik's cage with no idea if I'd ever see sunlight again.

One moment she was living and laughing, and the next she had death staring her in the face. Barely any time to do whatever things she might have left undone. Not even a chance to get in a few last days of happiness before it's all taken away from her.

The burn starts to form behind my eyes. I turn away from her, covering my face with my hands so my tears aren't obvious to the watching crowd either.

I imagine how my mother would have felt if she'd known she'd never be with her children again, never get to see them grow up—that they'd face so many torments without her. I think of all the hopes and dreams this woman might have had that the curse is wrenching from her.

I know what it's like to lose everything.

When the tears trickle out, I wipe them from my cheeks, the dampness cooling my fingers. Then I turn back toward the woman with an apologetic smile. She's staring at me, but I can't tell how much the tension in her expression is from the curse's rigidity and how much she's actually startled by the emotion I'm showing. By now, everyone here must have heard what my cure involves.

I reach out to her and stroke my tear-damp fingers over her cheek.

In that first instant when the cold of her skin seeps into my fingertips, my pulse lurches with the thought that the chill might not shift. But it never happens immediately.

"I want you to have all the life you were meant to," I say, just as a spot of warmth forms beneath my hand.

The warmth spreads over her face and through the rest of her body, the bluish cast and the frost fading away in its wake. Tentatively, she pushes her posture straighter. She inhales with a faint rattling sound and then again more clearly.

A joyful chuckle tumbles from her lips. She grins at me. "The cold is gone. It was in me right to my bones, and now everything is warm again."

My own joy sweeps through me. I find myself grinning back at her, barely aware of anyone else in the room. "I'm so glad I could help you."

To my surprise, her hand shoots out to grasp mine. None of the other fae I've tried to cure have offered any physical gesture of gratitude. She squeezes my fingers and gazes up at me with a softer smile. "It is an honor to have been blessed by the one the Heart blessed for us."

I'm not sure how to answer that remark. The words send a weird quiver through my chest. Then the fae who were standing by the chair before move forward to make sure the woman can get to her feet, and I ease back.

Corwin approaches me from behind and rests his hands on my shoulders. *There you go. You've mastered it now. The curse won't claim another while you're with us.*

Despite the pressure that comes with that statement, in that moment I'm only relieved that it worked. I haven't let anyone down today—not as far as I know, at least.

Then a voice rings out, echoing off the high ceiling. "All gratitude and grace to the Heart-blessed human!"

As my head jerks toward the speaker, several other voices rise up in a chorus of eager agreement. The crowd surges toward us, the nearest figures still keeping a respectful distance I'm sure is at least as much for Corwin's benefit as it is for mine, but approaching much closer than before. They stop just a few feet from me, wide-eyed as they take me in.

Under their scrutiny, my face flushes. But their gazes feel more awed than anything else. "The Heart-blessed human," a few of them murmur, using the same phrase the earlier voice did.

One young woman eases a little closer, her stance bashful. "Lady Talia, would you—would you touch my cheek as you did for Vinma? If I could receive your blessing, perhaps…" She glances down at her hands, shy about whatever it is she thinks my power can do for her.

Corwin speaks up as I grope for words in my confusion. "Talia's touch doesn't have any magic in itself. It won't stave off a curse that hasn't set in or accomplish anything else."

"But—the Heart shines so brightly on her—I'd just like to have been that close to the one it chose to conquer the curse." She peers at me again, her eyes shining with hope.

I don't have it in me to say no, as bewildered as the situation has made me. "All right."

I extend my hand, and she tips forward to meet me. My fingers barely graze her skin. She draws back, beaming as if I've given her some great gift. Immediately, several others start pushing forward, asking for me to "bless" them too.

Did you have any idea this would happen? I ask Corwin as I offer up my hand to each fae who wants it.

No. It never occurred to me… I suppose the healing at the ceremony was quite a spectacle, even though we didn't intend it to be. And my people have suffered from the curse for a long time—nearly everyone has lost at least an acquaintance to it if not a friend or family. I feel his smile even though I'm not looking at him. *If they're starting to see you as a savior, I can't say I blame them. As long as we make sure they understand the limits of your powers, I don't see the harm.*

Neither do I, but it doesn't exactly sit easy with me either.

I must touch the cheek of at least two dozen fae before they stop approaching me. When I wave goodbye, even more voices call out their thanks and other benedictions to me. By the time we reach the carriage, the whole flock appears to be out on their terraces again to see us off. I wave again, my heart somehow buoyant yet heavy at the same time.

This is the first time any fae beyond my lovers have seen me as just as worthy as their own kind. It's both exhilarating and reassuring.

The problem is, I can't help wondering how many expectations will follow on the heels of this new adoration.

CHAPTER SIX

Sylas

With a heaved breath and a low intonation of the true name, I urge the wood I'm shaping to expand out, filling out the walls of the room. It's slow, focused work, and after a few hours adding to the construction of the border castle without a break, a headache is starting to form at my temples. We're so close to completing the plans Corwin and I laid out that I haven't wanted to waste any moments I can spare on the project.

I step back, studying the outside of the building and rolling my shoulders. Whitt nods to me from across the field where he's been adding details to a room on the other side of our end of the castle.

At least we're no longer having to work immersed in the border haze. The farthest reaches of the structure now spill out into the grassy field on the summer side.

At the rustle of footsteps and the clearing of a throat, I turn to find one of our sentries striding across the grass toward me. He dips into a bow. "My lord, Lord Tristan has arrived and wishes to speak to you."

Wonderful. I can look forward to even more of a headache.

I manage not to grimace in front of the sentry, but it's a near thing.

"You can escort him to the front drawing room of Hearth-by-the-Heart's castle and tell him I'll be with him shortly."

Whitt is watching me, having followed the conversation with his sharp ears. When I catch his eyes, he gives me a questioning look.

I shake my head. I'd rather not have Tristan think I feel the need for backup when speaking to him. After all his conspiring with his cousin, the former arch-lord of this domain, I don't want him seeing anything in me but total confidence in my ability to defend myself and my people.

I take a moment to shake off the exertion of my conjuring, breathing in the warm fresh air, and then I stride toward the castle of my own domain to see what this mangy miscreant wants with me today.

Tristan hasn't bothered to take a seat despite the many chairs in the room. He's standing by one of the side tables, his pale, mint-green hair falling forward to shade his eyes, examining a vase that was a gift from a lady from one of the neighboring domains. Possibly a lady whose hopes for me have been dashed now that I've declared my devotion to Talia, but I haven't encouraged any interest beyond the professional, so she can't fault my behavior.

At my entrance, the younger lord turns. It'd be easy to underestimate him—to assume he's less of a threat than Ambrose was. His frame is trimmer, his features more delicate. But rancor emanates from his pose, and I've heard enough of his thoughts on various subjects in the past to be wary of him. Physical power is far from the worst threat a man can present.

His tone comes out tart. "I apologize if I interrupted you in the middle of important work, my lord. Thank you for attending to me."

I hold back a glower. Without saying the words, he's clearly indicated how *un*important he thinks the construction of our border castle is, and that he isn't sorry about it at all. But it's simpler to take the comment at face value.

"I'm here to serve all my people," I reply. Even wretched pissants like the man before me. I fold my arms over my chest. "What can I do for you, Lord Tristan?"

He purses his lips before going on. "Arch-Lord Ambrose had a great deal of possessions. I realize that due to his questionable actions, those were confiscated by the current arch-lords. But I was hoping that, as his kin, I might be able to request a couple of items that have been in our family for some time and would have greater value to me than you."

I raise an eyebrow. "We finished taking down Ambrose's castle weeks ago. Why are you only mentioning this now?"

Tristan spreads his hands. "Given the circumstances of his death, I felt it was more respectful to give you and the other arch-lords time to make your own assessment of his belongings first."

The circumstances which involved attempting to frame and then murder Arch-Lord Donovan—and nearly doing the same to me in the end. I smile tightly. Many of Ambrose's possessions were part of an illicit collection of artifacts and tools forbidden by fae law, which he'd amassed in preparation for the war he wanted to wage against the Unseelie. I don't know how much his cousin is aware of that, but I'm not about to inform him of the details he might not know.

"Many of the lesser items we dispersed among his pack-kin," I say. "I do still have some things stored that I hadn't decided what to do with yet. If you describe the items you hoped to collect, I'll check whether they're still here."

"I'd prefer to look for myself," Tristan says, pulling his spine straighter, though it still only brings him to half a head shorter than me.

I keep my tone even. "And given the nature of many of the items we discovered Ambrose had been gathering, I'd prefer to handle it myself." I wouldn't put it past this man to slip something we hadn't realized the malicious significance of into his pocket to secret it away. Anything he asks for, I intend to make a thorough inspection of first.

Tristan's lips twitch with a restrained frown, and a brief vision swims before my deadened eye—him lunging at me with fangs bared and claws free. He looks exactly as he does right now, down to every article of clothing, so even through the jolt of defensive adrenaline, I know it isn't a glimpse of some future attack. I'm seeing what he *wishes* he could do to me right now.

I offer him another thin smile and let a hint of wryness creep into my tone. "Such violent thoughts don't become a lord of your standing, especially when they're directed at one of your arch-lords."

Tristan stiffens, his eyes widening just slightly. I've told no one other than Talia about the unearthly glimpses my magic-struck eye offer, but Tristan doesn't need to know how I discerned his thoughts. Better he assumes I'm simply that perceptive with my regular senses.

"I'm not sure what you mean," he says.

"Ill intent has a way of showing through." When he doesn't remark on that, I lift my chin toward him. "Are you going to tell me what these heirlooms you're looking for are or not? I can see to them right now." And hopefully get him out of my domain for the rest of our long lives.

He hesitates for a few seconds longer but must realize I'm not budging on this matter. "There's a necklace, gold with several emeralds set in it, that was fashioned by my great-grandfather for my great-grandmother. The framing around the emeralds looks like shearvine leaves. And a cherry-wood puzzle box inlaid with pearls, about the size of my hand—he made that too."

The second description triggers a memory. "I believe Ambrose's mate took the box with her. We gave her the chance to gather the belongings that mattered most to her from the palace." Under careful supervision, of course. "You'll have to take that up with her. I can check for the necklace now. Please wait here. I'll have one of my staff bring you something to drink, as I'd imagine you'd appreciate after your journey."

As I leave the room, I make a discreet motion to the woman who was poised outside, listening in case she was needed. She bobs her head and hurries to the kitchen. Two guards have moved within view of the room to keep an eye on Tristan while I'm gone, not that I've set him up in a place containing anything significant he could interfere with.

Stepping into the storeroom where I set aside all of Ambrose's things that showed no offensive purpose and were too fine for me to feel comfortable simply discarding, my nose wrinkles. A hint of his scent, the acrid undertone that permeated his entire palace, still wafts off them.

It only takes a few minutes of pawing through the assortment to find the necklace in question. It is a lovely piece of craftsmanship. Everything in here has already been inspected, but I murmur words of magic over it anyway, testing it one more time for any enchantments or other hidden features.

There's nothing. Either it really is that meaningful to Tristan to have this family memento, or he was hoping that I'd give him a chance to search for it himself and that he'd be able to pocket some other item he wouldn't want me scrutinizing so carefully while he was at it.

I tuck the necklace into a silk bag and bring it back to where Tristan is now sipping the duskapple wine my pack-kin brought him. He opens the bag and checks the necklace as if he thinks I'd try to pass off some other trinket for the one he wanted.

"Well," he says, fixing the bag to his belt, "I'm glad to at least have that. After all the stories I've been hearing, I was a little concerned you might have gifted it to that human you're apparently so besotted with."

My hackles rise automatically, but I keep my voice mild. He's provoking me deliberately now, and I won't let him gain any higher ground by giving in to my frustration. "I would hardly have presented her with a token tied to the man who wished to wrench her from her home and treat her no better than an animal."

Tristan shrugs, a cruel glint coming into his eyes. "Fair enough. With her brother proving to be a dud, I give you my best wishes toward getting her with child in all haste, my lord. The more cures we have on hand, the better, as I'm sure all our people would agree. I'll take my leave."

He swivels without giving me a chance to respond, no doubt to add insult to injury. I grit my teeth, my fangs emerging despite my best attempt at reining my temper in. I'd love nothing more than to bite his head off quite literally for his insinuations, but he's framed them as a polite wish for the general well-being of the Seelie rather than the assault on Talia's honor we both know it is.

Back when Ambrose was still alive, Tristan pushed for us to use my soon-to-be mate as nothing more than a broodmare. That's the only value he sees in her.

The trouble is, he may be right that a significant number of the summer fae would believe the chances of Talia's children carrying the same power in their blood matter more than her choice about whether she has children or not and when. They wouldn't see the insult because they barely see her as more of a person than Ambrose did.

My headache has returned. Not even the thought of returning to the border castle to speed the time until my love will have a real home settles my spirits.

Talia's position among us has remained precarious for far too long. There must be *something* else I can do to free her from the weight of all our expectations. It'd be in the service of my people too, finding them a true cure that ends the curse for good rather than only for one moon.

I've already exhausted all the avenues I've been able to come up with on my own, but perhaps that means I need to push those with greater insight for more answers.

The idea that's sparked in my mind catches fire quickly. I only debate for a few minutes, considering the implications, before deciding there's no point in waiting.

In the hall, I catch the attention of one of the staff. "Tell Whitt and any other of my cadre who ask that I've taken up an expedition for the rest of the day. I should return by nightfall." They all know how to reach me should an emergency arise.

The carriage I conjure from a juniper is slim and small for maximum swiftness. As it rushes toward my destination, I sit back and contemplate the exact appeal I'm going to make.

Normally when approaching the great sage Nuldar, one is expected to request his consideration with a message and wait for his approval. But as old and respected as he may be, I'm an arch-lord now, and this is a matter of grave urgency. What does he have to pass the time with other than making vague proclamations for those who ask for them anyway?

Well, I'll leave out that last point when I'm actually speaking to him. But perhaps I'll get a straighter answer when he has less time to dwell on it and get his thoughts muddled up.

The field that lies at the edge of Nuldar's forest is vacant, much different from my last journey here with an entourage of arch-lords and their underlings. The drooping leaves of the starfall willows glitter beneath the sun, murmuring as the light breeze ripples through them.

As soon as I've brought my carriage to a halt, I spring out of it and set off through the trees.

When I come up on the tree Nuldar has become one with, I slow down, still wanting to show my respect. The aged fae, his skin melded into the pale, silvery gray of the trunk's bark, appears to be sleeping. The wizened face embedded in the tree doesn't stir as I kneel a few paces from the roots.

Then the eyelids twitch and open. The ancient sage peers down at me, his expression inscrutable.

I bow my head. "Great Nuldar, I apologize for arriving unannounced. I wish to speak to you about the gravest matter affecting our people, and I couldn't stand to delay my appeal. Would you be kind enough to hear me now?"

The aged fae is silent for a long stretch. Then he clears his throat with a rattling sound more wooden than fleshy. "You may speak, Arch-Lord Sylas," he rasps. "What I may answer remains to be heard."

I inhale deeply, steadying myself. "The human woman I brought before you last time, Talia, has proven to offer a temporary cure to both the Seelie curse and that of the Unseelie. But no action we've taken has revealed any way to make the cure permanent, nor have we uncovered any connection between Talia and any other party that has led us to other answers."

When I pause to be sure of my words, Nuldar lets out a rough sound. "What is your question, arch-lord?"

I'll only get one. I'm lucky he's been willing to speak with me at all. I doubt it would do any good asking him what the solution is outright—others have tried that before me and have gotten only riddles.

Sometimes asking for a method of finding an answer accomplishes more than requesting the answer itself. And now, with Talia, I have to assume we have more pieces of that method to help us interpret the sage's answer.

"What steps must we take, with what we currently have, to determine how to fully end the curse?" I ask.

Another long silence. Nuldar's eyes close. Has he decided to ignore me after all?

Then he blinks and fixes his deep blue eyes on me again. "You need do nothing at all," he says. "The answer is already on its way to you, soon to arrive if unimpeded. Giving it room to come will bring it faster than chasing after it—better a snare than a hunt. You must only be sure that your snare *is* a snare and not yet another caught in a trap. If it can capture a single heart, it will bring all you need to know back to you. Prepare well."

With that, he goes completely still. I wait, still kneeling, until I'm sure that's all he'll say. Then I straighten up with another dip of my head. "Thank you for your words of wisdom, honored sage."

I hurry back to my carriage, repeating his declaration in my head, my spirit unsettled. I'll have to see what Whitt makes of this talk of snares, but the first part was clear enough—I simply don't like it.

The fastest way to end the curse is to do nothing at all and wait for a solution to fall from the sky? Nuldar said we'd have the answer soon, but for a fae that old, the word is relative. He could mean decades more.

But if what Nuldar says is true, then anything we do to search for answers on our own could push them farther away from us rather than getting us closer to healing our people.

CHAPTER SEVEN

Talia

This is only my second time this deep in the fog-drenched territory at the fringes of the fae realm, and I find it just as eerie as the first. The cool haze drifts between the trees, which loom with their branches spread so broadly that only muted sunlight penetrates their leaves overhead. It gives the forest the feel of twilight even though it's actually midday. Here and there, distant rustling sounds reach my ears.

My fingers itch to curl around August's arm, to hold onto him as we venture through this haunted terrain, but I don't want to be in his way if he needs to quickly leap to our defense. Ferocious beasts prowl the edges of the summer realm just as they do in the winter lands. I have my dagger in its sheath at my hip, but I'm not exactly an expert with it.

I walk along between him and the Unseelie representative the arch-lords sent along for my second trip to the human world: the guard with human-like ears I saw Laoni sniping at on the night of the full moon. Now that we have a clearer idea of what to expect, both sides agreed that it was better to send fae who could pass for human. If we need to shed the magic keeping us unseen for some reason, they won't have to be as careful about how they appear.

The guard, who introduced himself to us as Kesral, peers into the depths of the fringe forest, the damp breeze stirring the short ponytail he's tied his dark brown hair into like before. Here, his stance is confident, his expression cautious but not particularly tense. He seemed a little wary of August on our journey by carriage out here, but by the end he'd relaxed enough to make a little small talk on August's favorite subjects: food and combat strategies.

I haven't seen anything that would explain Laoni's hostility toward him. Is it just because he has less fae blood than many of her other staff? She trusted him enough to give him this duty. Or is it a punishment in her mind to send him off as a sort of chaperone for my trip to the human world?

None of those questions seem right to ask, but curiosity itches at me.

August stops at a thicker patch of darkness between two tree trunks. It gleams with an almost liquid texture, just as Whitt described the portals between the worlds to me months ago.

August leans close and takes a sniff, then shakes his head. We know the one that'll lead us to the park not far from Jamie's house is in this general area, but apparently the portals sometimes shift around a little. He's already checked a few before without finding it.

"It shouldn't take too much longer," he assures us. "That one was almost right."

Kesral lets out a grunt that sounds dryly amused. "Never much of an exact science, is it, making the trip?"

That remark gives me an opening I can't resist. I glance at him, watching his reaction cautiously. "Have you traveled to the human world frequently?"

He shrugs, his gaze still scanning the forest around us for threats. "On the winter side, of course. When Arch-Lord Laoni requires something from those lands, it's often me she asks."

"Because you can blend in." I pause and then venture, "Was one of your parents human? August's mother was. And obviously both of mine." I bite my tongue, my cheeks flushing at my fumbling attempt to make the question less awkward. I don't think I succeeded.

Kesral just chuckles though, the warmth of the sound putting me back at ease. "It isn't so hard to tell, I suppose." He runs his fingers over the curve of one of his ears. "My blood father. My mother very much wanted a child, and when she and her mate hadn't been able to in a long time, they decided she would seek out a human to her liking at an opportune time. And here I am. I don't think of him as a father in any way other than that, though. My real father is the one who helped raise me."

He speaks about it easily enough—and I guess it is easier when his story isn't anywhere near as tragic as August's.

"It's pretty common in both realms," August says, leading the way to the next portal. "If fae never slipped out of the Mists to romance a human here and there, there'd be a lot fewer of us."

Kesral hums to himself. His voice drops as if he's not totally sure he wants his next words to be heard. "Unfortunate that more of our kin don't recognize that fact."

My gaze darts to him again. I grapple with my next words for a moment before spitting them out. "Do the other fae treat you badly because of it—because of your heritage?"

His expression stiffens, maybe with the fear he's said too much. "I wouldn't say badly. Only sometimes a little differently. I'm sure you've experienced some of the varied opinions on humankind during your time with us, though Arch-Lord Corwin is known for being sof—permissive with them."

He was going to say soft-hearted. I won't let myself be offended by that when I'd bet Kesral has overheard Laoni complaining about Corwin in much more insulting terms.

"That's different," I say. "I'm totally human, even if I have a few unexpected powers—powers that are nothing compared to what any fae can do, including you. And, I mean, your heritage obviously doesn't make that big a difference. August can serve on an arch-lord's cadre no problem."

My lover shoots a crooked smile over his shoulder at me. "Oh, there are a few who'd mutter about that, I promise you. And I do get some recognition from having a father who's not just fae but a true-blooded lord. I'd imagine Kesral has had a harder time of it than I have, if the winter realm is much like summer in that respect."

From the twist of Kesral's mouth, August must be right. The other man is silent for a stretch. Then he says, "I'm certain I'd never aspire to being part of my lord's coterie. She is clear on my place within her flock. I'm honored to support her rule in the ways assigned to me."

I want to ask about Laoni's harsh attitude toward him, but I'm not sure how without overstepping the tentative friendliness he's offered. And maybe it does just come down to how much human blood runs through his veins.

If she's like that with a fae man who's still very much fae despite his birth father, how does she treat whatever human servants she's brought to her domain? What about the other winter lords?

I haven't really had a chance to see how anyone other than Corwin interacts with humans besides me, and he's definitely considerate of his servants in a way I can tell is unusual. Sylas hasn't kept human servants at all in the time I've been with him… because of what he feared his former brother-in-law would do to them while Kellan was still around.

I've been so focused on saving the fae from their curse, I never considered all the other people here who might need my help. If I leave more permanently, who'll be left who would even think of speaking up for all the other humans kidnapped by the fae?

The question feels like a shackle tugging me in yet another direction. I shove aside those worries as well as I can, pushing on through the fog.

Then August lets out a triumphant exclamation by the portal he's stopped at. I hurry over, everything falling away except my need to see my brother again.

The whole reason I wanted to make this trip was to get a better idea of how he's living now. I only had a glimpse last time. How can I decide where I'm needed most, how much I owe who, when I know so little about his current situation? If I'm going to have to choose between all the responsibilities tugging at me, it'd better be an informed one.

August extends his hand to me, and I wrap my fingers around his. As we step through the portal together, Kesral follows close behind us.

The closest experience I can compare the trip to is walking through a hall in a mirror maze. The landscape around me shimmers and wavers as if undulating through water, although the air is perfectly still. I can't help closing my eyes for a moment like I did last time, dizziness scattering my thoughts.

When I open them again, we're just stepping onto the grass in the park. There's a tiny clearing amid several saplings where the undulating impression remains. We won't be perceivable to humans until we walk beyond that boundary.

August intones the words to wrap concealing magic around us. He was practicing with Whitt earlier today, and he motions to the air with more assurance now. A brief tingling washes over my skin and then fades away.

"All right," he says, looking pleased with the result, and nods to Kesral. "You were with one of the scouting parties that first located Talia's brother—I assume you remember the way?"

"Yes, the house that appears to be his main residence is north of here." Kesral sets off, and we fall into step behind him, letting him take the lead now.

We couldn't predict exactly what time of day we'd come out into, but the growing warmth in the air and the position of the sun suggest it's late morning. If it's a weekday, Jamie and our cousins will be at school and our aunt and uncle at work, so hopefully we'll be able to explore his current home without interruption or discovery.

Kesral picks up his pace as we reach the streets beyond the park, and I propel myself after him, my limp becoming more pronounced. An ache is starting to spread up from the warped arch into my ankle. August gives me a concerned glance, and I can tell he's struggling with the urge to offer to carry me. He doesn't want to embarrass me in front of company.

I reach for his hand again and squeeze, a silent reassurance that if I need him, I'll say so.

The house Kesral brings us to strikes a tiny chord of memory somewhere deep in my mind. A lifetime—or more than a dozen years

—ago, my parents drove us out here to visit Aunt Becca and Uncle Walter. I think they'd just moved into the house then? My memory is pretty fuzzy. We were only here for the weekend. Dad and Aunt Becca had a falling out several years before that and hadn't been talking much; I remember the atmosphere was still kind of tense.

How did she feel about suddenly taking in his grieving, savaged son?

We go around to the back door where we're mostly out of view of the neighboring houses. August casts a quick spell to confirm no one is in the house, and then Kesral steps in to magic the lock open. We slip quickly inside.

Sunlight streams from the window on the back door and through another bright pane in the kitchen we find ourselves in. It's a little messy, breakfast dishes piled in the sink and a box of cereal left out on the counter, but homey enough to bring a smile to August's lips.

I note a few photos attached to the fridge with magnets—two of my aunt and uncle with their own kids, but another with Jamie there too, on a dock at the edge of a lake. They all went on a cottage trip together?

He's grinning in the photograph, but I can't shake the sense that he looks a bit sad all the same.

August prowls through the room, opening and closing cupboards with eager interest. I guess he hasn't had a whole lot of chance to study the culinary habits of the average urban family.

"They appear to have plenty of ingredients on hand," he says. "And I can smell that they served a well-cooked roast chicken last night." He licks his lips so avidly I have to giggle.

We sneak down the hall to check out the other rooms. A few toys belonging to the younger kids dot the living room floor, and a game system that looks newer than the one August likes to play on is tucked away in the TV cabinet. My cousins appear to share the largest of the three bedrooms, with a set of bunkbeds and even more toys lying around. Nothing too fancy—I wouldn't say they're spoiled. But what about Jamie?

His bedroom turns out to be on the opposite side of the main hall. Whitt had told me it was small, but I'm still a little startled by the lack of space, only a few feet between the bed and desk and the wall opposite.

A crisp, citrusy smell laces the air that I don't associate with my brother at all. Has he started wearing cologne? I guess that wouldn't be so surprising at his age. He must be thinking about impressing girls.

It looks like he has a girlfriend right now. Between the band posters tacked to the wall, I spot several printed photos of him with his arm around a pretty teen with blue streaks in her fawn-brown hair and freckles across her cheeks. His smile in those looks relaxed and genuine, like he couldn't be happier. Some of the clenching sensation inside me releases.

He isn't an outcast or anything. Those guys at school might have harassed him, but he's found other people who care about him.

Mixed in with the girlfriend pics are a couple with a larger group, Jamie and the freckled girl and a couple other guys and girls. He's even got one from a Christmas that must have been a few years back, with him laughing and raising his arms defensively as the cousins shower him with torn wrapping paper.

Is he actually okay? Has he found a place where he can belong, just like I'm starting to among the fae?

August and Kesral have hung back by the door to give me space to make my investigation. "It all seems pretty good, actually," I tell August as I sit down at the desk. The room might be small, but Jamie has given it a sense of home. "He's doing well in school too." There are a couple of assignments off to the side of the desk, one with a B+ and the other with an A.

I open the drawers expecting to find more of the same, and instead stumble on a stack of charcoal sketches. The one on top is Jamie's girlfriend, a little rough but recognizable. He did love to doodle when he was a kid—I had no idea he'd gotten this good. He must be a little shy about them since he hasn't tacked them up.

Lifting the papers onto my lap, I start to sort through them. I've only gotten a few deep when my hands jerk to a halt.

I'm staring into a pair of glowering eyes in a darkly furred wolfish face with fangs bared. It sends a jolt of memory through me so strong that my heart is thumping twice as fast in an instant.

And loud enough that August can hear it. He leans into the room. “Is everything all right, Sweetness?”

“Y—yes. It’s just a picture.” But what a picture. And the next, and the next—black beasts slashing their claws across the pages, violently jagged lines, shaded puddles that make me think of blood. I swallow hard, my fingers shaking.

No, Jamie hasn’t left the past completely behind. If these drawings are anything to go by, it’s still stalking him even more determinedly than mine does me. But he’s hiding it away like he has no idea how to shake it.

How *could* he know how to deal with it? How could he understand what actually happened, let alone explain it to anyone else?

There’s no one in the world who has any idea what he’s going through… except me.

CHAPTER EIGHT

Talia

I know my fate matters a lot to the fae and their rulers, but I wasn't expecting such a huge welcoming party waiting for us on our return. Not just the summer arch-lords and some of their staff but all five of the winter arch-lords are standing around outside the castle of Hearth-by-the-Heart, waiting for August's carriage to draw to a halt.

I seek out Sylas's and Corwin's faces first. Both have schooled their expressions to a lordly calm, but I know Sylas well enough to read the tension in his jaw, and Corwin's uneasiness travels to me through our bond.

We tried to hold them off until you'd had a chance to catch your breath after your journey, he says. *But the others on both sides insisted. I suppose we should be a tiny bit grateful they've finally agreed on something so easily?*

No humor warms those words. I scramble out of the carriage to find out what's going on, wobbling when my feet hit the ground.

"Has something happened?" I ask as August joins me. "What's the matter?"

The arch-lords exchange a glance, and Celia speaks up. "Let us take the discussion to the Bastion. If the Heart objects to our proposal, it can do so there." The look she aims at Sylas suggests *he's* been objecting to whatever this is.

But he doesn't argue now, just inclines his head. His dark eye holds my gaze, his mouth twitching with just a trace of a grimace.

The whole gathering tramps across the fields and smatterings of forest to the building where the summer arch-lords conduct their business. *If there's been some new catastrophe, I'd like to know now,* I say to Corwin silently, my stomach knotting.

Nothing new, he says with a whiff of reassurance tempered by… sadness? *Only that our colleagues have come to some new conclusions after determining that your brother isn't a solution to our problems. They claim to have your best interests at heart, but I can't help suspecting they're actually tackling something else they see as a problem.*

Which is?

His inner voice takes on a bit of strain. *The fact that a human is bound to any of us in the first place, and that we've embraced that bond. And a human with unpredictable talents on top of that.*

This has something to do with separating me from my lovers? I bristle inwardly, but I try to keep my face as impassive as they have as we reach the tall stone palace with its gleaming veins of gold.

In the huge central room, cadre, coterie, and guards fall back to the rounded walls, leaving only me and the eight arch-lords in the center. Celia's lips are pursed, Donovan's forehead knit as if he's still working out where he stands on this subject. Of the winter arch-lords other than Corwin, only elderly Neve looks at all at ease with her vague smile. Laoni, Terisse, and Uzziah gaze down at me with an aura of authority.

"You've returned from visiting your brother," Laoni says without preamble.

I shift my weight from one foot to the other. "I didn't exactly visit with him. He still doesn't know I'm alive. I was just checking on his home, making sure he's been comfortable there." Discovering he hasn't really been. The memory of Jamie's violent sketches flashes behind my eyes.

Celia picks up the thread. "We understand that you've been somewhat torn. You've committed yourself to living among us here in the Mists, assuming there was nothing left for you in your own world. But now it turns out that's not true."

Are they going to question my loyalty to the fae like Laoni has tried to in the past? I fold my arms over my chest. "You don't have to worry about me taking off on you. I'm not sure yet how much I need to do for my brother, but I'll keep helping with the curse in every way I can."

Terisse dips her head. "But what if we could make it easier for you to accomplish both?"

I wasn't expecting them to offer to help *me*. I glance from one face to another warily. Corwin stays silent, only giving off a whiff of impatience that they're taking so long getting on with their point. He wants me to have room to make my own decision—about *what*?

"In what way?" I ask.

"Clearly, the Heart has seen fit to give you gifts that benefit us," Laoni says. "But you were born in the human world and would have remained there if not for your cruel kidnapping at the hands of that summer fae lord. It is your true home. We believe we could allow you to return there and make a life for yourself there while still drawing on your aid."

Return there… permanently? My gaze darts to my lovers—Sylas and Corwin around me, August and Whitt back by the wall. Corwin can't hide the pang of pain that shot through him at her suggestion.

It's your choice, he says, keeping his tone steady. *You can make it freely. You know how much you mean to me, my soul, but I wouldn't keep you from your world and your family if that's where you feel you should be.*

Neither would my Seelie men. They showed that much when we found out I was linked to Corwin, when we thought I might have to move to the winter realm permanently. But now—after all the ways we've struggled to find a compromise that lets us all stay together—

But I've considered it, haven't I? Not just about visiting the human world now and then but really going back, at least for a few months or even years, until I'm sure Jamie's okay. I just hadn't let myself think about it too deeply because I couldn't see how I'd be able to balance that with my duties to the fae.

"What about the curse?" I say tentatively. They can't mean to tackle it on their own again now that they have a cure in me. "How could I still heal people if I'm not here?"

Uzziah motions to the summer arch-lords. "The Seelie only need your blood one night a month. They could send someone to collect it from you—stealthily, so no one in your family would be aware. In the same way, we assume we could bring any new victims of our curse to you for you to offer your tears. The actual process only appears to take a few minutes."

"It would require a fair bit of effort on our part," Laoni says, as if they're making this proposal out of selfless generosity, "but we're willing to put in that effort to see you restored to your proper place."

Something in me hardens. That's what this is really about, isn't it? My "proper place." She and her two sycophants have never liked how devoted Corwin has become to me, and no doubt they like the fact that I'm staying so closely tied to three of my Seelie lovers at the same time even less. And I'd bet Celia would be happy to have me and all the complications I've brought into her life out of the way, so I only affect her when it's time to take my blood or tears.

They don't give a damn what my brother means to me. They're just seeing yet another opportunity to use him to serve their purposes.

But the worst part is, I'm not totally sure I shouldn't take them up on this offer anyway. After what I saw in Jamie's room today, maybe I should go back and reconnect with him for as long as it takes to heal *him*, regardless of the arch-lords' intentions.

I swallow thickly. "Thank you for making this offer. I'll need some time to think about it. I'm not sure yet what would really be best for everyone involved. There isn't any rush, is there?"

Laoni's lips flatten, but before she can say anything, Celia speaks up. "Of course not. We simply wanted you to know the opportunity is there so you can take one concern off your plate."

It hasn't really worked that way at all. Now I'm even more unsettled about the decision I have to make, knowing the arch-lords have their own agenda. In this moment, the weight of all the factors I need to consider feels almost suffocating.

Sylas steps in, setting his hand on my back with a little more familiarity than he might have before the rest of our audience was aware of our relationship. "Talia has had a long trip today, and she'll need her rest. You've made your proposal—now let's give her some peace to consider it."

"We're trying to do what's best for all parties involved too," Terisse says before the winter arch-lords step away, and I think she actually means that. I just don't agree with her assessment of what's "best."

Corwin hangs back as his colleagues leave. "Are you all right?" he asks, and flicks his gaze briefly toward Sylas. "I know it's your time in the summer realm now—I wish the border castle were already complete—but if you need me to stay to talk things over, or just to be here…"

And give the other arch-lords even more reason to think you're prioritizing me over your other responsibilities? I say through our bond, and sigh out loud. His affection wraps around me like an embrace, but I don't want to keep him from his people and his realm. I have three men here who can comfort me, after all. "I think I really do just need some rest. But if I need you after all, I know I can reach you in a moment."

"And I'll be with you immediately." He smiles and leans in to kiss me tenderly. The heat of his mouth, his own pleasure at the kiss, and the sense of my other men watching us with full approval all send a thrill through me despite my worries.

I clutch his shirt for just a second before letting him go. *I love you.*

And I love you. We'll see this through like we have so much else.

As he heads toward the border, Sylas guides me to one of the other exits, August and Whitt falling into step on either side of us. "What did you make of your trip, mite?" Whitt asks, his tone gentle. He can't be happy about the idea of me leaving the fae realm permanently any more than the others are, but he's kind enough not to push the subject.

I exhale raggedly. "I don't know. Jamie has obviously settled in with my aunt and uncle pretty well. It looks like they've accepted him into the family, and he's made at least a few friends… But I found some drawings of monsters and other dark things that I think must be from his memories of the attack. He hasn't totally gotten past it."

"The effects haven't completely left you either," August points out. "It isn't surprising—something that traumatic has a way of sticking in the brain."

"I just—I want to help him. But what if revealing myself brings up even more trauma or whatever? It's impossible to know. And I don't want to leave all of you." I rub my forehead. "Right now I think I just want to sleep. Maybe things will seem clearer after that."

"Let's get you right to bed then," August says, managing a teasing tone, and scoops me off my aching feet like he's probably been wanting to for hours now.

I let out a noise of protest that I don't mean all that much and then settle against his brawny chest. He carries me the rest of the way to the castle with swifter strides than I could have managed, his brothers matching his pace. But once we've stepped into the grand entrance hall and he sets me down, Sylas motions to me.

"If you can spare a few minutes before getting your rest, there's something I'd like to speak to you about first. It shouldn't take long."

I nod. "Of course."

He must make some gesture to the other men, because they don't follow us to Sylas's study. Inside, he motions for me to take what's become my favorite armchair in there and goes to his desk. But rather than taking a seat behind it, he retrieves something from one of the drawers and then sinks into the chair beside mine, tugging it around so he's facing me.

"A few days ago I went to see Nuldar again," he says.

I blink at him. "You didn't mention it."

"You were with Corwin then, and I hadn't decided what I was going to make of what he said yet. I'm still puzzling over it somewhat." He sighs, some of the tension he must be carrying just as I am leeching into his expression. "The main things he indicated were that the solution to the curse should become apparent to us without us needing to do anything but wait—in fact, attempting to speed it along might impede it instead—but we also must be prepared."

My mouth twists into a crooked smile, thinking of the first answer we got from Nuldar. "I don't suppose he bothered to mention *how* we should prepare?"

Sylas smiles back with a matching wryness. "He didn't. But I feel that there are some steps we can take that are general preparation against any harm—and that, as tied as you've been to the curse so far, it's particularly important that we equip you properly. Which is why I made this for you."

He holds out a loop of bronze like a wide, flat bracelet, a decorative pattern of flowers etched in its polished surface. "I tried to form it to interfere with your typical activities as little as possible. You could wear it on your wrist or your ankle. I'd have one on each if I wasn't concerned that having more than one would draw attention to their importance."

I take the bracelet from him, running my fingers over the smooth metal. It's too narrow for me to fit over my hand—but I could widen it with magic and then tell it to contract again once it's on so it hugs my wrist closely.

Oh. I glance up at him and find him studying me. "It's a hidden weapon," I say, checking that I've understood properly. "I can use the true name for bronze to change it into a blade or whatever else I might need to defend myself in an emergency."

"That was my thought. My fellow fae have only seen you make use of the true name for light—they won't immediately associate the bracelet with your potential powers, especially with it being so odd to think of a human using true names at all." Sylas runs his hand along his jaw. "I probably should have given you something like this when I first found out about your abilities in that area, but it's not the sort of strategy we'd generally use ourselves, so it didn't occur to me right away."

"Better now than never." I've mostly stopped carrying my pouch of salt—at first because we were worried it'd offend the Unseelie while I was finding my place there and now because I don't want to distress those who come to me for help—and my dagger could be snatched from me if I'm taken by surprise. But no enemy would think they had to remove a bracelet to fully disarm me.

With the images from Jamie's drawings lurking in the back of my mind, it's easy to summon the sense of terror that gives power to the true name. "*Fee-doom-ace-own,*" I murmur, willing the metal band to expand and then shrink against my skin. When it's resting around my wrist, it looks like nothing more than a pretty bangle. I doubt most of the fae would give it a second glance.

My sense of Corwin, nearly always with me, doesn't intrude, but a faint impression of gratitude toward Sylas trickles through our connection to me. I send a tendril of fondness back and gaze up at the man who offered this gift.

After all he's done for me, it's hard to doubt the summer arch-lord's feelings for me. Still, I can't help being filled with awe that a man with so much power and strength cares so deeply what happens to me. I might not agree with the fae dismissing or mistreating humans, but I know there are many ways I can't really match him.

But none of that matters to him. He loves me for what I *can* offer, and to him it's enough that he sees me as a better mate than any of the fine fae ladies who've vied for his attention. He's sheltered and protected me but also trusted and believed in me enough to let me stand up for myself when I've been able to. This bracelet is the perfect symbol of that love.

I slip off my chair. Sylas leans into my hug, pulling me right onto his lap and nestling my head against the crook of his neck. His earthy, smoky smell has never felt so welcoming.

"I love you," I say. "I really don't want to leave you. Any of you. If it wasn't for Jamie, I'd never even consider it. You know that, right?"

Sylas tightens his embrace, nuzzling my hair. His deep baritone comes out husky. "I do. And I hope you know how much I love you, Talia. You've healed so much more than just our curse. But part of loving you is letting you go if you believe you have to. Make your decision based on what feels right to *you*, not how the rest of us will feel about it."

Tears prick at the backs of my eyes. "There's just so much… So many things to consider that clash with each other. So many people counting on me, so many people I want to be there for."

"I know. I don't have to make the exact same choice you do, but

I've had plenty of hard ones in my time as a lord. Balancing my loyalties to my pack, my brothers, the rest of the realm, and my mate —both past and current." He presses a kiss to my forehead. "I don't envy you your position."

"Does it get easier?" I have to ask. "Figuring out what to do when you're pulled in different directions?"

He considers his answer for a long moment. "Maybe a little. You learn through trial and error which factors will matter most in which situations, which sacrifices will tear at you the least. And perhaps you get better at finding a way to compromise so that you don't end up torn at all. I think you've already proven quite adept at that."

"I've been trying to think of an option that means losing nothing," I mutter. "No luck so far. If you think of anything, let me know."

Sylas chuckles and ducks his head to seek out my lips. As our mouths meld together, the pressure on me doesn't exactly lighten, but it is a little easier to set it aside just for now, in the hopes that a better answer will come to me in the meantime.

If I don't find one soon enough, will the other arch-lords force the issue of me leaving? No bracelet will defend me against all of them if they set their minds to seeing me gone.

CHAPTER NINE

Corwin

With the sun lighting her pale face and beaming off her pink-and-violet hair, my mate is nothing short of gorgeous. She leans over the edge of the carriage, peering at the icy forest we're passing over, and then glances back at me with a sly glint in her eyes. "You said this is one of your favorite places in the realm. Why's it taken so long for you to show it to me, then?"

I make a vague motion with my hand, maintaining the casual atmosphere I've tried to set for this expedition. "It's a farther trek than places like the frostfire forest. And perhaps I wanted to save a few things to discover together once you were fully my mate."

The smile that crosses Talia's lips at that remark, both shy and sly, sends a bolt of desire straight to my groin. What a mate she is. My heart swells so much just looking at her that a tiny edge of fear creeps around the edges of my affection—the thought that it might be too much, that I might be too immersed in her to keep my head straight.

Especially when I might have to say goodbye to her sooner than I ever imagined.

But that's a fear driven by decades of sneers and judging glances, not by anything I truly believe. I simply have to keep reminding myself of that. What could be wrong with appreciating seeing the woman whose soul is twined with mine happy and relaxed for the first time in days, if not weeks? I can't remember the last time she showed this sort of playfulness, we've spent so much of our time together rushing from meeting to curse victim and back again.

Sylas sent a brief message to me before I came to meet Talia at the border that she could use any break I can provide from the responsibilities we fae have heaped on her. I can already tell his instincts were right.

Every part of me initially resisted the idea of sharing Talia's affections, but it's turned out that having other men who care so much for her in our lives benefits our own relationship as well. Now, I'd hate to lose their contributions to her happiness.

But today can be just about us. I took care of all my pressing responsibilities ahead of time, and my coterie can manage any new concerns that come up until my return. Even if another of my people falls victim to the curse, it doesn't take them so quickly that we need to be immediately available.

Talia has given so much of herself to my people, but she should be allowed a life that belongs just to her as well.

With a sweep of my hand, I direct the carriage toward a tall slope of rock so polished by natural forces that it gleams like marble. Around the other side, the top of the hill plunges into a sheer cliff. I bring the carriage to a stop some twenty feet above the ground where a crevice only a little wider than I am offers passage inside.

Curiosity hums through Talia and into our connection as I help her out of the carriage, which afterward I let sink to the ground where it won't require magic holding it up. She doesn't ask any questions though, knowing I wanted to show her rather than try to explain what we're about to experience with words and memories. Her fingers curl between mine, her gaze roving avidly over the glossy walls of the passage we step into.

"Not many venture out here since it isn't equipped to admit many visitors at once and it's rather distant from any village or other area of interest," I say. "But my father used to like to come out here to compose his thoughts, and as I got older he'd bring me as well. I find it has a way of both settling and lifting the spirits."

A faint melody is already seeping through the passage to our ears. Talia's gait begins to sway in time with it, perhaps without her even being aware of it. Her smile grows—she knows how fond I am of music. But this is more than a collection of lovely sounds.

We step out into a small cavern—about the size of my study in my palace but with a conical ceiling that rises many times higher to a pinprick of sunlight up above. Pointed stalactites of all sizes dangle from the slanted surface around the peak. A breeze winds through them, summoning the lilting notes and casting ripples of bright color across the rock. The hues seem to match the music, fiery reds and yellows when it skips along briskly, cool blues and purples when it smooths into more of a lull.

Talia steps carefully into the center of the space, inhaling with a gasp. "It's beautiful. And I see what you mean about it being calming but also uplifting at the same time. I think I could watch it for hours."

I beam at her. "We can stay here for hours if you'd like. I had Charles and Beth pack us some food, so we won't want for anything."

I spread a cloth over the stone floor that's thin but soft enough to provide a comfortable resting spot, and Talia sits down, still staring up at the dancing hues. A faint sheen of color touches her skin, making her look even more ethereal. After a bit, she lies right down on her back so she can watch the spectacle without straining her neck. I seat myself next to her and let my fingers drift idly over her fanned hair.

A sense of peace descends over me, as if this space is all that exists in the world, no troubles lurking in wait outside. Talia exhales with a shaky sound that stills my hand. With a pinch of concern, I rest my fingers against her temple. "Are you all right?"

"Yes," she said. "I mean, there's still a lot that's not exactly okay, but nothing I need to think about right now. This is a perfect escape."

She says that, but I can tell it isn't perfect because it isn't complete. Awe and delight emanate from her, but threads of tension still wind through them. She hasn't entirely relaxed. Which I suppose isn't unexpected, but I can't help feeling it means I've failed.

But there's more I can offer her, more that could wash those worries from her mind for a short time, isn't there?

I stroke my fingers down her cheek and drink in the giddy tingle that resonates through her body at my touch, skin-to-skin. We're even more attuned to each other's physical and emotional states now that we've confirmed our bond.

As I trail my hand farther down to the curve of her neck and shoulder, desire flickers between us, as much mine as hers. Her gaze slides from the ceiling to me, a hungry gleam shining in her eyes.

And yet something in me balks with a twinge of that earlier fear. We aren't in the privacy of my palace. This place isn't often frequented, but there is a chance that another party could stumble on us here. I've never done more than kiss her where we weren't safely behind a locked door.

Talia peers up at me, taking in my reaction, waiting patiently while I grapple with it. The heat of her longing courses into me, but she won't make any demands of me. If there's anything I know about my mate, it's that she'd never do anything she thought might harm or disturb me—well, unless there were worse consequences for *not* doing it.

I wet my lips, thinking of our interlude with Sylas just a couple of weeks ago. There is something to be said for the passions stirred by taking an unconventional route. What better way could there be to sweep her away from the troubles she hasn't been able to shake?

If someone *should* stumble on us, they'll simply see an arch-lord honoring his soul-twined mate in every way she deserves. I have nothing to be ashamed of in that.

I dip my hand lower to caress the swell of one of her breasts. Pleasure quivers from her into me, bringing my cock to half-mast before she's so much as touched me. With a murmur that's almost a purr, she arches into my palm as I swivel it over the tip. Her nipple hardens beneath the fabric, her breath already quickening.

It's an intoxicating sequence, generating bliss in her body that travels into me to inflame my own, and then my enjoyment spurring hers onward even more. The blessing of the soul-twined connection is that when we're so in sync, so devoted to each other, every bit of joy and desire the other feels sparks the same in us. It flows between us in a delicious cycle that in moments like these I never want to end.

Talia reaches up to tug on my jacket, and I lean in to claim her waiting lips. Her kiss is hard with longing, and I'm pleased to note that I can no longer sense any stress laced through her emotions. She's totally absorbed in the escape I'm creating for her.

I want to lose myself in her just as much. As I deepen our kiss, I loosen the ties down the front of yet another elegant dress her Seelie friend designed for her, that makes my mate look every bit the arch-lord's lady. Each inch of skin I uncover sends a heady thrill through me.

My fingers brush over the ridges of scar on her shoulder, and I give them the same gentle attention as the rest of her lovely body. She should know the only thing about them I regret is the pain that came with them. As far as I'm concerned, *she's* perfect.

I tug the dress farther down and can't resist lowering my head to kiss my way across her collarbone to her breasts. When I suck the pert peak of one into my mouth, the noise she makes shoots straight to my groin.

My erection is straining against my trousers now, but I'm not going to rush this. We came together so quickly at first with the urgency of our uncertain bond driving us. My beloved is meant to be savored.

Talia's fingers tangle in my hair, twining with the thick curls. The graze of her fingernails over my scalp sends an exquisite quiver through me. I work over one breast and then the other, lingering whenever her breath catches and her chest arches toward me again, until she yanks my lips back to hers.

As our mouths collide, she pulls at my jacket. Before I can finish stripping it off, she's already fumbling with the buttons on my shirt. I toss that aside as well, humming encouragingly as her slender hands trace over the planes of my chest and the true names marked there.

She charts me like a map, her fingers drawing heated lines in contrast with the cave's cool air. I delve my tongue into the sweetness of her mouth, cupping her breast at the same time, and swallow her moan. But as she squirms the rest of the way out of her dress with the help of my urging hands, a shiver travels through her that's not all pleasure.

Her human skin isn't as tolerant of the wintry chill as mine is. Without the warming spell on her clothes, goosebumps are rising over her skin.

Concern flashes through me before I latch onto an easy solution. With a smile, I sit us both up, guiding her onto my lap so she's straddling me in just her panties. Talia tips toward me, tucking herself close to my body's warmth, but I have more to offer.

The muscles on my back twitch with the release of my wings. I fold them forward around us, forming a sort of cocoon from the thickly-feathered appendages: a bubble of warmth that's all ours. Talia looks around at them and then grins at me with such genuine delight it sends a flutter through my pulse.

I draw her into another kiss, adjusting her against me. Her sex pushes against my rigid cock, and I have to swallow a groan. Not that holding it back can stop my mate from noticing. She kisses me back just as eagerly, rocking her hips at the same time in just the right way to increase that torturous pressure.

Tucking my fingers between her thighs from behind, I stroke them over her slit. The thin layer of cloth that separates us is already damp enough to drive me wild. I bring my hand around in front and delve it right beneath the fabric to tease her skin to skin. At Talia's whimper, I curl my forefinger right inside her.

I love being with you like this, she says in our private way, her inner voice as ragged as her breaths. *I love how you make me feel and tasting how good* you *feel too.*

Her words only stoke the flames of my passion higher. I add a second finger, pulsing them in and out of her, my own breath stuttering at the bliss I can feel coursing through her at my touch. *And what would you like from me next, my soul?* I ask, though the urgent need to be filled is already radiating from her body so strongly I might recognize it even without our bond.

Take me. Make me yours all over again. Show me all that fire you keep inside.

How can I deny a request like that? I wrench down my trousers and then divest her of her panties. Before I can make good on my intention, she reaches between us to grip my shaft. There's no restraining the groan that tumbles out of me as she works her hand up and down my length. She rubs herself against me, spreading her liquid to mingle with mine, and it's all I can do not to ram into her in one swift thrust.

Instead, I position her over me and ease her down inch by wonderful inch. I've been this close with lovers before, but there's nothing like her slickness closing around me in tandem with the heady sensation of fullness that emanates from her. It takes all my self-control not to give over to my most feral urges and drive us both to our peaks as quickly as I can.

Talia leans into me, rocking her hips up and down as I gradually increase my thrusts, welcoming me deeper and deeper. I wrap my wings tighter around her, and she strokes her fingers down the feathers. Her touch sends an electric current through the flesh beneath. A choked sound escapes me, and I pull her mouth to mine.

As our kisses become shakier and our pace more frantic, one of my hands slides around her ass to adjust her angle. Her head tips back with a moan when my cock hits that giddying spot within her channel, but a flash of memory reaches me at the same time: the ecstasy of her caught between two of her Seelie lovers, both inside her at the same time.

I tease my fingers over her other opening, and she gasps, clutching me harder. *Shall I satisfy that desire too, my mate?* I ask.

Her inner voice comes to me in fragments. *Yes. Oh. That's— so good.*

She starts to clench around my cock. I barely manage to hold the ache in my balls in check until the full tremor races through her body. Her sex clamps around me, and my own release races through me in a surge of molten bliss.

Talia sags against me, still enveloped in my wings, still impaled on my now-softening cock. I hold her there, unwilling to let her go just yet. As I loop my arms around her and tuck my chin against her temple, the thought passes through my mind that I wish I never had to let her go at all.

But I might have to in a nearly permanent way.

I've tried not to dwell on the decision I know my mate is struggling with. I try to shove it away now, but a glimmer of awareness passes from Talia into me. Awareness—and a nervousness that it might not be her choice after all.

I hug her even closer. *You will do what's right for you. And if what's right for you is staying here in the fae realm with us, then I'll fight to the death to defend that choice, even if it's against my own colleagues.*

Her response is a wordless mix of love, gratitude, and sadness that I have to say that at all. Then she dismisses those thoughts for the moment as I did, letting the joy of our intimacy wash the worries away. She nestles closer to me with a sigh that's all satisfaction.

We linger like that for quite a while, until hunger seeps into Talia's reverie. I bring out the snacks my kitchen staff packed for us, and we enjoy them under the warbling lights above.

It seems we've recovered the peace I hoped to bring Talia here. The whole journey back to Heart's Cadence under the sky darkening toward evening, a gentle smile plays on her lips like the breeze plays with her hair.

I knew we couldn't keep that peace forever, but my stomach knots when I see a messenger step out to meet us as soon as we've drawn up at my palace. I suppose it was too much to ask that we hold onto it for even a few minutes once we're back in the thick of our problems.

As we disembark, the man hustles over. He bobs into a bow. "I'm sorry to call on you so soon after your arrival, Arch-Lord Corwin. It's about Fina—the woman in Stonehaven your lady cured of the curse some weeks ago. The chill has come over her again."

CHAPTER TEN

Talia

"It's been about a month," I say, trying to count back through the weeks in my head as I peer over the side of the carriage, watching for the lights of the flock village to come into view through the night. Focusing on the practical details pushes back a little of the dread that keeps trying to strangle me. "A similar timeline to how often the summer fae need my cure."

Corwin nods, his normally impassive expression grim. "I'd hoped it might last longer for us, but I suppose we're lucky it isn't a shorter time span. Returning to one person is a lot less of an imposition than curing the entire Seelie population."

Of course, the real question is how easily I'll be able to cure Fina a second time.

Zelpha, the member of Corwin's coterie who's warmed up to me the most, gives me a gentle nudge with her muscular shoulder. "You're an old hat at this now. We zip over there, bring her out of the chill, and we'll be back not too long after bedtime."

I guess my worries aren't hard to pick up on even without a soul-twined bond. Her mention of bed makes my jaw twitch with the urge to yawn. Even though Corwin and I spent most of the day away from the bustle of his domain and the pressures of fae politics, I'm already feeling like curling up under a nice warm blanket and not coming out for a day or two.

But this woman needs me. Fina's the first winter fae I ever cured. I wonder how close she is to giving birth. It was her pregnancy that hit me with so much emotion I was brought to tears when I first met her —the thought of failing to save not just her but her unborn and obviously treasured child…

Zelpha's right, though. I know what I'm doing now. There's no reason it shouldn't work exactly the same way the second time.

I pull away from the biting wind and tuck myself against the crystalline windshield, still watching for the lights. The carriage bottom casts a pale glow over the snowy landscape below and just ahead of us. When I make out the edge of the valley that holds Fina's village, relief rushes through me even as my gut twists tighter.

I won't let anyone down. I can do this.

My sense of Corwin through our bond echoes those thoughts with additional reassurance. He directs the carriage down into the valley, and not just a few but many lights gleam into view up ahead. Several beam along a broad terrace at the foot of the lord's castle. The messenger said we're supposed to go there, even though last time I looked after Fina in her own home. Maybe because it was her second affliction, the lord wanted to keep a closer eye on her.

The terrace is wide enough for Corwin to land the carriage right on it. He takes my hand to help me out, and a slim man with hair a mix of mauve and dun brown comes hurrying out to meet us. I catch a murmur of voices trickling from the bright doorway behind him before it swings shut in his wake.

"Good, good, I'm glad you could make it here so quickly, my lord. And my lady." He dips into a bow for both of us, a sign of respect I'm not sure I'll ever be totally used to. With a sweep of his arm, he gestures us toward the castle, which is made out of jagged pinkish-gray stone like a more subdued version of the man's hair.

We walk through a small entry room into a vast space that must be intended for balls and other celebrations. Glowing gems dot the ceiling, filling the room with a hazy light, and beneath it a few dozen fae are gathered. Their conversations fall silent as we enter—they all turn to watch us.

To watch me. Their gazes prickle over my skin, and my chest constricts. It's like when I healed the man in the village common the other day, with most of his flock come to witness it—except that at least was the middle of the day when they might have been out and about anyway.

The lord confirms my suspicion. "Many of my flock wished to wait up to witness your curing. We are honored to have the first Unseelie to have received your blessing among us, Lady Talia, and look forward to seeing Fina twice blessed tonight."

I swallow hard, and Corwin squeezes my hand. *It's all right,* he says. *They're celebrating you and what you can do for us. I'm glad to see them recognizing how special you are.*

I guess that's one way of looking at it. I draw in a deep breath and let the lord usher me across the room to where Fina sits hunched on a large velvet cushion by the room's large hearth. As always with the curse victims, the heat of the flames doesn't appear to be reaching her at all. Her skin has grayed, her lips turned outright blue. Her arms have locked around her belly, which is even more rounded now than before.

It seems her neck has already frozen stiff, because she doesn't turn her head toward me, only managing to cast her gaze in my direction at an awkward angle. Her lips part, but the words she tries to form come out as a mumble.

An ache runs through me from throat to gut. It's worse than last time. Did the curse creep up on her that much longer ago, or has it taken hold so much faster?

The only good thing about her obvious distress is that I don't even need to work to summon tears. They're already welling up behind my eyes. I have to remind myself to turn away from her, to go through the motions of hiding my grief. The burning fills my eyes and seeps down to the back of my mouth.

Why can't I be enough? Why couldn't the curse have left her for good?

I have no answer to those questions, and they don't change what I have to do now. As the first tears trickle down my cheeks, I swipe them away. Our audience stands silent and mostly still, only swaying on their feet a bit as those farther back crane their necks to see. When I raise my head and turn back to Fina, a small gasp reaches my ears.

The winter fae are so unused to overt displays of emotion that my tears on their own are startling.

I walk up to Fina and touch her icy cheek like I did before. "Be well," I say, saying the first words that come to mind. "Both you and your baby."

There's a raspy intake of breath somewhere behind me, and then the warmth I'm waiting for blooms beneath my fingers.

Fina inhales with a shudder. Tentatively, she stretches out her arms and legs as the chill and the stiffness recede.

I move to step back, but she catches my hand. She peers up at me with eyes glistening with what might be a few tears of her own. *I've* never seen a winter fae cry before. I stop, lost for words.

"Thank you," she whispers, her voice still rough from her ordeal. "You've given me four blessings now, two for me and two for my baby. I don't know how to repay that generosity."

"You don't need to repay me," I say quickly. "I'm helping you—and everyone else the curse takes—because I want to. Because I can. I wish I could stop it completely."

Murmurs ripple through the crowd. "Heart bless Lady Talia as she blesses us!" one man calls out. I hear a woman remark in a hushed voice that this is a magic beyond any she's seen before. They all shuffle around, seemingly unwilling to be the first to leave my presence.

It's not so different from the last time, but their reverence doesn't feel any less strange. I'm still just… me, with powers I have no real control over. But I know Corwin is right, that it's better for them to appreciate me like this than for me to keep facing the same suspicion and disrespect they might have shown before.

The kind any other human in this world would face.

Corwin ends the spectacle by placing his hands on my shoulders and raising his voice to carry through the room. "It's late, and my lady needs her rest. We thank you all for paying your respects!"

The lord shoos his flock-folk off and ushers us back to our carriage. Even he stares at me a little wide-eyed as I clamber back into the vehicle. "It is a wonder to witness what you offer, but I hope we won't have need to call on you again," he says.

I bob my head in acknowledgment. "If you do need me, don't hesitate to send a message. I'll want to come."

But as I sink into the bench at the bow of the carriage with Corwin and Zelpha on either side of me, his statement starts to weigh on me. Corwin glances at me here and there as he focuses on navigating out the valley, but he doesn't push for me to open up.

Zelpha doesn't have the same qualms. She twists the tip of her loose braid around her forefinger and studies me. "What's eating at you, Talia?"

The fact that *she's* not overtly awed by me somehow makes it easier to open up. I rub my mouth. "I was just thinking—if the curse comes back every few weeks, and it keeps striking new people as well… This isn't like the Seelie curse where I just need to give my blood once a month and the fae can distribute it among themselves. I have to be with each Unseelie victim. Within a few months, I might need to be visiting someone every day. And after that…"

In a year, will all my time be taken up with traveling from one flock to another to heal those either newly cursed or succumbing for a second time—or a third, fourth, fifth time for that matter? How could the arch-lords really think that it'd work for them to bring all those fae to me in the human world? They'd be making the trip constantly.

My colleagues weren't aware of the exact timelines when they made that suggestion, Corwin says, sensing my thoughts. *But if you wished to remain with your brother for that long, we'd find a way to work around it.*

Out loud, he adds, "Now that we know how the cure works, and that the curse will return and the requests on your presence will multiply, we can start asking that the victims be brought to the border castle for you to work your cure on them there rather than us going to them."

That will make it easier. But it still means I'll essentially be on call every day at every hour someone might turn up. Especially if the curse continues to take hold faster and faster.

I press the heel of my hand to my temple and risk saying the words I know will cast a shadow over all the good we've done. "It won't be sustainable. Maybe for a few years, but eventually—" Eventually it'll be dozens a day. Will I even be able to summon that many tears over and over again?

Corwin and Zelpha exchange a look. Zelpha's mouth slants into a wry smile. "Well, we always knew your cure couldn't sustain us forever, right? This is a stopgap measure until we can find a more permanent solution."

"And hopefully we'll strike on that before the situation becomes overwhelming," Corwin says.

I touch the bronze bracelet Sylas gave me, thinking of the prediction Nuldar the sage gave him. The solution might be coming soon… whatever that means in fae terms. Nothing about this situation has been simple so far, though, so I'm not going to count on the next developments being any different.

What can I do about the problem now anyway? Fretting doesn't help anyone, least of all me.

When Corwin sits down on the bench next to me, I tuck myself under his arm and try to think about nothing but how lucky I am in so many other ways.

I doze for a bit during the trip back, and Corwin leaves me at my bedroom with a lingering kiss good night. But after I've washed up, I find I'm keyed up all over again. And hungry. We grabbed something to eat on the journey to Fina, but I didn't have a proper dinner.

I slip through the halls and limp into the kitchen, planning to put together a quick midnight snack. To my surprise, Beth is still there, eyeing several spice containers she's set in a row on the counter in front of her.

She startles at my entrance and then giggles, a blush coloring her cheeks. She hasn't seemed to know exactly how to relate to me after finding out I'm both human like her and not like her at all with the powers I can wield.

Seeing her reminds me of my earlier thoughts about how the fae treat most of their human and somewhat human companions. "What are you doing?" I ask as I grab a loaf of bread to cut off a slice.

Beth lets out another giggle and tugs an errant curl back from her face. "I want to come up with better flavoring for the moss-shoots. I feel like they're missing just a little something the way we prepare them now. I've been trying different combinations, just tasting them, to see if I can figure out the right one, but it hasn't really worked so far." She frowns at the spice containers.

I consider her as I spread a little butter and some preserved fruit on my bread. I carry the snack over to the island and perch on the stool across from her. "You really like doing this, don't you?" I ask. "Working in the kitchen for Corwin and everything?"

Beth shrugs, looking self-conscious all over again. "Yeah. It's kind of fun. Dad says they never had ingredients anything like we've got to work with back where he came from. And it's not like it's all work-work-work. I've gotten to see some pretty spectacular things."

I hesitate, not sure the question will come out right, and then push myself onward. "Corwin's very… kind with his human servants. I've gotten the impression that's not really the case with a lot of the fae lords. I'm not sure if you talk much with the staff in other domains or anything. Have you heard about anything—like people being mistreated or overworked?"

Beth freezes in place and drops her gaze. "I mean, Dad does say we're lucky to be in Heart's Cadence. I have heard a few things. But I don't know for sure—I mean, people might exaggerate or whatever. I wouldn't want to accuse any lords of anything."

Of course not. "I wouldn't want you to either," I assure her quickly. "I just… I've been thinking that because of what I can do, I've been able to get more recognition than humans normally do in this world. Maybe I can use that to help out other people who've ended up here. I think we all deserve some happiness."

Beth shivers. "There are definitely some people around the Heart who don't get a chance to be happy much at all." Then her gaze darts to me. "You won't tell any of the arch-lords I said that?"

"You don't have to worry," I say. But my hunger has been swallowed by a heavy lump in my stomach.

I told myself I needed to find out more about how Jamie's coping before I decided how much he needs me. How can I even think about abandoning this world without figuring out exactly what my fellow humans here are facing too?

CHAPTER ELEVEN

August

Seeing the border castle almost complete fills me with exhilaration. I can't keep the smile off my face as I move around the new kitchen—fully wood and on our side, as I requested—adding the last touches to the equipment. Talia watches me from a stool she's already made her own, perched there with her malformed foot dangling. She seems content just to watch me in silence.

But when I lean back against the counter to take in my work with a satisfied air, she straightens up on her seat. "August… Could I ask you about something it might be hard for you to talk about?"

Something catches in my chest that she even feels she needs to check first. I turn toward her. "Of course, Sweetness. Anything." We're in this together—all five of us now—and that means no secrets, no shying away from difficult conversations. And I know Talia would never bring up a potentially painful subject unless she believed it was important.

She looks down at her hands before meeting my eyes again. "It's just—I've started wondering about the other humans who are stuck here in the fae world. I know a few of them are here at least sort of by choice… Corwin would let any of his human servants go back to the human world if they asked… but from what I've heard, that's pretty rare. Obviously a lot of the fae I've had to deal with haven't seen me as anywhere near an equal."

"They're getting there," I say, sidling closer to take her hand. "As they see just how much you can do—"

She shakes her head. "It shouldn't matter how much I can *do*. Or any of the others. Just because they don't have magic, that doesn't mean they shouldn't get any say in what happens in their lives."

The anguish in her voice makes my heart ache. "Is this about your brother? I can tell you that the summer arch-lords have accepted that he can't help with the curse, and they won't push to bring him here anymore. If the Unseelie are still making demands, we'll deal with them."

"It's not really that either. Though I guess it's part of the same problem." Talia lowers her head, a few strands of her hair falling across her face. "I've barely been around other humans since I came to the fae realm, after being so isolated with Aerik and then Sylas not having any on his staff. But lots of the other packs have human servants, don't they? Their lives matter too."

She pauses, and I wait for her to decide where she's going with this topic. Her fingers tighten around mine. "You told me about how easily your father killed your mother when you were a kid. Was that how he treated all the humans in his domain? Like their lives didn't mean anything at *all*, and the only thing that mattered was what he felt like doing with them? Do *most* of the fae see us as that worthless?"

Now I understand why she hesitated to get into this subject. The memory of my mother's murder makes my stomach turn even now, hundreds of years later. But it's a reasonable question, one I might even have prompted with the things I've told Talia in the past. My early hesitations about taking Talia as a mate seem incredibly distant now that she's become so entwined in my life, but there was a time when I was wary of even how *I* might end up treating her.

I release her hand to stroke my fingers down her back. "Honestly, I don't completely know. As you can obviously tell, there are other fae like Aerik and Kellan who see humans as not much more than easy prey. But even when we did have human servants at Hearthshire, Sylas made sure that they were well cared for. I remember there was one woman who became pretty miserable, and he had her taken back. Donovan seems considerate in his treatment of his own servants."

I stop, frowning as I try to come up with a better answer. Finally, I have to admit, "I'm not sure which is more common. Even in Thundervale under my father, I didn't pay all that much attention to how any of the staff were treated other than my mother. And he's harsh to the fae who serve him too. I'd like to say he's one of the worst, that most are kinder…"

"But it could be that's how it goes in a lot of other packs too," Talia fills in.

I grimace. "Yes." Guilt twists through my gut, loosening only when a flicker of inspiration hits me. "Do you want to get a better idea with your own eyes? We could visit some of the nearby domains and ask to speak with the human servants… I wouldn't bother the arch-lords unnecessarily, but any of the lesser lords will kind of have to welcome an arch-lord's cadre-chosen." I smile a little slyly.

To my relief Talia smiles back. "I'd like that. I feel like I kind of owe it to the other humans here to speak up for them while *I'm* here, since some of the fae are starting to respect me more."

What a perfectly Talia thing to say. I press a kiss to her temple before she hops off the stool. "You're already doing so much, Sweetness. You don't need to take on more crusades."

Her expression turns serious. "But how can I spend all this time trying to heal the fae without doing anything for all the people like me who've ended up trapped here, maybe not much better off than I was in Aerik's cage? At least the fae are looking out for each other. The humans in this world… if I don't do anything, they have no one."

I can't argue that point. The fact that I hadn't considered it before myself brings back a pang of my earlier guilt.

I motion for her to follow me out of the kitchen. "Sylas hasn't given me any duties for the morning. We could pay a call on the domain that borders ours just beyond the Heart's hill right now if you'd like."

Talia heads for the door with a bit of a skip in her uneven steps. “Yes, please.”

I don’t have the carriage-summoning magic myself, so I direct her to the stable to pick out the steadiest horse we have. If I were traveling alone, I might simply shift, but arriving to request a favor with a woman riding on my wolfish back doesn’t seem like the most dignified approach, as much fun as it might be otherwise.

Fae horses aren’t exactly calm in temperament most of the time, but I pick out one I trust not to test the reins too much and scoop Talia up so she’s perched between my legs on the saddle. Thankfully, the skirt of her dress is loose enough that it only rides up to her knees. I wrap one arm around her waist to secure her. “Comfortable?”

She laughs, settling closer against me in a way that sends a pulse of heat through my groin. “I’m not sure I’d want to try this for a long trip, but for a short one it should be just fine.”

I can’t resist nipping the crook of her neck. Then I guide the horse toward the path that leads from our domain down the broad hill around the Heart.

For the first several minutes, cantering along with my love nestled against me and the sun beaming down on us through the trees, it’s a pretty enjoyable excursion. But as we reach the bottom of the slope and head on toward the border of the nearest neighboring domain, thoughts of the grim purpose of our visit rise back to the surface.

I don’t actually know what we’ll find here. Will it make Talia trust the fae even less? Make returning to the human world seem like a better option, no matter how much she cares for the few of us who’ve treated her well?

I swallow down those worries and focus on presenting an authoritative front for addressing the lady who rules this pack.

The sparse but vibrant forest we’ve been riding through falls away completely, and the castle comes into view up ahead. The lady must have a particular affinity for plant-life, because the tall, rippling structure looks as if it’s been created out of a mass of intertwined vines. The houses of the pack village look similarly woven, nearly blending into the grassy plain they’ve sprouted from.

Several members of the pack are out and about, tending to gardens or working their various crafts. At our arrival, a man polishing a bronze platter looks up and then stands. "Hey, there. What brings you to Petalrise?" His gaze moves to Talia, and he pauses. "You've come from Hearth-by-the-Heart?"

"We have," I say, helping Talia to the ground and then dismounting. "I'm from Arch-Lord Sylas's cadre. Our companion wished to speak with your lady about some of the workings of her domain, if she's present."

Won't it be sweet when I can call Talia my mate as Corwin does? Although if some of our brethren have their way, that day will never come.

Two attendants have already headed our way from the castle. One reaches for the horse's reins. "I'll see your steed to the stable. Lady Gullven will attend to you shortly."

The other attendant leads us into the castle. The rooms inside are filled with a greenish-gold light and a scent like newly grown leaves.

I've only had a few minutes to worry that the lady of the pack might find our visit a big imposition after all when she sweeps into the room and dips into a slight bow. I have to catch myself on the verge to bowing to *her*, still not totally used to the respects now paid to me as part of an arch-lord's cadre. Despite only being cadre-chosen, I'm now on a slightly higher level of authority than any regular lord or lady.

"What can I do for you, honored guests?" she asks.

I don't like the way her attention lingers on Talia with a slight furrow in her brow. I set my hand on Talia's shoulder. I can give her a proper title with her connection to Corwin, at least. "Lady Talia would like to learn more about the other humans living among us fae. I was hoping you'd give us permission to speak with whatever human servants you currently employ."

Employ isn't really the right word for it, since as Talia rightly pointed out, the humans in question won't have had much choice about making the journey to our world. They aren't being compensated for their work either. But I don't think saying "enslave" would encourage Gullven to agree.

More skepticism shows in her expression, but she nods. "I don't think they're so busy that it should be a problem. You can stay here in the sitting room, and I'll have them brought to you. And one of my staff will see about refreshments as well. I have another matter to attend to, but if you should have need of me, just send word."

"We appreciate it," Talia speaks up, her voice soft but confident in a way that makes my chest swell with pride. She really is finding her footing as a lady in her own right, regardless of what any of my fellow fae might think of her heritage.

Gullven slips away, and a few minutes later a young fae woman arrives with a tray of duskapple wine and pastries I can tell just on sight are a little under-baked. Talia nibbles at one as we wait for the human servants to arrive. "Not as good as yours," she murmurs to me with a hint of mischief in her voice.

Finally, another fae staff member appears, ushering four other figures into the room. There are two men and two women, all dressed in fae clothes that look a little rougher than what any of the fae staff we've seen have.

They come to a stop in the middle of the room, and the fae man gestures to us. "These are our guests," he tells the servants. "They would like to speak with you. Please answer their questions."

He steps back to the far wall to watch. One of the men stands still with obvious wariness in his stance, but the other man and both of the women gaze around them with vague bemused expressions I recognize in an instant. I'm so used to that demeanor that it didn't even occur to me to mention it when I was talking with Talia about the humans here.

"Why do they look so out of it?" Talia asks. Any cheerfulness in her mood has snuffed out at the sight of them.

"Their meals will include a regular dose of some kind of faerie drug," I say, my spirits sinking. "There are a few that have a calming and mildly euphoric effect. It helps keep them happy."

Talia shivers. "Because otherwise they'd be upset about being stolen from their homes."

The fae man speaks up hastily. "We only bring over those who've joined in our revels in the human lands. They come to us of their own accord."

Talia fixes her eyes on him. "But they can't know when they join a revel that they're giving their whole lives away. And it isn't exactly their 'own accord' when there's fae magic involved."

The man's gaze darts from her to me and back again, as if he's not sure who he should be addressing or how much he should even say. "It's how we've always done things," he says haltingly. "We see that they have everything they need."

Food and clothing and an occasional bath, he means. Talia doesn't need to speak for me to know what she'd be thinking—they're tended to much like our pack-kin Elliot tends to his sheep.

Talia's mouth has tightened, but she walks up to the row of figures, starting with the one at the farthest right. The woman's glazed eyes settle on her without any change in her vague expression.

"What work do you do in the castle?" Talia asks, her voice heart-wrenchingly gentle.

"I keep the kitchen clean," the woman says in a flat voice. "All the surfaces shining. That's what they ask, and that's what I do."

"And when the kitchen's already clean?"

The woman blinks as if she doesn't understand the question. "There's always something else that needs to be wiped down or polished. So much cooking and baking. When it's done for the night, then I sleep."

Talia's hands clench at her sides. I don't know whether I want more to yank her away from this confrontation or rage at the fae who've taken these humans. Neither is really an option.

She moves down the line, talking to a man who spends his days cleaning and mending clothes for the other servants and staff—because I'd imagine Lady Gullven sees that job as a waste of the Heart's magic—and the other woman, who alternates between fishing in a nearby lake and looking after the castle's garden. Scars from the hooks and lures she uses mottle her fingers.

She also has a bruise on her cheek. When Talia asks her about that, she raises her hand to it and only says, without a hint of emotion, "I wasn't listening well enough."

I wince inwardly.

When Talia reaches the one man who appears to still have his wits, his posture tenses even more than before. She studies him for a moment. "They don't make you take the faerie drugs."

"No," he says. "It would interfere with the work Lady Gullven expects me to do."

"And what's that?"

His jaw flexes. He might not be in the grips of a drug-induced haze, but I'm sure he's discovered the consequences of saying anything critical of his "employers."

He draws in a rough breath. "I'm an artist. I paint for her. Some of them she keeps; some I think she uses as gifts or similar purposes."

Talia seems to weigh her next words carefully. "You don't look all that happy about it. Did you *want* to come here? Why have you stayed?"

His mouth twists into a wry grimace. "I had a gallery, back home. Lady Gullven happened to wander into it one day—I'm not sure how she ended up there. She must have liked my style, because she invited me to come paint for her. She showed me how she could make the images I created come alive with magic, all the effects I could incorporate with the enchanted supplies she could give me… I made a deal with her. I don't think I totally understood—I can't go home until I've fulfilled it."

"What would fulfill it?" Talia asks.

"That's at Lady Gullven's discretion."

I'm familiar with those kinds of bargains. It's a common fae trick to stealthily make the terms dependent on their approval in a way that works in their favor, so they get to decide when the deal is over no matter what the other party does. Not a single one who extends an offer like that doesn't recognize that they're exploiting the person on the other end. They simply don't care.

Talia asks a few more questions of each of the servants and then tells the fae man that she doesn't want to bother them anymore. As we walk out to the stables, her face stays pensive. I long to reach for her, but I doubt there's any way to comfort her distress away.

And it's not just distress. I can see the determination forming behind her eyes at the same time. My chest tightens with unspoken thoughts.

I was afraid that seeing the way many of the fae treat her kind might drive her away. Maybe the real problem is the opposite. Now she has yet another cause she'll feel she has to champion, another duty weighing down on her… when she might be better off if we'd let *her* go home after all, away from the pressures and dangers of our world.

Am I showing my love by fighting to have her stay here, or would a truly loving mate be encouraging the opposite?

CHAPTER TWELVE

Talia

"There," Harper says, looking down at me with her hands on her hips. "You're not to move from that spot for at least an hour." She sets her slim frame down next to me on the grass with typical fae grace.

She led me out to this knoll overlooking the Shimmering Falls in Donovan's domain insisting that we needed a chance to talk after I've spent so much time running back and forth between the realms. I'm starting to think the walk was less a friendly excursion and more an intervention. Both my friends and my lovers seem to be dragging me away to some restful spot pretty often these days… I'm obviously not hiding the tension coiled inside me as well as I'd like to.

I lean back on my hands, letting myself take a moment to enjoy the soft grass beneath my palms and the faint, warm spray of the waterfall that reaches us even here. The rhythmic warble of the falling water soothes my nerves. And it occurs to me that I haven't just hung out and chatted with my closest fae friend since I found out about Jamie.

I make an apologetic face at Harper. "I'm sorry I haven't been around much lately. There've just been so many things going on…"

She waves off my apology. "I know. I'm not going to complain when you're running around taking care of so much and all I've got to do is keep making my dresses." She pauses and shoots a grin at me. "I got some ideas from the winter fae dresses you've brought back. I think I can combine elements of both styles to make some really striking designs."

Her enthusiasm is so infectious that it's easy to smile back. "I can't wait to see them."

"Oh, you'll probably be my first model for them after myself." She tucks her sleek blond hair behind her ears and peers out over the landscape ahead of us. Her next words come out more hesitant. "Is it true that you're thinking of going back to the human world? Like, to live there instead of here?"

I bite my lip, not sure what to say. Harper *is* my closest friend here, and I'm also hers. She's the only person who was born into Sylas's pack after they were banished a century ago. All her pack-kin are decades if not centuries older than her. I might be only twenty-one, but comparatively, from what I've gathered, that puts us at about the same point in our life-spans. And like her, I've spent most of my time in the fae world isolated and unsure of my place.

But now that the pack has risen to the most prominent position possible, I'm sure she'll make more friends among the other packs. Friends who'll have more in common with her than I do. Friends who won't age so much faster than she will. She'll be fine no matter what I choose.

"I'm not sure what I'm going to do yet," I say. "My brother's still having a bit of a hard time of it. It's just tricky to know whether me turning up out of the blue will really make things better for him or just confuse him. I have no idea how I'd even explain where I've been all this time." I rub my forehead.

Harper nods. "I understand why you'd want to help him. You basically always want to help everyone, and he's family on top of that. I wish our worlds weren't so far apart. It's not like with the winter realm where you can step across the border and be home in just a few minutes."

"Soon I'm going to have a home that's right there on the border." Sylas's pack and Corwin's flock were just putting the final touches on the joint castle this morning.

Will my lovers continue their alliance even if I'm gone for… however long I'd feel I need to be gone for? Corwin would wait for me —I know that for sure. He isn't going to find another soul-twined mate, as unfair as that might be to him. Sylas, August, and Whitt would wait for me too if I asked them. Somehow that knowledge reassures me and gnaws at me at the same time.

No matter what I do, it's definitely going to be unfair to *someone*. Maybe including me.

But the point of this excursion is to relax, not worry about all that. I slip off my boots and wiggle my toes in the grass. "Have you gotten any new customers for your dresses? I thought I saw one of Donovan's cadre-chosen wearing something in your style when some of them joined Whitt's last revel."

Harper giggles, a blush I don't totally understand coloring her cheeks. Does she think I'll be offended that she's making clothes for people other than me? "Yes, I got a few requests from the other arch-lords' packs. My goal is to see a ball where more than half of the ladies are wearing dresses I designed. I hope there's another one soon! Perhaps Arch-Lord Sylas will host one to celebrate the border castle."

"I think that would be a great idea. I'll mention it to him, since he's probably more focused on logistics and making sure the summer and winter fae don't go for each other's throats."

Harper giggles again, more openly this time, but there's still an odd gleam in her eyes as she glances at me. "He's really going to make you officially his mate, isn't he? And Whitt and August too. Four mates! I can't even imagine."

I laugh, my own cheeks heating. "I hardly can either most of the time. I definitely didn't plan for it to happen that way. And it's been complicated with the soul-twined bond and everything. I just hope the other arch-lords come around to accepting it." It isn't as if I'll be in their lives all that long by fae standards anyway, even if I stay here.

"They'll just have to," Harper says matter-of-factly. "It's what the Heart and your hearts want." Then she pauses with an air as if she's deciding whether to say something else. She looks down at her hands, which are fidgeting with a flower she's plucked. "When you felt the soul-twined bond with Corwin… They always say you know right away, the first time you see each other. Was it like that for you even though you're not—I mean, even though you're human?"

The moment when the bond seared through me is burned into my memory. "Yeah. The winter arch-lords had come to see Sylas as the new summer arch-lord during his coronation celebration. I'd never seen them before then. The first moment my gaze locked with Corwin's, I felt it. You definitely couldn't miss it."

I glance at her, a suspicion tickling at the edges of my mind. Why would she be wondering about that? "Is there someone you'd want to spark a soul-twined bond with?"

The bashful way Harper ducks her head confirms my guess before she even speaks. "I know it's silly. You're obviously a special case. No fae who isn't true-blooded ever had a soul-twined mate that we know of. But I just—it's a nice hope, right? It's *possible* even if not very likely. Of course, if the whole eyes meeting thing has already happened and nothing was there, I guess there isn't any possibility at all." She tosses the flower away.

If she's that concerned about it, I have to think the man she's interested in is true-blooded, or it wouldn't make any sense to be worrying about being his soul-twined mate. They could just become regular mates.

The trouble for her would be that, from what I understand, every true-blooded fae ends up forming a soul-twined bond eventually. They might strike up other relationships in the meantime—or sometimes even at the same time—but that one deep connection is always going to come first. And not being true-blooded herself, Harper couldn't be that one.

"Do you want to talk about it?" I ask tentatively.

My friend shakes her head quickly. "No. It's silly, honestly. I shouldn't even be thinking about it."

"I'm sure you'll have lots of chances to meet other potential mates as Sylas gets more settled in as arch-lord and starts hosting more events," I say, even though I know that comment wouldn't comfort me in the same position. There are millions of unattached human men back in the world that used to be my home, but that fact won't stop me from missing my fae lovers terribly if I have to leave them.

Before that melancholy thought can take hold any further, Corwin's voice carries abruptly through our bond. *I'm sorry to interrupt you when you're taking some time for yourself, beloved, but one of the flocks has brought a new cursed victim to Heart's Cadence for you to "bless," as they put it now. You don't need to come over immediately, but as soon as you've finished your visit with your friend...*

No, I'll come right away, I reply, despite—or maybe because of—the heaviness that wraps around my heart. *I won't be able to enjoy just sitting here chatting if I know someone's suffering while they wait for me.*

I pull my boots on and stand up. "I'm sorry. It hasn't been even an hour yet, but Corwin's just told me there's another winter fae hit by the curse. They're waiting in his domain for me to heal them."

"Of course." Harper scrambles up. "We'll have lots more time to talk later."

Will we? I don't voice that question out loud.

We hurry back across the forested terrain as quickly as my warped foot will allow. By the time we've passed Donovan's castle and the Bastion has come into sight, my foot is throbbing, and I'm wishing we brought a carriage or a horse.

That thought must travel to Corwin, because a second later he's telling me, *Stay where you are and give your foot a chance to recover. I'll come the rest of the way to you.*

It's all right, I try to say, but I can tell he isn't going to listen. He's already grabbing one of the carriages he keeps waiting in case someone needs one quickly.

Harper waits with me until he arrives. It's a bizarre sight, watching the pale, narrow vehicle with its crystalline features gliding through the vibrant summer landscape. Several Seelie outside of Donovan's castle stop to stare.

I scramble in with Corwin's helping hand and turn back to Harper. "Will you tell Sylas or one of his cadre-chosen where I've gone?"

She bobs her head, but Corwin interjects. "I've already talked to Whitt myself. We just finished the last essential pieces of the border castle." A soft smile touches his lips. "It's ready to be inhabited now. Not quite so much rushing back and forth from here on, I hope."

Knowing that buoys my spirits until we come up on the haze of the border. "I'm glad that they brought the latest victim to us instead of us having to travel across the realm," Corwin says. "But… it's a little more than I expected."

I tear my eyes away from the spectacle of the wooden end of the joint castle protruding from the fog and look at him. "More how?"

He hesitates, with an impression of awkwardness he can't hide from me. "You'll see. It isn't anything *bad*, just… You know how it's been the last couple of times."

I do, but somehow I'm still not prepared for us to emerge from the haze to find not just the curse victim and a few helpers but maybe three dozen figures gathered by the glow of the Heart. Maybe they think my power will work even better if I'm closer to it? But all these people…

How far did they come? I ask Corwin as we clamber out of the carriage and go to meet them.

A few hours' journey, Corwin says in a bemused tone. *That's at least a third of the flock, including a couple of their lord's coterie members. They weren't able to make it to our confirmation ceremony. They say they wanted to support their flock-fellow, but it's clear they're just as eager to see you work your cure with their own eyes.*

My "blessing," as they're calling it now. An uneasy itch travels over my skin.

I have to remember that it's a good thing the winter fae are so impressed with me now. Ever since August and I left Lady Gullven's domain, I've been wondering what I can do for the other humans on both sides of the border—and also those associated with them through birth, like Kesral, if that's possible. If they care so much about what I can do for them, will they care at least a little about what I have to say as well?

As Corwin ushers me over to where a fae man hunches right in front of the Heart's pulsing glow, I see other figures drifting toward us from Laoni's and Uzziah's castles. Noticing the commotion and coming to discover what it's about, presumably. It'd be hard to miss this gathering.

Excited murmurs carry through the crowd. "There she is!"

"Lady Talia is with us!"

"She came so swiftly."

I drag in a breath and give them all the best smile I can summon. The awed faces gaze back at me, some beaming in return, others more cautious. A woman I'm guessing is the cursed man's mate squeezes his shoulder, watching me too.

"It only struck him this morning," she says. "Whatever you can do for him, my lady..."

The man coughs out a croaked voice. "I'm honored to accept your blessing, Lady Talia."

Seeing them together, a lump is already rising in my throat. Turning away, I think of both them and me—of that woman losing her mate to the curse when she should have had so many more years with him, of me possibly leaving behind the men I've come to love so much.

As tears prick at the backs of my eyes, I sense Corwin's urge to reach out to me, but he knows I have to draw on whatever sadness I can to perform the cure.

When I picture the woman clinging to the man's frozen form if the curse completely takes hold, the tears begin to trickle out. I wipe them away and turn to face him. The motions come to me more confidently now that I've seen them work several times.

I can do this. The Heart has given me this power. It *wants* me to push back the curse. And maybe to accomplish other things too, that I don't fully understand yet.

As I stroke my fingers across the man's cheek, the fae gathered around us lean closer. There's a sense of a collective breath held. Then, as he shudders and starts to shake off the chill, that breath bursts into pleased gasps and sighs of relief.

"The blessed one!" someone calls out. "Thank the Heart for Lady Talia!"

At the voices echoing the same sentiment, I gather myself, gazing out over the small crowd. I can tell Corwin has picked up on my intention, but he doesn't dissuade me, offering a nudge of encouragement instead. His motion of support gives me the courage to speak up.

"I'm so glad that I can help all of the fae with the powers the Heart has given me, even though I'm a human," I say. "I hope that it helps you all see that the Heart can shine on humans just as well as the fae. It would make my own heart rest easier if I knew that you'll go back to your lives thinking better of the humans who've ended up in the fae realm—treating them with the same kindness and respect you'd offer me."

I get several nods from the gathered fae and some more called words of praise, but I have no idea how much they're just giving the appearance of being agreeable versus actually listening. It isn't as if I could change the entire culture around the fae treatment of humans in one day. Those words are a start though, even if it's a small one.

The fae from the curse victim's flock linger a while longer, many of them coming up to me to ask for a brief touch as its own sort of blessing, others just seeming to want a closer look. The cursed man bows in gratitude, and his mate bows even lower. "Thank you so much," she says, sounding a little choked up, which is startling from an Unseelie.

As they drift back toward the carriages they arrived on, Laoni and a couple of members of her coterie weave through the crowd to reach us. The dark expression on the arch-lord's face puts me immediately on guard, and Corwin tenses too.

"Meet us in the Hall of the Heart in one hour," she demands. "Both of you. It's time decisions were made."

Why is she upset? I ask Corwin as she strides off without waiting for an answer.

I'm not sure, he replies, but the realization is already rising up in me.

This is the first time any of the other arch-lords has seen how their people are responding to me now—how they're acting like I'm some kind of holy savior. And I don't think Laoni is happy about that development at all.

CHAPTER THIRTEEN

Talia

I've seen the Hall of the Heart many times through Corwin's eyes, but this is only my second time entering it. The high ceiling and the gleaming white marble all around take my breath away for a second. Seeing the stern expressions three of the arch-lords waiting for us are wearing, it's hard to catch it again.

I can't think of any valid reason they could have to complain about your behavior, Corwin reassures me as we walk together to his spot at the long marble table. *If you're uncertain of how to respond to anything they say, let me take the lead.*

I nod inwardly, although I hate letting anyone else fight my battles. Sometimes I need it—I know I can't face off with fae in every possible way on my own—but they're *never* going to respect me if they don't see me standing up for myself however I actually can.

Neve offers us a soft, dreamy smile. The others just eye us silently until we come to a stop at the table.

Laoni clears her throat, but Corwin jumps in before she can speak. "What is this about? What decisions were you talking about, Laoni?"

She glowers at him. "What do you think? Your mate has had quite a while to think on our proposal for her return to her own world. We would like to see that matter settled before it becomes any more fraught."

Fraught because the rest of the winter fae might protest me leaving their world now that they're becoming so impressed by me? Somehow I suspect Laoni is thinking more about ending whatever influence I might be gaining among her people than about how they'll feel about my absence.

"I didn't know there was a time limit on deciding," I say, keeping my voice as steady as possible. "There's more I want to understand about both worlds before I'm sure which would do the most good—not for me but for everyone involved."

Uzziah lets out a faint cough. "An honorable sentiment, but it does bring into question your motivations."

I sense Corwin bristling, though he doesn't show it other than in a slight terseness that creeps into his voice. "What exactly do you mean by that? Talia's 'motivations' have been nothing but pure. She's been selflessly helping us in a way none of us have been able to accomplish for weeks now."

"It may appear selfless, but who's to say the human isn't gaining something from it as well?" Laoni says archly. "She *can* lie after all, unlike the rest of us. Why else would she be so hesitant to do what's right for her family and for the brother she should owe the most loyalty to?"

Terisse's mouth twitches with a hint of discomfort, but she speaks up too. "Yes, how can we be so sure of her loyalty to us or even you if she'd abandon one of her own blood so easily?"

Guilt jabs through my stomach. "I haven't *abandoned* my brother," I retort. "I don't even know if suddenly jumping back into his life would be better for him than staying out of it. The situation isn't that simple."

Laoni studies me. "Or are you saying that because you don't want us to question why you're so intent on staying among us?"

I grit my teeth, but I'm not sure how to answer. "If I stay, it'll be because I can't stand the thought that people might end up suffering more without me right here to help with the curse." And because of all the suffering I might be able to save the other humans here from, though I don't think she'll want to hear about that. "And because I'm trying not to upend Jamie's life all over again."

Laoni folds her arms over her chest. "Take another day, then. I want us to be able to come up with a definite plan of action for handling our curse victims by then. We've been living in uncertainty long enough."

I'm not usually a violent person, but right then I'd like nothing more than to punch her right in her smug face. My fingers curl into my palms, but I hold my hands still at my sides. "Fine," I say. Corwin sets his hand on my back, and we walk back out of the building.

You don't need to agree to their demands, he says as we go. *We can insist on more time. We've been living in uncertainty for decades before now.*

I pause, but I can't ignore the constricting sensation in my chest that's been growing tighter since the first moment I found out Jamie was alive. *No. I think I do need to make a decision, not just for them but for me too. I'm not really getting any closer to an answer with all my fretting about it. I'd like to visit Jamie one more time before I'm sure, though.*

I'll make arrangements so that you can travel to the human world first thing in the morning. Corwin's hand moves to grasp my hand. *They were only trying to push their own agenda with their comments, you know. I have no doubts about your loyalty. I know how much you care about your brother.*

I squeeze his hand in return, but his reassurance doesn't erase the guilt still prickling through my gut. Laoni and the others might have been trying to shame me for their own reasons, but that doesn't mean their points were totally wrong. I *do* owe Jamie more than I owe anyone here in the fae realm, don't I? I should be able to find a way to help him when he's obviously struggling, even if it's hard at first.

Tomorrow I'll see him again, and hopefully it'll all become clearer.

"Sylas and the others should be waiting for us in your new home," Corwin reminds me as we set off across the icy fields toward his domain. "I could ask Charles and Beth to come over from the palace and make us all one of their fantastic dinners."

My insides are too tangled up for me to enjoy the thought of putting food inside me. I shake my head. "Not right now. I think I just want to be with all of you for a while, without anyone else there, without anything we're supposed to be doing."

The memory rises up of the time when I felt at my most despondent last month, when the answer to the winter curse was eluding me and I seemed to be failing everyone. I brought Corwin into my bed, and just cuddling against him melted some of my anguish.

Everything we did together *after* cuddling didn't hurt either…

I want to have all my lovers—my mates—around me, to be enveloped in their love. To see just how far we've come… even if we won't take our relationship any further after all.

Corwin takes in my emotions wordlessly. When we step over the threshold on the diamond side of the border castle, he sweeps me off my feet as August likes to do and tucks me against him.

As he heads through the halls to the central rooms where crystal and wood merge, my Seelie lovers emerge from their side of the castle to meet us. Sylas takes in our expressions and frowns.

"My colleagues have been especially hard on our mate today," Corwin says, his use of *our* setting off a glow of warmth inside me just like that. "I think the cure she needs is to be wrapped up in as much adoration as possible."

August's expression also turned solemn when he saw Corwin carrying me, but at that last remark, a grin springs to his face. "I'm all for that."

Whitt arches his eyebrows. "Let's break in that new bedroom of yours, mighty one."

A blush heats my cheeks even though I'm not sure just how thoroughly I want to break in the bedroom right at this moment. "That sounds perfect to me."

As we head up the stairs with their alternating wooden and diamond steps, Sylas draws up beside Corwin and me. "Should we be concerned about your colleagues' current demands, whatever they are?" he asks.

"No," I answer for Corwin. "Mostly they just want me to make a decision before much longer about whether I'm staying here or going back to Jamie. Which I probably should anyway. I've been putting it off, but it's only getting harder to sort out my thoughts, not easier."

A more somber mood settles over our group. Whitt slips his hand around one of my dangling feet and strokes his thumb over the arch. "If there's anything you need to know that would help you get a clearer picture of the situation, come to me without hesitation. And keep in mind that any decision you make now doesn't have to be final. They can't prevent you from changing your mind."

"We'd all fight for your right to return here or there if you wanted something different later on," August adds, the muscles in his shoulders flexing.

Knowing that should comfort me, but instead it only expands the melancholy ache in my chest. They're already preparing to say goodbye to me if that's what I insist on. The sorrow that lances through Corwin at that thought carries through our connection, and I know the other men must be similarly affected. Even considering the possibility of losing any of them hurts me just as much.

I swallow thickly and will down those emotions. Right now I want to be focused on this moment, in case it's the only chance I get to enjoy our shared home with the men I've been so looking forward to sharing it with. My decision can wait for tomorrow.

I haven't seen my fully finished bedroom before. When we step inside, a delighted laugh bubbles out of me. The walls are the same mix of diamond and wood as the other rooms in the middle of the castle, twined together here in delicate swirls. The furniture is a similar mix: a diamond washstand, a wooden wardrobe. The bedposts are wood with diamond spheres glinting at their peaks.

But what most delights me is the size of that bed. They've conjured one that's at least twice the size of those in either of my old bedrooms, more than large enough for all of us to comfortably fit on.

Corwin sets me down gently in the middle of the soft bedspread and then eases back. I can tell from the impressions trickling through our bond that he wants to show the other men he's not staking a greater claim on me, that he's willing to let them come to me first.

August and Whitt pause, studying him. They've never been part of any shared intimacies that involved my newest lover.

Sylas, who initiated our first shared encounter, settles next to me with his shoulders propped against the headboard, his fingers brushing over my hair. Seeing their lord make the first move, the other two climb onto the bed. August sprawls out at the opposite end of the bed and starts massaging my feet. Whitt presses a kiss to my belly and nestles his head against my hip.

Only then does Corwin properly join us, completing the ring of manly warmth around me with his head tucked against my shoulder. I kiss his forehead, run my hand down Sylas's chest, tease my fingers through Whitt's silky hair, and push my sole into August's touch encouragingly.

Just like that, we're all together as one unified collective. The lingering tension that stirred in Corwin at the prospect of navigating this situation fades away into contentment.

It's impossible not to feel like this is exactly where I belong—where we all belong. The love doesn't only pass between me and them but also between the men to each other, even if they share different sorts of affection and respect.

We brought the Seelie and Unseelie together after decades of war. We've challenged both societies' ideas of who could be a proper mate. So much trust and faith has grown between us. How can there be any problem we can't conquer?

But the problem of tomorrow's decision hasn't gone away. When my worries start gnawing at me again, I know just snuggling here in this ring of warmth won't be enough to chase them away. A starker desire ripples through me and collects between my thighs.

I want to know just how well all five of us can come together in every possible way, whether it's only the beginning or a memory I'll be able to hold on to tightly in days to come.

As often, my fae men's keen senses tip them off to the shift in my mood before I've given any purposeful sign. August's caresses become more provoking, traveling up my calf to the sensitive skin of my inner knee. Whitt traces his fingers across my abdomen, his breath spilling hot enough across my hip for me to feel it through my dress. Sylas slips his fingers under my chin and draws my face up to meet his kiss.

And through it all, my soul-twined mate watches with a weird mix of exhilaration and envy. His instinctive possessiveness hasn't totally left him, but he isn't letting it control him.

I want him to be a full part of this interlude. As I kiss Sylas back, I tug on Corwin's shirt. *I need you too, my soul.*

With the silent impression of a groan, he leans in to nip the curve of my neck. My breath hitches against Sylas's mouth.

No matter what happens, nothing can erase what I'm experiencing right now. Nothing can break the love we all share. That much I'm sure of.

The certainty comes with a joy that's bittersweet but also so potent I can't hold it back. I draw back from Sylas just enough to murmur a true name into the air. "*Sole-un-straw.*"

Light shimmers over us like a shower of tiny shooting stars. Corwin exhales sharply, and then he's guiding my mouth to his.

As he kisses me with more passion than I've ever felt from him before, my Seelie men intensify their attentions too. Sylas cups my breasts and nibbles the lobe of my ear. August and Whitt make a joint venture of guiding my dress up to my waist, kissing their way up my legs in tandem. By the time they reach my upper thighs, I'm squirming and soaking my panties.

August pauses for just an instant as if he's worried Corwin will change his mind if things get too intense. I tug on his hair, and he lowers his head to mouth me through the thin fabric over my sex. The heat of that intimate kiss sends a shudder of delight through me. A mewling sound escapes my throat, and Corwin's tongue delves between my lips at their parting, devouring me even more deeply.

Oh, God. I already feel like I'm on the verge of exploding, and not a single piece of clothing is off any of us.

As if sensing that thought, August yanks my panties right off and kisses me skin to skin. The slick of his tongue over my opening has me arching off the bed with a rush of pleasure. Whitt clasps my bottom and holds me up at an even better angle for his brother's attentions, dappling kisses across my hip bone at the same time. When August delves his tongue right inside me, Corwin has to swallow my cry.

But my soul-twined mate isn't selfish. He worships my mouth for a few moments longer and then releases me with a nod to Sylas. As my Seelie arch-lord reclaims my lips, Corwin opens the fastenings on my dress. As soon as he's gained access to my breasts, he lowers his mouth to them and works them over with just as much enthusiasm as August below.

With bliss burning through me from every direction, it's a miracle I keep enough of my head to know I want a little less clothing on the rest of them too. Picking up on that silent wish, Corwin straightens up to peel off his shirt. A tremor of discomforted modesty travels through our bond, but then he announces to the others, "Our mate would prefer not to be alone in her state of undress."

It's an awfully formal way of saying that I'd like them all naked, but it does the trick. Suddenly there are shirts and slacks being shed all around me. In the middle of it, they manage to completely remove my dress as well. I find myself kneeling between my four lovers with them wearing just their boxers, their erections straining against the fabric.

Another urge takes over me that I don't question. I reach for Corwin first, sliding my hand down his lean chest to the waist of his undergarment. "I want to taste all of you."

His breath stutters as I duck my head. I tug the waistband lower to free his shaft and take it into my mouth.

The salty flavor that mingles with his wintery forest scent is familiar now. I swirl my tongue around the corded length. Every twitch of his member, the desperate tensing of his fingers in my hair, and the echoes of the pleasure I'm offering him make me giddy. There are so many ways in which these men have more power than I do, but when it comes to the bedroom, I'm at least their equal. I don't have any more doubt that they want me just as much as I want them.

I move from Corwin to Whitt, freeing my sly strategist in turn. His eyes turn heavy-lidded as he strokes my cheek. "Taste as much as you like."

The scent that clings to every part of him is almost the opposite of Corwin, like sunbaked sand, but I relish it just as much. The groan that spills out of Whitt when I suck hard on his rigid length makes my own sex throb.

I'm tempted to stay there and see how long it takes to draw out Whitt's release with just my mouth, but I don't want to leave my other lovers neglected. I lap the head of his shaft and turn toward August.

The warrior's face has flushed, his eyes shining with both affection and lust. "I'm right here for you, Sweetness," he says in a husky voice.

And he is, his thick member nearly filling my hand as I draw it out. I lick around the tip and then take as much as I can into my mouth. His fingers drag over my scalp with just the right mix of tenderness and tension to set off a wave of sparks. I could drink in his sweetly musky flavor all day.

But I still have one more lover I want to include in this impromptu ritual. I give August a quick kiss on the mouth, our flavors mixing on our lips, and ease around to face Sylas.

The Seelie arch-lord watches me with nothing but love and desire in his dark eye. I tip forward so I can kiss a path down the middle of his chest, over several of his true-name tattoos, before I reach his boxers. When I delve inside them, he presses into my grasp as if he can't help himself. His earthy, smoky scent fills my lungs.

I suck him down slowly, tracing my tongue along the rigid shaft to find the spots that make his muscles tighten and his chest hitch. I'm learning how to make this man come undone. All of these men. They're mine, and I'm theirs, and that'll be true no matter how far away I am at any given moment.

As I draw a rough sound from Sylas's throat, one more hunger shivers through me. I've taken each of them one-by-one, but can I make our union completely literal and make love with all four of them at the same time? See us all reach our releases together?

I don't know, but I have to try. I've managed it with my three Seelie lovers before. One more should be possible.

I ease back, glancing around at the four men, my lips tingling from the use I've just put them to. Corwin shouldn't have to speak this desire for me.

"I want all of you… with me, together," I said. "I'm not sure exactly how…"

When I trail off awkwardly, Corwin smiles, his expression full of heat and affection. "I'd imagine we can accommodate that wish as well as the other," he says in a lower tone than he normally takes on. "I know you've already discovered many of the ways we can pleasure you and you us."

A sharper flare of heat surges through me. I think of him touching my other entrance when we made love in the cave, of Whitt penetrating me there weeks ago, and a heady tingling washes through me.

Through communication that's mostly unspoken, the men move around me, pausing to offer kisses and caresses as we navigate my request. I find myself braced over Sylas, my knees by his hips, my hands braced against his chest as he sprawls back on the bed. He holds my waist to steady me, not to control me. In answer to the question in his dark eye, I rock myself against him so the head of his member slides across my opening. It feels so good I quiver with eagerness.

As I sink down onto him, a deeper pleasure flares through my core. A whimper works its way from my throat.

Whitt gives August a lightly playful nudge. "Do you think you can see to our lady's other needs this time, whelp?"

August mock-glowers at him, any trace of rancor dissolved by the broad smile that stretches his mouth at the same time. "It would be my honor."

He kneels behind me, carefully straddling Sylas's legs, and kisses a scorching path from the middle of my back to the nape of my neck. His fingers work me over, spreading my own liquid and an added slickness he conjures with a murmured word to prepare my other opening.

With the blissful sensations swelling all through my core and up into my abdomen, it's hard to focus. I manage to tug Whitt and then Corwin closer on either side of me. I bow down to kiss Sylas hard and lift up again to kiss the men next to me, gasping against Whitt's mouth when August eases into me.

Oh, that sensation of being doubly filled makes me feel as if I'm soaring and burning up at the same time.

Corwin makes a strained noise as my delight passes into him. I curl my fingers around his jutting erection. As I begin to stroke up and down it, I lean the other way to take Whitt into my mouth for the second time. This time I'm going to see him all the way through to the end.

Relishing all of my men at once doesn't go perfectly smoothly with so many moving parts. Sometimes I become so overwhelmed with the pleasure racing through me that I lose myself in a momentary daze. I have to adjust my position a few times, taking the moment to steal more kisses. But as I sink into the rhythm of the two men thrusting into me, it drives my momentum with the other two until we're swaying together in a rush of heated delight that's swiftly becoming an inferno.

To my surprise, it's Whitt who topples over the edge first, with a hissed curse and a squeeze of my shoulder. After he's flooded my mouth, he pants for a moment and then turns closer attention to every area of my body he can reach to spark more pleasure in me. His thumb swivels over a nipple, both Sylas and August buck into me in unison, and my hand jerks around Corwin's shaft so hard I feel the surge of his impending release. I duck quickly enough to wrap my lips around him just as he reaches his peak.

I rest my hands on Sylas's chest again, sliding them over the sweat that's formed there. He lets out a growl and pumps into me faster. August matches his pace, and all at once I'm hurtling toward my own orgasm at top speed. All I can do is hang on through the tsunami of ecstasy until the final wave crashes over me.

I come apart with a cry that's almost a sob, shaking in my lovers' joint embrace. Sylas groans and August clutches me tighter as they both follow me over the edge.

I end up slumped on the covers in a nest formed by my four mates, their limbs tucked around mine, finding a comfortable space next to each other. When I catch Corwin's gaze, his eyes glitter with the same thrilled satisfaction that's resonating through our connection.

We are five, and we are one.

And tomorrow I have to decide whether keeping us together is the right thing or an avoidance of my true responsibilities.

CHAPTER FOURTEEN

Talia

We've gotten to the sports field outside Jamie's high school just as the last class of the day is getting out. Students are already streaming across the grass and the sidewalk around it. I pick up my pace, worried that I might have missed him. If he doesn't head to our aunt and uncle's house from here, I won't know where to find him.

August and Kesral have accompanied me for the same reasons as before. In a way, Corwin is following me too, sharply aware of my emotional state through our bond. I can tell he wants to know the second I've made a decision—and to be able to weigh in if I only find myself more confused.

I hurry over to the school building as fast as my limp allows, scanning the teens ambling around us. To my relief, it's only a minute or two before my gaze snags on a familiar head of curly brown hair.

Jamie is meandering around the side of the school, talking with another guy as they look at papers they're both holding. The vibe of their conversation strikes me as more businesslike than friendly—maybe they're supposed to work together on a project or something.

From seeing my brother eating on his own at lunch the other day, I don't get the impression he has much in the way of friends here at school. He must have met his girlfriend and the people they were hanging out with in his photos somewhere else.

There are so many other people around, it's hard to get close enough to him to pick up anything but fragments of what he and the other guy are saying. My fae companions and I have to weave between the dispersing students as we keep pace with the two of them. They head off across the field, where the other teens are starting to gather in clusters, leaving more room for us to maneuver. Would it be too much to ask for Jamie to stop walking and finish his conversation standing still?

A bunch of the teens nearby glance toward Jamie and his partner as they pass. I recognize a couple of the guys who hassled him at lunch the other day. One of them points to Jamie and makes a grossed-out expression for the benefit of the others, who titter with laughter.

Jamie keeps talking to the guy with him, but I can tell he's noticed the attention. His jaw has tightened, his gaze staying studiously on the paper he's motioning to.

I bristle on his behalf, glaring at the bullies, not that they can tell anyone's pissed off with them. Jamie's partner rubs his mouth, looking like he wants to be anywhere but with my brother.

A dog's bark reaches my ears from somewhere behind me. I don't pay much attention to it, too focused on my brother, until the pounding of heavy paws comes after it. A squirrel streaks past us over the grass, making for a tree at the other side of the field—and a big black hound charges after it, leash streaming, right into Jamie's path.

It doesn't look all that much like the massive wolves the Seelie can shift into. Its fur is shorter, its muzzle boxier, its ears floppy. As big as it is, I think the top of its head would only reach the level of Sylas's shoulders when he's in wolf form. But the sudden movement, the flash of bared teeth, and the general canine shape are enough to make my pulse hiccup in the first moment before I recognize what it is, even though I've had a lot of time and practice getting over my fears.

Jamie flinches so hard the papers he was holding and the book he had them propped on thump to the ground. He jerks back a couple of steps, a panicked sound escaping his mouth, a tremor running through his body.

He hugs himself but can't seem to stop shaking. My heart wrenches with the urge to run right to him, throw my arms around him, and tell him he'll be okay.

Before I can, a mocking laugh rings out. The bunch of teens who were giggling over Jamie's appearance are sauntering closer, the two guys from before in the lead.

"Monster boy is afraid of a pet dog?" one sneers, glancing over to where the dog's owner has finally caught up with the hound and grabbed its leash. "Pretty sad getting terrified over something that's a whole lot less terrifying to look at than you."

Now I want to wrap Jamie up in a hug *and* tell August to rip out that jerk's throat so he'll find out just how much reason my brother has to react like this. I step forward, my hands flexing, the words rising from my chest to ask August to take the magic off me so they can see me.

So what if I seem to come out of nowhere? It couldn't be more obvious that my brother needs me—he needs me right *now*.

"Wait!" Kesral says, probably with instructions not to jeopardize the secrecy of the fae world. He grabs my arm before I can get close enough that they'll feel my presence even if they can't see me.

I turn to tell him off, but my voice catches at Jamie's movement. His shoulders still rigid, he bends to pick up his things from the ground. There's a bit of a stutter to his next couple of breaths, but then it evens out. He's no longer shaking or cringing like I would have been just months ago when shocked into the memories of the past.

But then, I guess Jamie's had a chance to work through some of those fears too. Maybe he hasn't gotten to confront his attackers face to face, but he's had access to things *I* never got, like therapists and years of life outside a cage.

He straightens up and faces his bully. Even his partner is staring at him, having backed away as if to avoid any association with Jamie at all.

"You got a problem with me, McCarty?" the other guy says, folding his arms over his chest and raising his chin like a dare.

Jamie fixes him with a cool but cutting stare that I suspect Whitt would appreciate. "Not really. See, the thing is, I don't care if you think I look terrifying or whatever. Why the hell *should* I care what a dick like you thinks?"

The bully's jaw drops. His friends stay totally silent with varying expressions of shock. It takes a moment before the guy manages to speak, and then it comes out with a sputter. "Who the fuck do you figure you are? *Everyone* thinks you're a deformed loser who belongs in a freak show, you know."

Jamie shrugs. "Then 'everyone' can go fuck themselves. I don't need some stamp of approval from you. I've got a family and a girlfriend and friends who don't think I'm a loser, and they matter to me way more than a bunch of random idiots. And you know what? Because *I'm* not a prick, I hope you never have to go through what I did to end up looking like this."

He makes a swift gesture toward the scars on his face and then turns on his heel to walk away. I'm gaping now too, but with as much admiration as shock.

"Look at the spine on him," Kesral says with an approving chuckle.

August slips his arm around me and nuzzles my hair. "It must run in the family."

Maybe it does. My brother's stronger than I guessed. But I pull away from August to follow Jamie, my heart thumping harder. Was he really so confident in what he just said, or was it a bold front to cover up the pain he didn't want the bullies to see?

I doubt that their comments left him completely unscathed, but they don't appear to have done any major damage even to his mood. As Jamie leaves the schoolyard behind, he pulls out his phone. I manage to peek over and see he's texting the girl from the pictures in his room, who just sent him a selfie and a message asking him to meet up with her after dinner.

Sure, Jamie types back. *I can't wait. But I should warn you, I just told off the second most popular guy at school, so being seen with me is probably bad for your reputation.* He adds a winking emoji at the end and grins as he sends the message off.

His girlfriend replies a moment later with a laughing emoji and the words, *Who needs a reputation? I'd rather have you, thank you very much.*

They banter back and forth a bit more, and by the time Jamie tucks the phone into his pocket and slips into a convenience store to grab a snack, he looks totally relaxed.

He's okay.

The knowledge settles over me with a weirdly bittersweet sense of relief. He handled that situation all on his own, no need for a big sister to come running to his rescue. Maybe the trauma of the attack isn't gone, but he's obviously figuring out his way past that.

What could I do for him that he isn't already doing for himself? If I insisted on staying and pushing my way into his life, would it honestly be for his benefit, or would I only be looking to absolve my own guilt?

I can't completely walk away from him. I don't *want* to. But maybe… Maybe it would be all right for me to go back to the life I've made for myself away from here and just check in on him every now and then.

Something about that idea sends an uncomfortable twinge through my gut. If I only stop by once a month or something like that, a lot could change without me realizing it. If he was in serious trouble, I'd want to know right away.

As we trail after Jamie along the sidewalk, I worry at my lower lip. He heads into a bowling alley next, and ducking inside after him, I see him setting up behind the shoe counter. So he's got a part-time job too.

"The kid seems pretty independent," August remarks.

"Yeah." I grapple with my thoughts as we return to the street. If there's anyone who could help me with this, it'd be August, right?

I touch his arm. "You know a lot of medical and bodily magic, right? Is there some kind of spell you could cast that would sort of connect me to Jamie from a distance—that would alert me somehow if he was in major physical or emotional distress?"

August cocks his head. "I can think of a couple of strategies that might work. But they'd require a sort of token to attach the spell to. Something you'd keep close to you and something he would too."

I glance down at myself, and my gaze falls on the bronze bracelet Sylas gave me. As I trace my fingers over the smooth metal, an image sparks in my mind that brings a smile to my lips.

I don't have to leave my brother completely. I can give him a little piece of our family to hold onto. He might not totally understand it, but from what I've seen, I think there's a good chance he'll keep it nearby.

"You can conjure up some bronze even here, right?" I say. "I want to make him a cuff bracelet that matches mine. We'll use those."

August beams at me. "Whatever you need, Sweetness."

It only takes him a few minutes to construct a bracelet nearly identical to mine, just a little larger and more manly-looking, with a notch in the bottom so Jamie can slide it on if he decides to wear it since he can't magically expand it.

"I'll do the finishing touches," I say with a rush of exhilaration. It really will be a present from me.

Grasping the metal loop in my hands, I focus intently on it. "*Fee-doom-ace-own.*"

With my will and the syllables, I etch four names into the inside of the bracelet: Dad's, Mom's, *Talia*, and *Jamie*. Sweat has broken out on the back of my neck by the time I'm done, but I hand the bracelet to August with a deep sense of satisfaction.

He takes my own bracelet as well and sits down on a patch of lawn to work the more intensive magic I requested. I glance around, realizing there's one more thing I'd like to include.

"Do you have a piece of paper and something to write with?" I ask Kesral, figuring I can pilfer one from somewhere around here if not.

The winter fae man has been watching the proceedings with obvious curiosity. He looks almost pleased now to be brought in on our little mission.

"I can create them for you," he says, and murmurs a few magic-laced syllables of his own. In a matter of moments, he's offering me a slip of fine paper like the stuff in Whitt's books and a narrow stick of charcoal.

I debate the message for a while and finally settle on something short and to the point. *Always with you*, I scrawl on the paper.

By the time August has finished his spellwork, evening is descending on us. We sneak to my aunt and uncle's house, and I slip through the back door to Jamie's bedroom. Folding the note around the bracelet, I set it on his pillow for him to find when he gets back from his date.

I straighten up and look down at it, weighing my decision and the ache in my chest. Am I doing the right thing—for me? For him?

I won't know for sure until more time has passed, but after seeing his strength today, it feels right. I will be with him, just not every moment of every day. The fae *and* the humans back in the fae world need me so much more.

Taking a deep breath, I head back out to meet August and Kesral. "Okay," I say. "Let's go home."

As we head back to the park, a trace of dread creeps into my stomach. I rub my fingers over my bracelet, but my apprehension has nothing to do with Jamie.

The other arch-lords were very eager to see me gone from their world. How are they going to react when they find out they can't get rid of me so easily after all?

CHAPTER FIFTEEN

Corwin

"You're not normally this cheerful when we have to go talk to your colleagues," Talia says in a teasing tone, glancing at me over her shoulder from where she's standing in front of the full-length mirror. She called me into her bedroom to inspect the outfit she's chosen for the meeting. Rather than one of her Seelie friend's elaborate creations, she's gone with a subdued and practical gown completely in the winter fae style—one of my own craftsmen's creations.

"I suppose I don't typically have quite so much to be cheerful about," I reply, a smile tugging at my lips. As much practice as I've had keeping my emotions bottled up, it's hard not to grin like some kind of maniac.

She's staying. There'll be minor compromises to be made to allow her to watch over her brother, of course, but she isn't returning to the human world for any substantial length of time. I get to have my soul-twined mate by my side where she's meant to be.

I doubt my colleagues will be anywhere near as enthusiastic about that fact as I am, but I can't bring myself to care. She's *my* mate. The

Heart has willed it. Not even the most arrogant of arch-lords can put up much argument to that fact.

Talia smiles back at me. She does a slow twirl in front of the mirror, careful of her wounded foot in her usual boots, and smooths down the dress's skirt. "I thought if I go looking as much as possible like I belong here, they might be a little more open to my request."

Not just lovely to behold but so keen-minded as well. I nod. "I think that was the right choice. But we still want you to look an arch-lord's lady as well. Perhaps… Wait here a moment."

I duck out of the room and hurry to my own, where I left a jewelry box I meant to offer her when it seemed like a good time. I'm sure she'll appreciate it now when it'll support her goals as well as amplifying her beauty.

The box is cool against my fingers, a mix of ebony wood and silver not so different from the blend of oak and diamond making up this castle, wound together in an intricate pattern. It holds several treasures passed down through my family. When I step into Talia's bedroom with it, I open it up and take out the piece I was thinking of: a silver necklace dappled with tiny, pale blue diamonds that shimmer like sunlight on snow.

"This was my grandmother's," I tell her, going to her to clasp it around her neck. "The first arch-lord to rule from Heart's Cadence."

I adjust the necklace, resisting the urge to let my hands linger against Talia's smooth skin, and step back to take in the whole picture. The dress was only a little on the plain side, and that simple piece elevates her ensemble from professional to honor-worthy.

Talia touches the necklace, awed gratitude carrying through our bond. "Thank you. It looks perfect."

"It is perfect. I dare them to try to say no to you when you look like that."

She shoots me a wry glance. "Somehow I think they'll take that dare. They don't even like me when I'm helping them. They're definitely not going to be happy about me poking around seeing what they might be doing wrong."

She speaks easily enough, but I can sense the worries tangled inside her. She does have an accurate measure of the other arch-lords.

I rest my hands on her shoulders and press a quick kiss to the back of her head. "You have a reasonable request. I'll speak up for your right to make it, and so will Sylas—and perhaps even Neve and that Donovan fellow will support it too. If they resist, they'll only be admitting they have something untoward to hide."

Talia makes a disgruntled sound. "But they might prefer to admit that than to have it outright exposed." She sighs. "I wish we could at least have the meeting here instead of in the Hall."

"Laoni wanted everything to be 'equal,' and since we had the last joint meeting of the arch-lords on the summer side…" I give her an apologetic grimace in the mirror. "After this, it'll be balanced out, and perhaps we can convince them to make use of the border castle for all future collective conferences."

There's a knock on the door, and Whitt's dry voice carries through. "We're due across the way in a few minutes. Is the mite ready to go? Don't keep her all to yourself now."

My instinct is to bristle at the word "mite," but Talia's internal reaction is all warm amusement, so obviously the nickname isn't meant to offend.

"I'm coming," she calls out, giving her dress one last straightening tug, and clasps my hand to draw me with her to the door.

Sylas's strategist has dressed sharply for this meeting as well, although from what I've observed, Whitt is the most clothing-conscious of Talia's Seelie men at any time. His bright brown hair, though, is rumpled as if he hasn't done more than run his fingers through it. I suppose I should be glad it's Sylas who'll be doing any talking out of the bunch.

Whitt looks Talia over with an appreciative gleam in his eyes that raises my hackles all over again even though I approve of it. As I tamp down on the jealousy I've mostly but not entirely conquered, he takes Talia's other hand so we can lead her downstairs together.

"Let's go see what those feather-brained winter arch-lords can find to complain about today," he says breezily.

Talia mock-glowers at him. "It isn't as if all the summer arch-lords have been so welcoming. If you're coming along, you'd better play nice."

Whitt presses his free hand to his chest as if in shock. "Of all the things I may be called, I'd think you'd know by now that 'nice' isn't one of them."

My mate elbows him teasingly, and he grins. I keep my mouth shut, not sure how to respond to the ribbing banter.

Out of the three Seelie men, Whitt is the one I'm the least at ease with still. Sylas and I have formed a sort of understanding as equals, both dedicated to Talia and the fae folk we represent. August wears his emotions clearly on his face and is generally straightforward in his speaking. Whitt is the type of fae who'll happily weave a story that skirts the very edge of lying and laugh about it later. Which is the sort of temperament I suppose one would want in a spymaster, but that doesn't make me any surer of where anything stands with him.

He adores Talia, though. That much I'm certain of from the interactions I've observed both in person and through her memories. Even now, there's no missing the fondness that brightens his expression in her presence. That's all I really need to know.

Sylas and August are waiting downstairs. "Beautiful as always, my love," Sylas says to Talia, who beams at him, and we head out through the broad doorway on my side of the castle toward the Hall of the Heart.

The other Seelie arch-lords have come across the border from their own domains. We spot Donovan and a couple of his cadre-chosen crossing the icy plain and entering the Hall before we reach it. Halfway there, Zelpha and Verik catch up with us. The discussion today could affect a great deal about how things are run in both realms, and we want our closest associates quickly apprised.

Laoni and Uzziah are already at the table when we arrive, along with Celia and Donovan, who's just getting into his place. Terisse arrives a moment later, and Neve wanders in last, on her own and not appearing at all concerned about that fact. She grants Talia a smile that makes me more hopeful about her taking our side.

Laoni is scowling, her expression even sourer than it's been the last few times we spoke. "I understand your mate has come to a decision about her living situation," she says to me briskly. "Let's hear it."

I can tell from her tone that she's already reasonably certain what that decision is and she isn't pleased about it. My body tenses, but I let Talia speak for herself. The more she shows she can hold her own among them, the harder it'll be for them to dismiss her.

Talia raises her chin, looking impressively regal. "After further observation and reflection, I believe that it's in everyone's best interests, including mine and my brother's, if I stay here in the fae world. My brother has adapted fairly well to the trauma he's been through, and I don't want to risk dredging up the past by coming back into his life out of nowhere. And it'll be much easier for me to continue helping with the curse if I'm here."

Uzziah makes a scoffing sound that sets my teeth on edge.

Celia narrows her eyes. "Are you sure you've made that judgment with all the factors fully considered and not simply following the desires of your heart? I can understand you have many reasons you'd *want* to think it best to remain here."

Sylas stirs. "Neither I nor my cadre nor Arch-Lord Corwin, that I'm aware of, have done anything but support Talia's right to choose where she goes. We haven't swayed her in any direction."

I incline my head in acknowledgment, and Talia sets her hands firmly on the tabletop. "I've thought long and hard about this. I'm completely confident in my decision."

Laoni's lips curl. "And we're supposed to go by a human's reasoning rather than what we fae feel is best for our peoples? Are we the arch-lords here or is she?"

"We are," I say tersely. "And not all of those arch-lords feel she should leave. In fact, I haven't heard any clear explanation for why that is a more practical course of action. Are you sure those of you pushing for my mate to live elsewhere aren't being swayed by *your* emotions rather than reason?"

Laoni's eyes flash with anger as I knew they would, but I don't regret my remark one bit.

Before she can retort, Donovan shifts on his feet with a hint of discomfort. "It will definitely be easier tending to the curse with Talia close by. Especially for the Unseelie when each of the victims requires separate treatment."

"There are other factors to consider," Celia puts in. "This isn't truly her world. Her presence may have other effects that are less desirable."

"Like what?" Sylas asks, fixing her with a level stare. "I've asked before and never had any proof offered: has her relationship with any of us present affected us or anyone else negatively in any way?"

Terisse's jaw works. "We can't be certain that it won't in the future."

"But it hasn't yet," Talia breaks in. "It's because of the close relationship I've formed with fae on both sides of the border that you're able to have meetings like this rather than continuing to *kill* each other in the first place, isn't it? Why make up problems that don't exist yet when I can help so much with the biggest problem you do know about?"

I fight back a smile at her tart remarks. That would only enrage my colleagues who are against her decision even more. But all of them fall silent, obviously not having any real argument to push forward.

"Actually," Talia goes on, gathering confidence, "Arch-Lord Celia brought up a point that leads into the other subject I wanted to discuss today. I may not theoretically belong here, but it was fae who brought me here, and you've brought plenty of other humans into your world as well—humans you've kept for their entire lives."

"What of it?" Uzziah demands.

Talia gazes at him and then the others around the table, not letting her determined stance waver. "I've done a lot to help improve the lives of the fae by fending off the curse. I think I have a duty to step up for *my* people who are living among you too. I'd like to visit more of the domains on both sides of the border with a decree from the arch-lords that the lords and ladies are to allow me free access to talk to their human servants."

Laoni draws in a hiss of breath. "There we have it. Your dust-destined mate is looking for ways to make trouble already. What purpose could that mission serve us?"

"Watch how you speak to my lady," I say, just barely holding back the rancor I want to aim at her. I have to keep my cool in this company, but I can't stand by while they insult my mate either.

Talia turns to Laoni, her voice still even. "It will serve the people you've forced to become citizens of the fae world. When I've seen enough, I expect to have recommendations on improving the treatment they're currently facing. We can debate exactly which you'll agree to then, but I won't stand by quietly while others like me are being drugged and tricked into slavery."

A flare of pride warms my chest. How could anyone doubt that she's meant to stand beside me as my lady?

But naturally Laoni doesn't see it that way. Her shoulders go rigid, her jaw even tighter than before. When she speaks, it's in a tone venomous enough to kill. "It's not your place to question traditions that have been in place for thousands of years longer than you've been alive. Your freak circumstances might have given you the appearance of power, but don't forget that you're still a dung-body underneath."

An emotional wince travels from Talia into me, but my anger has already rushed to the front of my mind. All at once, my reserve seems ridiculous.

Why should I care what these people think any more than Talia does? What good is there in courting the favor of those who deal it out so grudgingly and unfairly? From the very start of this conversation—from the first moment Talia came among us, really—they've shown nothing but disrespect to her and our bond.

They're never going to change their views until they see some consequences for them.

I wrap my hand around one of Talia's and aim a glare at Laoni. "How you shame the Heart by speaking of the one it's blessed with so much—the one who's given us so much—with such insults. We don't need to stand here and listen to your hostility any longer. My mate has stated her request. Unless you can come up with a logical reason to deny it, not based on the prejudiced assumption that she matters less than the rest of us, I have no interest in hearing anything further spoken against it. We'll proceed whether we have your acceptance or not."

Talia glances at me, startled, but when I draw her away from the table, she walks with me as steadily as she can, her head held high. I catch a muffled chuckle from someone behind us, and then Sylas is striding to catch up. My coterie members and his cadre-chosen follow behind us.

"Corwin!" Uzziah calls, but I don't even look back. They need to do more than that to earn my attention again.

As we step out into the wintry air beyond the building's walls to head back to the border castle, Talia squeezes my hand. The emotions churning within her are a potent mix of amazement, trepidation, and… love. *I can't believe you told them off like that. That you walked right out on them.*

I know it might lead to more difficulties down the road, I start, but she shakes her head.

I was impressed. I don't know if it'll make any difference to how they treat me in the long run… but I appreciated that you'd stand up for me that much anyway.

A lump rises in my throat. *I always will, my soul.*

"Well," August says a little awkwardly, rubbing his hands together. "After that, I think we could all use a good meal to wash away the bad taste left in our mouths. Talia, do you want to join me in making the first epic dinner of your new home?"

A little more of the tension fades from my mate as she smiles at him. "That sounds wonderful."

When we reach the castle, Zelpha and Verik set off to fill the rest of my coterie in, Zelpha giving me a jaunty salute and an approving smile as she turns away. Talia and August make for the kitchen.

Sylas pauses in the winter front hall and studies me. "Should we be prepared for any fallout from that move?"

I manage a strained laugh. "I'm not sure. I've never defied my colleagues that blatantly before. I suppose we'll see. What about your own?"

He shrugs. "Donovan is already friendly to us. I can deal with Celia if she has any further concerns. I have a few things to see to with my pack, but I'll return in time for dinner." The corners of his mouth twitch upward. "Knowing August, it'll be at least a couple of hours before he can see through his full vision of this feast."

He strides off, leaving me in the hall—with Whitt, who's lingered nearby. He's eyeing me too, with a more appraising air than I felt from his lord. My skin prickles uneasily, but then an easy grin stretches across his face.

"You'd pick her over any of them, wouldn't you, Lord Bird?" he says.

The nickname irks me, but not enough that I'd focus on that rather than the important part of his question. "In an instant," I reply automatically.

Not one of my colleagues has earned more loyalty from me than Talia has. I'll do what's best for my people as well… but what's best for my people is having her with us, protected and free.

And loved.

Whitt tips his head to me. For the first time since I met him, I have the sense I'm seeing the real man, not a carefully constructed façade. "I'm glad," he says. "That'll make things easier for all of us. And it's what she deserves."

I allow myself a little smile in return. "I couldn't agree more about that."

He motions to me. "Come on then, you chilly raven. Let's see if we can't move this dinner along a little faster than those two can manage on their own. I could eat a horse already."

I've drawn a firm line with my fellow arch-lords for the first time since I took this position, and no doubt they're fuming about it. But as I walk with Whitt down the hall to the kitchen, a sense of peace settles over me greater than any I've felt before.

CHAPTER SIXTEEN

Talia

I'm woken by a gentle rapping on my door. August stirs next to me on the bed, looping his brawny arm around my waist and nuzzling the back of my neck. I rest my arm over his as I rub my eyes with my other hand. "Yes?"

Zelpha's voice carries through. "I'm sorry to disturb you, but we've got visitors. A woman struck by the curse… and rather a lot of her flock too." Her tone turns a bit dry with that last bit.

I bite back a groan, which really wouldn't be fair of me, and swipe the stray locks back from my face. "All right. I'll be down as soon as I can."

"You don't have to rush too much. Corwin's wrangling them for the moment, and they're pretty pleased just being attended to by an arch-lord."

Sensing our conversation through the bond, my soul-twined mate sends a tendril of confirmation, reassurance, and apology my way. I get the vague impression of him directing the carriages that've shown up over to the stretch of plain by the Heart where I offered my cure last time. I guess that's going to become the standard healing spot.

August hugs me closer and presses a kiss to my shoulder. "Always so busy, Sweetness."

"I'm the only one who can keep them alive." But my busy-ness is only going to get worse as the curse victims who need their cure repeated multiply.

Pushing aside that thought and the sinking sensation in my gut, I roll over to give August a quick kiss on the lips and then push myself upright.

The border castle is going to be my primary home from here on, and all of my mates decided I shouldn't be left alone there, especially when we can't be totally certain of good intentions from every other fae around. At least one of my men will be staying with me every night, and Corwin plans to have a coterie member on hand as much as possible. Both he and Sylas have also assigned a rotation of staff from their packs to see to cleaning and other basic needs… and a couple of guards to monitor the entrances.

No one can pass through those doorways without taking the border oath of non-violence, but we all know that fae are adept at finding loopholes.

I limp over to my wardrobe and grab a dress that'll look reasonably lady-like. Most of my clothes have been moved here already, but the bedroom still feels new, not quite home yet. I've only spent a few nights in it so far.

As I give my face a quick wash and dampen down flyaway hairs at the basin, August ducks out to return to his bedroom in the joint castle. By the time I've pulled on my boots, he's back and dressed, his handsome face ruddy from its own washing. "I'll walk you over," he says.

"I'm sure Zelpha would, if you need to get back to anything in Hearth-by-the-Heart," I say.

He shakes his head. "I'm supposed to run through some training exercises with a bunch of the pack later this morning, but at this time, I expected to still be sleeping." He winks at me to show he isn't at all bothered by the disruption, though. "And I owe you breakfast after you finish your curse-curing work."

"Corwin's kitchen staff have been sending meals over," I remind him.

He claps his hands together with a grin. "I'm sure I can come up with something fitting to accompany their spread. And you should eat a little before you get to work too."

His good cheer puts me in a better mood. He hustles ahead of me to grab some berries he brought from the summer realm, and I pop them into my mouth a few at a time as I make my way to the door, focusing on the tart sweetness and not the task ahead of me.

It isn't as if we're facing that much of an intrusion. I'll go out, see to the curse victim in a matter of minutes, and then there'll be the whole rest of the day ahead of us.

We step outside into the cool wind, and I'm grateful again that the weather is never too intense close to the Heart. A few sparkling flakes of snow tumble around us, the sky hazed with pale clouds overhead.

The crowd gathered around the Heart looks to be about the same size as the last one that arrived, a few dozen fae. Don't they have anything better to do than come all this way just to watch me brush a few tears to someone's cheek?

That thought sends a prick of guilt through my stomach when our guests turn to watch me approach, so many of their faces lit with eager hope. Maybe they're not ready to see all humans as anywhere near their equals, but they've been willing to see me as someone special—someone worthy of gratitude and awe.

Corwin raises his hand in greeting where he's standing right in front of the Heart. The pulsing glow makes the blue tone in his dark curls shift along their curves. He smiles at me with another tingle of apology through our connection.

It's fine, I say. *This is one of the reasons I stayed here.*

The folk must have hurried the cursed woman to us as soon as she showed the first signs of the curse. Her skin is eerily pale but not yet tinged with blue, and she's managing to keep her back fairly straight in the chair someone brought for her, though her shoulders are hunched. She takes in my approach with a weird mix of excitement and fear playing across her features.

I can't imagine what it must be like to be on the other end of the curse. To have to wonder whether the cure might not work this time, or whether the supernatural chill will really ever leave once it's taken hold.

Here I am worrying about how healing them affects *me* when they're the ones with their lives on the line.

Just like that, I'm a little choked up. I walk up to the woman and dip my head in acknowledgment. "I hope your journey here wasn't too long or uncomfortable. I'll do my best to see you back to your normal self as quickly as possible."

She manages a smile that seems to take some effort. "Thank you, my lady. The stories about your generosity are obviously true."

Ignoring the niggling of discomfort that comes with the idea of the fae spreading stories about me, even good ones, I focus on the ache of grief inside me. How must it feel to find yourself suddenly on the brink of death? Imagine all the things I'd be horrified at losing if some horrible illness struck me out of nowhere. There's so much more I want to do with the life I've only just gotten back…

She must have so many people she'll leave behind, so many dreams unfulfilled. And all her hopes of survival rest on me. Even a couple of months ago, she'd have had no hope at all. No choice but to slowly seize up until she was locked inside her own body even more thoroughly than Aerik locked me in that cage…

At the first burn of tears behind my eyes, I turn away. August stands at a careful distance without a word, Corwin silent too as he gives me the space to follow my instincts.

One tear and another slips down my cheeks, the cold air nipping at the wetness. I brush my fingers across my face, suck in a breath, and face the woman again.

Her posture stiffens as I step toward her, as if she's afraid to find out whether it'll actually work. Afraid that if it doesn't, that'll be her death sentence right there. But she holds still as my fingertips graze her cheek and inhales sharply when warmth spreads from the spot where I touched. When her gaze meets mine again, a glint that's almost watery is dancing in her eyes.

"Thank you," she murmurs, her voice gone rough. "You truly are a lady for us all."

"The Heart's lady!" someone calls out amid the crowd. Other voices rise in agreement. The folk of the woman's flock close in around us, checking her over to make sure she's recovering, peering at me with open amazement. I manage to smile back at them, not sure how to respond. What would they expect from me?

Most of them bow, some lower than I've ever seen anyone bow to Corwin or Sylas. Then a strident voice carries from the fringes of the crowd. "All right. The cure is done. You'd best get back to your homes and allow for a full healing."

I glance up to see Laoni has come over with several other fae. The visiting flock gives a few reluctant mutters, but they drift toward their carriages after offering me more praises.

They only make it halfway to the vehicles before someone near the front of the group points into the distance. "There are more coming!"

He's right. A few more large carriages are soaring into view, heading for our plateau around the Heart. Everyone stops to watch their arrival. Laoni frowns, her brow creasing, but she doesn't seem to want to be too forceful in shooing the first set of visitors away. She does still need to keep some good will as arch-lord.

What do you think this is about? I ask Corwin. *Were you expecting them?*

He gives an inward shake of his head. *It can't be another curse victim. There's never been two anywhere near this close together.*

The curse has been steadily intensifying in both severity and its pace, though. But when the carriages come to a stop and another crowd pours out, I recognize the man being carried over the side by his mate.

It isn't a new curse victim but an old one—the second fae I healed successfully, on the day of my confirmation ceremony. He's been hit a second time just like Fina was.

I suppose it works out that you're already here, Corwin says, but some concern carries through in his voice.

My chest has constricted. It *is* better that I help both victims one after the other rather than being called back hours later. But this is just a preview of what my life will become more and more like as the curse takes greater hold, isn't it? How will I be able to accomplish anything else I want to when they need me so much, so often?

How can I possibly complain when they're the ones freezing to death?

I swallow down my frustrations, not wanting to show my discomfort when both the new arrivals and the original visitors are gazing at me so adoringly... worshipfully. Without even looking at Laoni, I can feel her critical eyes fixed on me too. She doesn't like the standing I've gained among her people at all. Too bad for her she can't do anything about it.

I focus on the man who needs my help, my mouth slanting into a bittersweet smile. "I'm glad you could make it to me before you're too ill, but I'm sorry you needed to come back to me at all."

He manages to shrug with a bit of a hitch to the movement. "It is what it is. I'm grateful I have you to turn to, my lady."

His mate lowers him to the ground and sits next to him, even though she shivers being so close to his chilly body. The members of his flock who joined him gather around, and the other flock drifts back over to observe this new spectacle.

I think of all the fae who died before I came—of Corwin's father, of his former best friend and the lover who betrayed him, of the hundreds of others who succumbed to the cursed ice with no one to push it back. So many lives lost in such a horrible way.

And what will happen when I'm gone? To the fae, to the humans living here that I haven't even started to properly defend...

The tears return, hotter than before. I go through the same show of hiding them, wiping them away, and then reaching out to the cursed man. As my fingers slide over his cheek, he sighs in relief before the warmth even sparks beneath his skin. As if my touch on its own is enough to tell him everything will be all right.

Except it won't. The curse will come back for him again and again, until my days are full of crying these tears of temporary healing.

An unexpected sense of panic twists around my stomach, as if time is slipping through my fingers with every breath.

The man bows his head and his mate quickly squeezes my forearm in thanks. The two flocks exclaim to each other about what a marvel I am and how wonderful it is that the Heart has blessed me with this power… And my gaze settles on Laoni again.

Her face is stern and what I can hear of her voice is terse as she orders her staff to get the visitors moving toward their carriages. A muscle in her jaw flexes. She *hates* that I'm getting so much recognition, doesn't she?

But I have it all the same. And maybe—maybe I can use this new power in my favor like I have the others I've discovered. I tried to wield my possible influence once, just encouraging that other flock to consider their treatment of humans. What if I could turn the social pressure of their devotion to me into some kind of leverage here?

A flicker of uneasy excitement darts through my chest. The pieces of the idea click together in my head, and I step forward before the visiting flocks move any farther away. Corwin gives me an encouraging nod. I push the words out, not letting myself second-guess my impromptu plan.

"Thank you all for the honor you're offering me even though I'm not fae," I say, pitching my voice to carry. "It means so much to me to have your respect and admiration. I hope to discover how many of the other humans in your realm have talents and skills to offer that you might not have realized. If Arch-Lord Laoni will agree, I'd love to start by speaking with the humans she has seen fit with her keen judgment to bring into her domain."

Laoni's gaze jerks to me, sharpening into a glare for just an instant before a chorus of approval swells through the crowd. "Yes, of course, the blessed human lady should see to the others of her kind," someone near me says.

Another nods, beaming. "Who knows what other good Lady Talia may be able to do for us?"

I don't exactly like that I've had to frame it more about what the humans might be able to do for them than my fellow mortals deserving lives in their own right, but if it gets me to my goal, I'll take it.

I keep my eyes fixed on Laoni, waiting for her response. Corwin steps up beside me and sets his hand on my shoulder, signaling his support for my request. *She's going to be angry, but I have to say I think it'll be worth it.*

Everyone is watching Laoni expectantly now. She glances around, her lips pressing flat, and then forces her mouth into a smile. How can she say no to my request when it's phrased like that? And once she's given her word here before the Heart and so many of her own flock-folk and others, she won't want to shame herself by going back on it.

"An excellent idea," she says with just a slight edge to her tone. "We can certainly make arrangements for that."

Arrangements that might take the rest of my lifetime, she's probably thinking. I put on the sweetest smile I can manage myself. "Perfect. I could come by tomorrow. I wouldn't trouble you at all. You could simply leave instructions with your staff that they should show me to your human servants. I'll have someone from my mate's coterie attend to me."

Laoni manages to keep her expression impassive, but I have the feeling she'd be killing me with her stare right now if she could. "I suppose that would be acceptable," she replies grudgingly.

The gathered flock-folk let out a little cheer. Corwin dips his head graciously to his colleague. "We appreciate your openness, Arch-Lord Laoni."

I turn back toward my castle with lighter spirits. Even with my duties for the curse, I can still take a stand for the other humans here.

Now I just need to figure out what I'm going to do once I see just how horrible their situation is in Laoni's domain.

CHAPTER SEVENTEEN

Talia

"You're lucky I like you as much as I do, Talia," Zelpha remarks in a wry voice. "Because spending the day hanging out in Heart's Resilience is not my idea of a fun pastime."

"It's not mine either," I say, looking ahead to the glinting fortress of Laoni's castle. The pale metal walls and spires look elegant and intimidating at the same time. The building reminds me of a cage more than I like. "But if we can make a case for changing how the arch-lords are treating the humans in their domains, then we have a much better chance of getting the other lords and ladies on board. I guess Laoni's main strength is metalwork?"

Zelpha nods. "That place was her father's construction, though she's added bits to it here and there. Solid iridium. Not what I'd want to be surrounded by day in and day out, but we all have our own tastes." She makes a face as if to say she finds Laoni's particularly questionable.

We tramp the last short distance across the plain, our boots crunching in the thin layer of newly fallen snow. As we approach the front doors, our wavering reflections move to meet us. *That's* not unsettling at all. I restrain a shiver.

The door opens, and one of Laoni's guards ushers us inside. "We're ready for you, Lady Talia," he says stiffly. He doesn't sound any happier about my visit than his boss was. I hope she didn't take out too much of her frustration over my gambit on her staff.

I offer him a tentative smile. "Wonderful. Where can we speak to the human servants?"

He motions for us to follow him. "A few of them are still busy in the kitchen. The others we've gathered in their repose room to speak to you."

The walls inside the castle are just as reflective as those outside. Skewed echoes of our forms ripple across them on both sides of us as we make our way deeper into the castle. They give the eerie impression that you could never be alone in this place, that there could be people watching your every movement no matter where you go.

A soft light beams down from fixtures on the high, curved ceiling, amplified as it bounces across the metal surfaces. I wouldn't generally associate Laoni with anything soft, but a starker light would be nearly blinding.

It's a long walk with several turns and a trip up a flight of stairs. The dry air tickles my nose. By the time the guard stops outside a doorway, my warped foot has started to ache. I keep my limp as in check as I can when I ease past him into the room.

A woman I recognize from Laoni's coterie is waiting there, along with more human figures than I was expecting. At our entrance, a dozen of them get up from beds laid out in rows across the room as if on command.

Not just as if. They must have been commanded to do exactly that. One glance at them, and I can tell they're all in the same drugged haze as most of the humans in Petalrise, too spaced out to react that quickly to my arrival otherwise. I doubt they have much room to make any decisions for themselves in their muddled minds.

As I take in the room, my throat tightens. The floor and walls gleam, the beds are small but neatly made with blankets that look brand new. I can't help wondering how much work Laoni put into prettying up this space in anticipation of my arrival.

But there's nothing in the space other than those beds and a single wash basin by the far wall. No shelves, no cupboards, nothing hanging on the walls. No sign of any personal possessions. They don't even have storage for clothes. I suppose they wear the same outfits continuously, and the fae simply bring them replacements as needed.

The clothes they're all wearing now are of the simpler winter-fae style, fitted tunics and trousers in shades of gray. I don't spot any stains or wrinkles, and my suspicion grows that a lot of preparation has gone into making their situation appear as comfortable as possible. The servants can't have done much work in these clothes, which means they were given new outfits specifically for my visit.

From their glazed expressions, they don't have the capacity to care at the moment. The fae treat their *horses* better than the humans they've kidnapped.

"There, you can see them," the coterie woman says, and glances narrowly at Zelpha. "There's no need for you to remain. I can see to Lady Talia's needs."

A prickle of apprehension runs down my spine. I have ways of defending myself, including the new bronze bracelet with its delicate weight around my wrist, but I know I'm not a match for a fae when it comes to magic or physical strength. What would she do to ensure this visit goes well if I didn't have one of Corwin's people with me?

No doubt Zelpha has similar thoughts. She arches her eyebrows at the other woman. "That's all right. My lord instructed me to accompany Talia the entire time, and I intend to follow his orders."

Leaning on Corwin's authority seems to work. Laoni's coterie woman frowns but doesn't argue further. She sidles closer as I step toward the humans, her gaze fixed on me now. I wonder if she's watching for any excuse to complain about my behavior and kick me out of the castle after all.

I simply won't give her any excuses, then.

I smile at each of the servants, even though they're too out of it to smile back, and offer each a "Hello" and "It's good to meet you." When I hold out my hand to shake each of theirs, just to see how they move, I can't help noticing bruises that look like fingerprints clamped around one man's arm where his sleeve falls back. One slim woman's grasp feels so weak and brittle I'm afraid I'll break her fingers if I squeeze. Another man holds his shoulders awkwardly when he extends his arm, favoring one.

"What happened to your shoulder?" I ask him.

"I didn't finish quickly enough," he says in a dull tone, "and I—"

"It was an accident," the coterie woman breaks in. "A momentary clumsiness. We healed him as well as we could."

They healed him when it happened or only as well as they could *now*, who knows how long after it happened? And was he really just clumsy, or did it happen because of some kind of punishment?

I suspect pushing him to say more will get him in more trouble than it might be worth.

"How much time do they spend in this room?" I ask.

"It's only for sleeping," the fae woman replies.

I look around. "And what about when they have time off?"

Her mouth opens and closes again as she seems to grapple with her words.

"They don't get time off, most likely," Zelpha puts in. "Work them from waking until they're falling asleep on their feet."

"We aren't so hard on them," the other woman protests. "They have plenty of idle moments."

"And what do they do in those moments?" I say. "Just stand there like they are now?"

"That's all they want to do." She turns to the servants. "Are any of you unhappy with your situation here?"

I get a chorus of murmured "No"s in response, but no audible enthusiasm. I hold my tongue against pointing out that they haven't been allowed to feel unhappy. This woman isn't the one making the decisions about what happens here anyway.

I'm obviously not going to get anything more useful out of them while she's overseeing things, but I've seen enough anyway. I turn to her. "What about the kitchen servants? I'd like to see the space they're working in, even if they're not done with their jobs."

The coterie woman wavers and then nods. "Fine. They should be just finishing up as it is."

She stalks out ahead of us, clearly expecting us to follow her. The guard who brought us to the room has vanished.

As we trail behind the coterie woman, I glance at Zelpha, keeping my voice low. "Is there any reason fae would *need* to bring human servants in? I mean, Corwin only has a few. Sylas has managed to do without any for decades. There's nothing they can do that fae couldn't —and more easily, since the fae have magic—is there?"

Zelpha shakes her head. "Not that I can think of—other than giving the fae who wish it a better chance at having more children." She winces just as I cringe inwardly. I know in an instant that some of those fae must outright rape the human servants while they're in that drugged-up daze. There's no way they could really consent in that state. They'd barely understand what they're agreeing to.

"It's tradition, like the arch-lords said at the meeting the other day," Zelpha goes on. "Many think we shouldn't have to handle any sort of drudgework, magically or otherwise, if we can get humans to do it. And I'd bet a great deal of the ones who think that way also enjoy always having someone around they can lord it over, regardless of whether they're lords themselves."

It's not hard for me to believe that.

I exhale slowly, willing down the urge to squirm with horror. This isn't an insurmountable problem. The fae don't *need* the humans, so they could treat them better, or let them return to the human world, or—so many other possible compromises. I just have to find the compromise they'll agree to. And with so many of the Unseelie seeing me as some kind of blessed savior, hopefully I can manage that just like I managed to get myself invited into Laoni's castle.

We turn down a wider hall with a couple of painted portraits nearly as tall as I am hanging on the gleaming wall. The one we pass first shows Laoni with a slender, knob-chinned man I assume is her soul-twined mate. I've never met the man, but then, I'm not sure I've met any of the arch-lords' mates. They don't typically bring them around to the meetings.

The next painting shows a couple I assume are Laoni's parents.

The man looks as stern and brawny, and the woman has a turquoise tint to her hair like Laoni does. They sit straight and formal but with their hands clasped together in a way that seems to show genuine affection.

I pause, taking it in. Corwin said something about Laoni coming into her rule suddenly and early like he did, didn't he?

"These are the previous lord and lady, right?" I say. "What happened to them?"

The coterie woman stops in her tracks and swivels on her heel. "They are no longer with us," she says tersely. "As I don't think it right to remind the arch-lord of, should she happen to pass by."

It's hard to imagine Laoni actually grieving, but losing one's parents early can't be easy for anyone, even her. But why would it affect her that badly to hear someone mention it after all this time? Just what *did* happen to them?

The woman taps her foot at my hesitation. "Come along. Did you want to see the kitchen or not?"

I bite back the questions she obviously won't answer anyway and hurry after her. I'll get a straighter answer from Corwin. I could ask him right now, but I'd rather not divert my attention while I'm in the home of someone I already know wants me out of the picture.

We descend a staircase and walk into a large room even bigger than the kitchen in Corwin's palace. The pale iridium is broken by the darker metals used to form the ovens and countertops.

A few fae staff are setting some trays of pastries in the cold room to sit before baking. The coterie woman lifts her chin toward a man who's just taking a final dish out of the sink of wash water. "There's one you're looking for."

I limp over, and he turns toward me. His face is as vacant as the others upstairs.

"Hi," I say anyway. "I'm Talia. How long have you been working in the kitchen here?"

He sways a little as if to some melody only he can hear. "Oh, it's been… It's been a good long time."

A portly fae man with bushy eyebrows marches over to us. "What's this about, now?"

The coterie woman speaks up before I can. "You should have heard, Serev. Lady Talia has come to check up on our mortal helpers."

I look around. "Where are the others? We were told there were a few in the kitchen."

Serev lets out a huff. "What you'd want with those dust-destined—"

The coterie woman clears her throat, and his mouth snaps shut. He glances at me again, and understanding seems to click in his eyes. I smile back at him tightly. It isn't as if I'm surprised to find more fae with dismissive attitudes toward humans among Laoni's staff.

"They're sorting something out in the storeroom," he says. "I'll get them for you."

He bustles off and returns a minute later with an elderly man and woman. The second I look at their whitened hair and the wrinkles lining their faces, I can't help thinking that back in the world where they belong, they'd be retired by now. Instead, they're still working away day in and day out. The horror inside me clenches tighter.

When I ask them how they feel about their work, the woman blinks at me with confusion. "Always something to do," the man says in an unnervingly dreamy tone. "Keeps us busy."

The woman nods slowly. "It does that."

"What would you do if you weren't working here?" I venture, aware of the coterie woman watching us like a hawk. I'm treading on thin ice.

But the elderly couple aren't aware enough to really complain. "What is there but here?" the woman asks, sounding genuinely bewildered.

Beside me, Zelpha looks like she's biting back a grimace. I step aside and let Serev dismiss the couple, ideas about all the ways I want to help these people whirling in my head. All I know for sure is that things can't go on like this. Not while I'm here, not while I have some kind of leverage with which to stand up for people like me.

As I turn to tell the coterie woman I've seen enough, a few fae in guard uniforms barge into the kitchen. I don't know two of them by name, but the third, coming up behind them, is Kesral.

They go to a shelf where it appears the food is up for grabs. The first two grab hunks of dried meat, but when Kesral tries to push past them to take something for himself, they jostle him back with their shoulders. One lets out a cruel chuckle.

"First pickings for those who don't have dung in their veins," the other sneers.

Kesral's jaw tenses, but he steps back while they look over the offerings and grab a few more treats. "Have at it, son of dung," the first guard tosses over his shoulder as they bump past him on their way out.

My hands ball at my sides on his behalf. My gaze darts to Serev, expecting him to join in the jibes after the way he started to talk about the human servants, but his expression has clouded over.

When Kesral has ducked out, I risk a much more pointed question than I've tried before. "You don't think it's right that the fae who are more human get treated worse?"

Serev's head jerks around. His mouth works. "It isn't the same. He's still fae. Fae is fae. I don't know why our lord allows them to get away with it."

His lord *participates* in the harassment from what I've seen. I knit my brow. "What do you mean?"

He waves his thick hand in the air. "Ah, Kesral started hanging around the castle helping out where he could when he was a very young thing. He and Arch-Lord Laoni are close in age. They got up to rather a lot of exploits together, from what I saw. Back when they were children, you couldn't tear them apart."

What? I have to stop myself from staring at him. "I guess her opinion of him changed."

"An arch-lord has many responsibilities without worrying about every member of the staff," the coterie woman says tartly.

Serev shrugs. "True enough. They must have grown apart as they grew up. It happens. I just can't imagine her approving of that kind of talk toward him, faithful as he's been."

And yet when I saw them together, she seemed incapable of doing anything but snapping at him. I catch Zelpha's eye, but she makes a puzzled gesture in return.

Well, whatever's gone on between Laoni and her former friend, it doesn't change what I need to do. Maybe helping the humans in the fae world will help the human-leaning fae as well.

CHAPTER EIGHTEEN

Whitt

Sylas studies me for a long moment after I've finished speaking. It's difficult to tell which of his eyes, the dark one or the deadened one, is seeing more.

"You're sure about this," he says finally.

I lean back against the doorframe of his study, listening to reconfirm that no one's nearby in the hall outside. "I've been sure *I* want to since before this whole business with the Unseelie. I only needed to be sure of Corwin. But since it affects the cadre and my service to you as well, I wouldn't go forward without consulting you."

A hint of wryness curls my brother's lips. "And if I said no, would you heed me?"

The wryness stops me from bristling. It's still a new sensation, feeling this at ease with the man I serve. Knowing he's only teasing, that he trusts me and I trust him. A fleeting jab of irritation runs through me that his former mate stole that ease from us for so long, but what's done is done. At least we've ended up in a better place.

"I wouldn't have brought it up otherwise," I reply with a crooked grin. "You are my lord. And you've spent more time with Corwin than I have—it's possible you've seen reasons for concern that I've missed."

Sylas shakes his head. "My assessment is much the same as yours. His loyalty is to Talia above his colleagues, and to the alliance between our peoples over their self-interest. The fact that you've drawn the same conclusions reassures *me*."

He pauses and rubs his hand across his jaw, his gaze going momentarily distant before refocusing on me. "I think what you suggest could benefit us and is unlikely to harm us. I wish I were in a position to offer it myself. If you're confident in the decision, by all means, go ahead. But I would ask that you don't speak of it to anyone else, including August, unless absolutely necessary."

I don't need to ask him why, even though the thought of keeping something from our other brother sends a vague uneasiness through me. August isn't as adept at dissembling and subterfuge as either of us. He'd never let a crucial piece of information slip purposefully, but in an urgent situation where he didn't have much time to think, he could give something away. And the wrong person finding out about this could be disastrous.

I dip my head in acknowledgment. "I completely agree. Thank you."

Sylas gives me a softer smile. "I'm glad you've found a partner who brings you more peace than most ever achieve. I was starting to think you'd keep your bachelor ways forever."

The warmth of his words leaves me a bit awkward. It's true that I'm not often at ease with any sort of affection, brotherly or romantic. I let out a rough chuckle. "You well know what a spectacular mate she is."

After I leave the study, I gather a few items I wanted to stash in my new rooms in the border castle and then make my way over there at the agreed time. Talia has been with August and then Corwin for most of the day, but this evening and the night belong to me. As the accord between the realms becomes stronger, I expect we'll all spend more of our time working out of that space together, but I can't say I mind getting the mite to myself for a little while.

I speak my vow and go in through our entrance. Before I've made it more than a few steps inside, Talia appears at the other end of the front hall, which is nearly as grand as Hearth-by-the-Heart's. Her cheeks are nearly as ruddy as the pink strands of her windblown hair, suggesting she's just come in from outside in the winter realm. The hue makes her look so wildly alive that my heart skips a beat when she beams at me.

No, I never thought any woman would ever affect me so deeply either. What a marvel she is.

As she limps over and gives me a hug in greeting, Corwin peeks in from the hall. He offers me a nod of welcome and then heads off. The man is a bit of an odd duck, but it's become clear that his stiffness and formality are simply part of his general personality, not any reservations he still holds about our joint relationship—and he's willing to shed them as Talia needs him to. Unlike the rest of his jabbering colleagues.

Now that the moment is upon me, I'm not sure how to begin. But Talia pre-empts me anyway.

"There's something I wanted to ask you about," she says. "If you don't mind getting right into business the second you've gotten here."

I laugh. "If you're scheming something, I definitely want to be a part of that." I hold up the satchel I packed. "I need to bring this to my room—and if you'll join me, we can talk in there with some privacy." I'll want that for the subject I mean to speak about as well.

I grasp her hand, and she follows me upstairs to the bedrooms. As I put my belongings away, she perches on the edge of the bed—only half the size her new one is, but plenty lavish enough for my tastes. I don't plan on sharing this one with anyone other than her.

"This morning I went to see how the human servants in Laoni's castle are treated," she says.

I can't imagine that trip was very inspiring. I glance over my shoulder at her. "And?"

"It went about as well as you'd think, which isn't very well." She makes a face. "I'm going to see if I can check on some other domains on both sides of the border to get the full picture, but I feel like I have a pretty good idea of what's typical already... The hard part is going to be convincing anyone to go against the kinds of things they've been doing for thousands of years. I was hoping you might have some ideas for how to pitch the idea of better treatment for humans to the other fae."

"Me specifically?"

She shrugs with a small but sweet smile. "Strategy is your specialty, right? Who better to strategize with?"

It's a logical explanation, but nevertheless her words provoke a flutter of tenderness in my chest. She has two arch-lords ready to leap to her aid, but there are still things she'd rather turn to me for.

I sit next to her on the bed and slip my arm around her waist. "Let's see. What exactly do you want to convince my brethren to do?"

The way she nestles into my casual embrace so eagerly warms my heart even more.

"In a perfect situation, which I realize I might not get, at least not without a few stepping stones along the way?" she says. "The fae would stop taking any humans from their world at all, unless the humans are agreeing to come with a full understanding of what they're getting into and no trickery to hold them here."

I hum to myself. "That request would definitely meet quite a bit of resistance, but I'll put my mind to it. What of the mortals already among us?"

She tips her head to the side in thought. "For the humans already here, no more drugs should be forced on them. They should be given some time to clear their heads and see their true situation, and then get to choose whether they stay or go home. And if they choose to stay, they need to be respected and given a chance to have lives of their own as much as the fae staff."

I nod slowly. "Even the fae servants aren't always respected, but they're definitely better off than the humans nearly everywhere. Your biggest challenge is going to be convincing all the lords and ladies to do without their easily controlled workforce."

Talia grimaces. "They don't *need* human servants. Anything the humans are doing, fae could do it too. Probably faster in most cases. We can point to Sylas as an example of a lord who's managed with only fae on staff for, what, about a century now?"

"Having an arch-lord as an exemplar certainly can't hurt. And as our people's respect for *you* grows, I'd imagine it'll become easier to convince them that those like you deserve better as well." I rub my jaw, mulling it over. "We'll definitely want to approach the situation one piece at a time rather than trying to overhaul the system all in one go."

"Where do you think it'd be easiest to start?"

That's the big question. "Perhaps rather than focusing on one element at a time, we'd be best off tackling one domain at a time," I say. "Starting with the arch-lords. Hearth-by-the-Heart already operates without human help, and Corwin's human servants are all fully conscious and accepting of their situation, aren't they? We could go to Donovan next. I think he'd be our best bet for convincing."

Talia's eyes light up. "That makes sense. After him, maybe we could talk to Neve on the winter side. She seems like the most flexible of the other winter arch-lords."

"Perfect. If we have both of them, then half of us would be setting a new standard. Easier to start pressuring the others into following suit. And once the regular lords and ladies see that their arch-lords are making a change, they'll be more inclined to do the same themselves."

She taps her lips. "I should probably see how Donovan's human servants are doing in general before we make any suggestions to him. Do you think you or Sylas could speak to him about me making a visit there?"

"No problem at all." I ruffle her hair. "Is that a solid enough plan for you, at least as a start?"

"Definitely. Thank you." She leans into me again, and I tuck her tighter against me instinctively.

There's so much I want to say to her, so many ways I've imagined this, but now that I'm on the verge, the act feels so momentous it takes me a minute to gather myself. I trace my fingers over Talia's cheek and kiss her temple.

"Talia… A couple of months back I told you there was something I wanted to offer you when I felt I could do so without jeopardizing my other responsibilities. Do you remember that?"

She pulls back, her gaze snapping up to meet mine. I can tell right away that she does.

Her voice comes out quiet. "It's all right. I understand that with the situation with Corwin—accepting him as my soul-twined mate and having that unshakeable connection with him—it isn't totally secure. I never expected you to trust even *me* that much, let alone him as well."

Love swells inside me. I cup her chin, holding her gaze. "That's not why I'm bringing it up. I trusted you enough that I'd have offered you my true name back then if it'd only been about you. And having seen the strength of Corwin's will and his dedication to you… I trust him as well. If *you* don't find it too much of a responsibility to carry."

Talia blinks at me. "You want—you'd give me your true name now?" she says, a little breathless.

I want to wrap her in the tightest of embraces, but I can't do that and look her in the eyes at the same time. "I would. I want you to be able to call on me no matter where you are, no matter what's happening. You have Corwin, of course, but if I should be closer, or he should be incapacitated… From what Sylas heard from the sage, Heart only knows how much more complicated our lives may become in the coming years. And I'll be here for you in every way I can be—as you've been here for me."

Her eyes mist with tears, but her smile eliminates any fear that they're unhappy ones. "You really don't have to. I know what a big deal it is."

I give in to the urge to gather her up in my arms now, breathing in her tartly sweet scent. "I want to. I have no doubt about that. My only concern is whether you want to accept."

"Yes," she says without hesitation. "Yes. If I could have a soul-twined bond with all of you, I'd want it, and this is as close to that as I can get. I'd die before I let anyone use it against you."

My throat constricts. I believe she means that. "I intend to see it never comes to that, mite."

I dip my head so my lips brush the shell of her ear. The syllables I've never spoken to anyone before catch in the back of my mouth. I urge them onto my tongue. "*Wye-con-ell.*"

"*Wye-con-ell,*" Talia repeats in a murmur, and just like that, a tingle races through the center of my being. She looks up at me. "So if I need you, I just say it—the way I say the other true names—and I'll be able to reach out to you with my thoughts?"

"You can include a request with the name," I say. "Ask me to open my mind to you if you have something to tell me, ask me to answer a question, ask me to come to you— I have to obey. So, use it wisely."

"Of course." Her eyes shine with awe. "How will I know— With the other true names, I couldn't get a handle on them right away."

I was prepared for that question. "I thought we could play a little game of hide-and-seek," I say with a wink. "There's a spot in this castle it wouldn't be easy to get to without special guidance. Give me five minutes to reach it, and then speak my true name and focus on your awareness of me with as much concentration as you can. If you've got it right, you should be able to follow the route straight to me. Ready?"

Talia laughs, though she still looks a bit shy about it. "No time like the present."

"Then come to me as soon as you can." I kiss her once more, on the lips this time, reveling in the knowledge that I belong to this woman in every way that matters to me—that she *wanted* me to belong to her. Then I get up and leave the room.

I'm not sure when I'll have need of the office set aside for my use on the border castle's third floor. I'm reluctant to move my books and other supplies over just yet when I still need to do much of my work in Hearth-by-the-Heart. But it's here nonetheless, and during the construction I added a personal touch: one of my secret passageways.

By pressing the right spot on the built-in shelves, one section slides to the side to reveal a narrow hidden doorway. The spiral staircase beyond leads both down to a disguised exit at the base of the castle and up to a small terrace near the top of one of the turrets.

I head up, lifting my nose to the traces of fresh summer air that seep past the door above. The turret is set forward enough on our side of the castle that it escapes the haze of the border completely. I step out onto the wooden platform with its polished, waist-high railing to a view that encompasses nearly the entire hill around the Heart as well as some of the sprawling terrain beyond it.

Evening is creeping up on us. The shadows of the buildings below stretch long, and pinks and purples that echo Talia's hair glow in the scattered clouds. Even if this wasn't a particularly distinctive occasion, the sight would please me. I look forward to sharing it with my soon-to-be mate.

As I lean against the railing, the warm breeze ruffling over my hair with a faint smell of wildflowers, the same tingling sensation that ran through me before touches me again. Talia is calling on me.

I picture my path through the castle from leaving my bedroom, and the tingles condense inside my skull. I get the faintest impression of Talia from them—her slightly uneven gait, her eagerness to find me, her excitement that she's been able to sense my presence at all.

I linger on the bookshelves trick for the longest, until my ears catch the rasp of the hidden entrance opening from below. Talia's soft footsteps patter up the stairs. As she comes through the upper doorway, I turn to meet her.

Her whole face is glowing now. She throws herself into my arms, squeezing me close. "That was amazing. I just… knew which way to go, and then I could feel you guiding me when I needed it. It isn't like the soul-twined bond at all, but it's still wonderful."

"No matter where you or I go, you'll always be able to reach me," I say.

She tips her head up, seeking my lips. I have no problem at all giving her the kiss she's requesting.

This woman has never been short on passion, but there's a depth of ardor to her embrace now that tops any kiss we've shared before, as if she means to meld right into me. It stirs every nerve in my body to eager alertness.

"Thank you," she says when she draws back. "I know the words aren't really enough, but—thank you. I wish I could give the same thing back to you."

But she doesn't have a true name to give.

I tease my fingers along her jaw. "You've offered me plenty, Talia. In some ways I'd say more than I've yet offered you."

She snorts as if that's impossible. Then her gaze drifts from me to the view, and she sucks in an awed breath. "Wow. I didn't know you'd built a balcony up here."

"It's for my use only. And I suppose yours as well, should you have need of it. As spymaster, I enjoy having a good view over my surroundings." I smirk. "It has a spell around it to hide any sight of it from below, so no one will ever know they're being spied on."

"You think of everything," she says, amused. She moves to the railing, setting her hands on it and peering out into the distance.

We're so high up here that the fae moving about in the domains below look no larger than mice. Talia studies them and the vivid colors spreading across the darkening sky. When her eyes flick back to me, I catch a hint of slyness in them.

She turns her back to the railing and then boosts herself up with a hitch of her arms to sit on it. My pulse lurches. I lunge for her in the same instant, some part of my mind picturing her tumbling over the edge—but as my hands catch her waist, I can already feel that she was keeping her balance just fine.

"Trying to give me a heart attack there, mite?" I ask, bowing my head over hers.

She smiles sweetly up at me. "Showing that I trust you with my life just as you've trusted me with yours. I can't offer the same openness you did, but there are other ways I can bare myself to you."

Still gripping the railing with one hand, she raises the other to the collar of her dress. In the aftermath of my panic, it takes me a moment to realize she's loosening the ties that run down the center of the bodice. The fabric gapes open, gradually unveiling more and more pale skin over her collarbone and the swells of her breasts.

A jolt of lust shoots straight to my groin, and heat floods my body. I wrench my gaze from her chest to her face. My voice comes out rough. "Talia..."

She reaches lower and gives an extra tug to uncover her breasts completely. Her pert nipples pebble in the breeze. She watches me, avidly and yet still with a shy flush creeping across her cheeks.

"I want you," she says simply. "I know you won't let me fall."

"Never," I rasp, looping one arm around her to hold her firmly in place. She splays her legs so I can step closer between them, and Heart help me, my cock is already straining against the crotch of my slacks.

I understand the symbolism of this gesture, and I want to allow her it, but I can't possibly pretend I'm doing this all for her benefit. I doubt I've ever desired her more.

I lower my head to reclaim her lips. As our mouths lock together, I caress my fingers over her breasts, teasing one nipple into an even harder point and then doing the same to the other, drinking in the whimpers my touch provokes like fine wine.

Talia squirms close enough that her sex brushes my cock, her fingers interlacing behind my neck. She kisses me like she might never get to again, like she's starving for me, and that only makes me all the hungrier for her.

My patience is fraying fast. I slip my free hand between her legs, hefting up the skirt of her dress, and trace the dampness spreading across her panties. A groan escapes me. Kissing her harder, I delve my tongue between her lips to tangle with hers.

As I stroke her faster, her fingernails prick my neck with perfect nicks of pain. "Whitt," she gasps, arching into me.

I know what she wants now, but I intend to give her the highest pleasure I can before I take my own.

I tuck my fingers right inside her panties to fondle her skin to skin. My mouth captures every needy sound that slips from her lips. I pump one finger, then two, then three inside her as my thumb dances across her clit.

Talia's head falls back with an outright moan. The wind rises, tossing her hair around her. I sway with her on the railing, my other arm still firm around her back, her trust in me absolute. Her lack of fear brings an ache into my chest that's far more potent than my lust.

I swivel my thumb, increasing the pressure when she pushes into my touch. Her spine arches farther, and then her channel is clenching around my fingers, a tremor of release racing through her body.

Before it's even faded, she grasps my arm. "I want *you*," she says with the determination I admire so much. "All of you, inside me, coming with me."

I nuzzle her cheek. "Then you'll have your wish, mighty one."

She tugs at my slacks, and together we free my cock. I tear the panties right off her rather than carry out the gymnastics of peeling them off intact while I'm this close to her. I'll bring her a dozen replacements next time.

Her fingers close around my throbbing length, and just like that I'm panting against her hair. "You spark the hottest fire in me I've ever felt," I say. "I will never want anyone else but you."

She tugs me forward. "Then have me."

I don't need any further encouragement to plunge right into her wet heat.

Skies above, being joined with her like this is never less than glorious, but tonight tops every time before. She rocks to meet me, heedless of the height and her precarious position, knowing that even in my greatest rush of passion I'll protect her with all I have. The wind whips over us as if urging us on.

The intensity of the moment is too much for me to hold back for very long. I buck into her, and she reaches her second peak with a giddy cry. The bliss written all across her beautiful face brings my own body surging toward ecstasy. I hold her to me and thrust a few more times before all my desire spills inside her in a blaze of release.

We cling to each other there for a few minutes, catching our ragged breaths. Talia makes a pleased sound and nestles her head against my chest. I think her show of faith has been clear enough that I can now heft her off the railing and sit with her on my lap in a position where falling isn't a possibility.

"I think we should do that again sometime," Talia announces.

A laugh tumbles out of me. "I won't argue with that. You call, and I'll be at your side."

She peers up at me, abruptly serious. "I wouldn't ever use that power casually, you know. Only if it was an emergency."

I brush my fingers over her hair. "If it's just to convey a message, speak to me whenever you like. But yes, I'd prefer if you didn't order my immediate arrival unless necessary. If only because it would make it rather hard to keep our arrangement a secret. But I wasn't at all worried that you would."

"Good." She leans into me again, her face turned toward the view between the bars of the railing. Then, abruptly, she straightens up. "What's *that*?"

I follow her gaze, my spirits sinking at her tone before I've even spotted what she's reacting to.

In the near distance, coming from somewhere near the base of the hill around the Heart, a plume of smoke is rising, glinting bloody red against the darkening sky.

CHAPTER NINETEEN

Talia

By the time we make it to the front entrance, my dress hastily refastened as Whitt and I hurried down the stairs, shouts are carrying up the hill. Even though the eerie smoke I spotted looked far off, the breeze now carries an acrid, metallic scent that makes my nose wrinkle.

The smoke wasn't coming from anywhere near Hearth-by-the-Heart, at least. As far as I could tell, it was rising from some spot at the edge of Donovan's or Celia's domain.

Whitt glances at me, his expression taut with concern, and I brace myself for him to tell me he thinks I should stay back while he investigates. But he must realize I won't want to be left in the dark—and respect the fact that I'd rather risk a little danger than stay shut up in the castle unknowing—because he gives me a curt nod.

"We can get there fastest if I carry you," he says.

Without waiting for my response, he hunches forward, shifting into his tawny wolf form in a matter of seconds. Watching the transformation now is nothing but exhilarating. He crouches low, and

I clamber onto his back the way I did once before when he carried me through the woods to one of his favorite groves.

I don't think today's destination is going to be anywhere near as pleasant.

I lean against his muscular back, burying my fingers in the thick ruff of fur around his neck, and he sets off at a lope. The swift, rhythmic pace is easy to adapt to. I tighten my knees against his sides to keep my balance, but I have no more fear of falling than I did perched on the railing of his secret balcony.

He races across the grassy plain around the Bastion and into the forestland that surrounds the other arch-lords' castles. The smoky tang in the air thickens, and the shouts multiply. Other wolfish figures charge through the shadows between the trees around us, heading to the same spot the quickest way the summer fae are capable of.

As we veer along a well-beaten path down the hill, the forest thins into patches here and there. Whitt runs through another dense stretch of trees and bursts out at the edge of a darkened field of wildflowers.

The smoke is rising from a patch of burning vegetation in the middle of that field. I can't see any cause for the ruddy glow that's rippling through the billows all the way up to the sky, but it's hard to make out anything all that clearly in the deepening evening and the flickering light.

It doesn't even look like the actual spot that's burning should be big enough to produce all that smoke. When I squint, I can only make out a dark pile of soot surrounded by that wavering glow, about the size of a campfire pit.

But then, when fae magic is involved, all sorts of unusual things are possible.

Fae have gathered all around the burning spot, more arriving from all directions. None of them has gotten close, though, all hanging back several feet. Some in human form and some still wolves, they prowl around that invisible border, their eyes wary and their mouths curled into frowns.

Why isn't anyone putting it out?

Whitt pushes closer through the crowd and stops in the midst of it. As he lets me slide off his back, I spot a few familiar figures in the crowd: one of Celia's cadre-chosen and a couple of Donovan's. Not all of the fae around us have arrived from the arch-lords' domains, though. Many are hurrying over from farther beyond the hill, from the neighboring domains.

Whitt straightens up next to me, shaking off the transformation. He glances around. "We're right at the border of four different domains here. Whoever's responsible for this, they wanted to catch plenty of attention."

Corwin must catch my uneasy emotions, because his voice breaks through my thoughts. *What's going on over there?*

I'm not sure yet, I reply. *Don't worry—there are plenty of fae here. I'm sure we can deal with whatever it is.*

He accepts that answer with a twinge of concern but no protest.

"What *is* it?" I ask Whitt, peering at the smoking patch, which doesn't appear to have grown. "How is it making so much smoke—and why doesn't someone just throw some water on it or something?"

"There must be some magic to it that's complicating matters. Something about the scent..." Taking a step forward, Whitt inhales sharply, and his stance goes rigid.

"What?" I demand, catching up with him.

He nods toward the stream of smoke with a sickly grimace. "It's got iron in it. I can feel it prickling in my lungs. We *can't* get close enough to try to douse it, and it'll drain away the power of any spell. How in the lands...?"

His forehead furrows with confusion. I glance around at the other gathered fae again. They all look equally uncomfortable and puzzled, the shouts having dwindled into muttered conversation as they must be discussing how to tackle this strange intrusion.

The obvious answer is right here. "I can put it out," I say. "The iron isn't going to hurt *me*. Get me a bucket of water or whatever you think will do it, and I'll give it a shot."

Whitt hesitates. "We don't know what other effects it might produce, mite. No one could easily get to you to protect you."

"Then I'll be careful about it. We can't leave this thing polluting the air with toxic metals, can we? What else are you going to do?"

His jaw works, but he must know I'm right. If he hadn't brought me along, calling on human servants to deal with the problem would have been the obvious solution anyway. And I can at least think on my feet better than those in a drugged-up daze.

As he debates, I notice the darkened patch of soot creeping wider. More smoke billows up. The hairs on the back of my neck rise. "It's getting larger. If we wait, *I* might not be able to put it out either."

Whitt hisses through his teeth in annoyance, but I know it's not directed at me. "All right. You'll go in there carefully and withdraw as quickly as you can. I'm not sure water will do it on its own, though… Give me a moment."

He raises his voice to reach the other fae around us. "Did anyone see how this started?"

All we get are shaken heads and responses to the negative. One of Donovan's cadre-chosen comes over to us. "I was one of the first to get here. There was no one around except a couple of the fae from Saplight. By all appearances, it started spontaneously."

"That hardly seems likely," Whitt mutters. He narrows his eyes at the burning spot, which has stretched a little farther again in the time he's been talking, and lets out a growl. "I don't like this at all." He touches my shoulder. "Stay right here until I get back."

He moves to the fringes of the growing crowd and must work some conjuring there, because he returns carrying a thick, sodden blanket. He hands it to me gingerly. "This should be enough to smother and dampen the source of the smoke—it's the best I can come up with that doesn't rely on direct magical effects. We can hope it'll at least cut off the smoke for long enough that we fae can step in and handle anything remaining."

At my nod, Whitt ushers me to the edge of the inner ring. His hand twitches against my elbow as the metallic smoky scent deepens. He raises his other arm to catch the attention of the assembled fae. "Lady Talia, our human comrade, is going to attempt to smother the burning. Please keep careful watch for any signs of a threat to her while she takes on this task for us."

Dozens of pairs of eyes fix on me, hopeful murmurs traveling through the crowd.

I limp forward, scanning the area around the burning patch but refusing to hesitate. The spot is still small enough that I should be able to cover the whole thing with one heave of the wet fabric, but it won't stay that small for long.

The smoke stings my eyes and makes my lungs itch. When I'm just a couple of steps away, a cough erupts out of me. I choke it back as well as I can and heft up the blanket to toss it.

Just as I'm about to fling my arms forward, a tiny shape darts around the burning patch. Even as I register the rat-like shape, it's shooting up into that of a burly man—a man who's lunging right at me, needle-like claws jutting from his fingertips.

A yelp jolts from my throat. I drop the blanket, groping for the dagger at my hip, but the Murk fae is already on me. Still ducked down in a rat-like posture, his head slams into my stomach.

We topple over together. His claws rake across my thigh, and pain explodes through my leg. I smack my hands toward him in a reflexive gesture of defense—

—and a sudden burst of light blazes between us.

The fae man topples over and slumps on the ground next to me. I stare at him, my chest heaving for breath, agony searing through my thigh.

He doesn't move. His half-closed eyes look dull. Is he… dead?

What even happened?

Trembling fingers close around my shoulders. Whitt has made it to me, but the effects of the smoke are already sending tremors through his whole body. He coughs weakly and tries to drag me away, but my gaze jerks back to the smoke.

I haven't finished what I came here to do. The Murk man tried to stop me, but he failed—that's all that matters until this is done.

Talia, Corwin says. *Talia, are you all right?* But I can't find the concentration to answer him.

"Wait!" I shout over the tumult of voices around us, and push onto my hands and knees to grab the fallen blanket. Clenching my teeth against the pain in my leg, I yank the sodden fabric off the ground, lurch toward the burning patch, and manage to hurl the blanket right over it.

With a sputtering sound, the smoke vanishes, the last billow drifting off toward the sky. The center of the blanket quivers and goes still. All we're left with is that square of fabric and the dead Murk man in the middle of the ring of Seelie.

Fighting his wheezes, Whitt stumbles to me and manages to scoop me off my feet. As he hauls me farther from the burning spot, we both cough to clear our lungs. Other fae converge on the blanket, on the Murk fae, and on the two of us. My thigh feels as if a fire has caught within it.

I'm okay, I tell Corwin. *It's done.* The words seem to waver as they pass through our bond.

They mustn't be very convincing, because his only response is a surge of protectiveness and a brief declaration. *I'm coming to you.*

A voice rings out from what sounds like far away to my pain-addled mind. "Lady Talia has saved us again! The Heart worked through her to protect us and fend off the Murk."

"She's sacrificed her blood for us once more," someone else declares from a different direction. "The ravens have been calling her blessed. I think they're right about that one thing."

The only word that totally sinks in is *blood.* I stare down at my leg, recognizing the dark red blotch spreading across the whole front of my dress's skirt as just that.

So much blood. And the pain is like those claws are digging deeper into me with every second. Maybe I'm not okay after all.

Whitt tears right through the silky cloth up to just below my hip so he can uncover the wound. A snarl escapes him at the sight of my gouged flesh, but only for an instant before he's murmuring hasty true names.

The pain numbs just a little. There's too much blood already on me for me to tell whether he's been able to stop more from seeping out.

"Who here is skilled at healing?" he calls out, a note of desperation in his voice.

I want to tell him I'll be just fine, that I've been scratched up plenty before with the scars to prove it, but I can't seem to find my voice.

A woman hunches down beside us and hovers her hands over the wound. At her emphatic words, the agony searing through my leg pulls back even more. The claws of pain dwindle into pin-pricks. I glance down, the movement dizzying me, and see the skin sealing into pale pink lines marking my leg from just above my knee to halfway up my thigh.

"Will she be all right?" asks another woman I don't recognize from behind the healer. She sounds surprisingly concerned for a stranger. I realize a whole horde of fae are standing around us, peering down at me with worried eyes.

"She didn't bleed for long enough to put her in severe danger," the healer says. "Thank the Heart." She touches the side of my face. "And thank the Heart for you, coming here and foiling the Murk's plot. The cuts were deep, down to the bone. It'll still hurt for some time as the muscle fully heals. Be gentle with yourself, Lady Talia."

I think that's the first time a regular Seelie outside Sylas's pack has referred to me by my official title. Now... now many of the fae around us are bowing their heads and offering murmurs of consolation and hope with expressions that are oddly familiar.

It's the same kind of awe I've been seeing from the Unseelie after I cure a curse victim.

I don't feel as if I really did all that much just now. I'm not even sure what I *did* do, other than get my leg carved up and throw a blanket on the ground, which are hardly awe-worthy acts.

"I—I just wanted to help you all," I say.

That remark is met with another volley of murmurs—and some exclamations about "the light!" As Whitt helps me up, I rub my forehead.

Right, there was that flash of light when the Murk man attacked me. It almost seemed like it was the light that killed him. If he *did* die.

My pulse hiccups, and I turn to Whitt. "Is he dead? The Murk?"

Whitt inclines his head, studying me. "They checked him over thoroughly, as you can imagine. The body will be further inspected for any clues to his other intentions or associates and then disposed of. I've never seen you use light like that before."

Because I haven't. I'm not even sure I did use it now.

I bite my lip, aware of the audience all around us. It might not be a bad thing for the Seelie to start to see me as something more than a convenient tonic ingredient. The more they respect me, the more I can demand they respect the other humans here, just like I've started to sway the winter fae. But nothing about this situation sits quite right with me.

I sway on my feet, still a bit dizzy, and Whitt steadies me. "I think I'd better bring Lady Talia home to rest," he says. "If you discover anything notable about this fire or the ones who caused it, send word to Hearth-by-the-Heart at once."

The nearest fae offer their agreement, a few of them brushing their fingers over my arm as we pass them. I can't tell whether they're trying to offer me comfort or take something from my presence.

When we've made it to the edge of the crowd, Whitt scoops me off my feet as August likes to do and sets off up the hill, obviously deciding I'm in no condition to be riding wolves.

"Corwin's coming to us," I say, still a little dazed. I can sense my soul-twined mate hurrying across the border. "He'll meet us up the hill."

Whitt nods. As he tucks my head against his shoulder, he asks under his breath, "What exactly happened back there, mighty one? I would have gotten him off you if you hadn't managed it yourself so abruptly. I'm sorry I didn't get to you soon enough to stop him laying claws on you at all."

"Don't blame yourself," I say, leaning into his embrace. I run through what I can remember of those panicked moments. "I… don't actually know what happened. I didn't say any true names. The light just appeared."

I pause, my uneasiness spreading farther through my chest. "It didn't *feel* like it came from me. I didn't feel anything at all—no energy or power moving through me, the way I do when I've used true names before."

"Hmm." Whitt's mouth slants downward. "You know what's normal for you and what isn't better than I do, mite. I suppose it's possible one of my brethren cast a spell to intervene and then didn't want to distract attention from the heroics you did perform."

I *could* believe that, even though I'm not totally sure I do. I worry at my lip. "I thought you said your magic wouldn't work that close to the iron in the smoke."

"It shouldn't have been able to." He sighs. "I don't like it. Once you're someplace safe, I'll see what else I can find out. At least whatever it was worked in your favor."

That's true. Maybe it's silly to be fretting about the source of the strange light when it might have even saved my life.

I let my body totally relax against Whitt's, and my gaze wanders over the trees we're passing between. It catches on a fall of pearly-white hair half-dimmed by the deepening evening shadows.

Celia is coming down the hill along a course several paces away. Even as I notice her, her gaze stops on us. Her lips flatten into a stern line that looks disapproving. Then she moves on, leaving me even more unnerved than I was before.

CHAPTER TWENTY

Talia

I'd have thought that being in pain would make it easier to produce tears. As the healer warned me might happen, the wound on my thigh still throbs deep in the muscle when I'm moving around much. But even with that pulsing ache spreading through my flesh, I can't start weeping for the curse victim in front of me like flicking a switch.

I look at her, taking in the frail lines of her aged body turned even more brittle in the curse's grip, and think of the children and grandchildren she might be hoping to see grow older, that the curse would steal from her. Of my own grandparents who passed on, never knowing I was still alive, while I was trapped here in the fae realm. It takes a few minutes for the familiar burn to form.

Our audience, gathered in the glow of the Heart's rhythmic light, is nothing but patient. They might even like it when the spectacle takes a little longer, giving time for their anticipation to grow so their relief when I deliver the cure can be that much greater. When I turn away from the cursed woman, with Corwin's hand on my shoulder in case I need steadying, enough breaths draw in to form a collective gasp.

The fae who came to watch the healing are even more reverent than usual today. It might have something to do with the fact that after seeing how my limp was worsening as I moved around the castle, Corwin insisted on carrying me out to the Heart. There's no outward sign of my wound, but he had a few members of his coterie pass on word that people would need to be more patient with me for a little while. When he approached this group with me in his arms, we were met with a lot of widened eyes and murmurs of concern and appreciation.

I guess that makes sense. It's an even bigger generosity to put my time and energy toward healing the fae when I'm not fully healed myself. Still, the awed silence of the crowd feels even stranger than the eager murmurs I've gotten before.

It's a bigger audience than usual too. As before, the curse victim arrived with a large retinue of her flock-folk. But several others have drifted over from both Heart's Cadence and at least a couple of the other arch-lords' domains—and from across the border as well. One of Sylas's staff in the joint castle must have passed on word in the summer realm that I was being called to do a curing, because a dozen or so Seelie slipped through the haze around the Heart around the same time Corwin and I got here.

They've hung back from the Unseelie crowd, watching curiously from a respectful distance. Apparently yesterday's encounter with the Murk has drawn even more interest from the summer fae than I realized.

I focus harder on the sadness I stirred up, and my tears finally spill over. After a moment, I swipe them away and turn back toward the aged fae woman. When I reach for her cheek, her stiffened face manages to twitch to form a hint of a smile.

I might worry about how demanding my role will become as the curse intensifies, but moments like this are why I can't imagine backing down from it. No matter what fae like Aerik or Laoni think of me, every single one I've healed has been grateful beyond words.

None of them deserve to die, especially not in the curse's cruel way.

This time, when the woman straightens up and shows that the frigid chill has released her, the crowd around us keeps a careful distance from me, respectful of my injury. Many of them still call out words of thanks and of their hopes that my wound heals well and soon. As I nod and smile to them in return, my gaze slips past them to the distant form of Laoni's iridium castle.

After all the chaos last night, Whitt and I never got a chance to reach out to Donovan about a visit to see how his human servants are faring. And I still have so many questions to expand on what I learned about Laoni's past and family.

I don't have any immediate business to attend to after this, if there's something you want to talk about, Corwin says through our bond, raising his hand in farewell to the now-dispersing crowd. I know he's careful not to dig too deeply into thoughts I'm not purposefully sending his way, but he can't help picking up on my mood.

There is, actually, I say, but before we can head back to the border castle, one of his staff comes hurrying over from the palace at Heart's Cadence.

"My lord," the man says when he reaches us, with a low bow. "And lady," he adds hastily before focusing back on Corwin. "A messenger has come calling—she said she needs to pass on some news to you as soon as you're able to hear it."

Corwin frowns, apprehension trickling from him into me to join my own. *I'll come with you*, I say before he can suggest I go back to the border castle on my own. *I'd rather hear whatever it is myself—and maybe it'll be something that involves me.*

He nods and reaches for me to lift me up. I still feel a bit awkward being carried like an invalid, but my leg is hurting enough just from standing on my own for the last ten minutes that I'm not going to complain about it. The man from the palace doesn't appear to think it's odd.

"Did the messenger give any indication of what matter she wants to speak to me about?" Corwin asks him as he strides toward the palace. The melody the wind makes passing around the diamond spires shivers over us. "Or which domain she was sent from?"

The attendant shakes his head. "She said nothing other than what I've already conveyed. I assumed it was a message that required discretion."

"That's fine. I wouldn't want you to press in a situation like that. Thank you for summoning me."

At the entrance hall, the fae man heads off to whatever other duties he has to attend to. Corwin keeps carrying me all the way to the room next to the terrace where visitors from farther abroad tend to land. The attendant had said the messenger would be waiting for us there, but when we reach the sitting room with its scattered armchairs and tables, there's no one else there.

Frowning, Corwin sets me down and scans the space. I sink onto the nearest chair, puzzled myself.

After a moment, he walks over to the doors leading to the sparkling terrace and plucks a bit of pale bark that's been fixed to the wall there. "It appears she left a note." He studies it, and I catch the gist through our bond before he speaks again. "She apologizes and says she wanted to confirm one detail of the message, but that she should return within the hour."

"I guess that's not too long," I say. It seems a little strange that she'd have left like that, but I'd rather she delivered an accurate message than one she knew might not be factual. "We were going to talk anyway."

"Yes." Corwin tugs another chair closer and sits down next to me, reaching to take my hand. He runs his thumb gently over my knuckles. "How have you been feeling, my soul? You're sure your injury is on the mend?"

"It's already better than it was last night," I say, squeezing his fingers. He found me and Whitt before we'd even reached Hearth-by-the-Heart, flying to us in a panic despite my reassurances, and insisted on having his own healer check the wound over before he could relax. Then he sent out a few more guards from Heart's Cadence to patrol for any signs of the Murk around the Heart on this side of the border. "The healer did say it'd hurt for a while until it's fully healed."

"What's been concerning you, then?"

I look toward the broad windows, though I can't see Laoni's castle from here, only the sprawling icy landscape beyond the Heart's plateau. "I saw a painting of Laoni's parents when I visited her castle yesterday. Her coterie woman seemed uncomfortable when I asked about them. I wondered if you know what happened to them."

Corwin leans back in his chair, his gaze going distant with thought. "I was too young to participate in any direct discussions around their passings, but I did hear some talk of it, mostly from my own parents. Her mother died before I was born, when Laoni was still a young child. I gather they went on a trip to visit a domain that included a magical whirlpool among its striking features, and there was an accident in which her mother fell in and was sucked down too quickly for anyone to save her."

I shudder. "That's horrible."

"Yes. I think there was a lot of talk about it among the lords and ladies afterward, especially because her father hated to speak of it himself. But my parents said he'd always been strict and became even more so afterward. I suppose he was afraid any carelessness might result in someone else he cared about meeting a similar fate."

It's hard to imagine what "strict" or "even stricter" might look like from winter fae who are already so uptight in general. Maybe that explains a few things about how rigid Laoni is on certain subjects.

"Her father was the arch-lord, then?" I say. "So she didn't inherit it until he passed on?"

Corwin inclines his head. "I was still a child then, and she was… around the equivalent of the age you are now, in fae terms. That incident I know more of the details of. A lord from a domain near the fringes thought he'd better his flock's situation by taking over one of the arch-lordships. He picked Laoni's domain to target. Her father was able to fend off the attack and protect her, but in the process he took a wound that proved fatal. There was nothing the healers could do."

That's horrible too. I rub my mouth, not entirely comfortable with the sense of sympathy the story provokes. It doesn't really matter what awful things Laoni has been through if she's being awful herself. All of my men have been through traumatizing experiences themselves, and they've all kept their senses of fairness and compassion despite it.

Neither account explains why she'd have turned her back on her friendship with Kesral either. "Do you have any idea why she's so dismissive of humans—and fae with human heritage?" I ask.

"I'm not aware of any particular reason for it. I hadn't even noticed her being unusually harsh to staff of more dilute blood until the other day." Corwin grimaces. "But then, that might be my own failing. Before you came into my life, I wasn't quite as attentive to my colleagues' treatment of specific sorts of underlings."

His guilt travels through our connection. I twine my fingers with his. "I think that's understandable. It's such an accepted part of fae society." Which is going to make it even harder to challenge that part.

Before the gloomy thought can fully take hold, one of Corwin's guards bursts into the room. "My lord," she says, jerking into a brief bow, "I think you'd better come. The other arch-lords have marched on the new castle—they're demanding you hear them out."

"What?" Corwin springs to his feet, his forehead furrowing. "If they want to speak to me, they can come to me here—or meet me in the Hall of the Heart if they prefer that."

The guard shakes her head. "I—I don't think that'll be possible, my lord."

Corwin strides toward the doorway, and I hurry after him, gritting my teeth against the ache that wakes up within a few steps. When he stops to help me, I urge him onward silently. *Better they see me standing and walking on my own two feet, considering what they already think of me.*

He insists on scooping me up on the way to the main entrance and only putting me back on my feet there. We walk out side by side and halt just outside the diamond palace.

It isn't all of the arch-lords—I only see Laoni, Uzziah, and Terisse standing across the plain from us—but it isn't *only* them either. I understand now why the guard used the word "marched." Each arch-lord has a squadron of soldiers poised behind them, forming a semi-circle around the winter side of the border castle.

My gut twists. What the hell is going on?

Corwin strides over to them, slowing his pace just enough for me to keep up with my greater limp. I come to a halt right next to him, holding my head high despite the throbbing in my leg.

"What's the meaning of this?" he demands of his colleagues. "You look ready to stage an assault."

Laoni's eyes flash. "Perhaps we are. Consider yourself lucky that we're warning you before we take matters completely into our own hands."

Corwin looks from her to the other two and back again. "What are you talking about?"

Laoni jabs her forefinger in my direction. She pitches her voice loud enough to carry to all the assembled soldiers. "This human woman has been elevated beyond her station for too long already. No matter how 'blessed' she may be, it goes against the laws of the Heart for one who is not a lord or lady by inheritance to rule from a castle of his or her own. And 'Lady' Talia cannot be considered a lady in the same way as one of our own besides, since she isn't even fae. This structure stands in total defiance to the proper order of things."

I stare at her, trying to wrap my head around everything she's saying. Can she really support all those claims? She didn't bring any of that up while we were building the castle.

Maybe it took her this long to dig up some obscure law she felt she could twist to her ends. Or maybe she didn't bother digging until she saw just how avidly her people are starting to respond to me.

Maybe it's my fault for pushing my luck, forcing her hand to get my visit into *her* castle.

As I swallow thickly, Corwin sets a firm hand on my shoulder. "The Heart allowed it to be built. I think that's proof enough that we haven't—"

"You are hardly the sole judge of what is good for the Heart or for this realm," Laoni interrupts with a sneer. "We're giving you until the end of the day tomorrow to bring down your half of this unnatural building and salvage whatever you would of it. If you've failed to complete the task by then, our people will destroy it for you."

CHAPTER TWENTY-ONE

August

I'm not sure what agonizes me more: the anguish that's been etched on Talia's face since we started this voyage or the guilt she clearly feels over asking me to help her relieve that anguish.

"I'm sorry to be dragging you away from Sylas with everything that's going on," she says, her hands twisting together in her lap where she's sitting on the other side of the small carriage my brother conjured for us.

"I wouldn't be much use to him or the others right now anyway," I remind her. "The three of them can pore over plenty of books and records without any help from me. We'll be back well before tomorrow, when hopefully I *won't* need to be of use stopping those mangy raven arch-lords from carrying out their threat."

She rubs the bronze bangle fitted snugly around her wrist. "I don't actually feel that anything's wrong with Jamie."

"The spell I cast will only kick in if he's in severe distress," I say. "There are ways the arch-lords could have interfered with his life that wouldn't necessarily have caused that yet. After the way they tried to steal him away before, I can't blame you for being worried."

"And he might not even be wearing his bracelet, in which case I wouldn't be alerted even if he was in a horrible situation. I just… I have to know." She exhales slowly, but her expression stays just as pained.

I've been guiding the carriage slowly since we entered the foggy woods at the very edge of the fringelands. When we've finally reached the area where the portals are more numerous, I stop the vehicle and help Talia out. I mean to carry her while I check the nearest passages, but she shakes her head and slips from my arms. "I'll wait here while you check as quickly as you can. I don't want to slow you down. I'm sure I'll be fine."

As I glance around the hazy forest, my fangs itch in my gums. We haven't had the same incursions of fearsome beasts that the winter realm has experienced, probably because our population hasn't dwindled and our curse actually makes us *more* fearsome rather than less when it takes hold. But there are plenty that still lurk around the edges of the Mist.

I can't smell any of them at the moment. I just won't go too far.

Shifting into wolf form so I can travel even faster, I stretch into the new configuration of my muscles and lope to the nearest portal. All it takes is a sniff to determine whether the human lands on the other side hold the exact combination of unusual scents that marked the place where we found Talia's brother. I think I've narrowed down the patch of forest where we'll find it even more than last time, although the doorways to the human world do have a habit of drifting around some.

It only takes three tries to identify it. I sprint back to Talia, throwing myself into the shift before I've even halted, but when I reach for her she simply takes my hand. "I can walk. I'm not going to be a burden."

I let her limp along beside me, wincing inwardly at the much more pronounced unevenness to her steps with her recent wound. Those wretched Murk. I wish I'd been there to tear the one who did this to shreds.

"You haven't been a burden," I say firmly. "Whatever's gotten into the Unseelie arch-lords, it's them being pricks, not anything you've done wrong. They should be celebrating how much you've helped them like the rest of their people, not getting picky about who lives in what castle."

"I think it's a little more complicated than that," Talia mutters, which might be true, but I can't think of any way she's to blame for the current conflict.

At the right portal, I cast the spell to keep us hidden from mortal eyes. Talia finally lets me pick her up for the journey through, which is a bit disorienting even when you're in the best of health. The colors and shapes around us waver and twist, and all at once we're standing in the secluded clearing in the park.

The smells of burnt gasoline and sun-baked tar that trickle through the air mark this place as part of the human world even without anything in view other than trees and grass. With a few steps, the buildings of the city beyond show amid the greenery.

Talia starts to squirm in my arms, but I let out a mild growl of refusal. "You said you wanted to move quickly. I can walk faster carrying you than you can with your leg hurting you."

Talia grimaces, but she relaxes into me. I wish I could feel more triumphant about my victory. I'd rather she wasn't wounded in the first place.

The Unseelie arch-lords are attacking the first home she's had in our world that's been totally *hers*. It isn't a stretch to think they might come after her brother and use him as leverage for whatever it is they want to gain. I hate to think what they might do to Talia herself if they can find a way to justify it to themselves.

I want to believe that we could simply refuse their initial demands and it'll all die down, but few things in the fae world are ever actually simple. Whitt looked worried when we left, even surrounded by all his papers and with several of his associates among our pack-kin at his beck and call. If *he* thinks there's a reason for concern, then the situation has to be bad.

As I carry Talia through the park, avoiding a woman pushing a stroller and a man walking three boisterous dogs that bark in my direction even though they can't see me, I study the angle of the sun.

"It's early morning here. I'd say around breakfast time. Your brother should be at home around then, shouldn't he?"

"I think so." Talia peers around us. "I don't even know if it's a school day or the weekend. Or what month it is. I'm so out of touch." She lets out a little laugh, but it doesn't sound all that amused.

"I can't tell the exact month since we don't follow them," I say, "but it smells and looks like late spring to me. We could check a newspaper for the exact date."

Talia hesitates and then shakes her head. "No. All that's important is making sure Jamie's okay and then getting back to deal with the arch-lords as soon as possible. I shouldn't be worrying about that stuff anyway."

But she is. I can't blame her for that either. This world was meant to be hers before Aerik and his blasted cadre tore her away from it—why shouldn't she wonder about it? Her life would have been so much different if he'd never rampaged into it.

The pang that runs through my chest at the thought speaks of how much the idea of never having met her pains me. But that alternate path would have led to much *less* pain for her.

Even if we check on Jamie now, how can we be sure the Unseelie arch-lords won't target him later? I swallow that question, not wanting to disturb Talia further if she hasn't already thought of the possibility. The only way we could totally protect him is to, well, bring him under our protection, which would throw off his own life in ways I know she doesn't want.

I may not love the stink of human machines, but the neighborhood where Talia's aunt and uncle live isn't wholly unpleasant. Birds chirp in the many trees that loom from the well-tended lawns. I spot a vegetable garden in one front yard that I might have to examine more closely for curiosity's sake on a less urgent future visit. The breeze that washes over us is as pleasantly warm as it is in the summer realm near the Heart.

When we reach the house itself, I prowl around the structure, peeking through the windows and holding Talia so she can see in too. At the kitchen, I stop. She lets out a relieved sigh.

Her brother is sitting at the kitchen table with two younger children I assume are her cousins, all of them eating cereal from bowls. Another prickle of curiosity ripples over me to find out what exactly that tastes like. Cereal isn't really a thing in the fae world, and I've only sampled a few.

But we're not here for that either.

"He's wearing the bracelet," Talia murmurs, a smile crossing her face for the first time since we set off. The bronze band gleams at her brother's wrist.

I tighten my arms around her in a gentle hug. My mind scrambles to think of what else I could offer to reassure her even after we leave here again.

"I could set down a spell around the house to alert us if any fae come near," I say. "Around his school as well. It wouldn't prevent them from coming, and I can't cover everywhere he might go…"

Talia sucks her lower lip under her teeth as she considers. "No. That would take a lot of time that we don't really have right now, and if they did come to take him, they'd probably be sneaky about it anyway. A false sense of security is worse than not having it at all."

She rubs her forehead, her smile gone as quickly as it came. "I don't think there's any way I'd feel totally sure he's okay other than monitoring him every second, which obviously I can't. I'm just glad to know the arch-lords haven't gone that far yet."

Another possibility occurs to me. "I can ask Sylas to post a rotation of sentries in the area on the fringes near the portal. It wouldn't need to require much manpower, and then we'll have someone keeping an eye on things the one place they'd have to pass through to reach him."

Talia tucks her head against my neck. "There, that sounds perfect. Who says you can't be a strategist too? Thank you, August."

"Anything for you, Sweetness."

I'm about to say we should head back now when a sudden realization creeps up over me. Talia said it wasn't possible for her to stay here and watch over her brother… but technically it is. We were willing to let her stay in the human world for as long as she needed to if she'd decided to do just that.

She'd be safer here than in the fae world, where she's become a target of Seelie, Unseelie, and Murk alike. I tried to convince Sylas to send her here months ago, before we even knew her brother was alive, to protect her from the ongoing conflicts. And maybe if the Unseelie have to go without her healing abilities for a few days, their arch-lords will find reasons to respect her more.

She'd never agree to it, though. She felt guilty enough just asking to make this brief trip.

I adjust her in my arms, my gut knotting. Now that I've considered it, I know it would be so easy. Talia wouldn't be able to make the journey back to the fae realm without a guide. If I left her here, she'd have to go in to her aunt and uncle, reconnect with her brother, and stay here in the best sort of peace I can give her…

Talia stirs, glancing up at me. "Is everything okay?"

I open my mouth and close it again. There's a moment when I'm almost tempted. But only almost.

Those months ago, I was willing to send her away without consulting her about it. The way she reacted when she discovered I'd gone behind her back is burned into my memory. *That* hurt her, much more than any suffering she's shown from her wound.

No matter how much I might want to protect her, I can't do it by denying her own free will. I wouldn't be much better than Aerik then.

She decides what risks she can handle, not me.

I close my eyes, wishing for a better solution but knowing there isn't one. At least I can take a little joy in knowing that her choice keeps her close to me. I'll protect her from as much as I can with my claws and my fangs. Let's hope that's enough.

"Not at all, Sweetness," I say. "Let's go home and deal with those feather-brained winter arch-lords."

CHAPTER TWENTY-TWO

Talia

The forest along the fringes of the Mists is so desolate that the last thing I expect is to run into another fae the moment we step through the portal. Holding me, August jerks to a halt. We both stare at Kesral, who's poised as if he was about to walk through the portal we just came through, staring back at us.

"What are you doing here?" I blurt out with a lurch of my heart. Did Laoni send someone to kidnap Jamie after all?

He backs up a couple of steps, raising his hands in a peace-making gesture at August's instinctive flexing of his muscles. "My apologies for surprising you. Arch-Lord Laoni heard that you'd set off for the human world without any Unseelie accompaniment. She asked me to determine what you were doing."

I guess she really didn't have any plans for Jamie if it hadn't even occurred to her why I'd be checking on him.

Is everything all right, Talia? Corwin asks through our bond, having picked up on my initial reaction. I've been keeping a barrier up against our connection so I don't distract him while he's concentrating on finding counterarguments to Laoni's claims, but I was so startled they fell away.

It seems so, I tell him. *I was just surprised. Don't let me disturb you.*

I give him a moment to take stock of my well-being and then imagine the wall of light rising inside me again so I don't intrude on his work. Relaxing in August's arms, I nudge him to set me down.

"I was worried about my brother," I tell Kesral as I straighten out my dress. "I just wanted to look in on him. With tensions being so high right now… it was hard not to be concerned."

His jaw tightens at my reference to the arch-lords' threat. "I had no hand in any of the demands regarding your new castle. I won't speak against my lady, but—I have no wish to oppose you or your mates."

The fact that he's willing to call all my men "mates" even though only one of them officially is at the moment eases any lingering uneasiness I might have had about his presence. "I'm glad to hear that. We were going to be heading back now too. I assume you'll do the same."

He nods. "I'll tell my lady that you were simply taking a little comfort in being near to your family."

That's true enough, and doesn't outright give any ideas about the way Laoni might use my family. I hope I haven't drawn too much of her attention in Jamie's direction by checking up on him.

Kesral's small winter-style carriage sits next to ours. A glimmer around the wooden structure we arrived in suggests it's encased in some kind of spell. Kesral dismisses the magic with an apologetic air and glances at us again. "It'll be best if I escort you to Arch-Lord Laoni myself so she can see that you have returned—and much the same as you were before."

"All right." I don't want to get him in trouble.

"I'm staying with her," August says with a hint of a growl in his voice.

Kesral gives him a slight smile. "That would probably be preferable. She isn't all that trusting of the Seelie still either."

He turns to climb into his carriage, but a question bubbles up inside me—the one that's been stewing ever since I spoke to Laoni's kitchen manager. "Kesral… Is it true that you and Laoni used to be close friends when you were a lot younger, before she became an arch-lord?"

He swivels back around, his shoulders stiffening a bit. "Who did you hear that from?"

I shrug, trying to keep the atmosphere casual. "When I visited her castle to see about the human servants there, Serev in the kitchen mentioned it."

Kesral dips his head awkwardly. "Well, we did spend a lot of time together as children. But of course she had many responsibilities to prepare for and which she then had to take on far earlier than she should have needed to. She's had to face a great deal, mostly on her own… It's been my honor to continue supporting her however I can."

However much she even lets him these days. But clear affection rings through his voice, so unmistakeable it jars against my memories of the way *she* speaks to him.

I grapple with my next question and finally just spit it out. "She seems to be the opposite of friendly with you these days. She's always been cold and sometimes even harsh when I've heard her talking to you. And a couple of the other guards were hassling you about the human part of your heritage—she obviously doesn't intervene to speak up for you with your colleagues."

Kesral is silent for a long moment, his expression somber enough that my gut starts to twist. "I'm sorry," I add. "This is probably an uncomfortable subject. I shouldn't have pried."

"I suppose it's fair," he says with a rough chuckle. "Here I am chasing you down on your private business. All you're doing is asking questions." He runs his hand back over his hair, which is in its usual short ponytail. "I can't speak for her, of course. And I promise you she wasn't always so strict with me. When she could be more carefree, she was a good friend. But circumstances change…"

I wait patiently as he seems to consider his next words. He inhales slowly and continues. "I'm not sure how much you know about her family's history, but after my lady's mother died, her father who was arch-lord at the time became much more hostile toward humans and anyone associated with them. They'd brought a few human servants along on the trip where she died, and I think somehow he blamed them for not trying to save her, even though they would inevitably have drowned."

Yes, if the whirlpool Corwin mentioned was so strong a true-blooded fae could be overwhelmed by it in seconds, a human wouldn't stand a chance. And having seen the state of most human servants in this world, I'm not sure it'd even occur to them to spring to anyone's rescue, they're so dazed with the drugs the fae feed them.

But grief can warp people's minds in unfair ways. Look at what it's done to Corwin's mother, who's practically insane with it.

"And Laoni picked up the same attitude?" I venture.

"Not all at once, but over time, especially as her training intensified, she started keeping her distance and becoming more critical of my failings." Kesral makes a dismissive gesture. "I can't complain. It was unlikely we'd continue as we were once we grew up anyway."

His gaze flicks away from me for a second, and I get the sense he's suppressing more sadness than he's letting himself show. "I'm sorry," I say. "It's still got to be hard."

He meets my eyes again, something softening in his expression. "I consider myself lucky to have had her companionship as much as I did for as long as I did. I can still remember—" A gentle smile touches his lips. "I was there with her when she mastered her first true name, for silver. She was so pleased, and her first thought was that she wanted to help me master it too..."

He pauses and inclines his head. "I know she hasn't been the easiest on you either, but there's a good heart underneath. I'm sure that hasn't changed. And I'll be here for her as long as she needs me in whatever capacity."

As he speaks, a different impression takes a hold of me. Kesral isn't just talking fondly about a friendship of the past. He sounds like he's... in love with her.

A sharp pang shoots through my heart on his behalf. That's so much worse than facing insults from an old friend. Does Laoni have any idea how much she's hurting him, how devoted to her he is despite her harshness?

I don't want to bring Kesral any more pain by harping on the subject. "That's very admirable," I say after a brief fumble for words. "Thank you for putting up with my curiosity."

He gives me a small bow. "I serve my lady, but I can recognize that you've done impressive things for our people—including her and the rest of my flock—as well."

August rests his hand on my head. "*My* lady is hoping to get back to her pack and her flock quickly. I hope you won't mind if we make the trip back a speedy one."

"Not at all," Kesral says. "Let us be off."

I nestle myself on a couple of cushions in the base of our carriage to escape the wind generated by our swift flight. With the warbling of the rushing air passing over us and the wavering shapes of leaves and clouds whipping past overhead, the whole world seems to have gone into fast-forward.

The rocking of the carriage starts to lull me. I didn't sleep all that well last night with my wound aching and my head full of worries about the Murk and the humans living among the fae. Even with all the new worries added to that heap, at some point I drift off with August watching over me.

I wake up at the slowing of the carriage and a sudden shift in temperature. The chilly breeze that touches my cheek tells me we've passed into the winter realm. I sit up in time to see Laoni's iridium castle looming closer.

August stops outside it next to Kesral's vehicle. "Let's make this quick."

The Unseelie guard nods and beckons for us to follow him.

Laoni must have been alerted to our approach, because she strides into the entrance room just as we enter. "Well?" she says imperiously, looking at Kesral.

He bobs low with more respect than I think he really owes her. "There was no cause for concern. Lady Talia and her mate were simply making a routine check on her brother. They were in the human realm for less than an hour, and they readily agreed to present themselves to you to confirm it."

Her gaze darts over us, and her mouth pinches. "In the past, we've agreed to an Unseelie escort accompanying you on such trips. Why did you shirk that agreement this time?"

"I thought that condition was only for while we were still deciding what was going to happen with Jamie," I say. "Nothing important was happening today. And frankly, I didn't think your flock or either of the other arch-lords you trust would want to be bothered with the trip."

Laoni bristles. "I'll decide what's a bother and what's not. It's this sort of impertinence that makes trust difficult to come by."

"Talia's simply answering your question," August breaks in.

"It's the tone of her answer I object to."

Oh, she's one to talk about tone.

But before I can say as much, Kesral speaks up again in a more tender voice than I've heard from him before. Maybe our conversation has stirred up so many memories of the past that they've clouded his perception of the present. "My lady, from what I've seen of Lady Talia and her companions, they have no ill intentions toward us. I understand your leaning toward caution, and it's as commendable as always, but in this case—"

Laoni spins toward him, cutting him off with a snap. "It's not for you to commend me or not. I haven't asked for your opinion, and you should know better than to offer it as if it's wanted."

Kesral can't quite restrain a flinch. My hackles rise, but in the same moment, Laoni's face twitches, as if she's controlling some further reaction she didn't want to let out. As I pause, studying her, she raises her chin haughtily.

Kesral dips into an even lower bow this time. "I apologize for overstepping, my lady." He makes a movement toward her and halts when Laoni jerks a step backward, away from him. You'd think he had the plague from the way she recoiled. His mouth slants downward. "I'll take my leave."

As he slips away, his spine rigid but his shoulders just slightly slumped, Laoni's gaze follows him for a second. Her jaw flexes, and in that instant, I could swear I catch a hint of pain… or maybe regret.

The trace of emotion smooths away an instant later. I might have thought I'd imagined it if her hand didn't rise just then to the side of her neck.

To the true-name mark etched against her tan skin, the one I know from Corwin's teachings is for silver. The first one she earned, with Kesral by her side.

A lump rises in my throat. She obviously hasn't forgotten their past together either. Why in the world does she treat him so awfully if it hurts her to do it just like it hurts him?

My frustration with everything she's done to and around me over the past several weeks boils over. "How can you be so hard on him when he cares so much about supporting you?"

Laoni whirls on me. "What would you know about any of it?"

I glare right back at her. "I know that no matter what your father told you, you seem to be smart enough to have figured out that human beings aren't horrible just because a few didn't drown themselves trying to save your mother. And he isn't even human—he's just got a little more mixed in with the fae part than you do. But maybe you just like being a bully more than anything else."

"Talia," August says quietly, grasping my shoulder, but I'm done anyway.

Laoni gapes at me, her face turning splotchy with anger and maybe shock. "You—you have no idea about anything," she retorts in a rough undertone. "Not everything that happens has to do with how human or not someone is. And not everyone gets to have whatever they want regardless of who the Heart ties them to. We do our best with the duties we're given."

At the end of that tirade, she snaps her mouth shut, looking almost sick. "Never mind," she goes on brusquely. "Get out of my castle and see to yours."

My mind is still working over what she said, trying to fit it together with what I already knew and what I witnessed during this confrontation. Does she think I've gotten whatever I want—while she's here demanding my men tear down the home they made for me? What has *she* ever wanted that she didn't—

Regardless of who the Heart ties to them.

Understanding smacks into me like an ocean wave, the pieces colliding. Kesral's account of their history together. Laoni pushing him away and yet seeming to regret it. And that remark...

I'm not sure I'm right, but the suspicion swells in my chest too forcefully to be ignored. Is there any chance she'd admit it?

The more of an audience she has, the less likely.

"August," I say carefully, "would you let me speak to Laoni alone for a minute? I'll meet you outside."

August tenses beside me. He eyes the arch-lord warily. "Are you sure, Talia?"

"I don't think Arch-Lord Laoni wants to damage the woman who's curing her people." She might want to ruin my happiness, but she's accomplishing that by striking out at everyone and everything around me. Having me alone won't help her.

"I have nothing to say to you," Laoni sneers as August reluctantly heads for the door.

"But I have something to say to you," I reply. "And I respect *you* enough, in spite of everything, to do it privately."

She frowns, her hands balling at her sides, but she doesn't send me away. Looking into her eyes, I don't think she has any idea what I want to talk about, which may be the only reason she's listening.

The door thumps shut behind August. I glance around to confirm there are no other fae nearby. Then I fold my arms over my chest. "You wanted him to be your mate. Kesral. But it couldn't happen because he isn't true-blooded."

"What?" Laoni sputters, but she can't contain the panic that flashes across her expression, and I know I've hit the mark.

"It actually makes a lot more sense than you browbeating him just because he's got a human parent," I say, keeping my tone even. "You can use that as an excuse to be awful to him, and maybe you even believe it a little after whatever ideas your father passed on about humans, and that way there isn't much chance of anyone figuring out the truth. And you can keep him at a distance, so *you're* not as bothered by the truth."

Laoni draws her brawny frame tall, her eyes flashing. "You are the last person who should be talking to anyone about picking mates."

"Why, because I picked four?" *Not everyone gets to have whatever they want*, she said before. Another suspicion prickles up through my chest. "Is that why you're so awful to *me*? Because I'm getting to have all the men I love instead of only my soul-twined mate? Who says you couldn't too? Be with him if you want. Work it out with your mate. You could let yourself be happy instead of trying to make sure I can't be."

Laoni has completely hardened, though. Now I can't spot a trace of the concern that showed through in those brief moments around Kesral. "This is exactly why humans are better kept drugged into oblivion. Making up crazy stories to justify all the rules you're flouting—you're as insane as Corwin's mother. Get out of here before I have you locked up the way he's had to her."

I wince at the viciousness of her remark. "Arch-Lord Laoni, you know it doesn't have to be like—"

"Get *out*!" She jabs her finger toward the door. There's so much fury in her stance that I'm not completely sure she *wouldn't* hurt me if I refused.

I retreat, my chest constricting around my heart as I step out into the cold air outside.

There's still so much I don't understand. Other arch-lords have taken more than one lover. Is it that she feels it'd be shameful to have one who's half-human? Or one I'm guessing she's fallen for in a way she hasn't her actual soul-twined mate?

Does she believe, like Sylas did, in being faithful to her soul-twined mate no matter who they are or what happens?

But the answers to those questions don't really matter in the end. What matters is that regardless of the reasons for her resentment of me and my relationship with my mates, she's holding onto that resentment just as tightly as before.

I swallow hard. In fact, after what I just said to her, she might be even more eager to see our joint castle fall.

CHAPTER TWENTY-THREE

Sylas

No one has made a move toward the border castle yet, but a few soldiers from the Unseelie arch-lords' domains have taken up stations nearby, simply monitoring our activity. Or lack of activity, I suppose, given that we haven't taken down the smallest piece of the structure so far.

I study them from a high window in the winter side of the castle. Corwin added warming spells to these rooms, but being surrounded by all this cool diamond with that icy expanse outside still sends a chill over my skin. It's going to take some time getting used to the less familiar elements of our newly shared existence.

If I'm allowed the chance to get used to them. The winter arch-lords clearly aren't backing down. It's only late afternoon on the same day they made their announcement, the sun still blazing somewhere behind me, and in theory Corwin has until tomorrow to meet their demands, but they're already preparing for battle.

In theory, they've only asked for him to dismantle what part of the castle extends into winter territory—but the halves of the building are so entwined, that would require a complete restructuring regardless.

And there's little point to having it if it doesn't allow Talia access to both realms the way Corwin planned.

A heaviness settles over my heart. I turn and stride back through the castle to my own side of the border.

I don't bother to call an official meeting in the Bastion. Donovan's already informed me that if I have the law behind me, he'll back me up against the Unseelie challenge. So in the interests of time and making a more personal appeal, I go straight to Celia's castle.

The fae man who greets me at the door hustles off to inform her of my arrival. She can't have been too deeply occupied, because he returns a minute later to escort me to one of the sitting rooms, and she's already inside when I enter.

Celia makes a vague gesture toward the chairs scattered along the edges of the room, but she remains standing by the elegant fireplace, its frame as sleek and dark as her own form. She sweeps her luminescent hair back over her shoulders and fixes me with a pensive gaze. "I hear there's trouble with the ravens regarding your new castle, Lord Sylas."

Her formality doesn't bode well for my mission. I incline my head. "Three of the winter arch-lords have demanded that Arch-Lord Corwin tear the winter side of the structure down. They claim that it's primarily Talia's home, and that being neither a lady by birth nor fae, giving her a castle of her own goes against the will of the Heart."

"It is unusual."

"So is Talia," I have to say. "As is her situation. My strategist and I—and Corwin as well—have been going through what records we can find on related matters, and I don't believe they have true justification. There have been occasional eccentrics among the faded fae who've built grand homes for themselves, and while they were viewed with some derision, they were never forced to dismantle them. There was no sign of magical backlash from the Heart either. And as soul-twined mate to a true-blooded arch-lord, I think we have reasonable grounds to say Talia has been granted her title in every way she could need it by the Heart itself."

Celia folds her arms over her chest. "It sounds as if you have the matter well in hand then."

I restrain a grimace. "I'm not sure deflecting the claim will be as easy as presenting those arguments. Those arch-lords, Laoni in particular, have had a vendetta against Talia and her union with Corwin since the soul-twined bond first took effect. You've seen how they've spoken and behaved during our past negotiations. Whatever their motivations, they want to destabilize her position among the fae. No matter what we say about it, I suspect they'll force the subject."

"They have definitely proved to be difficult allies at times," Celia allows. "I should hope they aren't in such a hurry to return to a state of war, though."

"I wouldn't think they are, but I wouldn't have expected this move from them either."

"I can understand your concern. However, this seems to be a matter between the Unseelie arch-lords and those of you with a direct stake in the border castle. Why exactly have you called on me?"

The fact that she's making me spell it out is even less reassuring. I square my shoulders. "I would like the Seelie arch-lords to present a united front when the Unseelie come to carry out their demands tomorrow. Donovan has already agreed. If we stand together in defense of the border castle remaining whole, with Corwin on our side as well, we represent half of the Heart's chosen representatives. I believe that may be enough to dissuade them."

Celia hums to herself. "Perhaps. But for how long, if they carry as much animosity as you suggest?"

"I can't be certain, of course. I wouldn't be surprised if they attempt another gambit before too long. But the more times we stand firm against them, the shakier their position becomes."

"And you don't think it's unwise to intrude on the political decisions of the winter realm when they don't directly affect us?"

"They affect *me*," I say. "They affect the woman I mean to take as my mate, who holds back the curse for all of the Seelie. The border castle was meant to represent the cooperation between the realms. So we're already involved, even if Corwin's colleagues are putting on a show of focusing only on him. Giving in to their demands now will only open the door to more problems as they push their advantage, not fewer."

Celia steps away from me, pacing to one end of the room and back again with measured steps. She slides her fingers along the edge of her jaw in thought. "It is also possible that their animosity isn't entirely unreasonable. Talia has risen to a position of great prominence in a matter of months. I can understand some wariness."

I can't stop myself from bristling. "Talia has never done anything but give of herself to help the rest of us in every way she can. To suggest that there might be any maliciousness to her situation is an insult to both one who's saved us from so much suffering and me and my cadre as well."

"I didn't mean that she's intentionally out to harm us," Celia replies dryly. "Obviously not. But there's so much we don't understand about her origins or her connection to the Heart. Every few weeks some new unexpected aspect to her powers emerges. Where does it end?"

"What does it matter?" I ask. "She's only ever used those powers to help us."

"So far. Again, Sylas, I'm not saying she has any ill intentions, only that even *she* isn't fully in control of what role she plays here. And we have no way of knowing how that role may shift in the future."

I frown at her, uneasiness coiling in my gut. Celia is making her points sound perfectly logical, but I have to wonder how much she's guided by her own discomfort with Talia's "prominence," as she put it. Is she truly worried that Talia's presence will end up harming us in some way, or does she simply feel her own authority is threatened by our people's growing fondness for my mate-to-be?

"We will see what comes," I say. "We can only make our decisions now based on what's already true."

"Perhaps." Celia pauses. "But I think I will stay out of your present conflict rather than take a side. What the Heart wants will come to pass one way or another. Let what is right be decided between those of you so concerned. And while I can't prevent you and Donovan from supporting Arch-Lord Corwin's cause while you carry the majority, I do hope you won't bring the conflict back into the summer realm when we've finally gotten some semblance of peace."

She turns away. A protest rises in my throat, but I can see there's no swaying her. If I badger her about it, I'll only be making myself look oafish.

"I'm disappointed by your decision, but I accept it," I say with all the politeness I can muster, and stalk out of the room.

The uneasiness stays with me as I make my way out into the warm afternoon air. The shadows have stretched longer in the time while I was speaking with Celia. I wander between them, too restless to fix on a destination. My wolf stirs beneath my skin, itching to be released.

There's nothing more I can do here other than wait for tomorrow and see how we fare. We have all the evidence we *should* need to confirm our right to keep the border castle. Whitt and Corwin are still gathering more.

And Celia's words niggle at me. *There's so much we still don't understand about her…*

It's true. None of our investigations have explained how Talia ended up so tied to the fae and our curse. If I knew more about *that*, perhaps it would persuade Celia to support our cause—or even alleviate whatever worries are gripping the winter arch-lords.

I can't think of any avenue I haven't pursued that could tell me more about those origins, though.

No, that isn't strictly true. I stop in a patch of sunlight, inhaling deeply, a cedar scent flooding my lungs. There is one course I haven't taken yet, both out of a suspicion it wouldn't prove useful anyway and a reluctance to ask anything of those involved. Also a small bit of concern that I might end up saying or doing something I'd regret when faced with those villains, discussing the horror they carried out.

But I have nothing else. If there's even a slight chance reaching out will tip the balance in Talia's favor, I should take that chance.

Without waiting for trepidation to set in, I veer toward the grove of juniper trees where I usually conjure my carriages. It's too long a journey to take it at a wolfish run, as much as I'd enjoy letting out some of the tension wound through me by stretching my legs that way.

I send a brief note of explanation to Whitt and set off at the swiftest course I can urge the vehicle to. As I speed over the landscape, I consider the exact questions I want to ask and how to phrase them.

It seems as though barely any time at all has passed before the bone-white walls of Aerik's fortress come into view up ahead.

My muscles tense automatically. Memories trickle through my mind of the night months ago when my cadre and I slunk inside that building and discovered Talia starving and grimy in her cramped cage, with nothing but a dirty blanket to cover her. My fangs prick at my gums.

Aerik has never fully paid for what he did to my love, and perhaps having freed her from his clutches and brought her all due happiness is the best victory we can claim. But I can't help hoping that someday he gives me an excuse to deliver a bloodier consequence.

Today, though, I can't be on the attack. I need his cooperation.

As I draw the carriage to a halt, a few fae emerge from the castle. By the time I've leapt out onto the tall grass, the lord of the domain himself has come out to meet me.

The dwindling sunlight catches in Aerik's vividly yellow hair, which he rakes his fingers through before walking right up to me. Tension tugs at the corners of his mouth. "Arch-Lord Sylas. To what do I owe the pleasure?"

We both know there's no joy in this meeting for either of us. I offer a thin smile. "There's a matter I'd like to speak to you about, if you have a moment. It shouldn't take much of your time."

Aerik's gaze flicks over me, and I suspect he'd put me off if he were bolder. But this is a man who enjoys bullying beings far less powerful than himself, not standing up to those who rule over him. He dips his head. "I can spare you that. Why don't you come inside?"

I like stepping into that bone-white building even less than standing outside it. As Aerik leads me to a small sitting room, my skin crawls. I keep my expression impassive, taking the chair he motions to and waiting until he's settled into one across from me.

Neither of us will want this conversation drawn out. I get straight to the point. "I'd like to hear your full account of the night you found Talia."

Aerik blinks at me. Whatever he might have imagined this visit was about, it clearly wasn't that. "I beg your pardon?" he says cautiously.

I set my elbows on the arms of the chair and fold my hands together in my lap. "The night of the full moon, when you stumbled into the human world with your cadre and came upon Talia. When you discovered the curse-breaking effect of her blood." And mauled her brother and slaughtered her parents. I hold in those accusations. "I want to know everything you can remember about that incident. How did you end up so far from home when the curse took you? Did you see anything else of note after you came out of it?"

Aerik is silent for a long moment, braced as if he thinks this might be a trick, that I'm setting him up for some kind of punishment right now. When I simply wait patiently, he swipes his hand across his mouth. "There was nothing of note about the situation in which we found her or our collecting of her. As soon as I tasted her blood and snapped out of the curse, I realized the effect she had and how valuable that made her. My cadre had already torn through her family—I didn't order their murders, if you were thinking I had."

It had occurred to me that he might have to ensure no one remained who'd search for Talia, but whether he incited his cadre or not makes little difference to the outcome. "I assume you arranged for them to sample her blood and wake up as well."

He nodded. "We healed her wounds so that she'd survive the journey back to our world and set off straight for the nearest portal. It was a small town, quiet. I believe we saw a couple of cars passing on the roads as we made our way, but no one else on foot. Nothing stands out in my memory. Although it would have needed to be rather impressive to have distracted me from the discovery we'd just made."

I can only imagine the whirlwind of his thoughts in that moment. For him, it would have been not just the thought of how she could benefit all Seelie-kind but how he could use her to improve his own standing among us.

My claws twitch behind my fingertips, but I hold them in. "All right. But how did you end up in that small town to begin with? It's a long way from here to the fringes. Surely you didn't normally wander so far on the night of the curse?"

"No," Aerik says shortly, and then knits his brow as if he's having trouble recalling the events. "A distant niece of mine called in a favor that day. Her domain is close to the fringelands. We meant to return before sundown. But…" The furrow in his brow deepens. "Something caught our attention. We tracked it into the woods along the fringe…"

As he focuses on dredging up the memory, an after-image wavers up over his face before my deadened eye. For a few seconds, I'm seeing both the man in front of me and another version of him, scanning his surroundings with a predatory gleam in his eyes and his fangs bared. Whatever he was searching for back then, he meant to rip it apart.

Aerik snaps his fingers, and the ghostly image vanishes with the blink of my eyes. He taps the arm of his chair. "A rat," he says. "We were chasing down a rat we were sure we'd scented. Those stinking Murk."

"A rat," I repeat. A clammy sensation squeezes around my gut.

Aerik nods. "We didn't want to let the thing get away. I think we suspected it'd caused the mischief my niece called us in over. We must have figured it didn't matter if the moon rose, we'd deal with the vermin just as easily wild as sane."

And in the process they'd ended up rampaging through a portal onto Talia's doorstep.

"That's all you remember?" I ask, even though I'm sure of the answer. None of us holds memories of our savagery in the grip of the curse. That's part of the horror of it—not even being sure what violence you've carried out.

"That's all of it." Aerik considers me. "Did my answers meet your satisfaction?"

"I appreciate your humoring my curiosity," I say, getting up. I'm not going to tell him my real reasons for asking. I *can't* tell him what I've discerned from his answers, since I'm not even sure myself yet.

A rat in the woods by the portals years ago, drawing Aerik and his cadre on a chase. A rat blasting down the homes in the Unseelie summer settlement last month. A rat springing at Talia just yesterday by an iron-laced fire.

I don't know what it means, but the one thing I am certain of is that I don't like it at all.

CHAPTER TWENTY-FOUR

Talia

Laoni said Corwin had until the end of the day after she made her demand, but she doesn't wait quite that long. The sun hasn't yet dipped out of view when many more soldiers from her, Terisse's, and Uzziah's domains begin assembling around the border castle. The arch-lords themselves take positions at the front of their troops, standing tall and stern.

I wonder what Neve makes of all this. But then, Neve doesn't seem to be all that aware of what's going on right in front of her much of the time, so she may not even realize her colleagues have made this challenge. Corwin didn't want to force her into the conflict when it's doubtful she could turn the tide anyway.

As I watch from one of the winter-side windows, our own soldiers gather in a tighter ring around the Unseelie side of the castle. Being the ones most familiar with this realm, Corwin's flock stands at the front, swords at their hips, heads high. A large part of Sylas's pack fills out the area behind them, with some support from Donovan's domain as well.

Our force looks so much smaller than the one opposing us. My fingers tighten where I'm gripping the diamond window frame, and Corwin comes up behind me, setting his hands on my shoulders.

"I should go out there now. Sylas and I will speak to my colleagues and see what we can make of this."

I drag in a shaky breath. "Do you think there's any chance they'll listen to you at this point?"

His mouth tenses. "A peaceful approach is always worth trying."

I can tell from the turmoil of emotions that seeps through our bond that he isn't hopeful at all.

"Well, I'd better get ready for my part then," I say, stepping back.

A pang of concern splits through all the other uneasiness I sense from Corwin. "Are you sure about this? I don't think they'd do you any major harm, but if they succeed in striking at the castle, it could be rather frightening being in the middle of it."

I fold my arms over my chest. "I think they need to see who they're striking at when they try to destroy the home we built. It's more than just a castle. And I'm more than just some random, powerless woman."

He sighs but kisses my temple. "You are indeed. Let's go, then."

He walks with me to the sitting room that leads out onto a small terrace overlooking the winter realm on the castle's second floor. As I step outside, the cold breeze gusts over me, tossing my hair. Several of the heads among the arch-lords' troops twitch upward, noticing my arrival.

I'll do whatever I can to see that no particle of this structure is touched, Corwin says silently as he heads downstairs.

And so will I, I reply.

I stand right at the railing, resting my hands on it and giving those below a clear view of me. A lot of the fae in the throng know me. They've watched me heal their people. Maybe they've never talked to me, but they have to realize what I can do for them is more important than the arch-lords' petty complaints.

The question is whether that knowledge will override their loyalty to their lords.

I pick out Kesral in the crowd, standing a few paces back from where Laoni is poised. When my gaze catches his across the distance, I think his mouth curls into a brief grimace, but he holds his ground. He doesn't want to be there, but he won't let her down.

I don't know if I'll ever understand how awful she's been to him when all he wants to do is support her.

Sylas is already outside, standing among his pack-kin with his cadre flanking him. When Corwin appears below, Zelpha, Verik, and Olander join him. The two groups move through the guards together to the front of the ring. The three Unseelie arch-lords take a step forward to meet them, though still keeping a clear distance.

Corwin speaks loudly enough for his voice to reach my high perch. "Comrades, we have spoken on this matter, and I will put forward my case again. We have found numerous accounts of beings less honored than my mate who have dwelled in structures similar to this one without resistance from the Heart. Since our joint castle has been built, there's been no sign that the Heart or any other natural powers of our world objects to it. Talia has earned the right to a real home of her own that encompasses all her responsibilities."

"Is it her responsibilities she's concerned about or more private matters between the four of you?" Uzziah asks with a sneer, his gaze flicking up to me for an instant.

"I hardly think you can doubt her dedication to her duties after how much of her time she's already devoted to healing your people," Sylas replies. "As to how she chooses to spend what time she has to herself, and in what company, that is indeed a private matter that doesn't affect you at all."

I don't think the other arch-lords agree with his assessment, but they don't pursue that line of argument any further, maybe balking at airing their personal prejudices about my relationships in front of their people so openly. Terisse stirs on her feet, but it's Laoni who speaks next.

"We gave our orders. We disapprove of the shape this venture of yours has taken, the pedestal on which you have placed your mate above all others when she isn't even fae. The majority carries the rule. The summer fae can do as they wish, but we will see any part of this structure that intrudes on our lands fall."

"Our authority as arch-lords can't be thrown about on a whim but must remain subject to the laws and principles already established," Corwin protests.

Laoni has already backed up to rejoin her people. She motions to her soldiers. They and the other troops move in near-unison, a vast murmuring of voices rising up as true names and other words of magic fill the air.

But our side was prepared for a magical assault. The fae protecting the castle lift their own voices, and a tingling rushes over my skin. The air in front of me shimmers with the barrier they've conjured.

Not a second too soon. The shimmering surface quakes an instant later with the warbling impact of a surge of energy. My fingers curl around the railing as if I need to hold onto it to stay upright, even though I haven't felt more than a tremor in the atmosphere yet.

I know Corwin's right—the arch-lords wouldn't want to hurt the woman who's curing their people. Their soldiers will have been instructed to catch me with their magic and move me to safety as they dismantle the diamond section of the castle. I'm just hoping it doesn't come to that.

The barrier shudders again, but it holds against the onslaught, even when the opposing fae call out their spells louder. Are we that much stronger than them? They've got at least twice as much manpower—I don't see how—

But then I do. As I peer through the quivering air, I spot many fae standing in the winter arch-lords' troops who aren't speaking at all. They're standing silently, their hands by their sides, their expressions somberly stoic. A couple give me the slightest nod when they notice my attention on them.

They're refusing to follow their lords' commands. Have the arch-lords noticed that so many of their underlings are rebelling?

So many of the arch-lords' own people are willing to stand against their rulers on my behalf. A strange shiver runs through me, a sense of power that's unlike anything I've felt before. Somehow I've earned that much devotion, enough to turn flock-folk against their lords.

Maybe the arch-lords aren't wrong to be worried about how I could undermine their authority. I already am. How much more could

I accomplish, given the chance and the time for more loyalties to shift toward me?

I'm not sure the fae's dedication to me will be enough to win the day for us now, though. Someone must have sent word back to the arch-lords' castles, because more fae are swooping down in raven form to join the flocks. They add their voices to the chanting.

The barrier wavers. A lick of magic breaks through, streaking across the diamond surface next to me and opening a crack in the wall.

My throat constricts. "Stop it!" I call out. "Think about what you're doing! This castle represents the unity between the summer and winter fae, between our realms—that we can work together to conquer the curse. Isn't that what you want? What else is going to be ruined if you ruin this?"

I think I see a few more of the opposing fae falter. The arch-lords motion to their troops, rousing the others to greater efforts. The forces below me recite more magical words, but a raggedness is already coming into their voices.

It's taking all their energy just to fend off our attackers for another minute or two. How long can their strength last?

As my spirits start to sink, an abrupt motion draws my gaze to Laoni. She's still standing at the front line of her flock-folk, but her hands that were raised a moment ago have snapped to her belly. A strange expression has crossed her face, as if something has startled her, but I can't see anything around that would have caused her reaction.

She turns to one of the guards near her and mutters something. He nods, and in a blink, she leaps off the ground into the form of a raven. With a few swift flaps of her wings, listing slightly to one side, she soars off toward her domain.

What's that about? Has she gone to demand more help in person?

I can't dwell on the puzzle for very long. More ravens are flying toward us, dark specks against the gray sky expanding into clearly winged shapes.

But they don't drop down among the winter arch-lords' troops. They land alongside Sylas and Corwin. Several make quick gestures of respect toward me before they open their mouths to add their voices to the protective spell.

Folk from other flocks must have heard what was happening—and they've decided to stand with me too.

A swell of warmth fills my chest with another of those strange shivers. I don't know if I can live up to the blessed figure they see me as, but I'm glad to see they're showing their support not just with words but actual action. I've helped them, and now they've come to my aid in turn, regardless of my humanity.

Uzziah and Terisse glance at each other and at the vacant spot Laoni left. Uzziah's jaw clenches. He beckons to some of his soldiers, and they march up alongside him. The fae on our side rest their hands on the hilts of their swords or bring their arms up defensively. My fleeting happiness vanishes.

Is it really going to come to this—to the arch-lords ordering their flocks to outright attack the people they're supposed to be representing? How long will our allies stay with us against a direct offensive?

I don't want violence to break out, Corwin says, picking up on my anxiety. *There has to be another way we can settle this.*

He speaks out loud to his colleagues. "Please, can't you see this is going too far? Our own people refuse to watch Talia and her home harmed. Listen to them even if you won't listen to me."

"The blessed one should have everything she asks for," one of the newcomers shouts. "She's going to save us all—we should do everything we can to reward her!"

Another lifts her voice. "By attacking her, you're attacking our hope of a cure. You're traitors to your own people."

An increasingly angry murmur ripples through our side of the crowd. I suppress the urge to hug myself. They're not just willing to defend me—they'd go to war for me against their own arch-lords if it came to that.

The realization is both exhilarating and terrifying. Do I really want that much responsibility on top of all the rest?

Can I afford to turn it away when there's so much I could accomplish with these people on my side?

Terisse glares at our forces, though her expression looks more pained than defiant. "Who is a traitor isn't for you to decide. We've proven ourselves before the Heart and earned the right to guide the realm in the directions we feel are best for all our people. To doubt our judgment is to betray us."

"Lady Talia has done more to conquer the curse in the past month than you all have in decades," someone snaps back.

I catch a glint of metal as a few of the figures below draw their swords. My stomach balls tighter. "Please," I say, leaning over the railing. "I don't want to see anyone's blood spilled—here or anywhere else. This castle isn't hurting anyone. Why do we have to fight over it?"

I can't tell how well my appeal hit the troops who've continued to follow their lords' commands. A few of the folk-flock have unfurled their wings as if preparing to soar into battle. A snarl carries up from one of the Seelie below me.

All these fae might be willing to fight for me, but that doesn't mean I want to see them do it—not here, not like this. This confrontation could wreck not just the home my mates built for me, but the peace we worked so hard to construct between the realms as well.

But what if the alternative is letting the winter arch-lords win?

Before the conflict actually comes to blows, one more raven speeds into view. Flying toward us from the direction of Laoni's domain, it moves so swiftly it's little more than a dark streak against the sky. It dives down into the strip of empty terrain between the opposing factions, straightening into the form of a man at the same time.

I don't recognize him, but Corwin clearly does. The man makes a signal for truce, and Corwin motions him over begrudgingly. He raises his inner barriers so I don't hear exactly what the man says to him, probably worried it'll be some new threat or insult.

I prod him impatiently. Whatever's going on, I need to know.

When our connection comes back into full focus, the first things I sense from Corwin are shock and distress. *What?* I demand.

He looks up at me, his eyes even darker than usual. *Laoni requests that you attend to her at her castle, with full discretion and an oath from her that you'll be allowed safe passage back. Her coterie man will escort you. It appears… she's been struck by the curse.*

What? A wave of my own shock crashes through me. For a few seconds, I don't know what to do with myself.

If it's true—I have to go to her, don't I? It may even be a chance to settle this conflict. But I'm not risking all the people who'd stood by me to attend to her.

Tell him I'll come as long as her troops and the others stand down first, I say to Corwin. *No magic or blows should be exchanged while I'm gone. Otherwise I stay here.*

Corwin answers with a tendril of approval. He conveys my conditions to the coterie man, whose expression tenses before he nods. He goes to speak with Terisse and Uzziah. After a few minutes, the arch-lords' soldiers back up several paces, lowering their weapons and retracting their wings.

They've given their word, Corwin says. *I can come with you.*

His offer reverberates with worry. I shake my head. *No. You need to be here in case they find a way to go back on their word. Your people need you.*

And it seems Laoni, as much as she must hate the fact, needs me.

CHAPTER TWENTY-FIVE

Talia

As I limp alongside him across the icy plain, Laoni's coterie man lets out little huffs of breath that sound almost like grumbles, as if he's annoyed by my limited speed. As it is, my leg is already throbbing from the pace I've pushed myself to. I'm tempted to snap at him that this would go a lot faster if Laoni would come out to meet me or if he'd arrange a carriage, but my innards are tangled so tight I'm not sure I could form words anyway.

Laoni doesn't want to come out to meet me because apparently she doesn't want anyone to know she's come down with the cursed sickness. I'm not sure what to make of that. Does she not want the flocks to see me healing her, making me even more a hero in their eyes? Or is she not really sick at all, only carrying out some new scheme?

She gave an oath, one her coterie man was able to convey to Corwin. One Corwin trusts. He wouldn't let me go alone if he wasn't sure she has no ill intentions.

The fae don't lie. I can take some comfort in that, even if I have seen them talk their way around the truth plenty of times.

What could Laoni intend to accomplish with this gambit if it is a gambit anyway? It's the castle she wants destroyed, not me. Or at least, she's not so selfish that she'd let any desire she has to destroy me overwhelm what she knows is best for her people.

At the shining iridium castle, the coterie man ushers me in and leads me upstairs. I'm surprised by the thought that Laoni might be willing to let me into a space as private as her bedroom, but the room he directs me into is a small lounge. My reflection wavers on the smooth walls around me, looking paler and frailer on those not-quite-mirrors. A faint scent like dried flowers reaches my nose.

Laoni is sitting stiffly on an ivory settee at the far end of the room, her chin raised and her hands clasped on her lap. There are a couple of matching chairs near her, a side table and a bookcase and a picture window that offers a view over the nearby cliff. It's Spartan and uncluttered, which doesn't surprise me from what I've seen of Laoni's personality.

The air is cold against my skin. Even though the curse's chill must be seeping through her, she hasn't conjured a fire or any warming magic. I guess she's realized it wouldn't really help.

"You may leave us," Laoni says tightly. Her coterie man bobs his head and slips away, shutting the door behind him.

A prickling sensation runs over my skin. Other than yesterday in her front hall with August just outside, this is the first time I've been alone in a room with the most hostile of the Unseelie arch-lords.

I'm right here with you, Corwin says, softly but firmly through our bond. And I know that I could call on Whitt in a similar way if I really needed to. But Laoni is watching me as if she expects *me* to lash out at her somehow, even though it's always been the opposite.

I wet my lips, not sure what to do with myself, and sink gingerly onto one of the chairs. "Your coterie man said you're ill. Are you sure it's the curse?"

Laoni's jaw flexes. "I'd hardly call on you like this if I wasn't." She seems to catch herself and smooths the sharpness from her tone before she continues. "I felt some tightness in my limbs and a bit of a chill developing earlier this afternoon, but I dismissed it as mere tension.

Over the past few hours, it's become increasingly impossible to ignore. I—"

She glances down at her hands and lifts one of them, the fingers curled toward her palm. "I can no longer straighten my fingers. My skin is turning cold even against fabric that holds a warming spell. I know what the signs are."

When I look at her closely, I can see the hints of it in her skin, a bluish tinge that's starting to creep into the usual tan hue. And is that the beginnings of a frost pattern touching the edge of her dark irises?

But that could be an illusion, couldn't it? I swallow thickly and can't help pointing out, "You've claimed an arch-lord was cursed before, and it turned out to be a trick."

"I have no wish to play games at the moment," Laoni snaps, the edge coming back into her voice. "I want this ailment gone before it interferes with my work. If I'm *not* sick, your cure certainly won't do anything for me, so there'd be nothing to gain in tricking you. Just heal me."

Even now, she doesn't offer me so much as the basic respect of asking rather than demanding. I study her for a long moment, my stomach knotting.

A shiver Laoni tries to restrain passes through her frame. Her gaze darts away as if she's ashamed to have let even that much weakness show. Her fingers twitch and clench tighter.

I don't think she's faking it. She's right that there's no obvious reason for her to do so anyway. With no audience, this is between only her and me.

I still feel a little sick myself, a queasiness winding through my gut. Because this woman is asking me to cure her so that she can go back out there and get right back to trying to destroy one of the few good things I've gotten in this world—something that was for my benefit too, not just that of the fae.

"What happens after?" I ask quietly. "After you're cured—because of the power that as far as we know only I can wield. Are you going to go back to my new home and keep claiming that I don't deserve any special considerations, that there's something wrong with the love I share with my mates?"

Laoni narrows her eyes at me. "Are you trying to bargain for the cure? Not the selfless savior anymore when you have a personal vendetta?"

A laugh sputters out of me. "The only one here with a vendetta has been you. I don't care what you do with your castles or the men you love, whether you wish you didn't or not. I've never once acted against you except in my own defense."

And I could do that again now, couldn't I? If I *didn't* cure her, if I let the curse take her… would that be murder or merely self-defense?

The thought sends a shiver of my own through me, even stronger and more unnerving than what I felt watching the fae stand against their arch-lords, ready to draw blood on my behalf if need be. I don't fully understand this power, and I don't have any clue at all why I have it, but it's greater than anything Laoni can wield in this moment, when her life depends on the choices I make next. I'm her only hope of survival.

The possibilities slip through my mind as we stare each other down. I could refuse to heal her until she and her allies swear an oath to take no further action against me and my mates. That request would be justified by her actions, wouldn't it?

Or even better, since I'm not sure I trust her not to weasel out of any oath she takes eventually, I could pretend that I've tried to heal her but failed. Eventually she won't be able to hide her illness any longer. If I make a more public attempt and she dies anyway, I don't think the fae will blame me. They'll assume it's the Heart's punishment for Laoni's attacks on me.

Even as those ideas pass through my head, nausea twists around my gut. To barter over her life, over sparing her all the agony the curse will bring—let alone to abandon her to that agony completely… If I left her to die for my gain, would I be any better than she is?

I have more power right now than I ever recognized behind my eyes and in the tips of my fingers. The power to shape the rulership of the entire Unseelie realm. What's really *right* in this situation?

What kind of woman will I become as I dispense that power?

"I want to know what I can expect after we're done here," I say, pressing my earlier question.

Laoni manages to raise her chin at a haughty angle even now. “Why would you think this will change anything?”

At her sneer, a large part of me wants to spring to my feet and march straight out of the room. I even get some satisfaction out of imagining her hope snuffing out as I vanish out the door. Then my stomach lurches, and I feel even queasier.

Talia? Corwin says softly. All at once, I choke up.

I know what kind of woman he sees in me. That all four of my lovers see. I know what the fae who've raised me up as a savior expect of their blessed human.

That's the woman I want to be. Not a tyrant, not a murderer. I was given this power to heal, not to destroy. There's so much pain and death in this world already. I will *not* add any more to it.

My heart thumps hard, but I hold Laoni's gaze as steadily as I can, letting the certainty I'm slowly building drive the words up my throat. “Maybe it shouldn't change anything. I don't know why you're so set on tearing down the things I've built. But if you'll do just one thing for me, maybe you can set aside all that resentment for just a second and recognize who I actually am.”

“And what's that?” Laoni demands.

“Someone who's just trying to make things better for your people, not to hurt them. Someone who'll heal even you, despite all the ways you've tried to hurt me and may continue to after I've done this.”

“You expect me to be ever so grateful that you're serving the Heart's purpose for you?”

My spine stiffens, but I'm not going to let her insults change *me*. “I'd like you to see that I have a will of my own beyond the gifts the Heart has given me. I know I could refuse to heal you, or claim that I did and my powers failed me. How many of your people would still stand by you if it looks like the Heart itself has turned its back on you?”

Laoni's expression turns even more sour. “If you claim you're not going to do either of those things, why even bring them up?”

I lean forward in my chair. I'm a little afraid she's going to be provoked into quite literally attacking me, but I can't stop until I've done everything I can to make her understand.

"I need *you* to know that I know all that, but I'm choosing to help you anyway. My life would probably be so much easier if the curse took you, but I'm not and never will be the kind of person who'd make that trade. It doesn't matter how many ways you've insulted me or how horribly so many other fae have treated me—I'm helping you anyway. That's who you've decided is your enemy. That's who you've decided to fight when there are so many actual villains out there. If you can know that, and keep trying to knock me down however you can..."

What can I say after that? I spread my hands. "It's up to you. I just hope that when you go back out to your troops and decide what to do against me and my mates, you remember that I held your life in my hands and chose to do everything I could to save it. I don't worship the Heart of the Mists the same way you do, but I'm pretty sure I can tell which course of action it'd approve of more."

Laoni just stares at me, her eyes smoldering with restrained emotion, her expression increasingly tensed. I've made all the appeal I can to whatever goodness there is inside her. I shouldn't leave her in the curse's grip any longer, or it'll look like I really am out to torment her after all.

"Let's begin then," I say, and stand up.

Looking at the fae woman who's put so much effort into upending my hard-won happiness, it's hard to summon much sympathy. For a second, I wonder if I'll fail after all simply because I can't work up tears on her behalf in the first place.

But then I think instead of the people who'd suffer from her death. I don't know how much she cares for her soul-twined mate, but he might love her a great deal. Kesral definitely does. All those soldiers on the plain outside the border castle look to her for guidance and protection.

What turmoil would it throw the whole winter realm into if Laoni succumbed to the curse without an heir? How many more people might die in the scramble to claim this castle? What would become of her flock when they're ousted from their domain?

Imagining all those figures cast adrift without a home is what finally hits the mark. Heat wells up behind my eyes. I turn around, sure I need to go through the motions of hiding my sadness even when there's no one else here to see, and urge the tears to spill out.

One and then another trickles over my skin. That has to be enough. I wipe them away, inhale slowly, and return my attention to Laoni.

She holds perfectly still as I graze my fingertips over her cheek. I can't read the emotion in her eyes, and her face is too rigid to give a valid impression. Then she takes a sharp breath just as I feel the warmth racing away from my hand over her flesh.

She looks up at me, and just for that instant, I think I catch a glimmer of awe in her gaze.

Then it's gone. Laoni stretches her arms, working her fingers that she can now uncurl, and nods curtly to me. "You've done your duty. You may go."

The words aren't quite as brusque as I might have expected, but they aren't exactly friendly either. I've said all I need to, so I head out the door in silence.

The coterie man is waiting farther down the hall. He hurries over to me and guides me toward the stairs. "She's well again?" he asks, unable to disguise his urgency.

I nod. "I healed her. I'd imagine she'll be out here giving orders again very soon." My nausea wraps tighter around my gut at the thought of what those orders might be.

We step outside into the brisk air to find a carriage waiting for us, Zelpha at the helm.

"Corwin thought you might appreciate a smoother journey back," she says, giving Laoni's coterie man a cool glance. "I assume you don't mind me taking over her escort from here, now that she's attended to your lady."

"I—by all means, go ahead," the fae man says, awkward enough that I find myself forgiving him for his previous oversight. He must have been panicked over Laoni's situation.

Zelpha helps me into the carriage, and I slump onto one of the benches, feeling as if I've just run for miles. The short walk through the castle has reawakened the pain in my thigh. I rub the spot and look at Zelpha as she directs the carriage back toward the border castle. "Has anything changed since I left?"

"Other than Corwin just about pacing a ditch in the ground?" Zelpha asks, the corners of her lips quirking up. "Not really. They've all just stood around waiting. Uzziah and Terisse talked some. I think they were wondering what's going on with Laoni, since she dragged the two of them into this mess and then abandoned them."

I've been fine, Corwin says through our bond, obviously overhearing her remark about him through my ears. His concern rings through his inner voice all the same. *Do you think your words to Laoni made any difference?*

I don't know. She didn't seem very happy with me even after I healed her.

If it didn't, there's no moving her. You were incredible.

A blush warms my cheeks. He must have had some sense of the inner turmoil I was grappling with, but he thinks that anyway.

All I did was speak from my heart, and I don't think Laoni cares very much what my heart wants. But I guess we'll have to wait and see.

The assembled fae on both sides of the stand-off watch with open curiosity as Zelpha brings the carriage to my high terrace. I take my former position, catching the eyes of Corwin and then my Seelie mates below, taking reassurance from seeing them still standing firm and the castle unmarked other than the one crack. Uzziah and Terisse are standing close in consultation again. One and then the other glances toward Laoni's domain.

Several more minutes pass in the same holding pattern. The troops shuffle on their feet, trying to tamp down on a growing restlessness that's rippling through the air. I tamp down on the growing urge to vomit.

Finally, a raven with a turquoise sheen to its dark feathers flaps into view. Laoni lands a few paces from where her colleagues are standing in the space between the fae forces, shifting as soon as she touches the ground. She strides over to Uzziah and Terisse and joins their conversation.

Their voices are so low I can't make anything out from my perch or through Corwin's ears. At one point, Uzziah lets out a rough, wordless exclamation that sounds like a protest. Terisse rubs her mouth, her forehead furrowed. I have no idea what any of it means.

I know I made the right choice for my conscience, but was it the wrong one in every other way? Could I have saved more bloodshed if I'd let Laoni die?

But then she turns away from the other arch-lords, summoning a pedestal of ice with a quick word and a motion of her hand. She leaps onto it so everyone in the crowd around her can see her easily. There's still a hint of stiffness to her motions, but I don't think anyone who wasn't already aware of what she's been through would notice it.

"My people," she says in a commanding voice. "And those of the summer realm who've seen fit to be here today. I have meditated long with the pulse of the Heart, and I have come to the conclusion… that I was misguided here today."

My pulse hiccups, and a murmur spreads through the watching fae. Is she saying what I want to think she is?

Laoni clears her throat and goes on. "We don't yet know who our greatest enemies are, but I'm sure they're not among us at this moment. We'll be better if we stand together, prepared to meet them and see the final end of this curse than if we're at each other's throats. The castle may stand as long as the Seelie keep their peace with us and Lady Talia continues to gift us with her healing powers."

She tips her head in just the slightest nod toward me.

My heart fills with so much light I almost think I'll float away. A matching joy resonates through Corwin. August glances up at me and grins wide. I grip the railing, so dizzy with relief I need it to steady me.

I don't think this is the last battle I'll face with the winter arch-lords… but it may be the worst. And now it's behind us.

CHAPTER TWENTY-SIX

Talia

I've never seen so many fae gathered together in one place, not even for Sylas's coronation festivities.

We're holding tonight's ceremony in the same place—in the sprawling field around the Heart on the summer side of the border—and that entire space is filled with figures turned toward me with eager eyes. More are standing amid the trees along the edges of the field. There are even ravens perched in the branches and circling overhead to watch the proceedings from where they can get a better view.

It's a little startling to see how many of the Unseelie have crossed the border to witness the ceremony. They're not mingling with the Seelie all that much yet, mostly keeping to one section of the field, but I haven't noticed any hostile glances or words exchanged.

Tonight is about the unity between summer and winter symbolized in me, and everything about the event so far speaks of the healing divide between the realms.

At this point, there hasn't been much to see except me where I'm perched on a chair on the platform built for the ceremony, right in front of the Heart. Its rhythmic energy washes over me, and its glow casts a golden light over the darkening forest. Beaming orbs shine along the edges of the field and float over the crowd. The breeze, pleasantly warm, tickles over me with a soft scent of clover. I couldn't have asked for a more peaceful atmosphere for this moment.

Harper darts up onto the platform next to me and runs her fingers over the lacy sleeve of the dress she designed for this occasion. It doesn't cover the scars on my shoulder so much as turn them into part of the intricate pattern—into something almost beautiful. I think it's the most amazing gown she's crafted yet.

"Seeing you in this light, I can't help thinking I should have added a little more sheen to the skirt," she mutters, never totally satisfied with her own work.

I laugh. "It's a little late for adjustments, isn't it? It's already spectacular. I'll be surprised if you don't have a hundred orders by the end of the night."

Her cheeks flush, and she ducks her head bashfully. "I've actually already gotten a few."

Knowing her typical modesty, that means she's had at least a dozen requests. I squeeze her hand. "That's wonderful. I talked to Corwin about some of that fabric you were hoping to experiment with—the weavers from the domain that specializes in it should have a shipment to us in the next week."

"Oh, perfect." She claps her hands together with so much excitement I have to grin. Then she shakes herself. "But never mind about me. This evening is about *you*." Her gaze darts to our audience. "I shouldn't even be up here."

"It's fine. My arch-lords had some special arrangements they needed to finish up." I have no idea what Corwin and Sylas were up to, only that it required some intense discussions with the other arch-lords this morning. "Is the man you have your eye on here tonight? You should at least ask him to dance."

Harper's flush deepens. "No, I—I couldn't. It's silly." Her hands twitch over her own dress. It has a sleeker skirt and fewer embellishments than mine but still an eye-catching design that brings to mind a rushing waterfall.

I make a dismissive sound. "It wouldn't hurt to try, would it? I want to see everyone else happy tonight too."

She gives me a bright smile. "I will be happy because you are. Everything else—it'll happen as it's meant to be in time, I'm sure."

I wish I had that same sense of faith. But at least today, it does feel as if everything is coming together as it ought to be.

As Harper slips back into the crowd, I spot Corwin's colleagues in a tight cluster near the other end of the platform. Besides Neve, who's wearing her usual vague expression, none of the arch-lords look exactly *pleased*, but they don't appear to be as sour about the event as I was worried they'd be. I might even see a flicker of a smile cross Terisse's face at one point.

My gaze catches Laoni's for just a second, and she offers me the slightest nod like she did a week ago outside the border castle, her expression staying impassive. Since that day when I healed her and she called back the assault on my castle, she hasn't been anywhere near warm. But she seems to have accepted that I'm here to stay in the fae world and that it isn't a bad thing.

She even told Corwin that he should encourage the Seelie to get on with this ceremony—that if we're going to insist on doing things in such a strange way, we should hurry up and make it official. The corners of my mouth twitch upward at the memory of her exasperated tone.

Donovan and Celia are standing near them, looking more relaxed. Donovan is chatting animatedly with one of his cadre-chosen, his bright hair dancing like a flame in the undulating glow of the Heart.

Tomorrow I can get started on the work I want to do here for myself and those like me. Donovan has agreed to make a public announcement that he'll be offering many more freedoms to the humans in his domain, and I'm going to help determine what would be best for each of his servants.

If we can convince Celia and Neve to follow suit after that, tackling the other three arch-lords might not be so difficult. Maybe they'll *want* to stop relying on human servitude now that they've seen how much frustration just one human can cause them. Who knows what chaos might be brought by the next human who ends up here?

My amused thoughts fall to the wayside at the movement of four striking figures through the crowd.

My lovers have dressed up in as much finery as I have for this occasion. Sylas's gold-embroidered jacket and slacks are a deep burgundy that brings out the purple in his dark hair. Whitt has gone with a sapphire-blue that makes his eyes gleam even more brightly. August looks a bit uncomfortable in the formal clothes, but the supple maroon fabric shows off his muscular form to great effect. And Corwin, my wintry raven, is perfectly elegant among them in pale blue and silver.

My heart thumps faster, but it's more excitement than anxiety. Nothing else can go wrong in the little time that's left before the ceremony begins, can it? This is actually happening.

I don't know what my life will be like a month from now, let alone years, and the curse still casts its shadow over both realms. But no matter what else happens, I'll have my four men as my mates.

From what Whitt told me, regular mating ceremonies where there's no soul-twined bond aren't usually this elaborate or public. Still, he and my other Seelie men felt that it was important to make a clear statement about their commitment to me in front of their subjects and whoever of the winter realm would join us. I definitely won't mind if the public declaration makes it less likely that more fae ladies will make passes at them hoping to catch the new arch-lord's or one of his cadre-chosen's eye.

As they step onto the platform, I stand up. The ache in my thigh from the Murk man's claws has faded nearly completely now. Thanks to my warped foot, I can't completely erase my limp as I walk to the center of the stage, but I'm not so self-conscious of it now. Most of the fae watching have seen it before. They know who I am and the damage I carry.

But they still honor what I offer them. And tonight they're going to honor the love I've found here—celebrate it, even.

The chatter of the crowd dims to a murmur as I reach the center of the stage. Sylas, Whitt, and August meet me there, standing in a loose line facing me. Corwin positions himself between us, placing one hand on my shoulder. He's holding something in his other hand wrapped in a bundle of dark fabric.

He clears his throat, and the crowd falls completely silent.

"Tonight," he says, "I recognize the bonds of love my soul-twined mate has formed with these three men, who are just as deserving of her affections as I am. I welcome them as her mates into our lives, and I ask that you all do the same. Lady Talia has proven how much kindness and generosity she can offer all of us, and she should have just as much in return."

He steps back, stopping at the back of the platform.

August reaches for my hand first. He clasps it, smiling at me so brilliantly that I feel as if my heart is flying.

In a way, August *has* taught me to fly: showing me how to use my shaky magical powers, giving me control over light and air. I never feel quite so safe as when he's standing by me or so nurtured as when we're building a meal together.

Lifting my hand so the audience can see our entwined fingers, he holds my gaze but raises his voice so all of the assembled fae can hear him.

"Before the Heart, I declare my intent to take Talia of Hearth-by-the-Heart and Heart's Cadence as my mate. I swear to cherish and protect her with all my being."

A magical thrum carries through his words. I can't offer the same sort of vow in return, but I put all the emotion I can into my answering statement. "Before the Heart, I declare my intent to take August of Hearth-by-the-Heart as my mate. I swear to cherish and protect him with all my being."

August squeezes my hand, and a tingle of energy passes from his palm into mine. Our souls might not be tied together like mine is to Corwin's, but the depth of his devotion shines in his eyes. He leans in, and I bob up on my toes to kiss him.

A murmur of what sounds like approval ripples through our audience. I brace myself for a shout of protest, but it seems even the Unseelie have settled into the idea of one of their arch-lords openly sharing his soul-twined mate with the wolfish summer fae.

When August eases back, it's Sylas who steps forward next. He's the one who suggested we take the vows from youngest to oldest rather than political authority. I think he wanted to avoid implying that his claim overshadowed that of his cadre-chosen.

He takes my hand as August did, both of his mismatched eyes fixed on me. I wonder if his ghostly one is catching glimpses of our future together. If he sees anything that worries him, he gives no sign of it.

His lips curve into the gentle smile he reserves for me, and I find myself remembering the first day when I woke up in his keep in Oakmeet after he'd rescued me from Aerik's cage. How he came into my room and spoke to me so kindly, earning my trust rather than demanding it.

We've come so far since then. Through a lot of pain and struggle, but without fail, he's given me the space to take control over my own life. And every one of the painful moments was worth it to make it here tonight.

"Before the Heart, I declare my intent to take Talia of Hearth-by-the-Heart and Heart's Cadence as my mate," he says in his resonant voice. "I swear to cherish and protect her with all my being."

I smile back at him, lit up with a glow of happiness that could rival the Heart itself. "Before the Heart, I declare my intent to take Sylas of Hearth-by-the-Heart as my mate. I swear to cherish and protect him with all my being."

He cups my jaw as he kisses me, holding me steady with his commanding strength. Then he draws back to make room for Whitt.

The last of my Seelie mates, both now and when we started, shoots me one of his crooked grins, but there's nothing but fondness in it. Staring into his ocean-blue eyes brings me back to that moment not long ago when he told me he trusted me with his own true name. Of the impression of his presence those syllables summoned even at a distance, all wryness and hidden passion, leading me straight to him when I called out with my mind.

Of the passion he brought me to balanced on the edge of his secret terrace, his hold never wavering.

Whitt was once afraid that he'd ruin me somehow. I hope by now he's seen how much he's strengthened my will and my confidence instead.

His voice holds its usual hint of dryness, but there's no mistaking the genuine promise in his words. "Before the Heart, I declare my intent to take Talia of Hearth-by-the-Heart and Heart's Cadence as my mate. I swear to cherish and protect her with all my being."

My last vow spills out of me so fast I almost lose my breath. "Before the Heart, I declare my intent to take Whitt of Hearth-by-the-Heart as my mate. I swear to cherish and protect him with all my being."

He claims my mouth with a subtle flick of his tongue that makes me gasp. When he releases me, his smile a little more wicked now, Corwin raises his hands toward the crowd.

"Lady Talia will live between our realms, serving both and served by both. She has brought peace to our world, soothed old hurts, and healed current maladies. As mate to arch-lords of both seasons and our champion against our curse, all four of us bestow on her this marker of her esteemed place among the fae."

I have no idea what he's talking about. None of my men mentioned anything like this.

Then Corwin unfurls the cloth bundle and holds out a thin, glinting crown. The strands of silver and gold curl together like twined vines, gripping five small gems that I understand instinctively stand for me and the four men who stand with me. As he sets it on my head, my breath catches.

It's only a symbol, no extra authority granted with it, he says through our bond with a trace of apology. *But we felt it was appropriate all the same.*

Thank you, I say, too overwhelmed with emotion to manage more than that. I look to each of my Seelie men with the same gratitude, and from the way they beam back at me, I can tell I don't need to say it out loud.

The graceful weight of the crown settles into my hair. Corwin lowers his arms—and a flare of brighter light streams over us with the next pulse of the Heart. Its glow and its warmth flood the field, tingling like a melody across my skin. For a second, it seems to enfold me in an embrace.

A rush of giddiness fills my chest. As the light contracts to its usual softer glow, gasps and awed exclamations fill the clearing. Even the winter arch-lords are looking around in wonder.

I don't know if the Heart's power actually carried out some magical effect or whether it was merely a symbol of approval, but I'm not sure it matters. If there were any doubts about whether the Heart agreed with this union—and the collaboration between summer and winter—they've been laid to rest now.

"Let the celebration begin!" Sylas announces.

Along the fringes of the field, musicians begin to play. Fae bustle off to grab the food and drinks already prepared for the occasion. August scoops me off my feet and carries me off the platform to claim the first dance.

My body is humming with so much relief and joy that the next couple of hours pass in a blur. I whirl and sway with each of my lovers in turn, reveling in the ecstatic air that's flowing all around us. Sweet juice, tender morsels of meat, and buttery pastries pass over my lips. The hundreds of fae around us frolic, drink, and make merry as only fae can, many of them pausing when they pass near me to bow in respect and congratulate me on my new union.

After a time, even with so much happiness gripping me, I can't ignore the growing ache in my warped foot. I perch on the edge of the platform to watch the festivities go on. Astrid dances with Verik, and Donovan takes a spin with Zelpha before she returns to a slender, doe-eyed woman I've gathered is her mate. I catch glimpses of Harper's pale dress and hair amid the revelers, though I can't see if she's found a partner. It all just feels so *right.*

My mates have stuck close to me throughout the night, but I shoo them off briefly so they can get some food. I'm supposed to be looking out for them as much as they look out for me, after all.

It's just after that when an elderly fae who has a vague expression that reminds me of Neve approaches me from the crowd. It takes me a moment to recognize her—she's from Donovan's pack, one of the attendants who work in his castle. I spoke to her briefly when I came to his domain to meet with his human servants.

She looked more alert then, but who knows what faerie delights she's been eating and drinking tonight with their various special effects.

"Lady Talia," she says in an upbeat if slightly creaky voice. "If I could do you the honor—I have a gift I'd like to offer you. Would you let me show it to you?"

"Of course." I slip off the platform and follow her through the crowd to the surrounding forest.

I suspect Astrid and at least one of Corwin's coterie members will follow to keep an eye on me, but I wouldn't feel particularly worried regardless. Donovan's pack has always been friendly with ours, and it isn't as if the woman could lie so close to the Heart about why she wants me to come with her anyway.

Fae are still meandering between the trees as they take a break from the dancing, joyful voices echoing through the air. The woman walks just a little farther, toward the pack village in Donovan's domain. Maybe she's left her gift in her home there.

But after several more steps, she turns and gives me a little bow. I see nothing in this spot except the dim silhouettes of the trees and the underbrush around them.

"I don't understand," I say tentatively, not wanting to offend her.

The words have barely left my lips when an unfamiliar man steps from the shadows. His smooth, flaxen hair falls to the tips of his faintly pointed ears, and his heavy-lidded eyes gaze down at me from a height that matches August's.

His hand descends to my forehead. Before I can move or even send out a panicked alarm to Corwin, blackness sweeps through my mind.

Just as the darkness swallows me, the stranger's voice reaches me, low and slightly hoarse. "Hello, Talia. It's time you met the one who made you."

ABOUT THE AUTHOR

Eva Chase is an Amazon bestselling author of urban fantasy and paranormal romance. She grew up on a steady diet of magic, mayhem, and romantic angst, and brings plenty of all three to her stories. But no need to fear the dreaded love triangle—Eva's heroines never have to choose. She lives in Ontario, Canada with her family and one velcro-like cat.

Along with the Bound to the Fae series, she is the author of the Royal Spares series, the Rites of Possession series, the Shadowblood Souls series, the Heart of a Monster series, the Gang of Ghouls series, the Flirting with Monsters series, the Cursed Studies trilogy, the Royals of Villain Academy series, the Moriarty's Men series, the Looking Glass Curse trilogy, the Their Dark Valkyrie series, the Witch's Consorts series, the Dragon Shifter's Mates series, the Demons of Fame Romance series, the Legends Reborn trilogy, and the Alpha Project Psychic Romance series.

Connect with Eva online:
www.evachase.com
eva@evachase.com

www.ingramcontent.com/pod-product-compliance
Lightning Source LLC
Chambersburg PA
CBHW020347310726
48979CB00015B/2536/J

* 9 7 8 1 9 9 0 3 3 8 9 2 2 *